Philip Kerr lives in London with his wife and three children. He is the author of more than twenty-five books, most recently *Prague Fatale*, which features the character of Bernie Günther, who is the hero of the three novels which make up the *Berlin Noir* trilogy. As P. B. Kerr he is also the author of a highly successful series of novels for children.

Berlin Noir

March Violets
The Pale Criminal
A German Requiem

PHILIP KERR

PENGUIN BOOKS

PENGUIN BOOKS

Published by the Penguin Group
Penguin Books Ltd, 80 Strand, London WC2R ORL, England
Penguin Group (USA) Inc., 375 Hudson Street, New York, New York 10014, USA
Penguin Group (Canada), 90 Eglinton Avenue East, Suite 700, Toronto, Ontario, Canada M4P 2Y3
(a division of Pearson Penguin Canada Inc.)
Penguin Ireland, 25 St Stephen's Green, Dublin 2, Ireland
(a division of Penguin Books Ltd)
Penguin Group (Australia), 250 Camberwell Road,
Camberwell, Victoria 3124, Australia (a division of Pearson Australia Group Pty Ltd)
Penguin Books India Pvt Ltd, 11 Community Centre, Panchsheel Park, New Delhi – 110 017, India
Penguin Group (NZ), 67 Apollo Drive, Rosedale, Auckland 0632, New Zealand
(a division of Pearson New Zealand Ltd)
Penguin Books (South Africa) (Pty) Ltd, Block D, Rosebank Office Park,
181 Jan Smuts Avenue, Parktown North, Gauteng 2193, South Africa

Penguin Books Ltd, Registered Offices: 80 Strand, London WC2R ORL, England

www.penguin.com

March Violets first published by Viking 1989
Published in Penguin Books 1990
The Pale Criminal first published by Viking 1990
Published in Penguin Books 1991
A German Requiem first published by Viking 1991
Published in Penguin Books 1992

Published together as *Berlin Noir* in Penguin Books 1993
Reissued in this edition 2012
003

Copyright © Philip Kerr, 1989, 1990, 1991
All rights reserved

The moral right of the author has been asserted

Printed in England by Clays Ltd, St Ives plc

ISBN: 978-0-241-96235-0

www.greenpenguin.co.uk

Contents

MARCII VIOLETS

For my mother

BERLIN, 1936

FIRST MAN: Have you noticed how the March Violets have managed to completely overtake Party veterans like you and me?
SECOND MAN: You're right. Perhaps if Hitler had also waited a little before climbing on to the Nazi bandwagon he'd have become Führer quicker too.

Schwarze Korps, November 1935

I

Stranger things happen in the dark dreams of the Great Persuader . . .

This morning, at the corner of Friedrichstrasse and Jägerstrasse, I saw two men, SA men, unscrewing a red *Der Stürmer* showcase from the wall of a building. *Der Stürmer* is the anti-Semitic journal that's run by the Reich's leading Jew-baiter, Julius Streicher. The visual impact of these display cases, with their semi-pornographic line-drawings of Aryan maids in the voluptuous embraces of long-nosed monsters, tends to attract the weaker-minded reader, providing him with cursory titillation. Respectable people have nothing to do with it. Anyway, the two SA men placed the Stürmerkästen in the back of their lorry next to several others. They did their work none too carefully, because there were at least a couple which had broken glass covers.

An hour later I saw the same two men removing another one of these Stürmerkästen from outside a tram-stop in front of the Town Hall. This time I went up to them and asked what they were doing.

'It's for the Olympiad,' said one. 'We're ordered to take them all down so as not to shock the foreign visitors who will be coming to Berlin to see the Games.'

In my experience, such sensitivity on the part of the authorities is unheard of.

I drove home in my car — it's an old black Hanomag — and changed into my last good suit: made of light-grey flannel cloth, it cost me 120 marks when I bought it three years ago, and it is of a quality that is becoming increasingly rare in this country; like butter, coffee and soap, new wool material is ersatz, more often than not. The new material is serviceable enough, all right, just not very hard-wearing, and rather ineffective when it comes to keeping out the cold in winter. Or, for that matter, in summer.

I checked my appearance in the bedroom mirror and then picked up my best hat. It's a wide-brimmed hat of dark-grey felt, and is encircled by a black barathea band. Common enough. But like the Gestapo, I wear my hat differently from other men, with the brim lower in front than at the back. This has the effect of hiding my eyes of course, which makes it more difficult for people to recognize me. It's a style that originated with the Berlin Criminal Police, the Kripo, which is where I acquired it.

I slipped a packet of Murattis into my jacket pocket, and, tucking a gift-wrapped piece of Rosenthal porcelain carefully under my arm, I went out.

The wedding took place at the Luther Kirche on Dennewitz Platz, just south of Potsdamer Railway Station, and a stone's throw from the home of the bride's parents. The father, Herr Lehmann, was an engine driver out of Lehrter Station, and drove the 'D-Zug', the express train, to Hamburg and back four times a week. The bride, Dagmar, was my secretary, and I had no idea what I was going to do without her. Not that I cared to know, either: I'd often thought of marrying Dagmar myself. She was pretty and good at organizing me, and in my own odd way I suppose that I loved her; but then at thirty-eight I was probably too old for her, and maybe just a shade too dull. I'm not much given to having a wild time, and Dagmar was the sort of girl who deserved some fun.

So here she was, marrying this flyer. And on the face of it he was everything that a girl could have wished for: he was young, handsome and, in the grey-blue uniform of the National Socialist Flying Corps, he looked to be the epitome of the dashing young Aryan male. But I was disappointed when I met him at the wedding reception. Like most Party members, Johannes Buerckel had the look and the air of a man who took himself very seriously indeed.

It was Dagmar who made the introduction. Johannes, true to type, brought his heels together with a loud click and bowed his head curtly before shaking my hand.

'Congratulations,' I said to him. 'You're a very fortunate fellow. I'd have asked her to marry me, only I don't think I look as good as you in uniform.'

I took a closer look at his uniform: on the left breast-pocket he wore the silver SA Sports Badge and the Pilots Badge; above these two decorations was the ubiquitous 'Scary' Badge – the Party Badge; and on his left arm he wore the swastika armband. 'Dagmar told me you were a pilot with Lufthansa on temporary attachment to the Ministry of Aviation, but I had no idea . . . What did you say he was, Dagmar?'

'A Sports Flyer.'

'Yes, that's it. A Sports Flyer. Well, I had no idea you fellows were in uniform.'

Of course it didn't take a detective to work out that 'Sports Flyer' was one of those fancy Reich euphemisms, and that this particular one related to the secret training of fighter pilots.

'He does look splendid, doesn't he?' said Dagmar.

'And you look beautiful, my dear,' cooed the groom dutifully.

'Forgive me for asking, Johannes, but is Germany's air force now to be officially recognized?' I said.

'Flying Corps,' said Buerckel. 'It's a Flying Corps.' But that was the whole of his answer. 'And you, Herr Günther – a private detective, eh? That must be interesting.'

'Private investigator,' I said, correcting him. 'It has its moments.'

'What sort of things do you investigate?'

'Almost anything, except divorce. People act funny when they're being cheated by their wives or their husbands, or when they're the ones doing the cheating. I was once engaged by a woman to tell her husband that she was planning to leave him. She was afraid he'd pop her. So I told him, and, what do you know, the son of a bitch tried to pop me. I spent three weeks in St Gertrauden Hospital with my neck in a brace. That finished me with matrimonial work permanently. These days I do anything from insurance investigations to guarding wedding presents to finding missing persons – that's the ones the police don't already know about, as well as the ones they do. Yes, that's one area of my business that's seen a real improvement since the National Socialists took power.' I smiled as affably as I could, and wiggled my eyebrows suggestively. 'I guess we've all done well out of National Socialism, haven't we? Proper little March Violets.'

'You mustn't take any notice of Bernhard,' said Dagmar. 'He has an odd sense of humour.' I would have said more, but the band started to play and Dagmar wisely led Buerckel on to the dance-floor, where they were applauded warmly.

Bored with the sekt that was on offer, I went into the bar in search of a real drink. I ordered a Bock and a Klares chaser, which is a shot of the clear, colourless potato-based alcohol I have a taste for, and I drank these fairly quickly and ordered the same again.

'Thirsty work, weddings,' said the little man next to me: it was Dagmar's father. He turned his back to the bar and watched his daughter proudly. 'Looks a proper picture, doesn't she, Herr Günther?'

'I don't know what I'm going to do without her,' I said. 'Perhaps you can persuade her to change her mind and stay on with me. I'm sure they must need the money. Young couples always need money when they first marry.'

Herr Lehmann shook his head. 'I'm afraid that there is only one kind of labour for which Johannes and his National Socialist government think a woman is qualified, and that's the kind she has at the end of a nine-month term.' He lit his pipe and puffed philosophically. 'Anyway,' he said. 'I suppose they'll be applying for one of those Reich Marriage Loans, and that would stop her from working, wouldn't it?'

'Yes, I suppose you're right,' I said, and downed the chaser. I saw his face say that he never had me marked as a drunk and so I said, 'Don't let this stuff fool you, Herr Lehmann. I just use it as a mouthwash, only I'm too damned lazy to spit the stuff out.' He chuckled at that, and slapped me on the back and ordered us two large ones. We drank those and I asked him where the happy couple were going on their sparkle.

'To the Rhine,' he said. 'Wiesbaden. Frau Lehmann and myself went to Königstein for ours. It's a lovely part of the world. He's not long back, though, and then he's off on some Strength Through Joy trip, courtesy of the Reich Labour Service.'

'Oh? Where to?'

'Mediterranean.'

'You believe that?'

The old man frowned. 'No,' he said grimly. 'I haven't mentioned it to Dagmar, but I reckon he's off to Spain . . .'

'. . . and war.'

'And war, yes. Mussolini has helped Franco, so Hitler's not going to miss out on the fun, is he? He won't be happy until he's got us into another bloody war.'

After that we drank some more, and later on I found myself dancing with a nice little stocking-buyer from Grunfeld's Department Store. Her name was Carola and I persuaded her to leave with me and we went over to Dagmar and Buerckel to wish them luck. It was rather odd, I thought, that Buerckel should choose that moment to make a reference to my war record.

'Dagmar tells me that you were on the Turkish front.' Was he, I wondered, a little bit worried about going to Spain? 'And that you won an Iron Cross.'

I shrugged. 'Only a second class.' So that was it, I thought; the flyer was hungry for glory.

'Nevertheless,' he said, 'an Iron Cross. The Führer's Iron Cross was a second class.'

'Well, I can't speak for him, but my own recollection is that provided a soldier was honest – comparatively honest – and served at the front, it was really rather easy towards the end of the war to collect a second class. You know, most of the first-class medals were awarded to men in cemeteries. I got my Iron Cross for staying out of trouble.' I was warming to my subject. 'Who knows,'

I said. 'If things work out, you might collect one yourself. It would look nice on a handsome tunic like that.'

The muscles in Buerckel's lean young face tightened. He bent forwards and caught the smell of my breath.

'You're drunk,' he said.

'*Si*,' I said. Unsteady on my feet, I turned away. '*Adios, hombre.*'

2

It was late, gone one o'clock, when finally I drove back to my apartment in Trautenaustrasse, which is in Wilmersdorf, a modest neighbourhood, but still a lot better than Wedding, the district of Berlin in which I grew up. The street itself runs north-east from Güntzelstrasse past Nikolsburger Platz, where there is a scenic sort of fountain in the middle of the square. I lived, not uncomfortably, at the Prager Platz end.

Ashamed of myself for having teased Buerckel in front of Dagmar, and for the liberties I had taken with Carola the stocking-buyer in the Tiergarten near the goldfish pond, I sat in my car and smoked a cigarette thoughtfully. I had to admit to myself that I had been more affected by Dagmar's wedding than previously I would have thought possible. I could see there was nothing to be gained by brooding about it. I didn't think that I could forget her, but it was a safe bet that I could find lots of ways to take my mind off her.

It was only when I got out of the car that I noticed the large dark-blue Mercedes convertible parked about twenty metres down the street, and the two men who were leaning on it, waiting for someone. I braced myself as one of the men threw away his cigarette and walked quickly towards me. As he drew nearer I could see that he was too well-groomed to be Gestapo and that the other one was wearing a chauffeur's uniform, although he would have looked a lot more comfortable in a leopard-skin leotard, with his music-hall weightlifter's build. His less than discreet presence lent the well-dressed and younger man an obvious confidence.

'Herr Günther? Are you Herr Bernhard Günther?' He stopped in front of me and I shot him my toughest look, the sort that would make a bear blink: I don't care for people who solicit me outside my house at one in the morning.

'I'm his brother. He's out of town right now.' The man smiled broadly. He didn't buy that.

'Herr Günther, the private investigator? My employer would like a word with you.' He pointed at the big Mercedes. 'He's waiting in the car. I spoke to the concierge and she told me that you were expected back this evening. That was three hours ago, so you can see we've been waiting quite some time. It really is very urgent.'

I lifted my wrist and flicked my eyes at my watch.

'Friend, it's 1.40 in the morning, so whatever it is you're selling, I'm not interested. I'm tired and I'm drunk and I want to go to bed. I've got an office on Alexanderplatz, so do me a favour and leave it till tomorrow.'

The young man, a pleasant, fresh-faced fellow with a button-hole, blocked my path. 'It can't wait until tomorrow,' he said, and then smiled winningly. 'Please speak to him, just for a minute, I beg you.'

'Speak to whom?' I growled, looking over at the car.

'Here's his card.' He handed it over and I stared stupidly at it like it was a winning raffle-ticket. He leaned over and read it for me, upside-down. ' "Dr Fritz Schemm, German Lawyer, of Schemm & Schellenberg, Unter den Linden, Number 67." That's a good address.'

'Sure it is,' I said. 'But a lawyer out at this time of night and from a smart firm like that? You must think I believe in fairies.' But I followed him to the car anyway. The chauffeur opened the door. Keeping one foot on the running board, I peered inside. A man smelling of cologne leaned forward, his features hidden in the shadows, and when he spoke, his voice was cold and inhospitable, like someone straining on a toilet-bowl.

'You're Günther, the detective?'

'That's right,' I said, 'and you must be –' I pretended to read his business card, '– Dr Fritz Schemm, German Lawyer.' I uttered the word 'German' with a deliberately sarcastic emphasis. I've always hated it on business cards and signs because of the implication of racial respectability; and even more so now that – at least as far as lawyers are concerned – it is quite redundant, since Jews are forbidden to practise law anyway. I would no more describe myself as a 'German Private Investigator' than I would call myself a 'Lutheran Private Investigator' or an 'Antisocial Private Investigator' or a 'Widowed Private Investigator', even though I am, or was at one time, all of these things (these days I'm not often seen in church). It's true that a lot of my clients are Jews. Their business is very profitable (they pay on the nail), and it's always the same – Missing Persons. The results are pretty much the same too: a body dumped in the Landwehr Canal courtesy of the Gestapo or the SA; a lonely suicide in a rowboat on the Wannsee; or a name on a police list of convicts sent to a KZ, a Concentration Camp. So right away I didn't like this lawyer, this German Lawyer.

I said: 'Listen, Herr Doktor, like I was just telling your boy here, I'm tired and I've drunk enough to forget that I've got a bank manager who worries about my welfare.' Schemm reached into his jacket pocket and I didn't even shift, which shows you how blue I must have been. As it was he only took out his wallet.

'I have made inquiries about you and I am informed that you offer a reliable service. I need you now for a couple of hours, for which I will pay you 200 Reichsmarks: in effect a week's money.' He laid his wallet on his knee and thumbed two blues onto his trouser-leg. This couldn't have been easy, since he had only one arm. 'And afterwards Ulrich will drive you home.'

I took the notes. 'Hell,' I said, 'I was only going to go to bed and sleep. I can do that anytime.' I ducked my head and stepped into the car. 'Let's go, Ulrich.'

The door slammed and Ulrich climbed into the driver's seat, with Freshface alongside of him. We headed west.

'Where are we going?' I said.

'All in good time, Herr Günther,' he said. 'Help yourself to a drink, or a cigarette.' He flipped open a cocktail cabinet which looked as though it had been salvaged from the *Titanic* and produced a cigarette box. 'These are American.'

I said yes to the smoke but no to the drink: when people are as ready to part with 200 marks as Dr Schemm had been, it pays to keep your wits about you.

'Would you be so kind as to light me, please?' said Schemm, fitting a cigarette between his lips. 'Matches are the one thing I cannot manage. I lost my arm with Ludendorff at the capture of the fortress of Liège. Did you see any active service?' The voice was fastidious, suave even: soft and slow, with just a hint of cruelty. The sort of voice, I thought, that could lead you into incriminating yourself quite nicely, thank you. The sort of voice that would have done well for its owner had he worked for the Gestapo. I lit our cigarettes and settled back into the Mercedes's big seat.

'Yes, I was in Turkey.' Christ, there were so many people taking an interest in my war record all of a sudden, that I wondered if I hadn't better apply for an Old Comrades Badge. I looked out of the window and saw that we were driving towards the Grunewald, an area of forest that lies on the west side of the city, near the River Havel.

'Commissioned?'

'Sergeant.' I heard him smile.

'I was a major,' he said, and that was me put firmly in my place. 'And you became a policeman after the war?'

'No, not right away. I was a civil servant for a while, but I couldn't stand the routine. I didn't join the force until 1922.'

'And when did you leave?'

'Listen, Herr Doktor, I don't remember you putting me on oath when I got into the car.'

'I'm sorry,' he said. 'I was merely curious to discover whether you left of your own accord, or . . .'

'Or was pushed? You've got a lot of forehead asking me that, Schemm.'

'Have I?' he said innocently.

'But I'll answer your question. I left. I dare say if I'd waited long enough they'd have weeded me out like all the others. I'm not a National Socialist, but I'm not a fucking Kozi either; I dislike Bolshevism just like the Party does, or at least I think it does. But that's not quite good enough for the modern Kripo or Sipo or whatever it's called now. In their book if you're not for it you must be against it.'

'And so you, a Kriminalinspektor, left Kripo,' he paused, and then added in tones of affected surprise, 'to become the house detective at the Adlon Hotel.'

'You're pretty cute,' I sneered, 'asking me all these questions when you already know the answers.'

'My client likes to know about the people who work for him,' he said smugly.

'I haven't taken the case yet. Maybe I'll turn it down just to see your face.'

'Maybe. But you'd be a fool. Berlin has a dozen like you – private investigators.' He named my profession with more than a little distaste.

'So why pick me?'

'You have worked for my client before, indirectly. A couple of years ago you conducted an insurance investigation for the Germania Life Assurance Company, of which my client is a major shareholder. While the Kripo were still whistling in the dark you were successful in recovering some stolen bonds.'

'I remember it.' And I had good reason to. It had been one of my first cases after leaving the Adlon and setting up as a private investigator. I said: 'I was lucky.'

'Never underestimate luck,' said Schemm pompously. Sure, I thought: just look at the Führer.

By now we were on the edge of the Grunewald Forest in Dahlem, home to some of the richest and most influential people in the country, like the Ribbentrops. We pulled up at a huge wrought-iron gate which hung between massive walls, and Freshface had to hop out to wrestle it open. Ulrich drove on through.

'Drive on,' ordered Schemm. 'Don't wait. We're late enough as it is.' We drove along an avenue of trees for about five minutes before arriving at a wide gravel courtyard around which were set on three sides a long centre building and the two wings that comprised the house. Ulrich stopped beside a small fountain and jumped out to open the doors. We got out.

Circling the courtyard was an ambulatory, with a roof supported by thick beams and wooden columns, and this was patrolled by a man with a pair of evil-looking Dobermanns. There wasn't much light apart from the coachlamp by the front door, but as far as I could see the house was white with pebbledash walls and a deep mansard roof – as big as a decent-sized hotel of the sort that I couldn't afford. Somewhere in the trees behind the house a peacock was screaming for help.

Closer to the door I got my first good look at the doctor. I suppose he was quite a handsome man. Since he was at least fifty, I suppose you would say that he was distinguished-looking. Taller than he had seemed when sitting in the back of the car, and dressed fastidiously, but with a total disregard for fashion. He wore a stiff collar you could have sliced a loaf with, a pin-striped suit of a light-grey shade, a creamy-coloured waistcoat and spats; his only hand was gloved in grey kid, and on his neatly cropped square grey head he wore a large grey hat with a brim that surrounded the high, well-pleated crown like a castle moat. He looked like an old suit of armour.

He ushered me towards the big mahogany door, which swung open to reveal an ashen-faced butler who stood aside as we crossed the threshold and stepped into the wide entrance hall. It was the kind of hall that made you feel lucky just to have got through the door. Twin flights of stairs with gleaming white banisters led up to the upper floors, and on the ceiling hung a chandelier that was bigger than a church-bell and gaudier than a stripper's earrings. I made a mental note to raise my fees.

The butler, who was an Arab, bowed gravely and asked me for my hat.

'I'll hang on to it, if you don't mind,' I said, feeding its brim through my fingers. 'It'll help to keep my hands off the silver.'

'As you wish, sir.'

Schemm handed the butler his own hat as if to the manor born. Maybe he was, but with lawyers I always assume that they came by their wealth and position through avarice and by means nefarious: I never yet met one that I coul' trust. His glove he neatly removed with an almost double-jointed contortion of his fingers, and dropped it into his hat. Then he straightened his necktie and asked the butler to announce us.

We waited in the library. It wasn't big by the standards of a Bismarck or a Hindenburg, and you couldn't have packed more than six cars between the Reichstag-sized desk and the door. It was decorated in early Lohengrin, with its great beams, granite chimney-piece in which a log crackled quietly, and wall-mounted weaponry. There were plenty of books, of the sort you buy by the metre: lots of German poets and philosophers and jurists with whom I can claim a degree of familiarity, but only as the names of streets and cafés and bars.

I took a hike around the room. 'If I'm not back in five minutes, send out a search party.'

Schemm sighed and sat down on one of the two leather sofas that were positioned at right angles to the fire. He picked a magazine off the rack and pretended to read. 'Don't these little cottages give you claustrophobia?' Schemm sighed petulantly, like an old maiden aunt catching the smell of gin on the pastor's breath.

'Do sit down, Herr Günther,' he said.

I ignored him. Fingering the two hundreds in my trouser pocket to help me stay awake, I meandered over to the desk and glanced over its green-leather surface. There was a copy of the *Berliner Tageblatt*, well read, and a pair of half-moon spectacles; a pen; a heavy brass ashtray containing the butt of a well-chewed cigar and, next to it, the box of Black Wisdom Havanas from which it had been taken; a pile of correspondence and several silver-framed photographs. I glanced over at Schemm, who was making heavy weather of his magazine and his eyelids, and then picked up one of the framed photographs. She was dark and pretty, with a full figure, which is just how I like them, although I could tell that she might find my after-dinner conversation quite resistible: her graduation robes told me that.

'She's beautiful, don't you think?' said a voice that came from the direction of the library door and caused Schemm to get up off the sofa. It was a singsong sort of voice with a light Berlin accent. I turned to face its owner and found myself looking at a man of negligible stature. His face was florid and puffy and had something so despondent in it that I almost failed to recognize it. While Schemm was busy bowing I mumbled something complimentary about the girl in the photograph.

'Herr Six,' said Schemm with more obsequy than a sultan's concubine, 'may I introduce Herr Bernhard Günther.' He turned to me, his voice changing to suit my depressed bank balance. 'This is Herr Doktor Hermann Six.' It was funny, I thought, how it was that in more elevated circles everyone was a damned doctor. I shook his hand and found it held for an uncomfortably long time as my new client's eyes looked into my face. You get a lot of clients who do that: they reckon themselves as judges of a man's character, and after all they're not going to reveal their embarrassing little problems to a man who looks shifty and dishonest: so it's fortunate that I've got the look of someone who is steady and dependable. Anyway, about the new client's eyes: they were blue, large and prominent, and with an odd sort of watery brightness in them, as if he had just stepped out of a cloud of mustard gas. It was with some shock that it dawned on me that the man had been crying.

Six released my hand and picked up the photograph I'd just been looking at. He stared at it for several seconds and then sighed profoundly.

'She was my daughter,' he said, with his heart in his throat. I nodded patiently. He replaced the photograph face down on the desk, and pushed his monkishly-styled grey hair across his brow. 'Was, because she is dead.'

'I'm sorry,' I said gravely.

'You shouldn't be,' he said. 'Because if she were alive you wouldn't be here with the chance to make a lot of money.' I listened: he was talking my language. 'You see, she was murdered.' He paused for dramatic effect: clients do a lot of that, but this one was good.

'Murdered,' I repeated dumbly.

'Murdered.' He tugged at one of his loose, elephantine ears before thrusting his gnarled hands into the pockets of his shapeless navy-blue suit. I couldn't help noticing that the cuffs of his shirt were frayed and dirty. I'd never met a steel millionaire before (I'd heard of Hermann Six; he was one of the major Ruhr industrialists), but this struck me as odd. He rocked on the balls of his feet, and I glanced down at his shoes. You can tell a lot by a client's shoes. That's the only thing I've picked up from Sherlock Holmes. Six's were ready for the Winter Relief – that's the National Socialist People's Welfare Organization where you send all your old clothes. But then German shoes aren't much good anyway. The ersatz leather is like cardboard; just like the meat, and the coffee, and the butter, and the cloth. But coming back to Herr Six, I didn't have him marked as so stricken by grief that he was sleeping in his clothes. No; I decided he was one of these eccentric millionaires that you sometimes read about in the newspapers: they spend nothing on anything, which is how they come to be rich in the first place.

'She was shot dead, in cold blood,' he said bitterly. I could see we were in for a long night. I got out my cigarettes.

'Mind if I smoke?' I asked. He seemed to recover himself at that.

'Do excuse me, Herr Günther,' he sighed. 'I'm forgetting my manners. Would you like a drink or something?' The 'or something' sounded just fine, like a nice four-poster, perhaps, but I asked for a mocha instead. 'Fritz?'

Schemm stirred on the big sofa. 'Thank you, just a glass of water,' he said humbly. Six pulled the bell-rope, and then selected a fat black cigar from the box on the desk. He ushered me to a seat, and I dumped myself on the other sofa, opposite Schemm. Six

took a taper and pushed it at a flame. Then he lit his cigar and sat
down beside the man in grey. Behind him the library door opened
and a young man of about thirty-five came into the room. A pair
of rimless glasses worn studiously at the end of a broad, almost
negroid nose belied his athletic frame. He snatched them off, stared
awkwardly at me and then at his employer.

'Do you want me in this meeting, Herr Six?' he said. His accent
was vaguely Frankfurt.

'No, it's all right, Hjalmar,' said Six. 'You get off to bed, there's
a good fellow. Perhaps you'd ask Farraj to bring us a mocha and a
glass of water, and my usual.'

'Um, right away, Herr Six.' Again he looked at me, and I
couldn't work out whether my being there was a source of vex-
ation to him or not, so I made a mental note to speak to him when
I got the chance.

'There is one more thing,' said Six, turning round on the sofa.
'Please remind me to go through the funeral arrangements with
you first thing tomorrow. I want you to look after things while
I'm away.'

'Very well, Herr Six,' and with that he wished us goodnight
and left.

'Now then, Herr Günther,' said Six after the door had closed.
He spoke with the Black Wisdom stuck in the corner of his mouth,
so that he looked like a fairground barker and sounded like a child
with a piece of candy. 'I must apologize for bringing you here at
this unearthly hour; however, I'm a busy man. Most important of
all, you must understand that I am also a very private one.'

'All the same, Herr Six,' I said, 'I must have heard of you.'

'That is very probable. In my position I have to be the patron of
many causes and the sponsor of many charities – you know the
sort of thing I'm talking about. Wealth does have its obligations.'

So does an outside toilet, I thought. Anticipating what was
coming, I yawned inside myself. But I said: 'I can certainly believe
it,' with such an affectation of understanding that it caused him to
hesitate for a short moment before continuing with the well-worn

phrases I had heard so many times before. 'Need for discretion'; and 'no wish to involve the authorities in my affairs'; and 'complete respect for confidentiality', etc., etc. That's the thing about my job. People are always telling you how to conduct their case, almost as if they didn't quite trust you, almost as if you were going to have to improve your standards in order to work for them.

'If I could make a better living as a not-so-private investigator, I'd have tried it a long time ago,' I told him. 'But in my line of business a big mouth is bad for business. Word would get around, and one or two well-established insurance companies and legal practices who I can call regular clients would go elsewhere. Look, I know you've had me checked out, so let's get down to business, shall we?' The interesting thing about the rich is that they like being told where to get off. They confuse it with honesty. Six nodded appreciatively.

At this point, the butler cruised smoothly into the room like a rubber wheel on a waxed floor and, smelling faintly of sweat and something spicy, he served the coffee, the water and his master's brandy with the blank look of a man who changes his earplugs six times a day. I sipped my coffee and reflected that I could have told Six that my nonagenarian grandmother had eloped with the Führer and the butler would have continued to serve the drinks without so much as flexing a hair follicle. When he left the room I swear I hardly noticed.

'The photograph you were looking at was taken only a few years ago, at my daughter's graduation. Subsequently she became a schoolteacher at the Arndt Grammar School in Berlin-Dahlem.' I found a pen and prepared to take notes on the back of Dagmar's wedding invitation. 'No,' he said, 'please don't take notes, just listen. Herr Schemm will provide you with a complete dossier of information at the conclusion of this meeting.

'Actually, she was rather a good schoolteacher, although I ought to be honest and tell you that I could have wished for her to have done something else with her life. Grete – yes, I forgot to tell you her name – Grete had the most beautiful singing voice, and I wanted her to take up singing professionally. But in 1930 she married a young lawyer attached to the Berlin Provincial Court. His name was Paul Pfarr.'

'Was?' I said. My interruption drew the profound sigh from him once again.

'Yes. I should have mentioned it. I'm afraid he's dead too.'

'Two murders, then,' I said.

'Yes,' he said awkwardly. 'Two murders.' He took out his wallet and a snapshot. 'This was taken at their wedding.'

There wasn't much to tell from it except that, like most society wedding-receptions, it had been held at the Adlon Hotel. I recognized the Whispering Fountain's distinctive pagoda, with its carved elephants from the Adlon's Goethe Garden. I stifled a real yawn. It wasn't a particularly good photograph, and I'd had more than enough of weddings for one day and a half. I handed it back.

'A fine couple,' I said, lighting another Muratti. Six's black cigar lay smokeless and flat on the round brass ashtray.

'Grete was teaching until 1934 when, like many other women, she lost her job — a casualty of the government's general discrimination against working women in the employment drive. Meanwhile Paul landed a job at the Ministry of the Interior. Not long afterwards my first wife Lisa died, and Grete became very depressed. She started drinking and staying out late. But just a few weeks ago she seemed her old self again.' Six regarded his brandy morosely and then threw it back in one gulp. 'Three nights ago, however, Paul and Grete died in a fire at their home in Lichterfelde-Ost. But before the house caught fire they were each shot, several times, and the safe ransacked.'

'Any idea what was in the safe?'

'I told the fellows from Kripo that I had no idea what it contained.'

I read between the lines and said: 'Which wasn't quite true, right?'

'I have no idea as to most of the safe's contents. There was one item, however, which I did know about and failed to inform them of.'

'Why did you do that, Herr Six?'

'Because I would prefer that they didn't know.'

'And me?'

'The item in question affords you with an excellent chance of tracking down the murderer ahead of the police.'

'And what then?' I hoped he wasn't planning some private little execution, because I didn't feel up to wrestling with my conscience, especially when there was a lot of money involved.

'Before delivering the murderer into the hands of the authorities you will recover my property. On no account must they get their hands on it.'

'What exactly are we talking about?'

Six folded his hands thoughtfully, then unfolded them again, and then swathed himself with his arms like a party-girl's wrap. He looked quizzically at me.

'Confidentially, of course,' I growled.

'Jewels,' he said. 'You see, Herr Günther, my daughter died intestate, and without a will all her property goes to her husband's estate. Paul did make a will, leaving everything to the Reich.' He shook his head. 'Can you believe such stupidity, Herr Günther? He left everything. Everything. One can hardly credit it.'

'He was a patriot then.'

Six failed to perceive the irony in my remark. He snorted with derision. 'My dear Herr Günther, he was a National Socialist. Those people think that they are the first people ever to love the Fatherland.' He smiled grimly. 'I love my country. And there is nobody who gives more than I do. But I simply cannot stand the thought that the Reich is to be enriched even further at my expense. Do you understand me?'

'I think so.'

'Not only that, but the jewels were her mother's, so quite apart from their intrinsic value, which I can tell you is considerable, they are also of some sentimental account.'

'How much are they worth?'

Schemm stirred himself to offer up some facts and figures.

'I think I can be of some assistance here, Herr Six,' he said, delving into a briefcase that lay by his feet, and producing a buff-coloured file which he laid on the rug between the two sofas. 'I have here the last insurance valuations, as well as some photographs.' He lifted a sheet of paper and read off the bottom-line figure with no more expression than if it had been the amount of his monthly newspaper account. 'Seven hundred and fifty thousand Reichsmarks.' I let out an involuntary whistle. Schemm winced at that, and handed me some photographs. I had seen bigger stones, but only in photographs of the pyramids. Six took over with a description of their history.

'In 1925 the world jewel market was flooded with gems sold by Russian exiles or put on sale by the Bolsheviks, who had discovered a treasure trove walled up in the palace of Prince Youssoupov, husband to the niece of the Tsar. I acquired several pieces in Switzerland that same year: a brooch, a bracelet and, most precious of all, a diamond collet necklace consisting of twenty brilliants. It was made by Cartier and weighs over one hundred carats. It goes without saying, Herr Günther, that it will not be easy to dispose of such a piece.'

'No, indeed.' It might seem cynical of me, but the sentimental value of the jewels was now looking quite insignificant beside their monetary value. 'Tell me about the safe.'

'I paid for it,' said Six. 'Just as I paid for the house. Paul didn't have a great deal of money. When Grete's mother died I gave her the jewels, and at the same time I had a safe installed so that she could keep them there when they weren't in the vault at the bank.'

'So she had been wearing them quite recently?'

'Yes. She accompanied my wife and myself to a ball just a few nights before she was killed.'

'What kind of safe was it?'

'A Stockinger. Wall-mounted, combination lock.'

'And who knew the combination?'

'My daughter, and Paul, of course. They had no secrets from

each other, and I believe he kept certain papers to do with his work there.'

'Nobody else?'

'No. Not even me.'

'Do you know how the safe was opened, if there were any explosives used?'

'I believe there were no explosives used.'

'A nutcracker then.'

'How's that?'

'A professional safe-cracker. Mind you, it would have to be someone very good to puzzle it.' Six leaned forward on the sofa.

'Perhaps,' he said, 'the thief forced Grete or Paul to open it, then ordered them back to bed, where he shot them both. And afterwards he set fire to the house in order to cover his tracks — throw the police off the scent.'

'Yes, that's possible,' I admitted. I rubbed a perfectly circular area of smooth skin on my otherwise stubbly face: it's where a mosquito bit me when I was in Turkey, and ever since then I've never had to shave it. But quite often I find myself rubbing it when I feel uneasy about something. And if there's one thing guaranteed to make me feel uneasy, it's a client playing detective. I didn't rule out what he was suggesting might have happened, but it was my turn to play the expert: 'Possible, but messy,' I said. 'I can't think of a better way of raising the alarm than making your own private Reichstag. Playing Van der Lubbe and torching the place doesn't sound like the sort of thing a professional thief would do, but then neither does murder.' There were a lot of holes in that of course: I had no idea that it was a professional; not only that, but in my experience it's rare that a professional job also involves murder. I just wanted to hear my own voice for a change.

'Who would have known she had jewels in the safe?' I asked.

'Me,' said Six. 'Grete wouldn't have told anyone. I don't know if Paul had.'

'And did either of them have any enemies?'

'I can't answer for Paul,' he said, 'but I'm sure that Grete didn't have an enemy in the world.' While I could accept the possibility that Daddy's little girl always brushed her teeth and said her prayers at night, I found it hard to ignore how vague Six was about his son-in-law. That made the second time he was uncertain about what Paul would have done.

'What about you?' I said. 'A rich and powerful man like yourself must have his fair share of enemies.' He nodded. 'Is there anyone who might hate you bad enough to want to get back at you through your daughter?'

He re-kindled his Black Wisdom, puffed at it and then held it away from him between the tips of his fingers. 'Enemies are the inevitable corollary of great wealth, Herr Günther,' he told me. 'But these are business rivals I'm talking about, not gangsters. I don't think any of them would be capable of something as cold-blooded as this.' He stood up and went to attend to the fire. With a large brass poker he dealt vigorously with the log that was threatening to topple out of the grate. While Six was off-guard I jabbed him with one about the son-in-law.

'Did you and your daughter's husband get on?'

He twisted round to look at me, poker still in hand, and face slightly flushed. It was all the answer that I needed, but still he tried to throw some sand in my eyes. 'Why ever do you ask such a question?' he demanded.

'Really, Herr Günther,' said Schemm, affecting shock at my asking such an insensitive question.

'We had our differences of opinion,' said Six. 'But what man can be expected sometimes not to agree with his son-in-law?' He put down the poker. I kept quiet for a minute. Eventually he said: 'Now then, with regard to the conduct of your investigations, I would prefer it if you would confine your activities specifically to searching for the jewels. I don't care for the idea of you snooping around in the affairs of my family. I'll pay your fees, whatever they are –'

'Seventy marks a day, plus expenses,' I lied, hoping that Schemm hadn't checked it out.

'What is more, the Germania Life Assurance and Germania Insurance Companies will pay you a recovery fee of five per cent. Is that agreeable to you, Herr Günther?' Mentally I calculated the figure to be 37,500. With that sort of money I was set. I found myself nodding, although I didn't care for the ground rules he was laying down: but then for nearly 40,000 it was his game.

'But I warn you, I'm not a patient man,' he said. 'I want results, and I want them quickly. I have written out a cheque for your immediate requirements.' He nodded to his stooge, who handed me a cheque. It was for 1,000 marks and made out to cash at the Privat Kommerz Bank. Schemm dug into his briefcase again and handed me a letter on the Germania Life Assurance Company's notepaper.

'This states that you have been retained by our company to investigate the fire, pending a claim by the estate. The house was insured by us. If you have any problems you should contact me. On no account are you to bother Herr Six, or to mention his name. Here is a file containing any background information you may need.'

'You seem to have thought of everything,' I said pointedly.

Six stood up, followed by Schemm, and then, stiffly, by me. 'When will you start your investigations?' he said.

'First thing in the morning.'

'Excellent.' He clapped me on the shoulder. 'Ulrich will drive you home.' Then he walked over to his desk, sat down in his chair and settled down to go through some papers. He didn't pay me any more attention.

When I stood in the modest hall again, waiting for the butler to turn up with Ulrich, I heard another car draw up outside. This one was too loud to be a limousine, and I guessed that it was some kind of sports job. A door slammed, there were footsteps on the gravel and a key scraped in the lock of the front door. Through it came a woman I recognized immediately as the UFA Film Studio star, Ilse Rudel. She was wearing a dark sable coat and an evening dress of blue satin-organza. She looked at me, puzzled, while I just gawped back at her. She was worth it. She had the kind of body I'd only ever dreamed about, in the sort of dream I'd often dreamed of having again. There wasn't much I couldn't imagine it doing, except the ordinary things like work and getting in a man's way.

'Good morning,' I said, but the butler was there with his cat-burglar's steps to take her mind off me and help her out of the sable.

'Farraj, where is my husband?'

'Herr Six is in the library, madam.' My blue eyes popped a good deal at that, and I felt my jaw slacken. That this goddess should be married to the gnome sitting in the study was the sort of thing that bolsters your faith in Money. I watched her walk towards the library door behind me. Frau Six – I couldn't get over it – was tall and blonde and as healthy-looking as her husband's Swiss bank account. There was a sulkiness about her mouth, and my acquaintance with the science of physiognomy told me that she was used to having her own way: in cash. Brilliant clips flashed on her perfect ears, and as she got nearer the air was filled with the scent of 4711 cologne. Just as I thought she was going to ignore me, she glanced in my direction and said coolly: 'Goodnight, whoever you are.' Then the library swallowed her whole before I had a chance to do the same. I rolled my tongue up and tucked it back into my mouth. I looked at my watch. It was 3.30. Ulrich reappeared.

'No wonder he stays up late,' I said, and followed him through the door.

3

The following morning was grey and wet. I woke with a whore's drawers in my mouth, drank a cup of coffee and went through the morning's *Berliner Borsenzeitung*, which was even more difficult to understand than usual, with sentences as long and as hard-to-incomprehensible as a speech from Hess.

Shaved and dressed and carrying my laundry bag, I was at Alexanderplatz, the chief traffic centre of east Berlin, less than an hour later. Approached from Neue Königstrasse, the square is flanked by two great office blocks: Berolina Haus to the right, and Alexander Haus to the left, where I had my office on the fourth floor. I dropped off my laundry at Adler's Wet-Wash Service on the ground floor before going up.

Waiting for the lift, it was hard to ignore the small noticeboard that was situated immediately next to it, to which were pinned an appeal for contributions to the Mother and Child Fund, a Party exhortation to go and see an anti-Semitic film and an inspiring picture of the Führer. This noticeboard was the responsibility of the building's caretaker, Herr Gruber, a shifty little undertaker of a man. Not only is he the block air-defence monitor with police powers (courtesy of Orpo, the regular uniformed police), he is also a Gestapo informer. Long ago I decided that it would be bad for business to fall out with Gruber and so, like all the other residents of Alexander Haus, I gave him three marks a week, which is supposed to cover my contributions to whichever new money-making scheme the DAF, the German Labour Front, has dreamed up.

I cursed the lift's lack of speed as I saw Gruber's door open just enough to permit his peppered-mackerel of a face to peer down the corridor.

'Ah, Herr Günther, it's you,' he said, coming out of his office. He edged towards me like a crab with a bad case of corns.

'Good morning, Herr Gruber,' I said, avoiding his face. There was something about it that always reminded me of Max Schreck's screen portrayal of Nosferatu, an effect that was enhanced by the rodent-like washing movements of his skeletal hands.

'There was a young lady who came for you,' he said. 'I sent her up. I do hope that was convenient, Herr Günther.'

'Yes –'

'If she's still there, that is,' he said. 'That was at least half an hour ago. Only I knew Fräulein Lehmann is no longer working for you, so I had to say that there was no telling when you would turn up, you keeping such irregular hours.' To my relief the lift arrived and I drew open the door and stepped in.

'Thank you, Herr Gruber,' I said, and shut the door.

'Heil Hitler,' he said. The lift started to rise up the shaft. I called: 'Heil Hitler.' You don't miss the Hitler Salute with someone like Gruber. It's not worth the trouble. But one day I'm going to have to beat the crap out of that weasel, just for the sheer pleasure of it.

I share the fourth floor with a 'German' dentist, a 'German' insurance broker, and a 'German' employment agency, the latter having provided me with the temporary secretary who I now presumed was the woman seated in my waiting room. Coming out of the lift I hoped that she wasn't battle-scarred ugly. I didn't suppose for a minute that I was going to get a juicy one, but then I wasn't about to settle for any cobra either. I opened the door.

'Herr Günther?' She stood up, and I gave her the once-over: well, she wasn't as young as Gruber had led me to believe (I guessed her to be about forty-five) but not bad, I thought. A bit warm and cosy maybe (she had a substantial backside), but I happen to prefer them like that. Her hair was red with a touch of grey at the sides and on the crown, and tied back in a knot. She wore a suit of plain grey cloth, a white high-necked blouse and a black hat with a Breton brim turned up all around the head.

'Good morning,' I said, as affably as I could manage on top of the mewling tomcat that was my hangover. 'You must be my temporary secretary.' Lucky to get a woman at all, and this one looked half-reasonable.

'Frau Protze,' she declared, and shook my hand. 'I'm a widow.'

'Sorry,' I said, unlocking the door to my office. 'What part of Bavaria are you from?' The accent was unmistakable.

'Regensburg.'

'That's a nice town.'

'You must have found buried treasure there.' Witty too, I thought; that was good: she'd need a sense of humour to work for me.

I told her all about my business. She said it all sounded very exciting. I showed her into the adjoining cubicle where she was to sit on that backside.

'Actually, it's not so bad if you leave the door to the waiting room open,' I explained. Then I showed her the washroom along the corridor and apologized for the shards of soap and the dirty towels. 'I pay seventy-five marks a month and I get a tip like this,' I said. 'Damn it, I'm going to complain to that son-of-a-bitch of a landlord.' But even as I said it I knew I never would.

Back in my office I flipped open my diary and saw that the day's only appointment was Frau Heine, at eleven o'clock.

'I've an appointment in twenty minutes,' I said. 'Woman wants to know if I've managed to trace her missing son. He's a Jewish U-Boat.'

'A what?'

'A Jew in hiding.'

'What did he do that he has to hide?' she said.

'You mean apart from being a Jew?' I said. Already I could see that she had led quite a sheltered life, even for a Regensburger, and it seemed a shame to expose the poor woman to the potentially distressing sight of her country's evil-smelling arse. Still, she was all grown-up now, and I didn't have the time to worry about it.

'He just helped an old man who was being beaten up by some thugs. He killed one of them.'

'But surely if he was helping the old man –'

'Ah, but the old man was Jewish,' I explained. 'And the two thugs belonged to the SA. Strange how that changes everything, isn't it? His mother asked me to find out if he was still alive and still at liberty. You see, when a man is arrested and beheaded or sent to a KZ, the authorities don't always bother to inform his family. There are a lot of MPs – missing persons – from Jewish families these days. Trying to find them is a large part of my business.' Frau Protze looked worried.

'You help Jews?' she said.

'Don't worry,' I said. 'It's perfectly legal. And their money is as good as anyone's.'

'I suppose so.'

'Listen, Frau Protze,' I said. 'Jews, gypsies, Red Indians, it's all the same to me. I've got no reason to like them, but I don't have any reason to hate them either. When he walks through that door, a Jew gets the same deal as anyone else. Same as if he were the Kaiser's cousin. But it doesn't mean I'm dedicated to their welfare. Business is business.'

'Certainly,' said Frau Protze, colouring a little. 'I hope you don't think I have anything against the Jews.'

'Of course not,' I said. But of course that is what everybody says. Even Hitler.

'Good God,' I said, when the U-Boat's mother had left my office. 'That's what a satisfied customer looks like.' The thought depressed me so much that I decided to get out for a while.

At Loeser & Wolff I bought a packet of Murattis, after which I cashed Six's cheque. I paid half of it into my own account; and I treated myself to an expensive silk dressing-gown at Wertheim's just for being lucky enough to land as sweet an earner as Six.

Then I walked south-west, past the railway station from which a train now rumbled forth heading towards the Jannowitz Bridge, to the corner of Königstrasse where I had left my car.

Lichterfelde-Ost is a prosperous residential district in south-west Berlin much favoured by senior civil servants and members of the armed forces. Ordinarily it would have been way out of a young couple's price league, but then most young couples don't have a multi-millionaire like Hermann Six for a father.

Ferdinandstrasse ran south from the railway line. There was a policeman, a young Anwärter in the Orpo, standing guard outside Number 16, which was missing most of the roof and all of its windows. The bungalow's blackened timbers and brickwork told the story eloquently enough. I parked the Hanomag and walked up to the garden gate, where I flipped out my identification for the young bull, a spotty-looking youth of about twenty. He looked at it carefully, naively, and said redundantly: 'A private investigator, eh?'

'S'right. I've been retained by the insurance company to investigate the fire.' I lit a cigarette and watched the match suggestively as it burned towards my fingertips. He nodded, but his face appeared troubled. It cleared all of a sudden as he recognized me.

'Hey, didn't you use to be in Kripo up at the Alex?' I nodded, my nostrils trailing smoke like a factory chimney. 'Yes, I thought I recognized the name – Bernhard Günther. You caught Gormann, the Strangler, didn't you? I remember reading about it in the newspapers. You were famous.' I shrugged modestly. But he was right. When I caught Gormann I was famous for a while. I was a good bull in those days.

The young Anwärter took off his shako and scratched the top of his squarish head. 'Well, well,' he said; and then: 'I'm going to join Kripo. That is, if they'll have me.'

'You seem a bright enough fellow. You should do all right.'

'Thanks,' he said. 'Hey, how about a tip?'

'Try Scharhorn in the three o'clock at the Hoppegarten.' I shrugged. 'Hell, I don't know. What's your name, young fellow?'

'Eckhart,' he said. 'Wilhelm Eckhart.'

'So, Wilhelm, tell me about the fire. First of all, who's the pathologist on the case?'

'Some fellow from the Alex. I think he was called Upmann or Illmann.'

'An old man with a small chin-beard and rimless glasses?' He nodded. 'That's Illmann. When was he here?'

'Day before yesterday. Him and Kriminalkommissar Jost.'

'Jost? It's not like him to get his flippers dirty. I'd have thought it would take more than just the murder of a millionaire's daughter to get him off his fat arse.' I threw my cigarette away, in the opposite direction from the gutted house: there didn't seem any point in tempting fate.

'I heard it was arson,' I said. 'Is that true, Wilhelm?'

'Just smell the air,' he said.

I inhaled deeply, and shook my head.

'Don't you smell the petrol?'

'No. Berlin always smells like this.'

'Maybe I've just been standing here a long time. Well, they found a petrol can in the garden, so I guess that seals it.'

'Look, Wilhelm, would you mind if I just took a quick look around? It would save me having to fill out some forms. They'll have to let me have a look sooner or later.'

'Go right ahead, Herr Günther,' he said, opening the front gate. 'Not that there's much to see. They took bags of stuff away with them. I doubt there's anything that would be of interest to you. I don't even know why I'm still here.'

'I expect it's to watch out in case the murderer returns to the scene of the crime,' I said tantalizingly.

'Lord, do you think he might?' breathed the boy.

I pursed my lips. 'Who knows?' I said, although personally I had never heard of such a thing. 'I'll take a look anyway, and thanks, I appreciate it.'

'Don't mention it.'

He was right. There wasn't much to see. The man with the matches had done a proper job. I looked in at the front door, but there was so much debris I couldn't see anywhere for me to step. Round to the side I found a window that gave onto another room where the going wasn't so difficult underfoot. Hoping that I might at least find the safe, I climbed inside. Not that I needed to be there at all. I just wanted to form a picture inside my head. I work better that way: I've got a mind like a comic book. So I wasn't too disappointed when I found that the police had already taken the safe away, and that all that was left was a gaping hole in the wall. There was always Illmann, I told myself.

Back at the gate I found Wilhelm trying to comfort an older woman of about sixty, whose face was stained with tears.

'The cleaning woman,' he explained. 'She turned up just now. Apparently she's been away on holiday and hadn't heard about the fire. Poor old soul's had a bit of a shock.' He asked her where she lived.

'Neuenburger Strasse,' she sniffed. 'I'm all right now, thank you, young man.' From her coat pocket she produced a small lace handkerchief which seemed as improbable in her large, peasant hands as an antimacassar in those of Max Schmeling, the boxer, and quite inadequate for the task which lay before it: she blew her pickled-walnut of a nose with the sort of ferocity and volume that made me want to hold my hat on my head. Then she wiped her big, broad face with the soggy remnant. Smelling some information about the Pfarr household, I offered the old pork chop a lift home in my car.

'It's on the way,' I said.

'I wouldn't want to put you to any trouble.'

'It's no trouble at all,' I insisted.

'Well, if you are sure, that would be very kind of you. I have had a bit of a shock.' She picked up the box that lay at her feet, each one of which bulged over the top of its well-polished black walking shoe like a butcher's thumb in a thimble. Her name was Frau Schmidt.

'You're a good sort, Herr Günther,' said Wilhelm.

'Nonsense,' I said, and so it was. There was no telling what information I might glean from the old woman about her late employers. I took the box from her hands. 'Let me help you with that,' I said. It was a suit-box, from Stechbarth's, the official tailor to the services, and I had the idea that she might have been bringing it for the Pfarrs. I nodded silently at Wilhelm, and led the way to the car.

'Neuenburger Strasse,' I repeated as we drove off. 'That's off Lindenstrasse, isn't it?' She confirmed that it was, gave me some directions and was silent for a moment. Then she started weeping again.

'What a terrible tragedy,' she sobbed.

'Yes, yes, it's most unfortunate.'

I wondered how much Wilhelm had told her. The less the better, I thought, reasoning that the less shocked she was, at least at this stage, the more I would get out of her.

'Are you a policeman?' she asked.

'I'm investigating the fire,' I said evasively.

'I'm sure you must be too busy to drive an old woman like me across Berlin. Why don't you drop me on the other side of the bridge and I'll walk the rest. I'm all right now, really I am.'

'It's no trouble. Anyway, I'd quite like to talk to you about the Pfarrs – that is, if it wouldn't upset you.' We crossed the Landwehr Canal and came onto Belle-Alliance Platz, in the centre of which rises the great Column of Peace. 'You see, there will have to be an inquest, and it would help me if I knew as much about them as possible.'

'Yes, well I don't mind, if you think I can be of assistance,' she said.

When we got to Neuenburger Strasse, I parked the car and followed the old woman up to the second floor of an apartment building that was several storeys high.

Frau Schmidt's apartment was typical of the older generation of people in this city. The furniture was solid and elaborate – Berliners spend a lot of money on their tables and chairs – and there was a big porcelain-tiled stove in the living room. A copy of an engraving by Dürer, which was as common in the Berliner's home as an aquarium in a doctor's waiting room, hung dully above a dark red Biedermeier sideboard on which were placed various photographs (including one of our beloved Führer) and a little silk swastika mounted in a large bronze frame. There was also a drinks tray, from which I took a bottle of schnaps and poured a small glassful.

'You'll feel better after you've drunk this,' I said, handing her the glass, and wondering whether or not I dared take the liberty of pouring myself one too. Enviously, I watched her knock it back in one. Smacking her fat lips she sat down on a brocaded chair by the window.

'Feel up to answering a few questions?'

She nodded. 'What do you want to know?'

'Well for a start, how long had you known Herr and Frau Pfarr?'

'Hmm, let's see now.' A silent movie of uncertainty flickered on the woman's face. The voice emptied slowly out of the Boris Karloff mouth, with its slightly protruding teeth, like grit from a bucket. 'It must be a year, I suppose.' She stood up again and removed her coat, revealing a dingy, floral-patterned smock. Then she coughed for several seconds, tapping herself on the chest as she did so.

All this time I stood squarely in the middle of the room, my hat on the back of my head and my hands in my pockets. I asked her what sort of couple the Pfarrs had been.

'I mean, were they happy? Argumentative?' She nodded to both of these suggestions.

'When I first went to work there, they were very much in love,' she said. 'But it wasn't long after that that she lost her job as a schoolteacher. Quite cut up about it, she was. And before long they were arguing. Not that he was there very often when I was. But when he was, then more often than not they'd have words, and I don't mean squabbles, like most couples. No, they had loud, angry arguments, almost as if they hated each other, and a couple of times I found her crying in her room afterwards. Well, I really don't know what it was they had to be unhappy about. They had a lovely home – it was a pleasure to clean it, so it was. Mind you, they weren't flashy. I never once saw her spending lots of money on things. She had lots of nice clothes, but nothing showy.'

'Any jewellery?'

'I believe she had some jewellery, but I can't say as I remember her wearing it, but then I was only there in the daytime. On the other hand, there was an occasion when I moved his jacket and some earrings fell onto the floor, and they weren't the sort of earrings that she would have worn.'

'How do you mean?'

'These were for pierced ears, and Frau Pfarr only ever wore clips. So I drew my own conclusions, but said nothing. It was none of my business what he got up to. But I reckon she had her suspicions. She wasn't a stupid woman. Far from it. I believe that's what drove her to drink as much as she did.'

'Did she drink?'

'Like a sponge.'

'What about him? He worked at the Ministry of the Interior, didn't he?'

She shrugged. 'It was some government place, but I couldn't tell you what it was called. He was something to do with the law – he had a certificate on the wall of his study. All the same, he was very quiet about his work. And very careful not to leave papers lying around so that I might see them. Not that I would have read them, mind. But he didn't take the chance.'

'Did he work at home much?'

'Sometimes. And I know he used to spend time at that big office building on Bülowplatz – you know, the one that used to be the headquarters for them Bolsheviks.'

'You mean the DAF building, the headquarters of the German Labour Front. That's what it is now that the Kozis have been thrown out of it.'

'That's right. Now and again Herr Pfarr would give me a lift there, you see. My sister lives in Brunnenstrasse and normally I'd catch a Number 99 to Rosenthaler Platz after work. Now and then Herr Pfarr was kind enough to run me as far as Bülowplatz, where I'd see him go in the DAF building.'

'You saw them last – when?'

'It's two weeks yesterday. I've been on holiday, see. A Strength Through Joy trip to Rugen Island. I saw her, but not him.'

'How was she?'

'She seemed quite happy for a change. Not only that, but she didn't have a drink in her hand when she spoke to me. She told me that she was planning a little holiday to the spas. She often went there. I think she got dried out.'

'I see. And so this morning you went to Ferdinandstrasse via the tailors, is that correct, Frau Schmidt?'

'Yes, that's right. I often did little errands for Herr Pfarr. He was usually too busy to get to the shops, and so he'd pay me to get things for him. Before I went on holiday there was a note asking me to drop his suit off at his tailors and that they knew all about it.'

'His suit, you say.'

'Well, yes, I think so.' I picked up the box.

'Mind if I take a look?'

'I don't see why not. He's dead after all, isn't he?'

Even before I had removed the lid I had a pretty good idea of what was in the box. I wasn't wrong. There was no mistaking the midnight black that echoed the old élitist cavalry regiments of the Kaiser's army, the Wagnerian double-lightning flash on the right collar-patch and the Roman-style eagle and swastika on the left sleeve. The three pips on the left collar-patch denoted the wearer of the uniform as a captain, or whatever the fancy rank that captains were called in the SS was. There was a piece of paper pinned to the right sleeve. It was an invoice from Stechbarth's, addressed to Hauptsturmführer Pfarr, for twenty-five marks. I whistled.

'So Paul Pfarr was a black angel.'

'I'd never have believed it,' said Frau Schmidt.

'You mean you never saw him wearing this?'

She shook her head. 'I never even saw it hanging in his wardrobe.'

'Is that so.' I wasn't sure whether I believed her or not, but I could think of no reason why she should lie about it. It was not uncommon for lawyers — German lawyers, working for the Reich — to be in the SS: I imagined Pfarr wearing his uniform on ceremonial occasions only.

It was Frau Schmidt's turn to look puzzled. 'I meant to ask you how the fire started.'

I thought for a minute and decided to let her have it without any of the protective padding, in the hope that the shock would stop her asking some awkward questions that I couldn't answer.

'It was arson,' I said quietly. 'They were both murdered.' Her jaw dropped like a cat-flap, and her eyes moistened again, as if she had stepped into a draught.

'Good God,' she gasped. 'How terrible. Whoever could do such a thing?'

'That's a good question,' I said. 'Do you know if either of them had any enemies?' She sighed deeply and then shook her head. 'Did you ever overhear either of them arguing with someone other than each other? On the telephone, perhaps? Somebody at the door? Anything.' She continued to shake her head.

'Wait a minute, though,' she said slowly. 'Yes, there was one occasion, several months ago. I heard Herr Pfarr arguing with another man in his study. It was pretty heated and, I can tell you, some of the language they used was not fit to be heard by decent folk. They were arguing about politics. At least I think it was politics. Herr Six was saying some terrible things about the Führer which –'

'Did you say Herr Six?'

'Yes,' she said. 'He was the other man. After a while he came storming out of the study and through the front door with a face like pig's liver. Nearly knocked me over he did.'

'Can you remember what else was said?'

'Only that each accused the other of trying to ruin him.'

'Where was Frau Pfarr when all this happened?'

'She was away, on one of her trips, I think.'

'Thank you,' I said. 'You've been most helpful. And now I must be getting back to Alexanderplatz.' I turned towards the door.

'Excuse me,' said Frau Schmidt. She pointed to the tailor's box. 'What shall I do with Herr Pfarr's uniform?'

'Mail it,' I said, putting a couple of marks on the table. 'To Reichsführer Himmler, Prinz Albrecht Strasse, Number 9.'

4

Simeonstrasse is only a couple of streets away from Neuenburger Strasse, but where the windows of the buildings in the latter are lacking paint, in Simeonstrasse they are lacking glass. Calling it a poor area is a bit like saying that Joey Goebbels has a problem finding his size in shoes.

Tenement buildings five- and six-storeys high closed in on a narrow crocodile's back of deep cobblestones like two granite cliffs, linked only by the rope-bridges of washing. Sullen youths, each one of them with a roll-up hanging in ashes from his thin lips like a trail of shit from a bowl-bored goldfish, buttressed the ragged corners of gloomy alleyways, staring blankly at the colony of snot-nosed children who hopped and skipped along the pavements. The children played noisily, oblivious to the presence of these older ones and taking no notice of the crudely daubed swastikas, hammers and sickles and general obscenities that marked the street walls and which were their elders' dividing dogmas. Below the level of the rubbish-strewn streets and under the shadow of the sun-eclipsing edifices which enclosed them were the cellars that contained the small shops and offices that served the area.

Not that it needs much in the way of service. There is no money in an area like this, and for most of these concerns business is about as brisk as a set of oak floorboards in a Lutheran church hall.

It was into one of these small shops, a pawnbroker, that I went, ignoring the large Star of David daubed on the wooden shutters that protected the shop window from breakage. A bell rang as I opened and shut the door. Doubly deprived of daylight, the shop's only source of illumination was an oil lamp hanging from the low ceiling, and the general effect was that of the inside of an old sailing ship. I browsed around, waiting for Weizmann, the proprietor, to appear from the back of the shop.

There was an old Pickelhaube helmet, a stuffed marmot, in a glass case, that looked as if it had perished of anthrax, and an old Siemens vacuum-cleaner; there were several cases full of military medals – mostly second-class Iron Crosses like mine own, twenty odd volumes of Kohler's *Naval Calendar*, full of ships long since sunk or sent to the breaker's yard, a Blaupunkt radio, a chipped bust of Bismarck and an old Leica. I was inspecting the case of medals when a smell of tobacco, and Weizmann's familiar cough, announced his present appearance.

'You should look after yourself, Weizmann.'

'And what would I do with a long life?' The threat of Weizmann's wheezing cough was ever present in his speech. It lay in wait to trip him like a sleeping halberdier. Sometimes he managed to catch himself; but this time he fell into a spasm of coughing that sounded hardly human at all, more like someone trying to start a car with an almost flat battery, and as usual it seemed to afford him no relief whatsoever. Nor did it require him to remove the pipe from his tobacco-pouch of a mouth.

'You should try inhaling a little bit of air now and then,' I told him. 'Or at least something you haven't first set on fire.'

'Air,' he said. 'It goes straight to my head. Anyway, I'm training myself to do without it: there's no telling when they'll ban Jews from breathing oxygen.' He lifted the counter. 'Come into the back room, my friend, and tell me what service I can do for you.' I followed him round the counter, past an empty bookcase.

'Is business picking up then?' I said. He turned to look at me. 'What happened to all the books?' Weizmann shook his head sadly.

'Unfortunately, I had to remove them. The Nuremberg Laws –' he said with a scornful laugh, '– they forbid a Jew to sell books. Even secondhand ones.' He turned and passed on through to the back room. 'These days I believe in the law like I believe in Horst Wessel's heroism.'

'Horst Wessel?' I said. 'Never heard of him.'

Weizmann smiled and pointed at an old Jacquard sofa with the stem of his reeking pipe. 'Sit down, Bernie, and let me fix us a drink.'

'Well, what do you know? They still let Jews drink booze. I was almost feeling sorry for you back there when you told me about those books. Things are never as bad as they seem, just as long as there's a drink about.'

'That's the truth, my friend.' He opened a corner cabinet, found the bottle of schnaps and poured it carefully but generously. Handing me my glass he said, 'I'll tell you something. If it wasn't for all the people who drink, this country really would be in a hell of a state.' He raised his glass. 'Let us wish for more drunks and the frustration of an efficiently run National Socialist Germany.'

'To more drunks,' I said, watching him drink it, almost too gratefully. He had a shrewd face, with a mouth that wore a wry smile, even with the chimneystack. A large, fleshy nose separated eyes that were rather too closely set together, and supported a pair of thick, rimless glasses. The still-dark hair was brushed neatly to the right of a high forehead. Wearing his well-pressed blue pin-striped suit, Weizmann looked not unlike Ernst Lubitsch, the comic actor turned film director. He sat down at an old rolltop and turned sideways to face me.

'So what can I do for you?'

I showed him the photograph of Six's necklace. He wheezed a little as he looked at it, and then coughed his way into a remark.

'If it's real –' He smiled and nodded his head from side to side. 'Is it real? Of course it's real, or why else would you be showing me such a nice photograph. Well then, it looks like a very fine piece indeed.'

'It's been stolen,' I said.

'Bernie, with you sitting there I didn't think it was stuck up a tree waiting for the fire service.' He shrugged. 'But, such a fine-looking necklace – what can I tell you about it that you don't already know?'

'Come on, Weizmann. Until you got caught thieving you were one of Friedlaender's best jewellers.'

'Ah, you put it so delicately.'

'After twenty years in the business you know bells like you know your own waistcoat pocket.'

'Twenty-two years,' he said quietly, and poured us both another glass. 'Very well. Ask your questions, Bernie, and we shall see what we shall see.'

'How would someone go about getting rid of it?'

'You mean some other way than just dropping it in the Land-wehr Canal? For money? It would depend.'

'On what?' I said patiently.

'On whether the person in possession was Jewish or Gentile.'

'Come on, Weizmann,' I said. 'You don't have to keep wringing the yarmulke for my benefit.'

'No, seriously, Bernie. Right now the market for gems is at rock bottom. There are lots of Jews leaving Germany who, to fund their emigration, must sell the family jewels. At least, those who are lucky enough to have any to sell. And, as you might expect, they get the lowest prices. A Gentile could afford to wait for the market to become more buoyant. A Jew could not.' Coughing in small explosive bursts, he took another, longer look at Six's photograph and gave a chesty little shrug.

'Way out of my league, I can tell you that much. Sure, I buy some small stuff. But nothing big enough to interest the boys from the Alex. Like you, they know about me, Bernie. There's my time in the cement for a start. If I was to step badly out of line they'd have me in a KZ quicker than the drawers off a Kit-Kat showgirl.' Wheezing like a leaky old harmonium, Weizmann grinned and handed the photograph back to me.

'Amsterdam would be the best place to sell it,' he said. 'If you could get it out of Germany, that is. German customs officers are a smuggler's nightmare. Not that there aren't plenty of people in Berlin who would buy it.'

'Like who, for instance?'

'The two-tray boys – one tray on top and one under the counter – they might be interested. Like Peter Neumaier. He's got a nice little shop on Schlüterstrasse, specializing in antique jewellery.

This might be his sort of thing. I've heard he's got plenty of flea and can pay it in whatever currency you like. Yes, I'd have thought he'd certainly be worth checking out.' He wrote the name down on a piece of paper. 'Then we have Werner Seldte. He may appear to be a bit Potsdam, but he's not above buying some hot bells.' Potsdam was a word of faint opprobrium for people who, like the antiquated pro-Royalists of that town, were smug, hypocritical and hopelessly dated in both intellectual and social ideas. 'Frankly, he's got fewer scruples than a backstreet angelmaker. His shop is on Budapester Strasse or Ebertstrasse or Hermann Goering Strasse or whatever the hell the Party calls it now.

'Then there are the dealers, the diamond merchants who buy and sell from classy offices where a browser for an engagement ring is about as popular as a pork chop in a rabbi's coat pocket. These are the sort of people who do most of their business on the gabbler.' He wrote down some more names. 'This one, Laser Oppenheimer, he's a Jew. That's just to show that I'm fair and that I've got nothing against Gentiles. Oppenheimer has an office on Joachimsthaler Strasse. Anyway, the last I heard of him he was still in business.

'There's Gert Jeschonnek. New to Berlin. Used to be based in Munich. From what I've heard, he's the worst kind of March Violet – you know, climbing on board the Party wagon and riding it to make a quick profit. He's got a very smart set of offices in that steel monstrosity on Potsdamer Platz. What's it called –?'

'Columbus Haus,' I said.

'That's it. Columbus Haus. They say that Hitler doesn't much care for modern architecture, Bernie. Do you know what that means?' Weizmann gave a little chuckle. 'It means that he and I have something in common.'

'Is there anyone else?'

'Maybe. I don't know. It's possible.'

'Who?'

'Our illustrious Prime Minister.'

'Goering? Buying hot bells? Are you serious?'

'Oh yes,' he said firmly. 'That man has a passion for owning expensive things. And he's not always as fussy as he could be regarding how he gets hold of them. Jewels are one thing I know he has a weakness for. When I was at Friedlaender's he used to come into the shop quite often. He was poor in those days – at least, too poor to buy much. But you could see he would have bought a great deal if he had been able to.'

'Jesus Christ, Weizmann,' I said. 'Can you imagine it? Me dropping in at Karinhall and saying, "Excuse me, Herr Prime Minister, but you wouldn't happen to know anything about a valuable diamond necklace that some coat has clawed from a Ferdinandstrasse residence in the past few days? I trust you would have no objections to me taking a look down your wife Emmy's dress and seeing if she's got them hidden somewhere between the exhibits?"'

'You'd have the devil's own job to find anything down there,' wheezed Weizmann excitedly. 'That fat sow is almost as big as he is. I'll bet she could breastfeed the entire Hitler Youth and still have milk enough left for Hermann's breakfast.' He began a fit of coughing which would have carried off another man. I waited until it had found a lower gear, and then produced a fifty. He waved it away.

'What did I tell you?'

'Let me buy something, then.'

'What's the matter? Are you running out of crap all of a sudden?'

'No, but –'

'Wait, though,' he said. 'There is something you might like to buy. A finger lifted it at a big parade on Unter den Linden.' He got up and went into the small kitchen behind the office. When he came back he was carrying a packet of Persil.

'Thanks,' I said, 'but I send my stuff to the laundry.'

'No, no, no,' he said, pushing his hand into the powder. 'I hid it in here just in case I had any unwelcome visitors. Ah, here we are.' He withdrew a small, flat, silvery object from the packet, and polished it on his lapel before laying it flat on my palm. It was an oval-shaped disc about the size of a matchbox. On one side was the ubiquitous German eagle clutching the laurel crown that encircled the swastika; and on the other were the words Secret State Police, and a serial number. At the top was a small hole by which the bearer of the badge could attach it to the inside of his jacket. It was a Gestapo warrant-disc.

'That ought to open a few doors for you, Bernie.'

'You're not joking,' I said. 'Christ, if they caught you with this –'

'Yes, I know. It would save you a great deal of slip money, don't you think? So if you want it, I'll ask fifty for it.'

'Fair enough,' I said, although I wasn't sure about carrying it myself. What he said was true: it would save on bribes; but if I was caught using it I'd be on the first train to Sachsenhausen. I paid him the fifty. 'A bull without his beer-token. God, I'd like to have seen the bastard's face. That's like a horn-player without a mouthpiece.' I stood up to go.

'Thanks for the information,' I said. 'And in case you didn't know, it's summertime up on the surface.'

'Yes, I noticed that the rain was a little warmer than usual. At least a rotten summer is one thing they can't blame on the Jews.'

'Don't you believe it,' I said.

5

There was chaos back at Alexanderplatz, where a tram had derailed. The clock in the tall, red-brick tower of St George's was striking three o'clock, reminding me that I hadn't eaten anything since a bowl of Quaker Quick Flakes ('For the Youth of the Nation') for breakfast. I went to the Café Stock; it was close by Wertheim's Department Store, and in the shadow of the S-Bahn railway viaduct.

The Café Stock was a modest little restaurant with an even more modest bar in the far corner. Such was the size of the eponymous proprietor's bibulous belly that there was only just room for him to squeeze behind the bar; and as I came through the door it was there that I found him standing, pouring beers and polishing glasses, while his pretty little wife waited on the tables. These tables were often taken by Kripo officers from the Alex, and this had the effect of obliging Stock to play up his commitment to National Socialism. There was a large picture of the Führer on the wall, as well as a printed sign that said, 'Always give the Hitler Salute.'

Stock wasn't always that way, and before March 1933 he had been a bit of a Red. He knew that I knew it, and it always worried him that there were others who would remember it too. So I didn't blame him for the picture and the sign. Everyone in Germany was somebody different before March 1933. And as I'm always saying, 'Who isn't a National Socialist when there's a gun pointed at his head?'

I sat down at an empty table and surveyed the rest of the clientele. A couple of tables away were two bulls from the Queer Squad, the Department for the Suppression of Homosexuality: a bunch of what are little better than blackmailers. At a table next to them, and sitting on his own, was a young Kriminalassistent from the station at Werdersche Market, whose badly pock-marked face

I remembered chiefly for his having once arrested my informer, Neumann, on suspicion of theft.

Frau Stock took my order of pig's knuckle with sauerkraut briskly and without much in the way of pleasantry. A shrewish woman, she knew and disapproved of my paying Stock for small snippets of interesting gossip about what was going on at the Alex. With so many officers coming in and out of the place, he often heard quite a lot. She moved off to the dumb-waiter and shouted my order down the shaft to the kitchen. Stock squeezed out from behind his bar and ambled over. He had a copy of the Party newspaper, the *Völkischer Beobachter*, in his fat hand.

'Hallo, Bernie,' he said. 'Lousy weather we're having, eh?'

'Wet as a poodle, Max,' I said. 'I'll have a beer when you're ready.'

'Coming right up. You want to look at the paper?'

'Anything in it?'

'Mr and Mrs Charles Lindbergh are in Berlin. He's the fellow that flew across the Atlantic.'

'It sounds fascinating, really it does. I suppose the great aviator will be opening a few bomber factories while he's here. Maybe even take a test-flight in a shiny new fighter. Perhaps they want him to pilot one all the way to Spain.'

Stock looked nervously over his shoulder and gestured for me to lower my voice. 'Not so loud, Bernie,' he said, twitching like a rabbit. 'You'll get me shot.' Muttering unhappily, he went off to get my beer.

I glanced at the newspaper he had left on my table. There was a small paragraph about the 'investigation of a fire on Ferdinand-strasse, in which two people are known to have lost their lives', which made no mention of their names, or their relation to my client, or that the police were treating it as a murder investigation. I tossed it contemptuously onto another table. There's more real news on the back of a matchbox than there is in the *Völkischer Beobachter*. Meanwhile, the detectives from the Queer Squad were leaving; and Stock came back with my beer. He held the glass up for my attention before placing it on the table.

'A nice sergeant-major on it, like always,' he said.

'Thanks.' I took a long drink and then wiped some of the sergeant-major off my upper lip with the back of my hand. Frau Stock collected my lunch from the dumb-waiter and brought it over. She gave her husband a look that should have burned a hole in his shirt, but he pretended not to have seen it. Then she went to clear the table that was being vacated by the pockmarked Kriminalassistant. Stock sat down and watched me eat.

After a while I said, 'So what have you heard? Anything?'

'A man's body fished out of the Landwehr.'

'That's about as unusual as a fat railwayman,' I told him. 'The canal is the Gestapo's toilet, you know that. It's got so that if someone disappears in this goddamn city, it's quicker to look for him at the lighterman's office than police headquarters or the city morgue.'

'Yes, but this one had a billiard cue – up his nose. It penetrated the bottom of his brain they reckoned.'

I put down my knife and fork. 'Would you mind laying off the gory details until I've finished my food?' I said.

'Sorry,' said Stock. 'Well, that's all there is really. But they don't normally do that sort of thing, do they, the Gestapo?'

'There's no telling what is considered normal on Prinz Albrecht Strasse. Perhaps he'd been sticking his nose in where it wasn't wanted. They might have wanted to do something poetic.' I wiped my mouth and laid some change on the table which Stock collected up without bothering to count it.

'Funny to think that it used to be the Art School – Gestapo headquarters, I mean.'

'Hilarious. I bet the poor bastards they work over up there go to sleep as happy as little snowmen at the notion.' I stood up and went to the door. 'Nice about the Lindberghs though.'

I walked back to the office. Frau Protze was polishing the glass on the yellowing print of Tilly that hung on the wall of my waiting room, contemplating with some amusement the predicament of the hapless Burgomeister of Rothenburg. As I came through the door the phone started to ring. Frau Protze smiled at me and then stepped smartly into her little cubicle to answer it, leaving me to look afresh at the clean picture. It was a long time since I'd really looked at it. The Burgomeister, having pleaded with Tilly, the sixteenth-century commander of the Imperial German Army, for his town to be spared destruction, was required by his conqueror to drink six litres of beer without drawing breath. As I remembered the story, the Burgomeister had pulled off this prodigious feat of bibbing and the town had been saved. It was, as I had always thought, so characteristically German. And just the sort of sadistic trick some SA thug would play. Nothing really changes that much.

'It's a lady,' Frau Protze called to me. 'She won't give her name, but she insists on speaking to you.'

'Then put her through,' I said, stepping into my office. I picked up the candlestick and the earpiece.

'We met last night,' said the voice. I cursed, thinking it was Carola, the girl from Dagmar's wedding reception. I wanted to forget all about that little episode. But it wasn't Carola. 'Or perhaps I should say this morning. It was pretty late. You were on your way out and I was just coming back after a party. Do you remember?'

'Frau –' I hesitated, still not quite able to believe it.

'Please,' she said, 'less of the Frau. Ilse Rudel, if you don't mind, Herr Günther.'

'I don't mind at all,' I said. 'How could I not remember?'

'You might,' she said. 'You looked very tired.' Her voice was as sweet as a plate of Kaiser's pancakes. 'Hermann and I, we often forget that other people don't keep such late hours.'

'If you'll permit me to say so, you looked pretty good on it.'

'Well, thank you,' she cooed, sounding genuinely flattered. In my experience you can never flatter any woman too much, just as you can never give a dog too many biscuits.

'And how can I be of service?'

'I'd like to speak to you on a matter of some urgency,' she said. 'All the same, I'd rather not talk about it on the telephone.'

'Come and see me here, in my office?'

'I'm afraid I can't. I'm at the studios in Babelsberg right now. Perhaps you would care to come to my apartment this evening?'

'Your apartment?' I said. 'Well, yes, I'd be delighted. Where is it?'

'Badenschestrasse, Number 7. Shall we say nine o'clock?'

'That would be fine.' She hung up. I lit a cigarette and smoked it absently. She was probably working on a film, I thought, and imagined her telephoning me from her dressing room wearing only a robe, having just finished a scene in which she'd been required to swim naked in a mountain lake. That took me quite a few minutes. I've got a good imagination. Then I got to wondering if Six knew about the apartment. I decided he did. You don't get to be as rich as Six was without knowing your wife had her own place. She probably kept it on in order to retain a degree of independence. I guessed that there wasn't much she couldn't have had if she really put her mind to it. Putting her body to it as well probably got her the moon and a couple of galaxies on top. All the same, I didn't think it was likely that Six knew or would have approved of her seeing me. Not after what he had said about me not poking into his family affairs. Whatever it was she wanted to talk to me urgently about was certainly not for the gnome's ears.

I called Müller, the crime reporter on the *Berliner Morgenpost*, which was the only half-decent rag left on the news-stand. Müller was a good reporter gone to seed. There wasn't much call for the old style of crime-reporting; the Ministry of Propaganda had seen to that.

'Look,' I said after the preliminaries, 'I need some biographical information from your library files, as much as you can get and as soon as possible, on Hermann Six.'

'The steel millionaire? Working on his daughter's death, eh, Bernie?'

'I've been retained by the insurance company to investigate the fire.'

'What have you got so far?'

'You could write what I know on a tram ticket.'

'Well,' said Müller, 'that's about the size of the piece we've got on it for tomorrow's edition. The Ministry has told us to lay off it. Just to record the facts, and keep it small.'

'How's that?'

'Six has got some powerful friends, Bernie. His sort of money buys an awful lot of silence.'

'Were you onto anything?'

'I heard it was arson, that's about all. When do you need this stuff?'

'Fifty says tomorrow. And anything you can dig up on the rest of the family.'

'I can always use a little extra money. Be talking to you.'

I hung up and shoved some papers inside some old newspapers and then dumped them in one of the desk drawers that still had a bit of space. After that I doodled on the blotter and then picked up one of the several paperweights that were lying on the desk. I was rolling its cold bulk around my hands when there was a knock at the door. Frau Protze edged into the room.

'I wondered if there was any filing that needed to be done.' I pointed at the untidy stacks of files that lay on the floor behind my desk.

'That's my filing system there,' I said. 'Believe it or not, they are in some sort of order.' She smiled, humouring me no doubt, and nodded attentively as if I was explaining something that would change her life.

'And are they all work in progress?'

I laughed. 'This isn't a lawyer's office,' I said. 'With quite a few of them, I don't know whether they are in progress or not. Investigation isn't a fast business with quick results. You have to have a lot of patience.'

'Yes, I can see that,' she said. There was only one photograph on my desk. She turned it round to get a better look at it. 'She's very beautiful. Your wife?'

'She was. Died on the day of the Kapp Putsch.' I must have made that remark a hundred times. Allying her death to another event like that, well, it plays down how much I still miss her, even after sixteen years. Never successfully however. 'It was Spanish influenza,' I explained. 'We were together for only ten months.' Frau Protze nodded sympathetically.

We were both silent for a moment. Then I looked at my watch. 'You can go home if you like,' I told her.

When she had gone I stood at my high window a long time and watched the wet streets below, glistening like patent leather in the late afternoon sunlight. The rain had stopped and it looked as though it would be a fine evening. Already the office workers were making their ways home, streaming out of Berolina Haus opposite, and down into the labyrinth of underground tunnels and walkways that led to the Alexanderplatz U-Bahn station.

Berlin. I used to love this old city. But that was before it had caught sight of its own reflection and taken to wearing corsets laced so tight that it could hardly breathe. I loved the easy, carefree philosophies, the cheap jazz, the vulgar cabarets and all of the other cultural excesses that characterized the Weimar years and made Berlin seem like one of the most exciting cities in the world.

Behind my office, to the south-east, was Police Headquarters, and I imagined all the good hard work that was being done there to crack down on Berlin's crime. Villainies like speaking disrespectfully of the Führer, displaying a 'Sold Out' sign in your butcher's shop window, not giving the Hitler Salute, and homosexuality. That was Berlin under the National Socialist Government: a big, haunted house with dark corners, gloomy staircases, sinister cellars, locked rooms and a whole attic full of poltergeists on the loose, throwing books, banging doors, breaking glass, shouting in the night and generally scaring the owners so badly that there were times when they were ready to sell up and get out. But most of the time they just stopped up their ears, covered their blackened eyes and tried to pretend that there was nothing wrong. Cowed with fear, they spoke very little, ignoring the carpet moving underneath their feet, and their laughter was the thin, nervous kind that always accompanies the boss's little joke.

Policing, like autobahn construction and informing, is one of the new Germany's growth industries; and so the Alex is always busy. Even though it was past closing time for most of the departments that had dealings with the public, there were still a great many people milling about the various entrances to the building when I got there. Entrance Four, for the Passport Office, was especially busy. Berliners, many of them Jewish, who had queued all day for an exit visa, were even now emerging from this part of the Alex, their faces happy or sad according to the success of their enterprise.

I walked on down Alexanderstrasse and passed Entrance Three, in front of which a couple of traffic police, nicknamed 'white mice' because of their distinctive short white coats, were climbing off their powder-blue BMW motorcycles. A Green Minna, a police-van, came racing down the street, Martin-horn blaring, in the direction of Jannowitz Bridge. Oblivious to the noise, the two white mice swaggered in through Entrance Three to make their reports.

I went in by Entrance Two, knowing the place well enough to have chosen the entrance where I was least likely to be challenged by someone. If I was stopped, I was on my way to Room 32a, the Lost Property Office. But Entrance Two also serves the police morgue.

I walked nonchalantly along a corridor and down into the basement, past a small canteen to a fire exit. I pushed the bar on the door down and found myself in a large cobbled courtyard where several police cars were parked. One of these was being washed by a man wearing gumboots who paid me no attention as I crossed the yard and ducked into another doorway. This led to the boiler room, and I stopped there for a moment while I made a mental check of my bearings. I hadn't worked at the Alex for ten years not to know my way around. My only concern was that I might meet someone who knew me. I opened the only other door that led out of the boiler room and ascended a short staircase into a corridor, at the end of which was the morgue.

When I entered the morgue's outer office I encountered a sour smell that was reminiscent of warm, wet poultry flesh. It mixed with the formaldehyde to make a sickly cocktail that I felt in my stomach at the same time as I drew it into my nostrils. The office, barely furnished with a couple of chairs and a table, contained nothing to warn the unwary of what lay beyond the two glass doors, except the smell and a sign which simply read 'Morgue: Entrance Forbidden'. I opened the doors a crack and looked inside.

In the centre of a grim, damp room was an operating-table that was also part trough. On opposite sides of a stained ceramic gulley were two marble slabs, set slightly at an angle so that fluids from a corpse could drain into the centre and be washed down a drain by water from one of the two tall murmuring taps that were situated at each end. The table was big enough for two corpses laid head-to-toe, one on each side of the drain; but there was only one cadaver, that of a male, which lay under the knife and the surgical saw. These were wielded by a bent, slight man with thin dark hair, a high forehead, glasses, a long hooked nose, a neat moustache and a small chin-beard. He was wearing gumboots, a heavy apron, rubber gloves and a stiff collar and a tie.

I stepped quietly through the doors, and contemplated the corpse with professional curiosity. Moving closer I tried to see what had caused the man's death. It was clear that the body had been lying in water, since the skin was sodden and peeling away on the hands and feet, like gloves and socks. Otherwise it was in largely reasonable condition, with the exception of the head. This was black in colour and completely featureless, like a muddy football, and the top part of the cranium had been sawn away and the brain removed. Like a wet Gordian knot, it now lay in a kidney-shaped dish awaiting dissection.

Confronted with violent death in all its ghastly hues, contorted attitudes and porcine fleshiness, I had no more reaction than if I had been looking in the window of my local 'German' butcher's shop, except that this one had more meat on display. Sometimes I was surprised at the totality of my own indifference to the sight of the stabbed, the drowned, the crushed, the shot, the burned and the bludgeoned, although I knew well how that insensitivity had come about. Seeing so much death on the Turkish front and in my service with Kripo, I had almost ceased to regard a corpse as being in any way human. This acquaintance with death had persisted since my becoming a private investigator, when the trail of a missing person so often led to the morgue at St Gertrauden, Berlin's largest hospital, or to a salvage-man's hut near a levee on the Landwehr Canal.

I stood there for several minutes, staring at the gruesome scene in front of me, and puzzled as to what had produced the condition of the head and the differing one of the body, before eventually Dr Illmann glanced round and saw me.

'Good God,' he growled. 'Bernhard Günther. Are you still alive?' I approached the table, and blew a breath of disgust.

'Christ,' I said. 'The last time I came across body odour this bad, a horse was sitting on my face.'

'He's quite a picture, isn't he?'

'You're telling me. What was he doing, frenching a polar bear? Or maybe Hitler kissed him.'

'Unusual, isn't it? Almost as if the head were burned.'

'Acid?'

'Yes.' Illmann sounded pleased, like I was a clever pupil. 'Very good. It's difficult to say what kind, but most probably hydrochloric or sulphuric.'

'Like someone didn't want you to know who he was.'

'Precisely so. Mind you, it doesn't disguise the cause of death. He had a broken billiard cue forced up one of his nostrils. It pierced the brain, killing him instantly. Not a very common way of killing a man; indeed, in my experience it is unique. However, one learns not to be surprised at the various ways in which murderers choose to kill their victims. But I'm sure you're not surprised. You always did have a good imagination for a bull, Bernie. To say nothing of your nerve. You know, you've got a hell of a nerve just walking in here like this. It's only my sentimental nature that stops me from having you thrown out on your ear.'

'I need to talk to you about the Pfarr case. You did the PM, didn't you?'

'You're well informed,' he said. 'As a matter of fact the family reclaimed the bodies this morning.'

'And your report?'

'Look, I can't talk here. I'll be through with our friend on the slab in a while. Give me an hour.'

'Where?'

'How about the Künstler Eck, on Alt Kölln. It's quiet there and we won't be disturbed.'

'The Künstler Eck,' I repeated. 'I'll find it.' I turned back towards the glass doors.

'Oh, and Bernie. Make sure you bring a little something for my expenses?'

The independent township of Alt Kölln, long since absorbed by the capital, is a small island on the River Spree. Largely given up to museums, it has thus earned itself the sobriquet 'Museum Island'. But I have to confess that I have never seen the inside of one of them. I'm not much interested in The Past and, if you ask me, it is this country's obsession with its history that has partly put us where we are now: in the shit. You can't go into a bar without some arsehole going on about our pre-1918 borders, or harking back to Bismarck and when we kicked the stuffing out of the French. These are old sores, and to my mind it doesn't do any good to keep picking at them.

From the outside, there was nothing about the place that would have attracted the passer-by to drop in for a casual drink: not the door's scruffy paintwork, nor the dried-up flowers in the window-box; and certainly not the poorly handwritten sign in the dirty window which read: 'Tonight's speech can be heard here.' I cursed, for this meant that Joey the Cripp was addressing a Party rally that evening, and as a result there would be the usual traffic chaos. I went down the steps and opened the door.

There was even less about the inside of the Künstler Eck that would have persuaded the casual drinker to stay awhile. The walls were covered with gloomy wood carvings – tiny models of cannons, death's heads, coffins and skeletons. Against the far wall was a large pump-organ painted to look like a graveyard, with crypts and graves yielding up their dead, at which a hunchback was playing a piece by Haydn. This was as much for his own benefit as anyone else's, since a group of storm-troopers were singing 'My Prussia Stands So Proud and Great' with sufficient gusto as to almost completely drown the hunchback's playing. I've seen some odd things in Berlin in my time, but this was like something from a Conrad Veidt film, and not a very good one at that. I expected the one-armed police-captain to come in at any moment.

Instead I found Illmann sitting alone in a corner, nursing a bottle of Engelhardt. I ordered two more of the same and sat down as the storm-troopers finished their song and the hunchback commenced a massacre of one of my favourite Schubert sonatas.

'This is a hell of a place to choose,' I said grimly.

'I'm afraid that I find it curiously quaint.'

'Just the place to meet your friendly neighbourhood bodysnatcher. Don't you see enough of death during the day that you have to come to drink in a charnel-house like this?'

He shrugged unabashedly. 'It is only with death around me that I am constantly reminded that I am alive.'

'There's a lot to be said for necrophilia.' Illmann smiled, as if agreeing with me.

'So you want to know about the poor Hauptsturmführer and his little wife, eh?' I nodded. 'This is an interesting case, and, I don't mind telling you, the interesting ones are becoming increasingly rare. With all the people who wind up dead in this city you would think I was busy. But of course, there is usually little or no mystery about how most of them got that way. Half the time I find myself presenting the forensic evidence of a homicide to the very people who committed it. It's an upside down world that we live in.' He opened his briefcase and took out a blue ring-file. 'I brought the photographs. I thought you would want to see the happy couple. I'm afraid they're a pair of real stokers. I was only able to make the identification from their wedding rings, his and hers.'

I flicked through the file. The camera angles changed but the subject remained the same: two gun-metal grey corpses, bald like Egyptian pharaohs, lay on the exposed and blackened springs of what had once been a bed, like sausages left too long under the grill.

'Nice album. What were they doing, having a punch-up?' I said, noticing the way in which each corpse had its fists raised like a bare-knuckle fighter.

'A common enough observation in a death like this.'

'What about those cuts in the skin? They look like knife wounds.'

'Again, what one would expect,' said Illmann. 'The heat in a conflagration causes the skin to split open like a ripe banana. That is, if you can remember what a banana looks like.'

'Where did you find the petrol cans?'

He raised his eyebrows quizzically. 'Oh, you know about those, do you? Yes, we found two empty cans in the garden. I don't think they'd been there very long. They weren't rusted and there was still a small amount of petrol which remained unevaporated in the bottom of one of them. And according to the fire officer there was a strong smell of petrol about the place.'

'Arson, then.'

'Undoubtedly.'

'So what made you look for bullets?'

'Experience. With a post-mortem following a fire, one always keeps in mind the possibility that there has been an attempt to destroy evidence. It's standard procedure. I found three bullets in the female, two in the male and three in the headboard of the bed. The female was dead before the fire started. She was hit in the head and the throat. Not so the male. There were smoke particles in the air passages and carbon monoxide in the blood. The tissues were still pink. He was hit in the chest and in the face.'

'Has the gun been found yet?' I asked.

'No, but I can tell you that it was most probably a 7.65 mm automatic, and something quite hard on its ammunition, like an old Mauser.'

'And they were shot from what sort of distance?'

'I should say the murderer was about 150 cm from the victims when firing the weapon. The entry and exit wounds were consistent with the murderer having stood at the bottom of the bed; and, of course, there are the bullets in the headboard.'

'Just the one weapon, you think?' Illmann nodded. 'Eight bullets,' I said. 'That's a whole magazine for a pocket pistol, isn't it? Somebody was making very sure. Or else they were very angry. Christ, didn't the neighbours hear anything?'

'Apparently not. If they did, they probably thought it was just the Gestapo having a little party. The fire wasn't reported until 3.10 a.m., by which time there was no chance of bringing it under control.'

The hunchback abandoned his organ recital as the stormtroopers launched into a rendition of 'Germany, Thou Art Our Pride'. One of them, a big burly fellow with a scar on his face the length and consistency of a piece of bacon-rind walked round the bar, waving his beer and demanding that the rest of the Künstler Eck's customers join in the singing. Illmann did not seem to mind and sang in a loud baritone. My own singing showed a considerable want of key and alacrity. Loud songs do not a patriot make. The trouble with these fucking National Socialists, especially the young ones, is that they think they have got a monopoly on patriotism. And even if they don't have one now, the way things are going, they soon will.

When the song was over, I asked Illmann some more questions. 'They were both naked,' he told me, 'and had drunk a good deal. She had consumed several Ohio Cocktails, and he'd had a large amount of beer and schnaps. More than likely they were quite drunk when they were shot. Also, I took a high vaginal swab in the female and found recent semen, which was of the same blood type as the male. I think they'd had quite an evening. Oh yes, she was eight weeks pregnant. Ah, life's little candle burns but briefly.'

'Pregnant.' I repeated the word thoughtfully. Illmann stretched and yawned.

'Yes,' he said. 'Want to know what they had for dinner?'

'No,' I said firmly. 'Tell me about the safe instead. Was it open or shut?'

'Open.' He paused. 'You know, it's interesting, you didn't ask me how it was opened. Which leads me to suppose that you already knew that beyond a bit of scorching, the safe was undamaged; that if the safe was opened illegally, then it was done by someone who knew what he was doing. A Stockinger safe is no pushover.'

'Any piano players on it?' Illmann shook his head.

'It was too badly scorched to take any prints,' he said.

'Let us assume,' I said, 'that immediately prior to the deaths of the Pfarrs, the safe contained – what it contained, and that it was, as it should have been, locked up for the night.'

'Very well.'

'Then there are two possibilities: one is that a professional nut-cracker did the job and then killed them; and the other is that someone forced them to open it and then ordered them back to bed where he shot them. Still, it's not like a pro to have left the safe door open.'

'Unless he was trying hard to look like an amateur,' said Illmann. 'My own opinion is that they were both asleep when they were shot. Certainly from the angle of bullet entry I would say that both of them were lying down. Now if you were conscious, and someone had a gun on you, it's more than likely you would be sitting up in bed. And so I would conclude that your intimidation theory is unlikely.' He looked at his watch and finished his beer.

Patting my leg, he added warmly, 'It's been good, Bernie. Just like the old days. How pleasant to talk to someone whose idea of detective work does not involve a spotlight and a set of brass knuckles. Still, I won't have to put up with the Alex for much longer. Our illustrious Reichskriminaldirektor, Arthur Nebe, is retiring me, just as he's retired the other old conservatives before me.'

'I didn't know you were interested in politics,' I said.

'I'm not,' he said. 'But isn't that how Hitler got elected in the first place: too many people who didn't give a shit who was running the country? The funny thing is that I care even less now than I did before. Catch me joining those March Violets on the bandwagon. But I won't be sorry to leave. I'm tired of all the squabbling that goes on between Sipo and Orpo as to who controls Kripo. It gets very confusing when it comes to filing a report, not knowing whether or not one should be involving our uniformed friends in Orpo.'

'I thought Sipo and the Gestapo were in the Kripo driving seat.'

'At the higher levels of command that is the case,' Illmann confirmed. 'But at the middle and lower levels the old administrative chains of command still operate. At the municipal level, local police presidents, who are part of Orpo, are also responsible for Kripo. But the word is that Orpo's head is giving undercover encouragement to any police president who is prepared to frustrate the thumbscrew boys in Sipo. In Berlin, that suits our own police president. He and the Reichskriminaldirektor, Arthur Nebe, hate each other's guts. Ludicrous, isn't it? And now, if you don't mind, I really must be going.'

'What a way to run a fucking bullring,' I said.

'Believe me, Bernie, you're well out of it.' He grinned happily. 'And it can get a lot worse yet.'

Illmann's information cost me a hundred marks. I've never found that information comes cheap, but lately the cost of private investigation does seem to be going up. It's not difficult to see why. Everyone is making some sort of a twist these days. Corruption in one form or another is the most distinctive feature of life under National Socialism. The government has made several revelations about the corruption of the various Weimar political parties, but these were as nothing compared to the corruption that exists now. It flourishes at the top, and everyone knows it. So most people figure that they are due a share themselves. I don't know of anyone who is as fastidious about such things as they used to be. And that includes me. The plain truth of it is that people's sensitivity to corruption, whether it's black-market food or obtaining favours from a government official, is about as blunt as a joiner's pencil stub.

6

That evening it seemed as though almost all of Berlin was on its way to Neukölln to witness Goebbels conduct the orchestra of soft, persuasive violins and brittle, sarcastic trumpets that was his voice. But for those unlucky enough not to have sight of the Popular Enlightener, there were a number of facilities provided throughout Berlin to ensure that they could at least have the sound. As well as the radios required by law in restaurants and cafés, on most streets there were loudspeakers mounted on advertising pillars and lamp-posts; and a force of radio wardens was empowered to knock on doors and enforce the mandatory civic duty to listen to a Party broadcast.

Driving west on Leipzigerstrasse, I met the torchlight parade of Brownshirt legions as it marched south down Wilhelmstrasse, and I was obliged to get out of my car and salute the passing standard. Not to have done so would have been to risk a beating. I guess there were others like me in that crowd, our right arms extended like so many traffic policemen, doing it just to avoid trouble and feeling a bit ridiculous. Who knows? But come to think of it, political parties were always big on salutes in Germany: the Social Democrats had their clenched fist raised high above the head; the Bolshies in the KPD had their clenched fist raised at shoulder level; the Centrists had their two-fingered, pistol-shaped hand signal, with the thumb cocked; and the Nazis had fingernail inspection. I can remember when we used to think it was all rather ridiculous and melodramatic, and maybe that's why none of us took it seriously. And here we all were now, saluting with the best of them. Crazy.

Badenschestrasse, running off Berliner Strasse, is just a block short of Trautenau Strasse, where I have my own apartment. Proximity is their only common factor. Badenschestrasse, Number 7 is one of the most modern apartment blocks in the city, and about as exclusive as a reunion dinner for the Ptolemies.

I parked my small and dirty car between a huge Deusenberg and a gleaming Bugatti and went into a lobby that looked like it had left a couple of cathedrals short of marble. A fat doorman and a storm-trooper saw me, and, deserting their desk and their radio which was playing Wagner prior to the Party broadcast, they formed a human barrier to my progress, anxious that I might want to insult some of the residents with my crumpled suit and self-inflicted manicure.

'Like it says on the sign outside,' growled Fatso, 'this is a private building.' I wasn't impressed with their combined effort to get tough with me. I'm used to being made to feel unwelcome, and I don't bounce easily.

'I didn't see any sign,' I said truthfully.

'We don't want any trouble, Mister,' said the storm-trooper. He had a delicate-looking jaw that would have snapped like a dead twig with only the briefest of introductions to my fist.

'I'm not selling any,' I told him. Fatso took over.

'Well, whatever it is you're selling, they don't want any here.'

I smiled thinly at him. 'Listen, Fatso, the only thing that's stopping me from pushing you out of my way is your bad breath. It'll be tricky for you, I know, but see if you can work the telephone, and ring up Fräulein Rudel. You'll find she's expecting me.' Fatso pulled the huge brown-and-black moustache that clung to his curling lip like a bat on a crypt wall. His breath was a lot worse than I could have imagined.

'For your sake, swanktail, you'd better be right,' he said. 'It'd be a pleasure to throw you out.' Swearing under his breath he wobbled back to his desk and dialled furiously.

'Is Fräulein Rudel expecting someone?' he said, moderating his tone. 'Only, she never told me.' His face fell as my story checked out. He put the phone down and swung his head at the lift door.

'Third floor,' he hissed.

There were only two doors, at opposite ends of the third. There was a velodrome of parquet-floor between them and, as if I was expected, one of the doors was ajar. The maid ushered me into the drawing room.

'You'd better take a seat,' she said grumpily. 'She's still dressing and there's no telling how long she'll be. Fix yourself a drink if you want.' Then she disappeared and I examined my surroundings.

The apartment was no larger than a private airfield and looked about as cheap a set as something out of Cecil B. de Mille, of whom there was a photograph jostling for pride of place with all the others on the grand piano. Compared with the person who had decorated and furnished the place, the Archduke Ferdinand had been blessed with the taste of a troupe of Turkish circus dwarves. I looked at some of the other photographs. Mostly they were stills of Ilse Rudel taken from her various films. In a lot of them she wasn't wearing very much – swimming nude or peering coyly from behind a tree which hid the more interesting parts. Rudel was famous for her scantily clad roles. In another photograph she was sitting at a table in a smart restaurant with the good Dr Goebbels; and in another, she was sparring with Max Schmeling. Then there was one in which she was being carried in a workman's arms, only the 'workman' just happened to be Emil Jannings, the famous actor. I recognized it as a still from *The Builder's Hut*. I like the book a lot better than I had liked the film.

At the hint of 4711 I turned around, and found myself shaking the beautiful film star by the hand.

'I see you've been looking at my little gallery,' she said, re-arranging the photographs I had picked up and examined. 'You must think it terribly vain of me to have so many pictures of myself on display, but I simply can't abide albums.'

'Not at all,' I said. 'It's very interesting.' She flashed me the smile that made thousands of German men, myself included, go weak at the chin.

'I'm so glad you approve.' She was wearing a pair of green-velvet lounging pyjamas with a long, gold, fringed sash, and high-heeled green morocco slippers. Her blonde hair was done up in a braided knot at the back of her head, as was fashionable; but unlike most German women, she was also wearing makeup and smoking a cigarette. That sort of thing is frowned on by the BdM, the Women's League, as being inconsistent with the Nazi ideal of German Womanhood; however, I'm a city boy: plain, scrubbed, rosy faces may be just fine down on the farm, but like nearly all German men I prefer my women powdered and painted. Of course, Ilse Rudel lived in a different world to other women. She probably thought the Nazi Women's League was a hockey association.

'I'm sorry about those two fellows on the door,' she said, 'but you see, Josef and Magda Goebbels have an apartment upstairs, so security has to be extra tight, as you can imagine. Which reminds me, I promised Josef that I'd try and listen to his speech, or at least a bit of it. Do you mind?'

It was not the sort of question that you ever asked; unless you happened to be on first-name terms with the Minister of Propaganda and Popular Enlightenment, and his lady wife. I shrugged.

'That's fine by me.'

'We'll only listen for a few minutes,' she said, switching on the Philco that stood on top of a walnut drinks cabinet. 'Now then. What can I get you to drink?' I asked for a whisky and she poured me one that was big enough for a set of false teeth. She poured herself a glass of Bowle, Berlin's favourite summer drink, from a tall, blue-glass pitcher, and joined me on a sofa that was the colour and contours of an underripe pineapple. We clinked glasses and, as the tubes of the radio set warmed up, the smooth tones of the man from upstairs slipped slowly into the room.

First of all, Goebbels singled out foreign journalists for criticism, and rebuked their 'biased' reporting of life in the new Germany. Some of his remarks were clever enough to draw laughter and then applause from his sycophantic audience. Rudel smiled uncertainly, but remained silent, and I wondered if she understood what her club-footed neighbour from upstairs was talking about. Then he raised his voice and proceeded to declaim against the traitors – whoever they were, I didn't know – who were trying to sabotage the national revolution. Here she stifled a yawn. Finally, when Joey got going on his favourite subject, the glorification of the Führer, she jumped up and switched the radio off.

'Goodness me, I think we've heard enough from him for one evening.' She went over to the gramophone and picked up a disc. 'Do you like jazz?' she said, changing the subject. 'Oh, it's all right, it's not negro jazz. I love it, don't you?' Only non-negro jazz is permitted in Germany now, but I often wonder how they can tell the difference.

'I like any kind of jazz,' I said. She wound up the gramophone and put the needle into the groove. It was a nice relaxed sort of piece with a strong clarinet and a saxophonist who could have led a company of Italians across no man's land in a barrage.

I said: 'Do you mind me asking why you keep this place?'

She danced back to the sofa and sat down. 'Well, Herr Private Investigator, Hermann finds my friends a little trying. He does a lot of work from our house in Dahlem, and at all hours: I do most of my entertaining here, so as not to disturb him.'

'Sounds sensible enough,' I said. She blew a column of smoke at me from each exquisite nostril, and I took a deep breath of it; not because I enjoyed the smell of American cigarettes, which I do, but because it had come from inside her chest, and anything to do with that chest was all right by me. From the movement underneath her jacket I had already concluded that her breasts were large and unsupported.

'So,' I said, 'what was it that you wanted to see me about?' To my surprise, she touched me lightly on the knee.

'Relax,' she smiled. 'You're not in a hurry, are you?' I shook my head and watched her stub out her cigarette. There were already several butts in the ashtray, all heavily marked with lipstick, but none of them had been smoked for more than a few puffs, and it occurred to me that she was the one who needed to relax, and that maybe she was nervous about something. Me perhaps. As if confirming my theory she jumped up off the sofa, poured herself another glass of Bowle and changed the record.

'Are you all right with your drink?'

'Yes,' I said, and sipped some. It was good whisky, smooth and peaty, with no backburner in it. Then I asked her how well she had known Paul and Grete Pfarr. I don't think the question surprised her. Instead, she sat close to me, so that we were actually touching, and smiled in a strange way.

'Oh, yes,' she said whimsically. 'I forgot. You're the man who's investigating the fire for Hermann, aren't you?' She did some more grinning, and added: 'I suppose the case has the police baffled.' There was a note of sarcasm in her voice. 'And then you come along, the Great Detective, and find the clue that solves the whole mystery.'

'There's no mystery, Fräulein Rudel,' I said provocatively. It threw her only slightly.

'Why, surely the mystery is, who did it?' she said.

'A mystery is something that is beyond human knowledge and comprehension, which means that I should be wasting my time in even trying to investigate it. No, this case is nothing more than a puzzle, and I happen to like puzzles.'

'Oh, so do I,' she said, almost mocking me, I thought. 'And please, you must call me Ilse while you're here. And I shall call you by your Christian name. What is it?'

'Bernhard.'

'Bernhard,' she said, trying it for size, and then shortening it, 'Bernie.' She gulped a large mouthful of the champagne and sauterne mixture she was drinking, picked out a strawberry from the top of her glass and ate it. 'Well, Bernie, you must be a very good private investigator to be working for Hermann on something as important as this. I thought you were all seedy little men who followed husbands and looked through keyholes at what they got up to, and then told their wives.'

'Divorce cases are just about the one kind of business that I don't handle.'

'Is that a fact?' she said, smiling quietly to herself. It irritated me quite a bit, that smile; in part because I felt she was patronizing me, but also because I wanted desperately to stop it with a kiss. Failing that, the back of my hand. 'Tell me something. Do you make much money doing what you do?' Tapping me on the thigh to indicate that she hadn't finished her question, she added: 'I don't mean to sound rude. But what I want to know is, are you comfortable?'

I took note of my opulent surroundings before answering. 'Me, comfortable? Like a Bauhaus chair, I am.' She laughed at that. 'You didn't answer my question about the Pfarrs,' I said.

'Didn't I?'

'You know damn well you didn't.'

She shrugged. 'I knew them.'

'Well enough to know what Paul had against your husband?'

'Is that really what you're interested in?' she said.

'It'll do for a start.'

She gave an impatient little sigh. 'Very well. We'll play your game, but only until I get bored of it.' She raised her eyebrows questioningly at me, and although I had no idea what she was talking about, I shrugged and said:

'That's fine by me.'

'It's true, they didn't get on, but I haven't the haziest why. When Paul and Grete first met, Hermann was against their getting married. He thought Paul wanted a nice platinum tooth – you know, a rich wife. He tried to persuade Grete to drop him. But Grete wouldn't hear of it. After that, by all accounts they got on fine. At least until Hermann's first wife died. By then I'd been seeing him for some time. It was when we got married that things really started to cool off between the two of them. Grete started drinking. And their marriage seemed little more than a fig-leaf, for decency's sake – Paul being at the Ministry and all that.'

'What did he do there, do you know?'

'No idea.'

'Did he nudge around?'

'With other women?' She laughed. 'Paul was good-looking, but a bit lame. He was dedicated to his work, not another woman. If he did, he kept it very quiet.'

'What about her?'

Rudel shook her golden head, and took a large gulp of her drink. 'Not her style.' But she paused for a moment and looked more thoughtful. 'Although . . .' She shrugged. 'It probably isn't anything.'

'Come on,' I said. 'Unpack it.'

'Well, there was one time in Dahlem, when I was left with just the tiniest suspicion that Grete might have had something going with Haupthändler.' I raised an eyebrow. 'Hermann's private secretary. This would have been about the time when the Italians had entered Addis Ababa. I remember that only because I went to a party at the Italian Embassy.'

'That would have been early in May.'

'Yes. Anyway, Hermann was away on business, so I went by myself. I was filming at UFA the next morning and had to be up early. I decided to spend the night at Dahlem, so I would have a bit more time in the morning. It's a lot easier getting to Babelsberg from there. Anyway, when I got home I poked my head around the drawing-room door in search of a book I had left there, and who should I find sitting in the dark but Hjalmar Haupthändler and Grete.'

'What were they doing?'

'Nothing. Nothing at all. That's what made it so damned suspicious. It was two o'clock in the morning and there they were, sitting at opposite ends of the same sofa like a couple of school children on their first date. I could tell they were embarrassed to see me. They gave me some cabbage about just chatting and was that really the time. But I didn't buy it.'

'Did you mention it to your husband?'

'No,' she said. 'Actually, I forgot about it. And even if I hadn't, I wouldn't have told him. Hermann is not the sort of person who could have just left it alone to sort itself out. Most rich men are like that, I think. Distrustful, and suspicious.'

'I'd say he must trust you a great deal to let you keep your own apartment.'

She laughed scornfully. 'God, what a joke. If you knew what

I have to put up with. But then you probably know all about us, you being a private investigator.' She didn't let me answer. 'I've had to sack several of my maids because they were being bribed by him to spy on me. He's really a very jealous man.'

'Under similar circumstances I'd probably act the same way,' I told her. 'Most men would be jealous of a woman like you.' She looked me in the eye, and then at the rest of me. It was the sort of provocative look that only whores and phenomenally rich and beautiful film stars can get away with. It was meant to get me to climb aboard her bones like a creeper on to a trellis. A look that made me want to gore a hole in the rug. 'Frankly, you probably like to make a man jealous. You strike me as the kind of woman who holds out her hand to signal a left and then makes a right, just to keep him guessing. Are you ready to tell me why you asked me here tonight?'

'I've sent the maid home,' she said, 'so stop thrashing words and kiss me, you big idiot.' Normally I'm not too good at taking orders, but on this occasion I didn't quarrel. It's not every day that a film star tells you to kiss her. She gave me the soft, luscious inside of her lips, and I let myself equal their competence, just to be polite. After a minute I felt her body stir, and when she pulled her mouth away from my lamprey-like kiss her voice was hot and breathless.

'My, that was a real slow-burner.'

'I practise on my forearm.' She smiled and raised her mouth up to mine, kissing me like she intended to lose control of herself and so that I would stop holding something back from her. She was breathing through her nose, as if she needed more oxygen, gradually getting serious about it, and me keeping pace with her, until she said:

'I want you to fuck me, Bernie.' I heard each word in my fly. We stood up in silence, and taking me by the hand she led me to the bedroom.

'I've got to go to the bathroom first,' I said. She was pulling the pyjama-jacket over her head, her breasts wobbling: these were real film star's chicks and for a moment I couldn't take my eyes off them. Each brown nipple was like a British Tommy's helmet.

'Don't be too long, Bernie,' she said, dropping first her sash, and then the trousers, so that she stood there in just her knickers.

But in the bathroom I took a long, honest look in the mirror, which was one whole wall, and asked myself why a living goddess like the one turning down the white satin sheets needed me of all people to help justify an expensive laundry account. It wasn't my choirboy's face, or my sunny disposition. With my broken nose and my car-bumper of a jaw, I was handsome only by the stand-ards of a fairground boxing-booth. I didn't imagine for a minute that my blond hair and blue eyes made me fashionable. She wanted something else besides a brush, and I had a shrewd idea what it was. The trouble was I had an erection that, temporarily at least, was very firmly in command.

Back in the bedroom, she was still standing there, waiting for me to come and help myself. Impatient of her, I snatched her knickers down, pulling her onto the bed, where I prised her sleek, tanned thighs apart like an excited scholar opening a priceless book. For quite a while I pored over the text, turning the pages with my fingers and feasting my eyes on what I had never dreamed of possessing.

We kept the light on, so that finally I had a perfect view of myself as I plugged into the crisp fluff between her legs. And after-wards she lay on top of me, breathing like a sleepy but contented dog, stroking my chest almost as if she was in awe of me.

'My, but you're a well-built man.'

'Mother was a blacksmith,' I said. 'She used to hammer a nail into a horse's shoe with the flat of her hand. I get my build from her.' She giggled.

'You don't say much, but when you do you like to joke, don't you?'

'There are an awful lot of dead people in Germany looking very serious.'

'And so very cynical. Why is that?'

'I used to be a priest.'

She fingered the small scar on my forehead where a piece of shrapnel had creased me. 'How did you get this?'

'After church on Sundays I'd box with the choirboys in the sacristy. You like boxing?' I remembered the photograph of Schmeling on the piano.

'I adore boxing,' she said. 'I love violent, physical men. I love going to the Busch Circus and watching them train before a big fight, just to see if they defend or attack, how they jab, if they've got guts.'

'Just like one of those noblewomen in ancient Rome,' I said, 'checking up on her gladiators to see if they're going to win before she puts a bet on.'

'But of course. I like winners. Now you . . .'

'Yes?'

'I'd say you could take a good punch. Maybe take quite a few. You strike me as the durable, patient sort. Methodical. Prepared to soak up more than a little punishment. That makes you dangerous '

'And you?' She bounced excitedly on my chest, her breasts wobbling engagingly, although, for the moment at least, I had no more appetite for her body.

'Oh, yes, yes,' she cried excitedly. 'What sort of fighter am I?'

I looked at her from the corner of one eye. 'I think you would dance around a man and let him expend quite a bit of energy before coming back at him with one good punch to win on a knock-out. A win on points would be no sort of contest for you. You always like to put them down on the canvas. There's just one thing that puzzles me about this bout.'

'What's that?'

'What makes you think I'd take a dive?'

She sat up in bed. 'I don't understand.'

'Sure you do.' Now that I'd had her it was easy enough to say. 'You think your husband hired me to spy on you, isn't that right? You don't believe I'm investigating the fire at all. That's why you've been planning this little tryst all evening, and now I imagine

I'm supposed to play the poodle, so that when you ask me to lay off I'll do just what you say, otherwise I might not get any more treats. Well, you've been wasting your time. Like I said, I don't do divorce work.'

She sighed and covered her breasts with her arms. 'You certainly can pick your moments, Herr Sniffer Dog,' she said.

'It's true, isn't it?'

She sprang out of bed and I knew that I was watching the whole of her body, as naked as a pin without a hat, for the last time; from here on in I would have to go to the cinema to catch those tantalizing glimpses of it, like all the other fellows. She went over to the cupboard and snatched a gown from a hanger. From the pocket she produced a packet of cigarettes. She lit one and smoked it angrily, with one arm folded across her chest.

'I could have offered you money,' she said. 'But instead I gave you myself.' She took another nervous puff, hardly inhaling it at all. 'How much do you want?'

Exasperated, I slapped my naked thigh, and said: 'Shit, you're not listening, spoon-ears. I told you. I wasn't hired to go peeking through your keyhole and find out the name of your lover.'

She shrugged with disbelief. 'How did you know I had a lover?' she said.

I got out of bed, and started to dress. 'I didn't need a magnifying glass and a pair of tweezers to pick that one up. It stands to reason that if you didn't already have a lover, then you wouldn't be so damned nervous of me.' She gave me a smile that was as thin and dubious as the rubber on a secondhand condom.

'No? I bet you're the sort who could find lice on a bald head. Anyway, who said I was nervous of you? I just don't happen to care for the interruption of my privacy. Look, I think you had better push off.' She turned her back to me as she spoke.

'I'm on my way.' I buttoned up my braces and slipped my jacket on. At the bedroom door, I made one last try to get through to her.

'For the last time, I wasn't hired to check up on you.'

'You've made a fool of me.'

I shook my head. 'There's not enough sense in anything you've said to fill a hollow tooth. With all your milkmaid's calculations, you didn't need my help to make a fool of yourself. Thanks for a memorable evening.' As I left her room she started to curse me with the sort of eloquence you expect only from a man who has just hammered his thumb.

I drove home feeling like a ventriloquist's mouth ulcer. I was sore at the way things had turned out. It's not every day that one of Germany's great film stars takes you to bed and then throws you out on your ear. I'd like to have had more time to grow familiar with her famous body. I was a man who had won the big prize at the fair, only to be told there had been a mistake. All the same, I said to myself, I ought to have expected something like that. Nothing resembles a street snapper so much as a rich woman.

Once inside my apartment I poured myself a drink and then boiled some water for a bath. After that, I put on the dressing-gown I'd bought in Wertheim's and started to feel good again. The place was stuffy, so I opened a few windows. Then I tried reading for a while. I must have fallen asleep, because a couple of hours had passed by the time I heard the knock at the door.

'Who is it?' I said, going into the hall.

'Open up. Police,' said a voice.

'What do you want?'

'To ask you some questions about Ilse Rudel,' he said. 'She was found dead at her apartment an hour ago. Murdered.' I snatched the door open and found the barrel of a Parabellum poking me in the stomach.

'Back inside,' said the man with the pistol. I retreated, raising my hands instinctively.

He wore a Bavarian-cut sports coat of light-blue linen, and a canary-yellow tie. There was a scar on his pale young face, but it was neat and clean-looking, and probably self-inflicted with a razor in the hope that it might be mistaken for a student's duelling scar. Accompanied by a strong smell of beer, he advanced into my hallway, closing the door behind him.

'Anything you say, sonny,' I said, relieved to see that he looked less than comfortable with the Parabellum. 'You had me fooled there with that story about Fräulein Rudel. I shouldn't have fallen for it.'

'You bastard,' he snarled.

'Mind if I put my hands down? Only my circulation isn't what it used to be.' I dropped my hands to my sides. 'What's this all about?'

'Don't deny it.'

'Deny what?'

'That you raped her.' He adjusted his grip on the gun, and swallowed nervously, his Adam's apple tossing around like a honeymoon couple under a thin pink sheet. 'She told me what you did to her. So you needn't try and deny it.'

I shrugged. 'What would be the point? In your shoes I know who I would believe. But listen, are you sure you know what you're doing? Your breath was waving a red flag when you tiptoed in here. The Nazis may seem a bit liberal in some things, but they haven't done away with capital punishment, you know. Even if you're hardly old enough to be expected to hold your drink.'

'I'm going to kill you,' he said, licking his dry lips.

'Well, that's all right, but do you mind not shooting me in the belly?' I pointed at his pistol. 'It's by no means certain that you'd kill me, and I'd hate to spend the rest of my life drinking milk. No, if I were you I'd go for a head shot. Between the eyes if you can manage it. A difficult shot, but it would kill me for sure. Frankly, the way I feel right now, you'd be doing me a favour. It must be something I've eaten, but my insides feel like the wave machine at Luna Park.' I farted a great, meaty trombone of a fart in confirmation.

'Oh, Jesus,' I said, waving my hand in front of my face. 'See what I mean?'

'Shut up, you animal,' said the young man. But I saw him raise

the barrel and level it at my head. I remembered the Parabellum
from my army days, when it had been the standard service pistol.
The Pistol .08 relies on the recoil to fire the striker, but with the
first shot the firing mechanism is always comparatively stiff. My
head made a smaller target than my stomach, and I hoped that I'd
have enough time to duck.

I threw myself at his waist, and as I did so I saw the flash and felt
the air of the 9 mm bullet as it zipped over my head and smashed
something behind me. My weight carried us both crashing into
the front door. But if I had expected him to be less than capable of
putting up a stiff resistance, I was mistaken. I took hold of the
wrist with the gun and found the arm twisting towards me with a
lot more strength than I had credited it with. I felt him grab the
collar of my dressing-gown and twist it. Then I heard it rip.

'Shit,' I said. 'That does it.' I pushed the gun towards him, and
succeeded in pressing the barrel against his sternum. Putting my
whole weight onto it I hoped to break a rib, but instead there was
a muffled, fleshy report as it fired again, and I found myself covered
in his steaming blood. I held his limp body for several seconds
before I let it roll away from me.

I stood up and took a look at him. There was no doubt that he
was dead, although blood continued to bubble up from the hole in
his chest. Then I went through his pockets. You always want to
know who's been trying to kill you. There was a wallet containing
an ID card in the name of Walther Kolb, and 200 marks. It didn't
make sense to leave the money for the boys from Kripo, so I took
150 to cover the cost of my dressing-gown. Also, there were two
photographs; one of these was an obscene postcard in which a man
was doing things to a girl's bottom with a length of rubber tube;
and the other was a publicity still of Ilse Rudel, signed, 'with
much love'. I burned the photograph of my former bedmate,
poured myself a stiff one and, marvelling at the picture of the
erotic enema, I called the police.

A couple of bulls came down from the Alex. The senior officer,
Oberinspektor Tesmer, was a Gestapo man; the other, Inspektor

Stahlecker, was a friend, one of my few remaining friends in Kripo, but with Tesmer around there wasn't a chance of an easy ride.

'That's my story,' I said, having told it for the third time. We were all seated round my dining table on which lay the Parabellum and the contents of the dead man's pockets. Tesmer shook his head slowly, as if I had offered to sell him something he wouldn't have a chance of shifting himself.

'You could always part exchange it for something else. Come on, try again. Maybe this time you'll make me laugh.' With its thin, almost non-existent lips, Tesmer's mouth was like a slash in a length of cheap curtain. And all you saw through the hole were the points of his rodent's teeth, and the occasional glimpse of the ragged, grey-white oyster that was his tongue.

'Look, Tesmer,' I said. 'I know it looks a bit beat up, but take my word for it, it's really very reliable. Not everything that shines is any good.'

'Try shifting some of the fucking dust off it then. What do you know about the canned meat?'

I shrugged. 'Only what was in his pockets. And that he and I weren't going to get along.'

'That wins him quite a few extra points on my card,' said Tesmer.

Stahlecker sat uncomfortably beside his boss, and tugged nervously at his eyepatch. He had lost an eye when he was with the Prussian infantry, and at the same time had won the coveted 'pour le mérite' for his bravery. Me, I'd have hung onto the eye, although the patch did look rather dashing. Combined with his dark colouring and bushy black moustache, it served to give him a piratical air, although his manner was altogether more stolid: slow even. But he was a good bull, and a loyal friend. All the same, he wasn't about to risk burning his fingers while Tesmer was doing his best to see if I'd catch fire. His honesty had previously led him to express one or two ill-advised opinions about the NSDAP during the '33 elections. Since then he'd had the sense to keep his mouth shut, but he and I both knew that the Kripo Executive was just

looking for an excuse to hang him out to dry. It was only his outstanding war record that had kept him in the force this long.

'And I suppose he tried to kill you because he didn't like your
cologne,' said Tesmer.

'You noticed it too, huh?' I saw Stahlecker smile a bit at that,
but so did Tesmer, and he didn't like it.

'Günther, you've got more lip than a nigger with a trumpet.
Your friend here may think you're funny, but I just think you're a
cunt, so don't fuck me around. I'm not the sort with a sense of
humour.'

'I've told you the truth, Tesmer. I opened the door and there
was Herr Kolb with the lighter pointing at my dinner.'

'A Parabellum on you, and yet you still managed to take him.
I don't see any fucking holes in you, Günther.'

'I'm taking a correspondence course in hypnotism. Like I said,
I was lucky, he missed. You saw the broken light.'

'Listen, I don't mesmerize easy. This fellow was a professional.
Not the sort to let you have his lighter for a bag of sherbet.'

'A professional what – haberdasher? Don't talk out of your
navel, Tesmer. He was just a kid.'

'Well, that makes it worse for you, because he isn't going to do
any more growing up.'

'Young he may have been,' I said, 'but he was no weakling.
I didn't bite my lip because I find you so damned attractive. This is
real blood, you know. And my dressing-gown. It's torn, or hadn't
you noticed?'

Tesmer laughed scornfully. 'I thought you were just a sloppy
dresser.'

'Hey, this is a fifty-mark gown. You don't think I'd tear it just
for your benefit, do you?'

'You could afford to buy it, then you could also afford to lose it.
I always thought your kind made too much money.' I leaned back
in my chair. I remembered Tesmer as one of Police Major Walther
Wecke's hatchet-men, charged with rooting out conservatives and

Bolsheviks from the force. A mean bastard if ever there was one. I wondered how Stahlecker managed to survive.

'What is it you earn, Günther? Three? Four hundred marks a week? Probably make as much as me and Stahlecker put together, eh, Stahlecker?' My friend shrugged non-committally.

'I dunno.'

'See?' said Tesmer. 'Even Stahlecker doesn't have any idea how many thousands a year you make.'

'You're in the wrong job, Tesmer. The way you exaggerate, you should work for the Ministry of Propaganda.' He said nothing. 'All right, all right, I get it. How much is it going to cost me?' Tesmer shrugged, trying to control the grin that threatened to break out on his face.

'From a man with a fifty-mark gown? Let's say a round hundred.'

'A hundred? For that cheap little garter-handler? Go and take another look at him, Tesmer. He doesn't have a Charlie Chaplin moustache and a stiff right arm.'

Tesmer stood up. 'You talk too much, Günther. Let's hope your mouth begins to fray at the edges before it gets you into serious trouble.' He looked at Stahlecker and then back at me. 'I'm going for a piss. Your old pitman here has got until I come back into the room to persuade you, otherwise . . .' He pursed his lips and shook his head. As he walked out, I called after him:

'Make sure you lift the seat.' I grinned at Stahlecker.

'How are you doing, Bruno?'

'What is it, Bernie? Have you been drinking? You blue or something? Come on, you know how difficult Tesmer could make things for you. First you plum the man with all that smart talk, and now you want to play the black horse. Pay the bastard.'

'Look, if I don't black horse him a little and drag my heels about paying him that kind of mouse, then he'll figure I'm worth a lot more. Bruno, as soon as I saw that son of a bitch I knew that the evening was going to cost me something. Before I left Kripo he and Wecke had me marked. I haven't forgotten and neither has he. I still owe him some agony.'

'Well, you certainly made it expensive for yourself when you mentioned the price of that gown.'

'Not really,' I said. 'It cost nearer a hundred.'

'Christ,' breathed Stahlecker. 'Tesmer is right. You *are* making too much money.' He thrust his hands deep into his pockets and looked squarely at me. 'Want to tell me what really happened here?'

'Another time, Bruno. It was mostly true.'

'Excepting one or two small details.'

'Right. Listen, I need a favour. Can we meet tomorrow? The matinée at the Kammerlichtspiele in the Haus Vaterland. Back row, at four o'clock.'

Bruno sighed, and then nodded. 'I'll try.'

'Before then see if you can't find out something about the Paul Pfarr case.' He frowned and was about to speak when Tesmer returned from the lavatory.

'I hope you wiped the floor.'

Tesmer pointed a face at me in which belligerence was moulded like cornice-work on a Gothic folly. The set of his jaw and the spread of his nose gave him about as much profile as a piece of lead piping. The general effect was early-Paleolithic.

'I hope you decided to get wise,' he growled. There would have been more chance of reasoning with a water buffalo.

'Seems like I don't have much choice,' I said. 'I don't suppose there's any chance of a receipt?'

7

Just off Kronprinzenallee, on the edge of Dahlem, was the huge wrought-iron gate to Six's estate. I sat in the car for a while and watched the road. Several times I closed my eyes and found my head nodding. It had been a late night. After a short nap I got out and opened the gate. Then I ambled back to the car and turned onto the private road, down a long, gentle slope and into the cool shade cast by the dark pine trees lining its gravelled length.

In daylight Six's house was even more impressive, although I could see now that it was not one but two houses, standing close together: beautiful, solidly built Wilhelmine farmhouses.

I pulled up at the front door, where Ilse Rudel had parked her BMW the night I had first seen her, and got out, leaving the door open just in case the two Dobermanns put in an appearance. Dogs are not at all keen on private investigators, and it's an antipathy that is entirely mutual.

I knocked on the door. I heard it echo in the hall and, seeing the closed shutters, I wondered if I'd had a wasted journey. I lit a cigarette and stood there, just leaning on the door, smoking and listening. The place was about as quiet as the sap in a gift-wrapped rubber tree. Then I heard some footsteps, and I straightened up as the door opened to reveal the Levantine head and round shoulders of the butler, Farraj.

'Good morning,' I said brightly. 'I was hoping that I'd find Herr Haupthändler in.' Farraj looked at me with the clinical distaste of a chiropodist regarding a septic toenail.

'Do you have an appointment?' he asked.

'Not really,' I said, handing him my card. 'I was hoping he might give me five minutes, though. I was here the other night, to see Herr Six.' Farraj nodded silently, and returned my card.

'My apologies for not recognizing you, sir.' Still holding the door, he retreated into the hall, inviting me to enter. Having closed it behind him, he looked at my hat with something short of amusement.

'No doubt you will wish to keep your hat again, sir.'

'I think I had better, don't you?' Standing closer to him, I could detect the very definite smell of alcohol, and not the sort they serve in exclusive gentlemen's clubs.

'Very good, sir. If you'll just wait here for a moment, I'll find Herr Haupthändler and ask him if he can see you.'

'Thanks,' I said. 'Do you have an ashtray?' I held my cigarette ash aloft like a hypodermic syringe.

'Yes, sir.' He produced one made of dark onyx that was the size of a church Bible, and which he held in both hands while I did the stubbing out. When my cigarette was extinguished he turned away and, still carrying the ashtray, he disappeared down the corridor, leaving me to wonder what I was going to say to Haupthändler if he would see me. There was nothing in particular I had in mind, and not for one minute did I imagine that he would be prepared to discuss Ilse Rudel's story about him and Grete Pfarr. I was just poking around. You ask ten people ten dumb questions, and sometimes you hit a raw nerve somewhere. Sometimes, if you weren't too bored to notice, you managed to recognize that you were on to something. It was a bit like panning for gold. Every day you went down to the river and went through pan after pan of mud. And just occasionally, provided you kept your eyes peeled, you found a dirty little stone that was actually a nugget.

I went to the bottom of the stairs and looked up the stairwell. A large circular skylight illuminated the paintings on the scarlet-coloured walls. I was looking at a still life of a lobster and a pewter pot when I heard footsteps on the marble floor behind me.

'It's by Karl Schuch you know,' said Haupthändler. 'Worth a great deal of money.' He paused, and added: 'But very, very dull. Please, come this way.' He led the way into Six's library.

'I'm afraid I can't give you very long. You see, I still have a great many things to do for the funeral tomorrow. I'm sure you understand.' I sat down on one of the sofas and lit a cigarette. Haupthändler folded his arms, the leather of his nutmeg-brown sports jacket creaking across his sizeable shoulders, and leaned against his master's desk.

'Now what was it that you wished to see me about?'

'Actually, it's about the funeral,' I said, improvising on what he had given me. 'I wondered where it was to be held.'

'I must apologize, Herr Günther,' he said. 'I'm afraid it hadn't occurred to me that Herr Six would wish you to attend. He's left all the arrangements to me while he's in the Ruhr, but he didn't think to leave any instructions regarding a list of mourners.'

I tried to look awkward. 'Oh, well,' I said, standing up. 'Naturally, with a client such as Herr Six I should like to have been able to pay my respects to his daughter. It is customary. But I'm sure he will understand.'

'Herr Günther,' said Haupthändler, after a short silence. 'Would you think it terrible of me if I were to give you an invitation now, by hand?'

'Not at all,' I said. 'If you are sure it won't inconvenience your arrangements.'

'It's no trouble,' he said. 'I have some cards here.' He walked around the desk and pulled open a drawer.

'Have you worked for Herr Six long?'

'About two years,' he said absently. 'Prior to that I was a diplomat with the German Consular Service.' He took out a pair of glasses from his breast pocket and placed them on the end of his nose before writing out the invitation.

'And did you know Grete Pfarr well?'

He glanced up at me briefly. 'I really didn't know her at all,' he said. 'Other than to say hallo to.'

'Do you know if she had any enemies, jealous lovers, that sort of thing?' He finished writing the card, and pressed it on the blotter.

'I'm quite sure she didn't,' he said crisply, removing his glasses and returning them to his pocket.

'Is that so? What about him? Paul.'

'I can tell you even less about him, I'm afraid,' he said, slipping the invitation into an envelope.

'Did he and Herr Six get on all right?'

'They weren't enemies, if that's what you're implying. Their differences were purely political.'

'Well, that amounts to something quite fundamental these days, wouldn't you say?'

'Not in this case, no. Now if you'll excuse me, Herr Günther, I really must be getting on.'

'Yes, of course.' He handed me the invitation. 'Well, thanks for this,' I said, following him out into the hall. 'Do you live here too, Herr Haupthändler?'

'No, I have an apartment in town.'

'Really? Where?' He hesitated for a moment.

'Kurfürstenstrasse,' he said eventually. 'Why do you ask?'

I shrugged. 'I ask too many questions, Herr Haupthändler,' I said. 'Forgive me. It's habit, I'm afraid. A suspicious nature goes with the job. Please don't be offended. Well, I must be going.' He smiled thinly, and as he showed me to the door he seemed relaxed; but I hoped I had said enough to put a few ripples on his pond.

The Hanomag seems to take an age to reach any sort of speed, so it was with a certain amount of misplaced optimism that I took the Avus 'Speedway' back to the centre of town. It costs a mark to get on this highway, but the Avus is worth it: ten kilometres without a curve, all the way from Potsdam to Kurfürstendamm. It's the one road in the city on which the driver who fancies himself as Carraciola, the great racing driver, can put his foot down and hit speeds of up to 150 kilometres an hour. At least, they could in the days before BV Aral, the low-octane substitute petrol that's not much better than meths. Now it was all I could do to get ninety out of the Hanomag's 1.3 litre engine.

I parked at the intersection of Kurfürstendamm and Joachimsthaler Strasse, known as 'Grunfeld Corner' because of the department store of the same name which occupies it. When Grunfeld, a Jew, still owned his store, they used to serve free lemonade at the Fountain in the basement. But since the State dispossessed him, as it has with all the Jews who owned big stores, like Wertheim, Hermann Tietz and Israel, the days of free lemonade have gone. If that weren't bad enough, the lemonade you now have to pay for and once got free doesn't taste half as good, and you don't have to have the sharpest taste-buds in the world to realize that they're cutting down on the sugar. Just like they're cheating on everything else.

I sat drinking my lemonade and watching the lift go up and down the tubular glass shaft that allowed you to see out into the store as you rode from floor to floor, in two minds whether or not to go up to the stocking counter and see Carola, the girl from Dagmar's wedding. It was the sour taste of the lemonade that put me in mind of my own debauched behaviour, and that decided me against it. Instead I left Grunfeld's and walked the short distance down Kurfürstendamm and onto Schlüterstrasse.

A jewellers is one of the few places in Berlin where you can expect to find people queueing to sell rather than to buy. Peter Neumaier's Antique Jewellers was no exception. When I got there the line wasn't quite outside the door, but it was certainly rubbing the glass; and it was older and sadder looking than most of the queues that I was used to standing in. The people waiting there were from a mixture of backgrounds, but mostly they had two things in common: their Judaism and, as an inevitable corollary, their lack of work, which was how they came to be selling their valuables in the first place. At the top of the queue, behind a long glass counter, were two stone-faced shop assistants in good suits. They had a neat line in appraisal, which was to tell the prospective seller how poor the piece actually was and how little it was likely to fetch on the open market.

'We see stuff like this all the time,' said one of them, wrinkling his lips and shaking his head at the spread of pearls and brooches on the counter beneath him. 'You see, we can't put a price on sentimental value. I'm sure you understand that.' He was a young fellow, half the age of the deflating old mattress of a woman before him, and good-looking too, although in need of a shave, perhaps. His colleague was less forthcoming with his indifference: he sniffed so that his nose took on a sneer, he shrugged a half shrug of his coathanger-sized shoulders, and he grunted unenthusiastically. Silently, he counted out five one-hundred-mark notes from a roll in his skinny miser's hand that must have been worth thirty times as much. The old man he was buying from was undecided about whether or not he should accept what must have been a derisory offer, and with a trembling hand he pointed at the bracelet lying on the piece of cloth he had wrapped it up in.

'But look here,' said the old man, 'you've got one just like it in the window for three times what you're offering.'

The Coathanger pursed his lips. 'Fritz,' he said, 'how long has that sapphire bracelet been in the window?' It was an efficient double-act, you had to say that much.

'Must be six months,' responded the other. 'Don't buy another one, this isn't a charity you know.' He probably said that several times a day. Coathanger blinked with slow boredom.

'See what I mean? Look, go somewhere else if you think you can get more for it.' But the sight of the cash was too much for the old man, and he capitulated. I walked to the head of the line and said that I was looking for Herr Neumaier.

'If you've got something to sell, then you'll have to wait in line with all the rest of them,' muttered Coathanger.

'I have nothing to sell,' I said vaguely, adding, 'I'm looking for a diamond necklace.' At that Coathanger smiled at me like I was his long-lost rich uncle.

'If you'll just wait one moment,' he said unctuously, 'I'll just see if Herr Neumaier is free.' He disappeared behind a curtain for a minute, and when he returned I was ushered through to a small office at the end of the corridor.

Peter Neumaier sat at his desk, smoking a cigar that belonged properly in a plumber's tool-bag. He was dark, with bright blue eyes, just like our beloved Führer, and was possessed of a stomach that stuck out like a cash register. The cheeks of his face had a red, skinned look, as if he had eczema, or had simply stood too close to his razor that morning. He shook me by the hand as I introduced myself. It was like holding a cucumber.

'I'm pleased to meet you, Herr Günther,' he said warmly. 'I hear you're looking for some diamonds.'

'That's correct. But I should tell you that I'm acting on behalf of someone else.'

'I understand,' Neumaier grinned. 'Did you have a particular setting in mind?'

'Oh, yes indeed. A diamond necklace.'

'Well, you have come to the right place. There are several diamond necklaces I can show you.'

'My client knows precisely what he requires,' I said. 'It must be a diamond collet necklace, made by Cartier.' Neumaier laid his cigar in the ashtray, and breathed out a mixture of smoke, nerves and amusement.

'Well,' he said. 'That certainly narrows the field.'

'That's the thing about the rich, Herr Neumaier,' I said. 'They always seem to know exactly what they want, don't you think?'

'Oh, indeed they do, Herr Günther.' He leaned forwards in his chair and, collecting his cigar, he said: 'A necklace such as you describe is not the sort of piece that comes along every day. And of course it would cost a great deal of money.' It was time to stick the nettle down his trousers.

'Naturally, my client is prepared to pay a great deal of money. Twenty-five per cent of the insured value, no questions asked.'

He frowned. 'I'm not sure I understand what you're talking about,' he said.

'Come off it, Neumaier. We both know that there's a lot more to your operation than the heart-warming little scene you're putting on out front there.'

He blew some smoke and looked at the end of his cigar. 'Are you suggesting that I buy stolen merchandise, Herr Günther, because if you are —'

'Keep your ears stiff, Neumaier, I haven't finished yet. My client's flea is solid. Cash money.' I tossed the photograph of Six's diamonds at him. 'If some mouse walks in here trying to sell it, you give me a call. The number's on the back.'

Neumaier regarded it and me distastefully and then stood up. 'You are a joke, Herr Günther. With a few cups short in your cupboard. Now get out of here before I call the police.'

'You know, that's not a bad idea,' I said. 'I'm sure they'll be very impressed with your public spirit when you offer to open up your safe and invite them to inspect the contents. That's the confidence of honesty, I suppose.'

'Get out of here.'

I stood up and walked out of his office. I hadn't intended to handle it that way, but I hadn't liked what I'd seen of Neumaier's operation. In the shop Coathanger was half-way through offering an old woman a price for her jewel-box that was less than she might have got for it at the Salvation Army hostel. Several of the Jews waiting behind her looked at me with an expression that was a mixture of hope and hopelessness. It made me feel about as comfortable as a trout on a marble slab, and for no reason that I could think of, I felt something like shame.

Gert Jeschonnek was a different proposition. His premises were on the eighth floor of Columbus Haus, a nine-storeyed building on Potsdamer Platz which has a strong emphasis on the horizontal line. It looked like something a long-term prisoner might have made, given an endless supply of matches, and at the same time it put me in mind of the nearly eponymous building near Tempelhof Airport that is Columbia Haus – the Gestapo prison in Berlin. This country shows its admiration for the discoverer of America in the strangest ways.

The eighth floor was home to a whole country-club of doctors, lawyers and publishers, who were only just getting by on 30,000 a year.

The double entrance doors to Jeschonnek's office were made of polished mahogany, on which appeared in gold lettering, 'GERT JESCHONNEK. PRECIOUS STONE MERCHANT'. Beyond these was an L-shaped office with walls that were a pleasant shade of pink, on which were hung several framed photographs of diamonds, rubies and various gaudy little baubles that might have stimulated the greed of a Solomon or two. I took a chair and waited for an anaemic young man sitting behind a typewriter to finish on the telephone. After a minute he said:

'I'll call you back, Rudi.' He replaced the receiver and looked at me with an expression that was just a few centimetres short of surly.

'Yes?' he said. Call me old-fashioned, but I have never liked male secretaries. A man's vanity gets in the way of serving the needs of another male, and this particular specimen wasn't about to win me over.

'When you've finished filing your nails, perhaps you'd tell your boss that I'd like to see him. The name's Günther.'

'Do you have an appointment?' he said archly.

'Since when does a man who's looking for some diamonds need to make an appointment? Tell me that, would you?' I could see that he found me less amusing than a boxful of smoke.

'Save your breath to cool your soup,' he said, and came round the desk to go through the only other door. 'I'll find out if he can see you.' While he was out of the room I picked up a recent issue of *Der Stürmer* from the magazine rack. The front page had a drawing of a man in angel's robes holding an angel's mask in front of his face. Behind him was his devil's tail, sticking out from underneath his surplice, and his 'angel's' shadow, except that this now revealed the profile behind the mask to be unmistakably Jewish. Those *Der Stürmer* cartoonists love to draw a big nose, and this one was a real pelican's beak. A strange thing to find in a respectable businessman's office, I thought. The anaemic young man emerging from the other office provided the simple explanation.

'He won't keep you very long,' he said, adding, 'He buys that to impress the kikes.'

'I'm afraid I don't follow.'

'We get a lot of Jewish custom in here,' he explained. 'Of course, they only want to sell, never to buy. Herr Jeschonnek thinks that if they see that he subscribes to *Der Stürmer*, it will help him to drive a harder bargain.'

'Very shrewd of him,' I said. 'Does it work?'

'I guess so. You'd better ask him.'

'Maybe I will at that.'

There wasn't much to see in the boss's office. Across a couple of acres of carpet was a grey steel safe that had once been a small battleship, and a Panzer-sized desk with a dark leather top. The desk had very little on it except a square of felt, on which lay a ruby that was big enough to decorate a Maharajah's favourite elephant, and Jeschonnek's feet, wearing immaculate white spats, and these swung under the table as I came through the door.

Gert Jeschonnek was a burly hog of a man, with small piggy eyes and a brown beard cropped close to his sunburned face. He wore a light-grey double-breasted suit that was ten years too young for him, and in the lapel was a Scary Badge. He had March Violet plastered all over him like insect repellent.

'Herr Günther,' he said brightly, and for a moment he was almost standing at attention. Then he crossed the floor to greet me. A purplish butcher's hand pumped mine own, which showed patches of white when I let it go. He must have had blood like treacle. He smiled a sweet smile and then looked across my shoulder to his anaemic secretary who was about to close the door on us. Jeschonnek said:

'Helmut. A pot of your best strong coffee please. Two cups, and no delays.' He spoke quickly and precisely, beating time with his hand like a teacher of elocution. He led me over to the desk, and the ruby, which I figured was there to impress me, in the same way as the copies of *Der Stürmer* were there to impress his Jewish custom. I pretended to ignore it, but Jeschonnek was not to be denied his little performance. He held the ruby up to the light in his fat fingers, and grinned obscenely.

'An extremely fine cabochon ruby,' he said. 'Like it?'

'Red isn't my colour,' I said. 'It doesn't go with my hair.' He laughed and replaced the ruby on the velvet, which he folded up and returned to his safe. I sat down on a big armchair in front of his desk.

'I'm looking for a diamond necklace,' I said. He sat down opposite me.

'Well, Herr Günther, I'm the acknowledged expert on diamonds.' His head gave a proud little flourish, like a racehorse, and I caught a powerful whiff of cologne.

'Is that so?' I said.

'I doubt if there's a man in Berlin who knows as much about diamonds as I do.' He thrust his stubbly chin at me, as if challenging me to contradict him. I almost threw up.

'I'm glad to hear it,' I said. The coffee arrived and Jeschonnek glanced uncomfortably after his secretary as he minced out of the room.

'I cannot get used to having a male secretary,' he said. 'Of course, I can see that the proper place for a woman is in the home, bringing up a family, but I have a great fondness for women, Herr Günther.'

'I'd take a partner before I'd take on a male secretary,' I said. He smiled politely.

'Now then, I believe you're in the market for a diamond.'

'Diamonds,' I said, correcting him.

'I see. On their own, or in a setting?'

'Actually I'm trying to trace a particular piece which has been stolen from my client,' I explained, and handed him my card. He stared at it impassively. 'A necklace, to be precise. I have a photograph of it here.' I produced another photograph and handed it to him.

'Magnificent,' he said.

'Each one of the baguettes is one carat,' I told him.

'Quite,' he said. 'But I don't see how I can help you, Herr Günther.'

'If the thief should try and offer it to you, I'd be grateful if you would contact me. Naturally, there is a substantial reward. I have been authorized by my client to offer twenty-five per cent of the insured value for recovery, no questions asked.'

'May one know the name of your client, Herr Günther?'

I hesitated. 'Well,' I said. 'Ordinarily, a client's identity is confidential. But I can see that you are the kind of man who is used to respecting confidentiality.'

'You're much too kind,' he said.

'The necklace is Indian, and belongs to a princess who is in Berlin for the Olympiad, as the guest of the Government.' Jeschonnek began to frown as he listened to my lies. 'I have not met the princess myself, but I am told that she is the most beautiful creature that Berlin has ever seen. She is staying at the Adlon Hotel, from where the necklace was stolen several nights ago '

'Stolen from an Indian princess, eh?' he said, adding a smile to his features. 'Well, I mean, why was there nothing in the newspapers about this? And why are the police not involved?' I drank some of my coffee to prolong a dramatic pause.

'The management of the Adlon is anxious to avoid a scandal,' I said. 'It's not so very long ago that the Adlon suffered a series of unfortunate robberies committed there by the celebrated jewel-thief Faulhaber.'

'Yes, I remember reading about that.'

'It goes without question that the necklace is insured, but where the reputation of the Adlon is concerned, that is hardly the point, as I am sure you will understand.'

'Well, sir, I shall certainly contact you immediately if I come across any information that may help you,' said Jeschonnek, producing a gold watch from his pocket. He glanced at it deliberately. 'And now, if you'll excuse me, I really must be getting on.' He stood up and held out his pudgy hand.

'Thanks for your time,' I said. 'I'll see myself out.'

'Perhaps you'd be kind enough to ask that boy to step in here when you go out,' he said.

'Sure.'

He gave me the Hitler Salute. 'Heil Hitler,' I repeated dumbly.

In the outside office the anaemic boy was reading a magazine. My eyes caught sight of the keys before I'd finished telling him that his boss required his presence: they were lying on the desk next to the telephone. He grunted and wrenched himself out of his seat. I hesitated at the door.

'Oh, do you have a piece of paper?'

He pointed to the pad on which the keys were lying. 'Help yourself,' he said, and went into Jeschonnek's office.

'Thanks, I will.' The key-ring was labelled 'Office'. I took a cigarette case out of my pocket and opened it. In the smooth surface of the modelling clay I made three impressions – two sides and a vertical – of both keys. I suppose that you could say I did it on impulse. I'd hardly had time to digest everything that Jeschonnek had said; or rather, what he hadn't said. But then I always carry that piece of clay, and it seems a shame not to use it when the opportunity presents itself. You would be surprised how often a key that I've had made with that mould comes in useful.

Outside, I found a public telephone and called the Adlon. I still remembered lots of good times at the Adlon, and lots of friends, too.

'Hello, Hermine,' I said, 'it's Bernie.' Hermine was one of the girls on the Adlon's switchboard.

'You stranger,' she said. 'We haven't seen you in ages.'

'I've been a bit busy,' I said.

'So's the Führer, but he still manages to get around and wave to us.'

'Maybe I should buy myself an open-top Mercedes and a couple of outriders.' I lit a cigarette. 'I need a small favour, Hermine.'

'Ask.'

'If a man telephones and asks you or Benita if there is an Indian princess staying at the hotel, would you please say that there is? If he wants to speak to her, say she's not taking any calls.'

'That's all?'

'Yes.'

'Does this princess have a name?'

'You know the names of any Indian girls?'

'Well,' she said, 'I saw a film the other week which had this Indian girl in it. Her name was Mushmi.'

'Let it be Princess Mushmi then. And thanks, Hermine. I'll be speaking to you soon.'

I went into the Pschorr Haus restaurant and ate a plate of bacon and broad beans, and drank a couple of beers. Either Jeschonnek knew nothing about diamonds, or he had something to hide. I'd told him that the necklace was Indian, when he ought to have recognized it as being by Cartier. Not only that, but he had failed to contradict me when I described the stones incorrectly as baguettes. Baguettes are square or oblong, with a straight edge; but Six's necklace consisted of brilliants, which are round. And then there was the caratage; I'd said that each stone was a carat in weight, when they were obviously several times larger.

It wasn't much to go on; and mistakes are made: it's impossible always to pick up a stick by the right end; but all the same, I had this feeling in my socks that I was going to have to visit Jeschonnek again.

8

After leaving Pschorr Haus, I went into the Haus Vaterland, which as well as housing the cinema where I was to meet Bruno Stahlecker, is also home to an almost infinite number of bars and cafés. The place is popular with the tourists, but it's too old-fashioned to suit my taste: the great ugly halls, the silver paint, the bars with their miniature rainstorms and moving trains; it all belongs to a quaint old European world of mechanical toys and music-hall, leotarded strong-men and trained canaries. The other thing that makes it unusual is that it's the only bar in Germany that charges for admission. Stahlecker was less than happy about it.

'I had to pay twice,' he grumbled. 'Once at the front door, and again to come in here.'

'You should have flashed your Sipo pass,' I said. 'You'd have got in for nothing. That's the whole point of having it, isn't it?' Stahlecker looked blankly at the screen.

'Very funny,' he said. 'What is this shit, anyway?'

'Still the newsreel,' I told him. 'So what did you find out?'

'There's the small matter of last night to be dealt with yet.'

'My word of honour, Bruno, I never saw the kid before.' Stahlecker sighed wearily. 'Apparently this Kolb was a small-time actor. One or two bit-parts in films, in the chorus-line in a couple of shows. Not exactly Richard Tauber. Now why would a fellow like that want to kill you? Unless maybe you've turned critic and gave him a few bad notices.'

'I've got no more understanding of theatre than a dog has of laying a fire.'

'But you do know why he tried to kill you, right?'

'There's this lady,' I said. 'Her husband hired me to do a job for him. She thought that I'd been hired to look through her keyhole.

So last night she has me round to her place, asks me to lay off and accuses me of lying when I tell her that I'm not concerned who she's sleeping with. Then she throws me out. Next thing I know there's this pear-head standing in my doorway with a lighter poked in my gut, accusing me of raping the lady. We dance around the room a while, and in the process the gun goes off. My guess is that the kid was in a swarm about her, and that she knew it.'

'And so she put him up to it, right?'

'That's the way I see it. But try and make it stick and see how far you'd get.'

'I don't suppose you're going to tell me the name of this lady, or her husband, are you?' I shook my head. 'No, I thought not.'

The film was starting: called *The Higher Order*, it was one of those patriotic little entertainments that the boys in the Ministry of Propaganda had dreamed up on a bad day. Stahlecker groaned.

'Come on,' he said. 'Let's go and get a drink. I don't think I can stand watching this shit.'

We went to the Wild West Bar on the first floor, where a band of cowboys were playing *Home on the Range*. Painted prairies covered the walls, complete with buffalo and Indians. Leaning up against the bar, we ordered a couple of beers.

'I don't suppose any of this would have something to do with the Pfarr case, would it, Bernie?'

'I've been retained to investigate the fire,' I explained. 'By the insurance company.'

'All right,' he said. 'I'll tell you this just the once, and then you can tell me to go to hell. Drop it. It's a hot one, if you'll pardon the expression.'

'Bruno,' I said, 'go to hell. I'm on a percentage.'

'Just don't say I didn't warn you when they throw you into a KZ.'

'I promise. Now unpack it.'

'Bernie, you've got more promises than a debtor has for the bailiff.' He sighed and shook his head. 'Well, here's what there is.

'This Paul Pfarr fellow was a high-flyer. Passed his juridicial in 1930, saw preparatory service in the Stuttgart and Berlin Provincial

Courts. In 1933, this particular March Violet joins the SA, and by 1934 he is an assessor judge in the Berlin Police Court, trying cases of police corruption, of all things. The same year he is recruited into the SS and in 1935 he also joins the Gestapo, supervising associations, economic unions and of course the DAF, the Reich Labour Service. Later that year he is transferred yet again, this time to the Ministry of the Interior, reporting directly to Himmler, with his own department investigating corruption amongst servants of the Reich.'

'I'm surprised that they notice.'

'Apparently Himmler takes a very dim view of it. Anyway, Paul Pfarr was charged with paying particular attention to the DAF, where corruption is endemic.'

'So he was Himmler's boy, eh?'

'That's right. And his ex-boss takes an even dimmer view of people working for him getting canned than he does of corruption. So a couple of days ago the Reichskriminaldirektor appoints a special squad to investigate. It's an impressive team: Gohrmann, Schild, Jost, Dietz. You get mixed up in this, Bernie, and you won't last longer than a synagogue window.'

'They got any leads?'

'The only thing I heard was that they were looking for a girl. It seems as though Pfarr might have had a mistress. No name, I'm afraid. Not only that, but she's disappeared.'

'You want to know something?' I said. 'Disappearing is all the rage. Everyone's doing it.'

'So I heard. I hope you aren't the fashionable sort, then.'

'Me? I must be one of the only people in this city not to own a uniform. I'd say that makes me very unfashionable.'

Back at Alexanderplatz I visited a locksmith and gave him the mould to make a copy of Jeschonnek's office keys. I'd used him many times before, and he never asked any questions. Then I collected my laundry and went up to the office.

I wasn't half-way through the door before a Sipo pass had flashed in front of my face. In the same instant I caught sight of the Walther inside the man's unbuttoned grey-flannel jacket.

'You must be the sniffer,' he said. 'We've been waiting to speak to you.' He had mustard-coloured hair, coiffed by a competition sheepshearer, and a nose like a champagne cork. His moustache was wider than the brim on a Mexican's hat. The other one was the racial archetype with the sort of exaggerated chin and cheekbones he'd copied off a Prussian election poster. They both had cool, patient eyes, like mussels in brine, and sneers like someone had farted, or told a particularly tasteless joke.

'If I'd known, I'd have gone to see a couple of movies.' The one with the pass and the haircut stared blankly at me.

'This here is Kriminalinspektor Dietz,' he said.

The one called Dietz, who I guessed to be the senior officer, was sitting on the edge of my desk, swinging his leg and looking generally unpleasant.

'You'll excuse me if I don't get out my autograph-book,' I said, and walked over to the corner by the window where Frau Protze was standing. She sniffed and pulled out a handkerchief from the sleeve of her blouse, and blew her nose. Through the material she said:

'I'm sorry, Herr Günther, they just barged in here and started ransacking the place. I told them I didn't know where you were, or when you would be back, and they got quite nasty. I never knew that policemen could behave so disgracefully.'

'They're not policemen,' I said. 'More like knuckles with suits. You'd better run along home now. I'll see you tomorrow.'

She sniffed some more. 'Thank you, Herr Günther,' she said. 'But I don't think I'll be coming back. I don't think my nerves are up to this sort of thing. I'm sorry.'

'That's all right. I'll mail what I owe you.' She nodded, and having stepped round me she almost ran out of the office. The haircut snorted with laughter and kicked the door shut behind her. I opened the window.

'There's a bit of a smell in here,' I said. 'What do you fellows do when you're not scaring widows and searching for the petty-cash box?'

Dietz jerked himself off my desk and came over to the window. 'I heard about you, Günther,' he said, looking out at the traffic. 'You used to be a bull, so I know that you know the official paper on just how far I can go. And that's still a hell of a long way yet. I can stand on your fucking face for the rest of the afternoon, and I don't even have to tell you why. So why don't you cut the shit and tell me what you know about Paul Pfarr, and then we'll be on our way again.'

'I know he wasn't a careless smoker,' I said. 'Look, if you hadn't gone through this place like an earth-tremor, I might have been able to find a letter from the Germania Life Assurance Company engaging me to investigate the fire pending any claim.'

'Oh, we found that letter,' said Dietz. 'We found this, too.' He took my gun out of his jacket pocket and pointed it playfully at my head.

'I've got a licence for it.'

'Sure you have,' he said, smiling. Then he sniffed the muzzle, and spoke to his partner. 'You know, Martins, I'd say this pistol has been cleaned; and recently, too.'

'I'm a clean boy,' I said. 'Take a look at my fingernails if you don't believe me.'

'Walther PPK, 9 mm,' said Martins, lighting a cigarette. 'Just like the gun that killed poor Herr Pfarr and his wife.'

'That's not what I heard.' I went over to the drinks cabinet. I was surprised to see that they hadn't helped themselves to any of my whisky.

'Of course,' said Dietz, 'we were forgetting that you've still got friends over at the Alex, weren't we.' I poured myself a drink. A little too much to swallow in less than three gulps.

'I thought they got rid of all those reactionaries,' said Martins. I surveyed the last mouthful of whisky.

'I'd offer you boys a drink, only I wouldn't want to have to throw away the glasses afterwards.' I tossed the drink back.

Martins flicked away his cigarette and, clenching his fists, he stepped forward a couple of paces. 'This bum specializes in lip like a yid does in nose,' he snarled. Dietz stayed where he was, leaning on the window. But when he turned around there was tabasco in his eyes.

'I'm running out of patience with you, mulemouth.'

'I don't get it,' I said. 'You've seen the letter from the Assurance people. If you think it's a fake, then check it out.'

'We already did.'

'Then why the double act?' Dietz walked over and looked me up and down like I was shit on his shoe. Then he picked up my last bottle of good scotch, weighed it in his hand and threw it against the wall above the desk. It smashed with the sound of a canteen of cutlery dropping down a stairwell, and the air was suddenly redolent with alcohol. Dietz straightened his jacket after the exertion.

'We just wanted to impress you with the need to keep us informed of what you're doing, Günther. If you find out anything, and I mean anything, then you better speak to us. Because if I find out you've been giving us any fig-leaf, then I'll have you in a KZ so quick, your fucking ears will whistle.' He leaned towards me and I caught the smell of his sweat. 'Understand, mulemouth?'

'Don't stick your jaw too far out, Dietz,' I said, 'or I'll feel obliged to slap it.'

He smiled. 'I'd like that sometime. Really I would.' He turned to his partner. 'Come on,' he said. 'Let's get out of here before I kick him in the eggs.'

I'd just finished clearing up the mess when the phone rang. It was Müller from the *Berliner Morgenpost* to say that he was sorry, but beyond the sort of material that the obituaries people collected over the years, there really wasn't much in the files about Hermann Six to interest me.

'Are you giving me the up and down, Eddie? Christ, this fellow is a millionaire. He owns half the Ruhr. If he stuck his finger up his arse he'd find oil. Somebody must have got a look through his keyhole at some time.'

'There was a reporter a while back who did quite a bit of spade-work on all of those big boys on the Ruhr: Krupp, Voegler, Wolff, Thyssen. She lost her job when the Government solved the un-employment problem. I'll see if I can find out where she's living.'

'Thanks, Eddie. What about the Pfarrs? Anything?'

'She was really into spas. Nauheim, Wiesbaden, Bad Homburg, you name it, she'd splashed some there. She even wrote an article about it for *Die Frau*. And she was keen on quack medicine. There's nothing about him, I'm afraid.'

'Thanks for the gossip, Eddie. Next time I'll read the society page and save you the trouble.'

'Not worth a hundred, huh?'

'Not worth fifty. Find this lady reporter for me and then I'll see what I can do.'

After that I closed the office and returned to the key shop to collect my new set of keys and my tin of clay. I'll admit it sounds a bit theatrical; but honestly, I've carried that tin for several years, and short of stealing the actual key itself, I don't know of a better way of opening locked doors. A delicate mechanism of fine steel with which you can open any kind of lock, I don't have. The truth is that with the best modern locks, you can forget picking: there are no slick, fancy little wonder tools. That stuff is for the film-boys at UFA. More often than not a burglar simply saws off the bolt-head, or drills around it and removes a piece of the goddam door. And that reminded me: sooner or later I was going to have to check out just who there was in the fraternity of nutcrackers with the talent to have opened the Pfarrs' safe. If that was how it was done. Which meant that there was a certain scrofulous little tenor who was long overdue for a singing lesson.

I didn't expect to find Neumann at the dump where he lived in Admiralstrasse, in the Kottbusser Tor district, but I tried there anyway. Kottbusser Tor was the kind of area that had worn about as well as a music-hall poster, and Admiralstrasse, Number 43 was the kind of place where the rats wore ear-plugs and the cockroaches had nasty coughs. Neumann's room was in the basement at the back. It was damp. It was dirty. It was foul. And Neumann wasn't there.

The concierge was a snapper who was over the hill and down a disused mine-shaft. Her hair was every bit as natural as parade goose-stepping down the Wilhelmstrasse, and she'd evidently been wearing a boxing-glove when she'd applied the crimson lipstick to her paperclip of a mouth. Her breasts were like the rear ends of a pair of dray horses at the end of a long hard day. Maybe she still had a few clients, but I thought it was a better bet that I'd see a Jew at the front of a Nuremberg pork-butcher's queue. She stood in the doorway to her apartment, naked under the grubby towelling robe which she left open, and lit a half-smoked cigarette.

'I'm looking for Neumann,' I said, doing my level best to ignore the two coat-pegs and the Russian boyar's beard that were being displayed for my benefit. You felt the twang and itch of syphilis in your tail just looking at her. 'I'm a friend of his.' The snapper yawned cheesily and, deciding that I'd seen enough for free, she closed her robe and tied the cord.

'You a bull?' she sniffed.

'Like I said, I'm a friend.' She folded her arms and leaned on the doorway.

'Neumann doesn't have any friends,' she said, looking at her dirty fingernails and then back at my face. I had to give her that one. 'Except for me, maybe, and that's only because I feel sorry for the little twitcher. If you were a friend of his you'd tell him to see a doctor. He isn't right in the head, you know.' She took a long drag on her cigarette and then flicked the butt past my shoulder.

'He's not tapped,' I said. 'He just has a tendency to talk to himself. A bit strange, that's all.'

'If that's not tapped then I don't know what the hell is,' she said. There was something in that too.

'You know when he'll be back?'

The snapper shrugged. A hand that was all blue veins and knuckle-duster rings took hold of my tie; she tried to smile coyly, only it came out as a grimace. 'Maybe you'd care to wait for him,' she said. 'You know, twenty marks buys an awful lot of time.'

Retrieving my tie I took out my wallet and thumbed her a five. 'I'd like to. Really I would. But I must be getting on my way. Perhaps you'd tell Neumann that I was looking for him. The name is Günther. Bernhard Günther.'

'Thank you, Bernhard. You're a real gentleman.'

'Do you have any idea where he might be?'

'Bernhard, your guess is as good as mine. You could chase him from Pontius to Pilate and still not find him.' She shrugged and shook her head. 'If he's broke he'll be somewhere like the X Bar, or the Rucker. If he's got any mouse in his pocket he'll be trying to nudge a bit of plum at the Femina or the Café Casanova.' I started down the stairs. 'And if he's not at any of those places then he'll be at the racetrack.' She followed me out onto the landing and down some of the steps. I got into my car with a sigh of relief. It's always difficult getting away from a snapper. They never like to see trade walking out of the door.

I don't have much faith in experts; or, for that matter, in the statements of witnesses. Over the years I've come to belong to the school of detection that favours good, old-fashioned, circumstantial evidence of the kind that says a fellow did it because he was the type who'd do that sort of thing anyway. That, and information received.

Keeping a tenor like Neumann is something that requires trust and patience; and just as the first of these does not come naturally to Neumann, so the second does not come naturally to me: but only where he is concerned. Neumann is the best informer I've ever had, and his tips are usually accurate. There were no lengths to which I would not go to protect him. On the other hand, it does not follow that you can rely on him. Like all informers he would sell his own sister's plum. You get one to trust you, that's the hard bit; but you could no more trust one yourself than I could win the Sierstorpff Stakes at the Hoppegarten.

I started at the X Bar, an illegal jazz club where the band were sandwiching American hits between the opening and closing chords of whatever innocuous and culturally acceptable Aryan number took their fancy; and they did it well enough not to trouble any Nazi's conscience regarding so-called inferior music.

In spite of his occasionally strange behaviour, Neumann was one of the most nondescript, anonymous-looking people I had ever seen. It was what made him such an excellent informer. You had to look hard to see him, but that particular night, there was no sign of him at the X. Nor at the Allaverdi, nor the Rucker Bar in the rough end of the red-light district.

It wasn't yet dark, but already the dope dealers had surfaced. To be caught selling cocaine was to be sent to a KZ, and for my money they couldn't catch too many of them; but as I knew from experience, that wasn't easy: the dealers never carried coke on them; instead they would hide it in a stash nearby, in a secluded alley or doorway. Some of them posed as war cripples selling cigarettes; and some of them were war cripples selling cigarettes, wearing the yellow armlet with its three black spots that had persisted from Weimar days. This armlet conferred no official status, however; only the Salvation Army received official permission to peddle wares on street corners, but the laws against vagrancy were not strictly enforced anywhere except the more fashionable areas of the city, where the tourists were likely to go.

'Ssigars, and ssigarettes,' hissed a voice. Those familiar with this 'coke signal' would answer with a loud sniff; often they found that they had bought cooking salt and aspirin.

The Femina, on Nurnberger Strasse, was the sort of spot you went when you were looking for some female company if you didn't mind them big and florid and thirty marks for the privilege. Table telephones made the Femina especially suitable for the shy type, so it was just Neumann's sort of place, always presuming that he had some money. He could order a bottle of sekt and invite a girl to join him without so much as moving from his table. There were even pneumatic tubes through which small presents could be blown into the hand of a girl at the opposite end of the club. Apart from money, the only thing a man needed at the Femina was good eyesight.

I sat at a corner table and glanced idly at the menu. As well as the list of drinks, there was a list of presents that could be purchased from the waiter, for sending through the tubes: a powder compact for one mark fifty; a matchbox-container for a mark; and perfume for five. I couldn't help thinking that money was likely to be the most popular sort of present you could send rocketing over to whichever party girl caught your eye. There was no sign of Neumann, but I decided to stick it out for a while in case he showed up. I signalled the waiter and ordered a beer.

There was a cabaret, of sorts: a chanteuse with orange hair, and a twangy voice like a Jew's harp; and a skinny little comedian with joined-up eyebrows, who was about as risqué as a wafer on an ice-cream sundae. There was less chance of the crowd at the Femina enjoying the acts than there was of it rebuilding the Reichstag: it laughed during the songs; and it sang during the comedian's monologues; and it was no nearer the palm of anyone's hand than if it had been a rabid dog.

Looking round the room I found there were so many false eyelashes flapping at me that I was beginning to feel a draught. Several tables away a fat woman rippled the fingers of a pudgy hand at me, and misinterpreting my sneer for a smile, she started to struggle out of her seat. I groaned.

'Yessir?' answered the waiter. I pulled a crumpled note out of my pocket and tossed it on to his tray. Without bothering to wait for my change I turned and fled.

There's only one thing that unnerves me more than the company of an ugly woman in the evening, and that's the company of the same ugly woman the following morning.

I got into the car and drove to Potsdamer Platz. It was a warm, dry evening, but the rumbling in the purple sky told me that the weather was about to change for the worse. I parked on Leipziger

Platz in front of the Palast Hotel. Then I went inside and telephoned the Adlon.

I got through to Benita, who said that Hermine had left her a message, and that about half an hour after I had spoken to her a man had called asking about an Indian princess. It was all I needed to know.

I collected my raincoat and a flashlight from the car. Holding the flash under the raincoat I walked the fifty metres back to Potsdamer Platz, past the Berlin Tramway Company and the Ministry of Agriculture, towards Columbus Haus. There were lights on the fifth and seventh floors, but none on the eighth. I looked in through the heavy plate-glass doors. There was a security guard sitting at the desk reading a newspaper, and, further along the corridor, a woman who was going over the floor with an electric polisher. It started to rain as I turned the corner onto Hermann Goering Strasse, and made a left onto the narrow service alley that led to the underground car-park at the back of Columbus Haus.

There were only two cars parked – a DKW and a Mercedes. It seemed unlikely that either of them belonged to the security guard or the cleaner; more probably, their owners were still at work in offices on the floors above. Behind the two cars, and under a bulkhead light, was a grey, steel door with the word 'Service' painted on it; it had no handle, and was locked. I decided that it was probably the sort of lock that had a spring bolt that could be withdrawn by a knob on the inside, or by means of a key on the outside, and I thought that there was a good chance that the cleaner might leave the building through this door.

I checked the doors of the two parked cars almost absent-mindedly, and found that the Mercedes was not locked. I sat in the driver's seat, and fumbled for the light switch. The two huge lamps cut through the shadows like the spots at a Party rally in Nuremberg. I waited. Several minutes passed. Bored, I opened the glove-box. There was a road map, a bag of mints and a Party membership book with stamps up to date. It identified the bearer as one

Henning Peter Manstein. Manstein had a comparatively low Party number, which belied the youthfulness of the man in the photograph on the book's ninth page. There was quite a racket in the sale of early Party numbers, and there was no doubting that was how Manstein had come by his. A low number was essential to quick political advancement. His handsome young face had the greedy look of a March Violet stamped all over it, as clearly as the Party insignia embossed across the corner of the photograph.

Fifteen minutes passed before I heard the sound of the service door opening. I sprang out of the seat. If it was Manstein, then I was going to have to make a run for it. A wide pool of light spilled onto the floor of the garage, and the cleaning woman came through the door.

'Hold the door,' I called. I switched off the headlights and slammed the car door. 'I've left something upstairs,' I said. 'I thought for a minute I was going to have to walk all the way round to the front.' She stood there dumbly, holding the door open as I approached. When I drew near her she stepped aside, saying:

'I have to walk all the way to Nollendorf Platz. I don't have no big car to take me home.'

I smiled sheepishly, like the idiot I imagined Manstein to be. 'Thanks very much,' I said, and muttered something about having left my key in my office. The cleaning woman hovered a little and then released the door to me. I stepped inside the building and let it go. It closed behind me, and I heard the loud click of the cylinder lock as the bolt hit the chamber.

Two double doors with porthole windows led into a long, brightly lit corridor that was lined with stacks of cardboard boxes. At the far end was a lift, but there was no way of using it without alerting the guard. So I sat down on the stairs and removed my shoes and socks, putting them on again in reverse order, with the socks over the shoes. It's an old trick, favoured by burglars, for muffling the sound of shoe-leather on a hard surface. I stood up and began the long climb.

By the time I got to the eighth floor my heart was pounding

with the effort of the climb and having to breathe quietly. I waited at the edge of the stairs, but there was no sound from any of the offices next to Jeschonnek's. I shone the flash at both ends of the corridor, and then walked down to his door. Kneeling down I looked for some wires that might give a clue to there being an alarm, but there were none; I tried first one key, and then the other. The second one was almost turning, so I pulled it out and smoothed the points with a small file. I tried again, this time successfully. I opened the door and went in, locking it behind me in case the security guard decided to do his rounds. I pointed the flash onto the desk, over the pictures and across to the door to Jeschonnek's private office. Without the least resistance to the levers, the key turned smoothly in my fingers. Covering the name of my locksmith with mental blessings, I walked over to the window. The neon sign on top of Pschorr Haus cast a red glow over Jeschonnek's opulent office, so there wasn't much need for the flash. I turned it off.

I sat down at the desk and started to look for I didn't know what. The drawers weren't locked, but they contained little that was of any interest to me. I got quite excited when I found a red leather-bound address book, but I read it all the way through, recognizing just the one name: that of Hermann Goering, only he was care of a Gerhard Von Greis at an address on Derfflingerstrasse. I remembered Weizmann the pawnbroker saying something about Fat Hermann having an agent who sometimes bought precious stones on his behalf, so I copied out Von Greis's address and put it in my pocket.

The filing cabinet wasn't locked either, but again I drew a blank; plenty of catalogues of gems and semi-precious stones, a Lufthansa flight table, a lot of papers to do with currency exchange, some invoices and some life assurance policies, one of which was with the Germania Life.

Meanwhile, the big safe sat in the corner, impregnable, and mocking my rather feeble attempts to uncover Jeschonnek's secrets, if he had any. It wasn't difficult to see why the place wasn't fitted with an alarm. You couldn't have opened that box if you'd had a truck-load of dynamite. There wasn't much left, apart from the waste-paper basket. I emptied the contents on the desk, and started to poke through the scraps of paper: a Wrigley's chewing-gum wrapper, the morning's *Völkischer Beobachter*, two ticket-halves from the Lessing Theater, a till receipt from the KDW department store and some rolled-up balls of paper. I smoothed them out. On one of these was the Adlon's telephone number, and underneath the name 'Princess Mushmi', which had been question-marked and then crossed out several times; next to it was written my own name. There was another telephone number written next to my name, and this had been doodled around so that it looked like an illumination from a page in a medieval Bible. The number was a mystery to me, although I recognized it was Berlin West. I picked up the receiver and waited for the operator.

'Number please?' she said.

'J 1–90–33.'

'Trying to connect you.' There was a brief silence on the line, and then it started ringing.

I have an excellent memory when it comes to recognizing a face, or a voice, but it might have taken me several minutes to place the cultured voice with its light Frankfurt accent that answered the telephone. As it was, the man identified himself immediately he had finished confirming the number.

'I'm so sorry,' I mumbled indistinctly. 'I have the wrong number.' But as I replaced the receiver I knew that it was anything but.

9

It was in a grave close to the north wall of the Nikolai Cemetery on Prenzlauer Allee, and only a short distance away from the memorial to National Socialism's most venerated martyr, Horst Wessel, that the bodies were buried, one on top of the other, following a short service at Nikolai Kirche on nearby Molken Market.

Wearing a stunning black hat that was like a grand piano with the lid up, Ilse Rudel was even more beautiful in mourning than she was in bed. A couple of times I caught her eye, but tight-lipped, like she had my neck between her teeth, she looked straight through me as if I was a piece of dirty glass. Six himself maintained an expression that was more angry than grief-stricken: with eyebrows knotted and head bowed, he stared down into the grave as though he were trying by a supernatural effort of will to make it yield up the living body of his daughter. And then there was Haupthändler, who looked merely thoughtful, like a man for whom there were other matters that were more pressing, such as the disposal of a diamond necklace. The appearance on the same sheet of paper in Jeschonnek's waste-paper basket of Haupthändler's home telephone number with that of the Adlon Hotel, my own name and that of the bogus princess, demonstrated a possible chain of causation: alarmed by my visit, and yet puzzled by my story, Jeschonnek had telephoned the Adlon to confirm the existence of the Indian princess, and then, having done so, he had telephoned Haupthändler to confront him with a set of facts regarding the ownership and theft of the jewels which was at variance with that which might originally have been explained to him.

Perhaps. At least, it was enough to be going on with.

At one point Haupthändler stared impassively at me for several seconds; but I could read nothing in his features: no guilt, no fear, no ignorance of the connection I had established between him and Jeschonnek, nor any suspicion of it either. I saw nothing that made me think he was incapable of having committed a double murder. But he was certainly no cracksman; so had he somehow persuaded Frau Pfarr to open it for him? Had he made love to her in order to get at her jewels? Given Ilse Rudel's suspicion that they might have been having an affair, it had to be counted as one possibility.

There were some other faces that I recognized. Old Kripo faces: Reichskriminaldirektor Arthur Nebe; Hans Lobbe, the head of Kripo Executive; and one face which, with its rimless glasses and small moustache, looked more as if it belonged to a punctilious little schoolmaster than to the head of the Gestapo and Reichsführer of the SS. Himmler's presence at the funeral confirmed Bruno Stahlecker's impression – that Pfarr had been the Reichsführer's star pupil, and that he wasn't about to let the murderer get away with it.

Of a woman on her own, who might have been the mistress that Bruno had mentioned as having been kept by Paul Pfarr, there was no sign. Not that I really expected to see her, but you never can tell.

After the burial Haupthändler was ready with a few words of advice from his, and my employer, 'Herr Six sees little need for you to have concerned yourself in what is essentially a family affair. I'm also to remind you that you are being remunerated on the basis of a daily fee.'

I watched the mourners get into their big black cars, and then Himmler and the top bulls in Kripo get into theirs. 'Look, Haupthändler,' I said. 'Forget the sledge ride. Tell your boss that if he thinks he's getting a cat in a sack, then he can cut me loose now. I'm not here because I like fresh air and eulogies.'

'Then why are you here, Herr Günther?' he said.

'Ever read *The Song of the Niebelungen*?'

'Naturally.'

'Then you'll remember that the Niebelung warriors wished to avenge the murder of Siegfried. But they couldn't tell who they should hold to account. So the trial of blood was begun. The Burgundian warriors passed one by one before the bier of the hero. And when it was the murderer Hagen's turn, Siegfried's wounds flowed with blood again, so revealing Hagen's guilt.'

Haupthändler smiled. 'That's hardly the stuff of modern criminal investigation, is it?'

'Detection should observe the little ceremonies, Herr Haupthändler, be they apparently anachronistic. You might have noticed that I was not the only person involved in finding a solution to this case who attended this funeral.'

'Are you seriously suggesting that someone here could have killed Paul and Grete Pfarr?'

'Don't be so bourgeois. Of course it is possible.'

'It's preposterous, that's what it is. All the same, do you have someone in mind for the role of Hagen yet?'

'It's under consideration.'

'Then I trust you will be able to report your having identified him to Herr Six before very long. Good day to you.'

I had to admit one thing. If Haupthändler had killed the Pfarrs then he was as cool as a treasure chest in fifty fathoms of water.

I drove down Prenzlauer Strasse on to Alexanderplatz. I collected my mail and went up to the office. The cleaning woman had opened the window, but the smell of booze was still there. She must have thought I washed in the stuff.

There were a couple of cheques, a bill and a hand-delivered note from Neumann telling me to meet him at the Café Kranzler at twelve o'clock. I looked at my watch. It was almost 11.30.

In front of the German War Memorial a company of Reichswehr were making trade for chiropodists to the accompaniment of a brass band. Sometimes I think that there must be more brass bands in Germany than there are motor-cars. This one struck up with *The Great Elector's Cavalry March* and set off at a lick towards the Brandenburger Tor. Everyone who was watching was getting in some arm exercise, so I hung back, pausing in a shop doorway to avoid having to join them.

I walked on, following the parade at a discreet distance and reflecting on the last alterations to the capital's most famous avenue: changes that the Government has deemed to be necessary to make Unter den Linden more suitable for military parades like the one I was watching. Not content with removing most of the lime trees which had given the avenue its name, they had erected white Doric columns on top of which sat German eagles; new lime trees had been planted, but these were not even as tall as the street lamps. The central lane had been widened, so that military columns might march twelve abreast, and was strewn with red sand so that their jackboots did not slip. And tall white flagpoles were being erected for the imminent Olympiad. Unter den Linden had always been flamboyant, without much harmony in its mixture of architectural designs and styles; but that flamboyance was now made brutal. The bohemian's fedora had become a Pickelhaube.

The Café Kranzler, on the corner of Friedrichstrasse, was popular with the tourists and prices were accordingly high; so it was not the sort of place that I would have expected Neumann to have chosen for a meet. I found him twitching over a cup of mocha and an abandoned piece of cake.

'What's the matter?' I said, sitting down. 'Lost your appetite?'

Neumann sneered at his plate. 'Just like this Government,' he said. 'It looks damn good, but tastes of absolutely nothing. Lousy ersatz cream.' I waved to the waiter and ordered two coffees. 'Look, Herr Günther, can we make this quick? I'm going over to Karlshorst this afternoon.'

'Oh? Got a tip, have you?'

'Well, as a matter of fact –'

I laughed. 'Neumann, I wouldn't bet on a horse that you were going to back if it could out-pace the Hamburg Express.'

'So fuck off, then,' he snapped.

If he was a member of the human race at all, Neumann was its least attractive specimen. His eyebrows, twitching and curling like two poisoned caterpillars, were joined together by an irregular scribble of poorly matched hair. Behind thick glasses that were almost opaque with greasy thumbprints, his grey eyes were shifty and nervous, searching the floor as if he expected that at any moment he would be lying flat on it. Cigarette smoke poured out from between teeth that were so badly stained with tobacco they looked like two wooden fences.

'You're not in trouble, are you?' Neumann's face adopted a phlegmatic expression.

'I owe some people some flea, that's all.'

'How much?'

'Couple of hundred.'

'So you're going to Karlshorst to try and win some of it, is that it?'

He shrugged. 'And what if I am?' He put out his cigarette and searched his pockets for another. 'You got a nail? I've run out.' I tossed a packet across the table.

'Keep it,' I said, lighting us both. 'A couple of hundred, eh? You know, I just might be able to help you out there. Maybe even leave you some on top. That is, if I get the right information.'

Neumann raised his eyebrows. 'What sort of information?'

I drew on my cigarette, and held it deep within my lungs. 'The name of a puzzler. A first class professional nutcracker who might have done a job about a week ago; stolen some bells.'

He pursed his lips and shook his head slowly. 'I haven't heard anything, Herr Günther.'

'Well, if you do, make sure you let me know.'

'On the other hand,' he said, lowering his voice, 'I could tell you something that would put you well in with the Gestapo.'

'What's that?'

'I know where a Jewish U-Boat is hiding out.' He smiled smugly.

'Neumann, you know I'm not interested in that crap.' But as I spoke, I thought of Frau Heine, my client, and her son. 'Hold on a moment,' I said. 'What's the Jew's name?' Neumann gave me a name, and grinned, a disgusting sight. His was an order of life not much higher than the calcareous sponge. I pointed my finger squarely at his nose. 'If I get to hear that U-Boat's been pulled in, I won't have to know who informed on him. I promise you, Neumann, I'll come round and tear your fucking eyelids off.'

'What's it to you?' he whined. 'Since when have you been the knight in Goldberg armour?'

'His mother is a client of mine. Before you forget you ever heard about him, I want the address where he is so I can tell her.'

'All right, all right. But that's got to be worth something, hasn't it?' I took out my wallet and gave him a twenty. Then I wrote down the address that Neumann gave me.

'You'd disgust a dung-beetle,' I said. 'Now, what about this nutcracker?'

He frowned exasperatedly at me. 'Look, I said I didn't have anything.'

'You're a liar.'

'Honest, Herr Günther, I don't know nothing. If I did, I'd tell you. I need the money, don't I?' He swallowed hard and wiped the sweat from his brow with a public health-hazard of a handkerchief. Avoiding my eyes, he stubbed out his cigarette, which was only half-smoked.

'You don't act like someone who knows nothing,' I said. 'I think you're scared of something.'

'No,' he said flatly.

'Ever hear of the Queer Squad?' He shook his head. 'You might say they used to be colleagues of mine. I was thinking that if I found out you'd been holding out on me, I'd have a word with them. Tell them you were a smelly little para 175.' He looked at me with a mixture of surprise and outrage.

'Do I look like I suck lemons? I'm not queer, you know I'm not.'

'Yes, but they don't. And who are they going to believe?'

'You wouldn't do that.' He grabbed my wrist.

'From what I hear of it, left-handers don't have too good a time of it in the KZs.' Neumann stared glumly into his coffee.

'You evil bastard,' he sighed. 'A couple of hundred you said, and a bit more.'

'A hundred now, and two more if it's on the level.' He started to twitch.

'You don't know what you're asking, Herr Günther. There's a ring involved. They'd kill me for sure if they found out I'd fingered them.' Rings were unions of ex-convicts, dedicated officially to the rehabilitation of criminals; they had respectable club names, and their rules and regulations spoke of sporting activities and social gatherings. Not infrequently, a ring would host a lavish dinner (they were all very rich) at which defence lawyers and police officials would appear as guests of honour. But behind their semi-respectable façades the rings were nothing more than the institutions of organized crime in Germany.

'Which one is it?' I asked.

'The "German Strength".'

'Well, they won't find out. Anyway, none of them are as powerful as they used to be. There's only one ring that's doing good business these days and that's the Party.'

'Vice and drugs may have taken a bit of a hammering,' he said, 'but the rings still run the gambling, the currency rackets, the black market, new passports, loan-sharking and dealing in stolen goods.' He lit another cigarette. 'Believe me, Herr Günther, they're still strong. You don't want to get in their way.' He lowered his voice and leaned towards me. 'I've even heard a strong whisper that they canned some old Junker who was working for the Prime Minister. How do you like that, eh? The bulls don't even know that he's dead yet.'

I racked my brain and came across the name that I had copied from Gert Jeschonnek's address book. 'This Junker's name; it wouldn't have been Von Greis, would it?'

'I didn't hear no name. All I know is that he's dead, and that the bulls are still looking for him.' He flicked his ash negligently at the ashtray.

'Now tell me about the nutcracker.'

'Well, it seems like I did hear something. About a month ago, a fellow by the name of Kurt Mutschmann finishes two years' cement at Tegel Prison. From what I've heard about him, Mut-schmann is a real craftsman. He could open the legs of a nun with rigor mortis. But the polyps don't know about him. You see, he got put inside because he clawed a car. Nothing to do with his regular line of work. Anyway, he's a German Strength man, and when he came out the ring was there to look after him. After a while they set him up with his first job. I don't know what it was. But here's the interesting part, Herr Günther. The boss of German Strength, Red Dieter, has now got a contract out on Mutschmann, who is nowhere to be found. The word is that Mutschmann double-crossed him.'

'Mutschmann was a professional, you say.'

'One of the best.'

'Would you say murder was part of his portfolio?'

'Well,' said Neumann, 'I don't know the man myself. But from what I've heard, he's an artist. It doesn't sound like his number.'

'What about this Red Dieter?'

'He's a right bastard. He'd kill a man like someone else would pick their nose.'

'Where do I find him?'

'You won't tell him it was me who told you, will you, Herr Günther? Not even if he were to put a gun to your head.'

'No,' I lied; loyalty goes only so far.

'Well, you could try the Rheingold Restaurant on Potsdamer Platz. Or the Germania Roof. And if you take my advice you'll carry a lighter.'

'I'm touched by your concern for my well-being, Neumann.'

'You're forgetting the money,' he said, correcting me. 'You said I'd get another 200 if it checked out.' He paused, and then added: 'And a hundred now.' I took out my wallet again and thumbed him a couple of fifties. He held the two notes up to the window to scrutinize the watermarks.

'You must be joking.'

Neumann looked at me blankly. 'What about?' He pocketed the money quickly.

'Forget it.' I stood up and dropped some loose change onto the table. 'One more thing. Can you remember when you heard about the contract on Mutschmann?' Neumann looked as thoughtful as he could manage.

'Well, now that I come to think of it, it was last week, about the time that I heard about this Junker getting killed.'

I walked west down Unter den Linden towards Pariser Platz and the Adlon.

I went through the hotel's handsome doorway and into the sumptuous lobby with its square pillars of dark, yellow-clouded marble. Everywhere there were tasteful *objets d'art*; and in every corner there was the gleam of yet more marble. I went into the bar, which was full of foreign journalists and embassy people, and asked the barman, an old friend of mine, for a beer and the use of his telephone. I called Bruno Stahlecker at the Alex.

'Hallo, it's me, Bernie.'

'What do you want, Bernie?'

'How about Gerhard Von Greis?' I said. There was a long pause. 'What about him?' Bruno's voice sounded vaguely challenging, as if he was daring me to know more than I was supposed to.

'He's just a name on a piece of paper to me at the moment.'

'That all?'

'Well, I heard he was missing.'

'Would you mind telling me how?'

'Come on, Bruno, why are you being so coy about it? Look, my little song-bird told me, all right? Maybe if I knew a bit more I might be able to help.'

'Bernie, there are two hot cases in this department right now, and you seem to be involved in both of them. That worries me.'

'If it will make you feel better, I'll have an early night. Give me a break, Bruno.'

'This makes two in one week.'

'I owe you.'

'You're damn right you do.'

'So what's the story?'

Stahlecker lowered his voice. 'Ever heard of Walther Funk?'

'Funk? No, I don't think I have. Wait a minute, isn't he some big noise in the business world?'

'He used to be Hitler's economic advisor. He's now Vice-President of the Reich Chamber of Culture. It would seem that he and Herr Von Greis were a bit warm on each other. Von Greis was Funk's boyfriend.'

'I thought the Führer couldn't stand queers?'

'He can't stand cripples either, so what will he do when he finds out about Joey Goebbels's club foot?' It was an old joke, but I laughed anyway.

'So the reason for tiptoes is because it could be embarrassing for Funk, and therefore embarrassing for the Government, right?'

'It's not just that. Von Greis and Goering are old friends. They saw service together in the war. Goering helped Von Greis get his first job with I. G. Farben Chemicals. And lately he'd been acting as Goering's agent. Buying art and that sort of thing. The Reichs-kriminaldirektor is keen that we find Von Greis as soon as possible. But it's over a week now, and there's been no sign of him. He and Funk had a secret love-nest on Privatstrasse that Funk's wife didn't know about. But he hasn't been there for days.' From my pocket I removed the piece of paper on which I had copied down an address from the book in Jeschonnek's desk drawer: it was a number in Derfflingerstrasse.

'Privatstrasse, eh? Was there any other address?'

'Not as far as we know.'

'Are you on the case, Bruno?'

'Not any more I'm not. Dietz has taken over.'

'But he's working on the Pfarr case, isn't he?'

'I guess so.'

'Well, doesn't that tell you something?'

'I don't know, Bernie. I'm too busy trying to put a name to some guy with half a billiard cue up his nose to be a real detective like you.'

'Is that the one they fished out of the river?'

Bruno sighed irritatedly. 'You know, one time I'm going to tell you something you don't already know about.'

'Illmann was talking to me about it. I bumped into him the other night.'

'Yeah? Where was that?'

'In the morgue. I met your client there. Good-looking fellow. Maybe he's Von Greis.'

'No, I thought of that. Von Greis had a tattoo on his right forearm: an imperial eagle. Look, Bernie, I've got to go. Like I said a hundred times, don't hold out on me. If you hear anything, let me know. The way the boss is riding me, I could use a break.'

'Like I said, Bruno, I owe you one.'

'Two. You owe me two, Bernie.'

I hung up and made another call, this time to the governor of Tegel Prison. I made an appointment to see him and then ordered another beer. While I was drinking it I did some doodling on a piece of paper, the algebraic kind that you hope will help you think more clearly. When I finished doing that, I was more confused than ever. Algebra was never my strong subject. I knew I was getting somewhere, but I thought I would worry about where that was only when I arrived.

10

Derfflingerstrasse was convenient for the brand-new Air Ministry situated at the south end of Wilhelmstrasse and the corner of Leipzigerstrasse, not to mention the Presidential Palace on nearby Leipzigerplatz: convenient for Von Greis to wait upon his master in his capacities as Chief of the Luftwaffe and as Prime Minister of Prussia.

Von Greis's apartment was on the third floor of a smart apartment-block. There was no sign of a concierge, so I went straight on up. I hit the door-knocker and waited. After a minute or so had elapsed I bent down to look through the letter-box. To my surprise I found the door swinging open as I pushed back the flap on its tight spring.

I didn't need my deerstalker-hat to realize that the place had been turned over, from top to bottom. The long hallway's parquet floor was covered with books, papers, envelopes and empty wallet files, as well as a considerable amount of broken glass which was referable to the empty doors of a large secretaire bookcase.

I walked past a couple of doors and stopped dead as I heard a chair scrape in the grate of one of the rooms ahead of me. Instinctively I reached for my gun. The pity was, it was still in my car. I was going for a heavy cavalry sabre mounted on the wall when behind me I heard a piece of glass crack underneath someone's foot, and a stinging blow to the back of my neck sent me plunging through a hole in the earth.

For what seemed like hours, although it must only have been a few minutes, I lay at the bottom of a deep well. Fumbling my way back to consciousness I became aware of something in my pockets, and then a voice from a long way off. Then I felt someone lift me under the shoulders, drag me for a couple of miles and shove my face under a waterfall.

I shook my head and squinted up to look at the man who had hit me. He was almost a giant, with a lot of mouth and cheeks, like he'd stuffed each of them with a couple of slices of bread. There was a shirt round his neck, but it was the kind that belonged properly in a barber's chair, and the kind of neck that ought to have been harnessed to a plough. The arms of his jacket had been stuffed with several kilos of potatoes, and they ended prematurely, revealing wrists and fists that were the size and colour of two boiled lobsters. Breathing deeply, I shook my head painfully. I sat up slowly, holding my neck with both hands.

'Christ, what did you hit me with? A length of railway track?'

'Sorry about that,' said my attacker, 'but when I saw you going for that sabre I decided to slow you down a bit.'

'I guess I'm lucky you didn't decide to knock me out, otherwise . . .' I nodded at my papers which the giant was holding in his great paws. 'Looks like you know who I am. Mind telling me who you are? It seems like I ought to know you.'

'Rienacker, Wolf Rienacker. Gestapo. You used to be a bull, didn't you? Up at the Alex.'

'That's right.'

'And now you're a sniffer. So what brought you up here?'

'Looking for Herr Von Greis.' I glanced about the room. There was a lot of mess, but it didn't seem that there was much missing. A silver epergne stood immaculate on a sideboard, the empty drawers of which were lying on the floor; and there were several dozen oil paintings leaning in neat ranks against the walls. Clearly whoever had ransacked the place hadn't been after the usual variety of loot, but something in particular.

'I see.' He nodded slowly. 'You know who owns this apartment?'

I shrugged. 'I had supposed it was Herr Von Greis.'

Rienacker shook his bucket-sized head. 'Only some of the time. No, the apartment is owned by Hermann Goering. Few people know about it, very few.' He lit a cigarette and threw me the packet. I lit one and smoked it gratefully. I noticed that my hand was shaking.

'So the first mystery,' continued Rienacker, 'is how you did.

The second is why you wanted to speak to Von Greis at all. Could be that you were after the same thing that the first mob were after? The third mystery is where Von Greis is now. Maybe he's hiding, maybe someone's got him, maybe he's dead. I don't know. This place was done over a week ago. I came back here this afternoon to have another poke around in case there was something I missed the first time, and to do some thinking, and what do you know, you come through the door.' He took a long drag on his cigarette. In his enormous ham of a fist it looked like a baby's tooth. 'It's my first real break on this case. So how's about you start talking?'

I sat up and straightened my tie and tried to fix my sodden collar. 'Let me just figure this out,' I said. 'I've got this friend up at the Alex who told me that the police don't know about this place, and yet here you are staking it out. Which leads me to suppose that you, or whoever it is you're working for, likes it that way. You'd prefer to find Von Greis, or at least get your hands on what makes him so popular, before they do. Now, it wasn't the silver, and it wasn't the paintings, because they're still here.'

'Go on.'

'This is Goering's apartment, so I guess that makes you Goering's bloodhound. There's no reason Goering should have any regard for Himmler. After all, Himmler won control of the police and the Gestapo from him. So it would make sense for Goering to want to avoid involving Himmler's men more than was necessary.'

'Aren't you forgetting something? I work for the Gestapo.'

'Rienacker, I may be easy to slug, but I'm not stupid. We both know that Goering has lots of friends in the Gestapo. Which is hardly surprising, since he set it up.'

'You know, you should have been a detective.'

'My client thinks much the same way as yours about involving the bulls in his business. Which means that I can level with you, Rienacker. My man is missing a picture, an oil painting, which he acquired outside any of the recognized channels, so you see, it would be best if the police didn't know anything about it.' The big bull said nothing, so I kept on going.

'Anyway, a couple of weeks ago, it was stolen from his home. Which is where I fit in. I've been hanging around some of the dealers, and the word I hear is that Hermann Goering is a keen art buyer – that somewhere in the depths of Karinhall he has a collection of old masters, not all of them acquired legitimately. I heard that he had an agent, Herr Von Greis, in all matters relating to the purchase of art. So I decided to come here and see if I could speak to him. Who knows, the picture I'm looking for might very well be one of the ones stacked up against that wall.'

'Maybe it is,' said Rienacker. 'Always supposing I believe you. Who's the painting by, and what's the subject?'

'Rubens,' I said, enjoying my own inventiveness. 'A couple of nude women standing by a river. It's called *The Bathers*, or something like that. I've a photograph back at the office.'

'And who is your client?'

'I'm afraid I can't tell you that.'

Rienacker wielded a fist slowly. 'I could try persuading you perhaps.'

I shrugged. 'I still wouldn't tell you. It's not that I'm the honourable type, protecting my client's reputation, and all that crap. It's just that I'm on a pretty substantial recovery fee. This case is my big chance to make some real flea, and if it costs me a few bruises and some broken ribs then that's the way it will have to be.'

'All right,' said Rienacker. 'Take a look at the pictures if you want. But if it is there I'll have to clear it first.' I got back onto my wobbly legs and went over to the paintings. I don't know a great deal about Art. All the same, I recognize quality when I see it, and most of the pictures in Goering's apartment were the genuine article. To my relief there was nothing that had a nude woman in it, so I wasn't required to make a guess as to whether Rubens had done it or not.

'It's not here,' I said finally. 'But thanks for letting me take a look.' Rienacker nodded.

In the hallway I picked up my hat and placed it back on my throbbing head. He said: 'I'm at the station on Charlottenstrasse. Corner of Französische Strasse.'

'Yes,' I said, 'I know it. Above Lutter and Wegner's Restaurant, isn't it?' Rienacker nodded. 'And yes, if I hear anything, I'll let you know.'

'See that you do,' he growled, and let me out.

When I got back to Alexanderplatz, I found that I had a visitor in my waiting room.

She was well-built and quite tall, in a suit of black cloth that lent her impressive curves the contours of a well-made Spanish guitar. The skirt was short and narrow and tight across her ample behind, and the jacket was cut to give a high-waisted line, with the fullness gathered in to fit under her substantial bust. On her shiny black head of hair she wore a black hat with a brim turned up all the way round, and in her hands she held a black cloth bag with a white handle and clasp, and a book which she put down as I came into the waiting room.

The blue eyes and perfectly lipsticked mouth smiled with disarming friendliness.

'Herr Günther, I imagine.' I nodded dumbly. 'I'm Inge Lorenz. A friend of Eduard Müller. Of the *Berliner Morgenpost?*' We shook hands. I unlocked the door to my office.

'Come in and make yourself comfortable,' I said. She took a look around the room and sniffed the air a couple of times. The place still smelt like a bartender's apron.

'Sorry about the smell. I'm afraid I had a bit of an accident.' I went to the window and pushed it open. When I turned round I found her standing beside me.

'An impressive view,' she observed.

'It's not bad.'

'Berlin Alexanderplatz. Have you read Döblin's novel?'

'I don't get much time for reading nowadays,' I said. 'Anyway, there's so little that's worth reading.'

'Of course it's a forbidden book,' she said, 'but you should read it, while it's in circulation again.'

'I don't understand,' I said.

'Oh, but haven't you noticed? Banned writers are back in the bookshops. It's because of the Olympiad. So that tourists won't think things are quite as repressive here as has been made out. Of course, they'll disappear again as soon as it's all over but, if only because they are forbidden, you should read them.'

'Thanks. I'll bear it in mind.'

'Do you have a cigarette?'

I flipped open the silver box on the desk and held it up by the lid for her. She took one and let me light her.

'The other day, in a café on Kurfürstendamm, I absent-mindedly lit one, and some old busybody came up to me and reminded me of my duty as a German woman, wife or mother. Fat chance, I thought. I'm nearly thirty-nine, hardly the age to start producing new recruits for the Party. I'm what they call a eugenic dud.' She sat down in one of the armchairs and crossed her beautiful legs. I could see nothing that was dud about her, except maybe the cafés she frequented. 'It's got so that a woman can't go out wearing a bit of make-up for fear of being called a whore.'

'You don't strike me as being the type to worry much about what people call you,' I said. 'And as it happens, I like a woman to look like a lady, not a Hessian milkmaid.'

'Thank you, Herr Günther,' she said smiling. 'That's very sweet of you.'

'Müller says you used to be a reporter on the DAZ.'

'Yes, that's right. I lost my job during the Party's "Clear Women out of Industry" campaign. An ingenious way of solving Germany's unemployment problem, don't you think? You just say that a woman already has a job, and that's looking after the home and the family. If she doesn't have a husband then she'd better get one, if she knows what's good for her. The logic is frightening.'

'How do you support yourself now?'

'I did freelance a bit. But right now, well frankly, Herr Günther, I'm broke, which is why I'm here. Müller says you're digging for some information on Hermann Six. I'd like to try and sell what I know. Are you investigating him?'

'No. Actually, he's my client.'

'Oh.' She seemed slightly taken aback at this.

'There was something about the way he hired me that made me want to know a lot more about him,' I explained, 'and I don't just mean the school he went to. I suppose you could say that he irritated me. You see, I don't like being told what to do.'

'Not a very healthy attitude these days.'

'I guess not.' I grinned at her. 'Shall we say fifty marks then, for what you know?'

'Shall we say a hundred, and then you won't be disappointed?'

'How about seventy-five and dinner?'

'It's a deal.' She offered me her hand and we shook on it.

'Is there a file or something, Fräulein Lorenz?'

She tapped her head. 'Please call me Inge. And it's all up here, down to the last detail.'

And then she told me.

'Hermann Six was born, the son of one of the wealthiest men in Germany, in April 1881, eight years to the day before our beloved Führer entered this world. Since you mentioned school, he went to the König Wilhelm Gymnasium in Berlin. After that he went into the stock exchange, and then into his father's business, which, of course, was the Six Steel Works.

'Along with Fritz Thyssen, the heir to another great family fortune, young Six was an ardent nationalist, organizing the passive resistance to the French occupation of the Ruhr in 1923. For this both he and Thyssen were arrested and imprisoned. But there the similarity between the two ends, for unlike Thyssen, Six has never cared for Hitler. He was a Conservative Nationalist, never a National Socialist, and any support he may have given the Party has been purely pragmatic, not to say opportunistic.

'Meanwhile he married Lisa Voegler, a former State Actress in the Berlin State Theatre. They had one child, Grete, born in 1911. Lisa died of tuberculosis in 1934, and Six married Ilse Rudel, the actress.' Inge Lorenz stood up and started to walk about the room as she spoke. Watching her made it difficult to concentrate: when she turned away my eyes were on her behind; and when she turned to face me they were on her belly.

'I said that Six doesn't care for the Party. That's true. He is equally opposed, however, to the trade-union cause, and appreciated the way in which the Party set about neutralizing it when it first came to power. But it's the so-called Socialism of the Party that really sticks in his throat. And the Party's economic policy. Six was one of several leading businessmen present at a secret meeting in early 1933 held in the Presidential Palace, at which future National Socialist economic policy was explained by Hitler and Goering. Anyway, these businessmen responded by contributing several million marks to Party coffers on the strength of Hitler's promise to eliminate the Bolsheviks and restore the army. It was a courtship that did not last long. Like a lot of Germany's industrialists, Six favours expanding trade and increased commerce. Specifically, with regard to the steel industry he prefers to buy his raw materials abroad, because it's cheaper. Goering does not agree, however, and believes that Germany should be self-sufficient in iron ore, as in everything else. He believes in a controlled level of consumption and exports. It's easy to see why.' She paused, waiting for me to furnish her with the explanation that was so easy to see.

'Is it?' I said.

She tutted and sighed and shook her head all at once. 'Well, of course it is. The simple fact of the matter is that Germany is preparing for war, and so conventional economic policy is of little or no relevance.'

I nodded intelligently. 'Yes, I see what you mean.' She sat down on the arm of her chair, and folded her arms.

'I was speaking to someone who still works on the DAZ,' she said, 'and he says that there's a rumour that in a couple of months, Goering will assume control over the second four-year economic plan. Given his declared interest in the setting up of state-owned raw material plants to guarantee the supply of strategic resources, such as iron ore, one can imagine that Six is less than happy about that possibility. You see, the steel industry suffered from considerable over-capacity during the depression. Six is reluctant to sanction the investment that is required for Germany to become self-sufficient in iron ore because he knows that as soon as the re-armament boom finishes, he'll find himself massively over-capitalized, producing expensive iron and steel, itself the result of the high cost of producing and using domestic iron ore. He'll be unable to sell German steel abroad because of the high price. Of course, it goes without saying that Six wants business to keep the initiative in the German economy. And my guess is that he'll be doing his best to persuade the other leading businessmen to join him in opposing Goering. If they fail to back him, there's no telling what he's capable of. He's not above fighting dirty. It's my suspicion, and it's only a suspicion, mind, that he has contacts in the underworld.'

The stuff on German economic policy was of marginal consequence, I thought; but Six and the underworld, well that really got me interested.

'What makes you say that?'

'Well, first there was the strike-breaking that occurred during the steel strikes,' she said. 'Some of the men who beat up workers had gangland connections. Many of them were ex-convicts, members of a ring, you know, one of those criminal rehabilitation societies.'

'Can you remember the name of this ring?' She shook her head. 'It wasn't German Strength, was it?'

'I don't remember.' She thought some more. 'I could probably dig up the names of the people involved, if that would help.'

'If you can,' I said, 'and anything else you can produce on that strike-breaking episode, if you wouldn't mind.'

There was a lot more, but I already had my seventy-five-marks worth. Knowing more about my private, secretive client, I felt that I was properly in the driving seat. And now that I'd heard her out, it occurred to me that I could make use of her.

'How would you like to come and work for me? I need someone to be my assistant, someone to do the digging around in public records and to be here now and then. I think it would suit you. I could pay you, say, sixty marks a week. Cash, so we wouldn't have to inform the labour people. Maybe more if things work out. What do you say?'

'Well if you're sure . . .' She shrugged. 'I could certainly use the money.'

'That's settled then.' I thought for a minute. 'Presumably, you still have a few contacts on papers, in government departments?' She nodded. 'Do you happen to know anyone in the DAF, the German Labour Service?'

She thought for a minute, and fiddled with the buttons on her jacket. 'There was someone,' she said, ruminatively. 'An ex-boyfriend, an SA man. Why do you ask?'

'Give him a call, and ask him to take you out this evening.'

'But I haven't seen or spoken to him in months,' she said. 'And it was bad enough getting him to leave me alone the last time. He's a real leech.' Her blue eyes glanced anxiously at me.

'I want you to find out anything you can about what Six's son-in-law, Paul Pfarr, was so interested in that he was there several times a week. He had a mistress, too, so anything you can find out about her as well. And I mean anything.'

'I'd better wear an extra pair of knickers, then,' she said. 'The man has hands like he thinks he should have been a midwife.' For the briefest of moments I allowed myself a small pang of jealousy, as I imagined him making a pass at her. Perhaps in time I might do the same.

'I'll ask him to take me to see a show,' she said, summoning me from my erotic reverie. 'Maybe even get him a little drunk.'

'That's the idea,' I said. 'And if that fails, offer the bastard money.'

II

Tegal Prison lies to the north-west of Berlin and borders a small lake and the Borsig Locomotive Company housing-estate. As I drove onto Seidelstrasse, its red-brick walls heaved into sight like the muddy flanks of some horny-skinned dinosaur; and when the heavy wooden door banged shut behind me, and the blue sky vanished as though it had been switched off like an electric light, I began to feel a certain amount of sympathy for the inmates of what is one of Germany's toughest prisons.

A menagerie of warders lounged around the main entrance hall, and one of these, a pug-faced man smelling strongly of carbolic soap and carrying a bunch of keys that was about the size of the average car tyre, led me through a Cretan labyrinth of yellowing, toilet-bricked corridors and into a small cobbled courtyard in the centre of which stood the guillotine. It's a fearsome-looking object, and always sends a chill down my spine when I see it again. Since the Party had come to power, it had seen quite a bit of action, and even now it was being tested, no doubt in preparation for the several executions that were posted on the gate as scheduled for dawn the next morning.

The warder led me through an oak door and up a carpeted stairway, to a corridor. At the end of the corridor, the warder stood outside a polished mahogany door and knocked. He paused for a second or two and then ushered me inside. The prison governor, Dr Konrad Spiedel, rose from behind his desk to greet me. It was several years since I had first made his acquaintance, when he'd been governor of Brauweiler Prison, near Köln, but he had not forgotten the occasion:

'You were seeking information on the cellmate of a prisoner,' he recalled, nodding towards an armchair. 'Something to do with a bank robbery.'

'You've a good memory, Herr Doktor,' I said.

'I confess that my recall is not entirely fortuitous,' he said. 'The same man is now a prisoner within these walls, on another charge.' Spiedel was a tall, broad-shouldered man of about fifty. He wore a Schiller tie and an olive-green Bavarian jacket; and in his button-hole, the black-and-white silk bow and crossed swords that denoted a war veteran.

'Oddly enough, I'm here on the same sort of mission,' I explained. 'I believe that until recently you had a prisoner here by the name of Kurt Mutschmann. I was hoping that you could tell me something about him.'

'Mutschmann, yes, I remember him. What can I tell you except that he kept out of trouble while he was here, and seemed quite a reasonable fellow?' Spiedel stood up and went over to his filing cabinet, and rummaged through several sections. 'Yes, here we are. Mutschmann, Kurt Hermann, aged thirty-six. Convicted of car theft April 1934, sentenced to two years' imprisonment. Address given as Cicerostrasse, Number 29, Halensee.'

'Is that where he went on discharge?'

'I'm afraid your guess is as good as mine. Mutschmann had a wife, but during his imprisonment it would seem from his record that she visited him only the one time. It doesn't look like he had much to look forward to on the outside.'

'Did he have any other visitors?'

Spiedel consulted the file. 'Just the one, from the Union of Ex-Convicts, a welfare organization we are led to believe, although I have my doubts as to the authenticity of that organization. A man by the name of Kasper Tillessen. He visited Mutschmann on two occasions.'

'Did Mutschmann have a cellmate?'

'Yes, he shared with 7888319, Bock, H.J.' He retrieved another file from the drawer. 'Hans Jürgen Bock, aged thirty-eight. Convicted of assaulting and maiming a man in the old Steel Workers Union in March 1930, sentenced to six years' imprisonment.'

'Do you mean that he was a strike-breaker?'

'Yes, he was.'

'You wouldn't happen to have the particulars of that case, would you?'

Spiedel shook his head. 'I'm afraid not. The case file has been sent back to Criminal Records at the Alex.' He paused. 'Hmm. This might help you, though. On discharge Bock gave the address where he was intending to stay as "Care of Pension Tillessen, Chamisso-platz, Number 17, Kreuzberg". Not only that but this same Kasper Tillessen paid Bock a visit on behalf of the Union of Ex-Convicts.' He looked at me vaguely. 'That's about it, I'm afraid.'

'I think I've got enough,' I said brightly. 'It was kind of you to give me some of your time.'

Spiedel adopted an expression of great sincerity, and with some solemnity he said: 'Sir, it was my pleasure to help the man who brought Gormann to justice.'

I reckon that in ten years from now, I'll still be trading off that Gormann business.

When a man's wife visits him only once in two years' cement, then she doesn't bake him a sponge-cake to celebrate his freedom. But it was possible that Mutschmann had seen her after his release, if only to knock the shit out of her, so I decided to check her out anyway. You always eliminate the obvious. That's fundamental to detection.

Neither Mutschmann nor his wife lived at the address in Cice-rostrasse any more. The woman I spoke to there told me that Frau Mutschmann had re-married, and was living in Ohmstrasse on the Siemens housing-estate. I asked her if anyone else had been around looking for her, but she told me that there hadn't.

It was 7.30 by the time I got to the Siemens housing-estate. There are as many as a thousand houses on it, each of them built of the same whitewashed brick, and providing accommodation for the families of the employees of the Siemens Electrical Com-pany. I couldn't imagine anything less congenial than living in a house that had all the character of a sugar lump; but I knew that in the Third Reich there were many worse things being done in the name of progress than the homogenizing of workers' dwellings.

As I stood outside the front door, my nose caught the smell of cooking meat, pork I thought, and suddenly I realized how hungry I was; and how tired. I wanted to be at home, or seeing some easy, brainless show with Inge. I wanted to be anywhere other than confronting the flint-faced brunette who opened the door to me. She wiped her mottled pink hands on her grubby apron and eyed me suspiciously.

'Frau Buverts?' I said, using her new married name, and almost hoping she wasn't.

'Yes,' she said crisply. 'And who might you be? Not that I need to ask. You've got bull stapled to each dumb ear. So I'll tell you once, and then you can clear off. I haven't seen him in more than eighteen months. And if you should find him, then tell him not to come after me. He's as welcome here as a Jew's prick up Goering's arse. And that goes for you, too.'

It's the small manifestations of ordinary good humour and common courtesy that make the job so worthwhile.

Later that night, between 11 and 11.30, there was a loud knock at my front door. I hadn't had a drink, but the sleep I'd been having was deep enough to make me feel as if I had. I walked unsteadily into the hall, where the faint chalky outline of Walther Kolb's body on the floor brought me out of my sleepy stupor and prompted me to go back and get my spare gun. There was another knock, louder this time, followed by a man's voice.

'Hey, Günther, it's me, Rienacker. Come on, open up, I want to talk to you.'

'I'm still aching from our last little chat.'

'Aw, you're not still sore about that, are you?'

'I'm fine about it. But as far as my neck is concerned, you're strictly *persona non grata*. Especially at this time of night.'

'Hey, no hard feelings, Günther,' said Rienacker. 'Look, this is important. There's money in it.' There was a long pause, and when

Rienacker spoke again, there was an edge of irritation in his bass voice. 'Come on, Günther, open up, will you? What the fuck are you so scared of? If I was arresting you, I'd have busted the door down by now.' There was some truth in that, I thought, so I opened the door, revealing his massive figure. He glanced coolly at the gun in my hand, and nodded as if admitting that for the moment I still had an advantage.

'You weren't expecting me, then,' he said drily.

'Oh, I knew it was you all right, Rienacker. I heard your knuckles dragging on the stairs.'

He snorted a laugh that was mainly tobacco smoke. Then he said: 'Get dressed, we're going for a ride. And better leave the hammer.'

I hesitated. 'What's the matter?'

He grinned at my discomfiture. 'Don't you trust me?'

'Now why do you say that? The nice man from the Gestapo knocks on my door at midnight, and asks me if I'd like to take a spin in his big shiny-black motor-car. Naturally I just go weak at the knees because I know that you've booked us the best table at Horcher's.'

'Someone important wants to see you,' he yawned. 'Someone very important.'

'They've named me for the Olympic shit-throwing team, right?' Rienacker's face changed colour and his nostrils flared and contracted quickly, like two emptying hot-water bottles. He was starting to get impatient.

'All right, all right,' I said. 'I suppose I'm going whether I like it or not. I'll get dressed.' I went towards the bedroom. 'And no peeking.'

It was a big black Mercedes, and I climbed in without a word. There were two gargoyles in the front seat, and lying on the floor in the back, his hands cuffed behind him, was the semi-conscious body of a man. It was dark, but from his moans I could tell that he'd taken quite a beating. Rienacker got in behind me. With the movement of the car, the man on the floor stirred and made a half attempt to get up. It earned him the toe of Rienacker's boot against his ear.

'What did he do? Leave his fly button undone?'

'He's a fucking Kozi,' said Rienacker, outraged, as if he had arrested an habitual child molester. 'A midnight fucking postman. We caught him red-handed, pushing Bolshie leaflets for the KPD through letter-boxes in this area.'

I shook my head. 'I see the job is just as hazardous as it always was.'

He ignored me, and shouted to the driver. 'We'll drop this bastard off, and then go straight onto Leipzigerstrasse. Mustn't keep his majesty waiting.'

'Drop him off where? Schöneberger Bridge?'

Rienacker laughed. 'Maybe.' He produced a hip flask from his coat pocket and took a long pull from it. I'd had just such a leaflet put through my own letter-box the previous evening. It had been devoted largely to ridiculing no less a person than the Prussian Prime Minister. I knew that in the weeks leading up to the Olympiad, the Gestapo were making strenuous efforts to smash the communist underground in Berlin. Thousands of Kozis had been arrested and sent to KZ camps like Oranienburg, Columbia Haus, Dachau and Buchenwald. Putting two and two together, it suddenly came to me with a shock just who it was I was being taken to see.

At Grolmanstrasse Police Station, the car stopped, and one of the gargoyles dragged the prisoner out from under our feet. I didn't think much for his chances. If ever I saw a man destined for a late-night swimming lesson in the Landwehr, it was him. Then we drove east on Berlinerstrasse and Charlottenburger Chaussee, Berlin's east-west axis, which was decorated with a lot of black, white and red bunting in celebration of the forthcoming Olympiad. Rienacker eyed it grimly.

'Fucking Olympic Games,' he sneered. 'Waste of fucking money.'

'I'm forced to agree with you,' I said.

'What's it all for, that's what I'd like to know. We are what we are, so why pretend we're not? All this pretence really pisses me off. You know, they're even drafting in snappers from Munich and Hamburg because Berlin trade in female flesh has been so hard hit by the Emergency Powers. And nigger jazz is legal again. What do you make of that, Günther?'

'Say one thing, do another. That's this Government all over.'

He looked at me narrowly. 'I wouldn't go around saying that sort of thing, if I were you,' he said.

I shook my head. 'It doesn't matter what I say, Rienacker, you know that. Just as long as I can be of service to your boss. He wouldn't care if I were Karl Marx and Moses in one, if he thought I could be of use to him.'

'Then you'd better make the most of it. You'll never get another client as important as this one.'

'That's what they all say.'

Just short of the Brandenburger Tor, the car turned south onto Hermann Goering Strasse. At the British Embassy all the lights were burning and there were several dozen limousines drawn up out front. As the car slowed and turned into the driveway of the big building next door, the driver wound down the window to let the storm-trooper on guard identify us, and we heard the sound of a big party drifting across the lawn.

We waited, Rienacker and I, in a room the size of a tennis court. After a short while a tall thin man wearing the uniform of an officer in the Luftwaffe told us that Goering was changing, and that he would see us in ten minutes.

It was a gloomy palace: overbearing, grandiose and affecting a bucolic air that belied its urban location. Rienacker sat down in a medieval-looking chair, saying nothing as I took a look around, but watching me closely.

'Cosy,' I said, and stood in front of a Gobelin tapestry depicting several hunting scenes that could just as easily have accommodated a scene featuring a full-scale version of the Hindenburg. The room's only light came from a lamp on the huge Renaissance-style desk which was composed of two silver candelabra with parchment shades; it illuminated a small shrine of photographs: there was one of Hitler wearing the brown shirt and leather cross belt of an SA man, and looking more than a little like a boy scout; and there were photographs of two women, whom I guessed were Goering's dead wife Karin, and his living wife Emmy. Next to the photographs was a large leather-bound book, on the front of which was a coat of arms, which, I presumed, was Goering's own. This was a mailed fist grasping a bludgeon, and it struck me how much more appropriate than the swastika it would have been for the National Socialists.

I sat down beside Rienacker, who produced some cigarettes. We waited for an hour, perhaps longer, before we heard voices outside the door, and hearing it open, we both stood up. Two men in Luftwaffe uniform followed Goering into the room. To my astonishment, I saw that he was carrying a lion cub in his arms. He kissed it on the head, pulled its ears and then dropped it on to the silk rug.

'Off you go and play, Mucki, there's a good little fellow.' The cub growled happily, and gambolled over to the window, where he started to play with the tassel on one of the heavy curtains.

Goering was shorter than I had imagined, which made him seem that much bulkier. He wore a sleeveless green-leather hunting jacket, a white flannel shirt, white drill trousers and white tennis shoes.

'Hallo,' he said, shaking my hand and smiling broadly. There was something slightly animal about him, and his eyes were a hard, intelligent blue. The hand wore several rings, one of them a big ruby. 'Thank you for coming. I'm so sorry you've been kept waiting. Affairs of state, you understand.' I said that it was quite all right, although in truth I hardly knew what to say. Close up, I was struck by the smooth, almost babyish quality of his skin, and I wondered if it was powdered. We sat down. For several minutes he continued to appear delighted at my being there, almost childishly so, and after a while he felt obliged to explain himself.

'I've always wanted to meet a real private detective,' he said.

'Tell me, have you ever read any of Dashiell Hammett's detective stories? He's an American, but I think he's wonderful.'

'I can't say I have, sir.'

'Oh, but you should. I shall lend you a German edition of *Red Harvest*. You'll enjoy it. And do you carry a gun, Herr Günther?'

'Sometimes, sir, when I think I might need it.'

Goering beamed like an excited schoolboy. 'Are you carrying it now?'

I shook my head. 'Rienacker here thought it might scare the cat.'

'A pity,' said Goering. 'I should like to have seen the gun of a real shamus.' He leaned back in his chair, which looked as though it might once have belonged to a bumper-sized Medici pope, and waved his hand.

'Well then, to business,' he said. One of the aides brought forward a file and laid it before his master. Goering opened it and studied the contents for several seconds. I figured that it was about me. There were so many files on me around these days that I was beginning to feel like a medical case-history.

'It says here that you used to be a policeman,' he said. 'Quite an impressive record, too. You'd have been a kommissar by now. Why did you leave?' He removed a small lacquered pillbox from his jacket and shook a couple of pink pills onto his fat palm as he waited for me to reply. He took them with a glass of water.

'I didn't much care for the police canteen, sir.' He laughed loudly. 'But with respect, Herr Prime Minister, I'm sure you are well aware of why I left, since at that time you were yourself in command of the police. I don't recall making a secret of my opposition to the purging of so-called unreliable police officers. Many of those men were my friends. Many of them lost their pensions. A couple even lost their heads.'

Goering smiled slowly. With his broad forehead, cold eyes, low growling voice, predatory grin and lazy belly, he reminded me of nothing so much as a big, fat, man-eating tiger; and as if telepathically conscious of the impression he was making on me, he leaned forwards in his chair, scooped up the lion cub from off the rug and cradled it on his sofa-sized lap. The cub blinked sleepily, hardly stirring as its owner stroked its head and thumbed its ears. He looked like he was admiring his own child.

'You see,' he said. 'He is not in anyone's shadow. And he's not afraid to speak his mind. That is the great virtue of independence. There's no reason on earth why this man should do me a service. He's got the guts to remind me of that when another man would have stayed silent. I can trust a man like that.'

I nodded at the file on his desk. 'I'd lay a bet that it was Diels who put that little lot together.'

'And you'd be right. I inherited this file, your file, with a great many others, when he lost his position as Gestapo chief to that little shit of a chicken farmer. It was the last great service that he was to do for me.'

'Do you mind my asking what happened to him?'

'Not at all. He is still in my employment, although occupying a lesser position, as an inland-shipping administrator with the Hermann Goering Works in Cologne.' Goering repeated his own name without the least trace of hesitation or embarrassment; he must have thought it was the most natural thing in the world that a factory should bear his name.

'You see,' he said proudly, 'I look after the people who have done me a service. Isn't that so, Rienacker?'

The big man's answer came back with the speed of a pilota ball. 'Yes sir, Herr Prime Minister, you most certainly do.' Full marks, I thought as a servant bearing a large tray of coffee, Moselle and eggs Benedict for the Prime Minister came into the room. Goering tucked in as if he hadn't eaten all day.

'I may no longer be head of the Gestapo,' he said, 'but there are many in the security police, like Rienacker here, who are still loyal to me, rather than to Himmler.'

'A great many,' piped Rienacker loyally.

'Who keep me informed about what the Gestapo is doing.' He dabbed daintily at his wide mouth with a napkin. 'Now then,' he said. 'Rienacker tells me that you turned up at my apartment in

Derfflingerstrasse this afternoon. It is, as he may already have told you, an apartment that I have placed at the disposal of a man who in certain matters is my confidential agent. His name is, as I believe you know, Gerhard Von Greis, and he has been missing for over a week. Rienacker says that you thought that he might have been approached by someone trying to sell a stolen painting. A Rubens nude, to be precise. What made you think that my agent was worth contacting, and how you managed to track him down to that particular address I have no idea. But you impress me, Herr Günther.'

'Thank you very much, Herr Prime Minister.' Who knows? I thought; with a little practice I could sound just like Rienacker.

'Your record as a police officer speaks for itself, and I don't doubt that as a private investigator you are no less competent.' He finished eating, swallowed a glassful of Moselle and lit an enormous cigar. He showed no signs of weariness, unlike the two aides and Rienacker, and I was starting to wonder what the pink pills had been. He blew a doughnut-sized smoke-ring. 'Günther, I want to become your client. I want you to find Gerhard Von Greis, preferably before Sipo does. Not that he's committed any crime, you understand. It's just that he is the custodian of some confidential information which I have no wish to see fall into Himmler's hands.'

'What kind of confidential information, Herr Prime Minister?'

'I'm afraid I can't tell you that.'

'Look, sir,' I said. 'If I'm going to row the boat I like to know if there are any leaks in it. That's the difference between me and a regular bull. He doesn't get to ask why. It's the privilege of independence.'

Goering nodded. 'I admire directness,' he said. 'I don't just say that I'm going to do something, I do it and I do it properly. I don't suppose there's any point in hiring you unless I take you fully into my confidence. But you must understand, that imposes certain obligations on you, Herr Günther. The price of betraying my trust is a high one.'

I didn't doubt it for a minute. I got so little sleep these days,

I didn't think that losing some more on account of what I knew about Goering was going to make any difference. I couldn't back off. Besides, there was likely to be some good money in it, and I try not to walk away from money if I can possibly help it. He took another two of the little pink pills. He seemed to take them as often as I might have smoked a cigarette.

'Sir, Rienacker will tell you that when he and I met in your apartment this afternoon, he asked me to tell him the name of the man I was working for, the man who owns the Rubens nude. I wouldn't tell him He threatened to beat it out of me. I still wouldn't tell him.'

Rienacker leaned forwards. 'That's correct, Herr Prime Minister,' he offered.

I continued with my pitch. 'Every one of my clients gets the same deal. Discretion and confidentiality. I wouldn't stay in business for very long if it was any other way.'

Goering nodded. 'That's frank enough,' he said. 'Then let me be equally frank. Many positions in the bureaucracy of the Reich fall to my patronage. Consequently, I'm often approached by a former colleague, a business contact, to grant a small favour. Well, I don't blame people for trying to get on. If I can, I help them. But of course I will ask a favour in return. That is the way the world works. At the same time, I have built up a large store of intelligence. It is a reservoir of knowledge that I draw on to get things done. Knowing what I know, it is easier to persuade people to share my point of view. I have to take the larger view, for the good of the Fatherland. Even now there are many men of influence and power who do not agree with what the Führer and myself have identified as the priorities for the proper growth of Germany, so that this wonderful country of ours may assume its rightful place in the world.' He paused. Perhaps he was expecting me to jump up and give the Hitler Salute and burst into a couple of verses of *Horst Wessel*; but I stayed put, nodding patiently, waiting for him to come to the point.

'Von Greis was the instrument of my will,' he said silkily, 'as well as of my foible. He was both my purchasing agent, and my fund raiser.'

'You mean he was an up-market squeeze-artist.'

Goering winced and smiled at the same time. 'Herr Günther, it does you much credit to be so honest, and so objective, but please try not to make it compulsive. I am a blunt man myself, but I don't make a virtue out of it. Understand this: everything is justified in the service of the State. Sometimes one must be hard. It was, I think, Goethe who said that one must either conquer and rule, or serve and lose, suffer or triumph, be the anvil or the hammer. Do you understand?'

'Yes, sir. Look, it might help if I knew who Von Greis had dealings with.'

Goering shook his head. 'I really can't tell you that. It's my turn to get on the soapbox and talk about Discretion and Confidentiality. To that extent, you'll have to work in the dark.'

'Very well, sir, I'll do my best. Do you have a photograph of the gentleman?'

He reached into a drawer and produced a small snapshot which he handed to me. 'This was taken five years ago,' he said. 'He hasn't changed a great deal.'

I looked at the man in the picture. Like many German men, he wore his fair hair cropped relentlessly close to the skull, except for an absurd kiss-curl decorating his broad forehead. The face, crumpled in many places like an old cigarette-packet, wore a waxed moustache, and the general effect was of the cliché German Junker to be found in the pages of a back number of *Jugend*.

'Also, he has a tattoo,' added Goering. 'On his right arm. An imperial eagle.'

'Very patriotic,' I said. I put the photograph in my pocket, and asked for a cigarette. One of Goering's aides offered me one from the great silver box, and lit it with his own lighter. 'I believe that the police are working on the idea that his disappearance might have something to do with his being a homosexual.' I said nothing about the information that Neumann had given me concerning the German Strength ring having murdered a nameless aristocrat. Until I could check his story, there was no point in throwing away what might turn out to be a good card.

'That is indeed a possibility.' Goering's admission sounded uncomfortable. 'It's true, his homosexuality led him to some dangerous places and, on one occasion, it even brought him to the attention of the police. However, I was able to see that the charge was dropped. Gerhard was not deterred by what should have been a salutary experience. There was even a relationship with a prominent bureaucrat to contend with. Foolishly, I allowed it to continue in the hope that it would force Gerhard to become more discreet.'

I took this information with several pinches of salt. I thought it much more likely that Goering had allowed the relationship to continue in order that he might compromise Funk – a lesser political rival – with the aim of putting him into his back pocket. That is, if he wasn't there already.

'Did Von Greis have any other boyfriends?'

Goering shrugged and looked at Rienacker, who stirred, and said: 'There was nobody in particular, as far as we know. But it's difficult to say for sure. Most of the warm boys have been driven underground by the Emergency Powers. And most of the old queer clubs like the Eldorado have been closed. All the same, Herr Von Greis still managed to pursue a number of casual liaisons.'

'There is one possibility,' I said. 'That on a nocturnal visit to some out of the way corner of the city for sex, the gentleman was picked up by the local Kripo, beaten up and tossed into a KZ. You might not hear about it for several weeks.' The irony of the situation was not lost on me: that I should be discussing the disappearance of the servant of the man who was himself the architect of so many other disappearances. I wondered if he could see it too. 'Frankly, sir, one to two weeks is not a long time to be missing in Berlin these days.'

'Inquiries in that direction are already being made,' said Goering. 'But you are right to mention it. Apart from that, it's up to you now. From what inquiries Rienacker has made about you, missing persons would seem to be your speciality. My aide here will provide you with money, and anything else you may require. Is there anything else?'

I thought for a moment. 'I'd like to put a tap on a telephone.'

I knew that the Forschungsamt, the Directorate of Scientific Research, which took care of wire-taps, was subordinate to Goering. Housed in the old Air Ministry building, it was said that even Himmler had to obtain Goering's permission to put a wire-tap on someone, and I strongly suspected that it was through this particular facility that Goering continued to add to the 'reservoir of intelligence' that Diels had left to his erstwhile master.

Goering smiled. 'You are well-informed. As you wish.' He turned and spoke to his aide. 'See to it. It is to be given priority. And make sure that Herr Günther is given a daily transcript.'

'Yes, sir,' said the man. I wrote out a couple of numbers on a piece of paper and handed it to him. Then Goering stood up.

'This is your most important case,' he said, putting his hand lightly on my shoulder. He walked me to the door. Rienacker followed at a short distance. 'And if you are successful, you will not find me wanting in generosity.'

And if I wasn't successful? For the moment, I preferred to forget that possibility.

12

It was nearly light by the time I got back to my apartment. The 'painting-out' squad was hard at work on the streets, obliterating the nocturnal daubings of the KPD – 'Red Front will Win' and 'Long Live Thälmann and Torgler' – before the city awoke to the new day

I had been asleep for no more than a couple of hours when the sound of sirens and whistles wrenched me violently from my quiet slumbers. It was an air-raid practice.

I buried my head under the pillow and tried to ignore the area warden hammering on my door; but I knew that I would only have to account for my absence later on, and that failure to provide a verifiable explanation would result in a fine.

Thirty minutes later, when the whistles had blown and the sirens cranked to sound the all-clear, there seemed little point in going back to bed. So I bought an extra litre off the Bolle milkman and cooked myself an enormous omelette.

Inge arrived at my office at just after nine. Without much cere-mony she sat down on the other side of my desk and watched me finish making some case notes.

'Did you see your friend?' I asked her after a moment.

'We went to the theatre.'

'Yes? What did you see?' I found that I wanted to know every-thing, including details that had no bearing on the man's possible knowledge of Paul Pfarr.

'*The Base Wallah*. It was rather weak, but Otto seemed to enjoy it. He insisted on paying for the tickets, so I didn't need the petty cash.'

'Then what did you do?'

'We went to Baarz's beer restaurant. I hated it. A real Nazi place.

Everyone stood and saluted the radio when it played the *Horst Wessel Song* and *Deutschland Über Alles*. I had to do it too, and I hate to salute. It makes me feel like I'm hailing a taxi. Otto drank rather a lot and became very talkative. I drank quite a lot myself actually – I feel a bit rough this morning.' She lit a cigarette. 'Anyway, Otto was vaguely acquainted with Pfarr. He says that Pfarr was about as popular as a ferret in a gumboot at the DAF, and it's not difficult to see why. Pfarr was investigating corruption and fraud in the Labour Union. As a result of his investigations, two treasurers of the Transport Workers Union were dismissed and sent to KZs, one after the other; the chairman of the Koch Strasse shop-committee of Ullstein's, the big printing works, was found guilty of stealing funds and executed; Rolf Togotzes, the cashier of the Metal Workers Union, was sent to Dachau; and a lot more. If ever a man had enemies, it was Paul Pfarr. Apparently there were lots of smiling faces around the department when it became known that Pfarr was dead.'

'Any idea what he was investigating at the time of his death?'

'No. Apparently he played things very close to his chest. He liked to work through informers, amassing evidence until he was ready to make formal charges.'

'Did he have any colleagues there?'

'Just a stenographer, a girl by the name of Marlene Sahm. Otto, my friend, if you can call him that, took quite a shine to her, and asked her out a couple of times. Nothing much came of it. That's the story of his life, I'm afraid. But he remembered her address though.' Inge opened her handbag and consulted a small notebook. 'Nollendorfstrasse, Number 23. She'll probably know what he had been getting up to.'

'He sounds like a bit of a ladies' man, your friend Otto.'

Inge laughed. 'That's what he said about Pfarr. He was pretty sure that Pfarr was cheating on his wife, and that he had a mistress. He saw him with a woman on several occasions at the same nightclub. He said that Pfarr seemed embarrassed at being discovered.

Otto said she was quite a beauty, if a bit flashy. He thought her name was Vera, or Eva, or something like that.'

'Did he tell the police that?'

'No. He says that they never asked. On the whole he'd rather not get involved with the Gestapo unless he has to.'

'You mean that he hasn't even been questioned?'

'Apparently not.'

I shook my head. 'I wonder what they're playing at.' I thought for a minute, and then added, 'Thanks for doing that, by the way. I hope it wasn't too much of a nuisance.'

She shook her head. 'How about you? You look tired.'

'I was working late. And I didn't sleep all that well. Then this morning there was a damned air-raid practice.' I tried to massage some life into the top of my head. I didn't tell her about Goering. There was no need for her to know more than she had to. It was safer for her that way.

That morning she was wearing a dress of dark-green cotton with a fluted collar and cavalier cuffs of stiffened white lace. For a brief moment I fed myself on the fantasy that had me lifting her dress up and familiarizing myself with the curve of her buttocks and the depth of her sex.

'This girl, Pfarr's mistress. Are we going to try and find her?'

I shook my head. 'The bulls would be bound to hear about it. And then it could get awkward. They're quite keen on finding her themselves, and I wouldn't want to start picking that nostril with one finger already in there.' I picked up the phone and asked to be connected to Six's home telephone number. It was Farraj, the butler, who answered.

'Is Herr Six, or Herr Haupthändler, at home? It's Bernhard Günther speaking.'

'I'm sorry, sir, but they're both away at a meeting this morning. Then I believe they'll be attending the opening of the Olympic Games. May I give either of them a message, sir?'

'Yes, you can,' I said. 'Tell them both that I'm getting close.'

'Is that all, sir?'

'Yes, they'll know what I mean. And make sure that you tell both of them, Farraj, won't you.'

'Yes, sir.'

I put the phone down. 'Right,' I said. 'It's time we got going.'

It was a ten-pfennig ride on the U-Bahn to the Zoo Station, repainted to look especially smart for the Olympic fortnight. Even the walls of the houses backing on to the station had been given a new coat of white. But high above the city, and where the Hindenburg airship droned noisily back and forwards towing an Olympic flag, the sky had gathered a surly gang of dark-grey clouds. As we left the station, Inge looked upwards and said: 'It would serve them right if it rained. Better still, if it rained for the entire fortnight.'

'That's the one thing they can't control,' I said. We approached the top of Kurfürstenstrasse. 'Now then, while Herr Haupthändler is away with his employer, I propose to have a squint at his rooms. Wait for me at Aschinger's restaurant.' Inge began to protest, but I continued speaking: 'Burglary is a serious crime, and I don't want you around if the going gets tough. Understand?'

She frowned, and then nodded. 'Brute,' she muttered, as I walked away.

Number 120 was a five-storey block of expensive-looking flats, of the sort that had a heavy black door that was polished so keenly they could have used it as a mirror in a negro jazz-band's dressing room. I summoned the diminutive caretaker with the enormous stirrup-shaped brass door-knocker. He looked about as alert as a doped tree sloth. I flashed the Gestapo warrant disc in front of his rheumy little eyes. At the same time I snapped 'Gestapo' at him and, pushing him roughly aside, I stepped quickly into the hall. The caretaker oozed fear through every one of his pasty pores.

'Which is Herr Haupthändler's apartment?'

Realizing that he was not about to be arrested and sent to a KZ, the caretaker relaxed slightly. 'The second floor, apartment five. But he's not at home right now.'

I snapped my fingers at him. 'Your pass-key, give it to me.' With eager, unhesitating hands, he produced a small bunch of keys and removed one from the ring. I snatched it from his trembling fingers.

'If Herr Haupthändler returns, ring once on the telephone, and then replace the receiver. Is that clear?'

'Yes, sir,' he said, with an audible gulp.

Haupthändler's were an impressively large suite of rooms on two levels, with arched doorways and a shiny wooden floor covered with thick Oriental rugs. Everything was neat and well-polished, so much so that the apartment seemed hardly lived in at all. In the bedroom were two large twin beds, a dressing-table, and a pouffe. The colour scheme was peach, jade-green and mushroom, with the first colour predominating. I didn't like it. On each of the two beds was an open suitcase, and on the floor were empty carrier-bags from several large department stores including C & A, Grunfeld's, Gerson's and Tietz. I searched through the suitcases. The first one I looked in was a woman's, and I was struck by the fact that everything in it was, or at least looked, brand-new. Some of the garments still had the price tags attached, and even the soles of the shoes were unworn. By contrast the other suitcase, which I presumed must belong to Haupthändler himself, contained nothing that was new, except for a few toiletries. There was no diamond necklace. But lying on the dressing-table was a wallet-sized folder containing two Deutsche Lufthansa air-tickets, for the Monday evening flight to Croydon, London. The tickets were returns, and booked in the name of Herr and Frau Teich-müller.

Before leaving Haupthändler's apartment I called the Adlon Hotel. When Hermine answered I thanked her for helping me with the Princess Mushmi story. I couldn't tell if Goering's people in the Forschungsamt had tapped the telephone yet; there were no audible clicks, nor any extra resonance in Hermine's voice. But I knew that if they really had put a tap on Haupthändler's telephone, then I ought to see a transcript of my conversation with

Hermine later on that day. It was as good a way as any of testing the true extent of the Prime Minister's cooperation.

I left Haupthändler's rooms and returned to the ground floor. The caretaker emerged from his office and took possession of his pass-key again.

'You will say nothing of my being here to anyone. Otherwise it will go badly for you. Is that understood?' He nodded silently. I saluted smartly, something Gestapo men never do, preferring as they do, to remain as inconspicuous as possible, but I was laying it on for the sake of effect.

'Heil Hitler,' I said.

'Heil Hitler,' repeated the caretaker, and, returning the salute, he managed to drop the keys.

'We've got until Monday night to pull this one back,' I said, sitting down at Inge's table. I explained about the air-tickets and the two suitcases. 'The funny thing was that the woman's case was full of new things.'

'Your Herr Haupthändler sounds like he knows how to look after a girl.'

'*Everything* was new. The garter-belt, the handbag, the shoes. There wasn't one item in that case that looked as though it had been used before. Now what does that tell you?'

Inge shrugged. She was still slightly piqued at having been left behind. 'Maybe he's got a new job, going door-to-door, selling women's clothes.'

I raised my eyebrows.

'All right then,' she said. 'Maybe this woman that he's taking to London doesn't have any nice clothes.'

'More like, doesn't have any clothes at all,' I said. 'Rather a strange kind of woman, wouldn't you say?'

'Bernie, just you come home with me. I'll show you a woman without any clothes.'

For a brief second I entertained myself with the idea. But I went on, 'No, I'm convinced that Haupthändler's mystery girlfriend is starting out on this trip with a completely new wardrobe, from top to toe. Like a woman with no past.'

'Or,' said Inge, 'a woman who is starting afresh.' The theory was taking shape in her mind even as she was speaking. With greater conviction, she added, 'A woman who has had to sever contact with her previous existence. A woman who couldn't go home and pick up her things, because there wasn't time. No, that can't be right. She has until Monday night after all. So perhaps she's afraid to go home, in case there's someone waiting for her there.' I nodded approvingly, and was about to develop this line of reasoning, but found that she was there ahead of me. 'Perhaps,' she said, 'this woman was Pfarr's mistress, the one the police are looking for. Vera, or Eva, I forget which.'

'Haupthändler in this with her? Yes,' I said thoughtfully, 'that could fit. Maybe Pfarr gives his mistress the brush-off when he finds out that his wife is pregnant. The prospect of fatherhood has been known to bring some men to their senses. But it also happens to spoil things for Haupthändler, who might himself have had ambitions as far as Frau Pfarr was concerned. Maybe Haupthändler and this woman Eva got together and decided to play the part of the wronged lover – in tandem, so to speak – and also make a little money into the bargain. It's not unlikely that Pfarr might have told Eva about his wife's jewellery.' I stood up, finishing my drink.

'Then maybe Haupthändler is hiding Eva somewhere.'

'That makes three maybes. More than I'm used to having over lunch. Any more and I'll get sick.' I glanced at my watch. 'Come on, we can think about it some more on the way.'

'On the way where?'

'Kreuzberg.'

She levelled a well-manicured finger at me. 'And this time, I'm not being left somewhere safe while you get all the fun. Understood?'

I grinned at her, and shrugged. 'Understood.'

*

The Kreuzberg, the Hill of the Cross, lies to the south of the city, in Viktoria Park, near Tempelhof Airport. It's where Berlin's artists gather to sell their pictures. Just a block away from the park, Chamissoplatz is a square surrounded by high, grey, fortress-like tenements. Pension Tillessen occupied the corner of Number 17, but with its closed shutters pasted over with Party posters and KPD graffiti, it didn't look as though it had been taking guests since Bismarck grew his first moustache. I went to the front door and found it locked. Bending down, I peered through the letter-box, but there was no sign of anyone.

Next door, at the office of Heinrich Billinger, 'German' Accountant, the coalman was delivering some brown-coal briquets on what looked like a bakery tray. I asked him if he could recollect when the pension had closed. He wiped his smutty brow, and then spat as he tried to remember.

'It never was what you might call a regular pension,' he declared finally. He looked uncertainly at Inge, and choosing his words carefully, added: 'More what you might call a house of ill-repute. Not a regular out-and-out bawdy house, you understand. Just the sort of place where you used to see a snapper take her sledge. I remember as I saw some men coming out of there only a couple of weeks ago. The boss never bought coal regular like. Just the odd tray here and there. But as to when it closed, I couldn't tell you. If it is closed, mind. Don't judge it by the way it looks. Seems to me as how it's always been in that state.'

I led Inge round the back, to a small cobbled alleyway that was lined with garages and lock-ups. Stray cats sat mangily self-contained on top of brick walls; a mattress lay abandoned in a doorway, its iron guts spilling on to the ground; someone had tried to burn it, and I was reminded of the blackened bed-frames in the forensic photographs Illmann had shown me. We stopped beside what I took to be the garage belonging to the pension and looked through the filthy window, but it was impossible to see anything.

'I'll come back for you in a minute,' I said, and clambered up the drainpipe at the side of the garage and onto the corrugated iron roof.

'See that you do,' she called.

I walked carefully across the badly rusted roof on all fours, not daring to stand up straight and concentrate all my weight on one point. At the back of the roof I looked down into a small court-yard which led on to the pension. Most of the windows in the rooms were shrouded with dirty net curtains, and there was no sign of life at any of them. I searched for a way down, but there was no drainpipe, and the wall to the adjoining property, the German accountant's, was too low to be of any use. It was fortunate that the rear of the pension obscured the view to the garage of anyone who might have chanced to look up from poring over a dull set of accounts. There was no choice but to jump, although it was a height of over four metres. I made it, but it left the soles of my feet stinging for minutes afterwards, as if they had been beaten with a length of rubber hosing. The back door to the garage was not locked and, but for a pile of old car tyres, it was empty. I unbolted the double doors and admitted Inge. Then I bolted them again. For a moment we stood in silence, looking at each other in the half darkness, and I nearly let myself kiss her. But there are better places to kiss a pretty girl than a disused garage in Kreuzberg.

We crossed the yard, and when we came to the back door of the pension, I tried the handle. The door stayed shut.

'Now what?' said Inge. 'A lock-pick? A skeleton key?'

'Something like that,' I said, and kicked the door in.

'Very subtle,' she said, watching the door swing open on its hinges. 'I assume you've decided that there's nobody here.'

I grinned at her. 'When I looked through the letter-box I saw a pile of unopened mail on the mat.' I went in. She hesitated long enough for me to look back at her. 'It's all right. There's nobody here. Hasn't been for some time, I'd bet.'

'So what are we doing here?'

'We're having a look around, that's all.'

'You make it sound as if we were in Grunfeld's department store,' she said, following me down the gloomy stone corridor. The only sound was our own footsteps, mine strong and purposeful, and hers nervous and half on tiptoe.

At the end of the corridor I stopped and glanced into a large and extremely smelly kitchen. Piles of dirty dishes lay in untidy stacks. Cheese and meat lay flyblown on the kitchen table. A bloated insect buzzed past my ear. One step in, the stink was overpowering. Behind me I heard Inge cough so that it was almost a retch. I hurried to the window and pushed it open. For a moment we stood there, enjoying the clean air. Then, looking down at the floor, I saw some papers in front of the stove. One of the doors to the incinerator was open, and I bent forward to take a look. Inside, the stove was full of burnt paper, most of it nothing more than ash; but here and there were the edges or corners of something that had not quite been consumed by the flames.

'See if you can salvage some of this,' I said. 'It looks like someone was in a hurry to cover his tracks.'

'Anything in particular?'

'Anything legible, I suppose.' I walked over to the kitchen doorway.

'Where will you be?'

'I'm going to take a look upstairs.' I pointed to the dumbwaiter. 'If you need me, just shout up the shaft there.' She nodded silently, and rolled up her sleeves.

Upstairs, and on the same level as the front door, there was even more mess. Behind the front desk were empty drawers, their contents lying on the threadbare carpet; and the doors of every cupboard had been wrenched off their hinges. I was reminded of the mess in Goering's Derfflingerstrasse apartment. Most of the bedroom floorboards had been ripped up, and some of the chimneys showed signs of having been probed with a broom. Then I went into the dining room. Blood had spattered the white wallpaper like an enormous graze, and on the rug was a stain the size of a dinner-plate. I stood on something hard, and bent down to pick up what looked like a bullet. It was a lead weight, encrusted with blood. I tossed it in my hand and then put it in my jacket pocket.

More blood had stained the wooden sill of the dumb-waiter. I leaned into the shaft to shout down to Inge and found myself retching, so strong was the smell of putrefaction. I staggered away. There was something sticking in the shaft, and it wasn't a late breakfast. Covering my nose and mouth with my handkerchief, I poked my head back into the shaft. Looking down I saw that the lift itself was stuck between floors. Glancing upwards I saw that as it crossed the pulley, one of the ropes supporting the lift had been jammed with a piece of wood. Sitting on the sill, with the top half of my body in the shaft, I reached up and pulled the piece of wood away. The rope ran past my face and beneath me the lift plummeted down to the kitchen with a loud bang. I heard Inge's shocked scream; and then she screamed again, only this time it was louder and more sustained.

I sprinted out of the dining room, down the stairs to the basement and found her standing in the corridor, leaning weakly on the wall outside the kitchen. 'Are you all right?'

She swallowed loudly. 'It's horrible.'

'What is?' I went through the doorway. I heard Inge say: 'Don't go in there, Bernie.' But it was too late.

The body sat to one side in the lift, huddled foetally like a dare-devil ready to attempt Niagara Falls in a beer barrel. As I stared at it the head seemed to turn, and it took a moment for me to realize that it was covered with maggots, a glistening mask of worms feeding on the blackened face. I swallowed hard several times. Covering my nose and mouth once again, I stepped forward for a closer look, close enough so that I could hear the light rustling sound, like a gentle breeze through moist leaves, of hundreds of small mouth parts. From my small knowledge of forensics, I knew that soon after death, flies not only lay their eggs on a cadaver's moist parts such as the eyes and mouth, but also on open wounds. By the number of maggots feeding on the upper part of the cranium and on the right temple, it looked more than probable that the victim had been beaten to death. From the clothes I could tell that the body was that of a man, and judging by the obvious quality of his shoes, quite a wealthy one. I put my hand into the right-hand jacket pocket, and turned it inside out. Some loose change and scraps of paper fell to the floor, but there was nothing that might have identified him. I felt around the area of the breast pocket, but it seemed to be empty, and I didn't feel like squeezing my hand between his knee and the maggoty head to make sure. As I stepped back to the window to draw a decent breath, a thought occurred to me.

'What are you doing, Bernie?' Her voice seemed stronger now.

'Just stay where you are,' I told her. 'I won't be very long. I just want to see if I can find out who our friend is.' I heard her take a deep breath, and the scrape of a match as she lit a cigarette. I found a pair of kitchen scissors and went back to the dumb-waiter, where I cut the arm of the jacket lengthways up the man's forearm. Against the skin's greenish, purplish hue and marbled veining, the tattoo was still clearly visible, clinging to his forearm like a large, black insect which, rather than feast on the head with the smaller flies and worms, had chosen to dine alone, on a bigger piece of carrion. I've never understood why men get themselves tattooed. You would have thought there were better things to do than deface your own body. Still, it makes identifying someone relatively straightforward, and it occurred to me that it wouldn't be very long before every German citizen was the subject of compulsory tattooing. But right now, the imperial German eagle identified Gerhard Von Greis just as certainly as if I had been handed his Party card and passport.

Inge looked round the doorway. 'Do you have any idea who it is?' I rolled up my sleeve and put my arm into the incinerator. 'Yes, I do,' I said, feeling around in the cold ash. My fingers touched something hard and long. I drew it out, and regarded it objectively. It was hardly burnt at all. Not the sort of wood that burns easily. At the thicker end it was split, revealing another lead weight, and an empty socket for the one I had found on the carpet in the dining room upstairs. 'His name was Gerhard Von Greis, and he was a high-class squeeze-artist. Looks like he was paid off, permanently. Someone combed his hair with this.'

'What is it?'

'A length of broken billiard cue,' I said, and thrust it back into the stove.

'Shouldn't we tell the police?'

'We don't have the time to help them feel their way around. Not right now, anyway. We'd just spend the rest of the weekend answering stupid questions.' I was also thinking that a couple of days' more fees from Goering wouldn't go amiss, but I kept that one to myself.

'What about him – the dead man?'

I looked back at Von Greis's maggoty body, and then shrugged. 'He's in no hurry,' I said. 'Besides, you wouldn't want to spoil the picnic, would you?'

We collected up the scraps of paper that Inge had managed to salvage from the inside of the stove, and caught a cab back to the office. I poured us both large cognacs. Inge drank it gratefully, holding the glass with both hands like a small child who is greedy for lemonade. I sat down on the side of her chair and put my arm around her trembling shoulders, drawing her to me, Von Greis's death accelerating our growing need to be close.

'I'm afraid I'm not used to dead bodies,' she said with an embarrassed smile. 'Least of all badly decomposed bodies that appear unexpectedly in service-lifts.'

'Yes, it must have been quite a shock to you. I'm sorry you had to see that. I have to admit he'd let himself go a bit.'

She gave a slight shudder. 'It's hard to credit that it was ever human at all. It looked so . . . so vegetable; like a sack of rotten potatoes.' I resisted the temptation to make another tasteless remark. Instead I went over to my desk, laid out the scraps of paper from Tillessen's kitchen stove and glanced over them. Mostly they were bills, but there was one, almost untouched by the flames, that interested me a good deal.

'What is it?' said Inge.

I picked up the scrap of paper between finger and thumb. 'A pay-slip.' She stood up and looked at it more closely. 'From a pay-packet made up by the Gesellschaft Reichsautobahnen for one of its motorway-construction workers.'

'Whose?'

'A fellow by the name of Hans Jürgen Bock. Until recently, he was in the cement with somebody by the name of Kurt Mutschmann, a nutcracker.'

'And you think that this Mutschmann might have been the one who opened the Pfarrs' safe, right?'

'Both he and Bock are members of the same ring, as was the owner of the excuse for a hotel we just visited.'

'But if Bock is in a ring with Mutschmann and Tillessen, what's he doing working in motorway construction?'

'That's a good question.' I shrugged and added, 'Who knows, maybe he's trying to go straight? Whatever he's doing, we ought to speak to him.'

'Perhaps he can tell us where to find Mutschmann.'

'It's possible.'

'And Tillessen.'

I shook my head. 'Tillessen's dead,' I explained. 'Von Greis was killed, beaten with a broken billiard cue. A few days ago, in the police morgue, I saw what happened to the other half of that billiard cue. It was pushed up Tillessen's nose, into his brain.'

Inge grimaced uncomfortably. 'But how do you know it was Tillessen?'

'I don't for sure,' I admitted. 'But I know that Mutschmann is hiding, and that it was Tillessen who he went to stay with when he got out of prison. I don't think Tillessen would have left a body lying around his own pension if he could possibly have avoided it.

The last I heard, the police still hadn't made a positive ID on the corpse, so I'm assuming that it must be Tillessen.'

'But why couldn't it be Mutschmann?'

'I don't see it that way. A couple of days ago my informer told me that there was a contract out on Mutschmann, by which time the body with the cue up its nose had already been fished out of the Landwehr. No, it could only be Tillessen.'

'And Von Greis? Was he a member of this ring too?'

'Not this ring, but another one, and far more powerful. He worked for Goering. All the same, I can't explain why he should have been there.' I swilled some brandy around my mouth like a mouthwash, and when I had swallowed it, I picked up the telephone and called the Reichsbahn. I spoke to a clerk in the payroll department.

'My name is Rienacker,' I said. 'Kriminalinspektor Rienacker of the Gestapo. We are anxious to trace the whereabouts of an autobahn-construction worker by the name of Hans Jürgen Bock, pay reference 30–4–232564. He may be able to help us in apprehending an enemy of the Reich.'

'Yes,' said the clerk meekly. 'What is it that you wish to know?'

'Obviously, the section of the autobahn on which he is working, and whether or not he'll be there today.'

'If you will please wait one minute, I shall go and check the records.' Several minutes elapsed.

'That's quite a nice little act you have there,' said Inge.

I covered the mouthpiece. 'It's a brave man who refuses to cooperate with a caller claiming to be in the Gestapo.'

The clerk came back to the telephone and told me that Bock was on a work detail beyond the edge of Greater Berlin, on the Berlin-to-Hanover stretch. 'Specifically, the section between Brandenburg and Lehnin. I suggest that you contact the site-office a couple of kilometres this side of Brandenburg. It's about seventy kilometres. You drive to Potsdam, then take Zeppelin Strasse. After about forty kilometres you pick up the A-Bahn at Lehnin.'

'Thank you,' I said. 'And is he likely to be working today?'

'I'm afraid I don't know,' said the clerk. 'Many of them do work Saturdays. But even if he's not working, you'll probably find him in the workers' barracks. They live on site, you see.'

'You've been most helpful,' I said, and added with the pomposity that is typical of all Gestapo officers, 'I shall report your efficiency to your superior.'

13

'It's just typical of the bloody Nazis,' said Inge, 'to build the People's roads before the People's car.'

We were driving towards Potsdam on the Avus Speedway, and Inge was referring to the much delayed Strength Through Joy car, the KdF-Wagen. It was a subject she evidently felt strongly about.

'If you ask me, it's putting the cart before the horse. I mean, who needs these gigantic highways? It's not as if there's anything wrong with the roads we have now. It's not as if there are that many cars in Germany.' She turned sideways in her seat the better to see me as she continued speaking. 'I have this friend, an engineer, who tells me that they're building an autobahn right across the Polish Corridor, and that one is projected across Czechoslovakia. Now why else would that be but to move an army about?'

I cleared my throat before answering; it gave me a couple more seconds to think about it. 'I can't see the autobahns are of much military value, and there are none west of the Rhine, towards France. Anyway, on a long straight stretch of road, a convoy of trucks makes an easy target for an air attack.'

This last remark drew a short, mocking laugh from my companion. 'That's precisely why they're building up the Luftwaffe – to protect the convoys.'

I shrugged. 'Maybe. But if you're looking for the real reason why Hitler has built these roads, then it's much more simple. It's an easy way of cutting the unemployment figures. A man receiving state relief risks losing it if he refuses the offer of a job on the autobahns. So he takes it. Who knows, that may be what happened to Bock.'

'You should take a look at Wedding and Neukölln sometime,' she said, referring to Berlin's remaining strongholds of KPD sympathy.

'Well, of course, there are those who know all about the rotten

pay and conditions on the autobahns. I suppose a lot of them think
that it's better not to sign on for relief at all rather than risk being
sent to work on the roads.' We were coming into Potsdam on the
Neue Königstrasse. Potsdam. A shrine where the older residents of
the town light the candles to the glorious, bygone days of the
Fatherland, and to their youth; the silent, discarded shell of Imperial Prussia. More French-looking than German, it's a museum of a
place, where the old ways of speech and sentiment are reverently
preserved, where conservatism is absolute and where the windows
are as well polished as the glass on the pictures of the Kaiser.

A couple of kilometres down the road to Lehnin, the pictur-
esque gave way abruptly to the chaotic. Where once had been
some of the most beautiful countryside outside Berlin, there was
now the earth-moving machinery and the torn brown valley that
was the half built Lehnin–Brandenburg stretch of autobahn.
Closer to Brandenburg, at a collection of wooden huts and idle
excavating equipment, I pulled up and asked a worker to direct
me to the foreman's hut. He pointed at a man standing only a few
metres away.

'If you want him, that's the foreman there.' I thanked him, and
parked the car. We got out.

The foreman was a stocky, red-faced man of medium height,
and with a belly that was bigger than a woman who has reached
the full term of her pregnancy: it hung over the edge of his trousers like a climber's rucksack. He turned to face us as we approached,
and almost as if he had been preparing to square up to me, he
hitched up his trousers, wiped his stubbly jaw with the back of his
shovel-sized hand and transferred most of his weight on to his
back foot.

'Hallo there,' I called, before we were quite next to him. 'Are
you the foreman?' He said nothing. 'My name is Günther, Bernhard Günther. I'm a private investigator, and this is my assistant,
Fräulein Inge Lorenz.' I handed him my identification. The foreman nodded at Inge and then returned his gaze back to my licence.
There was a literalness about his conduct that seemed almost simian.

'Peter Welser,' he said. 'What can I do for you people?'

'I'd like to speak to Herr Bock. I'm hoping he can help us. We're looking for a missing person.'

Welser chuckled and hitched up his trousers again. 'Christ, that's a funny one.' He shook his head and then spat onto the earth. 'This week alone I've had three workers disappear. Perhaps I should hire you to try and find them, eh?' He laughed again.

'Was Bock one of them?'

'Good God, no,' said Welser. 'He's a damn good worker. Ex-convict trying to live an honest life. I hope you're not going to spoil that for him.'

'Herr Welser, I just want to ask him one or two questions, not rubber him and take him back to Tegel Prison in my trunk. Is he here now?'

'Yes, he's here. He's very probably in his hut. I'll take you over there.' We followed him to one of several long, single-storey wooden huts that had been built at the side of what had once been forest, and was now destined to be the autobahn. At the bottom of the hut steps the foreman turned and said, 'They're a bit rough-and-ready, these fellows. Maybe it would be better if the lady didn't come in. You have to take these men as you find them. Some of them might not be dressed.'

'I'll wait in the car, Bernie,' said Inge. I looked at her and shrugged apologetically, before following Welser up the steps. He raised the wooden latch and we went through the door.

Inside, the walls and floor were painted a washed-out shade of yellow. Against the walls were bunks for twelve workers, three of them without mattresses and three of them occupied by men wearing just their underwear. In the middle of the hut was a pot-bellied stove made of black cast-iron, its stove-pipe going straight through the ceiling, and next to it a big wooden table at which four men were seated, playing skat for a few pfennigs. Welser spoke to one of the card players.

'This fellow is from Berlin,' he explained. 'He'd like to ask you a few questions.'

A solid slab of man with a head the size of a tree stump studied the palm of his big hand carefully, looked up at the foreman, and then suspiciously at me. Another man got up off his bunk and started to sweep the floor nonchalantly with a broom.

I've had better introductions in my time, and I wasn't surprised to see that it didn't exactly put Bock at his ease. I was about to utter my own codicil to Welser's inadequate reference when Bock sprang out of his chair, and my jaw, blocking his exit, was duly hooked aside. Not much of a punch, but enough to set off a small steam kettle between my ears and knock me sideways. A second or two later I heard a short, dull clang, like someone striking a tin tray with a soup ladle. When I had recovered my senses, I looked around and saw Welser standing over Bock's half-conscious body. In his hand he held a coal shovel, with which he had evidently struck the big man's head. There was the scrape of chairs and table legs as Bock's card-playing friends jumped to their feet.

'Relax, all of you,' yelled Welser. 'This fellow isn't a fucking bull, he's a private investigator. He's not come to arrest Hans. He just wants to ask him a few questions, that's all. He's looking for a missing person.' He pointed at one of the men in the skat game. 'Here you, give me a hand with him.' Then he looked at me. 'You all right?' he said. I nodded vaguely. Welser and the other man bent down and lifted Bock from where he lay in the doorway. I could see it wasn't easy; the man looked heavy. They sat him in a chair and waited for him to shake his head clear. Meanwhile the foreman told the rest of the men in the hut to go outside for ten minutes. The men in the bunks didn't put up any resistance and I could see that Welser was a man who was used to being obeyed, and quickly.

When Bock came round, Welser told him what he had told the rest of the hut. I could have wished that he had done it at the beginning.

'I'll be outside if you need me,' said Welser, and pushing the last man from the hut, he left the two of us alone.

'If you're not a polyp then you must be one of Red's boys.' Bock spoke sideways out of his mouth, and I saw that his tongue was several sizes too big for his mouth. Its tip remained buried in his cheek somewhere, so that all I saw was the large pink-coloured chew that was his tongue's thickest part.

'Look, I'm not a complete idiot,' he said more vehemently. 'I'm not so stupid that I'd get killed to protect Kurt. I really have no idea where he is.' I took out my cigarette case and offered him one. I lit us both in silence.

'Listen, first off, I'm not one of Red's boys. I really am a private investigator, like the man said. But I've got a sore jaw and unless you answer all my questions your name will be the one the boys up at the Alex draw out of the hat to make the trip to the blade for canning the meat at Pension Tillessen.' Bock stiffened in his chair. 'And if you move from that chair, so help me I'll break your damned neck.' I drew up a chair and put one foot on its seat so that I could lean on my knee while looking at him.

'You can't prove I was near the place,' he said.

I grinned at him. 'Oh, can't I?' I took a long pull at my smoke, and blew it in his face. I said: 'On your last little visit to Tillessen's joint you kindly left your pay-slip behind. I found it in the incinerator, next to the murder weapon. That's how I managed to track you down here. Of course it's not there now, but I could easily put it back. The police haven't yet found the body, but that's only because I haven't had time to tell them. That pay-slip puts you in an awkward situation. Next to the murder weapon, it's more than enough to send you to the block.'

'What do you want?'

I sat down opposite him. 'Answers,' I said. 'Look, friend, if I ask you to name the capital of Mongolia you'd better give me an answer or I'll have your fucking head for it. Do you understand?' He shrugged. 'But we'll start with Kurt Mutschmann, and what the two of you did when you came out of Tegel.'

Bock sighed heavily and then nodded. 'I got out first. I decided to try and go straight. This isn't much of a job, but it's a job. I didn't want to go back in the cement. I used to go back to Berlin for the odd weekend, see? Stay at Tillessen's bang. He's a pimp, or was. Sometimes he fixed me up with a bit of plum.' He tucked the cigarette into the corner of his mouth and rubbed the top of his head. 'Anyway, a couple of months after I got out, Kurt finished his cement and went to stay with Tillessen. I went to see him, and he told me that the ring were going to fix him up with his first bit of thieving.

'Well, the same night I saw him, Red Dieter and a couple of his boys turn up. He more or less runs the ring, you understand. They've got this older fellow with them, and start working him over in the dining room. I stayed out of the way in my room. After a while Red comes in and tells Kurt that he wants him to do a safe, and that he wants me to drive. Well, neither of us was too happy about it. Me, because I'd had enough of all that sort of thing. And Kurt because he's a professional. He doesn't like violence, mess, you know. He likes to take his time, too. Not just go straight ahead and do a job without any real planning.'

'This safe: did Red Dieter find out about it from the man in the dining room, the man being beaten up?' Bock nodded. 'What happened then?'

'I decided that I wanted nothing to do with it. So I went out through the window, spent the night at the doss-house on Frobestrasse, and came back here. That fellow, the one they had beaten up, he was still alive when I left. They were keeping him alive until they found out if he had told them the truth.' He took the cigarette stub out of his mouth and dropped it on the wooden floor, grinding it under his heel. I gave him another.

'Well, the next thing I hear is that the job went wrong. Tillessen did the driving, apparently. Afterwards, Red's boys killed him. They would have killed Kurt too, only he got away.'

'Did they double-cross Red?'

'Nobody's that stupid.'

'You're singing, aren't you?'

'When I was in the cement, in Tegel, I saw lots of men die on that guillotine,' he said quietly. 'I'd rather take my chances with Red. When I go I want to go in one piece.'

'Tell me more about the job.'

' "Just crack a nut," ' said Red. 'Easy to a man like Kurt, he's a real professional. Could open Hitler's heart. The job was middle of the night. Puzzle the safe and take some papers. That's all.'

'No diamonds?'

'Diamonds? He never said nothing about no bells.'

'Are you sure of that?'

'Course I'm sure. He was just to claw the papers. Nothing else.'

'What were these papers, do you know?'

Bock shook his head. 'Just papers.'

'What about the killings?'

'Nobody mentioned killings. Kurt wouldn't have agreed to do the job if he thought he was going to have to can anyone. He wasn't that kind of fellow.'

'What about Tillessen? Was he the type to shoot people in their beds?'

'Not a chance. That wasn't his style at all. Tillessen was just a fucking garter-handler. Beating up snappers was all he was good for. Show him a lighter and he'd have been off like a rabbit.'

'Maybe they got greedy, and helped themselves to more than they were supposed to.'

'You tell me. You're the fucking detective.'

'And you haven't seen or heard from Kurt since?'

'He's too smart to contact me. If he's got any sense, he'll have done a U-Boat by now.'

'Does he have any friends?'

'A few. But I don't know who. His wife left him, so you can forget her. She spent every pfennig he had earned, and when she'd finished she took off with another man. He'd die before he'd ask that bitch for help.'

'Perhaps he's dead already,' I suggested.

'Not Kurt,' said Bock, his face set against the thought. 'He's a clever one. Resourceful. He'll find a way out of it.'

'Maybe,' I said, and then: 'One thing I can't figure is you going straight, especially when you end up working here. How much do you make a week?'

Bock shrugged. 'About forty marks.' He caught the quiet surprise in my face. It was even less than I had supposed. 'Not much, is it?'

'So what's the deal? Why aren't you breaking heads for Red Dieter?'

'Who says I ever did?'

'You went inside for beating up steel pickets, didn't you?'

'That was a mistake. I needed the money.'

'Who was paying it?'

'Red.'

'And what was in it for him?'

'Money, same as me. Just more of it. His sort never gets caught. I worked that one out in the cement. The worst of it is that now that I've decided to go straight it seems like the rest of the country has decided to go bent. I go to prison and when I come out I find that the stupid bastards have elected a bunch of gangsters. How do you like that?'

'Well, don't blame me, friend, I voted for the Social Democrats. Did you ever find out who was paying Red to break the steel strikes? Hear any names maybe?'

He shrugged. 'The bosses, I suppose. Doesn't take a detective to work that one out. But I never heard any names.'

'But it was definitely organized.'

'Oh yes, it was organized all right. What's more it worked. They went back, didn't they?'

'And you went to prison.'

'I got caught. Never have been very lucky. You turning up here is proof of that.'

I took out my wallet and thumbed a fifty at him. He opened his mouth to thank me.

'Skip it.' I got to my feet and made for the hut door. Turning round, I said, 'Was your Kurt the type of puzzler to leave a nut he'd cracked open?'

Bock folded the fifty and shook his head. 'Nobody was ever tidier round a job than Kurt Mutschmann.'

I nodded. 'That's what I thought.'

'You're going to have quite an eye in the morning,' said Inge. She took hold of my chin and turned my head to get a better look at the bruise on my cheekbone. 'You'd better let me put something on that.' She went into the bathroom. We had stopped off at my apartment on our way back from Brandenburg. I heard her run the tap for a while, and when she returned she pressed a cold flannel to my face. As she stood there I felt her breath caress my ear, and I inhaled deeply of the haze of perfume in which she moved.

'This might help to stop the swelling,' she said.

'Thanks. A jaw-whistler looks bad for business. On the other hand, maybe they'll just think that I'm the determined type – you know, the kind who never lets up on a case.'

'Hold still,' she said impatiently. Her belly brushed against me, and I realized with some surprise that I had an erection. She blinked quickly and I supposed that she had noticed it too; but she did not step back. Instead, almost involuntarily, she brushed against me once more, only with a greater pressure than before. I lifted my hand and cradled her ample breast on my open palm. After a minute or so of that I took her nipple in between my finger and thumb. It wasn't difficult to find. It was as hard as the lid on a teapot, and just as big. Then she turned away.

'Perhaps we should stop now,' she said.

'If you're intending to stop the swelling, you're too late,' I told her. Her eyes passed lightly over me as I said it. Colouring a little, she folded her arms across her breasts and flexed her long neck against her backbone.

Enjoying the very deliberateness of my own actions, I stepped close to her and looked slowly down from her face, across her breasts and her belly, over her thighs to the hem of the green cotton dress. Reaching down I caught hold of it. Our fingers brushed as she took the hem from me and held it at her waist where I had placed it. Then I knelt before her, my eyes lingering on her underthings for long seconds before I reached up and slipped her knickers round her ankles. She steadied herself with one hand on my shoulder and stepped out of them, her long smooth thighs trembling slightly as she moved. I looked up at the sight I had coveted, and then beyond, to a face that smiled and then vanished as the dress rose up over her head, revealing her breasts, her neck and then her head again, which shook its cascade of shiny black hair like a bird fluttering the feathers on its wings. She dropped the dress to the floor and stood before me, naked but for her garter-belt, her stockings and her shoes. I sat back on my haunches and with an excitement that ached to be liberated I watched her slowly turn herself in front of me, showing me the profile of her pubic hair and her erect nipples, the long chute of her back and the two perfectly matched halves of her bottom, and then once more the swell of her belly, the dark pennant that seemed to prick the air with its own excitement, and the smooth, quivering shanks.

I picked her up and took her into the bedroom where we spent the rest of the afternoon, caressing, exploring and blissfully enjoying a feast of each other's flesh.

The afternoon drifted lazily into evening, with light sleep and tender words; and when we rose from my bed having satisfied our lust, we found our appetites the more ravenous.

I took her to dinner at the Peltzer Grill, and then dancing at the Germania Roof, in nearby Hardenbergstrasse. The Roof was crowded with Berlin's smartest set, many of them in uniform. Inge looked around at the blue glass walls, the ceiling illuminated with small blue stars and supported with columns of burnished copper, and the ornamental pools with their water-lilies, and smiled excitedly.

'Isn't this simply wonderful?'

'I didn't think that this was your sort of place,' I said lamely. But she didn't hear me. She was taking me by the hand and pulling me on to the less crowded of the two circular dance-floors.

It was a good band, and I held her tight and breathed through her hair. I was congratulating myself on bringing her here instead of, one of the clubs with which I was better acquainted, such as Johnny's or the Golden Horseshoe. Then I remembered that Neumann had said that the Germania Roof was one of Red Dieter's chosen haunts. So when Inge went to the ladies' room I called the waiter over to our table and handed him a five.

'This gets me a couple of answers to a couple of simple questions, right?' He shrugged, and pocketed the cash. 'Is Dieter Helfferich in the joint tonight?'

'Red Dieter?'

'What other colours are there?' He didn't get that, so I left it. He looked thoughtful for a moment, as if wondering whether or not the ringleader of German Strength would mind his being identified in this way. He made the right decision.

'Yes, he's here tonight.' Anticipating my next question, he nodded over his shoulder in the direction of the bar. 'He's sitting in the booth furthest from the band.' He started to collect some empties from the table and, lowering his voice, added, 'It doesn't do to ask too many questions about Red Dieter. And that's for free.'

'Just one more question,' I said. 'What's his usual neck-oil?' The waiter, who had the lemon-sucking look of a warm boy, looked at me pityingly, as if such a question hardly needed to be asked.

'Red drinks nothing but champagne.'

'The lower the life the fancier the taste, eh? Send a bottle over to his table, with my compliments.' I handed him my card and a note. 'And keep the change if there is any.' He gave Inge the once-over as she came back from the ladies' room. I didn't blame him, and he wasn't the only one; there was a man sitting at the bar who also seemed to find her worthy of attention.

We danced again and I watched the waiter deliver the bottle of champagne to Red Dieter's table. I couldn't see him in his seat, but

I saw my card being handed over, and the waiter nodding in my direction.

'Look,' I said, 'there's something that I have to do. I won't be long, but I'll have to leave you for a short while. If there's anything you want just ask the waiter.' She looked at me anxiously as I accompanied her back to the table.

'But where are you going?'

'I have to see someone, someone here. I'll only be a few minutes.'

She smiled at me, and said: 'Please be careful.'

I bent forward and kissed her on the cheek. 'Like I was walking on a tightrope.'

There was a touch of the Fatty Arbuckle about the solitary occupant of the end booth. His fat neck rested on a couple of doughnut-sized rolls pressed tight against the collar of his evening shirt. The face was as red as a boiled ham, and I wondered if this was the explanation behind the nickname. Red Dieter Helfferich's mouth was set at a tough angle like it ought to have been chewing on a big cigar. When he spoke it was a medium-sized brown bear of a voice, growling from the inside of a short cave, and always on the edge of outrage. When he grinned, the mouth was a cross between early-Mayan and High Gothic.

'A private investigator, huh? I never met one.'

'That just goes to show there aren't enough of us around. Mind if I join you?'

He glanced at the label on the bottle. 'This is good champagne. The least I can do is hear you out. Sit down –' He lifted his hand and looked at my card again for effect '– Herr Günther.' He poured us both a glass, and raised his own in a toast. Cowled under brows the size and shape of horizontal Eiffel Towers were eyes that were too wide for my comfort, each revealing a broken pencil of an iris.

'To absent friends,' he said.

I nodded and drank my champagne. 'Like Kurt Mutschmann perhaps.'

'Absent, but not forgotten.' He uttered a brash, gloating laugh and sipped at his drink. 'It would seem that we'd both like to know where he is. Just to put our minds at rest, of course. To stop us worrying about him, eh?'

'Should we be worried?' I asked.

'These are dangerous times for a man in Kurt's line of work. Well, I'm sure I don't have to tell you that. You know all about that, don't you, fleabite, you being an ex-bull.' He nodded appreciatively. 'I've got to hand it to your client, fleabite, it showed real intelligence involving you rather than your former colleagues. All he wants is his bells back, no questions asked. You can get closer. You can negotiate. Perhaps he'll even pay a small reward, eh?'

'You're very well informed.'

'I am if that's all your client wants; and to that extent I'll even help you, if I can.' His face darkened. 'But Mutschmann – he's mine. If your fellow has got any misplaced ideas of revenge, tell him to lay off. That's my beat. It's simply a matter of good business practice.'

'Is that all you want? Just to tidy up the store? You're forgetting the small matter of Von Greis's papers, aren't you? You remember – the ones your boys were so anxious to talk to him about. Like where he'd hidden them or who he'd given them to. What were you planning to do with the papers when you got them? Try a little first-class blackmail? People like my client maybe? Or did you want to put a few politicians in your pocket for a rainy day?'

'You're quite well informed yourself, fleabite. Like I said, your client is a clever man. It's lucky for me he took you into his confidence instead of the police. Lucky for me, lucky for you; because if you were a bull sitting there telling me what you just told me, you'd be on your way to being dead.'

I leaned out of the booth to check that Inge was all right. I could see her shiny black head easily. She was freezing off a uniformed reveller who was wasting his best lines.

'Thanks for the champagne, fleabite. You took a fair-sized chance talking to me. And you haven't had much of a payout on your bet. But at least you're walking away with your stake-money.' He grinned.

'Well this time, the thrill of playing was all I wanted.'

The gangster seemed to find that funny. 'There won't be another. You can depend on it.'

I moved to go, but found him holding my arm. I expected him to threaten me, but instead he said:

'Listen, I'd hate you to think that I'd cheated you. Don't ask me why, but I'm going to do you a favour. Maybe because I like your nerve. Don't turn round, but sitting at the bar is a big, heavy fellow, brown suit, sea-urchin haircut. Take a good look at him when you go back to your table. He's a professional killer. He followed you and the girl in here. You must have stepped on someone's corns. It looks as though you must be this week's rent money. I doubt he'll try anything in here, out of respect for me, you understand. But outside . . . fact is, I don't much like cheap gunmen coming in here. Creates a bad impression.'

'Thanks for the tip. I appreciate it.' I lit a cigarette. 'Is there a back way out of here? I wouldn't want my girl to get hurt.'

He nodded. 'Through the kitchens and down the emergency stairs. At the bottom there's a door that leads onto an alley. It's quiet there. Just a few parked cars. One of them, the light-grey sports, belongs to me.' He pushed a set of keys towards me. 'There's a lighter in the glove-box if you need it. Just leave the keys in the exhaust pipe afterwards, and make sure you don't mark the paintwork.'

I pocketed the keys and stood up. 'It's been nice talking to you, Red. Funny things, fleabites; you don't notice one when you're first bitten, but after a while there's nothing more irritating.'

Red Dieter frowned. 'Get out of here, Günther, before I change my mind about you.'

On the way back to Inge I glanced over at the bar. The man in the brown suit was easy enough to spot, and I recognized him as the man who had been looking at Inge earlier on. At our table Inge was finding it easy, if not particularly pleasant, to resist the negligible charm of a good-looking but rather short SS officer. I hurried Inge to her feet and started to draw her away. The officer held my arm. I looked at his hand and then in his face.

'Slow down, shorty,' I said, looming over his diminutive figure like a frigate coming alongside of a fishing boat. 'Or I'll decorate your lip and it won't be with a Knight's Cross and oak leaves.' I pulled a crumpled five-mark note from out of a pocket and dropped it onto the tabletop.

'I didn't think you were the jealous type,' she said, as I moved her towards the door.

'Get into the lift and go straight down,' I told her. 'When you get outside, go to the car and wait for me. There's a gun under the seat. Better keep it handy, just in case.' I glanced over at the bar where the man was paying for his drink. 'Look, I haven't got time to explain now, but it's got nothing to do with our dashing little friend back there.'

'And where will you be?' she said. I handed her my car keys.

'I'm going out the other way. There's a big man in a brown suit who's trying to kill me. If you see him coming towards the car, go home and phone Kriminalinspektor Bruno Stahlecker at the Alex. Got that?' She nodded.

For a moment I pretended to follow her, and then turned abruptly away, walking quickly through the kitchens and out of the fire door.

Three flights down I heard footsteps behind me in the almost pitch dark of the stairwell. As I scampered blindly down I wondered if I could take him; but then I wasn't armed and he was. What was more, he was a professional. I tripped and fell, scrambling up again even as I hit the landing, reaching out for the banister and wrenching myself down another flight, ignoring the pain in my elbows and forearms, with which I had broken my fall. At the top of the last flight I saw a light underneath a door and jumped. It was further than I thought but I landed well, on all fours. I hit the bar on the door and crashed out into the alley.

There were several cars, all of them parked in a neat row, but it wasn't difficult to spot Red Dieter's grey Bugatti Royale. I unlocked the door and opened the glove-box. Inside there were several small paper twists of white powder and a big revolver with a long barrel, the sort that puts a window in an eight-centimetre-thick mahogany door. I didn't have time to check whether it was loaded, but I didn't think that Red was the sort who kept a gun because he liked playing Cowboys and Indians.

I dropped to the ground and rolled under the running-board of the car parked next to the Bugatti, a big Mercedes convertible. At that moment my pursuer came through the fire door, hugging the well-shadowed wall for cover. I lay completely still, waiting for him to step into the moonlit centre of the alley. Minutes passed, with no sound or movement in the shadows, and after a while I guessed that he had edged along the wall in the cover of the shadow, until he was far enough away from the cars to cross the alley in safety before doubling back. A heel scraped on a cobblestone behind me, and I held my breath. There was only my thumb which moved, slowly and steadily pulling back the revolver's hammer with a scarcely audible click, and then releasing the safety. Slowly I turned and looked down the length of my body. I saw a pair of shoes standing squarely behind where I was lying, framed neatly by the two rear wheels of the car. The man's feet took him away to my right, behind the Bugatti, and, realizing that he was on to its half-open door, I slid in the opposite direction, to my left, and out from underneath the Mercedes. Staying low, beneath the level of the car's windows, I went to the rear and peered around its enormous trunk. A brown-suited figure crouched beside the rear tyre of the Bugatti in almost exactly the same position as me, but facing in the opposite direction. He was no more than a couple of metres away. I stepped quietly forward, bringing the big revolver up to level it at arm's length at the back of his hat.

'Drop it,' I said. 'Or I'll put a tunnel through your goddamned head, so help me God.' The man froze, but the gun stayed put in his hand.

'No problem, friend,' he said, releasing the handle of his automatic, a Mauser, so that it dangled from his forefinger by the trigger guard. 'Mind if I put the catch on it? This little baby's got a hair-trigger.' The voice was slow and cool.

'First pull the brim of your hat down over your face,' I said.

'Then put the catch on like you had your hand in a bag of sand. Remember, at this range I can hardly miss. And it would be too bad to mess up Red's nice paintwork with your brains.' He tugged at his hat until it was well down over his eyes, and after he had seen to the Mauser's safety catch he let the gun drop to the ground where it clattered harmlessly on the cobbles.

'Did Red tell you I was following you?'

'Shut up and turn around,' I told him. 'And keep your hands in the air.' The brown suit turned and then dropped his head back onto his shoulders in an effort to see beyond the brim of his hat.

'You going to kill me?' he said.

'That depends.'

'On what?'

'On whether or not you tell me who's signing your expenses.'

'Maybe we can make a deal.'

'I don't see that you've got much to trade,' I said. 'Either you talk or I fit you with an extra pair of nostrils. It's that simple.'

He grinned. 'You wouldn't shoot me in cold blood,' he said.

'Oh, wouldn't I?' I poked the gun hard against his chin, and then dragged the barrel up across the flesh of his face to screw it under his cheekbone. 'Don't be so sure. You've got me in the mood to use this thing, so you'd better find your tongue now or you'll never find it again.'

'But if I sing, then what? Will you let me go?'

'And have you track me down again? You must think I'm stupid.'

'What can I do to convince you that I wouldn't?'

I stepped away from him, and thought for a moment. 'Swear on your mother's life.'

'I swear on my mother's life,' he said readily enough.

'Fine. So who's your client?'

'You'll let me go if I tell you?'

'Yes.'

'Swear on your mother's life.'

'I swear on my mother's life.'

'All right then,' he said. 'It was a fellow called Haupthändler.'

'How much is he paying you?'

'Three hundred now and —' He didn't finish the sentence. Stepping forward I knocked him cold with one blow of the revolver's butt. It was a cruel blow, delivered with sufficient power to render him insensible for a long time.

'My mother is dead,' I said. Then I picked up his weapon and pocketing both guns I ran back to the car. Inge's eyes widened when she saw the dirt and oil covering my suit. My best suit.

'The lift's not good enough for you? What did you do, jump down?'

'Something like that.' I felt around under the driver's seat for the pair of handcuffs I kept next to my gun. Then I drove the seventy or so metres back to the alley.

The brown suit lay unconscious where I had dropped him. I got out of the car and dragged him over to a wall a short way up the alley, where I manacled him to some iron bars protecting a window. He groaned a little as I moved him, so I knew I hadn't killed him. I went back to the Bugatti and returned Red's gun to the glove-box. At the same time I helped myself to the small paper twists of white powder. I didn't figure that Red Dieter was the type to keep cooking-salt in his glove-box, but I sniffed a pinch anyway. Just enough to recognize cocaine. There weren't many of the twists. Not more than a hundred marks' worth. And it looked like they were for Red's personal use.

I locked the car and slid the keys inside the exhaust, like he'd asked. Then I walked back to the brown suit and tucked a couple of the twists into his top pocket.

'This should interest the boys at the Alex,' I said. Short of killing him in cold blood, I could think of no more certain way of ensuring that he wouldn't finish the job he'd started.

Deals were for people that met you with nothing more deadly in their right hand than a shot of schnaps.

14

The next morning it was drizzling, a warm fine rain like the spray from a garden-sprinkler. I got up feeling sharp and rested, and stood looking out of the windows. I felt as full of life as a pack of sled-dogs.

We got up and breakfasted on a pot of Mexican mixture and a couple of cigarettes. I think I was even whistling as I shaved. She came into the bathroom and stood looking at me. We seemed to be doing a lot of that.

'Considering that someone tried to kill you last night,' she said, 'you're in a remarkably good frame of mind this morning.'

'I always say that there's nothing like a brush with the grim reaper to renew the taste for life.' I smiled at her, and added, 'That, and a good woman.'

'You still haven't told me why he did it.'

'Because he was paid to,' I said.

'By whom? The man in the club?' I wiped my face and looked for missed stubble. There wasn't any, so I put down my razor.

'Do you remember yesterday morning that I telephoned Six's house and asked the butler to give both his master and Haupthändler a message?'

Inge nodded. 'Yes. You said to tell them that you were getting close.'

'I was hoping it would spook Haupthändler into playing his hand. Well, it did. Only rather more quickly than I had expected.'

'So you think he paid that man to kill you?'

'I know he did.' Inge followed me into the bedroom where I put on a shirt, and watched me as I fumbled with the cuff-link on the arm that I had grazed, and that she had bandaged. 'You know,' I said, 'last night posed just as many questions as it answered.

There's no logic to anything, none at all. It's like trying to make up a jigsaw, with not one but two sets of pieces. There were two things stolen from the Pfarrs' safe; some jewels and some papers. But they don't seem to fit together at all. And then there are the pieces which have a picture of a murder on them, which can't be made to fit with those belonging to the theft.'

Inge blinked slowly like a clever cat, and looked at me with the sort of expression that makes a man feel *meschugge* for not having thought of it first. Irritating to watch, but when she spoke I realized just how stupid I really was.

'Perhaps there never was just one jigsaw,' she said. 'Perhaps you've been trying to put one together when there were two all along.' It took a moment or two to let that one sink all the way in, helped at the end with the flat of my hand smacking against my forehead.

'Shit, of course.' Her remark had the force of revelation. It wasn't one crime I was staring in the face, trying to understand. It was two.

We parked on Nollendorfplatz in the shadow of the S-Bahn. Overhead, a train thundered across the bridge with a noise that possessed the whole square. It was loud; but it wasn't enough to disturb the soot from the great factory chimneys of Tempelhof and Neukölln that caked the walls of the buildings which ringed the square, buildings which had seen many better days. Walking westwards into lower-middle-class Schöneberg, we found the five-storey block of apartments on Nollendorfstrasse where Marlene Sahm lived, and climbed up to the fourth floor.

The young man who opened the door to us was in uniform – some special company of SA that I failed to recognize. I asked him if Fräulein Sahm lived there and he replied that she did and that he was her brother.

'And who are you?' I handed him my card and asked if I might speak to his sister. He looked more than a little put out at the intrusion and I wondered if he had been lying when he said that she was his sister. He ran his hand through a large head of straw-coloured hair, and glanced back over his shoulder before standing aside.

'My sister is having a lie-down right now,' he explained. 'But I will ask her if she wishes to speak with you, Herr Günther.' He closed the door behind us, and tried to fix a more welcoming expression to his face. Broad and thick-lipped, the mouth was almost negroid. It smiled broadly now, but quite independently of the two cold blue eyes that flicked between Inge and myself as if they had been following a table-tennis ball.

'Please wait here a moment.'

When he left us alone in the hall, Inge pointed above the sideboard where there hung not one, but three pictures of the Führer. She smiled.

'Doesn't look like they're taking any chances as far as their loyalty is concerned.'

'Didn't you know?' I said. 'They're on special offer at Woolworth's. Buy two dictators, and you get one free.'

Sahm returned, accompanied by his sister Marlene, a big, handsome blonde with a drooping, melancholic nose and an underhung jaw that lent her features a certain modesty. But her neck was so muscular and well-defined as to appear almost inflexible; and her bronzed forearm was that of an archer or a keen tennis player. As she strode into the hallway I caught a glimpse of a well-muscled calf that was the shape of an electric lightbulb. She was built like a rococo fireplace.

They showed us into the modest little sitting room, and, with the exception of the brother, who stood leaning against the doorway and looking generally suspicious of myself and Inge, we all sat down on a cheap brown-leather suite. Behind the glass doors of a tall walnut cabinet were enough trophies for a couple of school prize-givings.

'That's quite an impressive collection you have there,' I said awkwardly, to no one in particular. Sometimes I think my small-talk falls a couple of centimetres short.

'Yes, it is,' said Marlene, with a disingenuous look that might have passed for modesty. Her brother had no such reserve, if that's what it was.

'My sister is an athlete. But for an unfortunate injury she would be running for Germany in the Olympiad.' Inge and I made sympathetic noises. Then Marlene held up my card and read it again.

'How can I help you, Herr Günther?' she said.

I sat back on the sofa and crossed my legs before launching into my patter. 'I've been retained by the Germania Life Assurance Company to make some investigations concerning the death of Paul Pfarr and his wife. Anyone who knew them might help us to find out just what did happen and enable my client to make a speedy settlement.'

'Yes,' said Marlene with a long sigh. 'Yes, of course.'

I waited for her to say something before eventually I prompted her. 'I believe you were Herr Pfarr's secretary at the Ministry of the Interior.'

'Yes, that's right I was.' She was giving no more away than a card-player's eyeshade.

'Do you still work there?'

'Yes,' she said with an indifferent sort of shrug.

I risked a glance at Inge, who merely raised a perfectly pencilled eyebrow at me by way of response. 'Does Herr Pfarr's department investigating corruption in the Reich and the DAF still exist?'

She examined the toes of her shoes for a second, and then looked squarely at me for the first time since I had seen her. 'Who told you about that?' she said. Her tone was even, but I could tell that she was taken aback.

I ignored her question, trying to wrong-foot her. 'Do you think that's why he was killed – because somebody didn't like him snooping and blowing the whistle on people?'

'I – I have no idea why he was killed. Look, here, Herr Günther, I think –'

'Have you ever heard of a man by the name of Gerhard Von Greis? He's a friend of the Prime Minister, as well as being a black-mailer. You know, whatever it was that he passed on to your boss cost him his life.'

'I don't believe that —' she said, and then checked herself. 'I can't answer any of your questions.'

But I kept on going. 'What about Paul's mistress, Eva or Vera, or whatever her name is? Any idea why she might be hiding? Who knows, maybe she's dead too.'

Her eyes quivered like a cup and saucer in an express dining-car. She gasped at me and stood up, her hands clenched tightly at her sides. 'Please,' she said, her eyes starting to well up with tears. The brother shouldered himself away from the doorway, and moved in front of me, much in the manner of a referee stopping a boxing-match.

'That's quite enough, Herr Günther,' he said. 'I see no reason why I should allow you to interrogate my sister in this fashion.'

'Why not?' I asked, standing up. 'I bet she sees it all the time in the Gestapo. And a lot worse besides that.'

'All the same,' he said, 'it seems quite clear to me that she does not wish to answer your questions.'

'Strange,' I said. 'I had come to much the same conclusion.' I took Inge by the arm and moved towards the door. But as we were leaving I turned and added, 'I'm not on anyone's side, and the only thing I'm trying to get is the truth. If you change your mind, please don't hesitate to contact me. I didn't get into this business to throw anyone to the wolves.'

'I never had you down as the chivalrous type,' Inge said when we were outside again.

'Me?' I said. 'Now wait a minute. I went to the Don Quixote School of Detection. I got a B-plus in Noble Sentiment.'

'Too bad you didn't get one for Interrogation,' she said. 'You know, she got really rattled when you suggested that Pfarr's mistress might be dead.'

'Well, what would you have me do — pistol-whip it out of her?'

'I just meant that it was too bad she wouldn't talk, that's all. Maybe she will change her mind.'

'I wouldn't bet on it,' I said. 'If she does work for the Gestapo then it stands to reason that she's not the sort who underlines verses in her Bible. And did you see those muscles? I bet she's their best man with a whip or a rubber truncheon.'

We picked up the car and drove east on Bülowstrasse. I pulled up outside Viktoria Park.

'Come on,' I said. 'Let's walk awhile. I could do with some fresh air.'

Inge sniffed the air suspiciously. It was heavy with the stink of the nearby Schultheis brewery. 'Remind me never to let you buy me any perfume,' she said.

We walked up the hill to the picture market where what passed for Berlin's young artists offered their irreproachably Arcadian work for sale. Inge was predictably contemptuous.

'Have you ever seen such absolute shit?' she snorted. 'From all these pictures of the muscle-bound peasants binding corn and ploughing fields you would think we were living in a story by the Brothers Grimm.'

I nodded slowly. I liked it when she became animated on a subject, even if her voice was too loud and her opinions of the sort that could have landed both of us in a KZ.

Who knows, with a bit more time and patience she might have obliged me to re-examine my own rather matter-of-fact opinion of the value of art. But as it was, I had something else on my mind. I took her by the arm and steered her to a collection of paintings depicting steel-jawed storm-troopers that was arranged in front of an artist who looked anything but the Aryan stereotype. I spoke quietly.

'Ever since leaving the Sahms' apartment, I've had the idea that we were being followed,' I said. She looked around carefully. There were a few people milling around, but none that seemed especially interested in the two of us.

'I doubt you'll spot him,' I said. 'Not if he's good.'

'Do you think it's the Gestapo?' she asked.

'They're not the only pack of dogs in this town,' I said, 'but I guess that's where the smart money is. They're aware of my interest in this case and I wouldn't put it past them to let me do some of their legwork.'

'Well, what are we going to do?' Her face looked anxious, but I grinned back at her.

'You know, I always think that there's nothing that's quite as much fun as trying to shake off a tail. Especially if it might turn out to be the Gestapo.'

15

There were only two items in the morning mail, and both had been delivered by hand. Away from Gruber's inquisitive, hungry-cat stare, I opened them, and found that the smaller of the two envelopes contained a solitary square of cardboard that was a ticket for the day's Olympic track-and-field events. I turned it over, and on the back were written the initials 'M.S.' and '2 o'clock'. The larger envelope bore the seal of the Air Ministry and contained a transcript of calls that Haupthändler and Jeschonnek had made and received on their respective telephones during Saturday, which, apart from the one I had made myself from Haupthändler's apartment, was none. I threw the envelope and its contents into the waste-paper basket and sat down, wondering if Jeschonnek had already bought the necklace, and just what I would do if I was obliged to follow Haupthändler to Tempelhof Airport that same evening. On the other hand, if Haupthändler had already disposed of the necklace I couldn't imagine that he would have been wait-ing for the Monday evening flight to London just for the hell of it. It seemed more likely that the deal involved foreign currency, and that Jeschonnek had needed the time to raise the money. I made myself a coffee and waited for Inge to arrive.

I glanced out of the window and, seeing that the weather was dull, I smiled as I imagined her glee at the prospect of another shower of rain falling upon the Führer's Olympiad. Except that now I was going to get wet too.

What had she called it? 'The most outrageous confidence-trick in the history of modern times.' I was searching in the cupboard for my old rubberized raincoat when she came through the door.

'God, I need a cigarette,' she said, tossing her handbag onto a chair and helping herself from the box on my desk. With some amusement she looked at my old coat and added, 'Are you planning to wear that thing?'

'Yes. Fräulein Muscles came through after all. There was a ticket for today's games in the mail. She wants me to meet her in the stadium at two.'

Inge looked out of the window. 'You're right,' she laughed, 'you'll need the coat. It's going to come down by the bucket.' She sat down and put her feet up on my desk. 'Well, I'll just stay here on my own, and mind the shop.'

'I'll be back by four o'clock at the latest,' I said. 'Then we have to go to the airport.'

She frowned. 'Oh yes, I was forgetting. Haupthändler is planning to fly to London tonight. Forgive me if I sound naive, but exactly what are you going to do when you get there? Just walk up to him and whoever it is he's taking with him and ask them how much they got for the necklace? Maybe they'll just open their suitcases and let you take a look at all their cash, right there in the middle of Tempelhof.'

'Nothing in real life is ever all that tidy. There never are neat little clues that enable you to apprehend the crook with minutes to spare.'

'You sound almost sad about it,' she said.

'I had one ace in the hole which I thought would make things a bit easier.'

'And the hole fell in, is that it?'

'Something like that.'

The sound of footsteps in the outer office made me stop. There was a knock at the door, and a motorcyclist, a corporal in the National Socialist Flying Corps, came in bearing a large buff-coloured envelope of the same sort as the one I had consigned earlier to the waste-paper basket. The corporal clicked his heels and asked me if I was Herr Bernhard Günther. I said that I was, took the envelope from the corporal's gauntleted hands and signed his receipt slip, after which he gave the Hitler Salute and walked smartly out again.

I opened the Air Ministry envelope. It contained several type-written pages that made up the transcript of calls Jeschonnek and Haupthändler had made the previous day. Of the two, Jeschonnek, the diamond dealer, had been the busier, speaking to various people regarding the illegal purchase of a large quantity of American dollars and British sterling.

'Bulls-eye,' I said, reading the transcript of the last of Jeschonnek's calls. This had been to Haupthändler, and of course it also showed up in the transcript of the other man's calls. It was the piece of evidence I had been hoping for: the evidence that turned theory into fact, establishing a definite link between Six's private secretary and the diamond dealer. Better than that, they discussed the time and place for a meeting.

'Well?' said Inge, unable to restrain her curiosity a moment longer.

I grinned at her. 'My ace in the hole. Someone just dug it out. There's a meet arranged between Haupthändler and Jeschonnek at an address in Grünewald tonight at five. Jeschonnek's going to be carrying a whole bagful of foreign currency.'

'That's a hell of an informant you have there,' she said, frowning. 'Who is it? Hanussen the Clairvoyant?'

'My man is more of an impresario,' I said. 'He books the turns, and this time, anyway, I get to watch the show.'

'And he just happens to have a few friendly storm-troopers on the staff to show you to the right seat, is that it?'

'You won't like it.'

'If I start to scowl it will be heartburn, all right?'

I lit a cigarette. Mentally I tossed a coin and lost. I would tell it to her straight. 'You remember the dead man in the service-lift?'

'Like I just found out I had leprosy,' she said, shuddering visibly.

'Hermann Goering hired me to try and find him.' I paused, waiting for her comment, and then shrugged under her bemused stare. 'That's it,' I said. 'He agreed to put a tap on a couple of telephones – Jeschonnek's and Haupthändler's.' I picked up the transcript and waved it in front of her face. 'And this is the result.

Amongst other things it means that I can now afford to tell his people where to find Von Greis.'

Inge said nothing. I took a long angry drag at my cigarette and then stubbed it out like I was hammering a lectern. 'Let me tell you something: you don't turn him down, not if you want to finish your cigarette with both lips.'

'No, I suppose not.'

'Believe me, he's not a client that I would have chosen. His idea of a retainer is a thug with a machine-pistol.'

'But why didn't you tell me about it, Bernie?'

'When Goering takes someone like me into his confidence, the table stakes are high. I thought it was safer for you that you didn't know. But now, well, I can't very well avoid it, can I?' Once again I brandished the transcript at her. Inge shook her head.

'Of course you couldn't refuse him. I didn't mean to appear awkward, it's just that I was, well, a bit surprised. And thank you for wanting to protect me, Bernie. I'm just glad that you can tell someone about that poor man.'

'I'll do it right now,' I said.

Rienacker sounded tired and irritable when I called him.

'I hope you've got something, pushbelly,' he said, 'because Fat Hermann's patience is worn thinner than the jam in a Jewish baker's sponge-cake. So if this is just a social call then I'm liable to come and visit you with some dog-shit on my shoes.'

'What's the matter with you, Rienacker?' I said. 'You having to share a slab in the morgue or something?'

'Cut the cabbage, Günther, and get on with it.'

'All right, keep your ears stiff. I just found your boy, and he's squeezed his last orange.'

'Dead?'

'Like Atlantis. You'll find him piloting a service-lift in a deserted hotel on Chamissoplatz. Just follow your nose.'

'And the papers?'

'There's a lot of burnt ash in the incinerator, but that's about all.'

'Any ideas on who killed him?'

'Sorry,' I said, 'but that's your job. All I had to do was find our aristocratic friend, and that's as far as it goes. Tell your boss he'll be receiving my account in the post.'

'Thanks a lot, Günther,' said Rienacker, sounding less than pleased. 'You've got —' I cut across him with a curt goodbye, and hung up.

I left Inge the keys to the car, telling her to meet me in the street outside Haupthändler's beach house at 4.30 that afternoon. I was intending to take the special S-Bahn to the Reich Sports Field via the Zoo Station; but first, and so that I could be sure of not being followed, I chose a particularly circuitous route to get to the station. I walked quickly up Königstrasse and caught a number two tram to Spittel Market where I strolled twice around the Spindler Brunnen Fountain before getting onto the U-Bahn. I rode one stop to Friedrichstrasse, where I left the U-Bahn and returned once more to street level. During business hours Friedrichstrasse has the densest traffic in Berlin, when the air tastes like pencil shavings. Dodging umbrellas and Americans standing huddled over their Baedekers, and narrowly missing being run over by a Rudesdorfer Peppermint van, I crossed Tauberstrasse and Jäger-strasse, passing the Kaiser Hotel and the head office of the Six Steel Works. Then, continuing up towards Unter den Linden, I squeezed between some traffic on Französische Strasse and, on the corner of Behrenstrasse, ducked into the Kaiser Gallery. This is an arcade of expensive shops of the sort that are much patronized by tourists and it leads onto Unter den Linden at a spot next to the Hotel Westminster, where many of them stay. If you are on foot it has always been a good place to shake a tail for good. Emerging on to Unter den Linden, I crossed over the road and rode a cab to the Zoo Station, where I caught the special train to the Reich Sports Field.

The two-storey-high stadium looked smaller than I had expected, and I wondered how all the people milling around its perimeter would ever fit in. It was only after I had gone in that I realized that it was actually bigger on the inside than on the outside, and this by virtue of an arena that was several metres below ground level.

I took my seat, which was close to the edge of the cinder track and next to a matronly woman who smiled and nodded politely as I sat down. The seat to my right, which I imagined was to be occupied by Marlene Sahm, was for the moment empty, although it was already past two o'clock. Just as I was looking at my watch the sky released the heaviest shower of the day, and I was only too glad to share the matron's umbrella. It was to be her good deed of the day. She pointed to the west side of the stadium and handed me a small pair of binoculars.

'That is where the Führer will be sitting,' she said. I thanked her, and although I wasn't in the least bit interested, I scanned a dais that was populated with several men in frock-coats, and the ubiquitous complement of SS officers, all of them getting as wet as I was. Inge would be pleased, I thought. Of the Führer himself, there was no sign.

'Yesterday he didn't come until almost five o'clock,' explained the matron. 'Although with weather as atrocious as this, he could be forgiven for not coming at all.' She nodded down at my empty lap. 'You don't have a programme. Would you care to know the order of events?' I said that I would, but found to my embarrassment that she intended not to lend me her programme but to read it aloud.

'The first events on the track this afternoon are the heats of the 400-metre hurdles. Then we have the semi-finals and final of the 100-metres. If you'll allow me to say so, I don't think the German has a chance against the American negro, Owens. I saw him running yesterday and he was like a gazelle.' I was just about to start out on some unpatriotic remark about the so-called Master Race when Marlene Sahm sat down next to me, so probably saving me from my own potentially treasonable mouth.

'Thank you for coming, Herr Günther. And I'm sorry about yesterday. It was rude of me. You were only trying to help, were you not?'

'Certainly.'

'Last night I couldn't sleep for thinking about what you said about —' and here she hesitated for a moment. 'About Eva.'

'Paul Pfarr's mistress?' She nodded. 'Is she a friend of yours?'

'Not close friends, you understand, but friends, yes. And so early this morning I decided to put my trust in you. I asked you to meet me here because I'm sure I'm being watched. That's why I'm late too. I had to make sure I gave them the slip.'

'The Gestapo?'

'Well, I certainly don't mean the International Olympic Committee, Herr Günther.' I smiled at that, and so did she.

'No, of course not,' I said, quietly appreciating the way in which modesty giving way to impatience made her the more attractive. Beneath the terracotta-coloured raincoat she was unbuttoning at the neck, she wore a dress of dark blue cotton, with a neckline that allowed me a view of the first few centimetres of a deep and well-sunburnt cleavage. She started to fumble inside her capacious brown-leather handbag.

'So then,' she said nervously. 'About Paul. After his death I had to answer a great many questions, you know.'

'What about?' It was a stupid question, but she didn't say so.

'Everything. I think that at one stage they even got round to suggesting that I might be his mistress.' From out of the bag she produced a dark-green desk diary and handed it to me. 'But this I kept back. It's Paul's desk diary, or, rather, the one he kept himself, his private one, and not the official one that I kept for him: the one that I gave to the Gestapo.' I turned the diary over in my hands, not presuming to open it. Six, and now Marlene, it was odd the way people held things back from the police. Or maybe it wasn't. It all depended on how well you knew the police.

'Why?' I said.

'To protect Eva.'

'Then why didn't you simply destroy it? Safer for her and for you too I would have thought.'

She frowned as she struggled to explain something she perhaps only half understood herself. 'I suppose I thought that in the proper hands, there might be something in it that would identify the murderer.'

'And what if it should turn out that your friend Eva had something to do with it?'

Her eyes flashed and she spoke angrily 'I don't believe it for a second,' she said. 'She wasn't capable of harming anyone.'

Pursing my lips, I nodded circumspectly. 'Tell me about her.'

'All in good time, Herr Günther,' she said, her mouth becoming compressed. I didn't think Marlene Sahm was the type ever to be carried away by her passion or her tastes, and I wondered whether the Gestapo preferred to recruit this kind of woman, or simply affected them that way.

'First of all, I'd like to make something clear to you.'

'Be my guest.'

'After Paul's death I myself made a few discreet inquiries as to Eva's whereabouts, but without success. But I shall come to that too. Before I tell you anything I want your word that if you manage to find her you will try to persuade her to give herself up. If she is arrested by the Gestapo it will go very badly for her. This isn't a favour I'm asking, you understand. This is my price for providing you with the information to help your own investigation.'

'You have my word. I'll give her every chance I can. But I have to tell you: right now it looks as though she is in it up to her hatband. I believe that she's planning to go abroad tonight, so you'd better start talking. There's not much time.'

For a moment Marlene chewed her lip thoughtfully, her eyes gazing emptily at the hurdlers as they came up to the starting line. She remained oblivious of the buzz of excitement in the crowd that gave way to silence as the starter raised his pistol. As he fired she began to tell me what she knew.

'Well, for a start there's her name: it's not Eva. That was Paul's name for her. He was always doing that, giving people new names. He liked Aryan names, like Siegfried, and Brünhilde. Eva's real name was Hannah, Hannah Roedl, but Paul said that Hannah was a Jewish name, and that he would always call her Eva.'

The crowd gave a great roar as the American won the first heat of the hurdles.

'Paul was unhappy with his wife, but he never told me why. He and I were good friends, and he confided in me a great deal, but I never heard him speak about his wife. One night he took me to a gaming club, and it was there that I ran across Eva. She was working there as a croupier. I hadn't seen her in months. We first met working for the Revenue. She was very good with figures. I suppose that's why she became a croupier in the first place. Twice the pay, and the chance to meet some interesting people.'

I raised my eyebrows at that one: I, for one, have never found the people who gamble in casinos to be anything less than dull; but I said nothing, not wishing to cut her thread.

'Anyway, I introduced her to Paul, and you could see they were attracted. Paul was a handsome man, and Eva was just as good-looking, a real beauty. A month later I met her again and she told me that she and Paul were having an affair. At first I was shocked; and then I thought it was really none of my business. For a while – maybe as long as six months – they were seeing quite a lot of each other. And then Paul was killed. The diary should provide you with dates and all that sort of thing.'

I opened the diary and turned to the date of Paul's murder. I read the entries written on the page.

'According to this he had an appointment with her on the night of his death.' Marlene said nothing. I started to turn back the pages. 'And here's another name I recognize,' I said. 'Gerhard Von Greis. What do you know about him?' I lit a cigarette and added: 'It's time you told me all about your little department in the Gestapo, don't you think?'

'Paul's department. He was so proud of it, you know.' She sighed profoundly. 'A man of great integrity.'

'Sure,' I said. 'All the time he was with this other woman, what he really wanted was to be back home with the wife.'

'In a funny way that's absolutely true, Herr Günther. That's exactly what he wanted. I don't think he ever stopped loving Grete. But for some reason he started hating her as well.'

I shrugged. 'Well, it takes all sorts. Maybe he just liked to wag his tail.' She stayed silent for a few minutes after that one, and they ran the next heat of the hurdles. Much to the delight of the crowd, the German runner, Nottbruch, won the race. The matron got very excited at that, standing up in her seat and waving her programme.

Marlene rummaged in her bag again, and took out an envelope.

'This is a copy of a letter originally empowering Paul to set up his department,' she said, handing it to me. 'I thought you might like to see it. It helps to put things in perspective, to explain why Paul did what he did.'

I read the letter. It went as follows:

The Reichsführer SS and	Berlin NW7
Chief of the German Police in	6 November 1935
the Reich Ministry of the	Unter den Linden, 74
Interior	Local Tel. 120 034
o–KdS g2(o/R V) No. 22 11/35	Trunk Call 120 037

Express letter to Hauptsturmführer Doktor Paul Pfarr

I write to you on a very serious matter. I mean corruption amongst the servants of the Reich. One principle must apply: public servants must be honest, decent, loyal and comradely to members of our own blood. Those individuals who offend against this principle – who take so much as one mark – will be punished without mercy. I shall not stand idly by and watch the rot develop.

As you know, I have already taken measures to root out corruption within the ranks of the SS, and a number of dishonest men have been eliminated accordingly. It is the will of the Führer that you should be empowered to investigate and root out corruption in the German Labour Front, where fraud is endemic. To this end you are promoted to the rank of Hauptsturmführer, reporting directly to me.

Wherever corruption forms, we shall burn it out. And at the end of the day, we shall say that we performed this task in love of our people.

Heil Hitler!
(signed)
Heinrich Himmler

'Paul was very diligent,' Marlene said. 'Arrests were made and the guilty punished.'

' "Eliminated",' I said, quoting the Reichsführer.

Marlene's voice hardened. 'They were enemies of the Reich,' she said.

'Yes, of course.' I waited for her to continue, and seeing her rather unsure of me I added, 'They had to be punished. I'm not disagreeing with you. Please go on.'

Marlene nodded. 'Finally, he turned his attention to the Steel Workers Union, and quite early on he became aware of certain rumours regarding his own father-in-law, Hermann Six. In the beginning he made light of it. And then, almost overnight, he was determined to destroy him. After a while, it was nothing short of an obsession.'

'When was this?'

'I can't remember the date. But I do remember that it was about the time that he started working late, and not taking telephone calls from his wife. And it wasn't long after that he started to see Eva.'

'And exactly how was Daddy Six misbehaving?'

'Corrupt DAF officials had deposited the Steel Workers Union and Welfare Fund in Six's bank –'

'You mean, he owns a bank as well?'

'A major shareholding, in the Deutsches Kommerz. In return, Six saw to it that these same officials were given cheap personal loans.'

'What did Six get out of it?'

'By paying low interest on the deposit to the detriment of the workers, the bank was able to improve the books.'

'Nice and tidy then,' I said.

'That's just the half of it,' she said with an outraged sort of chuckle. 'Paul also suspected that his father-in-law was skimming the union's funds. And that he was churning the union's investments.'

'Churning,' I said. 'What's that?'

'Repeatedly selling stocks and shares and buying others so that each time you can claim the legal percentages. The commission if you like. That would have been split between the bank and the union officials. But trying to prove it was a different story,' she said. 'Paul tried to get a tap on Six's telephone, but whoever it is that arranges these things refused. Paul said that somebody else was already tapping his phone and that they weren't about to share. So Paul looked for another way to get to him. He discovered that the Prime Minister had a confidential agent who had certain information that was compromising to Six, and for that matter to many others. His name was Gerhard Von Greis. In Six's case, Goering was using this information to make him toe the economic line. Anyway, Paul arranged to meet Von Greis and offered him a lot of money to let him take a look at what he had on Six. But Von Greis refused. Paul said he was afraid.'

She looked around as the crowd, anticipating the semi-final of the 100-metres, grew more excited. With the hurdles cleared off the track, there were now several sprinters warming up, including the man the crowd had come to see: Jesse Owens. For a moment, her attention was devoted entirely to the negro athlete.

'Isn't he superb?' she said. 'Owens I mean. In a class of his own.'

'But Paul did get hold of the papers, didn't he?'

She nodded. 'Paul was very determined,' she said, distractedly. 'At such times, he could be quite ruthless, you know.'

'I don't doubt it.'

'There is a department in the Gestapo at Prinz Albrecht Strasse, which deals with associations, clubs and the DAF. Paul persuaded them to issue a "red tab" on Von Greis, so that he could be arrested immediately. Not only that, but they saw to it that Von Greis was picked up by Alarm Command, and taken to Gestapo headquarters.'

'What is Alarm Command exactly?' I said.

'Killers.' She shook her head. 'You wouldn't want to fall into their hands. Their brief was to scare Von Greis: to scare him badly enough to convince him that Himmler was more powerful than Goering, that he should fear the Gestapo before he should fear the Prime Minister. After all, hadn't Himmler taken control of the Gestapo away from Goering in the first place? And then there was the case of Goering's former chief of Gestapo, Diels, being sold down the river by his former master. They said all of these things to Von Greis. They told him that the same would happen to him, and that his only chance was to cooperate, otherwise he would find himself facing the displeasure of the Reichsführer SS. That would mean a KZ for sure. Of course, Von Greis was convinced. What man in their hands would not have been? He gave Paul everything he had. Paul took possession of a number of documents which he spent several evenings examining at home. And then he was killed.'

'And the documents were stolen.'

'Yes.'

'Do you know something of what was in these documents?'

'Not in any detail. I never saw them myself. I only know what he told me. He said that they proved beyond all shadow of a doubt, that Six was in bed with organized crime.'

At the gun Jesse Owens was away to a good start, and by the first thirty metres he was powering fluently into a clear lead. In the seat next to me the matron was on her feet again. She had been wrong, I thought, to describe Owens as a gazelle. Watching the tall, graceful negro accelerate down the track, making a mockery of crackpot theories of Aryan superiority, I thought that Owens was nothing so much as a Man, for whom other men were simply a painful embarrassment. To run like that was the meaning of the earth, and if ever there was a master-race it was certainly not going to exclude someone like Jesse Owens. His victory drew a tremendous cheer from the German crowd, and I found it comforting that the only race they were shouting about was the one they had just seen.

Perhaps, I thought, Germany did not want to go to war after all. I looked towards that part of the stadium that was reserved for Hitler and other senior Party officials, to see if they were present to witness the depth of popular sentiment being demonstrated on behalf of the black American. But of the leaders of the Third Reich there was still no sign.

I thanked Marlene for coming, and then left the stadium. On the taxi-ride south towards the lakes, I spared a thought for poor Gerhard Von Greis. Picked up and terrified by the Gestapo, only to be released and almost immediately picked up, tortured and killed by Red Dieter's men. Now that's what I call unlucky.

We crossed Wannsee Bridge, and drove along the coast. A black sign at the head of the beach said, 'No Jews Here', which prompted the taxi-driver to an observation. 'That's a fucking laugh, eh? "No Jews Here." There's nobody here. Not with weather like this there isn't.' He uttered a derisive laugh for his own benefit.

Opposite the Swedish Pavilion restaurant a few die-hards still entertained hopes of the weather improving. The taxi-driver continued to pour scorn on them and the German weather as he turned into Koblanck Strasse, and then down Lindenstrasse. I told him to pull up on the corner of Hugo-Vogel Strasse.

It was a quiet, well-ordered and leafy suburb consisting of medium to large-sized houses, with neat front lawns and well-clipped hedges. I spotted my car parked on the pavement, but could see no sign of Inge. I looked around anxiously for her while I waited for my change. Feeling something was wrong, I managed to over-tip the driver, who responded by asking me if I wanted him to wait. I shook my head, and then stepped back as he roared off down the road. I walked down towards my car, which was parked about thirty metres down the road from Haupthändler's address. I checked the door. It wasn't locked, so I sat inside and waited a while, hoping that she might come back. I put the desk diary that Marlene Sahm had given me inside the glove-box, and then felt around under the seat for the gun I kept there. Putting it into my coat pocket, I got out of the car.

The address I had was a dirty-brown, two-storey affair with a run-down, dilapidated look about it. The paint was peeling from the closed shutters, and there was a 'For Sale' sign in the garden. The place looked as though it hadn't been occupied in a long time. Just the kind of place you'd choose to hide out in. A patchy lawn surrounded the house, and a short wall separated it from the pavement, on which a bright blue Adler was parked, facing downhill. I stepped over the wall, and went round the side, stepping carefully over a rusting lawnmower and ducking under a tree. Near the back corner of the house I took out the Walther and pulled back the slide to load the chamber and cock the weapon.

Bent almost double, I crept along beneath the level of the window, to the back door, which was slightly ajar. From somewhere inside the bungalow I could hear the sound of muffled voices. I pushed the door open with the muzzle of my gun and my eyes fell upon a trail of blood on the kitchen floor. I walked quietly inside, my stomach falling uncomfortably away beneath me like a coin dropped down a well, worried that Inge might have decided to take a look around on her own and been hurt, or worse. I took a deep breath and pressed the cold steel of the automatic against my cheek. The chill of it ran through the whole of my face, down the nape of my neck and into my soul. I bent down in front of the kitchen door to look through the keyhole. On the other side of the door was an empty, uncarpeted hallway and several closed doors. I turned the handle.

The voices were coming from a room at the front of the house and were clear enough for me to identify them as belonging to Haupthändler and Jeschonnek. After a couple of minutes there was a woman's voice too, and for a moment I thought it was Inge's, until I heard this woman laugh. Now that I was more impatient to know what had become of Inge than I was to recover Six's stolen diamonds and collect the reward, I decided that it was time I confronted the three of them. I'd heard enough to indicate that they weren't expecting any trouble, but as I came through the door,

I fired a shot over their heads in case they were in the mood to try something.

'Stay exactly where you are,' I said, feeling that I'd given them plenty of warning, and thinking that only a fool would pull a gun now. Gert Jeschonnek was just such a fool. It's difficult at the best of times to hit a moving target, especially one that's shooting back. My first concern was to stop him, and I wasn't particular how I did it. As it turned out, I stopped him dead. I could have wished not to have hit him in the head, only I wasn't given the opportunity. Having succeeded in killing one man, I now had the other to worry about, because by this time Haupthändler was on me, and wrestling for my gun. As we fell to the floor, he yelled to the girl who was standing lamely by the fireplace to get the gun. He meant the one which had fallen from Jeschonnek's hand when I blew his brains out, but for a moment the girl wasn't sure which gun it was that she was supposed to go for, mine or the one on the floor. She hesitated long enough for her lover to repeat himself, and in the same instant I broke free of his grasp and whipped the Walther across his face. It was a powerful backhand that had the follow-through of a match-winning tennis stroke, and it sent him sprawling, unconscious, against the wall. I turned to see the girl picking up Jeschonnek's gun. It was no time for chivalry, but then I didn't want to shoot her either. Instead I stepped smartly forward, and socked her on the jaw.

With Jeschonnek's gun safely in my coat pocket, I bent down to take a look at him. You didn't have to be an undertaker to see that he was dead. There are neater ways of cleaning a man's ears than a 9 mm bullet. I fumbled a cigarette into my dry mouth and sat down at the table to wait for Haupthändler and the girl to come round. I pulled the smoke through clenched teeth, kippering my lungs, and hardly exhaling at all, except in small nervous puffs. I felt like someone was playing the guitar with my insides.

The room was barely furnished, with only a threadbare sofa, a table and a couple of chairs. On the table, lying on a square of felt,

was Six's necklace. I threw the cigarette away, and tugged the diamonds towards me. The stones, clacking together like a handful of
marbles, felt cold and heavy in my hand. It was hard to imagine a
woman wearing them: they looked about as comfortable as a canteen of cutlery. Next to the table was a briefcase. I picked it up and
looked inside. It was full of money – dollars and sterling as I had
expected – and two fake passports in the names of a Herr and Frau
Rolf Teichmüller, the names that I had seen on the air-tickets in
Haupthändler's apartment. They were good fakes, but not hard to
obtain provided you knew someone at the passport office and were
prepared to pay some big expenses. I hadn't thought of it before,
but now it seemed that with all the Jews who had been coming to
Jeschonnek to finance their escapes from Germany, a fake-passport
service would have been a logical and highly profitable sideline.

The girl moaned and sat up. Cradling her jaw and sobbing
quietly, she went to help Haupthändler as he himself twisted over
on to his side. She held him by the shoulders as he wiped his bloody
nose and mouth. I flicked her new passport open. I don't know
that you could have described her, as Marlene Sahm had done, as a
beauty, but certainly she was good-looking, in a well-bred, intelligent sort of way – not at all the cheap party-girl I'd had in mind
when I'd been told that she was a croupier.

'I'm sorry I had to sock you, Frau Teichmüller,' I said. 'Or Hannah, or Eva, or whatever it is you or somebody else is calling you
at the moment.'

She glared at me with more than enough loathing to dry her
eyes, and mine besides. 'You're not so smart,' she said. 'I can't see
why these two idiots thought it was necessary to have you put out
of the way.'

'Right now I should have thought it was obvious.'

Haupthändler spat on the floor, and said, 'So what happens now?'

I shrugged. 'That depends. Maybe we can figure out a story:
crime of passion, or something like that. I've got friends down at
the Alex. Perhaps I can get you a deal, but first you've got to help
me. There was a woman working with me – tall, brown hair,

well-built, and wearing a black coat. Now there's some blood on the kitchen floor that's got me worried about her, especially as she seems to be missing. I don't suppose you would know anything about that, would you?'

Eva snorted with laughter. 'Go to hell,' said Haupthändler.

'On the other hand,' I said, deciding to scare them a little. 'Pre-meditated murder, well, that's a capital crime. Almost certain when there's a lot of money involved. I saw a man beheaded once – at Lake Ploetzen Prison. Goelpl, the state executioner, even wears white gloves and a tail-coat to do the job. That's rather a nice touch, don't you think?'

'Drop the gun, if you don't mind, Herr Günther.' The voice in the doorway was patient, but patronizing, as if addressing a naughty child. But I did as I was told. I knew better than to argue with a machine pistol, and a brief glance at his boxing-glove of a face told me that he wouldn't hesitate to kill me if I so much as told a bad joke. As he came into the room, two other men, both carry-ing lighters, followed.

'Come on,' said the man with the machine pistol. 'On your feet, you two.' Eva helped Haupthändler to stand. 'And face the wall. You too, Günther.'

The wallpaper was cheap flock. A bit too dark and sombre for my taste. I stared hard at it for several minutes while I waited to be searched.

'If you know who I am, then you know I'm a private investiga-tor. These two are wanted for murder.'

I didn't see the India Rubber so much as hear it sweep through the air towards my head. In the split second before I hit the floor and lost consciousness I told myself that I was getting tired of being knocked out.

16

Glockenspiel and big bass drum. What was that tune again? *Little Anna of Tharau is the One I Love*? No, not so much a tune as a number 51 tram to the Schönhauser Allee Depot. The bell clanged and the car shook as we raced through Schillerstrasse, Pankow, Breite Strasse. The giant Olympic bell in the great clock-tower tolling to the opening and closing of the Games. Herr Starter Miller's pistol, and the crowd yelling as Joe Louis sprinted up towards me and then put me on the deck for the second time in the round. A four-engined Junkers monoplane roaring through the night skies to Croydon taking my scrambled brains away with it. I heard myself say:

'Just drop me off at Lake Ploetzen.'

My head throbbed like a hot Dobermann. I tried raising it from the floor of the car, and found that my hands were handcuffed behind me; but the sudden, violent pain in my head made me oblivious to anything else but not moving my head again . . .

. . . a hundred thousand jackboots goose-stepping their way up Unter den Linden, with a man pointing a microphone down at them to pick up the awe-inspiring sound of an army crunching like an enormous great horse. An air-raid alarm. A barrage being laid down on the enemy trenches to cover the advance. Just as we were going over the top a big one exploded right above our heads, and blew us all off our feet. Cowering in a shell-hole full of incinerated frogs, with my head inside a grand piano, my ears ringing as the hammers hit the strings, I waited for the sound of battle to end . . .

Groggy, I felt myself being pulled out of the car, and then half carried, half dragged into a building. The handcuffs were removed, and I was sat down on a chair and held there so as to stop me falling off it. A man smelling of carbolic and wearing a uniform went through my pockets. As he pulled their linings inside out, I felt the collar of my jacket sticky against my neck, and when I touched it I found that it was blood from where I had been sapped. After that someone took a quick look at my head and said that I was fit enough to answer a few questions, although he might just as well have said I was ready to putt the shot. They got me a coffee and a cigarette.

'Do you know where you are?' I had to stop myself from shaking my head before mumbling that I didn't.

'You're at the Königs Weg Kripo Stelle, in the Grunewald.' I sipped some of my coffee and nodded slowly.

'I am Kriminalinspektor Hingsen,' said the man. 'And this is Wachmeister Wentz.' He jerked his head at the uniformed man standing beside him, the one who smelt of carbolic. 'Perhaps you'd care to tell us what happened.'

'If your lot hadn't hit me so hard I might find it easier to remember,' I heard myself croak.

The Inspektor glanced at the sergeant, who shrugged blankly. 'We didn't hit you,' he said.

'What's that?'

'I said, we didn't hit you.'

Gingerly, I touched the back of my head, and then inspected the dried blood on my fingers' ends. 'I suppose I did this when I was brushing my hair, is that it?'

'You tell us,' said the Inspektor. I heard myself sigh.

'What is going on here? I don't understand. You've seen my ID, haven't you?'

'Yes,' said the Inspektor. 'Look, why don't you start at the beginning? Assume we know absolutely nothing.'

I resisted the rather obvious temptation, and started to explain as best I was able. 'I'm working on a case,' I said. 'Haupthändler and the girl are wanted for murder –'

'Now wait a minute,' he said. 'Who's Haupthändler?'

I felt myself frown and tried harder to concentrate. 'No, I remember now. They're calling themselves the Teichmüllers now.

Haupthändler and Eva had two new passports, which Jeschonnek organized.'

The Inspektor rocked on his heels at that. 'Now we're getting somewhere. Gert Jeschonnek. The body we found, right?' He turned to his sergeant who produced my Walther PPK at the end of a piece of string from out of a paper bag.

'Is this your gun, Herr Günther?' said the sergeant.

'Yes, yes,' I said tiredly. 'It's all right, I killed him. It was self-defence. He was going for his gun. He was there to make a deal with Haupthändler. Or Teichmüller, as he's now calling himself.' Once again I saw the Inspektor and the sergeant exchange that look. I was starting to get worried.

'Tell us about this Herr Teichmüller,' said the sergeant.

'Haupthändler,' I said correcting him angrily. 'You have got him, haven't you?' The Inspektor pursed his lips and shook his head. 'The girl, Eva, what about her?' He folded his arms and looked at me squarely.

'Now look, Günther. Don't give us the cold cabbage. A neighbour reported hearing a shot. We found you unconscious, a dead body, and two pistols, each of them fired, and a lot of foreign currency. No Teichmüllers, no Haupthändler, no Eva.'

'No diamonds?' He shook his head.

The Inspektor, a fat, greasy, weary-looking man with tobacco-stained teeth, sat down opposite me and offered me another cigarette. He took one himself and lit us both in silence. When he spoke again his voice sounded almost friendly.

'You used to be a bull, didn't you?' I nodded, painfully. 'I thought I recognized the name. You were quite a good one too, as I recall.'

'Thanks,' I said.

'So I don't have to tell you of all people how this looks from my side of the charge-sheet.'

'Bad, eh?'

'Worse than bad.' The Inspektor rolled his cigarette between his lips for a moment, and winced as the smoke stung his eyeballs. 'Want me to call you a lawyer?'

'Thanks, no. But as long as you're in the mood to do an ex-bull a favour, there is one thing you could do. I've got an assistant, Inge Lorenz. Perhaps you would telephone her and let her know I'm being held.' He gave me a pencil and paper and I wrote down three phone numbers. The Inspektor seemed a decent sort of fellow, and I wanted to tell him that Inge had gone missing after driving my car to Wannsee. But that would have meant them searching my car and finding Marlene Sahm's diary, which would undoubtedly have incriminated her. Maybe Inge had been taken ill, and had caught a cab somewhere, knowing that I'd be along to pick up the car. Maybe.

'What about friends on the force? Somebody up at the Alex perhaps.'

'Bruno Stahlecker,' I said. 'He can vouch that I'm kind to children and stray dogs, but that's about it.'

'Too bad.' I thought for a moment. About the only thing that I could do was call the two Gestapo thugs who had ransacked my office, and throw them what I'd learned. It was a fair bet they'd be very unhappy with me, and I guessed that calling them would as likely win me an all-expenses trip to a KZ, as letting the local Inspektor charge me with Gert Jeschonnek's murder.

I'm not a gambling man, but they were the only cards I had.

Kriminalkommissar Jost drew thoughtfully on his pipe.

'It's an interesting theory,' he said. Dietz stopped playing with his moustache for long enough to snort contemptuously. Jost looked at his Inspektor for a moment, and then at me. 'But as you can see, my colleague finds it somewhat improbable.'

'That's putting it lightly, mulemouth,' muttered Dietz. Since scaring my secretary and smashing my last good bottle he seemed to have got uglier.

Jost was a tall, ascetic-looking man, with a face that wore a stag's permanently startled expression, and a scrawny neck that stuck out of his shirt collar like a tortoise in a rented shell. He allowed himself a little razor-blade of a smile. He was about to put his subordinate very firmly in his place.

'But then theory is not his strong point,' he said. 'He's a man of action, aren't you, Dietz?' Dietz glowered back, and the Kommissar's smile widened a fraction. Then he removed his glasses and began to clean them in such a way as might serve to remind anyone else in the interrogation-room that he regarded his own intellectualism as something superior to a vitality that was merely physical. Replacing his glasses he removed his pipe and gave way to a yawn that bordered on the effete.

'That's not to say that men of action do not have a place in Sipo. But after all is said and done, it is the men of thought who must make the decisions. Why do you suppose that the Germania Life Assurance Company did not see fit to inform us of the existence of this necklace?' The way he moved imperceptibly on to his question almost took me unawares.

'Perhaps nobody asked them,' I said hopefully. There was a long silence.

'But the place was gutted,' said Dietz in an anxious sort of way. 'Normally the insurance company would have informed us.'

'Why should they?' I said. 'There hadn't been a claim. But just to be neat they retained me, in case there should be.'

'Are you telling us that they knew that there was a valuable necklace in that safe,' said Jost, 'and yet were prepared not to pay out on it; that they were prepared to withhold valuable evidence?'

'But did you think to ask them?' I repeated again. 'Come now, gentlemen, these are businessmen we're talking about, not the Winter Relief. Why should they be in such a hurry to get rid of their money that they press someone to make a claim and take several hundred thousand Reichsmarks off their hands? And who should they pay out to?'

'The next of kin, surely,' said Jost.

'Without knowing who had title, and to what? Hardly,' I said.

'After all, there were other items of value in that safe which had nothing to do with the Six family, is that not so?' Jost looked blank. 'No, Kommissar, I think your men were too busy worrying about the papers belonging to Herr Von Greis to bother with finding out what else might have been in Herr Pfarr's safe.'

Dietz didn't like that one bit. 'Don't get smart with us, mulemouth,' he said. 'You're in no position to charge us with incompetence. We've got enough to kick you all the way to the nearest KZ.'

Jost pointed the stem of his pipe at me. 'In that at least he is right, Günther,' he said. 'Whatever our shortcomings were, you are the man with his neck on the block.' He sucked on his pipe, but it was empty. He started to fill it again.

'We'll check your story,' he said, and ordered Dietz to telephone the Lufthansa desk at Tempelhof to see if there was a reservation for the evening flight to London in the name of Teichmüller. When Dietz said there was, Jost lit his pipe; between puffs he said: 'Well then, Günther, you're free to leave.'

Dietz was beside himself, although that was only to be expected; but even the Grunewald station Inspektor seemed rather puzzled at the Kommissar's decision. For my part, I was as taken aback as either of them at this unexpected turn of events. Unsteadily I got to my feet, waiting for Jost to give Dietz the nod that would have him knock me down again. But he just sat there, puffing his pipe and ignoring me. I crossed the room to the door and turned the handle. As I went out I saw that Dietz had to look away, for fear that he might lose control and disgrace himself in front of his superior. Of the few pleasures that were left to me that evening, the prospect of Dietz's rage was sweet indeed.

As I was leaving the station, the desk-sergeant told me that there had been no reply from any of the telephone numbers that I'd given him.

Outside in the street, my relief at being released quickly gave way to anxiety for Inge. I was tired, and I thought I probably needed a few stitches in my head, but when I hailed a cab I found myself telling the driver to take me to where Inge had parked my car in Wannsee.

There was nothing in the car that gave any clue as to her where-abouts, and the police car parked in front of Haupthändler's beach house cancelled any hope I might have entertained of searching the place for some trace of her, always supposing that she had gone inside. All I could do was drive around Wannsee awhile on the chance that I might see her.

My apartment seemed especially empty, even with the radio and all the lights turned on. I telephoned Inge's apartment in Charlottenburg, but there was no reply. I called the office, I even called Müller, on the *Morgenpost*; but he knew as little about Inge Lorenz, who her friends were, if she had any family and where they lived, as it seemed I did myself.

I poured myself a massive brandy and drank it in one gulp, hoping to anaesthetize myself against a new kind of discomfort I was feeling – the kind that was deep in my gut: worry. I boiled up some water for a bath. By the time it was ready I'd had another large one, and was getting ready for my third. The tub was hot enough to parboil an iguana but, preoccupied with Inge and what might have happened, I hardly noticed.

Preoccupation submitted to puzzlement as I tried to fathom why it was that Jost had let me go on the strength of an interroga-tion lasting hardly as much as one hour. Nobody could have persuaded me that he believed everything that I had told him, des-pite his pretence to being something of a criminologist. I knew his reputation, and it wasn't that of a latter-day Sherlock Holmes. From what I had heard of him Jost had the imagination of a gelded carthorse. It went against everything he believed in to release me on such a desultory piece of cross-checking as a phone call to the Lufthansa desk at Tempelhof.

I dried myself and went to bed. For a while I lay awake, rum-maging through the ill-fitting drawers in the dilapidated cabinet of my head, hoping that I might find something that would make things appear clearer to me. I didn't find it, and I didn't think I was going to. But if Inge had been lying next to me, I might have told her that my guess was that I was free because Jost had superiors who wanted Von Greis's papers at any cost, even if that meant using a suspected double-murderer to do it.

I would also have told her that I was in love with her.

17

I awoke feeling hollower than a dug-out canoe, and disappointed that I didn't have a bad hangover to occupy my day.

'How do you like that?' I muttered to myself as I stood by my bed, and squeezed my skull in search of a headache. 'I suck the stuff up like a hole in the ground and I can't even get a decent tomcat.'

In the kitchen I made myself a pot of coffee that you could have eaten with a knife and fork, and then I had a wash. I made a bad job of shaving; slapping on some cologne, I nearly passed out.

There was still no reply from Inge's apartment. Cursing myself and my so-called speciality in finding missing persons, I called Bruno at the Alex and asked him to find out if the Gestapo might have arrested her. It seemed the most logical explanation. When a lamb is missing from the flock, there's no need to go hunting tiger if you live on the same mountain as a wolf pack. Bruno promised to ask around, but I knew that it might take several days to find out something. Nevertheless, I hung about my apartment for the rest of the morning in the hope that Bruno, or Inge herself, might call. I did a lot of staring at the walls and the ceiling, and I even got to thinking about the Pfarr case again. By lunchtime I was in the mood to start asking more questions. It didn't take a brick wall to fall on me to realize that there was one man who could provide a lot of the answers.

This time the huge wrought-iron gates to Six's property were locked. A length of chain had been wrapped and padlocked around the centre bars; and the small 'Keep Out' sign had been replaced with one that read: 'Keep Out. No Trespassers'. It was as if Six had suddenly grown more nervous about his own security.

I parked close to the wall and, having put the gun from my

bedside-drawer in my pocket, I got out of the car and climbed onto the roof. The top of the wall was easily reached, and I pulled myself up to sit astride the parapet. An elm tree provided an easy climb down to ground level.

There was little or no growl that I could recall, and I hardly heard the sound of the dogs' paws as they galloped across the fallen leaves. At the last second I heard a heavy, panting breath which made the hair on the back of my neck stand up on end. The dog was already leaping at my throat as I fired. The shot sounded small beneath the trees, almost too small to kill something as fierce as the Dobermann. Even as it fell dead at my feet the wind was already bearing the noise away, and in the opposite direction from the house. I let out the breath that unconsciously I had held while firing, and with my heart beating like a fork in a bowlful of egg-white, I turned instinctively, remembering that there had been not one, but two dogs. For a second or two, the leaves rustling in the trees overhead camouflaged the other's low growl. The dog came forward uncertainly, appearing in the clearing between the trees and keeping its distance from me. I stepped back as slowly it approached its dead brother, and when it dipped its head to sniff at the other's open wound, I raised my gun once more. In a sudden gust of wind, I fired. The dog yelped as the bullet kicked it off its feet. For a moment or two it continued breathing, and then it lay still.

Pocketing the gun, I moved into the trees and walked down the long slope in the direction of the house. Somewhere the peacock was calling, and I had half a mind to shoot that too if it were unlucky enough to be stumbled upon. Killing was very much on my mind. It is quite common in a homicide for the murderer to get warmed up for the main event by disposing of a few innocent victims, such as the family pets, along the way.

Detection is all about chain-making, manufacturing links: with Paul Pfarr, Von Greis, Bock, Mutschmann, Red Dieter Helfferich and Hermann Six, I had a length of something strong enough to put my weight on. Paul Pfarr, Eva, Haupthändler and Jeschonnek was shorter, and altogether different.

It wasn't that I intended killing Six. It was just that if I was unsuccessful in obtaining a few straight answers then I hadn't ruled it out as a possibility. So it was with some embarrassment then that, with these thoughts passing through my mind, I came across the millionaire himself, standing under a great fir tree, smoking a cigar and humming quietly.

'Oh, it's you,' he said, quite unperturbed to see me turn up on his property with a gun in my hand. 'I thought it was the groundsman. You'll want some money, I suppose.'

For a brief moment I didn't know what to say to him. Then I said: 'I shot the dogs.' I put the gun back into my pocket.

'Did you? Yes, I thought I heard a couple of shots.' If he felt any fear or irritation at this piece of information, he did not show it.

'You'd better come up to the house,' he said, and began to walk slowly towards the house, with me following a short way behind.

When we got within sight of the house I saw Ilse Rudel's blue BMW parked outside, and I wondered if I would see her. But it was the presence on the lawn of a large marquee that prompted me to break the silence between us.

'Planning a party?'

'Er, yes, a party. It's my wife's birthday. Just a few friends, you know.'

'So soon after the funeral?' My tone was bitter, and I saw that Six had noticed it too. As he walked along he searched first the sky and then the ground for an explanation.

'Well, I'm not –' he began. And then: 'One can't – one cannot mourn one's loss indefinitely. Life must go on.' Recovering some of his composure he added: 'I thought that it would be unfair to my wife to cancel her plans. And of course, we both have a position in society.'

'We mustn't forget that, must we?' I said. Leading us up to the front door, he said nothing, and I wondered if he was going to call for help. He pushed it open, and we stepped into the hall.

'No butler today?' I observed.

'It's his day off,' said Six, hardly daring to catch my eye. 'But there is a maid if you would like some refreshment. You must be quite warm after your little excitement.'

'Which one?' I said. 'Thanks to you I've had several "little excitements".'

He smiled thinly. 'The dogs, I mean.'

'Oh yes, the dogs. Yes, I am quite warm as it happens. They were big dogs. But I'm quite a shot, even though I say so myself.' We went in to the library.

'I enjoy shooting myself. But only for sport. I don't suppose I've ever shot anything bigger than a pheasant.'

'Yesterday, I shot a man,' I said. 'That's my second one in as many weeks. Since I started to work for you, Herr Six, it's become a bit of a habit with me, you know.' He stood awkwardly in front of me, his hands clasped behind his neck. He cleared his throat and threw the cigar butt into the cold fireplace. When eventually he spoke, he sounded embarrassed, as though he were about to dismiss an old and faithful servant who had been caught stealing.

'You know, I'm glad you came,' he said. 'As it happens I was going to speak to Schemm, my lawyer, this afternoon, and arrange for you to be paid. But since you are here I can write you a cheque.' And so saying he went over to his desk with such alacrity that I thought he might have a gun in the drawer.

'I'd prefer cash, if you don't mind.' He glanced up at my face, and then down at my hand holding the butt of the automatic in my jacket pocket.

'Yes, of course you would.' The drawer stayed shut. He sat down in his chair and rolled back a corner of the rug to reveal a small safe sunk in the floor.

'Now that's a handy little nut. You can't be too careful these days,' I said, relishing my own lack of tact. 'You can't even trust the banks, can you?' I peered innocently across the desk. 'Fireproof, is it?' Six's eyes narrowed.

'You'll forgive me, but I seem to have lost my sense of humour.' He opened the safe, and withdrew several packets of banknotes. 'I believe we said five per cent. Would 40,000 close our account?'

'You could try it,' I said, as he placed eight of the packets on the desk. Then he closed the safe, rolled back the carpet, and pushed the money towards me.

'They're all hundreds, I'm afraid.'

I picked up one of the bundles and tore the paper wrapping off. 'Just as long as they've got Herr Liebig's picture on them,' I said.

Smiling thinly, Six stood up. 'I don't think we need ever meet again, Herr Günther.'

'Aren't you forgetting something?'

He began to look impatient. 'I don't think so,' he said testily.

'Oh, but I'm sure you are.' I put a cigarette in my mouth and struck a match. Bending my head towards the flame I took a couple of quick puffs and then dropped the match into the ashtray. 'The necklace.' Six remained silent. 'But then, you already have it back, don't you?' I said. 'Or at least you know where it is, and who has got it.'

His nose wrinkled with distaste, as if it detected a bad smell. 'You're not going to be tiresome about this are you, Herr Günther? I do hope not.'

'And what about those papers? The evidence of your involvement with organized crime that Von Greis gave to your son-in-law. Or do you imagine that Red Dieter and his associates are going to persuade the Teichmüllers to tell them where they are? Is that it?'

'I've never heard of a Red Dieter, or —'

'Sure you have, Six. He's a crook, just like you. During the steel strikes he was the gangster you paid to intimidate your workers.'

Six laughed and lit his cigar. 'A gangster,' he said. 'Really, Herr Günther, your imagination is running away with you. Now, if you don't mind, you've been very handsomely paid, so if you will please leave I would be most grateful. I'm a very busy man, and I have a lot of things to do.'

'I guess things are difficult without a secretary to help. What if I were to tell you that the man calling himself Teichmüller, the one that Red's thugs are probably beating the shit out of right now, is really your private secretary, Hjalmar Haupthändler?'

'That is ridiculous,' he said. 'Hjalmar is visiting some friends in Frankfurt.'

I shrugged. 'It's a simple matter to get Red's boys to ask Teich-müller what his real name is. Perhaps he's already told them; but then, Teichmüller is the name on his new passport, so they could be forgiven for not believing him. He purchased it from the same man he was planning to sell the diamonds to. One for him and one for the girl.'

Six sneered at me. 'And does this girl have a real name too?' he said.

'Oh yes. Her name is Hannah Roedl, although your son-in-law preferred to call her Eva. They were lovers, at least they were until she murdered him.'

'That's a lie. Paul never had a mistress. He was devoted to my Grete.'

'Come off it, Six. What did you do to them that made him turn his back on her? That made him hate you bad enough to want to put you behind bars?'

'I repeat, they were devoted to each other.'

'I admit it's possible that they might have become reconciled to each other not long before they were killed, with the discovery that your daughter was pregnant.' Six laughed. 'And so Paul's mistress decided to get her own back.'

'Now you really are being ridiculous,' he said. 'You call yourself a detective and you don't know that my daughter was physically incapable of having children.'

I felt my jaw. 'Are you sure about that?'

'Good God, man, do you think it's something that I might have forgotten? Of course I'm sure.'

I walked round Six's desk and looked at the photographs that were arranged there. I picked one of them up, and stared grimly at the woman in the picture. I recognized her immediately. It was the woman from the beach house at Wannsee; the woman I had socked; the woman who I had thought was Eva, and was now call-ing herself Frau Teichmüller; the woman who in all probability had killed her husband and his mistress: it was Six's only daughter, Grete. As a detective, you have to expect to make mistakes; but it is nothing short of humiliating to come face to face with evidence of your own stupidity; and it is all the more galling when you discover that the evidence has been staring you in the face all along.

'Herr Six, this is going to sound crazy, I know, but I now believe that at least until yesterday afternoon your daughter was alive, and preparing to fly to London with your private secretary.'

Six's face darkened, and for a moment I thought he was going to attack me. 'What the hell are you babbling about now, you bloody fool?' he roared. 'What do you mean "alive"? My daughter is dead and buried.'

'I suppose that she must have come home unexpectedly and found Paul in bed with his bit of brush, both of them drunk as cats. Grete shot them both and then, realizing what she had done, she telephoned the only person she felt she could turn to, Haupthändler. He was in love with her. He would have done anything for her, and that included helping her to get away with murder.'

Six sat down heavily. He was pale and trembling. 'I don't believe it,' he said. But it was clear that he was finding my explanation only too plausible.

'I expect it was his idea to burn the bodies and make it look like it was your daughter who had died in bed with her husband, and not his mistress. He took Grete's wedding-ring and put it on the other woman's finger. Then he had the bright idea of taking the diamonds out of the safe and making it look like a burglary. That's why he left the door open. The diamonds were to stake their new life somewhere. New lives and new identities. But what Haupthändler didn't know was that somebody had already been in the safe that evening and removed certain papers that were compromising to you. This fellow was a real expert, a puzzler not long out of prison. A neat worker too. Not the sort to use explosives or do anything untidy like leave a safe door open. As drunk as they were, I'll bet that Paul and Eva never even heard him. One of Red's boys, of course. Red used to carry out all your dodgy little schemes, didn't he? While Goering's man Von Greis had these documents, things were merely inconvenient. The Prime Minister is a pragmatist. He could use the evidence of your previous criminality to ensure that you were useful to him, and make you toe the Party's economic line. But when Paul and the Black Angels got hold of them, that was altogether more uncomfortable. You knew that Paul wanted to destroy you. Backed into a corner you had to do something. So, as usual, you got Red Dieter to take care of it.

'But later on, with Paul and the girl dead, and the diamonds gone from the safe, it looked to you as though Red's man had been greedy, and that he'd taken more than he was supposed to. Not unreasonably you concluded that it was he who had killed your daughter, and so you told Red to put things right. Red managed to kill one of the two burglars, the man who had driven the car; but he missed the other, the one who had opened the safe, who therefore still had the papers and, you assumed, the diamonds. That's where I came in. Because you couldn't be sure that it wasn't Red himself who had double-crossed you, and so you probably didn't tell him about the diamonds, just as you didn't tell the police.'

Six took the dead cigar from out of the corner of his mouth and laid it, unsmoked, on the ashtray. He was starting to look very old.

'I have to hand it to you,' I said. 'Your reasoning was perfect: find the man with the diamonds and you would find the man with the documents. And when you found out that Helfferich hadn't hazed you, you put him on my tail. I led him to the man with the diamonds and, you thought, the documents too. At this very moment your German Strength associates are probably trying to persuade Herr and Frau Teichmüller to tell them where Mutschmann is. He's the man who really has the documents. And naturally they won't know what the hell he's talking about. Red won't like that. He's not a very patient man, and I'm sure I don't have to remind you of all people of what that means.'

The steel magnate stared into space, as if he had not heard one word I had said. I grabbed the lapels of his jacket, hauled him to his feet, and slapped him hard.

'Did you hear what I said? These murderers, these torturers, have your daughter.' His mouth went as slack as an empty douche-bag. I slapped it again.

'We've got to stop them.'

'So where's he got them?' I let him go and pushed him away from me.

'On the river,' he said. 'The Grosse Zug, near Schmöckwitz.'

I picked up the telephone. 'What's the number?'

Six swore. 'It's not on the phone,' he gasped. 'Oh Christ, what are we going to do?'

'We'll have to go there,' I said. 'We could drive there, but it would be quicker by boat.'

Six sprang round the desk. 'I've got a slipper at a mooring close by. We can drive there in five minutes.'

Stopping only to collect the boat keys and a can of petrol, we took the BMW and drove to the shores of the lake. The water was busier than on the previous day. A stiff breeze had encouraged the presence of a large number of small yachts, and their white sails covered the surface of the water like the wings of hundreds of moths.

I helped Six remove the green tarpaulin from the boat, and poured petrol into the tank while he connected the battery and started the engine. The slipper roared into life at the third time of asking, and the five-metre polished-wood hull strained at the mooring ropes, eager to be up-river. I threw Six the first line, and having untied the second I stepped quickly into the boat beside him. Then he wrenched the wheel to one side, punched the throttle lever and we jerked forwards.

It was a powerful boat and as fast as anything that even the river-police might have had. We raced up the Havel towards Spandau, Six holding the white steering-wheel grimly, oblivious to the effect that the slipper's enormous wake was having on the other waterway craft. It slapped against the hulls of boats moored under trees or beside small jetties, bringing their irate owners out on deck to shake their fists and utter shouts that were lost in the noise of the slipper's big engine. We went east on to the Spree.

'I hope to God we're not too late,' shouted Six. He had quite recovered his former vigour, and stared resolutely ahead of him, the man of action, with only a slight frown on his face to give a clue to his anxiety.

'I'm usually an excellent judge of a man's character,' he said, as if by way of explanation, 'but if it's any consolation to you, Herr Günther, I'm afraid I gravely underestimated you. I had not expected you to be as doggedly inquisitive. Frankly, I thought you'd do precisely what you were told. But then you're not the kind of man who takes kindly to being told what to do, are you?'

'When you get a cat to catch the mice in your kitchen, you can't expect it to ignore the rats in the cellar.'

'I suppose not,' he said.

We continued east, up-river, past the Tiergarten and Museum Island. By the time we turned south towards Treptower Park and Köpenick, I had asked him what grudge his son-in-law had had against him. To my surprise he showed no reluctance to answer my question; nor did he affect the indignant, rose-tinted viewpoint that had characterized all his previous remarks concerning members of his family, living and dead.

'As well-acquainted with my personal affairs as you are, Herr Günther, you probably don't need to be reminded that Ilse is my second wife. I married my first wife, Lisa, in 1910, and the following year she became pregnant. Unfortunately things went badly and our child was still-born. Not only that, but there was no possibility of her having another child. In the same hospital was an unmarried girl who had given birth to a healthy child at about the same time. She had no way of looking after it, so my wife and I persuaded her to let us adopt her daughter. That was Grete. We never told her she was adopted while my wife was alive. But after she died, Grete discovered the truth, and set about trying to trace her real mother.

'By this time of course Grete was married to Paul, and was devoted to him. For his part, Paul was never worthy of her. I suspect he was rather more keen on my family name and money than he was on my daughter. But to everyone else they must have seemed like a perfectly happy couple.

'Well, all that changed overnight when Grete finally tracked down her real mother. The woman was a gypsy from Vienna, working in a Bierkeller on Potsdamer Platz. If it was a shock to Grete it was the end of the world to that little shit Paul. Something called racial impurity, whatever that amounts to, gypsies running the Jews a close second for unpopularity. Paul blamed me for not having informed Grete earlier. But when I first saw her I didn't see a gypsy child, but a beautiful healthy baby, and a young mother who was as keen as Lisa and I that we should adopt her and give her the best in life. Not that it would have mattered if she'd been a rabbi's daughter. We'd still have taken her. Well, you remember what it was like then, Herr Günther. People didn't make distinctions like they do these days. We were all just Germans. Of course, Paul didn't see it that way. All he could think of was the threat Grete now posed to his career in the SS and the Party.' He laughed bitterly.

We came to Grünau, home of the Berlin Regatta Club. On a large lake on the other side of some trees, a 2,000-metre Olympic rowing course had been marked out. Above the noise of the slipper's engine could be heard the sound of a brass band, and a public-address system describing the afternoon's events.

'There was no reasoning with him. Naturally, I lost my temper with him, and called him and his beloved Führer all sorts of names. After that we were enemies. There was nothing I could do for Grete. I watched his hate breaking her heart. I urged her to leave him, but she wouldn't. She refused to believe that he wouldn't learn to love her again. And so she stayed with him.'

'But meanwhile he set out to destroy you, his own father-in-law.'

'That's right,' said Six. 'While all the time he sat there in the comfortable home that my money had provided for them. If Grete did kill him as you say, then he certainly had it coming. If she hadn't done it I might have been tempted to have arranged it myself.'

'How was he going to finish you?' I asked. 'What evidence was there that was so compromising to you?'

The slipper reached the junction of Langer See and Seddinsee. Six throttled back and steered the boat south in the direction of the hilly peninsula that was Schmöckwitz.

'Clearly your curiosity knows no bounds, Herr Günther. But I'm sorry to disappoint you. I welcome your assistance, but I see no reason why I should answer all your questions.'

I shrugged. 'I don't suppose it matters much now,' I said.

The Grosse Zug was an inn on one of the two islands between the marshes of Köpenick and Schmöckwitz. Less than a couple of hundred metres in length, and no more than fifty wide, the island was tightly packed with tall pine trees. Close to the water's edge there were more signs saying 'Private' and 'Keep Out' than on a fan-dancer's dressing-room door.

'What is this place?'

'This is the summer headquarters of the German Strength ring. They use it for their more secret meetings. You can see why, of course. It's so out of the way.' He started to drive the boat round the island, looking for somewhere to moor. On the opposite side we found a small jetty, to which were tied several boats. Up a short grassy slope was a cluster of neatly painted boathouses, and beyond it the Grosse Zug Inn itself. I collected up a length of rope and jumped off the slipper on to the jetty. Six cut the engine.

'We'd best be careful how we approach the place,' he said, joining me on the jetty, and tying up the front of the boat. 'Some of these fellows are inclined to shoot first and ask questions later.'

'I know just how they feel,' I said.

We walked off the jetty and up the slope towards the boathouses. Excepting the other boats, there was nothing to indicate that there was anyone else on the islet. But closer to the boathouses, two armed men emerged from behind an upturned boat.

Their faces wore expressions that were cool enough to cope with me telling them that I was carrying bubonic plague. It's the sort of confidence that only a sawn-off can give you.

'That's far enough,' said the taller of the two. 'This is private property. Who are you and what are doing here?' He didn't lift the gun from his forearm where it was cradled like a sleeping baby, but then he did not have to lift it very far to get off a shot. Six made the explanations.

'It's desperately important that I see Red.' He thumped his fist into the palm of his hand as he spoke. It made him seem rather melodramatic, I thought. 'My name is Hermann Six. I can assure you gentlemen he'll want to see me. But please hurry.'

They stood there shuffling uncertainly. 'The boss always tells us if he's expecting anyone. And he didn't say anything about you two.'

'Despite that, you can depend on it that there'll be hell to pay if he finds out you turned us away.'

Shotgun looked at his partner, who nodded and walked away towards the inn. He said: 'We'll wait here while we check it out.'

Wringing his hands nervously, Six called out after him: 'Please hurry. It's a matter of life or death.'

Shotgun grinned at that. I guessed he was used to matters of life and death where his boss was concerned. Six produced a cigarette and fed it nervously into his mouth. He snatched it out again without lighting it.

'Please,' he said to Shotgun. 'Are you holding a couple on the island, a man and a woman? The – the –'

'The Teichmüllers,' I said.

Shotgun's grin disappeared under a whole pantomine of dumb. 'I don't know nothing,' he said dully.

We kept looking anxiously at the inn. It was a two-storey affair, white-painted with neat, black shutters, a windowbox full of geraniums and a high mansard roof. As we watched, smoke started to come out of the chimney, and when the door finally opened

I half expected an old woman to come out carrying a tray of gingerbread. Shotgun's pitman beckoned us forward.

We moved Indian-file through the door, with Shotgun bringing up the rear. The two stumpy barrels gave me an itch in the back of my neck: if you have ever seen someone shot with a sawn-off at close range, you would know why. There was a small hallway with a couple of hatstands, only nobody had bothered to check his hat. Beyond that was a small room, where somebody was playing the piano like he had a couple of fingers missing. At the far end there was a round bar and some stools. Behind it were lots of sports trophies and I wondered who had won them and why. The Most Murders in One Year perhaps, or The Cleanest Knockout With an India Rubber – I had a nominee for that award myself if I could find him. But probably they had just bought them to make the place look more like what it was supposed to be – the headquarters of an ex-convicts' welfare association.

Shotgun's partner grunted. 'This way,' he said, and led us towards a door beside the bar.

Through the door the room was like an office. A brass lamp hung from one of the beams on the ceiling. There was a long walnut chaise-longue in the corner by the window, and next to it, a big bronze of a naked girl, the sort that looks as though the model must have had a bad accident with a circular saw. There was more art on the panelled walls, but of the sort that normally you only find in the pages of midwives' textbooks.

Red Dieter, his black shirt-sleeves rolled up, and his collar off, stood up from the green-leather sofa and flicked his cigarette into the fire. Glancing first at Six and then at me, he looked uncertain as to whether he ought to look welcoming or worried. He didn't get time to make a choice. Six stepped forwards, and caught him by the throat.

'For God's sake what have you done with her?' From a corner of the room another man came to my assistance, and each of us taking one of the old man's arms, we pulled him off.

'Hold up, hold up,' yelled Red. He straightened his jacket and tried to control his natural indignation. Then he glanced around his person, as if to check that his dignity was still intact.

Six continued to shout. 'My daughter, what have you done with my daughter?'

The gangster frowned and looked quizzically at me. 'What's he fucking talking about?'

'The two people your boys snatched from the beach house yesterday,' I said urgently. 'What have you done with them? Look, there's no time for an explanation now, but the girl is his daughter.'

He looked incredulous. 'You mean, she's not dead after all?' he said.

'Come on, man,' I said.

Red swore, his face darkened like dying gaslight, his lips quivering like he had just chewed on broken glass. A thin, blue vein stood off his square forehead like a piece of ivy on a brick wall. He pointed at Six.

'Keep him here,' he growled. Red shouldered his way through the men outside like an angry wrestler. 'If this is one of your tricks, Günther, I'll personally fillet your fucking nose.'

'I'm not that stupid. But as it happens, there is one thing that's puzzling me.'

At the front door Red stopped and glared at me. His face was the colour of blood, almost purple with rage. 'And what's that?'

'I had a girl working with me. Name of Inge Lorenz. She disappeared from the area of the beach house in Wannsee not long before your boys tapped me on the head.'

'So why ask me?'

'You've already kidnapped two people, so a third along the way might not be too much for your conscience to bear.'

Red almost spat in my face. 'What's a fucking conscience, then?' he said, and carried on through the door.

Outside the inn I hurried after him in the direction of one of the boathouses. A man came out, buttoning up his flies. Misinterpreting his boss's purposeful stride, he grinned.

'You come to give her one as well, boss?'

Red drew level with the man, looked blankly at him for a second, and then punched him hard in the stomach. 'Shut your stupid mouth,' he roared, and kicked his way through the boathouse door. I stepped over the man's gasping body and followed him inside.

I saw a long rack on which were laid several eight-oar boats, and tied to it was a man stripped to the waist. His head hung down, and there were numerous burns on his neck and shoulders. I guessed that it was Haupthändler, although as I came closer I could see that his face was so badly contused as to be unrecognizable. Two men stood idly by, paying no attention to their captive. They were both smoking cigarettes, and one of them wore a set of brass knuckles.

'Where's the fucking girl?' screamed Red. One of Haupthändler's torturers jabbed a thumb across his shoulder.

'Next door, with my brother.'

'Hey, boss,' said the other man. 'This coat still won't talk. Do you want us to work on him some more?'

'Leave the poor bastard alone,' he growled. 'He knows nothing.'

It was almost dark in the adjoining boathouse, and it took several seconds for our eyes to become accustomed to the gloom.

'Franz. Where the fuck are you?' We heard a soft groan, and the slap of flesh against flesh. Then we saw them: an enormous figure of a man, his trousers round his ankles, bent over the silent and naked body of Hermann Six's daughter, tied face down over an upturned boat.

'Get away from her, you big ugly bastard,' yelled Red.

The man, who was the size of a luggage locker, made no move to obey the order, not even when it was repeated at greater volume and at closer range. Eyes shut, his shoe-box of a head lying back on the parapet that was his shoulders, his enormous penis squeezing in and out of Grete Pfarr's anus almost convulsively, his knees bent like a man whose horse had escaped from underneath him, Franz stood his ground.

Red punched him hard on the side of the head. He might as well have been hitting a locomotive. The very next second he pulled out a gun and almost casually blew his man's brains out.

Franz dropped cross-legged to the ground, a collapsing chimney of a man, his head spurting a smoke-plume of burgundy, his still erect penis leaning to one side like the mainmast of a ship that has crashed onto the rocks.

Red pushed the body to one side with the toe of his shoe as I started to untie Grete. Several times he glanced awkwardly at the stripes that had been cut deep onto her buttocks and thighs with a short whip. Her skin was cold, and she smelt strongly of semen. There was no telling how many times she had been raped.

'Fuck, look at the state of her,' groaned Red, shaking his head. 'How can I let Six see her like this?'

'Let's hope she's alive,' I said, taking off my coat, and spreading it on the ground.

We laid her down, and I pressed my ear to her naked breast. There was a heartbeat, but I guessed that she was in deep shock.

'Is she going to be all right?' Red sounded naive, like a schoolboy asking about his pet rabbit. I looked up at him and saw that he was still holding the gun in his hand.

Summoned by the shot, several German Strength men were standing awkwardly at the back of the boathouse. I heard one of them say, 'He killed Franz'; and then another said, 'There was no call to do it,' and I knew we were going to have trouble. Red knew it too. He turned and faced them.

'The girl is Six's daughter. You all know Six. He's a rich and powerful man. I told Franz to leave her alone but he wouldn't listen. She couldn't have taken any more. He'd have killed her. She's only just alive now.'

'You didn't have to shoot Franz,' said a voice.

'Yeah,' said another. 'You could have slugged him.'

'What?' Red's tone was incredulous. 'His head was thicker than the oak on a nunnery door.'

'Not now it isn't.'

Red bent down beside me. With one eye on his men he murmured, 'You got a lighter?'

'Yes,' I said. 'Look, we don't stand a chance in here, nor does she. We've got to get to a boat.'

'What about Six?'

I buttoned the coat over Grete's naked body, and gathered her up in my arms. 'He can take his chances.'

Helfferich shook his head 'No, I'll go back for him. Wait for us on the jetty as long as you can. If they start shooting, then get the hell away. And in case I don't, I know nothing about your girl, fleabite.' We walked slowly towards the door, Red leading the way. His men stepped back sullenly to allow us through, and once outside we separated, and I walked back down the grassy slope to the jetty and to the boat.

I laid Six's daughter on the slipper's back seat. There was a rug in a locker and I took it out and put it over her still unconscious body. I wondered whether if she came round I might have another chance to ask her about Inge Lorenz. Would Haupthändler be any more cooperative? I was just thinking about going back to get him when from the direction of the inn I heard several pistol shots. I slipped the boat's line, started the engine and took the gun out of my pocket. With my other hand I held onto the jetty to stop the boat drifting. Seconds later I heard another volley of shots and what sounded like a riveter working along the stern of the boat. I rammed the throttle forwards and spun the wheel away from the jetty. Wincing with pain I glanced down at my hand, imagining that I had been hit, but instead I found an enormous splinter of wood from the jetty sticking out of the palm of my hand. Breaking off the largest part of it I turned and fired off the rest of my clip in the direction of the figures now appearing on the retreating jetty. To my surprise they threw themselves on their bellies. But behind me something heavier than a pistol had opened up. It was only a warning burst, but the big machine-gun cut through the trees and the wood of the jetty like metallic rain drops, sending up

splinters, chopping off branches and slicing through foliage. Looking to my front again, I had just enough time to pull the throttle
into reverse and steer away from the police-launch. Then I cut the
engine and instinctively raised my hands high above my head,
dropping my gun onto the floor of the boat as I did so.

It was then that I noticed the neat red caste-mark in the centre
of Grete's forehead, from which a hair's breadth trickle of blood
was now bisecting her lifeless features.

18

Listening to the systematic destruction of another human spirit has a predictably lowering effect on one's own fibre. I imagine that that was how it was intended to be. The Gestapo is nothing if not thoughtful. They let you eavesdrop on another's agony to soften you up on the inside; and only then do they get to work on the outside. There is nothing worse than a state of suspense about what is going to happen, whether it's waiting for the results of some tests at a hospital, or the headsman's axe. You just want to get it over with. In my own small way it was a technique I had used myself at the Alex when I'd let men, suspects, sweat themselves into a state where they were ready to tell you everything. Waiting for something lets your imagination step in to create your own private hell.

But I wondered what it was that they wanted from me. Did they want to know about Six? Did they hope that I knew where the Von Greis papers were? And what if they tortured me and I didn't know what they wanted me to tell them?

By the third or fourth day alone in my filthy cell, I was beginning to wonder if my own suffering was to be an end in itself. At other times I puzzled as to what had become of Six and Red Helfferich, who were arrested with me, and of Inge Lorenz.

Most of the time I just stared at the walls, which were a kind of palimpsest for those previous unfortunates who had been its occupants. Oddly enough there was little or no abuse for the Nazis. More common were recriminations between the Communists and the Social Democrats as to which of these two 'fallen women' was responsible for allowing Hitler to get elected in the first place: the Sozis blamed the Pukers, and the Pukers blamed the Sozis.

Sleep did not come easily. There was an evil-smelling pallet, which I avoided on my first night of incarceration, but as the days passed and the slop-bucket became more malodorous, I ceased to be so fastidious. It was only on the fifth day, when two SS guards came and hauled me out of my cell, that I realized just how badly I smelled: but it was nothing compared to their stink, which is of death.

They frog-marched me through a long urinous passage to a lift, and this took us up five floors to a quiet and well-carpeted corridor which, with its oak-panelled walls and gloomy portraits of the Führer, Himmler, Canaris, Hindenburg and Bismarck, had the air of an exclusive gentleman's club. We went through a double wooden door the height of a tram and into a large bright office where several stenographers were working. They paid my filthy person no attention at all. A young SS Hauptsturmführer came round an ornate sort of desk to look disinterestedly at me.

'Who's this?' With a click of his heels, one of the guards stood to attention and told the officer who I was.

'Wait there,' said the Hauptsturmführer and walked over to a polished mahogany door on the other side of the room, where he knocked and waited. Hearing a reply he poked his head round the door and said something. Then he turned and jerked his head at my guards who shoved me forwards.

It was a big, plush office with a high ceiling and some expensive leather furniture, and I saw that I wasn't going to get the routine Gestapo chat over the kind of script that would have to involve the twin prompts of blackjack and brass knuckles. Not yet anyway. They wouldn't risk spilling anything on the carpet. At the far end of the office was a French window, a set of bookshelves and a desk behind which, sitting in comfortable armchairs, were two SS officers. These were tall, sleek, well-groomed men with supercilious smiles, hair the colour of Tilsiter cheese and well-behaved Adam's apples. The taller of the pair spoke first, to order the guards and their adjutant out of the room.

'Herr Günther. Please sit down.' He pointed to a chair in front of the desk. I looked behind as the door shut, and then shuffled forwards, my hands in my pockets. Since they had taken away my shoelaces and braces at my arrest, it was the only way I had of keeping my trousers up.

I hadn't met senior SS officers before and so I was not certain as to the rank of the two who faced me; but I guessed that one was probably a colonel, and the other, the one who continued speaking, was possibly a general. Neither one of them seemed to be any older than about thirty-five.

'Smoke?' said the general. He held out a box and then tossed me some matches. I lit my cigarette and smoked it gratefully. 'Please help yourself if you want another.'

'Thanks.'

'Perhaps you would also like a drink?'

'I wouldn't say no to some champagne.' They both smiled simultaneously. The second officer, the colonel, produced a bottle of schnaps and poured a glassful.

'I'm afraid we don't run to anything so grand round here,' he said.

'Whatever you've got, then.' The colonel stood up and brought me the drink. I didn't waste any time with it. I jerked it back, cleaned my teeth and swallowed with every muscle in my neck and throat. I felt the schnaps flush right the way down to my corns.

'You'd better give him another,' said the general. 'He looks as though his nerves are a bit shaky.' I held out my glass for the refill.

'My nerves are just fine,' I said, nursing my glass. 'I just like to drink.'

'Part of the image, eh?'

'And what image would that be?'

'Why, the private detective of course. The shoddy little man in the barely furnished office, who drinks like a suicide who's lost his nerve, and who comes to the assistance of the beautiful but mysterious woman in black.'

'Someone in the SS perhaps,' I suggested.

He smiled. 'You might not believe it,' he said, 'but I have a passion for detective stories. It must be interesting.' His face was of an unusual construction. Its central feature was its protruding, hawk-like nose, which had the effect of making the chin seem weak; above the thin nose were glassy blue eyes set rather too close together, and slightly slanting, which lent him an apparently world-weary, cynical air.

'I'm sure that fairy-stories are a lot more interesting.'

'But not in your case, surely. In particular, the case you have been working on for the Germania Life Assurance Company.'

'For which,' the colonel chipped in, 'we may now substitute the name of Hermann Six.' The same type as his superior, he was better-looking if apparently less intelligent. The general glanced over a file that was open on the desk in front of him, if only to indicate that they knew everything there was to know about me and my business.

'Precisely so,' he murmured. After a short while he looked up at me and said: 'Why ever did you leave Kripo?'

'Coal,' I said.

He stared blankly at me. 'Coal?'

'Yeah, you know, mouse, gravel . . . money. Speaking of which, I had 40,000 marks in my pockets when I checked into this hotel. I'd like to know what's happened to it. And to a girl who was working with me. Name of Inge Lorenz. She's disappeared.'

The general looked at his junior officer, who shook his head. 'I'm afraid we know nothing about any girl, Herr Günther,' said the colonel. 'People are always disappearing in Berlin. You of all people should know that. As to your money, however, that is quite safe with us for the moment.'

'Thanks, and I don't mean to sound ungrateful, but I'd sooner leave it in a sock underneath my mattress.'

The general put his long, thin, violinist's hands together, as if he was about to lead us in prayer, and pressed their fingertips against his lips meditatively. 'Tell me, did you ever consider joining the Gestapo?' he said.

I figured it was my turn to try a little smile.

'You know, this wasn't a bad suit before I was obliged to sleep in it for a week. I may smell a bit, but not that badly.'

He gave an amused sort of sniff. 'The ability to talk as toughly as your fictional counterpart is one thing, Herr Günther,' he said. 'Being it is quite another. Your remarks demonstrate either an astonishing lack of appreciation as to the gravity of your situation, or real courage.' He raised his thin, gold leaf eyebrows and started to toy with the German Horseman's Badge on his left breast-pocket. 'By nature I am a cynical man. I think that all policemen are, don't you? So normally I would be inclined to favour the first assessment of your bravado. However, in this particular case it suits me to believe in the strength of your character. Please do not disappoint me by saying something really stupid.' He paused for a moment. 'I'm sending you to a KZ.'

My flesh turned as cold as a butcher's shop-window. I finished what was left of my schnaps, and then heard myself say: 'Listen, if it's about that lousy milk bill . . .'

They both started grinning a lot, enjoying my obvious discomfort.

'Dachau,' said the colonel. I stubbed out my cigarette and lit another. They saw my hand shake as I held the match up.

'Don't worry,' said the general. 'You'll be working for me.' He came round the desk and sat on its edge in front of me.

'And who are you?'

'I am Obergruppenführer Heydrich.' He waved his arm at the colonel and folded his arms. 'And this is Standartenführer Sohst of Alarm Command.'

'Pleased to meet you, I'm sure.' I wasn't. Alarm Command were the special Gestapo killers that Marlene Sahm had talked about.

'I've had my eye on you for some time,' he said. 'And after that unfortunate little incident at the beach house in Wannsee I have had you under constant observation, in the hope that you might lead us to certain papers. I'm sure you know the ones I mean. Instead you gave us the next best thing – the man who planned their theft. Over the past few days, while you've been our guest, we've been checking your story. It was the autobahn worker, Bock, who told us where to look for this Kurt Mutschmann fellow – the safecracker who now has the papers.'

'Bock?' I shook my head. 'I don't believe it. He wasn't the sort to turn informer about a friend.'

'It's quite true, I can assure you. Oh, I don't mean he told us exactly where to find him, but he put us on the right track, before he died.'

'You tortured him?'

'Yes. He told us that Mutschmann had once told him that if he were ever really wanted so that he was desperate, then he should probably think of hiding in a prison, or a KZ. Well, of course, with a gang of criminals looking for him, not to mention ourselves, then desperate is exactly what he must have been.'

'It's an old trick,' explained Sohst. 'You avoid arrest for one thing by having yourself arrested for another.'

'We believe that Mutschmann was arrested and sent to Dachau three nights after the death of Paul Pfarr,' said Heydrich. With a thin, smug smile he added: 'Indeed, he was almost begging to be arrested. It seems that he was caught red-handed, painting KPD slogans on the wall of a Kripo Stelle in Neukölln.'

'A KZ isn't so bad if you're a Kozi,' chuckled Sohst. 'In comparison with the Jews and the queers. He'll probably be out in a couple of years.'

I shook my head. 'I don't understand,' I told them. 'Why don't you simply have the commandant at Dachau question Mutschmann? What the hell do you need me for?'

Heydrich folded his arms and swung his jackbooted leg so that his toe was almost kicking my kneecap. 'Involving the commandant at Dachau would also mean having to inform Himmler, which I don't want to do. You see, the Reichsführer is an idealist. He would undoubtedly see it as his duty to use these papers to punish those he perceived to be guilty of crimes against the Reich.'

I recalled Himmler's letter to Paul Pfarr which Marlene Sahm had shown me at the Olympic Stadium and nodded.

'I, on the other hand, am a pragmatist, and would prefer to use the papers in a rather more tactical way, as and where I require.'

'In other words, you're not above a bit of blackmail yourself. Am I right?'

Heydrich smiled thinly. 'You see through me so easily, Herr Günther. But you must understand that this is to be an undercover operation. Strictly a matter for Security. On no account should you mention this conversation to anyone.'

'But there must be somebody among the SS at Dachau that you can trust?'

'Of course there is,' said Heydrich. 'But what do you expect him to do, march up to Mutschmann and ask him where he has hidden the papers? Come now, Herr Günther, be sensible.'

'So you want me to find Mutschmann, and get to know him.'

'Precisely so. Build his trust. Find out where he's hidden the papers. And having done so, you will identify yourself to my man.'

'But how will I recognize Mutschmann?'

'The only photograph is the one on his prison record,' said Sohst, handing me a picture. I looked at it carefully. 'It's three years old, and his head will have been shaved of course, so it doesn't help you much. Not only that, but he's likely to be a great deal thinner. A KZ does tend to change a man. There is, however, one thing that should help you to identify him: he has a noticeable ganglion on his right wrist, which he could hardly obliterate.'

I handed back the photograph. 'It's not much to go on,' I said. 'Suppose I refuse?'

'You won't,' said Heydrich brightly. 'You see, either way you're going to Dachau. The difference is that working for me, you'll be sure to get out again. Not to mention getting your money back.'

'I don't seem to have much choice.'

Heydrich grinned. 'That's precisely the point,' he said. 'You don't. If you had a choice, you'd refuse. Anyone would. Which is why I can't send one of my own men. That and the need for secrecy. No, Herr Günther, as an ex-policeman, I'm afraid you fit the bill perfectly. You have everything to gain, or to lose. It's really up to you.'

'I've taken better cases,' I said.

'You must forget who you are now,' said Sohst quickly. 'We have arranged for you to have a new identity. You are now Willy Krause, and you are a black-marketeer. Here are your new papers.' He handed me a new identity card. They'd used my old police photograph.

'There is one more thing,' said Heydrich. 'I regret that verisimilitude requires a certain amount of further attention to your appearance, consistent with your having been arrested and interrogated. It's rare for a man to arrive at Columbia Haus without the odd bruise. My men downstairs will take care of you in that respect. For your own protection, of course.'

'Very thoughtful of you,' I said.

'You'll be held at Columbia for a week, and then transferred to Dachau.' Heydrich stood up. 'May I wish you good luck.' I took hold of my trouser band and got to my feet.

'Remember, this is a Gestapo operation. You must not discuss it with anyone.' Heydrich turned and pressed a button to summon the guards.

'Just tell me this,' I said. 'What's happened to Six and Helfferich, and the rest of them?'

'I see no harm in telling you,' he said. 'Well then, Herr Six is under house-arrest. He is not charged with anything, as yet. He is still too shocked at the resurrection and subsequent death of his daughter to answer any questions. Such a tragic case. Unfortunately, Herr Haupthändler died in hospital the day before yesterday, having never recovered consciousness. As to the criminal known as Red Dieter Helfferich, he was beheaded at Lake Ploetzen at six o'clock this morning, and his entire gang sent to the KZ at Sachsenhausen.' He smiled sadly at me. 'I doubt that any harm will come to Herr Six. He's much too important a man to suffer any lasting damage because of what has happened. So you can see, of all the other leading players in this unfortunate affair, you are the only one who is left alive. It merely remains to be seen if you can conclude this case successfully, not only as a matter of professional pride, but also your personal survival.'

The two guards marched me back to the elevator, and then to my cell, but only to beat me up. I put up a struggle but, weak from lack of decent food and proper sleep, I was unable to put up more than a token resistance. I might have managed one of them alone, but together they were more than a match for me. After that I was taken to the SS guardroom, which was about the size of a meeting hall. Near the double-thick door sat a group of SS, playing cards and drinking beer, their pistols and blackjacks heaped on another table like so many toys confiscated by a strict schoolmaster. Facing the far wall, and standing at attention in a line, were about twenty prisoners whom I was ordered to join. A young SS Sturmmann swaggered up and down its length, shouting at some prisoners and booting many in the back or on the arse. When an old man collapsed onto the stone floor, the Sturmmann booted him into unconsciousness. And all the time new prisoners were joining the line. After an hour there must have been at least a hundred of us.

They marched us through a long corridor to a cobbled courtyard where we were loaded into Green Minnas. No SS men came with us inside the vans, but nobody said much. Each sat quietly, alone with his own thoughts of home and loved ones whom he might never see again.

When we got to Columbia Haus we climbed out of the vans. The sound of an aeroplane could be heard taking off from nearby Tempelhof Flying Field, and as it passed over the Trojan-grey walls of the old military prison, to a man we all glanced wistfully up into the sky, each of us wishing that he were among the plane's passengers.

'Move, you ugly bastards,' yelled a guard, and with many kicks, shoves and punches, we were herded up to the first floor and paraded in five columns in front of a heavy wooden door. A menagerie of warders paid us close and sadistic attention.

'See that fucking door?' yelled the Rottenführer, his face twisted to one side with malice, like a feeding shark. 'In there we finish you as men for the rest of your days. We put your balls in a vice, see? Stops you getting homesick. After all, how can you want to go home to your wives and girlfriends if you've nothing left to go home with?' He roared with laughter, and so did the menagerie, some of whom dragged the first man kicking and screaming into the room, and closed the door behind them.

I felt the other prisoners shake with fear; but I guessed that this was the corporal's idea of a joke, and when eventually it came to my own turn, I made a deliberate show of calm as they took me to the door. Once inside they took my name and address, studied my file for several minutes, and then, having been abused for my supposed black-marketeering, I was beaten up again.

Once in the main body of the prison I was taken, painfully, to my cell, and on the way there I was surprised to hear a large choir of men singing *If You Still Have a Mother*. It was only later on that I discovered the reason for the choir's existence: its performances were made at the behest of the SS to drown out the screams from the punishment cellar where prisoners were beaten on the bare buttocks with wet sjamboks.

As an ex-bull I've seen the inside of quite a few prisons in my time: Tegel, Sonnenburg, Lake Plœtzen, Brandenburg, Zellenge-fängnis, Brauweiler; every one of them is a hard place, with tough discipline; but none of them came close to the brutality and dehu-manizing squalor that was Columbia Haus, and it wasn't long before I was wondering if Dachau could be any worse.

There were approximately a thousand prisoners in Columbia. For some, like me, it was a short-stay transit prison, on the way to a KZ; for others, it was a long-stay transit camp on the way to a KZ. Quite a few were only ever to get out in a pine box.

As a newcomer on a short stay I had a cell to myself. But since it was cold at night and there were no blankets, I would have wel-comed a little human warmth around me. Breakfast was coarse rye wholemeal bread and ersatz coffee. Dinner was bread and potato gruel. The latrine was a ditch with a plank laid across it, and you were obliged to shit in the company of nine other prisoners at any one time. Once, a guard sawed through the plank and some of the prisoners ended up in the cesspit. At Columbia Haus they appreciated a sense of humour.

I had been there for six days when one night, at around midnight, I was ordered to join a vanload of prisoners for transport to Putlitzstrasse Railway Station, and from there to Dachau.

Dachau is situated some fifteen kilometres north-west of Munich. Someone on the train told me that it was the Reich's first KZ. This seemed to me to be entirely appropriate, given Munich's reputation as the birthplace of National Socialism. Built around the remains of an old explosives factory, it stands anomalously near some farmland in pleasant Bavarian countryside. Actually, the countryside is all there is that's pleasant about Bavaria. The people certainly aren't. I felt sure that Dachau wasn't about to disappoint me in this respect, or in any other. At Columbia Haus they said that Dachau was the model for all later camps: that there was even a special school there to train SS men to be more brutal. They didn't lie.

We were helped out of the wagons with the usual boots and rifle-butts, and marched east to the camp entrance. This was enclosed by a large guardhouse underneath which was a gate with the slogan 'Work Makes You Free' in the middle of the iron grille-work. The legend was the subject of some contemptuous mirth among the other prisoners, but nobody dared say anything for fear of getting a kicking.

I could think of lots of things that made you free, but work wasn't one of them: after five minutes in Dachau, death seemed a better bet.

They marched us to an open square which was a kind of parade ground, flanked to the south by a long building with a high-pitched roof. To the north, and running between seemingly endless rows of prison huts, was a wide, straight road lined with tall poplar trees. My heart sank as I began to appreciate the full magnitude of the task that lay before me. Dachau was huge. It might take months even to find Mutschmann, let alone befriend him convincingly enough to learn where he had hidden the papers. I was beginning to doubt whether the whole exercise simply wasn't the grossest piece of sadism on Heydrich's part.

The KZ commander came out of the long hut to welcome us. Like everybody in Bavaria, he had a lot to learn about hospitality. Mostly he had punishments on offer. He said that there were more than enough good trees around to hang every one of us. He finished by promising us hell, and I didn't doubt that he would be as good as his word. But at least there was fresh air. That's one of the two things you can say for Bavaria: the other has something to do with the size of their women's breasts.

They had the quaintest little tailor's shop at Dachau. And a barber's shop. I found a nice off-the-peg in stripes, a pair of clogs, and then had a haircut. I'd have asked for some oil on it but that would have meant pouring it on the floor. Things started to look up when I got three blankets, which was an improvement on Columbia, and was assigned to an Aryan hut. This was quarters for 150 men. Jewish huts contained three times that number.

It was true what they said: there's always somebody else who is worse off than you. That is, unless you were unfortunate enough to be Jewish. The Jewish population in Dachau was never large, but in all respects Jews were the worst off. Except maybe the questionable means of attaining freedom. In an Aryan hut the death rate was one per night; in a Jewish hut it was nearer seven or eight.

Dachau was no place to be a Jew.

Generally the prisoners reflected the complete spectrum of opposition to the Nazis, not to mention those against whom the Nazis were themselves implacably hostile. There were Sozis and Kozis, trade unionists, judges, lawyers, doctors, schoolteachers, army officers. Republican soldiers from the Spanish Civil War, Jehovah's Witnesses, Freemasons, Catholic priests, gypsies, Jews, spiritualists, homosexuals, vagrants, thieves and murderers. With

the exception of some Russians, and a few former members of the
Austrian cabinet, everyone in Dachau was German. I met a convict
who was a Jew. He was also a homosexual. And if that weren't
enough, he was also a Communist. That made three triangles. His
luck hadn't so much run out as jumped on a fucking motorcycle.

Twice a day we had to assemble at the Appellplatz for Parade, and
after roll-call came the Hindenburg Alms – floggings. They fastened the man or woman to a block and gave you an average of
twenty-five on the bare arse. I saw several shit themselves during a
beating. The first time I was ashamed for them; but after that
someone told me it was the best way you had of spoiling the concentration of the man wielding the whip.

Parade was my best chance for looking at all the other prisoners.
I kept a mental log of those men I had eliminated, and within a
month I had succeeded in ruling out over 300 men.

I never forget a face. That's one of the things that makes you a
good bull, and one of the things that had prompted me to join the
force in the first place. Only this time my life depended on it. But
always there were newcomers to upset my methodology. I felt like
Hercules trying to clean the shit out of the Aegean stables.

How do you describe the indescribable? How can you talk about
something that made you mute with horror? There were many
more articulate than me who were simply unable to find the words.
It is a silence born of shame, for even the guiltless are guilty. Shorn
of all human rights, man reverts back to the animal. The starving
steal from the starving, and personal survival is the only consideration, which overrides, even censors, the experience. Work sufficient
to destroy the human spirit was the aim of Dachau, with death the
unlooked-for by-product. Survival was through the vicarious suffering of others: you were safe for a while when it was another man
who was being beaten or lynched; for a few days you might eat the
ration of the man in the next cot after he had expired in his sleep.

★

To stay alive it is first necessary to die a little.

Soon after my arrival at Dachau I was put in charge of a Jewish work-company building a workshop on the north-western corner of the compound. This involved filling handcarts with rocks weighing anything up to thirty kilos and pushing them up the hill out of the quarry and to the building site, a distance of several hundred metres. Not all the SS in Dachau were bastards: some of them were comparatively moderate and managed to make money by running small businesses on the side, using the cheap labour and pool of skills that the KZ provided, so it was in their interest not to work the prisoners to death. But the SS supervising the building site were *real* bastards. Mostly Bavarian peasants, formerly unemployed, theirs was a less refined type of sadism than that which had been practised by their urban counterparts at Columbia. But it was just as effective. Mine was an easy job: as company leader I was not required myself to shift the blocks of stone; but for the Jews working in my kommando it was backbreaking work all the way. The SS were always setting deliberately tight schedules for the completion of a foundation, or a wall, and failure to meet the schedule meant no food or water. Those who collapsed through exhaustion were shot where they fell.

At first I took a hand myself, and the guards found this hugely amusing; and it was not as if the work grew any lighter as a result of my participation. One of them said to me:

'What, are you a Jew-lover or something? I don't get it. You don't have to help them, so why do you bother?'

For a moment I had no answer. Then I said: 'You don't get it. That's why I have to bother.'

He looked rather puzzled, and then frowned. For a moment I thought he was going to take offence, but instead he just laughed and said: 'Well, it's your fucking funeral.'

After a while I realized that he was right. The heavy work was killing me, just like it was killing the Jews in my kommando. And so I stopped. Feeling ashamed, I helped a convict who had collapsed, hiding him under a couple of empty handcarts until he had sufficiently recovered to continue working. And I kept on doing it, although I knew I was risking a flogging. There were informers everywhere in Dachau. The other convicts warned me about them, which seemed ironic since I was half way to being one myself.

I wasn't caught in the act of hiding a Jew who had collapsed, but they started questioning me about it, so I had to assume I'd been fingered, just like I'd been warned. I was sentenced to twenty-five strokes.

I didn't dread the pain so much as I dreaded being sent to the camp hospital after my punishment. Since the majority of its patients were suffering from dysentery and typhoid, it was a place to avoid at all costs. Even the SS never went there. It would be easy, I thought, to catch something and get sick. Then I might never find Mutschmann.

Parade seldom lasted longer than one hour, but on the morning of my punishment it was more like three.

They strapped me to the whipping frame and pulled down my trousers. I tried to shit myself, but the pain was so bad that I couldn't concentrate enough to do it. Not only that, but there was nothing to shit. When I'd collected my alms they untied me, and for a moment I stood free of the frame before I fainted.

For a long time I stared at the man's hand which dangled over the edge of the cot above me. It never moved, not even a twitch of fingers, and I wondered if he were dead. Feeling unaccountably impelled to get up and look at him I raised myself up off my stomach and yelled with pain. My cry summoned a man to the side of my cot.

'Jesus,' I gasped, feeling the sweat start out on my forehead. 'It hurts worse now than it did out there.'

'That's the medicine, I'm afraid.' The man was about forty, rabbit-toothed, and with hair that he'd probably borrowed from an old mattress. He was terribly emaciated, with the kind of body that looked as though it belonged properly in a jar of formaldehyde, and there was a yellow star sewn to his prison jacket.

'Medicine?' There was a loud note of incredulity in my voice as I spoke.

'Yes,' drawled the Jew. 'Sodium chloride.' And then more briskly: 'Common salt to you, my friend. I've covered your stripes with it.'

'Good God,' I said. 'I'm not a fucking omelette.'

'That may be so,' he said, 'but I am a fucking doctor. It stings like a condom full of nettles, I know, but it's about the only thing I can prescribe that will stop the weals going septic.' His voice was round and fruity, like a funny actor's.

'You're lucky. You I can fix. I wish I could say the same for the rest of these poor bastards. Unfortunately there's only so much that one can do with a dispensary that's been stolen from a cookhouse.'

I looked up at the bunk above me, and the wrist which dangled over the edge. Never had there been an occasion when I had looked upon human deformity with such pleasure. It was a right wrist with a ganglion. The doctor lifted it out of my sight, and stood on my cot to check on its owner. Then he climbed down again, and looked at my bare arse.

'You'll do,' he said.

I jerked my head upwards. 'What's wrong with him?'

'Why, has he been giving you trouble?'

'No, I just wondered.'

'Tell me, have you had jaundice?'

'Yes.'

'Good,' he said. 'Don't worry, you won't catch it. Just don't kiss him or try to fuck him. All the same, I'll see that he's moved onto another bunk, in case he pisses on you. Transmission is through excretory products.'

'Transmission?' I said. 'Of what?'

'Hepatitis. I'll get them to put you on the top bunk and him on the bottom. You can give him some water if he gets thirsty.'

'Sure,' I said. 'What's his name?'

The doctor sighed wearily. 'I really haven't the faintest idea.'

Later on, when, with a considerable degree of discomfort, I had been moved by the medical orderlies on to the bunk above, and its previous occupant had been moved below, I looked down over the edge of my pallet at the man who represented my only way out of Dachau. It was not an encouraging sight. From my memory of the photograph in Heydrich's office, it would have been impossible to identify Mutschmann but for the ganglion, so yellow was his pallor and so wasted his body. He lay shivering under his blanket, delirious with fever, occasionally groaning with pain as cramp racked his insides. I watched him for a while and to my relief he recovered consciousness, but only long enough to try, unsuccessfully, to vomit. Then he was away again. It was clear to me that Mutschmann was dying.

Apart from the doctor, whose name was Mendelssohn, and three or four medical orderlies, who were themselves suffering from a variety of ailments, there were about sixty men and women in the camp hospital. As hospitals went it was little more than a charnel-house. I learned that there were only two kinds of patient: the sick, who always died, and the injured, who sometimes also got sick.

That evening, before it grew dark, Mendelssohn came to inspect my stripes.

'In the morning I'll wash your back and put some more salt on,' he said. Then he glanced disinterestedly down below at Mutschmann.

'What about him?' I said. It was a stupid question, and only served to arouse the Jew's curiosity. His eyes narrowed as he looked at me.

'Since you ask, I've told him to keep off alcohol, spicy food and to get plenty of rest,' he said drily.

'I think I get the picture.'

'I'm not a callous man, my friend, but there is nothing I can do to help him. With a high-protein diet, vitamins, glucose and methionine, he might have had a chance.'

'How long has he got?'

'He still manages to recover consciousness from time to time?' I nodded. Mendelssohn sighed. 'Difficult to say. But once coma has set in, a matter of a day or so. I don't even have any morphine to give him. In this clinic death is the usual cure that is available to patients.'

'I'll bear it in mind.'

'Don't get sick, my friend. There's typhus here. The minute you find yourself developing a fever, take two spoonfuls of your own urine. It does seem to work.'

'If I can find a clean spoon, I'll do just that. Thanks for the tip.'

'Well, here's another, since you're in such a good mood. The only reason that the Camp Committee meets here is because they know the guards won't come unless they absolutely have to. Contrary to outward appearances, the SS are not stupid. Only a madman would stay here for any longer than he has to.

'As soon as you can get about without too much pain, my advice to you is to get yourself out of here.'

'What makes you stay? Hippocratic oath?'

Mendelssohn shrugged. 'Never heard of it,' he said.

I slept for a while. I had meant to stay awake and watch Mut-schmann in case he came round again. I suppose I was hoping for one of those touching little scenes that you see in the movies, when the dying man is moved to unburden his soul to the man crouching over his deathbed.

When I awoke it was dark, and above the sound of the other inmates of the hospital coughing, and snoring, I heard the unmis-takeable sound, coming from the cot underneath, of Mutschmann retching. I leaned over and saw him in the moonlight, leaning on one elbow, clutching his stomach.

'You all right?' I said.

'Sure,' he wheezed. 'Like a fucking Galapagos tortoise, I'm going to live for ever.' He groaned again, and painfully, through clenched teeth, said: 'It's these damned stomach cramps.'

'Would you like some water?'

'Water, yes. My tongue is as dry as –' He was overcome by

another fit of retching. I climbed down gingerly, and fetched the ladle from a bucket near the bed. Mutschmann, his teeth chattering like a telegraph button, drank the water noisily. When he'd finished he sighed and lay back.

'Thanks, friend,' he said.

'Don't mention it,' I said. 'You'd do the same for me.'

I heard him cough his way through what sounded like a chuckle. 'No I fucking wouldn't,' he rasped. 'I'd be afraid of catching something, whatever it is that I've got. I don't suppose you know, do you?'

I thought for a moment. Then I told him. 'You've got hepatitis.'

He was silent for a couple of minutes, and I felt ashamed. I ought to have spared him that agony. 'Thanks for being honest with me,' he said. 'What's up with you?'

'Hindenburg Alms.'

'What for?'

'Helped a Jew in my work kommando.'

'That was stupid,' he said. 'They're all dead anyway. Risk it for someone who's got half a chance, but not for a Jew. Their luck is long gone.'

'Well, yours didn't exactly win the lottery.'

He laughed. 'True enough,' he said. 'I never figured on going sick. I thought I was going to get through this fuck-hole. I had a good job in the cobbler's shop.'

'It's a tough break,' I admitted.

'I'm dying, aren't I?' he said.

'That's not what the doc says.'

'No need to give me the cold cabbage. I can see it in the lead. But thanks anyway. Jesus, I'd give anything for a nail.'

'Me too,' I said.

'Even a roll up would do.' He paused. Then he said: 'There's something I've got to tell you.'

I tried to conceal the urgency that was crowding my voice-box. 'Yes? What's that then?'

'Don't fuck any of the women in this camp. I'm pretty sure that's how I got sick.'

'No, I won't. Thanks for telling me.'

The next day I sold my food ration for some cigarettes, and waited for Mutschmann to come out of his delirium. It lasted most of the day. When eventually he regained consciousness he spoke to me as if our previous conversation had been only a few minutes earlier.

'How's it going? How are the stripes?'

'Painful,' I said, getting off my bunk.

'I'll bet. That bastard sergeant with the whip really lays it on like fuck.' He inclined his emaciated face towards me, and said: 'You know, it seems to me that I've seen you somewhere.'

'Well now, let's see,' I said. 'The Rot Weiss Tennis Club? The Herrenklub? The Excelsior, maybe?'

'You're putting me on.' I lit one of the cigarettes and put it between his lips.

'I'll bet it was at the Opera – I'm a big fan, you know. Or perhaps it was at Goering's wedding?' His thin yellow lips stretched into something like a smile. Then he breathed in the tobacco smoke as if it was pure oxygen.

'You are a fucking magician,' he said, savouring the cigarette. I took it from his lips for a second before putting it back again. 'No, it wasn't any of those places. It'll come to me.'

'Sure it will,' I said, earnestly hoping that it wouldn't. For a moment I thought of saying Tegel Prison, but rejected it. Sick or not, he might remember differently, and then I'd be finished with him.

'What are you? Sozi? Kozi?'

'Black-marketeer,' I said. 'How about you?'

The smile stretched so that it was almost a rictus. 'I'm hiding.'

'Here? From whom?'

'Everyone,' he said.

'Well, you sure picked one hell of a hiding place. What are you, crazy?'

'Nobody can find me here,' he said. 'Let me ask you something: where would you hide a raindrop?' I looked puzzled until he answered, 'Under a waterfall. In case you didn't know it, that's Chinese philosophy. I mean, you'd never find it, would you?'

'No, I suppose not. But you must have been desperate,' I said.

'Getting sick . . . was just unlucky . . . But for that I'd have been out . . . in a year or so . . . by which time . . . they'd have given up looking.'

'Who would?' I said. 'What are they after you for?'

His eyelids flickered, and the cigarette fell from his unconscious lips and onto the blanket. I drew it up to his chin and tapped out the cigarette in the hope that he might come round again for long enough to smoke the other half.

During the night, Mutschmann's breathing grew shallower, and in the morning Mendelssohn pronounced that he was on the edge of coma. There was nothing that I could do but lie on my stomach and look down and wait. I thought of Inge a lot, but mostly I thought about myself. At Dachau, the funeral arrangements were simple: they burned you in the crematorium and that was it. End of story. But as I watched the poisons work their dreadful effect on Kurt Mutschmann, destroying his liver and his spleen so that his whole body was filled with infection, mostly my thoughts were of my Fatherland and its own equally appalling sickness. It was only now, in Dachau, that I was able to judge just how much Germany's atrophy had become necrosis; and as with poor Mutschmann, there wasn't going to be any morphine for when the pain grew worse.

There were a few children in Dachau, born to women imprisoned there. Some of them had never known any other life than the camp. They played freely in the compound, tolerated by all the guards, and even liked by some, and they could go almost anywhere, with the exception of the hospital barrack. The penalty for disobedience was a severe beating.

Mendelssohn was hiding a child with a broken leg under one of the cots. The boy had fallen while playing in the prison quarry, and had been there for almost three days with his leg in a splint when the SS came for him. He was so scared he swallowed his tongue and choked to death.

When the dead boy's mother came to see him and had to be told the bad news, Mendelssohn was the very model of professional sympathy. But later on, when she had gone, I heard him weeping quietly to himself.

'Hey, up there.' I gave a start as I heard the voice below me. It wasn't that I'd been asleep; I just hadn't been watching Mutschmann as I should have been. Now I had no idea of the invaluable period of time for which he had been conscious. I climbed down carefully and knelt by his cot. It was still too painful to sit on my backside. He grinned terribly and gripped my arm.

'I remembered,' he said.

'Oh yes?' I said hopefully. 'And what did you remember?'

'Where I seen your face.' I tried to appear unconcerned, although my heart was thumping in my chest. If he thought that I was a bull then I could forget it. An ex-convict never befriends a bull. It could have been the two of us washed away on some desert island, and he would still have spat in my face.

'Oh?' I said nonchalantly. 'Where was that, then?' I put his half-smoked cigarette between his lips and lit it.

'You used to be the house-detective,' he croaked. 'At the Adlon. I once cased the place to do a job.' He chuckled hoarsely. 'Am I right?'

'You've got a good memory,' I said, lighting one myself. 'That was quite some time ago.'

His grip tightened. 'Don't worry,' he said. 'I won't tell anyone. Anyway, it's not like you were a bull, is it?'

'You said you were casing the place. What particular line of criminality were you in?'

'I was a nutcracker.'

'I can't say as I recall the hotel safe ever being robbed,' I said. 'At least, not as long as I was working there.'

'That's because I didn't take anything,' he said proudly. 'Oh, I opened it all right. But there was nothing worth taking. Seriously.'

'I've only got your word for that,' I said. 'There were always rich people at the hotel, and they always had valuables. It was very rare that there wasn't something in that safe.'

'It's true,' he said. 'Just my bad luck. There really was nothing that I could take that I could ever have got rid of. That's the point, you see. There's no point in taking something you can't shift.'

'All right, I believe you,' I said.

'I'm not boasting,' he said. 'I was the best. There wasn't anything I couldn't crack. Here, I bet you'd expect me to be rich, wouldn't you?'

I shrugged. 'Perhaps. I'd also expect you to be in prison, which you are.'

'It's because I am rich that I'm hiding here,' he said. 'I told you that, didn't I?'

'You mentioned something about that, yes.' I took my time before I added: 'And what have you got that makes you so rich and wanted? Money? Jewels?'

He croaked another short laugh. 'Better than that,' he said. 'Power.'

'In what shape or form?'

'Papers,' he said. 'Take my word for it, there's an awful lot of people who'd pay big money to get their hands on what I've got.'

'What's in these papers?'

His breathing was shallower than a *Der Junggeselle* cover-girl.

'I don't know exactly,' he said. 'Names, addresses, information. But you're a clever sort of fellow, you could work it.'

'You haven't got them here, have you?'

'Don't be stupid,' he wheezed. 'They're safe, on the outside.' I took the dead cigarette from his mouth and threw it onto the floor. Then I gave him the rest of mine.

'It'd be a shame . . . for it never to be used,' he said breathlessly. 'You've been good . . . to me. So I'm going to do you a favour . . . Make 'em sweat, won't you? This'll be worth . . . a lorry load . . . of gravel . . . to you . . . on the outside.' I bent forwards to hear him speak. 'Pick 'em up . . . by the nose.' His eyelids flickered. I took him by the shoulders and tried to shake him back to consciousness.

Back to life.

I knelt there by him for some time. In the small corner of me that still felt things, there was a terrible and terrifying sense of abandonment. Mutschmann had been younger than I was, and strong, too. It wasn't too difficult to imagine myself succumbing to illness. I had lost a lot of weight, I had bad ringworms and my teeth felt loose in their gums. Heydrich's man, SS Oberschutze Bürger, was in charge of the carpenter's shop, and I wondered what would happen to me if I went ahead and gave him the code-word that would get me out of Dachau. What would Heydrich do to me when he discovered that I didn't know where Von Greis's papers were? Send me back? Have me executed? And if I didn't blow the whistle, would it even occur to him to assume that I had been unsuccessful and that he should get me out? From my short meeting with Heydrich, and what little I had heard of him, it seemed unlikely. To have got so near and failed at the last was almost more than I could bear.

After a while I reached forwards and drew the blanket over Mutschmann's yellow face. A short stub of a pencil fell onto the floor, and I looked at it for several seconds before a thought crossed my mind and a glint of hope once more shone in my heart. I drew the blanket back from Mutschmann's body. The hands were tightly bunched into fists. One after the other I prised them open. In Mut-schmann's left hand was a piece of brown paper of the sort that the prisoners in the cobbler's shop used to wrap shoe repairs for the SS guards in. I was too afraid of there being nothing to open the paper immediately. As it was, the writing was almost illegible, and it took me almost an hour to decipher the note's contents. It said,

'Lost property office, Berlin Traffic Dept. Saarlandstr. You lost briefcase sometime July on Leipzigerstr. Made of plain brown hide, with brass lock, ink-stain on handle. Gold initials K.M. Contains postcard from America, Western novel, *Old Surehand*, Karl May and business papers. Thanks. K.M.'

It was perhaps the strangest ticket home that anyone ever had.

19

It seemed that there were uniforms everywhere. Even the newspaper-sellers were wearing SA caps and greatcoats. There was no parade, and certainly there was nothing Jewish on Unter den Linden that could be boycotted. Perhaps it was only now, after Dachau, that I fully realized the true strength of the grip that National Socialism had on Germany.

I was heading towards my office. Situated incongruously between the Greek Embassy and Schultze's Art Shop, and guarded by two storm-troopers, I passed the Ministry of the Interior from which Himmler had issued his memo to Paul Pfarr regarding corruption. A car drew up outside the front door, and from it emerged two officers and a uniformed girl whom I recognized as Marlene Sahm. I stopped and started to say hallo and then thought better of it. She passed me by without a glance. If she recognized me she did a good job disguising it. I turned and watched her as she followed the two men inside the building. I don't suppose I was standing there for more than a couple of minutes, but it was long enough for me to be challenged by a fat man with a low brimmed hat.

'Papers,' he said abruptly, not even bothering to show a Sipo pass or warrant disc.

'Says who?'

The man pushed his porky, poorly shaven face at me and hissed: 'Says me.'

'Listen,' I said, 'you're sadly mistaken if you think you are possessed of what is cutely known as a commanding personality. So cut the shit and let's see some ID.' A Sipo pass flashed in front of my nose.

'You boys are getting lazy,' I said, producing my papers. He snatched them away for examination.

'What are you doing hanging around here?'

'Hanging? Who's hanging?' I said. 'I stopped to admire the architecture.'

'Why were you looking at those officers who got out of the car?'

'I wasn't looking at the officers,' I said. 'I was looking at the girl. I love women in uniforms.'

'On your way,' he said, tossing my papers back at me.

The average German seems to be able to tolerate the most offensive behaviour from anyone wearing a uniform or carrying some sort of official insignia. In everything except that I consider myself to be a fairly typical German, because I have to admit that I am naturally disposed to be obstructive to authority. I suppose you would say that it's an odd attitude for an ex-policeman.

On Königstrasse the collectors for the Winter Relief were out in force, shaking their little red collecting-boxes under everyone's noses, although November was only a few days old. In the early days the Relief had been intended to help overcome the effects of unemployment and the depression, but now, and almost universally, it was regarded as nothing more than financial and psychological blackmail by the Party: the Relief raised funds but, just as importantly, it created an emotional climate in which people were trained to do without for the sake of the Fatherland. Each week the collection was the charge of a different organization, and this week it was the Railwaymen.

The only railwayman I ever liked was my former secretary Dagmar's father. I had no sooner bitten my lip and handed over 20 pfennigs to one of them, than farther up the road I was solicited by another. The small glass badge you got for contributing didn't so much protect you from further harassment as mark you out as a good prospect. Still, it wasn't that which made me curse the man, fat as only a railwayman can be, and push him out of my way, but the sight of Dagmar herself disappearing round the sacrificial column that stands outside the Town Hall.

Hearing my hurried footsteps she turned and saw me before

I reached her. We stood awkwardly in front of the urn-like monument with its huge white-lettered motto which read 'Sacrifice for the Winter Relief'.

'Bernie,' she said.

'Hallo,' I said. 'I was just thinking about you.' Feeling rather awkward, I touched her on the arm. 'I was sorry to hear about Johannes.' She gave me a brave smile, and drew her brown wool coat closer about her neck.

'You've lost a lot of weight, Bernie. Have you been ill?'

'It's a long story. Have you got time for a coffee?'

We went to the Alexanderquelle on Alexanderplatz where we ordered real mocha and real scones with real jam and real butter.

'They say that Goering's got a new process that makes butter from coal.'

'It doesn't look like he's eating any of it then.' I laughed politely. 'And you can't buy an onion anywhere in Berlin. Father reckons they're using them to make poison gas for the Japs to use against the Chinese.'

After a while I asked her if she was able to discuss Johannes. 'I'm afraid there's not really much to tell,' she said.

'How did it happen?'

'All I know is that he was killed in an air-raid on Madrid. One of his comrades came to tell me. From the Reich I received a one-line message which read: "Your husband died for Germany's honour." In a pig's eye, I thought.' She sipped her coffee. 'Then I had to go and see someone at the Air Ministry, and sign a promise that I wouldn't talk about what had happened, and that I wouldn't wear mourning. Can you imagine that, Bernie? I couldn't even wear black for my own husband. It was the only way I could get a pension.' She smiled bitterly, and added: ' "You are Nothing, Your Nation is Everything." Well, they certainly mean it.' She took out her handkerchief and blew her nose.

'Never underestimate the National Socialists when it comes to the pantheistic,' I said. 'Individuals are an irrelevance. These days your own mother takes your disappearance for granted. Nobody cares.'

Nobody except me, I thought. For several weeks after my release from Dachau, the disappearance of Inge Lorenz was my only case. But sometimes even Bernie Günther draws a blank.

Looking for someone in Germany in the late autumn of 1936 was like trying to find something in a great desk drawer that had crashed to the floor, the contents spilled and then replaced according to a new order so that things no longer came easily to hand, or even seemed to belong in there. Gradually my sense of urgency was worn away by the indifference of others. Inge's former colleagues on the newspaper shrugged and said that really, they hadn't known her all that well. Neighbours shook their heads and sug gested that one needed to be philosophical about such things. Otto, her admirer at the DAF, thought she'd probably turn up before very long. I couldn't blame any of them. To lose another hair from a head that's already lost so many seems merely inconvenient.

Sharing quiet, lonely evenings with a friendly bottle, I often tried to imagine what might have become of her: a car accident; some kind of amnesia perhaps; an emotional or mental breakdown; a crime she had committed which necessitated an immediate and permanent disappearance. But always I was led back to abduction and murder and the idea that whatever had happened had been related to the case I had been working on.

Even after two months had passed, when you might normally have expected the Gestapo to have admitted to something, Bruno Stahlecker, lately transferred out of the city to a little Kripo station of no account in Spreewald, failed to come up with any record of Inge having been executed or sent to a KZ. And no matter how many times I returned to Haupthändler's house in Wannsee, in the hope that I might find something that would provide me with a clue to what had happened, there never was anything.

Until Inge's lease expired I often went back to her apartment looking for some secret things she had not seen fit to share with me. Meanwhile, the memory of her grew more distant. Having no photograph, I forgot her face, and came to realize how little I had really known about her, beyond rudimentary pieces of information. There had always seemed to be so much time to find out all there was to know.

As the weeks turned into months, I knew my chances of finding Inge grew smaller as an almost arithmetically inverse proportion. And as the trail grew colder, so did hope. I felt – I knew – that I would never see her again.

Dagmar ordered some more coffee, and we talked about what each of us had been doing. But I said nothing of Inge, or of my time in Dachau. There are some things that can't be discussed over morning coffee.

'How's business?' she asked.

'I bought myself a new car, an Opel.'

'You must be doing all right then.'

'What about you?' I asked. 'How do you live?'

'I'm back home with my parents. I do a lot of typing at home,' she said. 'Students' theses, that sort of thing.' She managed a smile. 'Father worries about me doing it. You see, I like to type at night, and the sound of my typewriter has brought the Gestapo round three times in as many weeks. They're on the lookout for people writing opposition newspapers. Luckily the sort of stuff that I'm churning out is so worshipful of National Socialism that they're easy to get rid of. But Father worries about the neighbours. He says they'll start to believe that the Gestapo is after us for something.'

After a while I suggested that we go to see a film.

'Yes,' she said, 'but I don't think I could stand one of those patriotic films.'

Outside the café we bought a newspaper.

On the front page there was a photograph of the two Hermanns, Six and Goering, shaking hands: Goering was grinning broadly, and Six wasn't smiling at all: it looked like the Prime Minister was going to have his way regarding the supply of raw materials for the German steel industry after all. I turned up the entertainments section.

'How about *The Scarlet Empress* at the Tauentzienpalast?' I said. Dagmar said that she'd seen it twice.

'What about this one?' she said. '*The Greatest Passion*, with Ilse Rudel. That's her new picture, isn't it? You like her, don't you? Most men seem to.' I thought of the young actor, Walther Kolb, who Ilse Rudel had sent to do murder for her, and had himself been killed by me. The line-drawing on the newspaper advertisement showed her wearing a nun's veil. Even when I had discounted my personal knowledge of her, I thought the characterization questionable.

But nothing surprises me now. I've grown used to living in a world that is out of joint, as if it has been struck by an enormous earthquake so that the roads are no longer flat, nor the buildings straight.

'Yes,' I said, 'she's all right.'

We walked to the cinema. The red *Der Stürmer* showcases were back on the street corners and, if anything, Streicher's paper seemed more rabid than ever.

THE PALE CRIMINAL

To Jane

Much about your good people moves me to disgust, and it is not their evil I mean. How I wish they possessed a madness through which they could perish, like this pale criminal. Truly I wish their madness were called truth or loyalty or justice: but they possess their virtue in order to live long and in a miserable ease.

Nietzsche

PART ONE

You tend to notice the strawberry tart in Kranzler's Café a lot more when your diet forbids you to have any.

Well, lately I've begun to feel much the same way about women. Only I'm not on a diet, so much as simply finding myself ignored by the waitress. There are so many pretty ones about too. Women, I mean, although I could as easily fuck a waitress as any other kind of female. There was one woman a couple of years ago. I was in love with her, only she disappeared. Well, that happens to a lot of people in this city. But since then it's just been casual affairs. And now, to see me on Unter den Linden, head one way and then the other, you would think that I was watching a hypnotist's pendulum. I don't know, maybe it's the heat. This summer, Berlin's as hot as a baker's armpit. Or maybe it's just me, turning forty and going a bit coochie-coo near babies. Whatever the reason, my urge to procreate is nothing short of bestial, which of course women see in your eyes, and then leave you well alone.

Despite that, in the long hot summer of 1938, bestiality was callously enjoying something of an Aryan renaissance.

Friday, 26 August

'Just like a fucking cuckoo.'

'What is?'

Bruno Stahlecker looked up from his newspaper.

'Hitler, who else?'

My stomach sank as it sensed another of my partner's profound analogies to do with the Nazis. 'Yes, of course,' I said firmly, hoping that my show of total comprehension would deter him from a more detailed explanation. But it was not to be.

'No sooner has he got rid of the Austrian fledgling from the European nest than the Czechoslovakian one starts to look precarious.' He smacked the newspaper with the back of his hand. 'Have you seen this, Bernie? German troop movements on the border of the Sudetenland.'

'Yes, I guessed that's what you were talking about.' I picked up the morning mail and, sitting down, started to sort through it. There were several cheques, which helped to take the edge off my irritation with Bruno. It was hard to believe, but clearly he'd already had a drink. Normally a couple of stops away from being monosyllabic (which I prefer being a shade taciturn myself) booze always made Bruno chattier than an Italian waiter.

'The odd thing is that the parents don't notice. The cuckoo keeps throwing out the other chicks, and the foster parents keep on feeding it.'

'Maybe they hope that he'll shut up and go away,' I said pointedly, but Bruno's fur was too thick for him to notice. I glanced over the contents of one of the letters and then read it again, more slowly.

'They just don't want to notice. What's in the post?'

'Hmm? Oh, some cheques.'

'Bless the day that brings a cheque. Anything else?'

'A letter. The anonymous kind. Someone wants me to meet him in the Reichstag at midnight.'

'Does he say why?'

'Claims to have information about an old case of mine. A missing person that stayed missing.'

'Sure, I remember them like I remember dogs with tails. Very unusual. Are you going?'

I shrugged. 'Lately I've been sleeping badly, so why not?'

'You mean apart from the fact that it's a burnt-out ruin, and it isn't safe to go inside? Well, for one, it could be a trap. Someone might be trying to kill you.'

'Maybe you sent it, then.'

He laughed uncomfortably. 'Perhaps I should come with you. I could stay out of sight, but within earshot.'

'Or gunshot?' I shook my head. 'If you want to kill a man you don't ask him to the sort of place where naturally he'll be on his guard.' I tugged open the drawer of my desk.

To look at there wasn't much difference between the Mauser and the Walther, but it was the Mauser that I picked up. The pitch of the grip, the general fit of the pistol made it altogether more substantial than the slightly smaller Walther, and it lacked for nothing in stopping-power. Like a fat cheque, it was a gun that always endowed me with a feeling of quiet confidence when I slipped it into my coat pocket. I waved the gun in Bruno's direction.

'And whoever sent me the party invitation will know I'm carrying a lighter.'

'Supposing there's more than one of them?'

'Shit, Bruno, there's no need to paint the devil on the wall. I can see the risks, but that's the business we're in. Newspapermen get bulletins, soldiers get dispatches and detectives get anonymous letters. If I'd wanted sealing-wax on my mail I'd have become a damned lawyer.'

Bruno nodded, tugged a little at his eyepatch and then transferred his nerves to his pipe — the symbol of our partnership's failure.
I hate the paraphernalia of pipe-smoking: the tobacco-pouch, the
cleaner, the pocket-knife and the special lighter. Pipe-smokers are
the grandmasters of fiddling and fidgeting, and as great a blight on
our world as a missionary landing on Tahiti with a boxful of
brassières. It wasn't Bruno's fault, for, in spite of his drinking and
his irritating little habits, he was still the good detective I'd rescued
from the obscurity of an out-of-the-way posting to a Kripo station in Spreewald. No, it was me that was at fault: I had discovered
myself to be as temperamentally unsuited to partnership as I would
have been to the presidency of the Deutsche Bank.

But looking at him I started to feel guilty.

'Remember what we used to say in the war? If it's got your
name and address on it, you can be sure it'll be delivered.'

'I remember,' he said, lighting his pipe and returning to his
Völkischer Beobachter. I watched him reading it with bemusement.

'You could as well wait for the town-crier as get any real news
out of that.'

'True. But I like to read a paper in the morning, even if it is
a crock of shit. I've got into the habit.' We were both silent for a
moment or two. 'There's another one of those advertisements in
here: "Rolf Vogelmann, Private Investigator, Missing Persons a
speciality".'

'Never heard of him.'

'Sure you have. There was another ad in last Friday's classified.
I read it out to you. Don't you remember?' He took his pipe out of
his mouth and pointed the stem at me. 'You know, maybe we
should advertise, Bernie.'

'Why? We've got all the business we can handle, and more.
Things have never been better, so who needs the extra expense?
Anyway, it's reputation that counts in this line of business, not column inches in the Party's newspaper. This Rolf Vogelmann obviously
doesn't know what the hell he's doing. Think of all the Jewish
business that we get. None of our clients reads that kind of shit.'

'Well, if you don't think we need it, Bernie . . .'

'Like a third nipple.'

'Some people used to think that was a sign of luck.'

'And quite a few who thought it reason enough to burn you at the stake.'

'The devil's mark, eh?' He chuckled. 'Hey, maybe Hitler's got one.'

'Just as surely as Goebbels has a cloven hoof. Shit, they're all from hell. Every damn one of them.'

I heard my footsteps ringing on a deserted Königsplatz as I approached what was left of the Reichstag building. Only Bismarck, standing on his plinth, hand on sword, in front of the western doorway, his head turned towards me, seemed prepared to offer some challenge to my being there. But as I recalled he had never been much of an enthusiast for the German parliament – had never even set foot in the place – and so I doubted that he'd have been much inclined to defend the institution on which his statue had, perhaps symbolically, turned its back. Not that there was much about this rather florid, Renaissance-style building that looked worth fighting for now. Its façade blackened by smoke, the Reichstag looked like a volcano which had seen its last and most spectacular eruption. But the fire had been more than merely the burnt offering of the 1918 Republic; it was also the clearest piece of pyromancy that Germany could have been given as to what Adolf Hitler and his third nipple had in store for us.

I walked up to the north side and what had been Portal V, the public entrance, through which I had walked once before, with my mother, more than thirty years ago.

I left my flashlight in my coat pocket. A man with a torch in his hand at night needs only to paint a few coloured circles on his chest to make a better target of himself. And anyway, there was more than enough moonlight shining through what was left of the roof for me to see where I was going. Still, as I stepped through the north vestibule, into what had once been a waiting-room,

I worked the Mauser's slide noisily to let whoever was expecting me know that I was armed. And in the eerie, echoing silence, it sounded louder than a troop of Prussian cavalry.

'You won't need that,' said a voice from the galleried floor above me.

'All the same, I'll just hang on to it awhile. There might be rats about.'

The man laughed scornfully. 'The rats left here a long time ago.' A torch beam shone in my face. 'Come on up, Günther.'

'Seems like I should know your voice,' I said, starting up the stairs.

'I'm the same way. Sometimes I recognize my voice, but I just don't seem to know the man using it. There's nothing unusual in that, is there? Not these days.' I took out my flashlight and pointed it at the man I now saw retreating into the room ahead of me.

'I'm interested to hear it. I'd like to hear you say that sort of thing over at Prinz Albrecht Strasse.' He laughed again.

'So you do recognize me after all.'

I caught up with him beside a great marble statue of the Emperor Wilhelm I that stood in the centre of a great, octagonally-shaped hall, where my torch finally picked out his features. There was something cosmopolitan about these, although he spoke with a Berlin accent. Some might even have said that he looked more than a little Jewish, if the size of his nose was anything to go by. This dominated the centre of his face like the arm on a sundial, and tugged the upper lip into a thin sneer of a smile. His greying, fair hair he wore closely cropped, which had the effect of accentuating the height of his forehead. It was a cunning, wily sort of face, and suited him perfectly.

'Surprised?' he said.

'That the head of Berlin's Criminal Police should send me an anonymous note? No, that happens to me all the time.'

'Would you have come if I had signed it?'

'Probably not.'

'And if I had suggested that you come to Prinz Albrecht Strasse instead of this place? Admit you were curious.'

'Since when has Kripo had to rely on suggestion to get people down to headquarters?'

'You've got a point.' His smirk broadening, Arthur Nebe produced a hip flask from his coat pocket. 'Drink?'

'Thanks. I don't mind if I do.' I swigged a cheekful of the clear grain alcohol thoughtfully provided by the Reichskriminaldirektor, and then took out my cigarettes. After I had lit us both I held the match aloft for a couple of seconds.

'Not an easy place to torch,' I said. 'One man, acting on his own: he'd have to have been a fairly agile sort of bugger. And even then I reckon it would have taken Van der Lubbe all night to get this little campfire blazing.' I sucked at my cigarette and added: 'The word is that Fat Hermann had a hand in it. A hand holding a piece of burning tinder, that is.'

'I'm shocked, shocked to hear you make such a scandalous suggestion about our beloved prime minister.' But Nebe was laughing as he said it. 'Poor old Hermann, getting the unofficial blame like that. Oh, he went along with the arson, but it wasn't his party.'

'Whose was it, then?'

'Joey the Cripp. That poor fucking Dutchman was an added bonus for him. Van der Lubbe had the misfortune to have decided to set fire to this place on the same night as Goebbels and his lads. Joey thought it was his birthday, especially as Lubbe turned out to be a Bolshie. Only he forgot that the arrest of a culprit meant a trial, which meant that there would have to be the irritating formality of producing evidence. And of course right from the start it was obvious to a man with his head in a bag that Lubbe couldn't have acted on his own.'

'So why didn't he say something at the trial?'

'They pumped him full of some shit to keep him quiet, threatened his family. You know the sort of thing.' Nebe walked round a huge bronze chandelier that lay twisted on the dirty marble floor. 'Here. I want to show you something.'

He led the way into the great Hall of the Diet, where Germany had last seen some semblance of democracy. Rising high above us was the shell of what had once been the Reichstag's glass dome. Now all the glass was blown out and, against the moon, the copper girders resembled the web of some gigantic spider. Nebe pointed his torch at the scorched, split beams that surrounded the Hall.

'They're badly damaged by the fire, but those half figures supporting the beams – can you see how some of them are also holding up letters of the alphabet?'

'Just about.'

'Yes, well, some of them are unrecognizable. But if you look hard you can still see that they spell out a motto.'

'Not at one o'clock in the morning I can't.'

Nebe ignored me. 'It says "Country before Party".' He repeated the motto almost reverently, and then looked at me with what I supposed to be a meaning.

I sighed and shook my head. 'Oh, that really knocks over the heap. You? Arthur Nebe? The Reichskriminaldirektor? A beefsteak Nazi? Well, I'll eat my broom.'

'Brown on the outside, yes,' he said. 'I don't know what colour I am on the inside, but it's not red – I'm no Bolshevik. But then it's not brown either. I am no longer a Nazi.'

'Shit, you're one hell of a mimic, then.'

'I am now. I have to be to stay alive. Of course, it wasn't always that way. The police force is my life, Günther. I love it. When I saw it corroded by liberalism during the Weimar years I thought that National Socialism would restore some respect for law and order in this country. Instead, it's worse than ever. I was the one who helped get the Gestapo away from the control of Diels, only to find him replaced with Himmler and Heydrich, and . . .'

'. . . and then the rain really started to come in at the eaves. I get the picture.'

'The time is coming when everyone will have to do the same. There's no room for agnosticism in the Germany that Himmler and Heydrich have got planned for us. It'll be stand up and be counted or take the consequences. But it's still possible to change things from the inside. And when the time is right we'll need men like you. Men on the force who can be trusted. That's why I've asked you here – to try and persuade you to come back.'

'Me? Back in Kripo? You must be joking. Listen, Arthur, I've built up a good business, I make a very good living now. Why should I chuck all that away for the pleasure of being on the force again?'

'You might not have much choice in the matter. Heydrich thinks that you might be useful to him if you were back in Kripo.'

'I see. Any particular reason?'

'There's a case he wants you to handle. I'm sure I don't have to tell you that Heydrich takes his Fascism very personally. He generally gets what he wants.'

'What's this case about?'

'I don't know what he's got in mind; Heydrich doesn't confide in me. I just wanted to warn you, so that you'd be prepared, so that you didn't do anything stupid like tell him to go to hell, which might be your first reaction. We both have great respect for your abilities as a detective. It just happens that I also want somebody in Kripo that I can trust.'

'Well, what it is to be popular.'

'You'll give it some thought.'

'I don't see how I can avoid it. It'll make a change from the crossword, I suppose. Anyway, thanks for the red light, Arthur, I appreciate it.' I wiped my dry mouth nervously. 'You got any more of that lemonade? I could use a drink now. It's not every day you get such good news.'

Nebe handed me his flask and I went for it like a baby after its mother's tit. Less attractive, but damn near as comforting.

'In your love letter you mentioned you had some information about an old case. Or was that your equivalent of the child-molester's puppy?'

'There was a woman you were looking for a while back. A journalist.'

'That's quite a while back. Nearly two years. I never found her.

One of my all too frequent failures. Perhaps you ought to let Hey-drich know that. It might persuade him to let me off the hook.'

'Do you want this or not?'

'Well, don't make me straighten my tie for it, Arthur.'

'There's not much, but here it is. A couple of months ago, the landlord of the place where your client used to live decided to redecorate some of the apartments, including hers.'

'Big-hearted of him.'

'In her toilet, behind some kind of false panel, he found a doper's kit. No drugs, but everything you'd need to service a habit — needles, syringes, the works. Now, the tenant who took over the place from your client when she disappeared was a priest, so it didn't seem likely that these needles were his, right? And if the lady was using dope, then that might explain a lot, wouldn't you say? I mean, you never can predict what a doper will do.'

I shook my head. 'She wasn't the type. I'd have noticed some-thing, wouldn't I?'

'Not always. Not if she was trying to wean herself off the stuff. Not if she were a strong sort of character. Well then, it was reported and I thought you'd like to know. So now you can close that file. With that sort of secret there's no telling what else she might have kept from you.'

'No, it's all right. I got a good look at her nipples.'

Nebe smiled nervously, not quite sure if I was telling him a dirty joke or not.

'Good were they — her nipples?'

'Just the two of them, Arthur. But they were beautiful.'

2

Monday, 29 August

The houses on Herbertstrasse, in any other city but Berlin, would each have been surrounded by a couple of hectares of shrub-lined lawn. But as it was they filled their individual plots of land with little or no space for grass and paving. Some of them were no more than the front-gate's width from the sidewalk. Architecturally they were a mixture of styles, ranging from the Palladian to the neo-Gothic, the Wilhelmine and some that were so vernacular as to be impossible to describe. Judged as a whole, Herbertstrasse was like an assemblage of old field-marshals and grand-admirals in full-dress uniforms obliged to sit on extremely small and inadequate camp stools.

The great wedding-cake of a house to which I had been summoned belonged properly on a Mississippi plantation, an impression enhanced by the black cauldron of a maid who answered the door. I showed her my ID and told her that I was expected. She stared doubtfully at my identification, as if she were Himmler himself.

'Frau Lange didn't say nothing to me about you.'

'I expect she forgot,' I said. 'Look, she only called my office half an hour ago.'

'All right,' she said reluctantly. 'You'd better come in.'

She showed me into a drawing-room that you could have called elegant but for the large and only partially chewed dog-bone that was lying on the carpet. I looked around for the owner but there was no sign of one.

'Don't touch anything,' said the black cauldron. 'I'll tell her you're here.' Then, muttering and grumbling like I'd got her out of the bath, she waddled off to find her mistress. I sat down on a mahogany sofa with dolphins carved on the armrests. Next to it was a matching table, the top resting on dolphin-tails. Dolphins were a comic effect always popular with German cabinet-makers, but, personally, I'd seen a better sense of humour in a three-pfennig stamp. I was there about five minutes before the cauldron rolled back in and said that Frau Lange would see me now.

We went along a long, gloomy hallway that was home to a lot of stuffed fish, one of which, a fine salmon, I stopped to admire.

'Nice fish,' I said. 'Who's the fisherman?' She turned impatiently.

'No fisherman here,' she said. 'Just fish. What a house this is for fish, and cats, and dogs. Only the cats is the worst. At least the fish is dead. You can't dust them cats and dogs.'

Almost automatically I ran my finger along the salmon's cabinet. There didn't seem to be a great deal of evidence that any kind of dusting took place; and even on my comparatively short introduction to the Lange household, it was easy to see that the carpets were rarely, if ever, vacuumed. After the mud of the trenches a bit of dust and a few crumbs on the floor don't offend me that much. But all the same, I'd seen plenty of homes in the worst slums of Neukölln and Wedding that were kept cleaner than this one.

The cauldron opened some glass doors and stood aside. I went into an untidy sitting-room which also seemed to be part office, and the doors closed behind me.

She was a large, fleshy orchid of a woman. Fat hung pendulously on her peach-coloured face and arms, making her look like one of those stupid dogs that is bred to have a coat several sizes too large for it. Her own stupid dog was altogether more shapeless than the ill-fitting Sharpei she resembled.

'It's very good of you to come and see me at such short notice,' she said. I uttered a few deferential noises, but she had the sort of clout you can only get from living in a fancy address like Herbert-strasse.

Frau Lange sat down on a green-coloured chaise longue and spread her dog's fur on her generous lap like a piece of knitting she intended to work on while explaining her problem to me. I supposed her to be in her middle fifties. Not that it mattered. When women get beyond fifty their age ceases to be of interest to anyone other than themselves. With men the situation is entirely the opposite.

She produced a cigarette case and invited me to smoke, adding as a proviso: 'They're menthol.'

I thought it was curiosity that made me take one, but as I sucked my first lungful I winced, realizing that I had merely forgotten how disgusting a menthol tastes. She chuckled at my obvious discomfort.

'Oh, put it out man, for God's sake. They taste horrible. I don't know why I smoke them, really I don't. Have one of your own or I'll never get your attention.'

'Thanks,' I said, stubbing it out in a hub-cap of an ashtray, 'I think I will.'

'And while you're at it, you can pour us both a drink. I don't know about you but I could certainly do with one.' She pointed to a great Biedermeier secretaire, the top section of which, with its bronze Ionic columns, was an ancient Greek temple in miniature.

'There's a bottle of gin in that thing,' she said. 'I can't offer you anything but lime juice to put in it. I'm afraid it's the only thing I ever drink.'

It was a little early for me, but I mixed two anyway. I liked her for trying to put me at my ease, even though that was supposed to be one of my own professional accomplishments. Except that Frau Lange wasn't in the least bit nervous. She looked like the kind of lady who had quite a few professional accomplishments of her own. I handed her the drink and sat down on a creaking leather chair that was next to the chaise.

'Are you an observant man, Herr Günther?'

'I can see what's happening in Germany, if that's what you mean.'

'It wasn't, but I'm glad to hear it anyway. No, what I meant was, how good are you at seeing things?'

'Come now, Frau Lange, there's no need to be the cat creeping around the hot milk. Just walk right up and lap it.' I waited for a moment, watching her grow awkward. 'I'll say it for you if you like. You mean, how good a detective am I.'

'I'm afraid I know very little of these matters.'

'No reason why you should.'

'But if I am to confide in you I feel I ought to have some idea of your credentials.'

I smiled. 'You'll understand that mine is not the kind of business where I can show you the testimonials of several satisfied customers. Confidentiality is as important to my clients as it is in the confessional. Perhaps even more important.'

'But then how is one to know that one has engaged the services of someone who is good at what he does?'

'I'm very good at what I do, Frau Lange. My reputation is well-known. A couple of months ago I even had an offer for my business. Rather a good offer, as it happened.'

'Why didn't you sell?'

'In the first place the business wasn't for sale. And in the second I'd make as bad an employee as I would an employer. All the same, it's flattering when that sort of thing happens. Of course, all this is quite beside the point. Most people who want the services of a private investigator don't need to buy the firm. Usually they just ask their lawyers to find someone. You'll find that I'm recommended by several law firms, including the ones who don't like my accent or my manners.'

'Forgive me, Herr Günther, but in my opinion the law is a much overrated profession.'

'I can't argue with you there. I never met a lawyer yet that wasn't above stealing his mother's savings and the mattress she was keeping them under.'

'In nearly all business matters I have found my own judgement to be a great deal more reliable.'

'What exactly is your business, Frau Lange?'

'I own and manage a publishing company.'

'The Lange Publishing Company?'

'As I said, I haven't often been wrong by trusting my own judgement, Herr Günther. Publishing is all about taste, and to know what will sell one must appreciate something of the tastes of the people to whom one is selling. Now, I'm a Berliner to my fingertips, and I believe I know this city and its people as well as anyone does. So with reference to my original question, which was to do with your being observant, you will answer me this: if I were a stranger in Berlin, how would you describe the people of this city to me?'

I smiled. 'What's a Berliner, eh? That's a good question. No client's ever asked me to leap through a couple of hoops to see how clever a dog I am before. You know, mostly I don't do tricks, but in your case I'll make an exception. Berliners like people to make exceptions for them. I hope you're paying attention now because I've started my act. Yes, they like to be made to feel exceptional, although at the same time they like to keep up appearances. Mostly they've got the same sort of look. A scarf, hat and shoes that could walk you to Shanghai without a corn. As it happens, Berliners like to walk, which is why so many of them own a dog: something vicious if you're masculine, something cute if you're something else. The men comb their hair more than the women, and they also grow moustaches you could hunt wild pig in. Tourists think that a lot of Berlin men like dressing-up as women, but that's just the ugly women giving the men a bad name. Not that there are many tourists these days. National Socialism's made them as rare a sight as Fred Astaire in jackboots.

'The people of this town will take cream with just about anything, including beer, and beer is something they take very seriously indeed. The women prefer a ten-minute head on it, just like the men, and they don't mind paying for it themselves. Nearly everyone who drives a car drives much too fast, but nobody would ever dream of running a red light. They've got rotten lungs because the air is bad, and because they smoke too much, and a sense of humour that sounds cruel if you don't understand it, and even crueller if you do. They buy expensive Biedermeier cabinets as solid as blockhouses, and then hang little curtains on the insides of the glass doors to hide what they've got in there. It's a typically idio-syncratic mixture of the ostentatious and the private. How am I doing?'

Frau Lange nodded. 'Apart from the comment about Berlin's ugly women, you'll do just fine.'

'It wasn't pertinent.'

'Now there you're wrong. Don't back down or I shall stop lik-ing you. It was pertinent. You'll see why in a moment. What are your fees?'

'Seventy marks a day, plus expenses.'

'And what expenses might there be?'

'Hard to say. Travel. Bribes. Anything that results in informa-tion. You get receipts for everything except the bribes. I'm afraid you have to take my word for those.'

'Well, let's hope that you're a good judge of what is worth pay-ing for.'

'I've had no complaints.'

'And I assume you'll want something in advance.' She handed me an envelope. 'You'll find a thousand marks in cash in there. Is that satisfactory to you?' I nodded. 'Naturally I shall want a receipt.'

'Naturally,' I said, and signed the piece of paper she had prepared. Very businesslike, I thought. Yes, she was certainly quite a lady. 'Incidentally, how did you come to choose me? You didn't ask your lawyer, and,' I added thoughtfully, 'I don't advertise, of course.'

She stood up and, still holding her dog, went over to the desk.

'I had one of your business cards,' she said, handing it to me. 'Or at least my son did. I acquired it at least a year ago from the pocket of one of his old suits I was sending to the Winter Relief.' She referred to the welfare programme that was run by the Labour Front, the DAF. 'I kept it, meaning to return it to him. But when I mentioned it to him I'm afraid he told me to throw it away. Only I didn't. I suppose I thought it might come in useful at some stage. Well, I wasn't wrong, was I?'

It was one of my old business cards, dating from the time before my partnership with Bruno Stahlecker. It even had my previous home telephone number written on the back.

'I wonder where he got it,' I said.

'I believe he said that it was Dr Kindermann's.'

'Kindermann?'

'I'll come to him in a moment, if you don't mind.' I thumbed a new card from my wallet.

'It's not important. But I've got a partner now, so you'd better have one of my new ones.' I handed her the card, and she placed it on the desk next to the telephone. While she was sitting down her face adopted a serious expression, as if she had switched off something inside her head.

'And now I'd better tell you why I asked you here,' she said grimly. 'I want you to find out who's blackmailing me.' She paused, shifting awkwardly on the chaise longue. 'I'm sorry, this isn't very easy for me.'

'Take your time. Blackmail makes anyone feel nervous.' She nodded and gulped some of her gin.

'Well, about two months ago, perhaps a little more, I received an envelope containing two letters that had been written by my son to another man. To Dr Kindermann. Of course I recognized my son's handwriting, and although I didn't read them, I knew that they were of an intimate nature. My son is a homosexual, Herr Günther. I've known about it for some time, so this was not the terrible revelation to me that this evil person had intended. He made that much clear in his note. Also that there were several more letters like the ones I had received in his possession, and that he would send them to me if I paid him the sum of 1,000 marks. Were I to refuse he would have no alternative but to send them to the Gestapo. I'm sure I don't have to tell you, Herr Günther, that this government takes a less enlightened attitude towards these unfortunate young men than did the Republic. Any contact between men, no matter how tenuous, is these days regarded as punishable. For Reinhard to be exposed as a homosexual would undoubtedly result in his being sent to a concentration camp for up to ten years.

'So I paid, Herr Günther. My chauffeur left the money in the place I was told, and a week or so later I received not a packet of letters as I had expected, but only one letter. It was accompanied by another anonymous note which informed me that the author had changed his mind, that he was poor, that I should have to buy the letters back one at a time, and that there were still ten of them in his possession. Since then I have received four back, at a cost of almost 5,000 marks. Each time he asks for more than the last.'

'Does your son know about this?'

'No. And for the moment at least I can see no reason why we should both suffer.' I sighed, and was about to voice my disagreement when she stopped me.

'Yes, you're going to say that it makes catching this criminal more difficult, and that Reinhard may have information which might help you. You're absolutely right, of course. But listen to my reasons, Herr Günther.

'First of all, my son is an impulsive boy. Most likely his reaction would be to tell this blackmailer to go to the devil, and not pay. This would almost certainly result in his arrest. Reinhard is my son, and as his mother I love him very dearly, but he is a fool, with no understanding of pragmatism. I suspect that whoever is blackmailing me has a shrewd appreciation of human psychology. He understands how a mother, a widow, feels for her only son – especially a rich and rather lonely one like myself.

'Second, I myself have some appreciation of the world of the homosexual. The late Dr Magnus Hirschfeld wrote several books on the subject, one of which I'm proud to say I published myself. It's a secret and rather treacherous world, Herr Günther. A blackmailer's charter. So it may be that this evil person is actually acquainted with my son. Even between men and women, love can make a good reason for blackmail – more so when there is adultery involved, or race defilement, which seems to be more a cause for concern to these Nazis.

'Because of this, when you have discovered the blackmailer's identity, I will tell Reinhard, and then it will be up to him what is to be done. But until then he will know nothing of this.' She looked at me questioningly. 'Do you agree?'

'I can't fault your reasoning, Frau Lange. You seem to have thought this thing through very clearly. May I see the letters from your son?' Reaching for a folder by the chaise she nodded, and then hesitated.

'Is that necessary? Reading his letters, I mean.'

'Yes it is,' I said firmly. 'And do you still have the notes from the blackmailer?' She handed me the folder.

'Everything is in there,' she said. 'The letters and the anonymous notes.'

'He didn't ask for any of them back?'

'No.'

'That's good. It means we're dealing with an amateur. Someone who had done this sort of thing before would have told you to return his notes with each payment. To stop you accumulating any evidence against him.'

'Yes, I see.'

I glanced at what I was optimistically calling evidence. The notes and envelopes were all typewritten on good quality stationery without any distinctive features, and posted at various districts throughout west Berlin – W.35, W.40, W.50 – the stamps all commemorating the fifth anniversary of the Nazis coming to power. That told me something. This anniversary had taken place on 30 January, so it didn't look like Frau Lange's blackmailer bought stamps very often.

Reinhard Lange's letters were written on the heavier weight of paper that only people in love bother to buy – the kind that costs so much it just has to be taken seriously. The hand was neat and fastidious, even careful, which was more than could be said of the contents. An Ottoman bath-house attendant might not have found anything particularly objectionable about them, but in Nazi Germany, Reinhard Lange's love-letters were certainly sufficient to earn their cheeky author a trip to a KZ wearing a whole chestful of pink triangles.

'This Dr Lanz Kindermann,' I said, reading the name on the lime-scented envelope. 'What exactly do you know about him?'

'There was a stage when Reinhard was persuaded to be treated for his homosexuality. At first he tried various endocrine preparations, but these proved ineffective. Psychotherapy seemed to offer a better chance of success. I believe several high-ranking Party members, and boys from the Hitler Youth, have undergone the same treatment. Kindermann is a psychotherapist, and Reinhard first became acquainted with him when he entered Kindermann's clinic in Wannsee seeking a cure. Instead he became intimately involved with Kindermann, who is himself homosexual.'

'Pardon my ignorance, but what exactly is psychotherapy? I thought that sort of thing was no longer permitted.'

Frau Lange shook her head. 'I'm not exactly sure. But I think that the emphasis is on treating mental disorders as part of one's overall physical health. Don't ask me how that differs from that fellow Freud, except that he's Jewish, and Kindermann is German. Kindermann's clinic is strictly Germans only. Wealthy Germans, with drink and drug problems, those for whom the more eccentric end of medicine has some appeal – chiropracty and that sort of thing. Or those just seeking an expensive rest. Kindermann's patients include the Deputy Führer, Rudolf Hess.'

'Have you ever met Dr Kindermann?'

'Once. I didn't like him. He's a rather arrogant Austrian.'

'Aren't they all?' I murmured. 'Think he'd be the type to try a little blackmail? After all, the letters were addressed to him. If it isn't Kindermann, then it has to be somebody who knows him. Or at least somebody who had the opportunity to steal the letters from him.'

'I confess that I hadn't suspected Kindermann for the simple reason that the letters implicate both of them.' She thought for a moment. 'I know it sounds silly, but I never gave any thought as to how the letters came to be in somebody else's possession. But now you come to mention it, I suppose that they must have been stolen. From Kindermann I would think.'

I nodded. 'All right,' I said. 'Now let me ask you a rather more difficult question.'

'I think I know what you're going to say, Herr Günther,' she said, heaving a great sigh. 'Have I considered the possibility that my own son might be the culprit?' She looked at me critically, and added: 'I wasn't wrong about you, was I? It's just the sort of cynical question that I hoped you would ask. Now I know I can trust you.'

'For a detective being a cynic is like green fingers in a gardener, Frau Lange. Sometimes it gets me into trouble, but mostly it stops me from underestimating people. So you'll forgive me I hope if I suggest that this could be the best reason of all for not involving him in this investigation, and that you've already thought of it.' I saw her smile a little, and added: 'You see how I don't underestimate you, Frau Lange.' She nodded. 'Could he be short of money, do you think?'

'No. As a board director of the Lange Publishing Company he draws a substantial salary. He also has income from a large trust that was set up for him by his father. It's true, he likes to gamble. But worse than that, for me, is that he is the owner of a perfectly useless title called *Urania*.'

'Title?'

'A magazine. About astrology, or some such rubbish. It's done nothing but lose money since the day he bought it.' She lit another cigarette and sucked at it with lips puckered like she was going to whistle a tune. 'And he knows that if he were ever really short of money, then he would only have to come and ask me.'

I smiled ruefully. 'I know I'm not what you might call cute, but have you ever thought of adopting someone like me?' She laughed at that, and I added: 'He sounds like a very fortunate young man.'

'He's very spoiled, that's what he is. And he's not so young any more.' She stared into space, her eyes apparently following her cigarette smoke. 'For a rich widow like myself, Reinhard is what people in business call "a loss leader". There is no disappointment in life that begins to compare with one's disappointment in one's only son.'

'Really? I've heard it said that children are a blessing as one gets older.'

'You know, for a cynic you're beginning to sound quite sentimental. I can tell you've no children of your own. So let me put you right about one thing, Herr Günther. Children are the reflection of one's old age. They're the quickest way of growing old I know. The mirror of one's decline. Mine most of all.'

The dog yawned and jumped off her lap as if having heard it many times before. On the floor it stretched and ran towards the door where it turned and looked back expectantly at its mistress. Unperturbed at this display of canine hubris, she got up to let the brute out of the room.

'So what happens now?' she said, coming back to her chaise longue.

'We wait for another note. I'll handle the next cash delivery. But until then I think it might be a good idea if I were to check into Kindermann's clinic for a few days. I'd like to know a little more about your son's friend.'

'I suppose that's what you mean by expenses, is it?'

'I'll try to make it a short stay.'

'See that you do,' she said, affecting a schoolmistressy sort of tone. 'The Kindermann Clinic is a hundred marks a day.'

I whistled. 'Very respectable.'

'And now I must excuse myself, Herr Günther,' she said. 'I have a meeting to prepare for.' I pocketed my cash and then we shook hands, after which I picked up the folder she had given me and pointed my suit at the door.

I walked back along the dusty corridor and through the hall. A voice barked: 'You just hang on there. I got to let you out. Frau Lange don't like it if I don't see her guests out myself.'

I put my hand on the doorknob and found something sticky there. 'Your warm personality, no doubt.' I jerked the door open irritatedly as the black cauldron waddled across the hall. 'Don't trouble,' I said inspecting my hand. 'You just get on back to whatever it is that you do around this dustbowl.'

'Been a long time with Frau Lange,' she growled. 'She never had no complaints.'

I wondered if blackmail came into it at all. After all, you have to have a good reason to keep a guard-dog that doesn't bark. I couldn't see where affection might possibly fit into it either – not with this woman. It was more probable that you could grow attached to a river crocodile. We stared at each other for a moment, after which I said, 'Does the lady always smoke that much?'

The black thought for a moment, wondering whether or not it was a trick question. Eventually she decided that it wasn't. 'She always has a nail in her mouth, and that's a fact.'

'Well, that must be the explanation,' I said. 'With all that cigarette smoke around her, I bet she doesn't even know you're there.' She swore under her searing breath and slammed the door in my face.

I had lots to think about as I drove back along Kurfürstendamm towards the city centre. I thought about Frau Lange's case and then her thousand marks in my pocket. I thought about a short break in a nice comfortable sanitarium at her expense, and the opportunity it offered me, temporarily at least, to escape Bruno and his pipe; not to mention Arthur Nebe and Heydrich. Maybe I'd even sort out my insomnia and my depression.

But most of all I thought of how I could ever have given my business card and home telephone number to some Austrian flower I'd never even heard of.

3

Wednesday, 31 August

The area south of Königstrasse, in Wannsee, is home to all sorts of private clinics and hospitals – the smart shiny kind, where they use as much ether on the floors and windows as they do on the patients themselves. As far as treatment is concerned they are inclined to be egalitarian. A man could be possessed of the constitution of an African bull elephant and still they would be happy to treat him like he was shell-shocked, with a couple of lipsticked nurses to help him with the heavier brands of toothbrush and lavatory paper, always provided he could pay for it. In Wannsee, your bank balance matters more than your blood pressure.

Kindermann's clinic stood off a quiet road in a large but well-behaved sort of garden that sloped down to a small backwater off the main lake and included, among the many elm and chestnut trees, a colonnaded pier, a boathouse and a Gothic folly that was so neatly built as to take on a rather more sensible air. It looked like a medieval telephone kiosk.

The clinic itself was such a mixture of gable, half-timber, mullion, crenellated tower and turret as to be more Rhine castle than sanitarium. Looking at it I half expected to see a couple of gibbets on the rooftop, or hear a scream from a distant cellar. But things were quiet, with no sign of anyone about. There was only the distant sound of a four-man crew on the lake beyond the trees to provoke the rooks to raucous comment.

As I walked through the front door I decided that there would probably be more chance of finding a few inmates creeping around outside about the time when the bats were thinking of launching themselves into the twilight.

My room was on the third floor, with an excellent view of the kitchens. At eighty marks a day it was the cheapest they had, and skipping around it I couldn't help but wonder if for an extra fifty marks a day I wouldn't have rated something a little bigger, like a laundry-basket. But the clinic was full. My room was all they had available, said the nurse who showed me up there.

She was a cute one. Like a Baltic fishwife but without the quaint country conversation. By the time she had turned down my bed and told me to get undressed I was almost breathless with excitement. First Frau Lange's maid, and then this one, as much a stranger to lipstick as a pterodactyl. It wasn't as if there weren't prettier nurses about. I'd seen plenty downstairs. They must have figured that with a very small room the least they could do would be to give me a very large nurse in compensation.

'What time does the bar open?' I said. Her sense of humour was no less pleasing than her beauty.

'There's no alcohol allowed in here,' she said, snatching the unlit cigarette from my lips. 'And strictly no smoking. Dr Meyer will be along to see you presently.'

'So what's he, the second-class deck? Where's Dr Kindermann?'

'The doctor is at a conference in Bad Neuheim.'

'What's he doing there, staying at a sanitarium? When does he come back here?'

'The end of the week. Are you a patient of Dr Kindermann, Herr Strauss?'

'No, no I'm not. But for eighty marks a day I had hoped I would be.'

'Dr Meyer is a very capable physician, I can assure you.' She frowned at me impatiently, as she realized that I hadn't yet made a move to get undressed, and started to make a tutting noise that sounded like she was trying to be nice to a cockatoo. Clapping her hands sharply, she told me to hurry up and get into bed as Dr Meyer would wish to examine me. Judging that she was quite capable of doing it for me, I decided not to resist. Not only was my nurse

ugly, but she was also possessed of a bedside manner that must
have been acquired in a market garden.

When she'd gone I settled down to read in bed. Not the kind of
read you would describe as gripping, so much as incredible. Yes,
that was the word: incredible. There had always been weird, occult
magazines in Berlin, like *Zenit* and *Hagal*, but from the shores of
the Maas to the banks of the Memel there was nothing to compare
with the grabbers that were writing for Reinhard Lange's magazine, *Urania*. Leafing through it for just fifteen minutes was enough
to convince me that Lange was probably a complete spinner. There
were articles entitled 'Wotanism and the Real Origins of Chris-
tianity', 'The Superhuman Powers of the Lost Citizens of Atlantis',
'The World Ice Theory Explained', 'Esoteric Breathing Exercises
for Beginners', 'Spiritualism and Race Memory', 'The Hollow-
Earth Doctrine', 'Anti-Semitism as Theocratic Legacy', etc. For a
man who could publish this sort of nonsense, the blackmail of a
parent, I thought, was probably the sort of mundane activity that
occupied him between ariosophical revelations.

Even Dr Meyer, himself no obvious testament to the ordinary,
was moved to remark upon my choice of reading matter.

'Do you often read this kind of thing?' he asked, turning the
magazine over in his hands as if it had been a variety of curious
artefact dug from some Trojan ruin by Heinrich Schliemann.

'No, not really. It was curiosity that made me buy it.'

'Good. An abnormal interest in the occult is often an indication
of an unstable personality.'

'You know, I was just thinking the same thing myself.'

'Not everyone would agree with me in that, of course. But the
visions of many modern religious figures – St Augustine, Luther –
are most probably neurotic in their origins.'

'Is that so?'

'Oh yes.'

'What does Dr Kindermann think?'

'Oh, Kindermann holds some very unusual theories. I'm not

sure I understand his work, but he's a very brilliant man.' He picked up my wrist. 'Yes indeed, a very brilliant man.'

The doctor, who was Swiss, wore a three-piece suit of green tweed, a great moth of a bow-tie, glasses and the long white chin-beard of an Indian holy man. He pushed up my pyjama sleeve and hung a little pendulum above the underside of my wrist. He watched it swing and revolve for a while before pronouncing that the amount of electricity I was giving off indicated that I was feeling abnormally depressed and anxious about something. It was an impressive little performance, but none the less bullet-proof, given that most of the folk who checked into the clinic were probably depressed or anxious about something, even if it was only their bill.

'How are you sleeping?' he said.

'Badly. Couple of hours a night.'

'Do you ever have nightmares?'

'Yes, and I don't even like cheese.'

'Any recurring dreams?'

'Nothing specific.'

'And what about your appetite?'

'I don't have one to speak of.'

'Your sex life?'

'Same as my appetite. Not worth mentioning.'

'Do you think much about women?'

'All the time.'

He scribbled a few notes, stroked his beard, and said: 'I'm prescribing extra vitamins and minerals, especially magnesium. I'm also going to put you on a sugar-free diet, lots of raw vegetables and kelp. We'll help get rid of some of the toxins in you with a course of blood-purification tablets. I also recommend that you exercise. There's an excellent swimming-pool here, and you may even care to try a rainwater bath, which you'll find to be most invigorating. Do you smoke?' I nodded. 'Try giving up for a while.' He snapped his notebook shut. 'Well, that should all help with your physical well-being. Along the way we'll see if we can't effect some improvement in your mental state with psychotherapeutic treatment.'

'Exactly what is psychotherapy, Doctor? Forgive me, but I thought that the Nazis had branded it as decadent.'

'Oh no, no. Psychotherapy is not psychoanalysis. It places no reliance on the unconscious mind. That sort of thing is all right for Jews, but it has no relevance to Germans. As you yourself will now appreciate, no psychotherapeutic treatment is ever pursued in isolation from the body. Here we aim to relieve the symptoms of mental disorder by adjusting the attitudes that have led to their occurrence. Attitudes are conditioned by personality, and the relation of a personality to its environment. Your dreams are only of interest to me to the extent that you are having them at all. To treat you by attempting to interpret your dreams, and to discover their sexual significance is, quite frankly, nonsensical. Now that is decadent.' He chuckled warmly. 'But that's a problem for Jews, and not you, Herr Strauss. Right now, the most important thing is that you enjoy a good night's sleep.' So saying he picked up his medical bag and took out a syringe and a small bottle which he placed on the bedside table.

'What's that?' I said uncertainly.

'Hyoscine,' he said, rubbing my arm with a pad of surgical spirit.

The injection felt cold as it crept up my arm, like embalming fluid. Seconds after recognizing that I would have to find another night on which to snoop around Kindermann's clinic, I felt the ropes mooring me to consciousness slacken, and I was adrift, moving slowly away from the shore, Meyer's voice already too far away for me to hear what he was saying.

After four days in the clinic I was feeling better than I had felt in four months. As well as my vitamins, and my diet of kelp and raw vegetables, I'd tried hydrotherapy, naturotherapy and a solarium treatment. My state of health had been further diagnosed through examination of my irises, my palms and my fingernails, which revealed me as calcium-deficient; and a technique of autogenic relaxation had been taught to me. Dr Meyer was making progress with his Jungian 'totality approach', as he called it, and was proposing to attack my depression with electrotherapy. And although I hadn't yet managed to search Kindermann's office, I did have a new nurse, a real beauty called Marianne, who remembered Reinhard Lange staying at the clinic for several months, and had already demonstrated a willingness to discuss her employer and the affairs of the clinic.

She woke me at seven with a glass of grapefruit juice and an almost veterinary selection of pills.

Enjoying the curve of her buttocks and the stretch of her pendulous breasts, I watched her draw back the curtains to reveal a fine sunny day, and wished that she could have revealed her naked body as easily.

'And how are you this beautiful day?' I said.

'Awful,' she grimaced.

'Marianne, you know it's supposed to be the other way around, don't you? I'm the one who is supposed to feel awful, and you're the one who should ask after my health.'

'I'm sorry, Herr Strauss, but I am bored as hell with this place.'

'Well, why don't you jump in here beside me and tell me all about it. I'm very good at listening to other people's problems.'

'I'll bet you're very good at other things as well,' she said, laughing. 'I shall have to put bromide in your fruit-juice.'

'What would be the point of that? I've already got a whole pharmacy swilling around inside of me. I can't see that another chemical would make much difference.'

'You'd be surprised.'

She was a tall, athletic-looking blonde from Frankfurt with a nervous sense of humour and a rather self-conscious smile that indicated a lack of personal confidence. Which was strange, given her obvious attractiveness.

'A whole pharmacy,' she scoffed. 'A few vitamins and something to help you sleep at night. That's nothing compared with some of the others.'

'Tell me about it.'

She shrugged. 'Something to help them wake up, and stimulants to help combat depression.'

'What do they use on the pansies?'

'Oh, them. They used to give them hormones, but it didn't work. So now they try aversion therapy. But despite what they say at the Goering Institute about it being a treatable disorder, in private all the doctors say that the basic condition is hard to influence. Kindermann should know. I think he might be a bit warm himself. I've heard him tell a patient that psychotherapy is only helpful in dealing with the neurotic reactions that may arise from homosexuality. That it helps the patient to stop deluding himself.'

'So then all he has to worry about is Section 175.'

'What's that?'

'The section of the German penal code which makes it a criminal offence. Is that what happened to Reinhard Lange? He was just treated for associated neurotic reactions?' She nodded, and sat herself on the edge of my bed. 'Tell me about this Goering Institute. Any relation to Fat Hermann?'

'Matthias Goering is his cousin. The place exists to provide psychotherapy with the protection of the Goering name. If it weren't for him there would be very little mental health in Germany worthy of the name. The Nazis would have destroyed psychiatric medicine merely because its leading light is a Jew. The whole thing is the most enormous piece of hypocrisy. A lot of them continue privately to subscribe to Freud, while denouncing him in public. Even the so-called Orthopaedic Hospital for the SS near Ravensbrück is nothing but a mental hospital for the SS. Kindermann is a consultant there, as well as being one of the Goering Institute's founding members.'

'So who funds the Institute?'

'The Labour Front, and the Luftwaffe.'

'Of course. The prime minister's petty-cash box.'

Marianne's eyes narrowed. 'You know, you ask a lot of questions. What are you, a bull or something like that?'

I got out of bed and slipped into my dressing-gown. I said: 'Something like that.'

'Are you working on a case here?' Her eyes widened with excitement. 'Something Kindermann could be involved in?'

I opened the window and leant out for a moment. The morning air was good to breathe, even the stuff coming up from the kitchens. But a cigarette was better. I brought my last packet in from the window ledge and lit one. Marianne's eyes lingered disapprovingly on the cigarette in my hand.

'You shouldn't be smoking, you know.'

'I don't know if Kindermann is involved or not,' I said. 'That's what I was hoping to find out when I came here.'

'Well, you don't have to worry about me,' she said fiercely. 'I couldn't care what happens to him.' She stood up with her arms folded, her mouth assuming a harder expression. 'The man is a bastard. You know, just a few weeks ago I worked a whole weekend because nobody else was available. He said he'd pay me double-time in cash. But he still hasn't given me my money. That's the kind of pig he is. I bought a dress. It was stupid of me, I should have waited. Well, now I'm behind with the rent.'

I was debating with myself whether or not she was trying to sell me a story when I saw the tears in her eyes. If it was an act it was a damn good one. Either way it deserved some kind of recognition.

She blew her nose, and said: 'Would you give me a cigarette, please?'

'Sure.' I handed her the pack and then thumbed a match.

'You know, Kindermann knew Freud,' she said, coughing a little with her first smoke. 'At the Vienna Medical School, when he was a student. After graduating he worked for a while at the Salzburg Mental Asylum. He's from Salzburg originally. When his uncle died in 1930, he left him this house, and he decided to turn it into a clinic.'

'It sounds like you know him quite well.'

'Last summer his secretary was sick for a couple of weeks. Kindermann knew I had some secretarial experience and asked me to fill in a while while Tarja was away. I got to know him reasonably well. Well enough to dislike him. I'm not going to stay here much longer. I've had enough, I think. Believe me, there are plenty of others here who feel much the same way.'

'Oh? Think anyone would want to get back at him? Anyone who might have a grudge against him?'

'You're talking about a serious grudge, aren't you? Not just a bit of unpaid overtime.'

'I suppose so,' I said, and flicked my cigarette out of the open window.

Marianne shook her head. 'No, wait,' she said. 'There was someone. About three months ago Kindermann dismissed one of the male nurses for being drunk. He was a nasty piece of work, and I don't think anyone was sad to see him go. I wasn't there myself, but I heard that he used some quite strong language to Kindermann when he left.'

'What was his name, this male nurse?'

'Hering, Klaus Hering I think.' She looked at her watch. 'Hey, I've got to be getting on with my work. I can't stay talking to you all morning.'

'One more thing,' I said. 'I need to take a look around Kindermann's office. Can you help?' She started to shake her head. 'I can't do it without you, Marianne. Tonight?'

'I don't know. What if we get caught?'

'The "we" part doesn't come into it. You keep a look-out, and if someone finds you, you say that you heard a noise, and that you were investigating. I'll have to take my chances. Maybe I'll say I was sleepwalking.'

'Oh, that's a good one.'

'Come on, Marianne, what do you say?'

'All right, I'll do it. But leave it until after midnight, that's when we lock up. I'll meet you in the solarium at around 12.30.'

Her expression changed as she saw me slide a fifty from my wallet. I crushed it into the breast pocket of her crisp white uniform. She took it out again.

'I can't take this,' she said. 'You shouldn't.' I held her fist shut to stop her returning the note.

'Look, it's just something to help tide you over, at least until you get paid for your overtime.' She looked doubtful.

'I don't know,' she said. 'It doesn't seem right somehow. This is as much as I make in a week. It'll do a lot more than just tide me over.'

'Marianne,' I said, 'it's nice to make ends meet, but it's even nicer if you can tie a bow.'

4

Monday, 5 September

'The doctor told me that the electrotherapy has the temporary side-effect of disturbing the memory. Otherwise I feel great.'

Bruno looked at me anxiously. 'You're sure?'

'Never felt better.'

'Well, rather you than me, being plugged in like that.' He snorted. 'So whatever you managed to find out while you were in Kindermann's place is temporarily mislaid inside your head, is that it?'

'It's not quite that bad. I managed to take a look around his office. And there was a very attractive nurse who told me all about him. Kindermann is a lecturer at the Luftwaffe Medical School, and a consultant at the Party's private clinic in Bleibtreustrasse. Not to mention his membership of the Nazi Doctors Association, and the Herrenklub.'

Bruno shrugged. 'The man is gold-plated. So what?'

'Gold-plated, but not exactly treasured. He isn't very popular with his staff. I found out the name of someone who he sacked and who might be the type to bear him a grudge.'

'It's not much of a reason, is it? Being sacked?'

'According to my nurse, Marianne, it was common knowledge that he got the push for stealing drugs from the clinic dispensary. That he was probably selling them on the street. So he wasn't exactly the Salvation Army type, was he?'

'This fellow have a name?'

I thought hard for a moment, and then produced my notebook from my pocket. 'It's all right,' I said, 'I wrote it down.'

'A detective with a crippled memory. That's just great.'

'Slow your blood down, I've got it. His name is Klaus Hering.'

'I'll see if the Alex has anything on him.' He picked up the telephone and made the call. It only took a couple of minutes. We paid a bull fifty marks a month for the service. But Klaus Hering was clean.

'So where is the money supposed to go?'

He handed me the anonymous note which Frau Lange had received the previous day and which had prompted Bruno to telephone me at the clinic.

'The lady's chauffeur brought it round here himself,' he explained, as I read over the blackmailer's latest composition of threats and instructions. 'A thousand marks to be placed in a Gerson carrier-bag and left in a wastepaper basket outside the Chicken House at the Zoo, this afternoon.'

I glanced out of the window. It was another warm day, and without a doubt there would be plenty of people at the Zoo.

'It's a good place,' I said. 'He'll be hard to spot and even harder to tail. There are, as far as I remember, four exits to the Zoo.' I found a map of Berlin in my drawer and spread it out on the desk. Bruno came and stood over my shoulder.

'So how do we play it?' he asked.

'You handle the drop, I'll play the sightseer.'

'Want me to wait by one of the exits afterwards?'

'You've got a four-to-one chance. Which way would you choose?'

He studied the map for a minute and then pointed to the canal exit. 'Lichtenstein Bridge. I'd have a car waiting on the other side in Rauch Strasse.'

'Then you'd better have a car there yourself.'

'How long do I wait? I mean, the Zoo's open until nine o'clock at night, for Christ's sake.'

'The Aquarium exit shuts at six, so my guess is that he'll show up before then, if only to keep his options open. If you haven't seen us by then, go home and wait for my call.'

I stepped out of the airship-sized glass shed that is the Zoo Station, and walked across Hardenbergplatz to Berlin Zoo's main entrance, which is just a short way south of the Planetarium. I bought a ticket that included the Aquarium, and a guidebook to make myself look more plausibly a tourist, and made my way first to the Elephant House. A strange man sketching there covered his pad secretively and shied away at my approach. Leaning on the rail of the enclosure I watched this curious behaviour repeated again and again as other visitors came over, until by and by the man found himself standing next to me again. Irritated at the presumption that I should be at all interested in his miserable sketch, I craned my neck over his shoulder, waving my camera close to his face.

'Perhaps you should take up photography,' I said brightly. He snarled something and cowered away. One for Dr Kindermann, I thought. A real spinner. At any kind of show or exhibition, it is always the people that present you with the most interesting spectacle.

It was another fifteen minutes before I saw Bruno. He hardly seemed to see me or the elephants as he walked by, holding the small Gerson store carrier-bag that contained the money under his arm. I let him get well in front, and then followed.

Outside the Chicken House a small red-brick, half-timbered building covered in ivy, which looked more like a village beer-cellar than a home to wild fowl, Bruno stopped, glanced around him, and then dropped the bag into a wastepaper basket that was beside a garden-seat. He walked quickly away, east, and in the direction of his chosen station at the exit on the Landwehr Canal.

A high crag of sandstone, the habitat of a herd of Barbary sheep, was situated opposite the Chicken House. According to the guidebook it was one of the Zoo's landmarks, but I thought it looked too theatrical to be a good imitation of the sort of place that would have been inhabited by these trotting rags in the wild. It was more like something you would have found on the stage of some grossly overblown production of *Parsifal*, if such a thing were humanly possible. I hovered there awhile, reading about the sheep and finally taking several photographs of these supremely uninteresting creatures.

Behind Sheep Rock was a high viewing tower from which it was possible to see the front of the Chicken House, indeed the whole of the Zoo, and I thought it looked like ten pfennigs well-spent for anyone wanting to make sure that he wasn't about to walk into a trap. With this thought in mind I was meandering away from the Chicken House, and towards the lake when a youth of about eighteen, with dark hair and a grey sports jacket, appeared from the far side of the Chicken House. Without even looking around he quickly picked the Gerson bag out of the wastepaper basket and dropped it into another carrier, this one from the Ka-De-We store. Then he walked briskly past me and, after a decent interval, I followed.

Outside the Moorish-style Antelope House the youth paused briefly beside the group of bronze centaurs that stood there, and, giving the appearance of one engrossed in his guidebook, I walked straight on to the Chinese Temple, where, hidden by several people, I stopped to watch him out of the corner of my eye. He came on again, and I guessed that he was making for the Aquarium and the south exit.

Fish were the last thing that you expected to see in the great green building that connects the Zoo with Budapester Strasse. A life-sized stone Iguanadon towered predatorily beside the door, above which was the head of yet another dinosaur. Elsewhere, the walls of the Aquarium were covered with murals and stone reliefs that depicted the kind of prehistoric beasts which would have swallowed a shark whole. It was to the Aquarium's other inhabitants, the reptiles, that these antediluvian decorations were in fact preferable.

Seeing my man disappear through the front door, and realizing that the Aquarium's dark interior would make it easy to lose him, I quickened my pace. Once inside I saw how much more probable than possible this actually was, since the sheer number of visitors made it difficult to see where he had gone.

Assuming the worst, I hurried towards the other door that led out on to the street, and almost collided with the youth as he turned away from a tank that contained a creature that looked more like a floating mine than a fish. For a few seconds he hesitated at the foot of the great marble stairs that led up to the reptiles before walking down to the exit, and out of the Aquarium and the Zoo.

Outside on Budapester Strasse I fell in behind a group of school-children as far as Ansbacher Strasse, where I got rid of the guidebook, slipped into the raincoat I was carrying, and turned up the brim of my hat. Minor alterations to your appearance are essential when following someone. There's that, and staying in the open. It's only when you start to cower in doorways that your man will get suspicious. But this fellow never even looked back as he crossed Wittenberg Platz, and went through the front door of Kaufhaus des Westens, the Ka-De-We, Berlin's biggest department store.

I had thought that he had used the other carrier only to throw a tail off, somebody who might have been waiting at one of the exits on the look out for a man carrying a Gerson bag. But now I realized that we were also in for a switch.

The beer-restaurant on Ka-De-We's third floor was full of lunchtime drinkers. They sat stolidly facing plates of sausage, and glasses of beer that were the height of table lamps. The youth carrying the money wandered among the tables as if looking for someone, and finally sat down opposite a man wearing a blue suit, sitting alone. He placed the carrier-bag with the money beside another just like it on the floor.

Finding an empty table I sat down just in sight of them, and picked up a menu which I affected to study. A waiter appeared. I told him I hadn't made up my mind, and he went away again.

Now the man in the blue suit stood up, laid some coins on the table and, bending down, picked up the carrier bag with the money. Neither one of them said a word.

When the blue suit went out of the restaurant I followed him, obeying the cardinal rule of all cases involving ransom: you always go after the money.

★

With its massive arched portico and twin, minaret-like towers, there was a monolithic, almost Byzantine quality about the Metropol Theatre on Nollendorfplatz. Appearing on reliefs at the foot of the great buttresses were intertwined as many as twenty naked figures, and it seemed like the ideal kind of place to try your hand at a spot of virgin sacrifice. On the righthand side of the theatre was a big wooden gateway, and through it the car park, as big as a football pitch, which backed on to several tall tenements.

It was to one of these buildings that I followed Blue Suit and the money. I checked the names on the mailboxes in the downstairs hall, and was pleased to find a K. Hering residing at number nine. Then I called Bruno from a phone box at the U-Bahn station across the road.

When my partner's old DKW pulled up at the wooden gate, I got into the passenger seat and pointed across to the other side of the car park, nearest to the tenements, where there were still quite a few spaces left, the ones nearer the theatre itself having been taken by those going to the eight o'clock show.

'That's our man's place there,' I said. 'On the second floor. Number nine.'

'Did you get a name?'

'It's our friend from the clinic, Klaus Hering.'

'That's nice and tidy. What does he look like?'

'He's about my height, thin, wiry build, fair hair, rimless glasses, aged about thirty. When he went in he was wearing a blue suit. If he leaves see if you can't get in there and find the pansy's love letters. Otherwise just stay put. I'm going to see the client for further instructions. If she's got any I'll be back tonight. If not, then I'll relieve you at six o'clock tomorrow morning. Any questions?' Bruno shook his head. 'Want me to ring the wife?'

'No thanks. Katia's used to my odd hours by now, Bernie. Anyway, me not being there will help to clear the air. I had another argument with my boy Heinrich when I got back from the Zoo.'

'What was it this time?'

'He's only gone and joined the motorized Hitler Youth, that's all.'

I shrugged. 'He would have to have joined the regular Hitler Youth sooner or later.'

'The little swine didn't have to be in such a damned hurry to join, that's all. He could have waited to be taken in, like the rest of the lads in his class.'

'Come on, look on the bright side. They'll teach him how to drive and look after an engine. They'll still turn him into a Nazi, of course, but at least he'll be a Nazi with a skill.'

Sitting in a taxi back to Alexanderplatz where I had left my car, I reflected that the prospect of his son acquiring mechanical skills probably wasn't much of a consolation to a man who, at the same age as Heinrich, had been a junior cycling champion. And he was right about one thing: Heinrich really was a perfect little swine.

I didn't call Frau Lange to let her know I was coming, and although it was only eight o'clock by the time I got to Herbertstrasse, the house looked dark and uninviting, as if those living there were out, or had retired to bed. But that's one of the more positive aspects of this job. If you've cracked the case then you are always assured of a warm welcome, no matter how unprepared they are for your arrival.

I parked the car, went up the steps to the front door and pulled the bell. Almost immediately a light came on in the window above the door, and after a minute or so the door opened to reveal the black cauldron's ill-tempered face.

'Do you know what time it is?'

'It's just gone eight,' I said. 'The curtains are going up at theatres all over Berlin, diners in restaurants are still scrutinizing the menu and mothers are just thinking that it's about time their children were in bed. Is Frau Lange at home?'

'She's not dressed for no gentlemen callers.'

'Well that's all right. I haven't brought her any flowers or chocolates. And I'm certainly not a gentleman.'

'You spoke the truth there all right.'

'That one was for free. Just to put you in a good enough mood to do as you're told. This is business, urgent business, and she'll want to see me or know the reason why I wasn't let in. So why don't you run along and tell her I'm here.'

I waited in the same room on the sofa with the dolphin armrests. I didn't like it any better the second time, not least because it was now covered with the ginger hairs of an enormous cat, which lay asleep on a cushion underneath a long oak sideboard. I was still picking the hairs off my trousers when Frau Lange came into the room. She was wearing a green silk dressing-gown of the sort that left the tops of her big breasts on show like the twin humps of some pink sea-monster, matching slippers, and she carried an unlit cigarette in her fingers. The dog stood dumbly at her corn-plastered heel, its nose wrinkling at the overpowering smell of English lavender that trailed off Frau Lange's body like an old feather-boa. Her voice was even more masculine than I had remembered.

'Just tell me that Reinhard had nothing to do with it,' she said imperiously.

'Nothing at all,' I said.

The sea-monster sank a little as she breathed a sigh of relief. 'Thank God for that,' she said. 'And do you know who it is that has been blackmailing me, Herr Günther?'

'Yes. A man who used to work at Kindermann's clinic. A male nurse called Klaus Hering. I don't suppose that the name will mean much to you, but Kindermann had to dismiss him a couple of months ago. My guess is that while he was working there he stole the letters that your son wrote to Kindermann.'

She sat down and lit her cigarette. 'But if his grudge was against Kindermann, why pick on me?'

'I'm just guessing, you understand, but I'd say that a lot has to do with your wealth. Kindermann's rich, but I doubt he's a tenth as rich as you, Frau Lange. What's more, it's probably mostly tied up in that clinic. He's also got quite a few friends in the SS, so Hering may have decided that it was simply safer to squeeze you. On the other hand, he may have already tried Kindermann and failed to get anywhere. As a psychotherapist he could probably easily explain your son's letters as the fantasies of a former patient. After all, it's not uncommon for a patient to grow attached to his doctor, even somebody as apparently loathsome as Kindermann.'

'You've met him?'

'No, but that's what I hear from some of the staff working at the clinic.'

'I see. Well, now what happens?'

'As I remember, you said that would be up to your son.'

'All right. Supposing that he wants you to go on handling things for us. After all, you've made pretty short work of it so far. What would your next course of action be?'

'Right now my partner, Herr Stahlecker, is keeping our friend Hering under surveillance at his apartment on Nollendorfplatz. As soon as Hering goes out, Herr Stahlecker will try and break in and recover your letters. After that you have three possibilities. One is that you can forget all about it. Another is that you can put the matter in the hands of the police, in which case you run the risk of Hering making allegations against your son. And then you can arrange for Hering to get a good old-fashioned hiding. Nothing too severe, you understand. Just a good scare to warn him off and teach him a lesson. Personally I always favour the third choice. Who knows? It might even result in your recovering some of your money.'

'Oh, I'd like to get my hands on that miserable man.'

'Best leave that sort of thing to me, eh? I'll call you tomorrow and you can tell me what you and your son have decided to do. With any luck we may even have recovered the letters by then.'

I didn't exactly need my arm twisted to have the brandy she offered me by way of celebration. It was excellent stuff that should have been savoured a little. But I was tired, and when she and the sea-monster joined me on the sofa I felt it was time to be going.

About that time I was living in a big apartment on Fasanenstrasse, a little way south of Kurfürstendamm, and within easy reach of all the theatres and better restaurants I never went to.

It was a nice quiet street, all white, mock porticoes and Atlantes supporting elaborate façades on their well-muscled shoulders. Cheap it wasn't. But that apartment and my partner had been my only two luxuries in two years.

The first had been rather more successful for me than the second. An impressive hallway with more marble than the Pergamon Altar led up to the second floor where I had a suite of rooms with ceilings that were as high as trams. German architects and builders were never known for their penny-pinching.

My feet aching like young love, I ran myself a hot bath.

I lay there for a long time, staring up at the stained-glass window which was suspended at right angles to the ceiling, and which served, quite redundantly, to offer some cosmetic division of the bathroom's higher regions. I had never ceased to puzzle as to what possible reason had prompted its construction.

Outside the bathroom window a nightingale sat in the yard's solitary but lofty tree. I felt that I had a lot more confidence in his simple song than the one that Hitler was singing.

I reflected that it was the kind of simplistic comparison my beloved pipe-smoking partner might have relished.

5

Tuesday, 6 September

In the darkness the doorbell rang. Drunk with sleep I reached across to the alarm clock and picked it off the bedside table. It said 4.30 in the morning with still nearly an hour to go before I was supposed to wake up. The doorbell rang again, only this time it seemed more insistent. I switched on a light and went out into the hall.

'Who is it?' I said, knowing well enough that generally it's only the Gestapo who take a pleasure in disturbing people's sleep.

'Haile Selassie,' said a voice. 'Who the fuck do you think it is? Come on, Günther, open up, we haven't got all night.'

Yes, it was the Gestapo all right. There was no mistaking their finishing-school manners.

I opened the door and allowed a couple of beer barrels wearing hats and coats to barge past me.

'Get dressed,' said one. 'You've got an appointment.'

'Shit, I am going to have to have a word with that secretary of mine,' I yawned. 'I forgot all about it.'

'Funny man,' said the other.

'What, is this Heydrich's idea of a friendly invitation?'

'Save your mouth to suck on your cigarette, will you? Now climb into your suit or we'll take you down in your fucking pyjamas.'

I dressed carefully, choosing my cheapest German Forest suit and an old pair of shoes. I stuffed my pockets with cigarettes. I even took along a copy of the *Berlin Illustrated News*. When Heydrich invites you for breakfast it's always best to be prepared for an uncomfortable and possibly indefinite visit.

★

Immediately south of Alexanderplatz, on Dircksenstrasse, the Imperial Police Praesidium and the Central Criminal Courts faced each other in an uneasy confrontation: legal administration versus justice. It was like two heavyweights standing toe to toe at the start of a fight, each trying to stare the other down.

Of the two, the Alex, also sometimes known as 'Grey Misery', was the more brutal looking, having a Gothic-fortress design with a dome-shaped tower at each corner, and two smaller towers atop the front and rear façades. Occupying some 16,000 square metres it was an object lesson in strength if not in architectural merit.

The slightly smaller building that housed the central Berlin courts also had the more pleasing aspect. Its neo-Baroque sandstone façade possessed something rather more subtle and intelligent than its opponent.

There was no telling which one of these two giants was likely to emerge the winner; but when both fighters have been paid to take a fall it makes no sense to stick around and watch the end of the contest.

Dawn was breaking as the car drew into Alex's central courtyard. It was still too early for me to have asked myself why Heydrich should have had me brought here, instead of Sipo, the Security Service headquarters in the Wilhelmstrasse, where Heydrich had his own office.

My two male escorts ushered me to an interview room and left me alone. There was a good deal of shouting going on in the room next door and that gave me something to think about. That bastard Heydrich. Never quite did it the way you expected. I took out a cigarette and lit it nervously. With the cigarette burning in a corner of my sour-tasting mouth I stood up and went over to the grimy window. All I could see were other windows like my own, and on the rooftop the aerial of the police radio station. I ground the cigarette into the Mexico Mixture coffee-tin that served as an ashtray and sat down at the table again.

I was supposed to get nervous. I was meant to feel their power. That way Heydrich would find me all the more inclined to agree with him when eventually he decided to show up. Probably he was still fast asleep in his bed.

If that was how I was supposed to feel I decided to do it differently. So instead of breakfasting on my fingernails and wearing out my cheap shoes pacing round the room, I tried a little self relaxation, or whatever it was that Dr Meyer had called it. Eyes closed, breathing deeply through my nose, my mind concentrated on a simple shape, I managed to remain calm. So calm I didn't even hear the door. After a while I opened my eyes and stared into the face of the bull who had come in. He nodded slowly.

'Well, you're a cool one,' he said, picking up my magazine.

'Aren't I just?' I looked at my watch. Half an hour had gone by. 'You took your time.'

'Did I? I'm sorry. Glad you weren't bored though. I can see you expected to be here a while.'

'Doesn't everyone?' I shrugged, watching a boil the size of a wheel-nut rub at the edge of his greasy collar.

When he spoke his voice came from deep within him, his scarred chin dipping down to his broad chest like a cabaret tenor.

'Oh yes,' he said. 'You're a private detective, aren't you? A professional smart-ass. Do you mind me asking, what kind of a living do you people make?'

'What's the matter, the bribes not coming in regular enough for you?' He forced himself to smile through that one. 'I do all right.'

'Don't you find that it gets lonely? I mean, you're a bull down here, you've got friends.'

'Don't make me laugh. I've got a partner, so I get all the friendly shoulder to cry on I need, right?'

'Oh yes. Your partner. That would be Bruno Stahlecker, wouldn't it?'

'That's right. I could give you his address if you like, but I think he's married.'

'All right, Günther. You've proved you're not scared. No need to make a performance out of it. You were picked up at 4.30. It's now seven —'

'Ask a policeman if you want the right time.'

'– but you still haven't asked anyone why you're here.'

'I thought that's what we were talking about.'

'Were we? Assume I'm ignorant. That shouldn't be too difficult for a smart-ass like you. What did we say?'

'Oh shit, look, this is your sideshow, not mine, so don't expect me to bring up the curtain and work the fucking lights. You go right ahead with your act and I'll just try to laugh and clap in the right places.'

'Very well,' he said, his voice hardening. 'So where were you last night?'

'At home.'

'Got an alibi?'

'Yeah. My teddy bear. I was in bed, asleep.'

'And before that?'

'I was seeing a client.'

'Mind telling me who?'

'Look, I don't like this. What are we trawling for? Tell me now, or I don't say another lousy word.'

'We've got your partner downstairs.'

'What's he supposed to have done?'

'What he's done is get himself killed.'

I shook my head. 'Killed?'

'Murdered, to be rather more precise. That's what we usually call it in these sort of circumstances.'

'Shit,' I said, closing my eyes again.

'That's my act, Günther. And I do expect you to help me with the curtain and the lights.' He jabbed a forefinger against my numb chest. 'So let's have some fucking answers, eh?'

'You stupid bastard. You don't think I had anything to do with it, do you? Christ, I was the only friend he had. When you and all your cute friends here at the Alex managed to have him posted out to some backwater in Spreewald, I was the one who came through for him. I was the one who appreciated that despite his awkward lack of enthusiasm for the Nazis, he was still a good bull.' I shook my head bitterly, and swore again.

'When did you last see him?'

'Last night, around eight o'clock. I left him in the car park behind the Metropol on Nollendorfplatz.'

'Was he working?'

'Yes.'

'Doing what?'

'Tailing someone. No, keeping someone under observation.'

'Someone working in the theatre or living in the apartments?' I nodded.

'Which was it?'

'I can't tell you. At least, not until I've discussed it with my client.'

'The one you can't tell me about either. Who do you think you are, a priest? This is murder, Günther. Don't you want to catch the man who killed your partner?'

'What do you think?'

'I think that you ought to consider the possibility that your client had something to do with it. And then suppose he says, "Herr Günther, I forbid you to discuss this unfortunate matter with the police." Where does that get us?' He shook his head. 'No fucking deal, Günther. You tell me or you tell the judge.' He stood up and went to the door. 'It's up to you. Take your time. I'm not in any hurry.'

He closed the door behind him, leaving me with my guilt for ever having wished ill to Bruno and his harmless pipe.

About an hour later the door opened and a senior SS officer came into the room.

'I was wondering when you'd show up,' I said.

Arthur Nebe sighed and shook his head.

'I'm sorry about Stahlecker,' he said. 'He was a good man. Naturally you'll want to see him.' He motioned me to follow him. 'And then I'm afraid you'll have to see Heydrich.'

Beyond an outer office and an autopsy-theatre where a pathologist stood working on the naked body of an adolescent girl was a
long, cool room with rows of tables stretching out in front of me.
On a few of them lay human bodies, some naked, some covered
with sheets, and some like Bruno still clothed and looking more
like items of lost luggage than anything human.

I walked over and took a long hard look at my dead partner.
The front of his shirt looked as though he had spilt a whole bottle
of red wine on himself, and his mouth gaped open like he'd been
stabbed sitting in a dentist's chair. There are lots of ways of winding up a partnership, but they didn't come much more permanent
than this one.

'I never knew he wore a plate,' I said absently, catching the glint
of something metallic inside Bruno's mouth. 'Stabbed?'

'Once, through the pump. They reckon under the ribs and up
through the pit of the stomach.'

I picked up each of his hands and inspected them carefully. 'No
protection cuts,' I said. 'Where did they find him?'

'Metropol Theatre car park,' said Nebe.

I opened his jacket, noticing the empty shoulder-holster, and
then unbuttoned the front of his shirt, which was still sticky with
his blood, to inspect the wound. It was difficult to tell without seeing him cleaned up a bit, but the entry looked split, as if the knife
had been rocked inside him.

'Whoever did it knew how to kill a man with a knife,' I said.
'This looks like a bayonet wound.' I sighed and shook my head.
'I've seen enough. There's no need to put his wife through this, I'll
make the formal identification. Does she know yet?'

Nebe shrugged. 'I don't know.' He led the way back through the
autopsy-theatre. 'But I expect someone will tell her soon enough.'

The pathologist, a young fellow with a large moustache, had
stopped work on the girl's body to have a smoke. The blood from
his gloved hand had stained the cigarette paper and there was some
of it on his lower lip. Nebe stopped and regarded the scene before
him with more than a little distaste.

'Well?' he said angrily. 'Is it another one?'

The pathologist exhaled lazily and pulled a face. 'At this early stage, it certainly looks that way,' he said. 'She's wearing all the right accessories.'

'I see.' It was easily apparent that Nebe didn't much care for the young pathologist. 'I trust your report will be rather more detailed than the last one. Not to mention more accurate.' He turned abruptly and walked quickly away, adding loudly over his shoulder, 'And make sure I have it as soon as possible.'

In Nebe's staff-car, on the way to the Wilhelmstrasse, I asked him what it was all about. 'Back there, in the autopsy-theatre, I mean.'

'My friend,' he said, 'I think that's what you're about to find out.'

The headquarters of Heydrich's SD, the Security Service, at number 102 Wilhelmstrasse, seemed innocuous enough from the outside. Even elegant. At each end of an Ionic colonnade was a square, two-storey gatehouse and an archway that led into a court-yard behind. A screen of trees made it difficult to see what lay beyond, and only the presence of two sentries told you that here was an official building of some sort.

We drove through the gate, past a neat shrub-lined lawn about the size of a tennis-court, and stopped outside a beautiful, three-storey building with arched windows that were as big as elephants. Stormtroopers jumped to open the car doors and we got out.

The interior wasn't quite what I had expected of Sipo HQ. We waited in a hall, the central feature of which was an ornate gilt staircase, decorated with fully-formed caryatids, and enormous chandeliers. I looked at Nebe, allowing my eyebrows to inform him that I was favourably impressed.

'It's not bad, is it?' he said, and taking me by the arm he led me to the French windows which looked out on to a magnificent landscaped garden. Beyond this, to the west, could be seen the modern outline of Gropius's Europa Haus, while to the north, the southern wing of Gestapo headquarters on Prinz Albrecht Strasse was clearly visible. I had good reason to recognize it, having once been detained there awhile at Heydrich's order.

At the same time, appreciating the difference between the SD, or Sipo as the Security Service was sometimes called, and the Gestapo was a rather more elusive matter, even for some of the people who worked for these two organizations. As far as I could understand the distinction, it was just like Bockwurst and Frankfurter: they have their special names, but they look and taste exactly the same.

What was easy to perceive was that with this building, the Prinz Albrecht Palais, Heydrich had done very well for himself. Perhaps even better than his putative master, Himmler, who now occupied the building next door to Gestapo headquarters, in what was formerly the Hotel Prinz Albrecht Strasse. There was no doubt that the old hotel, now called SS-Haus, was bigger than the Palais. But as with sausage, taste is seldom a question of size.

I heard Arthur Nebe's heels click, and looking round I saw that the Reich's crown prince of terror had joined us at the window.

Tall, skeletally thin, his long, pale face lacking expression, like some plaster of Paris death-mask, and his Jack Frost fingers clasped behind his ramrod-straight back, Heydrich stared outside for a moment or two, saying nothing to either of us.

'Come, gentlemen,' he said eventually, 'it's a beautiful day. Let's walk a bit.' Opening the windows he led the way into the garden, and I noticed how large were his feet and how bandy his legs, as if he had been riding a lot: if the silver Horseman's Badge on his tunic pocket was anything to go by, he probably had.

In the fresh air and sunshine he seemed to become more animated, like some kind of reptile.

'This was the summer house of the first Friedrich Wilhelm,' he said expansively. 'And more recently the Republic used it for important guests such as the King of Egypt, and the British prime minister. Ramsay MacDonald of course, not that idiot with the umbrella. I think it's one of the most beautiful of all the old palaces. I often walk here. This garden connects Sipo with Gestapo headquarters, so it's actually very convenient for me. And it's especially pleasant at this time of year. Do you have a garden, Herr Günther?'

'No,' I said. 'They've always seemed like a lot of work to me. When I stop work, that's exactly what I do – stop work, not start digging in a garden.'

'That's too bad. At my home in Schlactensee we have a fine garden with its own croquet lawn. Are either of you familiar with the game?'

'No,' we said in unison.

'It's an interesting game; I believe it's very popular in England. It provides an interesting metaphor for the new Germany. Laws are merely hoops through which the people must be driven, with varying degrees of force. But there can be no movement without the mallet – croquet really is a perfect game for a policeman.' Nebe nodded thoughtfully, and Heydrich himself seemed pleased with this comparison. He began to talk quite freely. In brief about some of the things he hated – Freemasons, Catholics, Jehovah's Witnesses, homosexuals and Admiral Canaris, the head of the Abwehr, German Military Secret Intelligence; and at length about some of the things that gave him pleasure – the piano and the cello, fencing, his favourite nightclubs and his family.

'The new Germany,' he said, 'is all about arresting the decline of the family, you know, and establishing a national community of blood. Things are changing. For instance, there are now only 22,787 tramps in Germany, 5,500 fewer than at the start of the year. There are more marriages, more births and half as many divorces. You might well ask me why the family is so important to the Party. Well, I'll tell you. Children. The better our children, the better the future for Germany. So when something threatens those children, then we had better act quickly.'

I found a cigarette and started to pay attention. It seemed like he was coming to the point at last. We stopped at a park bench and sat down, me between Heydrich and Nebe, the chicken-liver in the black-bread sandwich.

'You don't like gardens,' he said thoughtfully. 'What about children? Do you like them?'

'I like them.'

'Good,' he said. 'It's my own personal opinion that it is essential to like them, doing what we do – even the things we must do that are hard because they seem distasteful to us – for otherwise we can find no expression for our humanity. Do you understand what I mean?'

I wasn't sure I did, but I nodded anyway.

'May I be frank with you?' he said. 'In confidence?'

'Be my guest.'

'A maniac is loose on the streets of Berlin, Herr Günther.'

I shrugged. 'Not so as you would notice,' I said.

Heydrich shook his head impatiently.

'No, I don't mean a stormtrooper beating up some old Jew. I mean a murderer. He's raped and killed and mutilated four young German girls in as many months.'

'I haven't seen anything in the newspapers about it.'

Heydrich laughed. 'The newspapers print what we tell them to print, and there's an embargo on this particular story.'

'Thanks to Streicher and his anti-Semitic rag, it would only get blamed on the Jews,' said Nebe.

'Precisely so,' said Heydrich. 'The last thing I want is an anti-Jewish riot in this city. That sort of thing offends my sense of public order. It offends me as a policeman. When we do decide to clear out the Jews it will be in a proper way, not with a rabble to do it. There are the commercial implications too. A couple of weeks ago some idiots in Nuremberg decided to tear down a synagogue. One that just happened to be well-insured with a German insurance company. It cost them thousands of marks to settle the claim. So you see, race riots are very bad for business.'

'So why tell me?'

'I want this lunatic caught, and caught soon, Günther.' He looked drily at Nebe. 'In the best traditions of Kripo a man, a Jew, has already confessed to the murders. However, since he was almost certainly in custody at the time of the last murder, it seems that he might actually be innocent, and that an overzealous element in Nebe's beloved police force may quite simply have framed this man.

'But you, Günther, you have no racial or political axe to grind. And what is more you have considerable experience in this field of criminal investigation. After all it was you, was it not, who apprehended Gormann, the strangler? That may have been ten years ago, but everyone still remembers the case.' He paused and looked me straight in the eye – an uncomfortable sensation. 'In other words, I want you back, Günther. Back in Kripo, and tracking down this madman before he kills again.'

I flicked my cigarette-butt into the bushes and stood up. Arthur Nebe stared at me dispassionately, almost as if he disagreed with Heydrich's wish to have me back on the force and leading the investigation in preference to any of his own men. I lit another cigarette and thought for a moment.

'Hell, there must be other bulls,' I said. 'What about the one who caught Kürten, the Beast of Dusseldorf. Why not get him?'

'We've already checked up on him,' said Nebe. 'It would seem that Peter Kürten just gave himself up. Prior to that it was hardly the most efficient investigation.'

'Isn't there anyone else?'

Nebe shook his head.

'You see, Günther,' said Heydrich, 'we come back to you again. Quite frankly I doubt that there is a better detective in the whole of Germany.'

I laughed and shook my head. 'You're good. Very good. That was a nice speech you made about children and the family, General, but of course we both know that the real reason you're keeping the lid on this thing is because it makes your modern police force look like a bunch of incompetents. Bad for them, bad for you. And the real reason you want me back is not because I'm such a good detective, but because the rest are so bad. The only sort of crimes that today's Kripo is capable of solving are things like race-defilement, or telling a joke about the Führer.'

Heydrich smiled like a guilty dog, his eyes narrowing.

'Are you refusing me, Herr Günther?' he said evenly.

'I'd like to help, really I would. But your timing is poor. You see, I've only just found out that my partner was murdered last night. You can call me old-fashioned, but I'd like to find out who killed him. Ordinarily I'd leave it to the boys in the Murder Commission, but given what you've just told me it doesn't sound too promising, does it? They've all but accused me of killing him, so who knows, maybe they'll force me to sign a confession, in which case I'll have to work for you in order to escape the guillotine.'

'Naturally I'd heard about Herr Stahlecker's unfortunate death,' he said, standing up again. 'And of course you'll want to make some inquiries. If my men can be of any assistance, no matter how incompetent, then please don't hesitate. However, assuming for a moment that this obstacle were removed, what would be your answer?'

I shrugged. 'Assuming that if I refused I would lose my private investigator's licence –'

'Naturally . . .'

'– gun permit, driving licence –'

'No doubt we'd find some excuse . . .'

'– then probably I would be forced to accept.'

'Excellent.'

'On one condition.'

'Name it.'

'That for the duration of the investigation, I be given the rank of Kriminalkommissar and that I be allowed to run the investigation any way I want.'

'Now wait a minute,' said Nebe. 'What's wrong with your old rank of inspector?'

'Quite apart from the salary,' said Heydrich, 'Günther is no doubt keen that he should be as free as possible from the interference of senior officers. He's quite right of course. He'll need that kind of rank in order to overcome the prejudices that will undoubtedly accompany his return to Kripo. I should have thought of it myself. It is agreed.'

We walked back to the Palais. Inside the door an SD officer handed Heydrich a note. He read it and then smiled.

'Isn't that a coincidence?' he smiled. 'It would seem that my incompetent police force has found the man who murdered your partner, Herr Günther. I wonder, does the name Klaus Hering mean anything to you?'

'Stahlecker was keeping a watch on his apartment when he was killed.'

'That is good news. The only sand in the oil is that this Hering fellow would appear to have committed suicide.' He looked at Nebe and smiled. 'Well, we had better go and take a look, don't you think, Arthur? Otherwise Herr Günther here will think that we have made it up.'

It is difficult to form any clear impression of a man who has been hanged that is not grotesque. The tongue, turgid and protruding like a third lip, the eyes as prominent as a racing dog's balls – these things tend to colour your thoughts a little. So apart from the feeling that he wouldn't be winning the local debating-society prize, there wasn't much to say about Klaus Hering except that he was about thirty years old, slimly built, fair-haired and, thanks in part to his necktie, getting on for tall.

The thing looked clear-cut enough. In my experience hanging is almost always suicide: there are easier ways to kill a man. I have seen a few exceptions, but these were all accidental cases, where the victim had encountered the mishap of vagal inhibition while going about some sado-masochistic perversion. These sexual non-conformists were usually found naked or clothed in female underwear with a spread of pornographic literature to sticky hand, and were always men.

In Hering's case there was no such evidence of death by sexual misadventure. His clothes were such as might have been chosen by his mother; and his hands, which were loose at his sides, were unfettered eloquence to the effect that his homicide had been self-inflicted.

Inspector Strunck, the bull who had interrogated me back at the Alex, explained the matter to Heydrich and Nebe.

'We found this man's name and address in Stahlecker's pocket,' he said. 'There's a bayonet wrapped in newspaper in the kitchen. It's covered in blood, and from the look of it I'd say it was the knife that killed him. There's also a bloodstained shirt that Hering was probably wearing at the time.'

'Anything else?' said Nebe.

'Stahlecker's shoulder-holster was empty, General,' said Strunck. 'Perhaps Günther might like to tell us if this was his gun or not. We found it in a paper bag with the shirt.'

He handed me a Walther PPK. I put the muzzle to my nose and sniffed the gun-oil. Then I worked the slide and saw that there wasn't even a bullet in the barrel, although the magazine was full. Next I pulled down the trigger-guard. Bruno's initials were scratched neatly on the black metal.

'It's Bruno's gun, all right,' I said. 'It doesn't look like he even got his hand on it. I'd like to see that shirt please.'

Strunck glanced at his Reichskriminaldirektor for approval.

'Let him see it, Inspector,' said Nebe.

The shirt was from C & A, and heavily bloodstained around the stomach area and the right cuff, which seemed to confirm the general set-up.

'It does look as though this was the man who murdered your partner, Herr Günther,' said Heydrich. 'He came back here and, having changed his clothes, had a chance to reflect upon what he'd done. In a fit of remorse he hanged himself.'

'It would seem so,' I said, without much uncertainty. 'But if you don't mind, General Heydrich, I'd like to take a look round the place. On my own. Just to satisfy my curiosity about one or two things.'

'Very well. Don't be too long, will you?'

With Heydrich, Nebe and the police gone from the apartment, I took a closer look at Klaus Hering's body. Apparently he had tied a length of electrical cord to the banister, slipped a noose over his head, and then simply stepped off the stair. But only an inspection of Hering's hands, wrists and neck itself could tell me if that had really been what happened. There was something about the circumstances of his death, something I couldn't quite put my finger on, that I found questionable. Not least was the fact that he had chosen to change his shirt before hanging himself.

I climbed over the banister on to a small shelf that was made by the top of the stairwell's wall, and knelt down. Leaning forward, I had a good view of the suspension point behind Hering's right ear. The level of tightening of the ligature is always higher and more vertical with a hanging than with a case of strangulation. But here there was a second and altogether more horizontal mark just below the noose which seemed to confirm my doubts. Before hanging himself, Klaus Hering had been strangled to death.

I checked that Hering's shirt collar was the same size as the bloodstained shirt I had examined earlier. It was. Then I climbed back over the banister and stepped down a few stairs. Standing on tiptoe I reached up to examine his hands and wrists. Prising the right hand open I saw the dried blood and then a small shiny object, which seemed to be sticking into the palm. I pulled it out of Hering's flesh and laid it carefully on to the flat of my hand. The pin was bent, probably from the pressure of Hering's fist, and although encrusted with blood, the death's-head motif was unmistakable. It was an SS cap badge.

I paused briefly, trying to imagine what might have happened, certain now that Heydrich must have had a hand in it. Back in the garden at the Prinz Albrecht Palais, had he not asked me himself what my answer to his proposition would be if 'the obstacle' that was my obligation to find Bruno's murderer, were 'removed'? And wasn't this as completely removed as it was possible to achieve? No doubt he had anticipated what my answer would be and had already ordered Hering's murder by the time we went for our stroll.

With these and other thoughts I searched the apartment. I was quick but thorough, lifting mattresses, examining cisterns, rolling back rugs and even leafing through a set of medical textbooks. I managed to find a whole sheet of the old stamps commemorating the fifth anniversary of the Nazis coming to power which had consistently appeared on the blackmail notes to Frau Lange. But of her son's letters to Dr Kindermann there was no sign.

6

Friday, 9 September

It felt strange being back in a case-meeting at the Alex, and even stranger hearing Arthur Nebe refer to me as Kommissar Günther. Five years had elapsed since the day in June 1933 when, no longer able to tolerate Goering's police purges, I had resigned my rank of Kriminalinspektor in order to become the house detective at the Adlon Hotel. Another few months and they would have probably fired me anyway. If anyone had said then that I'd be back at the Alex as a member of Kripo's upper officer class while a National Socialist government was still in power, I'd have said that he was crazy.

Most of the people seated round the table would almost certainly have expressed the same opinion, if their faces were anything to go by now: Hans Lobbes, the Reichskriminaldirektor's number three and head of Kripo Executive; Count Fritz von der Schulenberg, deputy to Berlin's Police President, and representing the uniformed boys of Orpo. Even the three officers from Kripo, one from Vice and two from the Murder Commission who had been assigned to a new investigating team that was, at my own request, to be a small one, all regarded me with a mixture of fear and loathing. Not that I blamed them much. As far as they were concerned I was Heydrich's spy. In their position I would probably have felt much the same way.

There were two other people in attendance at my invitation, which compounded the atmosphere of distrust. One of these, a woman, was a forensic psychiatrist from the Berlin Charité Hospital. Frau Marie Kalau vom Hofe was a friend of Arthur Nebe, himself something of a criminologist, and attached officially to police headquarters as a consultant in matters of criminal psychology. The other guest was Hans Illmann, Professor of Forensic Medicine at the Friedrich Wilhelm University in Berlin, and formerly senior pathologist at the Alex until his cool hostility to Nazism had obliged Nebe to retire him. Even by Nebe's own admission, Illmann was better than any of the pathologists currently working at the Alex, and so at my request he had been invited to take charge of the forensic medical aspects of the case.

A spy, a woman and a political dissident. It needed only the stenographer to stand and sing 'The Red Flag' for my new colleagues to believe that they were the subject of a practical joke.

Nebe finished his long-winded introduction of me and the meeting was in my hands.

I shook my head. 'I hate bureaucracy,' I said. 'I loathe it. But what is required here is a bureaucracy of information. What is relevant will become clear later on. Information is the lifeblood of any criminal investigation, and if that information is contaminated then you poison the whole investigative body. I don't mind if a man's wrong about something. In this game we're nearly always wrong until we're right. But if I find a member of my team knowingly submitting wrong information, it won't be a matter for a disciplinary tribunal. I'll kill him. That's information you can depend on.

'I'd also like to say this. I don't care who did it. Jew, nigger, pansy, stormtrooper, Hitler Youth Leader, civil servant, motorway construction worker, it's all the same to me. Just as long as he did do it. Which leads me to the subject of Josef Kahn. In case any of you have forgotten, he's the Jew who confessed to the murders of Brigitte Hartmann, Christiane Schulz, and Zarah Lischka. Currently he's a Paragraph Fifty-one in the municipal lunatic asylum at Herzeberge, and one of the purposes of this meeting is to evaluate that confession in the light of the fourth murdered girl, Lotte Winter.

'At this point let me introduce you to Professor Hans Illmann, who has kindly agreed to act as the pathologist in this case. For

those of you who don't know him, he's one of the best pathologists in the country, so we're very fortunate to have him working
with us.'

Illmann nodded by way of acknowledgement, and carried on
with his perfect roll-up. He was a slight man with thin, dark hair,
rimless glasses and a small chin beard. He finished licking the paper
and poked the roll-up into his mouth, as good as any machine-
made cigarette, I marvelled quietly. Medical brilliance counted for
nothing beside this kind of subtle dexterity.

'Professor Illmann will take us through his findings after Kriminalassistent Korsch has read the relevant case note.' I nodded at
the dark, stocky young man sitting opposite me. There was something artificial about his face, as if it had been made up for him by
one of the police artists from Sipo Technical Services, with three
definite features and very little else: eyebrows joined in the middle
and perched on his overhanging brows like a falcon preparing for
flight; a wizard's long, crafty chin; and a small, Fairbanks-style
moustache. Korsch cleared his throat and began speaking in a voice
that was an octave higher than I was expecting.

'Brigitte Hartmann,' he read. 'Aged fifteen, of German parents.
Disappeared 23 May 1938. Body found in a potato sack on an allotment in Siesdorf, 10 June. She lived with her parents on the Britz
Housing Estate, south of Neukölln, and had walked from her
home to catch the U-Bahn at Parchimerallee. She was going to
visit her aunt in Reinickdorf. The aunt was supposed to meet her
at Holzhauser Strasse station, only Brigitte never arrived. The station master at Parchimer didn't remember her getting on the train,
but said that he'd had a night on the beer and probably wouldn't
have remembered anyway.' This drew a guffaw from along the table.

'Drunken bastard,' snorted Hans Lobbes.

'This is one of the two girls who have since been buried,' said
Illmann quietly. 'I don't think there's anything I can add to the
findings of the autopsy there. You may proceed, Herr Korsch.'

'Christiane Schulz. Aged sixteen, of German parents. Disappeared 8 June 1938. Body found 2 July, in a tramway tunnel that

connects Treptower Park on the righthand bank of the Spree, with the village of Stralau on the other. Half way along the tunnel there's a maintenance point, little more than a recessed archway. That's where the trackman found her body, wrapped in an old tarpaulin.

'Apparently the girl was a singer and often took part in the BdM, the League of German Girls, evening radio programme. On the night of her disappearance she had attended the Funkturm Studios on Masuren-Strasse, and sang a solo – the Hitler Youth song – at seven o'clock. The girl's father works as an engineer at the Arado Aircraft Works in Brandenburg-Neuendorf, and was supposed to pick her up on his way home, at eight o'clock. But the car had a flat tyre and he was twenty minutes late. By the time he got to the studios Christiane was nowhere to be seen and, supposing that she had gone home on her own, he drove back to Spandau. When by 9.30 she still hadn't arrived, and having contacted her closest friends, he called the police.'

Korsch glanced up at Illmann, and then myself. He smoothed the vain little moustache and turned to the next page in the file that lay open in front of him.

'Zarah Lischka,' he read. 'Aged sixteen, of German parents. Disappeared 6 July 1938, body found 1 August, down a drain in the Tiergarten, close to the Siegessäule. The family lived in Anton-strasse, Wedding. The father works at the slaughterhouse on Landsbergerallee. The girl's mother sent her down to some shops located on Lindowerstrasse, close to the S-Bahn station. The shop-keeper remembers serving her. She bought some cigarettes, although neither one of her parents smokes, some Blueband and a loaf of bread. Then she went to the pharmacy next door. The owner also remembers her. She bought some Schwarzkopf Extra Blonde hair colourant.'

Sixty out of every hundred German girls use it, I told myself almost automatically. It was funny the sort of junk I was remembering these days. I don't think I could have told you much of what was really important in the world other than what was happening in the German Sudeten areas – the riots, and the nationality conferences in Prague. It remained to be seen whether or not what was happening in Czechoslovakia was the only thing that really mattered after all.

Illmann stubbed out his cigarette and began to read his findings.

'The girl was naked, and there were signs that her feet had been bound. She had sustained two knife wounds to the throat. Nevertheless there existed strong indications that she had also been strangled, probably to silence her. It is likely that she was unconscious when the murderer cut her throat. The bruising bisected by the wounds suggests as much. And this is interesting. From the amount of blood still in her feet, and the crusted blood found inside her nose and on her hair, as well as the fact that the feet had been very tightly bound, it is my finding that the girl was hanging upside down when her throat was cut. Like a pig.'

'Jesus,' said Nebe.

'From my examination of the case notes of the previous two victims, it seems highly probable that the same *modus operandi* was applied there too. The suggestion made by my predecessor that these girls had their throats cut while they lay flat on the ground is patently nonsense, and takes no account of the abrasions to the ankles, or the amount of blood left in the feet. Indeed, it seems nothing short of negligent.'

'That is noted,' said Arthur Nebe, writing. 'Your predecessor is, in my opinion also, an incompetent.'

'The girl's vagina was undamaged and not penetrated,' continued Illmann. 'However, the anus gaped wide, permitting the passage of two fingers. Tests for spermatozoa proved positive.'

Somebody groaned.

'The stomach was flacid and was empty. Apparently Brigitte ate apfelkraut and bread-and-butter for lunch before going to the station. All food had been digested at the time of death. But apple is not easily digested, absorbing water as it does. Thus I would put this girl's death at between six and eight hours after she ate lunch, and therefore a couple of hours after she was reported missing. The obvious conclusion is that she was abducted and then later killed.'

I looked at Korsch. 'And the last one please, Herr Korsch.'

'Lotte Winter,' he said. 'Aged sixteen, of German parents. Disappeared 18 July 1938, her body found 25 August. She lived in Pragerstrasse, and attended the local grammar school where she was studying for her Middle Standard. She left home to have a riding lesson with Tattersalls at the Zoo, and never arrived. Her body was found inside the length of an old canoe in a boathouse near Muggel Lake.'

'Our man gets around, doesn't he?' said Count von der Schulenberg quietly.

'Like the Black Death,' said Lobbes.

Illmann took over once again.

'Strangled,' he said. 'Resulting in fractures of voice box, hyoid, thyroid cornua and alae, indicating a greater degree of violence than in the case of the Schulz girl. This girl was stronger, being more athletically inclined in the first place. She may have put up more of a fight. Suffocation was the cause of death here, although the carotid artery on the right side of her neck had been slashed. As before, the feet showed signs of having been tied together, and there was blood in the hair and nostrils. Undoubtedly she was hanging upside down when her throat was cut, and similarly her body was almost drained of blood.'

'Sounds like a fucking vampire,' exclaimed one of the detectives from the Murder Commission. He glanced at Frau Kalau vom Hofe. 'Sorry,' he added. She shook her head.

'Any sexual interference?' I asked.

'Because of the disagreeable odour, the girl's vagina had to be irrigated,' announced Illmann to more groans, 'and so no sperm could be found. However, the vaginal entrance did show scratch marks, and there was a trace of bruising to the pelvis, indicating that she had been penetrated – and forcibly.'

'Before her throat was cut?' I asked. Illmann nodded. The room was silent for a moment. Illmann set about fixing another roll-up.

'And now another girl has disappeared,' I said. 'Is that not correct, Inspector Deubel?'

Deubel shifted uncomfortably in his chair. He was a big, blond fellow with grey, haunted eyes that looked as though they had seen too much late-night police-work of the kind that requires you to wear thick leather protective gloves.

'Yes, sir,' he said. 'Her name is Irma Hanke.'

'Well, since you are the investigating officer, perhaps you would care to tell us something about her.'

He shrugged. 'She's from a nice German family. Aged seventeen, lives in Schloss Strasse, Steglitz.' He paused as his eye flicked down his notes. 'Disappeared Wednesday, 24 August, having left the house to collect for the Reich Economy Programme, on behalf of the BdM.' He paused again.

'And what was she collecting?' said the count.

'Old toothpaste tubes, sir. I believe that the metal is —'

'Thank you, Inspector, I know what the scrap value of toothpaste tubes is.'

'Yes, sir.' He glanced at his notes again. 'She was reported as having been seen on Feuerbachstrasse, Thorwaldsenstrasse, and Munster Damm. Munster Damm runs south beside a cemetery, and the sexton there says he saw a BdM girl answering Irma's description walking there at about 8.30 p.m. He thought she was heading west, in the direction of Bismarckstrasse. She was probably returning home, having said to her parents that she would be back at around 8.45. She never arrived, of course.'

'Any leads?' I asked.

'None, sir,' he said firmly.

'Thank you, Inspector.' I lit a cigarette, and then held the match to Illmann's roll-up. 'Very well then,' I puffed. 'So what we have are five girls, all of them about the same age, and all of them conforming to the Aryan stereotype that we know and love so well. In other words, they all had blonde hair, naturally or otherwise.

'Now, after our third Rhine maiden is murdered, Josef Kahn gets himself arrested for the attempted rape of a prostitute. In other words, he tried to leave without paying.'

'Typical Jew,' said Lobbes. There were a few laughs at that.

'As it happened, Kahn was carrying a knife, quite a sharp one at that, and he even has a minor criminal record for small theft and indecent assault. Very convenient. So the arresting officer at Grolmanstrasse Police Station, namely one Inspector Willi Oehme, decides to turn a few cards and see if he can't make twenty-one. He has a chat with young Josef, who's a bit soft in the head, and what with his honey-tongue and his thick knuckles, Willi manages to persuade Josef to sign a confession.

'Gentlemen, here I'd like to introduce you all to Frau Kalau vom Hofe. I say "Frau", as she's not allowed to call herself a doctor, although she is one, because she is very evidently a woman, and we all know, don't we, that a woman's place is in the home, producing recruits for the Party, and cooking the old man's dinner. She is in fact a psychotherapist, and is an acknowledged expert on that unfathomable little mystery that we refer to as the Criminal Mind.'

My eyes looked and licked at the creamy woman who sat at the far end of the table. She wore a magnolia skirt and a white marocain blouse, and her fair hair was pinned up in a tight bun at the back of her finely sculpted head. She smiled at my introduction and took a file out of her briefcase and opened it in front of her.

'When Josef Kahn was a child,' she said, 'he contracted acute encephalitis lethargica, which occurred in epidemic form among children in Western Europe between 1915 and 1926. This produced a gross change in his personality. After the acute phase of the illness, children may become increasingly restless, irritable, aggressive even, and appear to lose all moral sense. They beg, steal, lie and are often cruel. They talk incessantly and become unmanageable at school and at home. Abnormal sexual curiosity and sexual problems are often observed. Post-encephalitic adolescents sometimes show certain features of this syndrome, especially the lack of sexual restraint, and this is certainly true in Josef Kahn's case. He is also developing Parkinsonism, which will result in his increased physical debilitation.'

Count von der Schulenberg yawned and looked at his wrist-watch. But the doctor was not deterred. Instead she seemed to find his bad manners amusing.

'Despite his apparent criminality,' she said, 'I do not think that Josef killed any of these girls. Having discussed the forensic evidence with Professor Illmann, I am of the opinion that these killings show a level of premeditation of which Kahn is simply incapable. Kahn is capable only of the kind of frenzied murder that would have had him leave the victim where she fell.'

Illmann nodded. 'An analysis of his statement reveals a number of discrepancies with the known facts,' he said. 'His statement says that he used a stocking for the strangulations. The evidence, however, shows quite clearly that bare hands were used. He says that he stabbed his victims in the stomach. The evidence shows that none of them was stabbed, that they were all slashed across the throat. Then there is the fact that the fourth murder must have occurred while Kahn was in custody. Could this murder be the work of a different killer, someone copying the first three? No. Because there has been no press coverage of the first three to copy. And no, because the similarities between all four murders are too strong. They are all the work of the same man.' He smiled at Frau Kalau vom Hofe. 'Is there anything you wish to add to that, madam?'

'Only that that man could not possibly be Josef Kahn,' she said. 'And that Josef Kahn has been the subject of a form of fraud that one might have thought was impossible in the Third Reich.' There was a smile on her mouth as she closed her file and sat back in her chair, opening her cigarette case. Smoking, like being a doctor, was something else that women weren't supposed to do, but I could see that it wasn't the sort of thing that would have given her too many qualms.

It was the count who spoke next.

'In the light of this information, may one inquire of the

Reichskriminaldirektor if the ban on news-reporting that has applied in this case will now be lifted?' His belt creaked as he leant across the table, apparently eager to hear Nebe's reply. The son of a well-known general who was now the ambassador to Moscow, young von der Schulenberg was impeccably well-connected. When Nebe didn't answer, he added: 'I don't see how one can possibly impress upon the parents of girls in Berlin the need for caution without some sort of official statement in the newspapers. Naturally I will make sure that every Anwärter on the force is made aware of the need for vigilance on the street. However, it would be easier for my men in Orpo if there were some assistance from the Reich Ministry of Propaganda.'

'It's an accepted fact in criminology,' said Nebe smoothly, 'that publicity can act as an encouragement to a murderer like this, as I'm sure Frau Kalau vom Hofe will confirm.'

'That's correct,' she said. 'Mass murderers do seem to like to read about themselves in the newspapers.'

'However,' Nebe continued, 'I will make a point of telephoning the Muratti building today, and asking them if there is not some propaganda that can be directed towards young girls being made more aware of the need to be careful. At the same time, any such campaign would have to receive the blessing of the Obergruppenführer. He is most anxious that there is nothing said which might create a panic amongst German women.'

The count nodded. 'And now,' he said, looking at me, 'I have a question for the Kommissar.'

He smiled, but I wasn't about to place too much reliance on it. He gave every impression of having attended the same school in supercilious sarcasm as Obergruppenführer Heydrich. Mentally I lifted my guard in readiness for the first punch.

'As the detective who ingeniously solved the celebrated case of Gormann the strangler, will he share with us now his initial thoughts in this particular case?'

The colourless smile persisted beyond what might have seemed comfortable, as if he was straining at his tight sphincter. At least,

I assumed it was tight. As the deputy of a former SA man, Count Wolf von Helldorf, who was reputed to be as queer as the late SA boss Ernst Röhm, Schulenberg might well have had the kind of arse that would have tempted a short-sighted pickpocket.

Sensing that there was even more to be made of this disingenuous line of inquiry, he added· 'Perhaps an indication as to the kind of character we might be looking for?'

'I think I can help the administrative president there,' said Frau Kalau vom Hofe. The count's head jerked irritatedly in her direction.

She reached down into her briefcase and laid a large book on to the table. And then another, and another, until there was a pile as high as one of von der Schulenberg's highly polished jackboots.

'Anticipating just such a question, I took the liberty of bringing along several books dealing with the psychology of the criminal,' she said. 'Heindl's *Professional Criminal*, Wulffen's excellent *Handbook of Sexual Delinquency*, Hirschfeld's *Sexual Pathology*, F. Alexander's *The Criminal and his Judges* –'

This was too much for him. He collected his papers off the table and stood up, smiling nervously.

'Another time perhaps, Frau vom Hofe,' he said. Then he clicked his heels, bowed stiffly to the room and left.

'Bastard,' muttered Lobbes.

'It's quite all right,' she said, adding some copies of the German Police Journal to the pile of textbooks. 'You can't teach Hans what he won't learn.' I smiled, appreciating her cool resilience, as well as the fine breasts which strained at the material of her blouse.

After the meeting was concluded, I lingered there a little in order to be alone with her.

'He asked a good question,' I said. 'One to which I didn't have much of an answer. Thanks for coming to my assistance when you did.'

'Please don't mention it,' she said, starting to return some of her books to the briefcase. I picked one of them up and glanced at it.

'You know, I'd be interested to hear your answer. Can I buy you a drink?'

She looked at her watch. 'Yes,' she smiled. 'I'd like that.'

Die Letze Instanz, at the end of Klosterstrasse on the old city wall, was a local bar much favoured by bulls from the Alex and court officials from the nearby court of last instance, from which the place took its name.

Inside it was all dark-brown wood-panelled walls and flagged floors. Near the bar, with its great draught pump of yellow ceramic, on top of which stood the figure of a seventeenth-century soldier, was a large seat made of green, brown and yellow tiles, all with moulded figures and heads. It had the look of a very cold and uncomfortable throne, and on it sat the bar's owner, Warnstorff, a pale-skinned, dark-haired man wearing a collarless shirt and a capacious leather apron that was also his bag of change. When we arrived he greeted me warmly and showed us to a quiet table in the back, where he brought us a couple of beers. At another table a man was dealing vigorously with the biggest piece of pig's knuckle either of us had ever seen.

'Are you hungry?' I asked her.

'Not now I've seen him,' she said.

'Yes, I know what you mean. It does put you off rather, doesn't it? You'd think he was trying to win the Iron Cross the way he's battling that joint.'

She smiled, and we were silent for a moment. Eventually she said, 'Do you think there's going to be a war?'

I stared into the top of my beer as if expecting the answer to float to the surface. I shrugged and shook my head.

'I haven't really been keeping that close an eye on things lately,' I said, and explained about Bruno Stahlecker and my return to Kripo. 'But shouldn't I be asking you? As the expert on criminal psychology you should have a better appreciation of the Führer's mind than most people. Would you say his behaviour was compulsive or irresistible within the definition of Paragraph Fifty-one of the Criminal Code?'

It was her turn to search for inspiration in a glass of beer.

'We don't really know each other well enough for this kind of conversation, do we?' she said.

'I suppose not.'

'I will say this, though,' she said lowering her voice. 'Have you ever read *Mein Kampf*?'

'That funny old book they give free to all newlyweds? It's the best reason to stay single I can think of.'

'Well, I have read it. And one of the things I noticed was that there is one passage, as long as seven pages, in which Hitler makes repeated references to venereal disease and its effects. Indeed, he actually says that the elimination of venereal disease is The Task that faces the German nation.'

'My God, are you saying that he's syphilitic?'

'I'm not saying anything. I'm just telling you what is written in the Führer's great book.'

'But the book's been around since the mid-twenties. If he's had a hot tail since then his syphilis would have to be tertiary.'

'It might interest you to know,' she said, 'that many of Josef Kahn's fellow inmates at the Herzeberge Asylum are those whose organic dementia is a direct result of their syphilis. Contradictory statements can be made and accepted. The mood varies between euphoria and apathy, and there is general emotional instability. The classic type is characterized by a demented euphoria, delusions of grandeur and bouts of extreme paranoia.'

'Christ, the only thing you left out was the crazy moustache,' I said. I lit a cigarette and puffed at it dismally. 'For God's sake change the subject. Let's talk about something cheerful, like our mass-murdering friend. Do you know, I'm beginning to see his point, I really am. I mean, these are tomorrow's young mothers he's killing. More childbearing machines to produce new Party recruits. Me, I'm all for these by-products of the asphalt civilization they're always on about – the childless families with eugenically dud women, at least until we've got rid of this regime of rubber truncheons. What's one more psychopath among so many?'

'You say more than you know,' she said. 'We're all of us capable of cruelty. Every one of us is a latent criminal. Life is just a battle to maintain a civilized skin. Many sadistic killers find that it's only occasionally that it comes off. Peter Kurten for example. He was apparently a man of such a kindly disposition that nobody who knew him could believe that he was capable of such horrific crimes as he committed.'

She rummaged in her briefcase again and, having wiped the table, she laid a thin blue book between our two glasses.

'This book is by Carl Berg, a forensic pathologist who had the opportunity of studying Kurten at length following his arrest. I've met Berg and respect his work. He founded the Düsseldorf Institute of Legal and Social Medicine, and for a while he was the medico-legal officer of the Düsseldorf Criminal Court. This book, *The Sadist*, is probably one of the best accounts of the mind of the murderer that has ever been written. You can borrow it if you like.'

'Thanks, I will.'

'That will help you to understand,' she said. 'But to enter into the mind of a man like Kurten, you should read this.' Again she dipped into the bag of books.

'*Les Fleurs du mal*,' I read, 'by Charles Baudelaire.' I opened it and looked over the verses. 'Poetry?' I raised an eyebrow.

'Oh, don't look so suspicious, Kommissar. I'm being perfectly serious. It's a good translation, and you'll find a lot more in it than you might expect, believe me.' She smiled at me.

'I haven't read poetry since I studied Goethe at school.'

'And what was your opinion of him?'

'Do Frankfurt lawyers make good poets?'

'It's an interesting critique,' she said. 'Well, let's hope you think better of Baudelaire. And now I'm afraid I must be going.' She stood up and we shook hands. 'When you've finished with the books

you can return them to me at the Goering Institute on Budapes-
terstrasse. We're just across the road from the Zoo Aquarium. I'd
certainly be interested to hear a detective's opinion of Baudelaire,'
she said.

'It will be my pleasure. And you can tell me your opinion of
Dr Lanz Kindermann.'

'Kindermann? You know Lanz Kindermann?'

'In a way.'

She gave me a judicious sort of look. 'You know, for a police
Kommissar you are certainly full of surprises. You certainly are.'

7

Sunday, 11 September

I prefer my tomatoes when they've still got some green left in them. Then they're sweet and firm, with smooth, cool skins, the sort you would choose for a salad. But when a tomato has been around for a while, it picks up a few wrinkles as it grows too soft to handle, and even begins to taste a little sour.

It's the same with women. Only this one was perhaps a shade green for me, and possibly rather too cool for her own good. She stood at my front door and gave me an impertinent sort of north-to-south-and-back-again look, as if she was trying to assess my prowess, or lack of it, as a lover.

'Yes?' I said. 'What do you want?'

'I'm collecting for the Reich,' she explained, playing games with her eyes. She held a bag of material out, as if to corroborate her story. 'The Party Economy Programme. Oh, the concierge let me in.'

'I can see that. Exactly what would you like?'

She raised an eyebrow at that and I wondered if her father thought she wasn't still young enough for him to spank.

'Well, what have you got?' There was a quiet mockery in her tone. She was pretty, in a sulky, sultry sort of way. In civilian clothes she might have passed for a girl of twenty, but with her two pigtails, and dressed in the sturdy boots, long navy skirt, trim white blouse and brown leather jacket of the BdM – the League of German Girls – I guessed her to be no more than sixteen.

'I'll have a look and see what I can find,' I said, half amused at her grown-up manner, which seemed to confirm what you some-times heard of BdM girls, which was that they were sexually promiscuous and just as likely to get themselves pregnant at Hitler Youth Camp as they were to learn needlework, first aid and German folk history. 'I suppose you had better come in.'

The girl sauntered through the door as if she were trailing a mink wrap and gave the hall a cursory examination. She didn't seem to be much impressed. 'Nice place,' she murmured quietly.

I closed the door and laid my cigarette in the ashtray on the hall table. 'Wait here,' I told her.

I went into the bedroom and foraged under the bed for the suitcase where I kept old shirts and threadbare towels, not to mention all my spare house dust and carpet fluff. When I stood up and brushed myself off she was leaning in the doorway and smoking my cigarette. Insolently she blew a perfect smoke-ring towards me.

'I thought you Faith-and-Beauty girls weren't supposed to smoke,' I said, trying to conceal my irritation.

'Is that a fact?' she smirked. 'There are quite a few things we're not encouraged to do. We're not supposed to do this, we're not supposed to do that. Just about everything seems to be wicked these days, doesn't it? But what I always say is, if you can't do the wicked things when you're still young enough to enjoy them, then what's the point of doing them at all?' She jerked herself away from the wall and stalked out.

Quite the little bitch, I thought, following her into the sitting-room next door.

She inhaled noisily, like she was sucking at a spoonful of soup, and blew another smoke-ring in my face. If I could have caught it I would have wrapped it round her pretty little neck.

'Anyway,' she said, 'I hardly think one little drummer is going to knock over the heap, do you?'

I laughed. 'Do I look like the sort of dog's ear who would smoke cheap cigarettes?'

'No, I suppose not,' she admitted. 'What's your name?'

'Plato.'

'Plato. It suits you. Well, Plato, you can kiss me if you want.'

'You don't creep around it, do you?'

'Haven't you heard the nicknames they have for the BdM? The German Mattress League? Commodities for German Men?' She put her arms about my neck and performed a variety of coquettish expressions she'd probably practised in front of her dressing-table mirror.

Her hot young breath tasted stale, but I let myself equal the competence in her kiss, just to be affable, my hands squeezing at her young breasts, kneading the nipples with my fingers. Then I cupped her chubby behind in both my moistening palms, and drew her closer to what was increasingly on my mind. Her naughty eyes went round as she pressed herself against me. I can't honestly say I wasn't tempted.

'Do you know any good bedtime stories, Plato?' she giggled.

'No,' I said, tightening my grip on her. 'But I know plenty of bad ones. The kind where the beautiful but spoilt princess gets boiled alive and eaten up by the wicked troll.'

A vague glimmer of doubt began to grow in the bright blue iris of each corrupt eye, and her smile was no longer wholly confident as I hauled up her skirt and started to tug her pants down.

'Oh, I could tell you lots of stories like that,' I said darkly. 'The sort of stories that policemen tell their daughters. Horrible gruesome stories that give girls the kind of nightmares which their fathers can be glad of.'

'Stop it,' she laughed nervously. 'You're frightening me.' Certain now that things weren't going quite to plan, she reached desperately for her pants as I yanked them down her legs, exposing the fledgling that nestled in her groin.

'They're glad because it means that their pretty little daughters will be much too scared to ever go into a strange man's house, just in case he should turn into a wicked troll.'

'Please, mister, don't,' she said.

I smacked her bare bottom and pushed her away.

'So it's lucky for you, princess, that I'm a detective and not a troll, otherwise you'd be ketchup.'

'You're a policeman?' she gulped, tears welling up in her eyes.

'That's right, I'm a policeman. And if I ever find you playing the apprentice snapper again, I'll see to it that your father takes a stick to you, understand?'

'Yes,' she whispered, and quickly pulled up her pants.

I picked up the pile of old shirts and towels from where I had dropped them on the floor, and pushed them into her arms.

'Now get out of here before I do the job myself.' She ran into the hall and out of the apartment in terror, as if I had been Niebelung himself.

After I'd closed the door on her, the smell and touch of that delicious little body, and the frustrated desire of it, remained with me for as long as it took to pour myself a drink and take a cold bath.

That September it seemed that passion everywhere, already smouldering like a rotten fuse-box, was easily ignited, and I wished that the hot blood of Sudeten Germans in Czechoslovakia could have been as easily dealt with as was my own excitation.

As a bull you learn to expect an increase in crime during hot weather. In January and February even the most desperate criminals stay home in front of the fire.

Reading Professor Berg's book, *The Sadist*, later on that same day, I wondered how many lives had been saved simply because it was too cold or too wet for Kürten to venture out of doors, Still, nine murders, seven attempted murders and forty acts of arson was an impressive enough record.

According to Berg, Kürten, the product of a violent home, had come to crime at an early age, committing a string of petty larcenies and enduring several periods of imprisonment until, at the age of thirty-eight, he had married a woman of strong character. He had always had sadistic impulses, being inclined to torture cats and other dumb animals, and now he was obliged to keep these tendencies in a mental straitjacket. But when his wife was not at home Kürten's evil demon at times grew too powerful to restrain, and he was driven to commit the terrible and sadistic crimes for which he was to become infamous.

This sadism was sexual in its origin, Berg explained. Kürten's home circumstances had rendered him predisposed to a deviation of the sexual urge, and his early experiences had all helped to condition the direction of that urge.

In the twelve months that separated Kürten's capture and his execution, Berg had met frequently with Kürten and found him to be a man of notable character and talent. He was possessed of considerable charm and intelligence, an excellent memory and keen powers of observation. Indeed, Berg was moved to remark upon the man's accessibility. Another outstanding characteristic was Kürten's vanity, which manifested itself in his smart, well-cared for appearance and in his delight at having outwitted the Düsseldorf police for as long as he had cared to do so.

Berg's conclusion was not a particularly comfortable one for any civilized member of society: Kürten was not mad within the terms of Paragraph Fifty-one, in that his acts were neither completely compulsive nor wholly irresistible, so much as pure, unadulterated cruelty.

If that wasn't bad enough, reading Baudelaire left me feeling as comfortable in my soul as a bullock in an abattoir. It didn't require a superhuman effort of imagination to accept Frau Kalau vom Hofe's suggestion that this rather Gothic French poet provided an explicit articulation of the mind of a Landru, a Gormann or a Kürten.

Yet there was something more here. Something deeper and more universal than merely a clue as to the psyche of the mass murderer. In Baudelaire's interest in violence, in his nostalgia for the past and through his revelation of the world of death and corruption, I heard the echo of a Satanic litany that was altogether more contemporary, and saw the pale reflection of a different kind of criminal, one whose spleen had the force of law.

I don't have much of a memory for words. I can barely remember the words of the national anthem. But some of these verses stayed in my head like the persistent smell of mingled musk and tar.

*

That evening I drove down to see Bruno's widow Katia at their home in Berlin-Zehlendorf. This was my second visit since Bruno's death, and I brought some of his things from the office, as well as a letter from my insurance company acknowledging receipt of the claim I had made on Katia's behalf.

There was even less to say now than before, but nevertheless I stayed for a full hour, holding Katia's hand and trying to swallow the lump in my throat with several glasses of schnaps.

'How's Heinrich taking it?' I said uncomfortably, hearing the unmistakable sound of the boy singing in his bedroom.

'He hasn't talked about it yet,' said Katia, her grief giving way a little to embarrassment. 'I think he sings because he wants to escape from having to face up to it.'

'Grief affects people very differently,' I said, scraping around for some sort of excuse. But I didn't think this was true at all. To my own father's premature death, when I hadn't been much older than Heinrich was now, had been appended as its brutal corollary the inescapable logic that I was myself not immortal. Ordinarily I would not have been insensitive to Heinrich's situation. 'But why must he sing that song?'

'He's got it into his head that the Jews had something to do with his father's death.'

'That's absurd,' I said.

Katia sighed and shook her head. 'I've told him that, Bernie. But he won't listen.'

On my way out I lingered at the boy's doorway, listening to his strong young voice.

' "Load up the empty guns, And polish up the knives, Let's kill the Jewish bastards, Who poison all our lives." '

For a moment I was tempted to open the door and belt the young thug on the jaw. But what was the point? What was the point of doing anything but leave him alone? There are so many ways of escaping from that which one fears, and not the least of these is hatred.

8

Monday, 12 September

A badge, a warrant card, an office on the third floor and, apart from the number of SS uniforms there were about the place, it almost felt like old times. It was too bad that there were not many happy memories, but happiness was never an emotion in plentiful supply at the Alex, unless your idea of a party involved working on a kidney with a chair-leg. A couple of times men I knew from the old days stopped me in the corridor to say hallo, and how sorry they were to hear about Bruno. But mostly I got the kind of looks that might have greeted an undertaker in a cancer ward.

Deubel, Korsch and Becker were waiting for me in my office. Deubel was explaining the subtle technique of the cigarette punch to his junior officers.

'That's right,' he said. 'When he's putting the nail in his guzzler, you give him the uppercut. An open jaw breaks real easy.'

'How nice to hear that criminal investigation is keeping up with modern times,' I said as I came through the door. 'I suppose you learned that in the Freikorps, Deubel.'

The man smiled. 'You've been reading my school-report, sir.'

'I've been doing a lot of reading,' I said, sitting down at my desk.

'Never been much of a reader myself,' he said.

'You surprise me.'

'You've been reading that woman's books, sir?' said Korsch. 'The ones that explain the criminal mind?'

'This one doesn't take much explanation,' said Deubel. 'He's a fucking spinner.'

'Maybe,' I said. 'But we're not about to catch him with blackjacks and brass knuckles. You can forget all your usual methods –

cigarette punches and things like that.' I stared hard at Deubel. 'A killer like this is difficult to catch because, for most of the time at least, he looks and behaves like an ordinary citizen. And with none of the hallmarks of criminality, and no obvious motive, we can't rely on informers to help us get on his track.'

Kriminalassistent Becker, on loan from Department VB3 – Vice – shook his head.

'If you'll forgive me, sir,' he said, 'that's not quite true. Dealing with sexual deviants, there are a few informers. Butt-fuckers and dolly-boys, it's true, but now and again they do come up with the goods.'

'I'll bet they do,' Deubel muttered.

'All right,' I said. 'We'll talk to them. But first there are two aspects to this case that I want us all to consider. One is that these girls disappear and then their bodies are found all over the city. Well, that tells me that our killer is using a car. The other aspect is that as far as I am aware, we've never had any reports of anyone witnessing the abduction of a victim. No reports of a girl being dragged kicking and screaming into the back of a car. That seems to me to indicate that maybe they went willingly with the killer. That they weren't afraid. Now it's unlikely that they all knew the killer, but quite possibly they might have trusted him because of what he was.'

'A priest, maybe,' said Korsch. 'Or a youth leader.'

'Or a bull,' I said. 'It's quite possible he could be any one of those things. Or all of them.'

'You think he might be disguising himself?' said Korsch.

I shrugged. 'I think that we have to keep an open mind about all of these things. Korsch, I want you to check through the records and see if you can't match anyone with a record for sexual assault with either a uniform, a church or a car licence plate.' He sagged a little. 'It's a big job, I know, so I've spoken to Lobbes in Kripo Executive, and he's going to get you some help.' I looked at my wristwatch. 'Kriminaldirektor Müller is expecting you over in VC1 in about ten minutes, so you'd better get going.'

'Nothing on the Hanke girl yet?' I said to Deubel, when Korsch had gone.

'My men have looked everywhere,' he said. 'The railway embankments, the parks, waste ground. We've dragged the Teltow Canal twice. There's not a lot more we can do.' He lit a cigarette and grimaced. 'She's dead by now. Everyone knows it.'

'I want you to conduct a door-to-door inquiry throughout the area where she disappeared. Speak to everyone, and I mean everyone, including the girl's schoolfriends. Somebody must have seen something. Take some photographs to jog a few memories.'

'If you don't mind me saying, sir,' he growled, 'that's surely a job for the uniformed boys in Orpo.'

'Those mallet-heads are good for arresting drunks and garter-handlers,' I said. 'But this is a job requiring intelligence. That's all.'

Pulling another face, Deubel stubbed out his cigarette in a way that let me know he wished the ashtray could have been my face, and dragged himself reluctantly out of my office.

'Better mind what you say about Orpo to Deubel, sir,' said Becker. 'He's a friend of Dummy Daluege's. They were in the same Stettin Freikorps regiment.' The Freikorps were paramilitary organizations of ex-soldiers which had been formed after the war to destroy Bolshevism in Germany and to protect German borders from the encroachments of the Poles. Kurt 'Dummy' Daluege was the chief of Orpo.

'Thanks, I read his file.'

'He used to be a good bull. But these days he works an easy shift and then pushes off home. All Eberhard Deubel wants out of life is to live long enough to collect his pension and see his daughter grow up to marry the local bank manager.'

'The Alex has got plenty like him,' I said. 'You've got children, haven't you, Becker?'

'A son, sir,' he said proudly. 'Norfried. He's nearly two.'

'Norfried, eh? That sounds German enough.'

'My wife, sir. She's very keen on this Aryan thing of Dr Rosenberg's.'

'And how does she feel about you working in Vice?'

'We don't talk much about what happens in my job. As far as she is concerned, I'm just a bull.'

'So tell me about these sexual-deviant informers.'

'While I was in Section M2, the Brothel Surveillance Squad, we only used one or two,' he explained. 'But Meisinger's Queer Squad use them all the time. He depends on informers. A few years ago there was a homosexual organization called the Friendship League, with about 30,000 members. Well, Meisinger got hold of the entire list and still leans on a name now and then for information. He also has the confiscated subscription lists of several pornographic magazines, as well as the names of the publishers. We might try a couple of them, sir. Then there is Reichsführer Himmler's ferris-wheel. It's an electrically powered rotating card-index with thousands and thousands of names on it, sir. We could always see what came up on that.'

'It sounds like something a gypsy fortune-teller would use.'

'They say that Himmler's keen on that shit.'

'And what about a man who's keen on nudging something? Where are all the bees in this city now that all the brothels have been closed down?'

'Massage parlours. You want to give a girl some bird, you've got to let her rub your back first. Kuhn – he's the boss of M2 – he doesn't bother them much. You want to ask a few snappers if they'd had to massage any spinners lately, sir?'

'It's as good a place to start as any I can think of.'

'We'll need an E-warrant, a search for missing persons.'

'Better go and get one, Becker.'

Becker was tall, with small, bored, blue eyes, a thin straw-hat of yellow hair, a doglike nose, and a mocking, almost manic smile. His looked a cynical sort of face, which was indeed the case. In Becker's everyday conversation there was more blasphemy against the divine beauty of life than you would have found among a pack of starving hyenas.

Reasoning that it was still too early for the massage-trade, we decided to try the dirty-book brigade first, and from the Alex we drove south to Hallesches Tor.

Wende Hoas was a tall, grey building close to the S-Bahn railway. We went up to the top floor where, with manic smile firmly in place, Becker kicked in one of the doors.

A tubby, prim little man with a monocle and a moustache looked up from his chair and smiled nervously as we walked into his office. 'Ah, Herr Becker,' he said. 'Come in, come in. And you've brought a friend with you. Excellent.'

There wasn't much room in the musty-smelling room. Tall stacks of books and magazines surrounded the desk and filing cabinet. I picked up a magazine and started to flick through it.

'Hallo, Helmut,' Becker chuckled, picking up another. He grunted with satisfaction as he turned the pages. 'This is filthy,' he laughed.

'Help yourselves, gentlemen,' said the man called Helmut. 'If there's anything special you're looking for, just ask. Don't be shy.' He leant back in his chair and from the pocket of his dirty grey waistcoat he produced a snuff box which he opened with a flick of his dirty thumbnail. He helped himself to a pinch, an indulgence which was effected with as much offence to the ear as any of the printed matter that might have been available was to the eye.

In close but poorly photographed gynaecological detail, the magazine I was looking at was partly given over to text that was designed to strain the fly-buttons. If it was to be believed, young German nurses copulated with no more thought than the average alley-cat.

Becker tossed his magazine on to the floor and picked up another. ' "The Virgin's Wedding Night",' he read.

'Not your sort of thing, Herr Becker,' Helmut said.

' "The Story of a Dildo"?'

'That one's not at all bad.'

' "Raped on the U-Bahn".'

'Ah, now that is good. There is a girl in that one with the juiciest plum I've ever seen.'

'And you've seen a few, haven't you, Helmut?'

The man smiled modestly, and looked over Becker's shoulder as he gave the photographs close attention.

'Rather a nice girl-next-door type, don't you think?'

Becker snorted. 'If you happen to live next door to a fucking dog kennel.'

'Oh, very good,' Helmut laughed, and started to clean his monocle. As he did so, a long and extremely grey length of his lank brown hair disengaged itself from a poorly disguised bald-patch, like a quilt slipping off a bed, and dangled ridiculously beside one of his transparent red ears.

'We're looking for a man who likes mutilating young girls,' I said. 'Would you have anything catering for that sort of pervert?'

Helmut smiled and shook his head sadly. 'No, sir, I'm afraid not. We don't much care to deal for the sadistic end of the market. We leave the whipping and bestiality to others.'

'Like hell you do,' Becker sneered.

I tried the filing cabinet, which was locked.

'What's in here?'

'A few papers, sir. The petty-cash box. The account books, that sort of thing. Nothing to interest you, I think.'

'Open it.'

'Really, sir, there's nothing of any interest –' The words dried in his mouth as he saw the cigarette lighter in my hand. I thumbed the bezel and held it underneath the magazine I'd been reading. It burned with a slow blue flame.

'Becker. How much would you say this magazine was?'

'Oh, they're expensive, sir. At least ten Reichsmarks each.'

'There must be a couple of thousands' worth of stock in this rat-hole.'

'Easily. Be a shame if there was a fire.'

'I hope he's insured.'

'You want to see inside the cabinet?' said Helmut. 'You only had to ask.' He handed Becker the key as I dropped the blazing magazine harmlessly into the metal wastepaper bin.

There was nothing in the top drawer besides a cash box, but in the bottom drawer was another pile of pornographic magazines. Becker picked one up and turned back the plain front cover.

' "Virgin Sacrifice",' he said, reading the title page. 'Take a look at this, sir.'

He showed me a series of photographs depicting the degradation and punishment of a girl, who looked to be of high-school age, by an old and ugly man wearing an ill-fitting toupee. The weals his cane had left on her bare backside seemed very real indeed.

'Nasty,' I said.

'You understand, I am merely the distributor,' Helmut said, blowing his nose on a filthy handkerchief, 'not the manufacturer.'

One photograph was particularly interesting. In it the naked girl was bound hand and foot, and lying on a church altar like a human sacrifice. Her vagina had been penetrated with an enormous cucumber. Becker looked fiercely at Helmut.

'But you know who produced it, don't you?' Helmut remained silent only until Becker grabbed him by the throat and started to slap him across the mouth.

'Please don't hit me.'

'You're probably enjoying it, you ugly little pervert,' he snarled, warming to his work. 'Come on, talk to me, or you'll talk to this.' He snatched a short rubber truncheon from his pocket, and pressed it against Helmut's face.

'It was Poliza,' shouted Helmut. Becker squeezed his face.

'Say again?'

'Theodor Poliza. He's a photographer. He has a studio on Schiffbauerdamm, next to the Comedy Theatre. He's the one you want.'

'If you're lying to us, Helmut,' said Becker, grinding the rubber against Helmut's cheek, 'we'll be back. And we'll not only set fire to your stock, but you with it. I hope you've got that.' He pushed him away.

Helmut dabbed at his bleeding mouth with the handkerchief, 'Yes, sir,' he said, 'I understand.'

When we were outside again I spat into the gutter.

'Gives you a nasty taste in the mouth, doesn't it, sir? Makes me glad I didn't have a daughter, really it does.'

I'd like to have said that I agreed with him there. Only I didn't. We drove north.

What a city it was for its public buildings, as immense as grey granite mountains. They built them big just to remind you of the importance of the state and the comparative insignificance of the individual. That just shows you how this whole business of National Socialism got started. It's hard not to be overawed by a government, any government, that is accommodated in such grand buildings. And the long wide avenues that ran straight from one district to another seemed to have been made for nothing else but columns of marching soldiers.

Quickly recovering my stomach I told Becker to stop the car at a cooked-meat shop on Friedrichstrasse and bought us both a plate of lentil soup. Standing at one of the little counters, we watched Berlin housewives lining up to buy their sausage, which lay coiled on the long marble counter like the rusted springs from some enormous motor car, or grew off the tiled walls in great bunches, like overripe bananas.

Becker may have been married, but he hadn't lost his eye for the ladies, passing some sort of nearly obscene comment about most of the women who came into the shop while we were there. And it hadn't escaped my attention that he'd helped himself to a couple of pornographic magazines. How could it have? He didn't try to hide them. Slap a man's face, make his mouth bleed, threaten him with an india rubber, call him a filthy degenerate and then help yourself to some of his dirty books – that's what being in Kripo was all about.

We went back to the car.

'Do you know this Poliza character?' I said.

'We've met,' he said. 'What can I tell you about him except that he's shit on your shoe?'

The Comedy Theatre on Schiffbauerdamm was on the north

side of the Spree, a tower-topped relic ornamented with alabaster tritons, dolphins and assorted naked nymphs, and Poliza's studio was in a basement nearby.

We went down some stairs and into a long alleyway. Outside the door to Poliza's studio we were met by a man wearing a cream-coloured blazer, a pair of green trousers, a cravat of lime silk and a red carnation. No amount of care or expense had been spared with his appearance, but the overall effect was so lacking in taste that he looked like a gypsy grave.

Poliza took one look at us and decided that we weren't there selling vacuum-cleaners. He wasn't much of a runner. His bottom was too big, his legs were too short and his lungs were probably too hard. But by the time we realized what was happening he was nearly ten metres down the alley.

'You bastard,' muttered Becker.

The voice of logic must have told Poliza he was being stupid, that Becker and I were easily capable of catching him, but it was probably so hoarsened by fear that it sounded as disquietingly unattractive as we ourselves must have appeared.

There was no such voice for Becker, hoarse or otherwise. Yelling at Poliza to stop, he broke into a smooth and powerful running action. I struggled to keep up with him, but after only a few strides he was well ahead of me. Another few seconds and he would have caught the man.

Then I saw the gun in his hand, a long-barrelled Parabellum, and yelled at both men to stop.

Almost immediately Poliza came to a halt. He began to raise his arms as if to cover his ears against the noise of the gunshot, turning as he collapsed, blood and aqueous humour spilling gelatinously from the bullet's exit wound in his eye, or what was left of it.

We stood over Poliza's dead body.

'What is it with you?' I said breathlessly. 'Have you got corns? Are your shoes too tight? Or maybe you didn't think your lungs were up to it? Listen, Becker, I've got ten years on you and I could have caught this man if I'd been wearing a deep-sea-diver's suit.'

Becker sighed and shook his head.

'Christ, I'm sorry, sir,' he said. 'I only meant to wing him.' He glanced awkwardly at his pistol, almost as if he didn't quite believe it could have just killed a man.

'Wing him? What were you aiming at, his earlobe? Listen, Becker, when you try and wing a man, unless you're Buffalo Bill you aim at his legs, not try and give him a fucking haircut.' I looked around, embarrassed, almost expecting a crowd to have gathered, but the alley stayed empty. I nodded down at his pistol. 'What is that cannon, anyway?'

Becker raised the gun. 'Artillery Parabellum, sir.'

'Shit, haven't you ever heard of the Geneva Convention? That's enough gun to drill for oil.'

I told him to go and telephone the canned-meat wagon, and while he was away I took a look around Poliza's studio.

There wasn't much to see. An assortment of open-crotch shots drying on a line in the darkroom. A collection of whips, chains, manacles and an altar complete with candlesticks, of the sort that I had seen in the photographed series of the girl with the cucumber. A couple of piles of magazines like the ones we had found back at Helmut's office. Nothing to indicate that Poliza might have murdered five schoolgirls.

When I went outside again I found that Becker had returned with a uniformed policeman, a sergeant. The pair of them stood looking at Poliza's body like two small boys regarding a dead cat in the gutter, the sergeant even poking at Poliza's side with the toe of his boot.

'Right through the window,' I heard the man say, with what sounded like admiration. 'I never realized there was so much jelly in there.'

'It's a mess, isn't it?' said Becker without much enthusiasm.

They looked up as I walked towards them.

'Wagon coming?' Becker nodded. 'Good. You can make your report later.' I spoke to the sergeant. 'Until it arrives, you'll stay here with the body, sergeant?'

He straightened up. 'Yes, sir.'

'You finished admiring your handiwork?'

'Sir,' said Becker.

'Then let's go.'

We walked back to the car.

'Where are we going?'

'I'd like to check on a couple of these massage parlours.'

'Evona Wylezynska's the one to talk to. She owns several places. Takes 25 per cent of everything the girls make. Most likely she'll be at her place on Richard Wagner Strasse.'

'Richard Wagner Strasse?' I said. 'Where the hell is that?'

'It used to be Sesenheimerstrasse, running on to Spreestrasse. You know, where the Opera House is.'

'I suppose that we should count ourselves lucky that it's opera Hitler loves, and not football.'

Becker grinned. Driving there he seemed to recover some of his spirits.

'Do you mind if I ask you a really personal question, sir?'

I shrugged. 'Go right ahead. But if it works out, I might have to put my answer in an envelope and mail it to you instead.'

'Well it's this: have you ever fucked a Jew, sir?'

I looked at him, trying to catch his eye, but he kept both of them determinedly on the road.

'No, I can't say I have. But it certainly wasn't the race laws that prevented it. I guess I just never met one who wanted to fuck me.'

'So you wouldn't object if you got the chance?'

I shrugged. 'I don't suppose I would.' I paused, waiting for him to go on, but he didn't, so I said, 'Why do you ask, as a matter of fact?'

Becker smiled over the steering-wheel.

'There's a little Jewish snapper at this rub-joint we're going to,' he said enthusiastically. 'A real scorcher. She's got a plum that's like the inside of a conger-eel, just one long piece of suction muscle. The kind to suck you in like a minnow and blow you right out of her arse. Best bit of damned plum I've ever had.' He shook his head doubtfully. 'I don't reckon there's anything to beat a nice ripe Jewess. Not even a nigger-woman, or a Chink.'

'I never knew you were so broad-minded, Becker,' I said, 'or so damned cosmopolitan. Christ, I bet you've even read Goethe.'

Becker laughed at that one. He seemed to have quite forgotten Poliza. 'One thing about Evona,' he said. 'She won't talk unless we relax a little, if you know what I mean. Have a drink, take things easy. Act like we're not in a hurry. The minute we start to act like a couple of official stiffs in our trousers she'll haul down the shutters and start polishing the mirrors in the bedrooms.'

'Well, there's a lot of people like that these days. Like I always say, people won't put their fingers near the stove if they figure you're stewing a broth.'

Evona Wylezynska was a Pole with an Eton crop smelling lightly of Macassar oil, and a dangerous crevasse of cleavage. Although it was only the mid-afternoon she wore a peignoir of peach-coloured voile over a matching heavy satin slip, and high-heeled slippers. She greeted Becker like he was there with a rent rebate.

'Darling Emil,' she cooed. 'Such a long time since we seen you here. Where have you been hiding?'

'I'm off Vice now,' he explained, kissing her on the cheek.

'What a shame. And you were so good at it.' She gave me a litmus-paper sort of look, as if I was something that might stain the expensive carpet. 'And who is this you've brought us?'

'It's all right, Evona. He's a friend.'

'Does your friend have a name? And does he not know to take his hat off when he comes into a lady's house?'

I let that one go, and took it off. 'Bernhard Günther, Frau Wylezynska,' I said, and shook her hand.

'Pleased to meet you, darling, I'm sure.' Her thickly accented, languorous voice seemed to start somewhere near the bottom of her corset, the faint outline of which I could just about make out underneath her slip. By the time it got to her pouting mouth it had more tease than a fairy's kitten. The mouth was giving me quite a few problems too. It was the kind of mouth that can eat a five-course dinner at Kempinski's without spoiling its lipstick, only on this occasion I seemed to be the preoccupation of its taste-buds.

She ushered us into a comfortable sitting-room that wouldn't have embarrassed a Potsdam lawyer, and stalked towards the enormous drinks tray.

'What will you have, gentlemen? I have absolutely everything.'

Becker guffawed loudly. 'There's no doubt about that,' he said.

I smiled thinly. Becker was starting to irritate me badly. I asked for a scotch whisky, and as Evona handed me my glass her cold fingers touched mine.

She took a mouthful of her own drink as if it were unpleasant medicine to be hurried down, and tugged me on to a big leather sofa. Becker chuckled and sat down on an armchair beside us.

'And how is my old friend Arthur Nebe?' she asked. Noting my surprise, she added: 'Oh yes, Arthur and I have known each other for many years. Ever since 1920 in fact, when he first joined Kripo.'

'He's much the same,' I said.

'Tell him to come and visit me sometime,' she said. 'He can storm free with me any time he wants. Or just a nice massage. Yes, that's it. Tell him to come here for a nice rub. I give it to him myself.' She laughed loudly at the idea and lit a cigarette.

'I'll tell him,' I said, wondering if I would, and wondering if she really cared one way or the other.

'And you, Emil. Maybe you would like a little company? Maybe you would both like a rub yourselves, eh?'

I was about to broach the real purpose of our visit, but found that Becker was already clapping his hands and chuckling some more.

'That's it,' he said, 'let's relax a little. Be nice and friendly.' He glanced at me meaningfully. 'We're not in a hurry are we, sir?'

I shrugged and shook my head.

'Just as long as we don't forget why we came,' I said, trying not to sound like a prig.

Evona Wylezynska stood up and pressed a bell on the wall behind a curtain. She made a tutting noise, and said: 'Why not just forget everything? That's why most of my gentlemen come here, to forget about their cares.'

While her back was turned Becker frowned and shook his head at me. I wasn't sure exactly what he meant.

Evona took the nape of my neck in the palm of her hand and began to knead the flesh there with fingers that were as strong as blacksmith's pincers.

'There's a lot of tension here, Bernhard,' she informed me seductively.

'I don't doubt it. You should see the cart they've got me pulling down at the Alex. Not to mention the number of passengers I've been asked to take.' It was my turn to glance meaningfully at Becker. Then I took Evona's fingers away from my neck and kissed them amicably. They smelt of iodine soap, and there are better olfactory aphrodisiacs than that.

Evona's girls walked slowly into the room like a troupe of circus horses. Some were wearing just slips and stockings, but mostly they were naked. They took up positions around Becker and myself, and started to smoke or to help themselves to drinks, almost as if we hadn't been there at all. It was more female flesh than I had seen in a long time, and I have to admit that my eyes would have branded the bodies of any ordinary women. But these girls were used to being eyed, and remained coolly undisturbed by our prurient stares. One picked up a dining chair and, setting it down in front of me, sat astride it so that I had as perfect a view of her genitals as I could have been expected to have wished for. She started flexing her bare buttocks against the seat of the chair for good measure.

Almost immediately Becker was on his feet and rubbing his hands together like the keenest of street-traders.

'Well, this is very nice, isn't it?' Becker put his arms around a couple of the girls, his face growing redder with excitement. He glanced around the room and, not finding the face he was looking for, said: 'Tell me, Evona, where is that lovely little child-bearing machine of a Jewess who used to work for you?'

'You mean Esther. I'm afraid she had to go away.' We waited, but there was no sign of anything other than smoke coming from Evona's mouth to expand upon what she had said.

'That's too bad,' said Becker. 'I was telling my friend here just how nice she was.' He shrugged. 'Never mind. Plenty more where she came from, eh?' Ignoring the look on my face, and still supported like a drunk by the two snappers, he turned and walked down the creaking corridor and into one of the bedrooms, leaving me alone with the rest of them.

'And what is your preference, Bernhard?' Evona snapped her fingers and waved one of her girls forward. 'This one and Esther are very much alike,' she said, taking hold of the girl's bare backside and turning it towards my face, smoothing it with the palm of her hand. 'She has two vertebrae too many, so that her behind is a long way from her waist. Very beautiful, do you not think?'

'Very beautiful,' I said, and patted the girl's marble-cool bottom politely. 'But to be honest, I'm the old-fashioned type. I like a girl to have all her mind on me and not my wallet.'

Evona smiled. 'No, I did not think you were the type.' She smacked the girl's behind like a favourite dog. 'Go on, off you go. All of you.'

I watched them troop silently out of the room and felt something close to disappointment that I wasn't more like Becker. She seemed to sense this ambivalence.

'You are not like Emil. He is attracted to any girl who will show him her fingernails. I think that one would fuck a cat with a broken back. How's your drink?'

I swirled it demonstratively. 'Just fine,' I said.

'Well, is there anything else that I can get you?'

I felt her bosom press against my arm and smiled down at what was hanging in the gallery. I lit a cigarette and looked her in the eye.

'Don't pretend to be disappointed if I say that all I'm after is some information.'

She smiled, checking her advance, and reached for her drink. 'What kind of information?'

'I'm looking for a man, and before you rip a hole for the joke, the man I'm after is a killer, with four goals on the score-sheet.'

'How can I help you? I run a whorehouse, not a private detective agency.'

'It's not uncommon for a man to use one of your girls roughly.'

'There's none of them wears velvet gloves, Bernhard, I'll tell you that much. Quite a lot of them figure that just because they've paid for the privilege, it gives them a licence to tear a girl's underwear.'

'Someone who went beyond what is considered to be a normal hazard of the profession, then. Maybe one of your girls has had such a client. Or heard of someone who has.'

'Tell me more about your killer.'

'I don't know much,' I sighed. 'I don't know his name, where he lives, where he came from or what he looks like. What I do know is that he likes tying up schoolgirls.'

'Lots of men like tying girls up,' Evona said. 'Don't ask me what they get out of it. There are even some who like to whip girls, although I don't permit that sort of thing. That kind of pig should be locked away.'

'Look, anything might help. Right now there's not a great deal to go on.'

Evona shrugged, and stubbed out her cigarette. 'What the hell,' she said. 'I was a schoolgirl myself once. You said four girls.'

'It may even be five. All aged about fifteen or sixteen. Nice families, and bright futures until this maniac kidnaps them, rapes them, cuts their throats and then dumps their naked bodies.'

Evona looked thoughtful. 'There was something,' she said carefully. 'Of course you realize that it's unlikely that the sort of man who comes to my place or any place like it is the sort of man who preys on young girls. I mean, the point of a place like this is to take care of a man's needs.'

I nodded, but I was thinking of Kürten, and of how his case contradicted her. I decided not to press the point.

'Like I said, it's a long shot.'

Evona stood up and excused herself for a moment. When she returned she was accompanied by the girl whose elongated backside I had been obliged to admire. This time she was wearing a gown, and seemed more nervous clothed than she had been while naked.

'This is Helene,' Evona said, sitting down again. 'Helene, sit down and tell the Kommissar about the man who tried to kill you.'

The girl sat down on the chair where Becker had been sitting. She was pretty in a tired sort of way, as if she didn't sleep enough, or was using some sort of drug. Hardly daring to look me in the eye she chewed her lip and tugged at a length of her long red hair.

'Well, go on,' Evona urged. 'He won't eat you. He had that chance earlier on.'

'The man we're looking for likes to tie girls up,' I told her, leaning forward encouragingly. 'Then he strangles them, or cuts their throats.'

'I'm sorry,' she said after a minute. 'This is hard for me. I wanted to forget all about it, but Evona says that some schoolgirls have been murdered. I want to help, really I do, but it's hard.'

I lit a cigarette and offered her the packet. She shook her head. 'Take your time, Helene,' I said. 'Is this a customer we're talking about? Someone who came for a massage?'

'I won't have to go to court, will I? I'm not saying anything if it means standing up in front of a magistrate and saying I'm a party-girl.'

'The only person you'll have to tell is me.'

The girl sniffed without much enthusiasm.

'Well, you seem all right, I suppose.' She shot a look at the cigarette in my hand. 'Can I change my mind about that nail?'

'Sure,' I said, and held out the packet.

The first drag seemed to galvanize her. She smarted as she told the story, embarrassed a little, and probably a bit scared as well.

'About a month ago I had a client in one evening. I gave him a massage and when I asked him if he wanted me to dial his number he asked me if he could tie me up and then get himself frenched. I said that it would cost him another twenty, and he agreed. So there I was, trussed up like a roast chicken, having finished frenching him, and I ask him to untie me. He gets this funny look in his eye, and calls me a dirty whore, or something like that. Well you get used to men going mean on you when you've finished, like they're ashamed of themselves, but I could see that this one was different, so I tried to stay calm. Then he got the knife out and started to lay it flat on my neck like he wanted me to be scared. Which I was. Fit to scream my lungs out of my throat, only I didn't want to scare him into cutting me right away, thinking that I might be able to talk him out of it.' She took another tremulous drag on her cigarette.

'But that was just his cue to start throttling me, him thinking that I was about to scream, I mean. He grabbed hold of my windpipe and starts to choke me. If one of the other girls hadn't walked in there by mistake he'd have scratched me out and no mistake. I had the bruises on my neck for almost a week afterwards.'

'What happened when the other girl came in?'

'Well, I couldn't say for sure. I was more concerned with drawing breath than seeing that he got a taxi home all right, you know what I mean? As far as I know he just snatched up his things and got his smell out the door.'

'What did he look like?'

'He had a uniform on.'

'What kind of uniform? Can you be a little more specific?'

She shrugged. 'Who am I, Hermann Goering? Shit, I don't know what kind of uniform it was.'

'Well was it green, black, brown or what? Come on, girl, think. It's important.'

She took a fierce drag and shook her head impatiently.

'An old uniform. The sort they used to wear.'

'You mean like a war veteran?'

'Yes, that's the sort of thing, only a bit more – Prussian, I suppose. You know, the waxed moustache, the cavalry boots. Oh yes, I nearly forgot, he had spurs on.'

'Spurs?'

'Yes, like to ride a horse.'

'Anything else you remember?'

'He had a wineskin, on a string which he slung over his shoulder, so that it looked like a bugle at his hip. Only he said that it was full of schnaps.'

I nodded, satisfied, and leant back on the sofa, wondering what it would have been like to have had her after all. For the first time I noticed the yellowish discoloration of her hands which wasn't nicotine, jaundice or her temperament, but a clue that she'd been working in a munitions factory. In the same way I'd once identified a body pulled out of the Landwehr. Another thing I had learned from Hans Illmann.

'Hey, listen,' said Helene, 'if you get this bastard, make sure that he gets all the usual Gestapo hospitality, won't you? Thumbscrews and rubber truncheons?'

'Lady,' I said, standing up, 'you can depend on it. And thanks for helping.'

Helene stood up, her arms folded, and shrugged. 'Yes, well, I was a schoolgirl myself once, you know what I mean?'

I glanced at Evona and smiled. 'I know what you mean.' I jerked my head at the bedrooms along the corridor. 'When Don Juan's concluded his investigations, tell him that I went to question the head-waiter at Peltzers. Then maybe I thought I'd talk to the manager at the Winter Garden and see what I could get out of him. After that I might just head back to the Alex and clean my gun. Who knows, I may even find time to do a little police work along the way.'

9

Friday, 16 September

'Where are you from, Gottfried?'

The man smiled proudly. 'Eger, in the Sudetenland. Another few weeks and you can call it Germany.'

'Foolhardy is what I call it,' I said. 'Another few weeks and your Sudetendeutsche Partei will have us all at war. Martial law has already been declared in most SDP districts.'

'Men must die for what they believe in.' He leant back on his chair and dragged a spur along the floor of the interrogation room. I stood up, loosening my shirt collar, and moved out of the shaft of sunlight that shone through the window. It was a hot day. Too hot to be wearing a jacket, let alone the uniform of an old Prussian cavalry officer. Gottfried Bautz, arrested early that same morning, didn't seem to notice the heat, although his waxed moustache was beginning to show signs of a willingness to stand easy.

'What about women?' I asked. 'Do they have to die as well?'

His eyes narrowed. 'I think that you had better tell me why I have been brought here, don't you, Herr Kommissar?'

'Have you ever been to a massage parlour on Richard Wagner Strasse?'

'No, I don't think so.'

'You're a difficult man to forget, Gottfried. I doubt that you could have made yourself look any easier to remember than if you had rode up the stairs on a white stallion. Incidentally, why do you wear the uniform?'

'I served Germany, and I'm proud of it. Why shouldn't I wear a uniform?'

I started to say something about the war being over, but there didn't seem like much point, what with another one on the way, and Gottfried being such a spinner.

'So,' I said. 'Were you at the massage parlour on Richard Wagner Strasse, or not?'

'Maybe. One doesn't always remember the exact locations of places like that. I don't make a habit of –'

'Spare me the character reference. One of the girls there says that you tried to kill her.'

'That's preposterous.'

'She's quite adamant, I'm afraid.'

'Has this girl made a complaint against me?'

'Yes, she has.'

Gottfried Bautz chuckled smugly. 'Come now, Herr Kommissar. We both know that's not true. In the first place there hasn't been an identification parade. And in the second, even if there was, there's not a snapper in the whole of Germany who would report so much as a lost poodle. No complaint, no witness, and I fail to see why we're having this conversation at all.'

'She says that you tied her up like a hog, nudged her mouth and then tried to strangle her.'

'She says, she says. Look, what is this shit? It's my word against hers.'

'You're forgetting the witness, aren't you, Gottfried? The girl who came in while you were squeezing the shit out of the other one? Like I said, you're not an easy man to forget.'

'I'm prepared to let a court decide who is telling the truth here,' he said. 'Me, a man who fought for his country, or a couple of stupid little honeybees. Are they prepared to do the same?' He was shouting now, sweat starting off his forehead like pastry-glaze. 'You're just pecking at vomit, and you know it.'

I sat down again and aimed my forefinger at the centre of his face.

'Don't get smart, Gottfried. Not in here. The Alex breaks more skin that way than Max Schmeling, and you don't always get to go back to your dressing-room at the end of the fight.' I folded my hands behind my head, leant back and looked nonchalantly up at the ceiling. 'Take my word for it, Gottfried. This little bee isn't so dumb that she won't do exactly what I tell her to do. If I tell her to french the magistrate in open court she'll do it. Understand?'

'You can go fuck yourself, then,' he snarled. 'I mean, if you're going to custom-build me a cage then I don't see that you need me to cut you a key. Why the hell should I answer any of your questions?'

'Please yourself. I'm not in any hurry. Me, I'll go back home, take a nice hot bath, get a good night's sleep. Then I'll come back here and see what kind of an evening you've had. Well, what can I say? They don't call this place Grey Misery for nothing.'

'All right, all right,' he groaned. 'Go ahead and ask your lousy questions.'

'We searched your room.'

'Like it?'

'Not as much as the bugs you share with. We found some rope. My inspector thinks it's the special strangling kind you buy at Ka-De-We. On the other hand it could be the kind you use to tie someone up.'

'Or it could be the sort of rope I use in my job. I work for Rochling's Furniture Removals.'

'Yes, I checked. But why take a length of rope home with you? Why not just leave it in the van?'

'I was going to hang myself.'

'What changed your mind?'

'I thought about it awhile, and then things didn't seem quite so bad. That was before I met you.'

'What about the bloodstained cloth we found in a bag underneath your bed?'

'That? Menstrual blood. An acquaintance of mine, she had a small accident. I meant to burn it, but I forgot.'

'Can you prove that? Will this acquaintance corroborate your story?'

'Unfortunately I can't tell you very much about her, Kommissar. A casual thing, you understand.' He paused. 'But surely there are scientific tests which will substantiate what I say?'

'Tests will determine whether or not it is human blood. But I don't think there's anything as precise as you are suggesting. I can't say for sure, I'm not a pathologist.'

I stood up again and went over to the window. I found my cigarettes and lit one.

'Smoke?' He nodded and I threw the packet on to the table. I let him get his first breath of it before I tossed him the grenade. 'I'm investigating the murders of four, possibly five young girls,' I said quietly. 'That's why you're here now. Assisting us with our inquiries, as they say.'

Gottfried stood up quickly, his tongue tamping down his lower lip, the cigarette rolling on the table where he had thrown it. He started to shake his head and didn't stop.

'No, no, no. No, you've got the wrong man. I know absolutely nothing of this. Please, you've got to believe me. I'm innocent.'

'What about that girl you raped in Dresden, in 1931? You were in the cement for that, weren't you, Gottfried? You see, I've checked your record.'

'It was statutory rape. The girl was under age, that's all. I didn't know. She consented.'

'Now let's see, how old was she again? Fifteen? Sixteen? That's about the same age as the girls who've been murdered. You know, maybe you just like them young. You feel ashamed of what you are, and transfer your guilt to them. How can they make you do these things?'

'No, it's not true, I swear it –'

'How can they be so disgusting? How can they provoke you so shamelessly?'

'Stop it, for Christ's sake –'

'You're innocent. Don't make me laugh. Your innocence isn't worth shit in the gutter, Gottfried. Innocence is for decent, law-abiding citizens, not the kind of sewer-rat like you who tries to strangle a girl in a massage parlour. Now sit down and shut up.'

He rocked on his heels for a moment, and then sat down heavily.

'I didn't kill anyone,' he muttered. 'Whichever way you want to cut it, I'm innocent, I tell you.'

'That you may be,' I said. 'But I'm afraid I can't plane a piece of wood without dropping a few shavings. So, innocent or not, I've got to keep you for a while. At least until I can check you out.' I picked up my jacket and walked to the door.

'One last question for the moment,' I said. 'I don't suppose you own a car, do you?'

'On my pay? You are joking, aren't you?'

'What about the furniture van. Are you the driver?'

'Yes. I'm the driver.'

'Ever use it in the evenings?' He stayed silent. I shrugged and said: 'Well, I suppose I can always ask your employer.'

'It's not allowed, but sometimes I do use it, yes. Do a bit of private contracting, that sort of thing.' He looked squarely at me. 'But I never used it to kill anyone in, if that's what you were suggesting.'

'It wasn't, as it happens. But thanks for the idea.'

I sat in Arthur Nebe's office and waited for him to finish his telephone call. His face was grave when finally he replaced the receiver. I was about to say something when he raised his finger to his lips, opened his desk drawer and took out a tea-cosy with which he covered the phone.

'What's that for?'

'There's a wire on the telephone. Heydrich's, I suppose, but who can tell? The tea-cosy keeps our conversation private.' He leant back in his chair underneath a picture of the Führer and uttered a long and weary sigh. 'That was one of my men calling from the Berchtesgaden,' he said. 'Hitler's talks with the British prime minister don't seem to be going particularly well. I don't think our beloved Chancellor of Germany cares if there's war with England or not. He's conceding absolutely nothing.

'Of course he doesn't give a damn about these Sudeten Germans.

This nationalist thing is just a cover. Everyone knows it. It's all that Austro-Hungarian heavy industry that he wants. That he needs, if he's going to fight a European war. God, I wish he had to deal with someone stronger than Chamberlain. He brought his umbrella with him you know. Bloody little bank manager.'

'Do you think so? I'd say the umbrella denotes quite a sensible sort of man. Can you really imagine Hitler or Goebbels ever managing to stir up a crowd of men carrying umbrellas? It's the very absurdity of the British which makes them so impossible to radicalize. And why we should envy them.'

'It's a nice idea,' he said, smiling reflectively. 'But tell me about this fellow you've arrested. Think he might be our man?'

I glanced around the room for a moment, hoping to find greater conviction on the walls and the ceiling, and then lifted my hands almost as if I meant to disclaim Gottfried Bautz's presence in a cell downstairs.

'From a circumstantial point of view, he could fit the laundry list.' I rationed myself to one sigh. 'But there's nothing that definitely connects him. The rope we found in his room is the same type as the rope that was used to bind the feet of one of the dead girls. But then it's a very common type of rope. We use the same kind here at the Alex.

'Some cloth we found underneath his bed could be stained with blood from one of his victims. Equally, it could be menstrual blood, as he claims. He has access to a van in which he could have transported and killed his victims relatively easily. I've got some of the boys checking it over now, but so far it appears to be as clean as a dentist's fingers.

'And then of course there is his record. We've locked his door once before for a sexual offence – a statutory rape. More recently he probably tried to strangle a snapper he'd first persuaded to be tied up. So he could fit the psychological bill of the man we're looking for.' I shook my head. 'But that's more "could-be" than Fritz fucking Lang. What I want is some real evidence.'

Nebe nodded sagely and put his boots on the desk. Tapping

his fingers' ends together, he said: 'Could you build a case? Break him?'

'He's not stupid. It will take time. I'm not that good an interrogator, and I'm not about to take any short-cuts either. The last thing I want on this case is broken teeth on the charge sheet. That's how Josef Kahn got himself folded away and put in the costume-hire hospital.' I helped myself from the box of American cigarettes on Nebe's desk and lit one with an enormous brass table lighter, a present from Goering. The prime minister was always giving away cigarette lighters to people who had done him some small service. He used them like a nanny uses boiled sweets.

'Incidentally, has he been released yet?'

Nebe's lean face adopted a pained expression. 'No, not yet,' he said.

'I know it's considered only a small detail, the fact that he hasn't actually murdered anyone, but don't you think it's time he should be let out? We still have some standards left, don't we?'

He stood up and came round the desk to stand in front of me.

'You're not going to like this, Bernie,' he said. 'No more than I do myself.'

'Why should this be an exception? I figure that the only reason there aren't any mirrors in the lavatories is so that nobody has to look himself in the eye. They're not going to release him, right?'

Nebe leant against the side of the desk, folded his arms and stared at the toes of his boots for a minute.

'Worse than that, I'm afraid. He's dead.'

'What happened?'

'Officially?'

'You can give it a shot.'

'Josef Kahn took his own life while the balance of his mind was disturbed.'

'I can see how that would read nicely. But you know different, right?'

'I don't know anything for certain.' He shrugged. 'So call it informed guesswork. I hear things, I read things and I make a few reasonable conclusions. Naturally as Reichskriminaldirektor I have access to all kinds of secret decrees in the Ministry of the Interior.' He took a cigarette and lit it. 'Usually these are camouflaged with all sorts of neutral-sounding bureaucratic names.

'Well then, at the present moment there's a move to establish a new committee for the research of severe constitutional disease –'

'You mean like what this country is suffering from?'

'– with the aim of encouraging "positive eugenics, in accordance with the Führer's thoughts on the subject".' He waved his cigarette at the portrait on the wall behind him. 'Whenever you read that phrase "the Führer's thoughts on the subject", one knows to pick up one's well-read copy of his book. And there you will find that he talks about using the most modern medical means at our disposal to prevent the physically degenerate and mentally sick from contaminating the future health of the race.'

'Well, what the hell does that mean?'

'I had assumed it meant that such unfortunates would simply be prevented from having families. I mean, that does seem sensible, doesn't it? If they are incapable of looking after themselves then they can hardly be fit to bring up children.'

'It doesn't seem to have deterred the Hitler Youth leaders.'

Nebe snorted and went back round his desk. 'You're going to have to watch your mouth, Bernie,' he said, half-amused.

'Get to the funny bit.'

'Well, it's this. A number of recent reports, complaints if you like, made to Kripo by those related to institutionalized people leads me to suspect that some sort of mercy-killing is already being unofficially practised.'

I leant forward and grasped the bridge of my nose.

'Do you ever get headaches? I get headaches. It's smell that really sets them off. Paint smells pretty bad. So does formaldehyde in the mortuary. But the worst are those rotten pissing places you get where the dozers and rum-sweats sleep rough. That's a smell I can recall in my worst nightmares. You know, Arthur, I thought I knew every bad smell there was in this city. But that's last month's shit fried with last year's eggs.'

Nebe pulled open a drawer and took out a bottle and two glasses. He said nothing as he poured a couple of large ones.

I threw it back and waited for the fiery spirit to seek out what was left of my heart and stomach. I nodded and let him pour me another. I said: 'Just when you thought that things couldn't get any worse, you find out that they've always been a lot worse than you thought they were. And then they get worse.' I drained the second glass and then surveyed its empty shape. 'Thanks for telling me straight, Arthur.' I dragged myself to my feet. 'And thanks for the warmer.'

'Please keep me informed about your suspect,' he said. 'You might consider letting a couple of your men work a friend-and-foe shift on him. No rough stuff, just a bit of the old-fashioned psychological pressure. You know the sort of thing I mean. Incidentally, how are you getting on with your team? Everything working out there? No resentments, or anything like that?'

I could have sat down again and given him a list of faults there that were as long as a Party rally, but really he didn't need it. I knew that Kripo had a hundred bulls who were worse than the three I had in my squad. So I merely nodded and said that everything was fine.

But at the door to Nebe's office I stopped and uttered the words automatically, without even thinking. I said it, and not out of obligation, in response to someone else, in which situation I might have consoled myself with the excuse that I was just keeping my head down and avoiding the trouble of giving offence. I said it first.

'Heil Hitler.'

'Heil Hitler.' Nebe didn't look up from whatever it was that he had started writing as he mumbled his reply, so he didn't see my expression. I couldn't say what it would have looked like. But whatever my expression, it was born of the realization that the only real complaint I had at the Alex was going to be against myself.

10

Monday, 19 September

The telephone rang. I wrestled my way across from the other side of the bed and answered it. I was still registering the time while Deubel was speaking. It was two a.m.

'Say that again.'

'We think we've found the missing girl, sir.'

'Dead?'

'Like a mouse in a trap. There's no positive identification yet, but it looks like all the rest of them, sir. I've called Professor Illmann. He's on his way now.'

'Where are you, Deubel?'

'Zoo Bahnhof.'

It was still warm outside when I went down to the car, and I opened the window to enjoy the night air, as well as to help wake me up. For everyone but Herr and Frau Hanke asleep at their home in Steglitz, it promised to be a nice day.

I drove east along Kurfürstendamm with its geometric-shaped, neon-lit shops, and turned north up Joachimstaler Strasse, at the top of which loomed the great luminous greenhouse that was the Zoo Station. In front were several police vans, a redundant ambulance and a few drunks still intent on making a night of it, being moved on by a bull.

Inside, I walked across the floor of the central ticket hall towards the police barrier that had been erected in front of the lost property and left-luggage areas. I flashed my badge at the two men guarding the barrier and carried on through. As I rounded the corner Deubel met me half way.

'What have we got?' I said.

'Body of a girl in a trunk, sir. From the look and smell of her she's been in there sometime. The trunk was in the left-luggage office.'

'The professor here yet?'

'Him and the photographer. They haven't done much more than give her a dirty look. We wanted to wait for you.'

'I'm touched by your thoughtfulness. Who found the mortal remains?'

'I did, sir, with one of the uniformed sergeants in my squad.'

'Oh? What did you do, consult a medium?'

'There was an anonymous telephone call, sir. To the Alex. He told the desk sergeant where to find the body, and the desk sergeant told my sergeant. He rang me and we came straight down here. We located the trunk, found the girl and then I called you.'

'An anonymous caller you say. What time was this?'

'About twelve. I was just going off shift.'

'I'll want to speak to the man who took that call. You better get someone to check he doesn't go off duty either, at least not until he's made his report. How did you get in here?'

'The night station-master, sir. He keeps the keys in his office when they close the left luggage.' Deubel pointed at a fat greasy-looking man standing a few metres away, chewing the skin on the palm of his hand. 'That's him over there.'

'Looks like we're keeping him from his supper. Tell him I want the names and addresses of everyone who works in this section, and what time they start work in the morning. Regardless of what hours they work, I want to see them all here at the normal opening time, with all their records and paperwork.' I paused for a moment, steeling myself for what was about to follow.

'All right,' I said. 'Show me where.'

In the left-luggage office, Hans Illmann sat on a large parcel labelled 'Fragile', smoking one of his roll-ups and watching the police photographer set up his flashlights and camera-tripods.

'Ah, the Kommissar,' he said, eyeing me and standing. 'We're not long here ourselves, and I knew you'd want us to wait for you.

Dinner's a little overcooked, so you'll need these.' He handed me a pair of rubber gloves, and then looked querulously at Deubel. 'Are you sitting down with us, inspector?'

Deubel grimaced. 'I'd rather not, if you don't mind, sir. Normally I would, but I've got a daughter about that age myself.'

I nodded. 'You'd better wake up Becker and Korsch and get them down here. I don't see why we should be the only ones to lose our rat.'

Deubel turned to go.

'Oh, inspector,' said Illmann, 'you might ask one of our uniformed friends to organize some coffee. I work a great deal better when I'm awake. Also, I need someone to take notes. Can your sergeant write legibly, do you think?'

'I assume he does, sir.'

'Inspector, the one assumption that it is safe to make with regard to the educational standards that prevail in Orpo is that which allows only of the man being capable of completing a betting-slip. Find out for sure, if you wouldn't mind. I'd rather do it myself than later have to decipher the Cyrillic scrawl of a more primitive life-form.'

'Yes, sir.' Deubel smiled thinly and went to carry out his orders.

'I didn't think he was the sensitive type,' Illmann commented, watching him go. 'Imagine a detective not wanting to see the body. It's like a wine merchant declining to try a Burgundy he's about to purchase. Unthinkable. Wherever do they find these face-slappers?'

'Simple. They just go out and shanghai all the men wearing leather shorts. It's what the Nazis call natural selection.'

On the floor at the back of the left-luggage office lay the trunk containing the body, covered with a sheet. We pulled up a couple of large parcels and sat down.

Illmann drew back the sheet, and I winced a little as the animal-house smell rose up to greet me, turning my head automatically towards the better air that lay behind my shoulder.

'Yes, indeed,' he murmured, 'it's been a warm summer.'

It was a full-sized steamer trunk, and made of good quality blue leather, with brass locks and studs – the kind you see being loaded on to those high-class passenger liners that sail between Hamburg and New York. For its solitary occupant, a naked girl of about sixteen years old, there was only one kind of journey, the more final kind, which remained to be embarked upon. Partly swathed in what looked like a length of brown curtain material, she lay on her back with her legs folded to the left, a bare breast arching upwards as if there was something underneath her. The head lay at an impossibly contradictory angle to the rest of her body, the mouth open and almost smiling, the eyes half closed and, but for the dried blood in her nostrils and the rope around her ankles, you might almost have thought the girl was in the first stages of awakening from a long sleep.

Deubel's sergeant, a burly fellow with less neck than a hipflask and a chest like a sandbag, arrived with a notebook and pencil, and sat a little way apart from Illmann and me, sucking a sweet, his legs crossed almost nonchalantly, apparently undisturbed at the sight which lay before us.

Illmann looked appraisingly at him for a moment and then nodded, before beginning to describe what he saw.

'An adolescent female,' he said solemnly, 'about sixteen years of age, naked, and lying inside a large trunk of quality manufacture. The body is covered partially with a length of brown cretonne, and the feet are bound with a piece of rope.' He spoke slowly, with pauses between the phrases in order to allow the sergeant's handwriting to keep pace with him.

'Pulling the fabric away from the body reveals the head almost completely severed from the torso. The body itself shows signs of advancing decomposition, consistent with it having been in the trunk for at least four to five weeks. The hands show no signs of defence wounds, and I'm wrapping them for further examination of the fingers in the laboratory, although since she clearly bit her nails I expect I'll be wasting my time.' He took two thick paper bags out of his case and I helped him secure them over the dead girl's hands.

'Hallo, what's this? Do my eyes deceive me, or is this a blood-stained blouse which I see before me?'

'It looks like her BdM uniform,' I said, watching him pick up first the blouse, and then a navy skirt.

'How extraordinarily thoughtful of our friend to send us her laundry. And just when I thought he was becoming just a little bit predictable. First an anonymous telephone call to the Alex, and now this. Remind me to consult my diary and check that it's not my birthday.'

Something else caught my eye, and I leant forward and picked the small square piece of card out of the trunk.

'Irma Hanke's identity card,' I said.

'Well that saves me the trouble, I suppose.' Illmann turned his head towards the sergeant. 'The trunk also contained the dead girl's clothing and her identity card,' he dictated.

Inside the card was a smudge of blood.

'Could that be a fingermark, do you think?' I asked him.

He took the card out of my hand and looked carefully at the mark. 'Yes, it could. But I don't see the relevance. An actual fingerprint would be a different story. That would answer a lot of our prayers.'

I shook my head. 'It's not an answer. It's a question. Why would a psycho bother to look at his victim's identity? I mean, the blood indicates that she was probably already dead, assuming it's hers. So why does our man feel obliged to find out her name?'

'Perhaps in order that he might name her in his anonymous call to the Alex?'

'Yes, but then why wait several weeks before making the call? Doesn't that strike you as strange?'

'You have a point there, Bernie.' He bagged the identity card and placed it carefully in his case, before looking back into the trunk. 'And what have we here?' He lifted up a small but heavy-looking sack and glanced inside. 'How's this for strange?' He held it open for my inspection. It was the empty toothpaste tubes that Irma Hanke had been collecting for the Reich Economy Programme. 'Our killer does seem to have thought of everything.'

'It's almost as if the bastard were defying us to catch him. He gives us everything. Think how smug he'll be if we still can't nail him.'

Illmann dictated some more notes to the sergeant and then pronounced that he was finished with the preliminary scene-of-crime investigation, and that it was now the photographer's turn. Pulling our gloves off we moved away from the trunk and found that the station-master had provided coffee. It was hot and strong and I needed it to take away the taste of death that was coating my tongue. Illmann rolled a couple of cigarettes and handed me one. The rich tobacco tasted like barbecued nectar.

'Where does this leave your crazy Czech?' he said. 'The one who thinks he's a cavalry officer.'

'It seems that he really was a cavalry officer,' I said. 'Got a bit shell-shocked on the Eastern Front and never quite recovered. All the same, he's no hop and skip, and frankly, unless I get some hard evidence I'm not confident of making anything stick to him. And I'm not about to send anyone up on an Alexanderplatz-style confession. Not that he's saying anything, mind. He's been questioned the whole weekend and still maintains his innocence. I'll see if somebody from the left-luggage office here can identify him as the coat that left the trunk, but if not then I'll have to let him go.'

'I imagine that will upset your sensitive inspector,' chuckled Illmann. 'The one with the daughter. From what he was saying to me earlier, he was quite sure that it was only a matter of time before you had a case against him.'

'Almost certainly. He views the Czech's conviction for statutory rape as the best reason why I should let him take the fellow into a quiet cell and tap dance all over him.'

'So strenuous, these modern police methods. Wherever do they find the energy?'

'That's all they find energy for. This is well past Deubel's bedtime, as he's already reminded me. Some of these bulls think they're working banking hours.' I waved him over. 'Have you ever noticed how most of Berlin's crimes seem to happen during the day?'

'Surely you're forgetting the early-morning knock-up from your friendly neighbourhood Gestapo man.'

'You never get anyone more senior than a Kriminalassistent doing the A1 Red Tabs. And only then if it's someone important.'

I turned to face Deubel, who was doing his best to act dog-tired and ready for a hospital bed.

'When the photographer has finished his portrait, tell him I want a couple of shots of the trunk with the lid closed. What's more I want the prints ready by the time the left-luggage staff turns up. It'll be something to help refresh their memories. The professor here will be taking the trunk back to the Alex as soon as the snaps are done.'

'What about the girl's family, sir? It is Irma Hanke, isn't it?'

'They'll need to make a formal identification, of course, but not until the professor's had his way with her. Maybe even smartened her up a bit for her mother?'

'I'm not a mortician, Bernie,' he said coolly.

'Come on. I've seen you sew up a bag of minced beef before now.'

'Very well,' Illmann sighed. 'I'll see what I can do. I shall need most of the day, however. Possibly until tomorrow.'

'Have as long as you like, but I want to tell them the news this evening, so see if at least you can nail her head back on to her shoulders by then will you?'

Deubel yawned loudly.

'All right, inspector, you've passed the audition. The role of the tired man in need of his bed is yours. God knows you've worked hard enough for it. As soon as Becker and Korsch turn up you can go home. But I want you to set up an identity parade later on this morning. See if the men who work in this office can't remember our Sudeten friend.'

'Right, sir,' he said, already more alert now that his going home was imminent.

'What's the name of that desk sergeant? The one who took the anonymous call.'

'Gollner.'

'Not old Tanker Gollner?'

'Yes, sir. You'll find him at the police barracks, sir. Apparently he said he'd wait for us there as he'd been pissed around by Kripo before and didn't want to have to sit around all night waiting for us to show up.'

'Same old Tanker,' I smiled. 'Right, I'd best not keep him waiting, had I?'

'What shall I tell Korsch and Becker to do when they arrive?' Deubel asked.

'Get Korsch to go through the rest of the junk in this place. See if we might not have been left any other kind gifts.'

Illmann cleared his throat. 'It might be an idea if one of them were present to observe the autopsy,' he said.

'Becker can help you. He seems to enjoy being around the female body. Not to mention his excellent qualifications in the matter of violent death. Just don't leave him alone with your cadaver, Professor. He's just liable to shoot her or fuck her, depending on the way he's feeling.'

Kleine Alexander Strasse ran north-east towards Horst Wessel Platz and was where the police barracks for those stationed at the nearby Alex was situated. It was a big building, with small apartments for married men and senior officers, and single rooms for the rest.

Despite the fact that he was no longer married, Wachmeister Fritz 'Tanker' Gollner had a small one-bedroom apartment at the back of the barracks on the third floor, in recognition of his long and distinguished service record.

A well-tended window box was the apartment's only concession to homeliness, the walls being bare of anything except a couple of photographs in which Gollner was being decorated. He waved me to the room's solitary armchair and sat himself on the edge of the neatly made bed.

'Heard you was back,' he said quietly. Leaning forwards he pulled out a crate from under the bed. 'Beer?'

'Thanks.'

He nodded reflectively as he pushed off the bottle-tops with his bare thumbs.

'And it's Kommissar now, I hear. Resigns as an inspector. Reincarnated as a Kommissar. Makes you believe in fucking magic, doesn't it? If I didn't know you better I'd say you were in somebody's pocket.'

'Aren't we all? In one way or another.'

'Not me. And unless you've changed, not you either.' He swigged his beer thoughtfully.

Tanker was an East Fresian from Emsland where, it is said, brains are as rare as fur on fish. While he may not have been able to spell Wittgenstein, let alone explain his philosophy, Tanker was a good policeman, one of the old school of uniformed bulls, the firm but fair sort, enforcing the law with a friendly box on the ear for young rowdies, and less inclined to arrest a man and haul him off to the cells than give him an effective and administratively simple bedtime-story with his encyclopaedia-sized fist. It was said of Tanker that he was the toughest bull in Orpo and, looking at him sitting opposite me now, in his shirt sleeves, his great belt creaking under the weight of his even greater belly, I didn't find this hard to believe. Certainly time had stood still with his prognathous features – somewhere around one million years BC. Tanker could not have looked less civilized than if he had been wearing the skin of a sabre-toothed tiger.

I found my cigarettes and offered him one. He shook his head and took out his pipe.

'If you ask me,' I said, 'we're every one of us in the back pocket of Hitler's trousers. And he means to slide down a mountain on his arse.'

Tanker sucked at the bowl of his pipe and started to fill it with tobacco. When he'd finished he smiled and raised his bottle.

'Then here's to stones under the fucking snow.'

He belched loudly and lit his pipe. The clouds of pungent smoke that rolled towards me like Baltic fog reminded me of Bruno. It even smelt like the same foul mixture that he had smoked.

'You knew Bruno Stahlecker, didn't you, Tanker?'

He nodded, still drawing on the pipe. Through clenched teeth, he said: 'That I did. I heard about what happened. Bruno was a good man.' He removed the pipe from his leathery old mouth and surveyed the progress of his smoke. 'Knew him quite well, really. We were both in the infantry together. Saw a fair bit of action, too. Of course, he wasn't much more than a spit of a lad then, but it never seemed to bother him much, the fighting I mean. He was a brave one.'

'The funeral was last Thursday.'

'I'd have gone too if I could have got the time.' He thought for a moment. 'But it was all the way down in Zehlendorf. Too far.' He finished his beer and opened another two bottles. 'Still, they got the piece of shit who killed him I hear, so that's all right then.'

'Yes, it certainly looks like it,' I said. 'Tell me about this telephone call tonight. What time was this?'

'Just before midnight, sir. Fellow asks for the duty sergeant. You're speaking to him, I says. Listen carefully, he says. The missing girl, Irma Hanke, he says, is to be found in a large blue-leather trunk in the left-luggage at Zoo Bahnhof. Who's this, I asks, but he'd hung up.'

'Can you describe his voice?'

'I'd say it was an educated sort of voice, sir. And used to giving an order and having it carried out. Rather like an officer.' He shook his large head. 'Couldn't tell you how old, though.'

'Any accent?'

'Just the trace of Bavarian.'

'You sure about that?'

'My late wife was from Nuremberg, sir. I'm sure.'

'And how would you describe his tone? Agitated? Disturbed at all?'

'He didn't sound like a spinner, if that's what you mean, sir. He was as cool as the piss out of a frozen eskimo. As I said, just like an officer.'

'And he asked to speak to the duty sergeant?'

'Those were his actual words, sir.'

'Any background noise? Traffic? Music? That sort of thing?'

'Nothing at all.'

'What did you do then? After the call.'

'I telephoned the operator at the Central Telephone Office on Französische Strasse. She traced the number to a public telephone box outside Bahnhof West Kreuz. I sent a squad car round there to seal it off until a team from 5D could get down there and have it checked out for piano players.'

'Good man. And then you called Deubel?'

'Yes, sir.'

I nodded and started on my second bottle of beer.

'I take it Orpo knows what this is all about?'

'Von der Schulenberg had all the Hauptmanns into the briefing-room at the start of last week. They passed on to us what a lot of the men already suspected. That there was another Gormann on the streets of Berlin. Most of the lads figure that's why you're back on the force. Most of the civils we've got now couldn't detect coal on a slag heap. But that Gormann case. Well, it was a good piece of work.'

'Thanks, Tanker.'

'All the same, sir, it doesn't look like this little Sudeten spinner you're holding could have done it, does it? If you don't mind me saying so.'

'Not unless he had a telephone in his cell, no. Still, we'll see if the left-luggage people at Zoo Bahnhof like the look of him. You never know, he might have had an associate on the outside.'

Tanker nodded. 'That's true enough,' he said. 'Anything is possible in Germany just as long as Hitler shits in the Reich Chancellery.'

Several hours later I was back at Zoo Bahnhof, where Korsch had already distributed photographs of the trunk to the assembled left-luggage staff. They stared and stared, shook their heads and scratched their grizzly chins, and still none of them could remem-ber anyone leaving a blue-leather trunk.

The tallest of them, a man wearing the longest khaki-coloured boiler coat, and who seemed to be in charge of the rest, collected a notebook from under the metal-topped counter and brought it over to me.

'Presumably you record the names and addresses of those leaving luggage with you,' I said to him, without much enthusiasm. As a general rule, killers leaving their victims as left-luggage at railway stations don't normally volunteer their real names and addresses.

The man in the khaki coat, whose bad teeth resembled the blackened ceramic insulators on tram cables, looked at me with quiet confidence and tapped the hard cover of his register with the quick of a fingernail.

'It'll be in here, the one who left your bloody trunk.'

He opened his book, licked a thumb that a dog would have refused, and began to turn the greasy pages.

'On the trunk in your photograph there's a ticket,' he said. 'And on that ticket is a number, same one as what's chalked on the side of the item. And that number will be in this book, alongside a date, a name and an address.' He turned several more pages and then traced down the page with his forefinger.

'Here we are,' he said. 'The trunk was deposited here on Friday, 19 August.'

'Four days after she disappeared,' Korsch said quietly.

The man followed his finger along a line to the facing page. 'Says here that the trunk belongs to a Herr Heydrich, initial "R", of Wilhelmstrasse, number 102.'

Korsch snorted with laughter.

'Thank you,' I said to the man. 'You've been most helpful.'

'I don't see what's funny,' grumbled the man as he walked away.

I smiled at Korsch. 'Looks like someone has a sense of humour.'

'Are you going to mention this in the report, sir?' he grinned.

'It's material, isn't it?'

'It's just that the general won't like it.'

'He'll be beside himself, I should think. But you see, our killer isn't the only one who enjoys a good joke.'

★

Back at the Alex I received a call from the head of what was ostensibly Illmann's department – VD1, Forensics. I spoke to an SS-Hauptsturmführer Dr Schade, whose tone was predictably obsequious, no doubt in the belief that I had some influence with General Heydrich.

The doctor informed me that a fingerprint team had removed a number of prints from the telephone box at West Kreuz in which the killer had apparently called the Alex. These were now a matter for VC1, the Records Department. As to the trunk and its contents, he had spoken to Kriminalassistent Korsch and would inform him immediately if any fingerprints were discovered there.

I thanked him for his call, and told him that my investigation was to receive top priority, and that everything else would have to take second place.

Within fifteen minutes of this conversation, I received another telephone call, this time from the Gestapo.

'This is Sturmbannführer Roth here,' he said. 'Section 4B1. Kommissar Günther, you are interfering with the progress of a most important investigation.'

'4B1? I don't think I know that department. Are you calling from within the Alex?'

'We are based at Meinekestrasse, investigating Catholic criminals.'

'I'm afraid I know nothing of your department, Sturmbannführer. Nor do I wish to. Nevertheless, I cannot see how I can possibly be interfering with one of your investigations.'

'The fact remains that you are. It was you who ordered SS-Hauptsturmführer Dr Schade to give your own investigation priority over any other?'

'That's right, I did.'

'Then you, a Kommissar, should know that the Gestapo takes precedence over Kripo where the services of VD1 are required.'

'I know of no such thing. But what great crime has been committed that might require your department to take precedence over a murder investigation? Charging a priest with a fraudulent transubstantiation perhaps? Or trying to pass off the communion wine as the blood of Christ?'

'Your levity is quite out of order, Kommissar,' he said. 'This department is investigating most serious charges of homosexuality among the priesthood.'

'Is that so? Then I shall certainly sleep more soundly in my bed tonight. All the same, my investigation has been given top priority by General Heydrich himself.'

'Knowing the importance that he attaches to apprehending religious enemies of the state, I find that very hard to believe.'

'Then may I suggest that you telephone the Wilhelmstrasse and have the general explain it to you personally.'

'I'll do that. No doubt he will also be greatly disturbed at your failure to appreciate the menace of the third international conspiracy dedicated to the ruin of Germany. Catholicism is no less a threat to Reich security than Bolshevism and World Jewry.'

'You forgot men from outer space,' I said. 'Frankly, I don't give a shit what you tell him. VD1 is part of Kripo, not the Gestapo, and in all matters relating to this investigation Kripo is to take priority in the services of our own department. I have it in writing from the Reichskriminaldirektor, as does Dr Schade. So why don't you take your so-called case and shove it up your arse. A little more shit in there won't make much of a difference to the way you smell.'

I slammed the receiver down on to its cradle. There were, after all, a few enjoyable aspects to the job. Not least of these was the opportunity it afforded to piss on the Gestapo's shoes.

At the identity parade later that same morning, the left-luggage staff failed to identify Gottfried Bautz as the man who had deposited the trunk containing Irma Hanke's body, and to Deubel's disgust I signed the order releasing him from custody.

It's the law that all strangers arriving in Berlin must be reported to a police station by their hotelier or landlord within six days. In this

way the Resident Registration Office at the Alex is able to give out
the address of anyone resident in Berlin for the price of fifty pfennigs. People imagine that this law must be part of the Nazi
Emergency Powers, but in truth it has existed for a while. The
Prussian police was always so efficient.

My office was a few doors down from the Registration Office in
room 350, which meant that the corridor was always noisy with
people, and obliged me to keep my door shut. No doubt this had
been one of the reasons why I had been put here, as far away from
the offices of the Murder Commission as it was possible to be. I
suppose the idea was that my presence should be kept out of the
way of other Kripo personnel, for fear that I might contaminate
them with some of my more anarchic attitudes to police investigation. Or perhaps they had hoped that my insubordinate spirit might
be broken by first being dramatically lowered. Even on a sunny day
like this one was, my office had a dismal aspect. The olive-green
metal desk had more thread-catching edges than a barbed-wire
fence, and had the single virtue of matching the worn linoleum
and the dingy curtains, while the walls were a couple of thousand
cigarettes' shade of yellow.

Walking in there after snatching a few hours of sleep back at my
apartment, and presented with the sight of Hans Illmann waiting
patiently for me with a dossier of photographs, I didn't think that
the place was about to get any more pleasant. Congratulating myself
on having had the foresight to eat something before what promised to be an unappetizing meeting, I sat down and faced him.

'So this is where they've been hiding you,' he said.

'It's supposed to be only temporary,' I explained, 'just like me.
But frankly, it suits me to be out of the way of the rest of Kripo.
There's less chance of becoming a permanent fixture here again.
And I dare say that suits them too.'

'One would not have thought it possible to cause such aggrava-
tion throughout Kripo Executive from such a bureaucratic dungeon
as this.' He laughed, and stroking his chin-beard added: 'You, and
a Sturmbannführer from the Gestapo, have caused all sorts of

problems for poor Dr Schade. He's had telephone calls from lots of important people. Nebe, Müller, even Heydrich. How very satisfying for you. No, don't shrug modestly like that. You have my admiration, Bernie, you really do.'

I pulled open a drawer in my desk and took out a bottle and a couple of glasses.

'Let's drink to it,' I said.

'Gladly. I could use one after the day I've had.' He picked up the full glass and sipped it gratefully. 'You know, I had no idea that there was a special department in the Gestapo to persecute Catholics.'

'Nor had I. But I can't say that it surprises me much. National Socialism permits only one kind of organized belief.' I nodded at the dossier on Illmann's lap. 'So what have you got?'

'Victim number five is what we have got.' He handed me the dossier and started to roll himself a cigarette.

'These are good,' I said flicking through its contents. 'Your man takes a nice photograph.'

'Yes, I thought you'd appreciate them. That one of the throat is particularly interesting. The right carotid artery is almost completely severed thanks to one perfectly horizontal knife cut. That means that she was flat on her back when he cut her. All the same, the greater part of the wound is on the right-hand side of the throat, so in all probability our man is right-handed.'

'It must have been some knife,' I said, observing the depth of the wound.

'Yes. It severed the larynx almost completely.' He licked his cigarette paper. 'Something extremely sharp, like a surgical curette I should say. At the same time, however, the epiglottis was strongly compressed, and between that and the oesophagus on the right were haematomas as big as an orange pip.'

'Strangled, right?'

'Very good,' Illmann grinned. 'But half-strangled, in actual fact. There was a small quantity of blood in the girl's partially inflated lungs.'

'So he throttled her into silence, and later cut her throat?'

'She bled to death, hanging upside down like a butchered calf. Same as all the others. Do you have a match?'

I tossed my book across the desk. 'What about her important little places? Did he fuck her?'

'Fucked her, and tore her up a bit in the process. Well, you'd expect that. The girl was a virgin, I should imagine. There were even imprints of his fingernails on the mucous membrane. But more importantly I found some foreign pubic hairs, and I don't mean that they were imported from Paris.'

'You've got a hair colour?'

'Brown. Don't ask me for a shade, I can't be that specific.'

'But you're sure they're not Irma Hanke's?'

'Positive. They stood out on her perfectly Aryan fair-haired little plum like shit in a sugar-bowl.' He leaned back and blew a cloud into the air above his head. 'You want me to try and match one with a cutting from the bush of your crazy Czech?'

'No, I released him at lunchtime. He's in the clear. And as it happens his hair was fair.' I leafed through the typewritten pages of the autopsy report. 'Is that it?'

'Not quite.' He sucked at his cigarette and then crushed it into my ashtray. From his tweed hunting-jacket pocket he produced a sheet of folded newspaper which he spread out on the desk. 'I thought you ought to see this.'

It was the front page of an old issue of *Der Stürmer*, Julius Streicher's anti-Semitic publication. A flash across the top left-hand corner of the paper advertised it as 'A Special Ritual Murder Number'. Not that one needed reminding. The pen-and-ink illustration said it eloquently enough. Eight naked, fair-haired German girls hanging upside down, their throats slit, and their blood spilling into a great Communion plate that was held by an ugly caricature Jew.

'Interesting, don't you think?' he said.

'Streicher's always publishing this sort of crap,' I said. 'Nobody takes it seriously.'

Illmann shook his head, and reclaimed his cigarette. 'I'm not for one minute saying that it should be. I no more believe in ritual murder than I believe in Adolf Hitler the Peacemaker.'

'But there is this drawing, right?' He nodded. 'Which is remarkably similar to the method with which five German girls have already been killed.' He nodded again.

I glanced down the page at the article that accompanied the drawing, and read: 'The Jews are charged with enticing Gentile children and Gentile adults, butchering them and draining their blood. They are charged with mixing this blood into their masses (unleavened bread) and using it to practise superstitious magic. They are charged with torturing their victims, especially the children; and during this torture they scream threats, curses and cast magic spells against the Gentiles. This systematic murder has a special name. It is called Ritual Murder.'

'Are you suggesting that Streicher might have had something to do with these murders?'

'I don't know that I'm suggesting anything, Bernie. I merely thought I ought to bring it to your attention.' He shrugged. 'But why not? After all, he wouldn't be the first district Gauleiter to commit a crime. Governor Kube of Kurmark for example.'

'There are quite a few stories about Streicher that one hears,' I said.

'In any other country Streicher would be in prison.'

'Can I keep this?'

'I wish you would. It's not the sort of thing that one likes to leave lying on the coffee-table.' He crushed out yet another cigarette and stood up to leave. 'What are you going to do?'

'About Streicher? I don't exactly know.' I looked at my watch. 'I'll think about it after the formal ID. Becker's on his way back here with the girl's parents by now. We'd better get down to the mortuary.'

It was something that Becker said that made me drive the Hankes home myself after Herr Hanke had positively identified the remains of his daughter.

'It's not the first time I've had to break bad news to a family,' he had explained. 'In a strange way they always hope against hope, clinging on to the last straw right up until the end. And then when you tell them, that's when it really hits them. The mother breaks down, you know. But somehow these two were different. It's difficult to explain what I mean, sir, but I got the impression that they were expecting it.'

'After four weeks? Come on, they had just resigned themselves to it, that's all.'

Becker frowned and scratched the top of his untidy head.

'No,' he said slowly, 'it was stronger than that, sir. Like they already knew, for sure. I'm sorry, sir, I'm not explaining it very well. Perhaps I shouldn't have mentioned it at all. Perhaps I am imagining it.'

'Do you believe in instinct?'

'I suppose so.'

'Good. Sometimes it's the only thing a bull has got to go on. And then he's got no choice but to trust in it. A bull that doesn't trust a few hunches now and then doesn't ever take any chances. And without taking them you can't ever hope to solve a case. No, you were right to tell me.'

Sitting beside me now, as I drove south-west to Steglitz, Herr Hanke, an accountant with the AEG works on Seestrasse, seemed anything but resigned to his only daughter's death. All the same, I didn't discount what Becker had told me. I was keeping an open mind until I could form my own opinion.

'Irma was a clever girl,' Hanke sighed. He spoke with a Rhineland accent, with a voice that was just like Goebbels'. 'Clever enough to stay on at school and get her Abitur, which she'd wanted to do. But she was no book-buffalo. Just bright, and pretty with it. Good at sports. She had just won her Reich Sports Badge and her swimming certificate. She never did any harm to anyone.' His voice was breaking as he added: 'Who could have killed her, Kommissar? Who would do such a thing?'

'That's what I intend to find out,' I said. But Hanke's wife sitting in the back seat believed she already had the answer.

'Isn't it obvious who is responsible?' she said. 'My daughter was a good BdM girl, praised in her racial-theory class as the perfect example of the Aryan type. She knew her Horst Wessel and could quote whole pages of the Führer's great book. So who do you think killed her, a virgin, but the Jews? Who else but the Jews would have done such things to her?'

Herr Hanke turned in his seat and took his wife by the hand.

'We don't know that, Silke, dear,' he said. 'Do we, Kommissar?'

'I think it's very unlikely,' I said.

'You see, Silke? The Kommissar doesn't believe it, and neither do I.'

'I see what I see,' she hissed. 'You're both wrong. It's as plain as the nose on a Jew's face. Who else but the Jews? Don't you realize how obvious it is?'

'The accusation is loudly raised immediately, anywhere in the world, when a body is found which bears the marks of ritual murder. This accusation is raised only against the Jews.' I remembered the words of the article in *Der Stürmer* which I had folded in my pocket, and as I listened to Frau Hanke it occurred to me that she was right, but in a way she could hardly have dreamt of.

II

Thursday, 22 September

A whistle shrieked, the train jolted, and then we pulled slowly out of Anhalter Station on the six-hour journey that would take us to Nuremberg. Korsch, the compartment's only other occupant, was already reading his newspaper.

'Hell,' he said, 'listen to this. It says here that the Soviet foreign minister, Maxim Litvinoff declared in front of the League of Nations in Geneva that his government is determined to fulfil its existing treaty of alliance with Czechoslovakia, and that it will offer military help at the same time as France. Christ, we'll really be in for it then, with an attack on both fronts.'

I grunted. There was less chance of the French offering any real opposition to Hitler than there was of them declaring Prohibition. Litvinoff had chosen his words carefully. Nobody wanted war. Nobody but Hitler, that is. Hitler the syphilitic.

My thoughts returned to a meeting I had had the previous Tuesday with Frau Kalau vom Hofe at the Goering Institute.

'I brought your books back,' I explained. 'The one by Professor Berg was particularly interesting.'

'I'm glad you thought so,' she said. 'How about the Baudelaire?'

'That too, although it seemed much more applicable to Germany now. Especially the poems called "Spleen".'

'Maybe now you're ready for Nietzsche,' she said, leaning back in her chair.

It was a pleasantly furnished, bright office with a view of the Zoo opposite. You could just about hear the monkeys screaming in the distance.

Her smile persisted. She was better looking than I remembered.

I picked up the solitary photograph that sat on her desk and stared at a handsome man and two little boys.

'Your family?'

'Yes.'

'You must be very happy.' I returned the picture to its position. 'Nietzsche,' I said, changing the subject. 'I don't know about that. I'm not really much of a reader, you see. I don't seem to be able to find the time. But I did look up those pages in *Mein Kampf* – the ones about venereal disease. Mind you, it meant that for a while I had to use a brick to wedge the bathroom window open.' She laughed. 'Anyway, I think you must be right.' She started to speak but I raised my hand. 'I know, I know, you didn't say anything. You were just telling me what is written in the Führer's marvellous book. Not offering a psychotherapeutic analysis of him through his writing.'

'That's right.'

I sat down and faced her across the desk.

'But that sort of thing is possible?'

'Oh, yes indeed.'

I handed her the page from *Der Stürmer*.

'Even with something like this?'

She looked at me levelly, and then opened her cigarette box. I helped myself to one, and then lit us both.

'Are you asking me officially?' she said.

'No, of course not.'

'Then I should say that it would be possible. In fact I should say that *Der Stürmer* is the work of not one but several psychotic personalities. The so-called editorials, these illustrations by Fino – God only knows what effect this sort of filth is having on people.'

'Can you speculate a little? The effect, I mean.'

She pursed her beautiful lips. 'Hard to evaluate,' she said after a pause. 'Certainly for weaker personalities, this sort of thing, regularly absorbed, could be corrupting.'

'Corrupting enough to make a man a murderer?'

'No,' she said, 'I don't think so. It wouldn't make a killer out of a normal man. But for a man already disposed to kill, I think it's quite possible that this kind of story and drawing might have a profound effect on him. And as you know from your own reading of Berg, Kürten himself was of the opinion that the more salacious kind of crime reporting had very definitely affected him.'

She crossed her legs, the sibilance of her stockings drawing my thoughts to their tops, to her garters and finally to the lacy paradise that I imagined existed there. My stomach tightened at the thought of running my hand up her skirt, at the thought of her stripped naked before me, and yet still speaking intelligently to me. Exactly where is the beginning of corruption?

'I see,' I said. 'And what would be your professional opinion of the man who published this story? I mean Julius Streicher.'

'A hatred like this is almost certainly the result of a great mental instability.' She paused for a moment. 'Can I tell you something in confidence?'

'Of course.'

'You know that Matthias Goering, the chairman of this institute, is the prime minister's cousin?'

'Yes.'

'Streicher has written a lot of poisonous nonsense about medicine as a Jewish conspiracy, and psychotherapy in particular. For a while the future of mental health in this country was in jeopardy because of him. Consequently Dr Goering has good reason to wish Streicher out of the way, and has already prepared a psychological evaluation of him at the prime minister's orders. I'm sure that I could guarantee the cooperation of this institute in any investigation involving Streicher.'

I nodded slowly.

'Are you investigating Streicher?'

'In confidence?'

'Of course.'

'I don't honestly know. Right now let's just say that I'm curious about him.'

'Do you want me to ask Dr Goering for help?'

I shook my head. 'Not at this stage. But thanks for the offer. I'll certainly bear it in mind.' I stood up, and went to the door. 'I'll bet you probably think quite highly of the prime minister, him being the patron of this institute. Am I right?'

'He's been good to us, it's true. Without his help I doubt there would be an institute. Naturally we think highly of him for that.'

'Please don't think I'm blaming you, I'm not. But hasn't it ever occurred to you that your beneficent patron is just as likely to go and shit in someone else's garden, as Streicher is in yours? Have you ever thought about that? It stikes me as how it's a dirty neighbourhood we're living in, and that we're all going to keep finding crap on our shoes until someone has the sense to put all the stray dogs in the public kennel.' I touched the brim of my hat to her. 'Think about it.'

Korsch twisted his moustache absently as he continued reading his newspaper. I supposed that he had grown it in an effort to look more of a character, in the same way as some men will grow a beard: not because they dislike shaving – a beard requires just as much grooming as a clean-shaven face – but because they think it will make them seem like someone to be taken seriously. But with Korsch the moustache, little more than the stroke of an eyebrow-pencil, merely served to underscore his shifty mien. It made him look like a pimp, an effect at odds with his character however, which in a period of less than two weeks, I had discovered to be a willing and reliable one.

Noticing my attention, he was moved to inform me that the Polish foreign minister, Josef Beck, had demanded a solution to the problem of the Polish minority in the Olsa region of Czecho-slovakia.

'Just like a bunch of gangsters, isn't it, sir?' he said. 'Everyone wants his cut.'

'Korsch,' I said, 'you missed your vocation. You should have been a newsreader on the radio.'

'Sorry, sir,' he said, folding away his paper. 'Have you been to Nuremberg before?'

'Once. Just after the war. I can't say I like Bavarians much, though. How about you?'

'First time. But I know what you mean about Bavarians. All that quaint conservatism. It's a lot of nonsense, isn't it?' He looked out of the window for a minute at the moving picture that was the German countryside. Facing me again he said: 'Do you really think Streicher could have something to do with these killings, sir?'

'We're not exactly tripping over the leads in this case, are we? Nor would it appear that the Gauleiter of Franconia is what you would call popular. Arthur Nebe even went so far as to tell me that Julius Streicher is one of the Reich's greatest criminals, and that there are already several investigations pending against him. He was keen that we should speak to the Nuremberg Police President personally. Apparently there's no love lost between him and Streicher. But at the same time we have to be extremely careful. Streicher runs his district like a Chinese warlord. Not to mention the fact that he's on first-name terms with the Führer.'

When the train reached Leipzig a young SA naval company leader joined our compartment, and Korsch and I went in search of the dining car. By the time we had finished eating the train was in Gera, close to the Czech border, but despite the fact that our SA travelling companion got off at that stop, there was no sign of the troop concentrations we had heard about. Korsch suggested that the naval SA man's presence there meant that there was going to be an amphibious attack, and this, we both agreed, would be the best thing for everyone, given that the border was largely mountainous.

It was early evening by the time that the train got into the Haupt Station in central Nuremberg. Outside, by the equestrian statue of some unknown aristocrat, we caught a taxi which drove us eastwards along Frauentorgraben and parallel to the walls of the old city. These are as high as seven or eight metres, and dominated at intervals by big square towers. This huge medieval wall, and a great, dry, grassy moat that is as wide as thirty metres, help to distinguish the old Nuremberg from the new, which, with a singular lack of obtrusion, surrounds it.

Our hotel was the Deutscher Hof, one of the city's oldest and best, and our rooms commanded excellent views across the wall to the steep, pitched rooftops and regiments of chimney-pots which lay beyond.

At the beginning of the eighteenth century, Nuremberg was the largest city in the ancient kingdom of Franconia, as well as one of the principal marts of trade between Germany, Venice and the East. It was still the chief commercial and manufacturing city of southern Germany, but now it had a new importance, as the capital of National Socialism. Every year, Nuremberg played host to the great Party rallies which were the brainchild of Hitler's architect, Speer.

As thoughtful as the Nazis were, naturally you didn't have to go to Nuremberg to see one of these over-orchestrated events, and in September people stayed away from cinemas in droves for fear of having to sit through the newsreels which would be made up of virtually nothing else.

By all accounts, sometimes there were as many as a hundred thousand people at the Zeppelin Field to wave their flags. Nuremberg, like any city in Bavaria as I recall, never did offer much in the way of real amusement.

Since we weren't appointed to meet Martin, the Nuremberg Chief of Police, until ten o'clock the following morning, Korsch and I felt obliged to spend the evening in search of whatever entertainment there was. Especially because Kripo Executive was footing the bill. It was a thought that had particular appeal for Korch.

'This isn't bad at all,' he said enthusiastically. 'Not only is the Alex paying for me to stay in a cock-smart hotel, but I'm also getting the overtime.'

'Make the most of it,' I said. 'It's not often that fellows like you and me get to play the Party bigshot. And if Hitler gets his war, we may have to live on this little memory for quite a while.'

A lot of bars in Nuremberg had the look of places which might have been the headquarters of smaller trade guilds. These were filled with militaria and other relics of the past, and the walls were often adorned with old pictures and curious souvenirs collected by generations of proprietors, which were of no more interest to us than a set of logarithm tables. But at least the beer was good, you could always say that about Bavaria, and at the Blaue Flasche on Hall Platz, where we ended up for dinner, the food was even better.

Back at the Deutscher Hof we called in at the hotel's café restaurant for a brandy and were met by an astonishing sight. Sitting at a corner table, loudly drunk, was a party of three that included a couple of brainless-looking blondes and, wearing the single-breasted light-brown tunic of an NSDAP political leader, the Gauleiter of Franconia, Julius Streicher himself.

The waiter returning with our drinks smiled nervously when we asked him to confirm that it was indeed Julius Streicher sitting in the corner of the café. He said that it was, and quickly left as Streicher started to shout for another bottle of champagne.

It wasn't difficult to see why Streicher was feared. Apart from his rank, which was powerful enough, the man was built like a bare-fist fighter. With hardly any neck at all, his bald head, small ears, solid-looking chin and almost invisible eyebrows, Streicher was a paler version of Benito Mussolini. His apparent belligerence was given greater force by an enormous rhino-whip which lay on the table before him like some long black snake.

He thumped the table with his fist so that all the glasses and cutlery rattled loudly.

'What the fuck does a man have to do to get some fucking service around here?' he yelled at the waiter. 'We're dying of thirst.' He pointed at another waiter. 'You, I told you to keep a fucking eye on us, you little cunt, and the minute you saw an empty bottle to bring us another. What, are you stupid or something?' Once again he banged the table with his fist, much to the amusement of his two companions, who squealed with delight, and persuaded Streicher to laugh at his own ill-temper.

'Who does he remind you of?' said Korsch.

'Al Capone,' I said without thinking, and then added: 'Actually, they all remind me of Al Capone.' Korsch laughed.

We sipped our brandies and watched the show, which was more than we could have hoped for so early in our visit, and by midnight Streicher's and our own were the only parties left in the café, the others having been driven away by the Gauleiter's incessant cursing. Another waiter came to wipe our table and empty our ashtray.

'Is he always this bad?' I asked him.

The waiter laughed bitterly. 'This? This is nothing,' he said. 'You should have seen him ten days ago after the Party rallies were finally over. He tore hell out of this place.'

'Why do you let him come in here, then?' said Korsch.

The waiter looked at him pityingly. 'Are you kidding? You just try stopping him. The Deutscher is his favourite watering-hole. He'd soon find some pretext on which to close us down if we ever kicked him out. Maybe worse than that, who knows? They say he often goes up to the Palace of Justice on Furtherstrasse and whips young boys in the cells there.'

'Well, I'd hate to be a Jew in this town,' said Korsch.

'Too right,' said the waiter. 'Last month he persuaded a crowd of people to burn down the synagogue.'

Streicher now began to sing, and accompanied himself with a percussion that was provided with his knife and fork and the table-top, from which he had thoughtfully removed the tablecloth. The combination of his drumming, accent, drunkenness and complete inability to hold a tune, not to mention the screeches and giggles of his two guests, made it impossible for either Korsch or myself to recognize the song. But you could bet that it wasn't by Kurt Weill, and it did have the effect of driving the two of us off to bed.

The next morning we walked a short way north to Jakob's Platz, where opposite a fine church stands a fortress built by the old order of Teutonic knights. At its south-eastern point, it includes a domed edifice that is the Elisabeth-Kirche, while at the south-western point, on the corner of Schlotfegergasse, is the old barracks, now police headquarters. As far as I was aware, there wasn't another police HQ in the whole of Germany which had the facility of its own Catholic church.

'That way they're sure to wring a confession out of you one way or the other,' Korsch joked.

SS-Obergruppenführer Dr Benno Martin, whose predecessors as police president of Nuremberg included Heinrich Himmler, greeted us in his baronial top-storey office. The look of the place was such that I half expected him to have a sabre in his hand; and indeed, when he turned to one side I noticed that he had a duelling scar on his cheek.

'And how is Berlin?' he asked quietly, offering us a cigarette from his box. His own smoke he fitted into a rosewood holder that was more like a pipe and which held the cigarette vertically, at a right-angle to his face.

'Things are quiet,' I said. 'But that's because everyone is holding their breath.'

'Quite so,' he said, and waved at the newspaper on his desk. 'Chamberlain has flown to Bad Godesberg for more talks with the Führer.'

Korsch pulled the paper towards him and glanced at the headline. He pushed it back again.

'There's too much damned talk, if you ask me,' said Martin.

I grunted non-committally.

Martin grinned and laid his square chin on his hand. 'Arthur Nebe tells me that you've got a psychopath stalking the streets of Berlin, raping and cutting the flower of German maidenhood. He also tells me that you've a mind to take a look at Germany's most infamous psychopath and see if they might at least be holding hands. I refer of course to that pig's sphincter, Streicher. Am I right?'

I met his cold, penetrating gaze and held it. I was willing to bet that the general was no altar boy himself. Nebe had described Benno Martin as an extremely capable administrator. For a police chief in Nazi Germany that could have meant just about anything up to, and including, a Torquemada.

'That's right, sir,' I said, and showed him the *Der Stürmer* front page. 'This illustrates exactly how five girls have been murdered. With the exception of the Jew catching the blood in the plate of course.'

'Of course,' said Martin. 'But you haven't ruled out the Jews as a possibility.'

'No, but –'

'But it's the very theatricality of this same mode of killing that makes you doubt that it could be them. Am I right?'

'That and the fact that none of the victims has been Jewish.'

'Maybe he just prefers more attractive girls,' Martin grinned. 'Maybe he just prefers blonde, blue-eyed girls to depraved Jewish mongrels. Or maybe it's just coincidence.' He caught my raised eyebrow. 'But you're not the kind of man who believes much in coincidence, Kommissar, are you?'

'Not where murder is concerned, sir, no. I see patterns where other people see coincidence. Or at least I try to.' I leant back in my chair, crossing my legs. 'Are you acquainted with the work of Carl Jung on the subject, sir?'

He snorted with derision. 'Good God, is that what Kripo gets up to in Berlin these days?'

'I think he'd have made rather a good policeman, sir,' I said, smiling affably, 'if you don't mind me saying so.'

'Spare me the psychology lecture, Kommissar,' Martin sighed. 'Just tell me which particular pattern you see that might involve our beloved Gauleiter here in Nuremberg.'

'Well sir, it's this. It has crossed my mind that someone might be trying to sew the Jews into a very nasty body-bag.'

Now the general raised an eyebrow.

'Do you really care what happens to the Jews?'

'Sir, I care what happens to fifteen-year-old girls on their way home from school tonight.' I handed the general a sheet of type-written paper. 'These are the dates on which the five girls disappeared. I hoped that you might be able to tell me if Streicher or any of his associates were in Berlin on any of these occasions.'

Martin glanced down the page. 'I suppose that I can find out,' he said. 'But I can tell you now that he is virtually *persona non grata* there. Hitler keeps him down here, out of harm's way, so that the only people he can annoy are the ones of no account, like myself. Of course, that's not to say that Streicher doesn't visit Berlin in secret sometimes. He does. The Führer enjoys Streicher's after-dinner conversation, though I cannot imagine why, since he also apparently enjoys my own.'

He turned to the trolley of telephones that stood by his desk and called up his adjutant, telling him to establish Streicher's whereabouts on the dates I had provided.

'I was given to understand that you also had certain information regarding Streicher's criminal behaviour,' I said.

Martin got up and went over to his filing cabinet. Laughing quietly he took out a file that was as thick as a shoe box, and brought it back to the desk.

'There's virtually nothing I don't know about that bastard,' he snarled. 'His SS guards are my men. His telephone is tapped, and I have listening devices in all of his homes. I even have photographers on constant vigil in a shop opposite a room where he sees a prostitute from time to time.'

Korsch breathed a curse that was both admiration and surprise.

'So, where do you want to start? I could occupy one whole department with what that bastard gets up to in this town. Rape charges, paternity suits, assaults on young boys with that whip he carries, bribery of public officials, misappropriation of Party funds, fraud, theft, forgery, arson, extortion – we are talking about a gangster, gentlemen. A monster, terrorizing the people of this town, never paying his bills, driving businesses into bankruptcy, wrecking the careers of honourable men who had the courage to cross him.'

'We had a chance to see him for ourselves,' I said. 'Last night, at the Deutscher Hof. He was boozing it up with a couple of ladies.'

The general's look was scathing. 'Ladies. You're joking, of course. They'd have certainly been nothing more than common prosti-tutes. He introduces them to people as actresses, but prostitutes is what they are. Streicher is behind most of the organized prostitution in this city.' He opened his box-file and started to leaf through the complaint-sheets.

'Indecent assaults, criminal damage, hundreds of charges of corruption – Streicher runs this city like his personal kingdom, and gets away with it.'

'The rape charges sound interesting,' I said. 'What happened there?'

'No evidence offered. The victims were either bullied or bought. You see, Streicher is a very rich man. Quite apart from what he makes as a district governor, selling favours, offices even, he makes a fortune off that lousy newspaper of his. It's got a circulation of half a million, which at thirty pfennigs a copy adds up to 150,000 Reichsmarks a week.' Korsch whistled. 'And that's not counting what he makes from the advertising. Oh yes, Streicher can buy himself an awful lot of favours.'

'Anything more serious than the rape charges?'

'You mean, has he murdered anyone?'

'Yes.'

'Well, we won't count the lynchings of the odd Jew here and there. Streicher likes to organize a nice pogrom for himself now and then. Quite apart from anything else, it gives him a chance to pick up a bit of extra loot. And we'll discount the girl who died in his house at the hands of a backstreet angel-maker. Streicher wouldn't be the first senior Party member to procure an illegal abortion. That leaves two unsolved homicides which point the finger at his having been involved.

'One, a waiter at a party Streicher went to, who decided to choose that occasion to commit suicide. A witness saw Streicher walking in the grounds with the waiter less than twenty minutes before the man was found drowned in the pond. The other, a young actress acquainted with Streicher, whose naked body was found in Luitpoldhain Park. She had been flogged to death with a leather whip. You know, I saw the body. There wasn't a centimetre of skin left on her.'

He sat down again, apparently satisfied with the effect his

revelations had had on Korsch and myself. Even so he could not resist adding a few more salacious details as they occurred to him.

'And then there is Streicher's collection of pornography, which he boasts is the largest in Nuremberg. Boasting is what Streicher is best at: the number of illegitimate children he has fathered, the number of wet-dreams he's had that week, how many boys he has whipped that day. It's even the sort of detail he includes in his public speeches.'

I shook my head and heard myself sigh. How did it ever get to be this bad? How was it that a sadistic monster like Streicher got to a position of virtually absolute power? And how many others like him were there? But perhaps the most surprising thing was that I still had the capacity to be surprised at what was happening in Germany.

'What about Streicher's associates?' I said. 'The writers on *Der Stürmer*. His personal staff. If Streicher is trying to hang one on the Jews he could be using someone else to do the dirty work.'

General Martin frowned. 'Yes, but why do it in Berlin? Why not do it here?'

'I can think of a couple of good reasons,' I said. 'Who are Streicher's main enemies in Berlin?'

'With the exception of Hitler, and possibly Goebbels, you can take your pick.' He shrugged. 'Goering most of all. Then Himmler, and Heydrich.'

'That's what I thought you'd say. There's your first reason. Five unsolved murders in Berlin would cause maximum embarrassment to at least two of his worst enemies.'

He nodded. 'And your second reason?'

'Nuremberg has a history of Jew-baiting,' I said. 'Pogroms are common enough here. But Berlin is still comparatively liberal in its treatment of Jews. So if Streicher were to bring down the blame for these murders on to the heads of Berlin's Jewish community, then that would make things even harder for them as well. Perhaps for Jews all over Germany.'

'There might be something in that,' he admitted, picking another cigarette and screwing it into his curious little holder. 'But it's going to take time to organize this kind of investigation. Naturally I assume that Heydrich will ensure the full cooperation of the Gestapo. I think that the highest level of surveillance is warranted, don't you, Kommissar?'

'That's certainly what I'll be writing in my report, sir.'

The telephone rang. Martin answered it and then handed me the receiver.

'Berlin,' he said. 'For you.'

It was Deubel.

'There's another girl missing,' he said.

'When?'

'Around nine last night. Blonde, blue-eyed, same age as the others.'

'No witnesses?'

'Not so far.'

'We'll catch the afternoon train back.' I handed the receiver to Martin.

'It looks as if our killer was busy again last night,' I explained. 'Another girl disappeared around the time that Korsch and myself were sitting in the café at the Deutscher Hof giving Streicher an alibi.'

Martin shook his head. 'It would have been too much to hope that Streicher could have been absent from Nuremberg on all your dates,' he said. 'But don't give up. We may even yet manage to establish some sort of coincidence affecting Streicher and his associates which satisfies you, and me, not to mention this fellow Jung.'

12

Saturday, 24 September

Steglitz is a prosperous, middle-class suburb in south-west Berlin. The red bricks of the town hall mark its eastern side, and the Botanical Gardens its west. It was at this end, near the Botanical Museum and the Planzen Physiological Institute, that Frau Hildegard Steininger lived with her two children, Emmeline aged fourteen, and Paul aged ten.

Herr Steininger, the victim of a fatal car crash, had been some brilliant bank official with the Privat Kommerz, and the type that was insured up to his hair follicles, leaving his young widow comfortably off in a six-room apartment in Lepsius Strasse.

At the top of a four-storey building, the apartment had a large wrought-iron balcony outside a small, brown-painted French window, and not one but three skylights in the sitting-room ceiling. It was a big, airy sort of place, tastefully furnished and decorated, and smelling strongly of the fresh coffee she was making.

'I'm sorry to make you go through all this again,' I told her. 'I just want to make absolutely sure we didn't miss anything.'

She sighed and sat down at the kitchen table, opening her crocodile-leather handbag and finding a matching cigarette box. I lit her and watched her beautiful face tense a little. She spoke like she'd rehearsed what she was saying too many times to play the part well.

'On Thursday evenings Emmeline goes to a dancing class with Herr Wiechert in Potsdam. Grosse Weinmeisterstrasse if you want to know the address. That's at eight o'clock, so she always leaves here at seven, and catches a train from Steglitz Station which takes thirty minutes. There's a change at Wannsee I think. Well, at exactly ten minutes past eight, Herr Wiechert telephoned me to see if Emmeline was sick, as she hadn't arrived.'

I poured the coffee and set two cups down on the table before sitting opposite her.

'Since Emmeline is never, ever late, I asked Herr Wiechert to call again as soon as she arrived. And indeed he did call again, at 8.30, and at nine o'clock, but on each occasion it was to tell me that there was still no sign of her. I waited until 9.30 and called the police.'

She sipped her coffee with a steady hand, but it wasn't hard to see that she was upset. There was a wateriness in her blue eyes, and in the sleeve of her blue-crepe dress could be seen a sodden-looking lace handkerchief.

'Tell me about your daughter. Is she a happy sort of girl?'

'As happy as any girl can be who's recently lost her daddy.' She moved her blonde hair away from her face, something she must have done not once but fifty times while I was there, and stared blankly into her coffee cup.

'It was a stupid question,' I said. 'I'm sorry.' I found my cigarettes and filled the silence with the scrape of a match and my embarrassed breath of satisfying tobacco smoke. 'She attends the Paulsen Real Gymnasium School, doesn't she? Is everything all right there? No problems with exams, or anything like that? No school bullies giving her any trouble?'

'She's not the brightest in her class, perhaps,' said Frau Steininger, 'but she's very popular. Emmeline has lots of friends.'

'And the BdM?'

'The what?'

'The League of German Girls.'

'Oh, that. Everything's fine there too.' She shrugged, and then shook her head exasperatedly. 'She's a normal child, Kommissar. Emmeline isn't the kind to run away from home, if that's what you're implying.'

'Like I said, I'm sorry to have to ask these questions, Frau Steininger. But they have to be asked, I'm sure you understand. It's best that we know absolutely everything.' I sipped my coffee and then contemplated the grounds on the bottom of my cup. What did a shape like a scallop shell denote? I wondered. I said: 'What about boyfriends?'

She frowned. 'She's fourteen years old, for God's sake.' Angrily, she stubbed out her cigarette.

'Girls grow up earlier than boys. Earlier than we like, perhaps.' Christ, what did I know about it? Listen to me, I thought, the man with all the goddamned children.

'She's not interested in boys yet.'

I shrugged. 'Just tell me when you get tired of answering these questions, lady, and I'll get out of your way. I'm sure you've got lots more important things to do than help me to find your daughter.'

She stared at me hard for a minute, and then apologized.

'Can I see Emmeline's room, please?'

It was a normal room for a fourteen-year-old girl, at least normal for one who attended a fee-paying school. There was a large bill-poster for a production of *Swan Lake* at the Paris Opéra in a heavy black frame above the bed, and a couple of well-loved teddy bears sitting on the pink quilt. I lifted the pillow. There was a book there, a ten-pfennig romance of the sort you could buy on any street corner. Not exactly *Emil and the Detectives*.

I handed the book to Frau Steininger.

'Like I said, girls grow up early.'

'Did you speak to the technical boys?' I came through the door of my office at the same time as Becker was coming out. 'Is there anything on that trunk yet? Or that length of curtain material?'

Becker turned on his heel and followed me to my desk.

'The trunk was made by Turner & Glanz, sir.' Finding his notebook, he added, 'Friedrichstrasse, number 193a.'

'Sounds cock-smart. They keep a sales list?'

'I'm afraid not, sir. It's a popular line apparently, especially with all the Jews leaving Germany for America. Herr Glanz reckons that they must sell three or four a week.'

'Lucky him.'

'The curtain material is cheap stuff. You can buy it anywhere.'
He started to search through my in-tray.

'Go on, I'm listening.'

'You haven't read my report yet then?'

'Does it sound like I have?'

'I spent yesterday afternoon at Emmeline Steininger's school – the Paulsen Real Gymnasium.' He found his report and waved it in front of my face.

'That must have been nice for you. All those girls.'

'Perhaps you should read it now, sir.'

'Save me the trouble.'

Becker grimaced and looked at his watch.

'Well actually, sir, I was just about to go off. I'm supposed to be taking my children to the funfair at Luna Park.'

'You're getting as bad as Deubel. Where's he, as a matter of interest? Doing a bit of gardening? Shopping with the wife?'

'I think he's with the missing girl's mother, sir.'

'I've just come from seeing her myself. Never mind. Tell me what you found out and then you can clear off.'

He sat down on the edge of my desk and folded his arms.

'I'm sorry, sir, I was forgetting to tell you something else first.'

'Were you indeed? It seems to me that bulls forget quite a lot round the Alex these days. In case you need reminding, this is a murder investigation. Now get off my desk and tell me what the hell is going on.'

He sprang off my desk and stood to attention.

'Gottfried Bautz is dead, sir. Murdered, it looks like. His landlady found the body in his apartment early this morning. Korsch has gone over there to see if there's anything in it for us.'

I nodded quietly. 'I see.' I cursed, and then glanced up at him again. Standing there in front of my desk like a soldier, he was managing to look quite ridiculous. 'For God's sake, Becker, sit down before rigor mortis sets in and tell me about your report.'

'Thank you, sir.' He drew up a chair, turned it around and sat with his forearms leaning on the back.

'Two things,' he said. 'First, most of Emmeline Steininger's classmates thought she had spoken about running away from home on more than one occasion. Apparently she and her stepmother didn't get along too well –'

'Her stepmother? She never mentioned that.'

'Apparently her real mother died about twelve years ago. And then the father died recently.'

'What else?'

Becker frowned.

'You said that there were two things.'

'Yes, sir. One of the other girls, a Jewish girl, remembered something that happened a couple of months back. She said that a man wearing a uniform stopped his car near the school gate and called her over. He said that if she answered some questions he'd give her a lift home. Well, she says that she went and stood by his car, and the man asked her what her name was. She said that it was Sarah Hirsch. Then the man asked her if she was a Jew, and when she said that she was he just drove off without another word.'

'Did she give you a description?'

He pulled a face and shook his head. 'Too scared to say much at all. I had a couple of uniformed bulls with me and I think they put her off.'

'Can you blame her? She probably thought you were going to arrest her for soliciting or something. Still, she must be a bright one if she's at a Gymnasium. Maybe she would talk if her parents were with her, and if there weren't any dummies with you. What do you think?'

'I'm sure of it, sir.'

'I'll do it myself. Do I strike you as the avuncular type, Becker? No, you'd better not answer that.'

He grinned amiably.

'All right, that's all. Enjoy yourself.'

'Thank you, sir.' He stood up and went to the door.

'And Becker?'

'Yes, sir?'

'Well done.'

When he'd gone I sat staring into space for quite a while wishing that it was me who was going home to take my children out for a Saturday afternoon at Luna Park. I was overdue for some time off myself, but when you're alone in the world, that sort of thing doesn't seem to matter as much. I was balanced precariously on the edge of a pool of self-pity when there was a knock at my door and Korsch came into the room.

'Gottfried Bautz has been murdered, sir,' he said immediately.

'Yes, I heard. Becker said you went to take a look. What happened?'

Korsch sat down on the chair recently occupied by Becker. He was looking more animated than I had ever seen him before, and clearly something had got him very excited.

'Someone thought his brains were lacking a bit of air, so they gave him a special blow-hole. A real neat job. Between the eyes. The forensic they had down there reckoned it was probably quite a small gun. Probably a six millimetre.' He shifted on his chair. 'But this is the interesting part, sir. Whoever plugged him first knocked him cold. Gottfried's jaw was broken clean in two. And there was a cigarette end in his mouth. Like he'd bitten his smoke in half.' He paused, waiting for me to pass it between my ears a little. 'The other half was on the floor.'

'Cigarette punch?'

'Looks like it, sir.'

'Are you thinking what I'm thinking?'

Korsch nodded deliberately. 'I'm afraid I am. And here's another thing. Deubel keeps a six-shot Little Tom in his jacket pocket. He says that it's just in case he ever loses his Walther. A Little Tom fires the same size of round as killed the Czech.'

'Does he?' I raised my eyebrows. 'Deubel was always convinced that even if Bautz had had nothing to do with our case, he still belonged in the cement.'

'He tried to persuade Becker to have a word with some of his old friends in Vice. He wanted Becker to get them to red tab Bautz on some pretext and have him sent to a KZ. But Becker wasn't having any of it. He said that they couldn't do it, not even on the evidence of the snapper he tried to cut.'

'I'm very glad to hear it. Why wasn't I told about this before?' Korsch shrugged. 'Have you mentioned any of this to the team investigating Bautz's death? I mean about Deubel's cigarette punch and the gun?'

'Not yet, sir.'

'Then we'll handle it ourselves.'

'What are you going to do?'

'That all depends on whether or not he still has that gun. If you'd pierced Bautz's ears, what would you do with it?'

'Find the nearest pig-iron smelter.'

'Precisely. So if he can't show me that gun for examination then he's off this investigation. That might not be enough for a court, but it will satisfy me. I've no use for murderers on my team.'

Korsch scratched his nose thoughtfully, narrowly avoiding the temptation to pick it.

'I don't suppose you've any idea where Inspector Deubel is, do you?'

'Someone looking for me?' Deubel sauntered through the open door. The beery stink that accompanied him was enough to explain where he had been. An unlit cigarette in the corner of his crooked mouth, he stared belligerently at Korsch and then, with unsteady distaste, at me. He was drunk.

'Been in the Café Kerkau,' he said, his mouth refusing to move quite as he would have normally expected. 'It's all right, you know. It's all right, I'm off duty. Least for another hour, anyway. Be fine by then. Don't you worry about me. I can take care of myself.'

'What else have you been taking care of?'

He straightened like a puppet jerking back on its unsteady legs.

'Been asking questions at the station where the Steininger girl went missing.'

'That's not what I meant.'

'No? No? Well, what did you mean, Herr Kommissar?'

'Someone murdered Gottfried Bautz.'

'What, that Czech bastard?' He uttered a laugh that was part belch and part spit.

'His jaw was broken. There was a cigarette end in his mouth.'

'So? What's that to do with me?'

'That's one of your little specialities, isn't it? The cigarette punch? I've heard you say so yourself.'

'There's no fucking patent on it, Günther.' He took a long drag on the dead cigarette and narrowed his bleary eyes. 'You accusing me of canning him?'

'Can I see your gun, Inspector Deubel?'

For several seconds Deubel stood sneering at me before reaching for his shoulder holster. Behind him Korsch was slowly reaching for his own gun, and he kept his hand on its handle until Deubel had laid the Walther PPK on my desk. I picked it up and sniffed the barrel, watching his face for some sign that he knew Bautz had been killed with a gun of a much smaller calibre.

'Shot, was he?' He smiled.

'Executed, more like,' I said. 'It looks like someone put one between his eyes while he was out cold.'

'I'm choked.' Deubel shook his head slowly.

'I don't think so.'

'You're just pissing on the wall, Günther, and hoping that some of it will splash my fucking trousers. Sure, I didn't like that little Czech, just like I hate every pervert that touches kids and hurts women. But that doesn't mean that I had anything to do with his murder.'

'There's an easy way of convincing me of that.'

'Oh? And what's that?'

'Show me that garter-gun you keep on you. The Little Tom.'

Deubel raised his hands innocently.

'What garter-gun? I haven't got a gun like that. The only lighter I'm carrying is there on the table.'

'Everyone who's worked with you knows about that gun. You've bragged about it often enough. Show me the gun and you're in the clear. But if you're not carrying it, then I'll figure it's because you had to get rid of it.'

'What are you talking about? Like I said, I don't have —'

Korsch stood up. He said: 'Come on, Eb. You showed that gun to me only a couple of days ago. You even said that you were never without it.'

'You piece of shit. Take his side against one of your own, would you? Can't you see? He's not one of us. He's one of Heydrich's fucking spies. He doesn't give two farts about Kripo.'

'That's not the way I see it,' Korsch said quietly. 'So how about it? Do we get to see the gun or not?'

Deubel shook his head, smiled and wagged a finger at me.

'You can't prove anything. Not a thing. You know that, don't you?'

I pushed my chair away with the backs of my legs. I needed to be on my feet to say what I was going to say.

'Maybe so. All the same, you're off this case. I don't particularly give a damn what happens to you, Deubel, but as far as I'm concerned you can slither back to whichever excremental corner of this place you came from. I'm choosy about who I have to work with. I don't like killers.'

Deubel bared his yellow teeth even further. His grin looked like the keyboard of an old and badly out of tune piano. Hitching up his shiny flannel trousers he squared his shoulders and pointed his belly in my direction. It was all I could do to resist slamming my fist right into it, but starting a fight like that would probably have suited him very well.

'You want to open your eyes, Günther. Take a walk down to the cells and the interrogation rooms and see what's happening in this place. Choosy about who you work with? You poor swine. There are people being beaten to death here, in this building. Probably as we speak. Do you think anyone really gives a damn about what happens to some cheap little pervert? The morgue is full of them.'

I heard myself reply, with what sounded even to me like almost hopeless naïveté, 'Somebody has to give a damn, otherwise we're no better than criminals ourselves. I can't stop other people from wearing dirty shoes, but I can polish my own. Right from the start you knew that was the way I wanted it. But you had to do it your own way, the Gestapo way, that says a woman's a witch if she floats and innocent if she sinks. Now get out of my sight before I'm tempted to see if my clout with Heydrich goes as far as kicking your arse out of Kripo.'

Deubel sniggered. 'You're a renthole,' he said, and having stared Korsch out until his boozy breath obliged him to turn away, Deubel lurched away.

Korsch shook his head. 'I never liked that bastard,' he said, 'but I didn't think he was —' He shook his head again.

I sat down wearily and reached for the desk drawer and the bottle I kept there.

'Unfortunately he's right,' I said, filling a couple of glasses. I met Korsch's quizzical stare and smiled bitterly. 'Charging a Berlin bull with murder . . .' I laughed. 'Shit, you might just as well try and arrest drunks at the Munich beer festival.'

13

Sunday, 25 September

'Is Herr Hirsch at home?'

The old man answering the door straightened and then nodded. 'I am Herr Hirsch,' he said.

'You are Sarah Hirsch's father?'

'Yes. Who are you?'

He must have been at least seventy, bald, with white hair growing long over the back of his collar, and not very tall, stooped even. It was hard to imagine this man having fathered a fifteen-year-old daughter. I showed him my badge.

'Police,' I said. 'Please don't be alarmed. I'm not here to make any trouble for you. I merely wish to question your daughter. She may be able to describe a man, a criminal.'

Recovering a little of his colour after the sight of my credentials, Herr Hirsch stood to one side and silently ushered me into a hall that was full of Chinese vases, bronzes, blue-patterned plates and intricate balsa-wood carvings in glass cases. These I admired while he closed and locked the front door, and he mentioned that in his youth he had been in the German navy and had travelled widely in the Far East. Aware now of the delicious smell that filled the house, I apologized and said that I hoped I wasn't disturbing the family meal.

'It will be a while yet before we sit down and eat,' said the old man. 'My wife and daughter are still working in the kitchen.' He smiled nervously, no doubt unaccustomed to the politeness of public officials, and led me into a reception room.

'Now then,' he said, 'you said that you wished to speak to my daughter Sarah. That she may be able to identify a criminal.'

'That's right,' I said. 'One of the girls from your daughter's school has disappeared. It's quite possible she was abducted. One of the men, questioning some of the girls in your daughter's class, discovered that several weeks ago Sarah was herself approached by a strange man. I should like to see if she can remember anything about him. With your permission.'

'But of course. I'll go and fetch her,' he said, and went out.

Evidently this was a musical family. Beside a shiny black Bechstein grand were several instrument cases, and a number of music-stands. Close to the window which looked out on to a large garden was a harp, and in most of the family photographs on the sideboard, a young girl was playing a violin. Even the oil painting above the fire-place depicted something musical – a piano recital I supposed. I was standing looking at it and trying to guess the tune when Herr Hirsch returned with his wife and daughter.

Frau Hirsch was much taller and younger than her husband, perhaps no more than fifty – a slim, elegant woman with a set of pearls to match. She wiped her hands on her pinafore and then grasped her daughter by her shoulders, as if wishing to emphasize her parental rights in the face of possible interference from a state which was avowedly hostile to her race.

'My husband says that a girl is missing from Sarah's class at school,' she said calmly. 'Which girl is it?'

'Emmeline Steininger,' I said.

Frau Hirsch turned her daughter towards her a little.

'Sarah,' she scolded, 'why didn't you tell us that one of your friends had gone missing?'

Sarah, an overweight but healthy, attractive adolescent, who could not have conformed less to Streicher's racist stereotype of the Jew, being blue-eyed and fair-haired, gave an impatient toss of her head, like a stubborn little pony.

'She's run away, that's all. She was always talking about it. Not that I care much what's happened to her. Emmeline Steininger's no friend of mine. She's always saying bad things about Jews. I hate her, and I don't care if her father is dead.'

'That's enough of that,' her father said firmly, probably not caring to hear much about fathers who were dead. 'It doesn't matter what she said. If you know something that will help the Kommissar to find her, then you must tell him. Is that clear?'

Sarah pulled a face. 'Yes, Daddy,' she yawned, and threw herself down into an armchair.

'Sarah, really,' said her mother. She smiled nervously at me. 'She's not normally like this, Kommissar. I must apologize.'

'That's all right,' I smiled, sitting down on the footstool in front of Sarah's chair.

'On Friday, when one of my men spoke to you, Sarah, you told him you remembered seeing a man hanging around near your school, perhaps a couple of months ago. Is that right?' She nodded. 'Then I'd like you to try and tell me everything that you can remember about him.'

She chewed her fingernail for a moment, and inspected it thoughtfully. 'Well, it was quite a while ago,' she said.

'Anything you might recall could help me. For instance, what time of day was it?' I took out my notebook and laid it on my thigh.

'It was going-home time. As usual I was going home by myself.' She turned her nose up at the memory of it. 'Anyway, there was this car near the school.'

'What kind of car?'

She shrugged. 'I don't know makes of cars, or anything like that. But it was a big, black one, with a driver in the front.'

'Was he the one who spoke to you?'

'No, there was another man in the back seat. I thought they were policemen. The one sitting in the back had the window down and he called to me as I came through the gate. I was by myself. Most of the other girls had gone already. He asked me to come over, and when I did he told me that I was –' She blushed a little and stopped.

'Go on,' I said.

'– that I was very beautiful, and that he was sure my father and mother were very proud to have a daughter like me.' She glanced awkwardly at her parents. 'I'm not making it up,' she said with something approaching amusement. 'Honestly, that's what he said.'

'I believe you, Sarah,' I said. 'What else did he say?'

'He spoke to his driver and said, wasn't I a fine example of German maidenhood, or something stupid like that.' She laughed. 'It was really funny.' She caught a look from her father that I didn't see, and settled down again. 'Anyway, it was something like that. I can't remember exactly.'

'And did the driver say anything back to him?'

'He suggested to his boss that they could give me a ride home. Then the one in the back asked me if I'd like that. I said that I'd never ridden in one of those big cars before, and that I'd like to –'

Sarah's father sighed loudly. 'How many times have we told you, Sarah, not to –'

'If you don't mind, sir,' I said firmly, 'perhaps that can wait until later.' I looked back at Sarah. 'Then what happened?'

'The man said that if I answered some questions correctly, he'd give me a ride, just like a movie-star. Well, first he asked me my name, and when I told him he just sort of looked at me, as if he were shocked. Of course it was because he realized that I was Jewish, and that was his next question: was I Jewish? I almost told him I wasn't, just for the fun of it. But I was scared he would find out and that I would get into trouble, and so I told him I was. Then he leant back in his seat, and told the chauffeur to drive on. Not another word. It was very strange. As if I had vanished.'

'That's very good, Sarah. Now tell me: you said you thought they were policemen. Were they wearing uniforms?'

She nodded hesitantly.

'Let's start with the colour of these uniforms.'

'Sort of green-coloured, I suppose. You know, like a policeman, only a bit darker.'

'What were their hats like? Like policemen's hats?'

'No, they were peaked hats. More like officers. Daddy was an officer in the navy.'

'Anything else? Badges, ribbons, collar insignia? Anything like that?' She kept shaking her head. 'All right. Now the man who spoke to you. What was he like?'

Sarah pursed her lips and then tugged at a length of her hair. She glanced at her father. 'Older than the driver,' she said. 'About fifty-five, sixty. Quite heavy-looking, not much hair, or maybe it was just closely cropped, and a small moustache.'

'And the other one?'

She shrugged. 'Younger. A bit pale-looking. Fair-haired. I can't remember much about him at all.'

'Tell me about his voice, this man sitting in the back of the car.'

'You mean his accent?'

'Yes, if you can.'

'I don't know for sure,' she said. 'I find accents quite difficult to place. I can hear that they're different, but I can't always say where the person is from.' She sighed deeply, and frowned as she tried hard to concentrate. 'It could have been Austrian. But I suppose it could just as easily have been Bavarian. You know, old-fashioned.'

'Austrian or Bavarian,' I said, writing in my notebook. I thought about underlining the word 'Bavarian' and then thought better of it. There was no point in giving it more emphasis than she had done, even if Bavarian suited me better. Instead I paused, saving my last question until I was sure that she had finished her answer.

'Now think very clearly, Sarah. You're standing by the car. The window is down and you're looking straight into the car. You see the man with the moustache. What else can you see?'

She shut her eyes tight, and licking her lower lip she bent her brain to squeeze out one last detail.

'Cigarettes,' she said after a minute. 'Not like Daddy's.' She opened her eyes and looked at me. 'They had a funny smell. Sweet, and quite strong. Like bay-leaves, or oregano.'

I scanned my notes and when I was sure that she had nothing left to add I stood up.

'Thank you, Sarah, you've been a great help.'

'Have I?' she said gleefully. 'Have I really?'

'You certainly have.' We all smiled, and for a moment the four of us forgot who and what we were.

Driving from the Hirsch home, I wondered if any of them realized that for once Sarah's race had been to her advantage – that being Jewish had probably saved her life.

I was pleased with what I had learned. Her description was the first real piece of information in the case. In the matter of accents her description tallied with that of Tanker, the desk sergeant who had taken the anonymous call. But what was more important it meant that I was going to have to get the dates on which Streicher had been in Berlin from General Martin in Nuremberg, after all.

14

Monday, 26 September

I looked out of the window of my apartment at the backs of the adjoining buildings, and into several sitting-rooms where each family was already grouped expectantly round the radio. From the window at the front of my apartment I could see that Fasanen-strasse was deserted. I walked into my own sitting-room and poured myself a drink. Through the floor I could hear the sound of classical music coming from the radio in the pension below. A little Beethoven provided a nice top and tail for the radio speeches of the Party leaders. It's just what I always say: the worse the picture, the more ornate the frame.

Ordinarily I'm no listener to Party broadcasts. I'd sooner listen to my own wind. But tonight's was no ordinary Party broadcast. The Führer was speaking at the Sportspalast on Potsdamerstrasse, and it was widely held that he would declare the true extent of his intentions towards Czechoslovakia and the Sudetenland.

Personally, I had long ago come to the conclusion that for years Hitler had been deceiving everyone with his speeches about peace. And I'd seen enough westerns at the cinema to know that when the man in the black hat picks on the little fellow standing next to him at the bar, he's really spoiling for a fight with the sheriff. In this case the sheriff just happened to be French, and it didn't take much to see that he wasn't much inclined to do anything but stay indoors and tell himself that the gunshots he could hear across the street were just a few firecrackers.

In the hope that I was wrong about this, I turned on the radio, and like 75 million other Germans, waited to find out what would become of us.

A lot of women say that whereas Goebbels merely seduces, Hitler positively fascinates. It's difficult for me to comment on this. All the same, there is no denying the hypnotic effect that the Führer's speeches seem to have on people. Certainly the crowd at the Sportspalast seemed to appreciate it. I expect you had to be there to get the real atmosphere. Like a visit to a sewage plant.

For those of us listening at home, there was nothing to appreciate, no hope in anything that the number one carpet-chewer said. There was only the dreadful realization that we were a little closer to war than we had been the day before.

Tuesday, 27 September

The afternoon saw a military parade on Unter den Linden, one which looked more ready for war than anything ever seen before on the streets of Berlin. This was a mechanized division in full field equipment. But to my astonishment, there were no cheers, no salutes and no waving of flags. The reality of Hitler's belligerence was in everyone's mind and seeing this parade, people just turned and walked away.

Later that same day, when at his own request I met Arthur Nebe away from the Alex, at the offices of Günther & Stahlecker, Private Investigators – the door was still awaiting the sign-writer to come and change the name back to the original – I told him what I had seen.

Nebe laughed. 'What would you say if I told you that the division you saw were this country's probable liberators?'

'Is the army planning a *putsch*?'

'I can't tell you very much except to say that high officers of the Wehrmacht have been in contact with the British prime minister. As soon as the British give the order, the army will occupy Berlin and Hitler will be brought to trial.'

'When will that be?'

'As soon as Hitler invades Czechoslovakia the British will

declare war. That will be the time. Our time, Bernie. Didn't I tell you that Kripo would be needing men like you?'

I nodded slowly. 'But Chamberlain has been negotiating with Hitler, hasn't he?'

'That's the British way, to talk, to be diplomatic. It wouldn't be cricket if they didn't try to negotiate.'

'Nevertheless, he must believe that Hitler will sign some sort of treaty. More importantly, both Chamberlain and Daladier must themselves be prepared to sign some sort of treaty.'

'Hitler won't walk away from the Sudeten, Bernie. And the British aren't about to renege on their own treaty with the Czechs.'

I went over to the drinks cabinet and poured a couple.

'If the British and French intended to keep their treaty, then there would be nothing to talk about,' I said, handing Nebe a glass. 'If you ask me, they're doing Hitler's work for him.'

'My God, what a pessimist you are.'

'All right, let me ask you this. Have you ever been faced with the prospect of fighting someone you didn't want to fight? Someone larger than you, perhaps? It may be that you think you'll get a good hiding. It may be that you simply haven't got the stomach for it. You try and talk your way out of the situation, of course. The man who talks too much doesn't want to fight at all.'

'But we are not larger than the British and the French.'

'But they don't have the stomach for it.'

Nebe raised his glass. 'To the British stomach, then.'

'To the British stomach.'

Wednesday, 28 September

'General Martin has supplied the information about Streicher, sir.' Korsch looked at the telegraph he was holding. 'On the five dates in question it would seem that Streicher was known to be in Berlin on at least two of them. With regard to the other two that we don't know about, Martin has no idea where he was.'

'So much for his boast about his spies.'

'Well, there is one thing, sir. Apparently on one of the dates, Streicher was seen coming from the Furth aerodrome in Nuremberg.'

'What's the flying time between here and Nuremberg?'

'Couple of hours at the most. Do you want me to check with Tempelhof airport?'

'I've got a better idea. Get on to the propaganda boys at the Muratti. Ask them to supply you with a nice photograph of Streicher. Better ask for one of all the Gauleiters so as not to draw too much attention to yourself. Say it's for security up at the Reichs Chancellery, that always sounds good. When you've got it, I want you to go and talk to the Hirsch girl. See if she can't identify Streicher as the man in the car.'

'And if she does?'

'If she does, then you and I are going to find that we have made a lot of new friends. With one notable exception.'

'That's what I was afraid of.'

Thursday, 29 September

Chamberlain returned to Munich. He wanted to talk again. The Sheriff came too but it seemed that he was only going to look the other way when the shooting started. Mussolini polished his belt and his head and turned up to offer support to his spiritual ally.

While these important men came and went, a young girl, of little or no account in the general scheme of things, disappeared while doing the family shopping at the local market.

Moabit Market was on the corner of Bremerstrasse and Arminius Strasse. A large red-brick building, about the same size as a warehouse, it was where the working class of Moabit – which means everyone who lived in the area – bought their cheese, fish, cooked meats and other fresh provisions. There were even one or two places where you could stand and drink a quick beer and eat a sausage. The place was always busy and there were at least six ways in and out of the place. It's not somewhere that you just wander round. Most people are in a hurry, with little time to stand and stare at things they cannot afford; and anyway, there is none of those sort of goods in Moabit. So my clothes and unhurried demeanour marked me out from the rest.

We knew that Liza Ganz had disappeared from there because that was where a fishmonger had found a shopping bag which Liza's mother later identified as belonging to her.

Apart from that, nobody saw a damn thing. In Moabit, people don't pay you much attention unless you're a policeman looking for a missing girl, and even then it's just curiosity.

Friday, 30 September

In the afternoon I was summoned to Gestapo headquarters on Prinz Albrecht Strasse.

Glancing up as I passed through the main door, I saw a statue sitting on a truck-tyre of a scroll, working at a piece of embroidery. Flying over her head were two cherubs, one scratching his head and the other wearing a generally puzzled sort of expression. My guess was that they were wondering why the Gestapo should have chosen that particular building to set up shop. On the face of it, the art school formerly occupying number eight Prinz Albrecht Strasse and the Gestapo, who were currently resident there, didn't seem to have much in common beyond the rather obvious joke that everyone made about framing things. But that particular day I was more puzzled as to why Heydrich should have summoned me there, instead of to the Prinz Albrecht Palais on nearby Wilhelmstrasse. I didn't doubt that he had a reason. Heydrich had a reason for doing everything, and I felt sure that I would dislike this one just as much as all the others I'd ever heard.

Beyond the main door you went through a security check, and walking on again you found yourself at the foot of a staircase that was as big as an aqueduct. At the top of the flight you were in a vaulted waiting hall, with three arched windows that were of locomotive proportions. Beneath each window was a wooden bench of the kind you see in church and it was there that I waited, as instructed.

Between each window, on plinths, sat busts of Hitler and Goering. I wondered a bit at Himmler leaving Fat Hermann's head there, knowing how much they hated each other. Maybe Himmler just admired it as a piece of sculpture. And then maybe his wife was the Chief Rabbi's daughter.

After nearly an hour Heydrich finally emerged from the two double doors facing me. He was carrying a briefcase and shooed away his SS adjutant when he caught sight of me.

'Kommissar Günther,' he said, appearing to find some amusement at the sound of my rank in his own ears. He ushered me forwards along the gallery. 'I thought we could walk in the garden once again, like the last time. Do you mind accompanying me back to the Wilhelmstrasse?'

We went through an arched doorway and down another massive set of stairs to the notorious south wing, where what had once been sculptors' workshops were now Gestapo prison cells. I had good reason to remember these, having once been briefly detained there myself, and I was quite relieved when we emerged through a door and stood in the open air once again. You never knew with Heydrich.

He paused there for a moment, glancing at his Rolex. I started to say something, but he raised his forefinger and, almost conspiratorially, pressed his finger to his thin lips. We stood and waited, but for what I had no idea.

A minute or so later a volley of shots rang out, echoing away across the gardens. Then another; and another. Heydrich checked his watch again, nodded and smiled.

'Shall we?' he said, striding on to the gravel pathway.

'Was that for my benefit?' I said, knowing full well that it was.

'The firing squad?' He chuckled. 'No, no, Kommissar Günther. You imagine too much. And anyway, I hardly think that you of all people require an object lesson in power. It's just that I am particular about punctuality. With kings this is said to be a virtue, but with a policeman this is merely the hallmark of administrative efficiency. After all, if the Führer can make the trains run on time, the least I ought to be able to do is make sure that a few priests are liquidated at the proper appointed hour.'

So it was an object lesson after all, I thought. Heydrich's way of letting me know that he was aware of my disagreement with Sturmbannführer Roth from 4B1.

'Whatever happened to being shot at dawn?'

'The neighbours complained.'

'You did say priests, didn't you?'

'The Catholic Church is no less of an international conspiracy than Bolshevism or Judaism, Günther. Martin Luther led one Reformation, the Führer will lead another. He will abolish Roman authority over German Catholics, whether the priests permit him or not. But that is another matter, and one best left to those who are well versed in its implementation.

'No, I wanted to tell you about the problem I have, which is that I am under a certain amount of pressure from Goebbels and his Muratti hacks that this case you are working on be given publicity. I'm not sure how much longer I can stave them off.'

'When I was given this case, General,' I said, lighting a cigarette, 'I was against a ban on publicity. Now I'm convinced that publicity is exactly what our killer has been after all along.'

'Yes, Nebe said you were working on the theory that this might be some sort of conspiracy engineered by Streicher and his Jew-baiting pals to bring down a pogrom on the heads of the capital's Jewish community.'

'It sounds fantastic, General, only if you don't know Streicher.'

He stopped, and thrusting his hands deep inside his trouser pockets, he shook his head.

'There is nothing about that Bavarian pig that could possibly surprise me.' He kicked at a pigeon with the toe of his boot, and missed. 'But I want to hear more.'

'A girl has identified a photograph of Streicher as possibly the man who tried to pick her up outside a school from which another girl disappeared last week. She thinks that the man might have had a Bavarian accent. The desk sergeant who took an anonymous call tipping us off where exactly to find the body of another missing girl said that the caller had a Bavarian accent.

'Then there's motive. Last month the people of Nuremberg burnt down the city's synagogue. But here in Berlin there are only ever a few broken windows and assaults at the very worst. Streicher would love to see the Jews in Berlin getting some of what they've had in Nuremberg.

'What is more, *Der Stürmer*'s obsession with ritual murder leads me to make comparisons with the killer's *modus operandi*. You add all that to Streicher's reputation and it starts to look like something.'

Heydrich accelerated ahead of me, his arms stiff at his sides as if he were riding in the Vienna Riding School, and then turned to face me. He was smiling enthusiastically.

'I know one person who would be delighted to see Streicher's downfall. That stupid bastard has been making speeches all but accusing the prime minister of being impotent. Goering is furious about it. But you don't really have enough yet, do you?'

'No, sir. For a start my witness is Jewish.' Heydrich groaned. 'And of course the rest is largely theoretical.'

'Nevertheless, I like your theory, Günther. I like it very much.'

'I'd like to remind the general that it took me six months to catch Gormann the Strangler. I haven't yet spent a month on this case.'

'We don't have six months, I'm afraid. Look here, get me a shred of evidence and I can keep Goebbels off my back. But I need something soon, Günther. You've got another month, six weeks at the outside. Do I make myself clear?'

'Yes, sir.'

'Well, what do you need from me?'

'Round the clock Gestapo surveillance of Julius Streicher,' I said. 'A full undercover investigation of all his business activities and known associates.'

Heydrich folded his arms and took his long chin in his hand. 'I'll have to speak to Himmler about that. But it should be all right. The Reichsführer hates corruption even more than he loathes the Jews.'

'Well, that's certainly comforting, sir.'

We walked on towards the Prinz Albrecht Palais.

'Incidentally,' he said, as we neared his own headquarters, 'I've just had some important news that affects us all. The British and French have signed an agreement at Munich. The Führer has got the Sudeten.' He shook his head in wonder. 'A miracle, isn't it?'

'Yes indeed,' I muttered.

'Well, don't you understand? There isn't going to be a war. At least, not for the present time.'

I smiled awkwardly. 'Yes, it's really good news.'

I understood perfectly. There wasn't going to be a war. There wasn't going to be any signal from the British. And without that, there wasn't going to be any army *putsch* either.

PART TWO

15

Monday, 17 October

The Ganz family, what remained of it following a second anonymous call to the Alex informing us where the body of Liza Ganz was to be found, lived south of Wittenau in a small apartment on Birkenstrasse, just behind the Robert Koch Hospital where Frau Ganz was employed as a nurse. Herr Ganz worked as a clerk at the Moabit District Court, which was also nearby.

According to Becker they were a hard-working couple in their late thirties, both of them putting in long hours, so that Liza Ganz had often been left by herself. But never had she been left as I had just seen her, naked on a slab at the Alex, with a man stitching up those parts of her he had seen fit to cut open in an effort to determine everything about her, from her virginity to the contents of her stomach. Yet it had been the contents of her mouth, easier of access, which had confirmed what I had begun to suspect.

'What made you think of it, Bernie?' Illmann had asked.

'Not everyone rolls up as good as you, Professor. Sometimes a little flake will stay on your tongue, or under your lip. When the Jewish girl who said she saw our man said he was smoking something sweet-smelling, like bay-leaves or oregano, she had to be talking about hashish. That's probably how he gets them away quietly. Treats them all grown-up by offering them a cigarette. Only it's not the kind they're expecting.'

Illmann shook his head in apparent wonder.

'And to think that I missed it. I must be getting old.'

Becker slammed the car door and joined me on the pavement. The apartment was above a pharmacy. I had a feeling I was going to need it.

We walked up the stairs and knocked on the door. The man who opened it was dark and bad-tempered looking. Recognizing Becker he uttered a sigh and called to his wife. Then he glanced back inside and I saw him nod grimly.

'You'd better come in,' he said.

I was watching him closely. His face remained flushed, and as I squeezed past him I could see small beads of perspiration on his forehead. Further into the place I caught a warm, soapy smell, and I guessed that he'd only recently finished taking a bath.

Closing the door, Herr Ganz overtook and led us into the small sitting-room where his wife was standing quietly. She was tall and pale, as if she spent too much time indoors, and clearly she had not long stopped crying. The handkerchief was still wet in her hand. Herr Ganz, shorter than his wife, put his arm around her broad shoulders.

'This is Kommissar Günther, from the Alex,' said Becker.

'Herr and Frau Ganz,' I said, 'I'm afraid you must prepare yourselves for the worst possible news. We found the body of your daughter Liza early this morning. I'm very sorry.' Becker nodded solemnly.

'Yes,' said Ganz. 'Yes, I thought so.'

'Naturally there will have to be an identification,' I told him. 'It needn't be right away. Perhaps later on, when you've had a chance to draw yourselves together.' I waited for Frau Ganz to dissolve, but for the moment at least she seemed inclined to remain solid. Was it because she was a nurse, and rather more immune to suffering and pain? Even her own? 'May we sit down?'

'Yes, please do,' said Ganz.

I told Becker to go and make some coffee for us all. He went with some alacrity, eager to be out of the grief-stricken atmosphere, if only for a moment or two.

'Where did you find her?' said Ganz.

It wasn't the sort of question I felt comfortable answering. How do you tell two parents that their daughter's naked body was found inside a tower of car tyres in a disused garage on Kaiser Wilhelm

Strasse? I gave him the sanitized version, which included no more than the location of the garage. At this there occurred a very definite exchange of looks.

Ganz sat with his hand on his wife's knee. She herself was quiet, vacant even, and perhaps less in need of Becker's coffee than I was.

'Have you any idea who might have killed her?' he said.

'We're working on a number of possibilities, sir,' I said, finding the old police platitudes coming back to me once again. 'We're doing everything we can, believe me.'

Ganz's frown deepened. He shook his head angrily. 'What I fail to understand is why there has been nothing in the newspapers.'

'It's important that we prevent any copy-cat killings,' I said. 'It often happens in this sort of case.'

'Isn't it also important that you stop any more girls from being murdered?' said Frau Ganz. Her look was one of exasperation. 'Well, it's true, isn't it? Other girls have been murdered. That's what people are saying. You may be able to keep it out of the papers, but you can't stop people from talking.'

'There have been propaganda drives warning girls to be on their guard,' I said.

'Well, they obviously didn't do any good, did they?' said Ganz. 'Liza was an intelligent girl, Kommissar. Not the kind to do anything stupid. So this killer must be clever too. And the way I see it, the only way to put girls properly on their guard is to print the story, in all its horror. To scare them.'

'You may be right, sir,' I said unhappily, 'but it's not up to me. I'm only obeying orders.' That was the typically German excuse for everything these days, and I felt ashamed using it.

Becker put his head round the kitchen door.

'Could I have a word, sir?'

It was my turn to be glad to leave the room.

'What's the matter?' I said bitterly. 'Forgotten how to boil a kettle?'

He handed me a newspaper cutting, from the *Völkischer Beobachter*. 'Take a look at this, sir. I found it in the drawer here.'

It was an advertisement for a 'Rolf Vogelmann, Private Investigator, Missing Persons a Speciality', the same advertisement that Bruno Stahlecker had used to plague me with.

Becker pointed to the date at the top of the cutting: '3 October,' he said. 'Four days after Liza Ganz disappeared.'

'It wouldn't be the first time that people got tired waiting for the police to come up with something,' I said. 'After all, that's how I used to make a comparatively honest living.'

Becker collected some cups and saucers and put them on to a tray with the coffee pot. 'Do you suppose that they might have used him, sir?'

'I don't see any harm in asking.'

Ganz was unrepentant, the sort of client I wouldn't have minded working for myself.

'As I said, Kommissar, there was nothing in the newspapers about our daughter, and we saw your colleague here only twice. So as time passed we wondered just what efforts were being made to find our daughter. It's the not knowing that gets to you. We thought that if we hired Herr Vogelmann then at least we could be sure that someone was doing his best to try and find her. I don't mean to be rude, Kommissar, but that's the way it was.'

I sipped my coffee and shook my head.

'I quite understand,' I said. 'I'd probably have done the same thing myself. I just wish this Vogelmann had been able to find her.'

You had to admire them, I thought. They could probably ill-afford the services of a private investigator and yet they had still gone ahead and hired one. It might even have cost them whatever savings they had.

When we had finished our coffee and were leaving I suggested that a police car might come round and bring Herr Ganz down to the Alex to identify the body early the following morning.

'Thank you for your kindness, Kommissar,' said Frau Ganz, attempting a smile. 'Everyone's been so kind.'

Her husband nodded his agreement. Hovering by the open door, he was obviously keen to see the back of us.

'Herr Vogelmann wouldn't take any money from us. And now you're arranging a car for my husband. I can't tell you how much we appreciate it.'

I squeezed her hand sympathetically, and then we left.

In the pharmacy downstairs I bought some powders and swallowed one in the car. Becker looked at me with disgust.

'Christ, I don't know how you can do that,' he said, shuddering.

'It works faster that way. And after what we just went through I can't say that I notice the taste much. I hate giving bad news.' I swept my mouth with my tongue for the residue. 'Well? What did you make of that? Get the same hunch as before?'

'Yes. He was giving her all sorts of meaningful little looks.'

'So were you, for that matter,' I said, shaking my head in wonder. Becker grinned broadly. 'She wasn't bad, was she?'

'I suppose you're going to tell me what she'd be like in bed, right?'

'More your type I'd have thought, sir.'

'Oh? What makes you say that?'

'You know, the type that responds to kindness.'

I laughed, despite my headache. 'More than she responds to bad news. There we are with our big feet and long faces and all she can do is look like she was in the middle of her period.'

'She's a nurse. They're used to handling bad news.'

'That crossed my mind, but I think she'd done her crying already, and quite recently. What about Irma Hanke's mother? Did she cry?'

'God, no. As hard as Jew Süss that one. Maybe she did sniff a little when I first showed up. But they were giving off the same sort of atmosphere as the Ganzes.'

I looked at my watch. 'I think we need a drink, don't you?'

We drove to the Café Kerkau, on Alexanderstrasse. With sixty billiard tables, it was where a lot of bulls from the Alex went to relax when they came off duty.

I bought a couple of beers and carried them over to a table where Becker was practising a few shots.

'Do you play?' he said.

'Are you stretching me out? This used to be my sitting-room.'
I picked up a stick and watched Becker shoot the cue ball. It hit the
red, banked off the cushion and hit the other white ball square.

'Care for a little bet?'

'Not after that shot. You've got a lot to learn about working a
line. Now if you'd missed it —'

'Lucky shot, that's all,' Becker insisted. He bent down and cued
a wild one which missed by half a metre.

I clicked my tongue. 'That's a billiard cue you're holding, not a
white stick. Stop trying to lay me down, will you? Look, if it
makes you happy, we'll play for five marks a game.'

He smiled slightly and flexed his shoulders.

'Twenty points all right with you?'

I won the break and missed the opening shot. After that I might
just as well have been baby-sitting. Becker hadn't been in the Boy
Scouts when he was young, that much was certain. After four
games I tossed a twenty on to the felt and begged for mercy.
Becker threw it back.

'It's all right,' he said. 'You let me lay you down.'

'That's another thing you've got to learn. A bet's a bet. You
never ever play for money unless you mean to collect. A man that
lets you off might expect you to let him off. It makes people nervous, that's all.'

'That sounds like good advice.' He pocketed the money.

'It's like business,' I continued. 'You never work for free. If you
won't take money for your work then it can't have been worth
much.' I returned my cue to the rack and finished my beer. 'Never
trust anyone who's happy to do the job for nothing.'

'Is that what you've learnt as a private detective?'

'No, it's what I've learnt as a good businessman. But since you
mention it, I don't like the smell of a private investigator who tries
to find a missing schoolgirl and then waives his fee.'

'Rolf Vogelmann? But he didn't find her.'

'Let me tell you something. These days a lot of people go missing in this town, and for lots of different reasons. Finding one is

the exception, not the rule. If I'd torn up the bill of every disappointed client I had, I'd have been washing dishes by now. When you're private, there's no room for sentiment. The man who doesn't collect, doesn't eat.'

'Maybe this Vogelmann character is just more generous than you were, sir.'

I shook my head. 'I don't see how he can afford to be,' I said, unfolding Vogelmann's advertisement and looking at it again. 'Not with these overheads.'

16

Tuesday, 18 October

It was her, all right. There was no mistaking that golden head and those well-sculpted legs. I watched her struggle out of Ka-De-We's revolving door, laden with parcels and carrier-bags, looking like she was doing her last-minute Christmas shopping. She waved for a taxi, dropped a bag, bent down to retrieve it and looked up to find that the driver had missed her. It was difficult to see how. You'd have noticed Hildegard Steininger with a sack over your head. She looked as though she lived in a beauty parlour.

From inside my car I heard her swear and, drawing up at the kerb, I wound down the passenger window.

'Need a lift somewhere?'

She was still looking around for another taxi when she answered. 'No, it's all right,' she said, as if I had cornered her at a cocktail party and she had been glancing over my shoulder to see if there might be someone more interesting coming along. There wasn't, so she remembered to smile, briefly, and then added: 'Well, if you're sure it's no trouble.'

I jumped out to help her load the shopping. Millinery stores, shoe shops, a perfumers, a fancy Friedrichstrasse dress-designer, and Ka-De-We's famous food hall: I figured she was the type for whom a cheque-book provided the best kind of panacea for what was troubling her. But then, there are lots of women like that.

'It's no trouble at all,' I said, my eyes following her legs as they swung into the car, briefly enjoying a view of her stocking tops and garters. Forget it, I told myself. This one was too pricey. Besides, she had other things on her mind. Like whether the shoes matched the handbag, and what had happened to her missing daughter.

'Where to?' I said. 'Home?'

She sighed like I'd suggested the Palme doss-house on Frobel-strasse, and then, smiling a brave little smile, she nodded. We drove east towards Bülowstrasse.

'I'm afraid that I don't have any news for you,' I said, fixing a serious expression to my features and trying to concentrate on the road rather than the memory of her thighs.

'No, I didn't think you did,' she said dully. 'It's been almost four weeks now, hasn't it?'

'Don't give up hope.'

Another sigh, rather more impatient. 'You're not going to find her. She's dead, isn't she? Why doesn't somebody just admit it?'

'She's alive until I find out different, Frau Steininger.' I turned south down Potsdamerstrasse and for a while we were both silent. Then I became aware of her shaking her head and breathing like she had walked up a flight of stairs.

'Whatever must you think of me, Kommissar?' she said. 'My daughter missing, probably murdered, and here I am spending money as if I hadn't a care in the world. You must think me a heartless sort of woman.'

'I don't think anything of the kind,' I said, and started telling her how people dealt with these things in different ways, and that if a bit of shopping helped to take her mind off her daughter's dis-appearance for a couple of hours then that was perfectly all right, and that nobody would blame her. I thought I made a convincing case, but by the time we reached her apartment in Steglitz, Hilde-gard Steininger was in tears.

I took hold of her shoulder and just squeezed it, letting her go a bit before I said, 'I'd offer you my handkerchief if I hadn't wrapped my sandwiches in it.'

Through her tears she tried a smile. 'I have one,' she said, and tugged a square of lace from out of her sleeve. Then she glanced over at my own handkerchief and laughed. 'It does look as if you'd wrapped your sandwiches in it.'

After I'd helped to carry her purchases upstairs, I stood outside her door while she found her key. Opening it, she turned and smiled gracefully.

'Thank you for helping, Kommissar,' she said. 'It really was very kind of you.'

'It was nothing,' I said, thinking nothing of the sort.

Not even an invitation in for a cup of coffee, I thought when I was sitting in the car once more. Lets me drive her all this way and not even invited inside.

But then there are lots of women like that, for whom men are just taxi-drivers they don't have to tip.

The heavy scent of the lady's Bajadi perfume was pulling quite a few funny faces at me. Some men aren't affected by it at all, but a woman's perfume smacks me right in the leather shorts. Arriving back at the Alex some twenty minutes later, I think I must have sniffed down every molecule of that woman's fragrance like a vacuum cleaner.

I called a friend of mine who worked at Dorlands, the advertising agency. Alex Sievers was someone I knew from the war.

'Alex. Are you still buying advertising space?'

'For as long as the job doesn't require one to have a brain.'

'It's always nice to talk to a man who enjoys his work.'

'Fortunately I enjoy the money a whole lot better.'

It went on like that for another couple of minutes until I asked Alex if he had a copy of that morning's *Völkischer Beobachter*. I referred him to the page with Vogelmann's ad.

'What's this?' he said. 'I can't believe that there are people in your line of work who have finally staggered into the twentieth century.'

'That advertisement has appeared at least twice a week for quite a few weeks now,' I explained. 'What's a campaign like that cost?'

'With that many insertions there's bound to be some sort of discount. Listen, leave it with me. I know a couple of people on the *Völkischer Beobachter*. I can probably find out for you.'

'I'd appreciate it, Alex.'

'You want to advertise yourself, maybe?'

'Sorry, Alex, but this is a case.'

'I get it. Spying on the competition, eh?'

'Something like that.'

I spent the rest of that afternoon reading Gestapo reports on Streicher and his *Der Stürmer* associates: of the Gauleiter's affair with one Anni Seitz, and others, which he conducted in secret from his wife Kunigunde; of his son Lothar's affair with an English girl called Mitford who was of noble birth; of *Stürmer* editor Ernst Hiemer's homosexuality; of *Stürmer* cartoonist Philippe Rupprecht's illegal activities after the war in Argentina; and of how the *Stürmer* team of writers included a man called Fritz Brand, who was really a Jew by the name of Jonas Wolk.

These reports made fascinating, salacious reading, of the sort that would no doubt have appealed to *Der Stürmer*'s own following, but they didn't bring me any nearer to establishing a connection between Streicher and the murders.

Sievers called back at around five, and said that Vogelmann's advertising was costing something like three or four hundred marks a month.

'When did he start spending that kind of mouse?'

'Since the beginning of July. Only he's not spending it, Bernie.'

'Don't tell me he's getting it for nothing.'

'No, somebody else is picking up the bill.'

'Oh? Who?'

'Well that's the funny thing, Bernie. Can you think of any reason why the Lange Publishing Company should be paying for a private investigator's advertising campaign?'

'Are you sure about that?'

'Absolutely.'

'That's very interesting, Alex. I owe you one.'

'Just make sure that if you ever decide to do some advertising it's me you speak to first, all right?'

'You bet.'

I put down the receiver and opened my diary. My account for work done on Frau Gertrude Lange's behalf was at least a week overdue. Glancing at my watch I thought I could just about beat the westbound traffic.

They had the painters in at the house in Herbertstrasse when I called, and Frau Lange's black maid complained bitterly about people coming and going all the time so that she was never off her feet. You wouldn't have thought it to look at her. She was even fatter than I remembered.

'You'll have to wait here in the hall while I go and see if she's available,' she told me. 'Everywhere else is being decorated. Don't touch anything, mind.' She flinched as an enormous crash echoed through the house and, mumbling about men with dirty overalls disrupting the place, she went off in search of her mistress, leaving me to tap my heels on the marble floor.

It seemed to make sense, their decorating the place. They probably did it every year, instead of spring cleaning. I ran my hand over an art-deco bronze of a leaping salmon that occupied the middle of a great round table. I might have enjoyed its tactile smoothness if the thing hadn't been covered in dust. I turned, grimacing, as the black cauldron waddled back into the hall. She grimaced back at me and then down at my feet.

'You see what your boots has gone and done to my clean floor?' she said pointing at the several black marks my heels had left.

I tutted with theatrical insincerity.

'Perhaps you can persuade her to buy a new one,' I said. I was certain she swore under her breath before telling me to follow her.

We went along the same hallway that was a couple of coats of paint above gloomy, to the double doors of the sitting-room office. Frau Lange, her chins and her dog were waiting for me on the same chaise longue, except that it had been recovered with a shade of material that was easy on the eye only if you had a piece of grit in there on which to concentrate. Having lots of money is no guarantee of good taste, but it can make the lack of it more glaringly obvious.

'Don't you own a telephone?' she boomed through her cigarette smoke like a fog-horn. I heard her chuckle as she added: 'I think you must have once been a debt-collector or something.' Then, realizing what she had said, she clutched at one of her sagging jowls. 'Oh God, I haven't paid your bill, have I?' She laughed again, and stood up. 'I'm most awfully sorry.'

'That's all right,' I said, watching her go to the desk and take out her cheque-book.

'And I haven't yet thanked you properly for the speedy way in which you handled things. I've told all my friends about how good you were.' She handed me the cheque. 'I've put a small bonus on there. I can't tell you how relieved I was to have done with that terrible man. In your letter you said that it appeared as if he had hanged himself, Herr Günther. Saved somebody else the trouble, eh?' She laughed again, loudly, like an amateur actress performing rather too vigorously to be wholly credible. Her teeth were also false.

'That's one way of looking at it,' I said. I didn't see any point in telling her about my suspicion that Heydrich had had Klaus Hering killed with the aim of expediting my re-joining Kripo. Clients don't much care for loose ends. I'm not all that fond of them myself.

It was now that she remembered that her case had also happened to cost Bruno Stahlecker his life. She let her laughter subside, and fixing a more serious expression to her face she set about expressing her condolences. This also involved her cheque-book. For a moment I thought about saying something noble to do with the hazards of the profession, but then I thought of Bruno's widow and let her finish writing it.

'Very generous,' I said. 'I'll see that this gets to his wife and family.'

'Please do,' she said. 'And if there's anything else that I can do for them, you will let me know, won't you?'

I said that I would.

'There is something you can do for me, Herr Günther,' she said. 'There are still the letters I gave you. My son asked me if those last few could be returned to him.'

'Yes, of course. I'd forgotten.' But what was that she said? Was it possible that she meant the letters I still held in the file back at my office were the only surviving letters? Or did she mean that Reinhard Lange already had the rest? In which case, how had he come by them? Certainly I had failed to find any more of the letters when I searched Hering's apartment. What had become of them?

'I'll drop them round myself,' I said. 'Thank goodness he has the rest of them back safely.'

'Yes, isn't it?' she said.

So there it was. He did have them.

I began to move towards the door. 'Well, I'd better be getting along, Frau Lange.' I waved the two cheques in the air and then slipped them into my wallet. 'Thanks for your generosity.'

'Not at all.'

I frowned as if something had occurred to me.

'There is one thing that puzzles me,' I said. 'Something I meant to ask you about. What interest does your company have in the Rolf Vogelmann Detective Agency?'

'Rolf Vogelmann?' she repeated uncomfortably.

'Yes. You see I learnt quite by accident that the Lange Publishing Company has been funding an advertising campaign for Rolf Vogelmann since July of this year. I was merely wondering why you should have hired me when you might with more reason have hired him?'

Frau Lange blinked deliberately and shook her head.

'I'm afraid that I have absolutely no idea.'

I shrugged and allowed myself a little smile. 'Well, as I say, it just puzzled me, that's all. Nothing important. Do you sign all the company cheques, Frau Lange? I mean, I just wondered if this might be something your son could have done on his own without informing you. Like buying that magazine you told me about. Now what was its name? *Urania*.'

Clearly embarrassed, Frau Lange's face was beginning to redden. She swallowed hard before answering.

'Reinhard has signing power over a limited bank account which is supposed to cover his expenses as a company director. However, I'm at a loss to explain what this might relate to, Herr Günther.'

'Well, maybe he got tired of astrology. Maybe he decided to become a private investigator himself. To tell the truth, Frau Lange, there are times when a horoscope is as good a way of finding something out as any other.'

'I shall make a point of asking Reinhard about this when I next see him. I'm indebted to you for the information. Would you mind telling me where you got it from?'

'The information? Sorry, I make it a strict rule never to breach confidentiality. I'm sure you understand.'

She nodded curtly, and bade me good evening.

Back in the hall the black cauldron was still simmering over her floor.

'You know what I'd recommend?' I said.

'What's that?' she said sullenly.

'I think you should give Frau Lange's son a call at his magazine. Maybe he can work up a magic spell to shift those marks.'

17

Friday, 21 October

When I first suggested the idea to Hildegard Steininger, she had been less than enthusiastic.

'Let me get this straight. You want to pose as my husband?'

'That's right.'

'In the first place, my husband is dead. And in the second you don't look anything like him, Herr Kommissar.'

'In the first place I'm counting on this man not knowing that the real Herr Steininger is dead; and in the second, I don't suppose that he would have any more idea of what your husband might have looked like than I do.'

'Exactly who is this Rolf Vogelmann, anyway?'

'An investigation like this one is nothing more than a search for a pattern, for a common factor. Here the common factor is that we've discovered Vogelmann was retained by the parents of two other girls.'

'Two other victims, you mean,' she said. 'I know that other girls have disappeared and then been found murdered, you know. There may be nothing about it in the papers, but one hears things all the time.'

'Two other victims, then,' I admitted.

'But surely that's just a coincidence. Listen, I can tell you that I've thought of doing it myself, you know, paying someone to look for my daughter. After all, you still haven't found a trace of her, have you?'

'That's true. But it may be more than just a coincidence. That's what I'd like to find out.'

'Supposing that he is involved. What could he hope to gain from it?'

'We're not necessarily talking about a rational person here. So I don't know that gain will come into the equation.'

'Well, it all sounds very dubious to me,' she said. 'I mean, how did he get in touch with these two families?'

'He didn't. They got in touch with him after seeing his newspaper advertisement.'

'Doesn't that show that if he is a common factor, then it's not been through his own making?'

'Perhaps he just wants it to look that way. I don't know. All the same I'd like to find out more, even if it's just to rule him out.'

She crossed her long legs and lit a cigarette.

'Will you do it?'

'Just answer this question first, Kommissar. And I want an honest answer. I'm tired of all the evasions. Do you think that Emmeline can still be alive?'

I sighed and then shook my head. 'I think she's dead.'

'Thank you.' There was silence for a moment. 'Is it dangerous, what you're asking me to do?'

'No, I don't think so.'

'Then I agree.'

Now, as we sat in Vogelmann's waiting-room in his offices on Nürnburgerstrasse, under the eye of his matronly secretary, Hildegard Steininger played the part of the worried wife to perfection, holding my hand, and occasionally smiling at me smiles of the kind that are normally reserved for a loved one. She was even wearing her wedding-ring. So was I. It felt strange, and tight, on my finger after so many years. I'd needed soap to slide it on.

Through the wall could be heard the sound of a piano being played.

'There's a music school next door,' explained Vogelmann's secretary. She smiled kindly and added: 'He won't keep you waiting for very long.' Five minutes later we were ushered into his office.

In my experience the private investigator is prone to several common ailments: flat feet, varicose veins, a bad back, alcoholism and, God forbid, venereal disease; but none of them, with the possible exception of the clap, is likely to influence adversely the impression he makes on a potential client. However, there is one disability, albeit a minor one, which if found in a sniffer must give the client pause for thought, and that is short-sightedness. If you are going to pay a man fifty marks a day to trace your missing grandmother, at the very least you want to feel confident that the man you are engaging to do the job is sufficiently eagle-eyed to find his own cuff-links. Spectacles of bottle-glass thickness such as those worn by Rolf Vogelmann must therefore be considered bad for business.

Ugliness, on the other hand, where it stops short of some particular and gross physical deformity, need be no professional disadvantage, and so Vogelmann, whose unpleasant aspect was something more general, was probably able to peck at some sort of a living. I say peck, and I choose my words carefully, because with his unruly comb of curly red hair, his broad beak of a nose and his great breast-plate of a chest, Vogelmann resembled a breed of prehistoric cockerel, and one that had positively begged for extinction.

Hitching his trousers on to his chest, Vogelmann strode round the desk on big policeman's feet to shake our hands. He walked as if he had just dismounted a bicycle.

'Rolf Vogelmann, pleased to meet you both,' he said in a high, strangulated sort of voice, and with a thick Berlin accent.

'Steininger,' I said. 'And this is my wife Hildegard.'

Vogelmann pointed at two armchairs that were ranged in front of a large desk-table, and I heard his shoes squeak as he followed us back across the rug. There wasn't much in the way of furniture. A hat stand, a drinks trolley, a long and battered-looking sofa and, behind it, a table against the wall with a couple of lamps and several piles of books.

'It's good of you to see us this quickly,' Hildegard said graciously.

Vogelmann sat down and faced us. Even with a metre of desk between us I could still detect his yoghurt-curdling breath.

'Well, when your husband mentioned that your daughter was

missing, naturally I assumed there would be some urgency.' He wiped a pad of paper with the flat of his hand and picked up a pencil. 'Exactly when did she go missing?'

'Thursday, 22 September,' I said. 'She was on her way to dancing class in Potsdam and had left home – we live in Steglitz – at seven-thirty that evening. Her class was due to commence at eight, only she never arrived.' Hildegard's hand reached for mine, and I squeezed it comfortingly.

Vogelmann nodded. 'Almost a month, then,' he said ruminatively. 'And the police –?'

'The police?' I said bitterly. 'The police do nothing. We hear nothing. There is nothing in the papers. And yet one hears rumours that other girls of Emmeline's age have also disappeared.' I paused. 'And that they have been murdered.'

'That is almost certainly the case,' he said, straightening the knot in his cheap woollen tie. 'The official reason for the press moratorium on the reporting of these disappearances and homicides is that the police wish to avoid a panic. Also, they don't wish to encourage all the cranks which a case like this has a habit of producing. But the real reason is that they are simply embarrassed at their own persistent inability to capture this man.'

I felt Hildegard squeeze my hand more tightly.

'Herr Vogelmann,' she said, 'it's not knowing what's happened to her that is so hard to bear. If we could just be sure of whether or not –'

'I understand, Frau Steininger.' He looked at me. 'Am I to take it then that you wish me to try and find her?'

'Would you, Herr Vogelmann?' I said. 'We saw your advertisement in the *Völkischer Beobachter*, and really, you're our last hope. We're tired of just sitting back and waiting for something to happen. Aren't we, darling?'

'Yes. Yes, we are.'

'Do you have a photograph of your daughter?'

Hildegard opened her handbag and handed him a copy of the picture that she had earlier given to Deubel.

Vogelmann regarded it dispassionately. 'Pretty. How did she travel to Potsdam?'

'By train.'

'And you believe that she must have disappeared somewhere between your house in Steglitz and the dancing school, is that right?' I nodded. 'Any problems at home?'

'None,' Hildegard said firmly.

'At school, then?'

We both shook our heads and Vogelmann scribbled a few notes. 'Any boyfriends?'

I looked across at Hildegard.

'I don't think so,' she said. 'I've searched her room, and there's nothing to indicate that she had been seeing any boys.'

Vogelmann nodded sullenly and then was subject to a brief fit of coughing for which he apologized through the material of his handkerchief, and which left his face as red as his hair.

'After four weeks, you'll have checked with all her relations and schoolfriends that she hasn't been staying with them.' He wiped his mouth with his handkerchief.

'Naturally,' Hildegard said stiffly.

'We've asked everywhere,' I said. 'I've been along every metre of that journey looking for her and found nothing.' This was almost literally true.

'What was she wearing when she disappeared?'

Hildegard described her clothes.

'What about money?'

'A few marks. Her savings were untouched.'

'All right. I'll ask around and see what I can find out. You had better give me your address.'

I dictated it for him, and added the telephone number. When he'd finished writing he stood up, arched his back painfully, and then walked around a bit with his hands thrust deep into his pockets like an awkward schoolboy. By now I had guessed him to be no more than forty.

'Go home and wait to hear from me. I'll be in touch in a couple of days, or earlier if I find something.'

We stood up to leave.

'What do you think are the chances of finding her alive?' Hildegard said.

Vogelmann shrugged dismally. 'I've got to admit that they're not good. But I will do my best.'

'What's your first move?' I said, curious.

He checked the knot of his tie again, and stretched his Adam's apple over the collar stud. I held my breath as he turned to face me.

'Well, I'll start by getting some copies made of your daughter's photograph. And then put them into circulation. This city has a lot of runaways, you know. There are a few children who don't much care for the Hitler Youth and that sort of thing. I'll make a start in that direction, Herr Steininger.' He put his hand on my shoulder and accompanied us to the door.

'Thank you,' said Hildegard. 'You've been most kind, Herr Vogelmann.'

I smiled and nodded politely. He bowed his head, and as Hildegard passed out of the door in front of me I caught him glancing down at her legs. You couldn't blame him. In her beige wool bolero, dotted foulard blouse and burgundy wool skirt, she looked like a year's worth of war reparations. It felt good just pretending to be married to her.

I shook Vogelmann's hand and followed Hildegard outside, thinking to myself that if I were really her husband I would be driving her home to undress her and take her to bed.

It was an elegantly erotic daydream of silk and lace that I was conjuring up for myself as we left Vogelmann's offices and went out into the street. Hildegard's sexual appeal was something altogether more streamlined than steamy imaginings of bouncing breasts and buttocks. All the same, I knew that my little husband fantasy was short on probability since, in all likelihood, the real Herr Steininger, had he been alive, would almost certainly have driven his beautiful young wife home for nothing more stimulating than a cup of fresh coffee before returning to the bank where he worked. The simple fact of the matter is that a man who wakes alone will think of having a woman just as surely as a man who wakes with a wife will think of having breakfast.

'So what did you make of him?' she said when we were in the car driving back to Steglitz. 'I thought he wasn't as bad as he looked. In fact, he was quite sympathetic, really. Certainly no worse than your own men, Kommissar. I can't imagine why we bothered.'

I let her go on like that for a minute or two.

'It struck you as perfectly normal that there were so many obvious questions that he didn't ask?'

She sighed. 'Like what?'

'He never mentioned his fee.'

'I dare say that if he thought we couldn't have afforded it, then he would have brought it up. And by the way, don't expect me to take care of the account for this little experiment of yours.'

I told her that Kripo would pay for everything.

Seeing the distinctive dark-yellow of a cigarette-vending van, I pulled up and got out of the car. I bought a couple of packs and threw one in the glove-box. I tapped one out for her, then myself and lit us both.

'It didn't seem strange that he also neglected to ask how old Emmeline was, which school she attended, what the name of her dancing teacher was, where I worked, that sort of thing?'

She blew smoke out of both nostrils like an angry bull. 'Not especially,' she said. 'At least, not until you mentioned it.' She thumped the dashboard and swore. 'But what if he had asked which school Emmeline goes to? What would you have done if he'd turned up there and found out that my real husband is dead? I'd like to know that.'

'He wouldn't have.'

'You seem very sure of that. How do you know?'

'Because I know how private detectives operate. They don't like to walk right in after the police and ask all the same questions. Usually they like to come at a thing from the other side. Walk round it a bit before they see an opening.'

'So you think that this Rolf Vogelmann is suspicious?'

'Yes, I do. Enough to warrant detailing a man to keep an eye on his premises.'

She swore again, rather more loudly this time.

'That's the second time,' I said. 'What's the matter with you?'

'Why should anything be the matter? No indeed. Single ladies never mind people giving out their addresses and telephone numbers to those whom the police believe to be suspicious. That's what makes living on one's own so exciting. My daughter is missing, probably murdered, and now I have to worry that that horrible man might drop round one evening for a little chat about her.' She was so angry she almost sucked the tobacco out of the cigarette paper. But even so, this time when we arrived at her apartment in Lepsius Strasse, she invited me inside.

I sat down on the sofa and listened to the sound of her urinating in the bathroom. It seemed strangely out of character for her not to be at all self-conscious about such a thing. Perhaps she didn't care if I heard or not. I'm not sure that she even bothered to close the bathroom door.

When she came back into the room she asked me peremptorily for another cigarette. Leaning forwards I waved one at her which she snatched from my fingers. She lit herself with the table lighter, and puffed like a trooper in the trenches. I watched her with interest as she paced up and down in front of me, the very image of parental anxiety. I selected a cigarette myself, and tugged a book of matches from my waistcoat pocket. Hildegard glanced fiercely at me as I bent my head towards the flame.

'I thought detectives were supposed to be able to light matches with their thumbnails.'

'Only the careless kind, who don't pay five marks for a manicure,' I said yawning.

I guessed that she was working up to something, but had no more idea of what it could be than I had of Hitler's taste in soft-furnishings. I took another good look at her.

She was tall – taller than the average man, and in her early thir-ties, but with the knock-knees and turned-in toes of a girl half her age. There wasn't much of a chest to speak of, and even less behind. The nose was maybe a bit too broad, the lips a shade too thick, and the cornflower-blue eyes rather too close together; and with the possible exception of her temper, there was certainly nothing deli-cate about her. But there was no doubting her long-limbed beauty which had something in common with the fastest of fillies out at the Hoppegarten. Probably she was just as difficult to hold on the rein; and if you ever managed to climb into the saddle, you could have done no more than hope that you got the trip as far as the winning-post.

'Can't you see that I'm scared?' she said, stamping her foot on the polished wood floor. 'I don't want to be on my own now.'

'Where is your son Paul?'

'He's gone back to his boarding-school. Anyway, he's only ten, so I can't see him coming to my assistance, can you?' She dropped on to the sofa beside me.

'Well I don't mind sleeping in his room for a few nights,' I said, 'if you really are scared.'

'Would you?' she said happily.

'Sure,' I said, and privately congratulated myself. 'It would be my pleasure.'

'I don't want it to be your pleasure,' she said, with just a trace of a smile, 'I want it to be your duty.'

For a moment I almost forgot why I was there. I might even have thought that she had forgotten. It was only when I saw the tear in the corner of her eye that I realized she really was afraid.

18

Wednesday, 26 October

'I don't get it,' said Korsch. 'What about Streicher and his bunch? Are we still investigating them or not?'

'Yes,' I said. 'But until the Gestapo surveillance throws up something of interest to us, there's not a lot we can do in that direction.'

'So what do you want us to do while you're looking after the widow?' said Becker, who was on the edge of allowing himself a smile I might have found irritating. 'That is, apart from checking the Gestapo reports.'

I decided not to be too sensitive about the matter. That would have been suspicious in itself.

'Korsch,' I said, 'I want you to keep your eye on the Gestapo inquiry. Incidentally, how's your man getting on with Vogelmann?'

He shook his head. 'There's not a lot to report, sir. This Vogelmann hardly ever leaves his office. Not much of a detective if you ask me.'

'It certainly doesn't look like it,' I said. 'Becker, I want you to find me a girl.' He grinned and looked down at the toe of his shoe. 'That shouldn't be too difficult for you.'

'Any particular kind of girl, sir?'

'Aged about fifteen or sixteen, blonde, blue-eyed, BdM and,' I said, feeding him the line, 'preferably a virgin.'

'That last part might be a bit difficult, sir.'

'She'll have to have plenty of nerve.'

'Are you thinking of staking her out, sir?'

'I believe it's always been the best way to hunt tiger.'

'Sometimes the goat gets killed though, sir,' said Korsch.

'As I said, this girl will have to have guts. I want her to know as much as possible. If she is going to risk her life then she ought to know why she's doing it.'

'Where exactly are we going to do this, sir?' said Becker.

'You tell me. Think about a few places where our man might notice her. A place where we can watch her without being seen ourselves.' Korsch was frowning. 'What's troubling you?'

He shook his head with slow distaste. 'I don't like it, sir. Using a young girl as bait. It's inhuman.'

'What do you suggest we use? A piece of cheese?'

'A main road,' Becker said, thinking out loud. 'Somewhere like Hohenzollerndamm, but with more cars, to increase our chances of him seeing her.'

'Honestly, sir, don't you think it's just a bit risky?'

'Of course it is. But what do we really know about this bastard? He drives a car, he wears a uniform, he has an Austrian or Bavarian accent. After that everything is a maybe. I don't have to remind you both that we are running out of time. That Heydrich has given me less than four weeks to solve this case. Well, we need to get closer, and we need to do it quickly. The only way is to take the initiative, to select his next victim for him.'

'But we might wait for ever,' said Korsch.

'I didn't say that it would be easy. You hunt tiger and you can end up sleeping in a tree.'

'What about the girl?' Korsch continued. 'You don't propose to keep her at it night and day, do you?'

'She can do it in the afternoons,' said Becker. 'Afternoons and early evenings. Not in the dark, so we can make sure he sees her, and we see him.'

'You're getting the idea.'

'But where does Vogelmann fit in?'

'I don't know. A feeling in my socks, that's all. Maybe it's nothing, but I just want to check it out.'

Becker smiled. 'A bull has to trust a few hunches now and then,' he said.

I recognized my own uninspired rhetoric. 'We'll make a detective out of you yet,' I told him.

She listened to her Gigli gramophone records with the avidity of someone who is about to go deaf, offering and requiring no more conversation than a railway ticket-collector. By now I had realized that Hildegard Steininger was about as self-contained as a fountain-pen, and I figured that she probably preferred the kind of man who could think of himself as little more than a blank sheet of writing paper. And yet, almost in spite of her, I continued to find her attractive. For my taste she was too much concerned with the shade of her gold-spun hair, the length of her fingernails and the state of her teeth, which she was forever brushing. Too vain by half, and too selfish twice over. Given a choice between pleasing herself and pleasing someone else she would have hoped that pleasing herself would have made everyone happy. That she should have thought that one would almost certainly result from the other was for her as simple a reaction as a knee jerking under a patella-hammer.

It was my sixth night staying at her apartment, and as usual she had cooked a dinner that was nearly inedible.

'You don't have to eat it, you know,' she had said. 'I was never much of a cook.'

'I was never much of a dinner guest,' I had replied, and eaten most of it, not for politeness' sake, but because I was hungry and had learnt in the trenches not to be too fussy about my food.

Now she closed the gramophone cabinet and yawned.

'I'm going to bed,' she said.

I tossed aside the book I was reading and said that I was going to turn in myself.

In Paul's bedroom I spent a few minutes studying the map of Spain that was pinned to the boy's wall, documenting the fortunes of the Condor Legions, before turning out the light. It seemed that every German schoolboy these days wanted to be a fighter-pilot. I was just settling down when there was a knock at the door.

'May I come in?' she said, hovering naked in the doorway. For a moment or two she just stood there, framed in the light from the hallway like some marvellous madonna, almost as if she were allowing me to assess her proportions. My chest and scrotum tightening, I watched her walk gracefully towards me.

Whereas her head and back were small, her legs were so long that she seemed to have been created by a draughtsman of genius. One hand covered her sex and this small shyness excited me very much. I allowed it for a short time while I looked upon the rounded simple volumes of her breasts. These were lightly, almost invisibly nippled, and the size of perfect nectarines.

I leant forwards, pushed that modest hand away, and then, taking hold of her smooth flanks, I pressed my mouth against the sleek filaments that mantled her sex. Standing up to kiss her I felt her hand reach down urgently for me, and winced as she peeled me back. It was too rough to be polite, to be tender, and so I responded by pushing her face first on to the bed, pulling her cool buttocks towards me and moulding her into a position that pleased me. She cried out at the moment when I plunged into her body, and her long thighs trembled wonderfully as we played out our noisy pantomime to its barnstorming denouement.

We slept until dawn came creeping through the thin material of the curtains. Awake before her, I was struck by her colour, which was every bit as cool as her awakening expression which changed not a bit as she sought to find my penis with her mouth. And then, turning on to her back, she pulled herself up the bed and laid her head on the pillow, her thighs yawning open so that I could see where life begins, and again I licked and kissed her there before acquainting it with the full rank of my ardour, pressing myself into her body until I thought that only my head and shoulders would remain unconsumed.

Finally, when there was nothing left in either of us, she wrapped herself round me and wept until I thought that she would melt.

19

Saturday, 29 October

'I thought you'd like the idea.'

'I'm not sure that I don't. Just give me a second to swill it around my head.'

'You don't want her hanging around somewhere just for the hell of it. He'll smell that shit in minutes and won't go near her. It's got to look natural.'

I nodded without a great deal of conviction and tried to smile at the BdM girl Becker had found. She was an extraordinarily pretty adolescent and I wasn't sure what Becker had been more impressed with, her bravery or her breasts.

'Come on, sir, you know what it's like,' he said. 'These girls are always hanging around the *Der Stürmer* display cases on street corners. They get a cheap thrill reading about Jewish doctors interfering with mesmerized German virgins. Look at it this way. Not only will it stop her from getting bored, but also, if Streicher or his people are involved, then they're more than likely going to take notice of her here, in front of one of these Stürmerkästen, than anywhere else.'

I stared uncomfortably at the elaborate, red-painted case, probably built by some loyal readers, with its vivid slogans proclaiming: 'German Women: The Jews are your Destruction', and the three double-page spreads from the paper under glass. It was bad enough to ask a girl to act as bait, without having to expose her to this kind of trash as well.

'I suppose you're right, Becker.'

'You know I am. Look at her. She's reading it already. I swear she likes it.'

'What's her name?'

'Ulrike.'

I walked over to the Stürmerkästen where she was standing, singing quietly to herself.

'You know what to do, Ulrike?' I said quietly, not looking at her now that I was beside her, but staring at the Fips cartoon with its mandatory ugly Jew. No one could look like that, I thought. The nose was as big as a sheep's muzzle.

'Yes, sir,' she said brightly.

'There are lots of policemen around. You can't see them, but they are all watching you. Understand?' I saw her head nod in the reflection on the glass. 'You're a very brave girl.'

At that she started to sing again, only louder, and I realized that it was the Hitler Youth song:

> 'Our flag see before us fly,
> Our flag means an age without strife,
> Our flag leads us to eternity,
> Our flag means more to us than life.'

I walked back to where Becker was standing and got back into the car.

'She's quite a girl, isn't she, sir?'

'She certainly is. Just make sure that you keep your flippers off her, do you hear?'

He was all innocence. 'Come on, sir, you don't think I'd try to bird that one, do you?' He got into the driving seat and started the engine.

'I think you'd fuck your great-grandmother, if you really want my opinion.' I glanced over each shoulder. 'Where are your men?'

'Sergeant Hingsen's on the first floor of that apartment building there,' he said, 'and I've got a couple of men on the street. One is tidying up the graveyard on the corner, and the other's cleaning windows over there. If our man does show up, we'll have him.'

'Do the girl's parents know about this?'

'Yes.'

'Rather public-spirited of them to give their permission, wouldn't you say?'

'They didn't exactly do that, sir. Ulrike informed them that she had volunteered to do this in the service of the Führer and the Fatherland. She said that it would be unpatriotic to try and stop her. So they didn't have much choice in the matter. She's a forceful sort of girl.'

'I can imagine.'

'Quite a swimmer, too, by all accounts. A future Olympic prospect, her teacher reckons.'

'Well, let's just hope for a bit of rain in case she has to try and swim her way out of trouble.'

I heard the bell in the hall and went to the window. Pulling it up I leant out to see who was working the bell-pull. Even three storeys up I could recognize Vogelmann's head of distinctive red hair.

'That's a very common thing to do,' said Hildegard. 'Lean out of a window like a fishwife.'

'As it happens, I might just have caught a fish. It's Vogelmann. And he's brought a friend.'

'Well, you had better go and let them in, hadn't you?'

I walked out on to the landing and operated the lever that pulled the chain to open the street door, and watched the two men climb up the stairs. Neither one of them said anything.

Vogelmann came into Hildegard's apartment wearing his best undertaker's face, which was a blessing since the grim set to his halitosic mouth meant that, for a while at least, it stayed mercifully shut. The man with him was shorter than Vogelmann by a head, and in his mid-thirties, with fair hair, blue eyes and an intense, even academic air about him. Vogelmann waited until we were all seated before introducing the other man as Dr Otto Rahn, and promised to say more about him presently. Then he sighed loudly and shook his head.

'I'm afraid that I have had no luck in the search for your daughter Emmeline,' he said. 'I've asked everyone I could possibly have asked, and looked everywhere I could possibly have looked. With no result. It has been most disappointing.' He paused, and added: 'Of course, I realize that my own disappointment must count as nothing besides your own. However, I thought I might at least find some trace of her.

'If there was anything, anything at all, that gave some clue as to what might have become of her, then I would feel justified in recommending to you that I continue with my inquiries. But there's nothing that gives me any confidence that I wouldn't be wasting your time and money.'

I nodded with slow resignation. 'Thank you for being so honest, Herr Vogelmann.'

'At least you can say we tried, Herr Steininger,' Vogelmann said. 'I'm not exaggerating when I say that I have exhausted all the usual methods of inquiry.' He stopped to clear his throat and, excusing himself, dabbed at his mouth with a handkerchief.

'I hesitate to suggest this to you, Herr and Frau Steininger, and please don't think me facetious, but when the usual has proved itself to be unhelpful, there can surely be no harm in resorting to the unusual.'

'I rather thought that was why we consulted you in the first place,' Hildegard said stiffly. 'The usual, as you put it, was something that we expected from the police.'

Vogelmann smiled awkwardly. 'I've expressed it badly,' he said. 'I should perhaps have been talking in terms of the ordinary and the extraordinary.'

The other man, Otto Rahn, came to Vogelmann's assistance.

'What Herr Vogelmann is trying to suggest, with as much good taste as he can in the circumstances, is that you consider enlisting the services of a medium to help you find your daughter.' His accent was educated and he spoke with the speed of a man from somewhere like Frankfurt.

'A medium?' I said. 'You mean spiritualism?' I shrugged. 'We're not believers in that sort of thing.' I wanted to hear what Rahn might have to say in order to sell us on the idea.

He smiled patiently. 'These days it's hardly a matter of belief. Spiritualism is now more of a science. There have been some quite amazing developments since the war, especially in the last decade.'

'But isn't this illegal?' I asked meekly. 'I'm sure I read somewhere that Count Helldorf had banned all professional fortune-telling in Berlin, why, as long ago as 1934.'

Rahn was smooth and not at all deflected by my choice of phrase.

'You're very well informed, Herr Steininger. And you're right, the Police President did ban them. Since then, however, the situation has been satisfactorily resolved, and racially sound practitioners in the psychic sciences are incorporated in the Independent Professions sections of the German Labour Front. It was only ever the mixed races, the Jews and the gypsies, that gave the psychic sciences a bad name. Why, these days the Führer himself employs a professional astrologer. So you see, things have come a long way since Nostradamus.'

Vogelmann nodded and chuckled quietly.

So this was the reason Reinhard Lange was sponsoring Vogelmann's advertising campaign, I thought. To drum up a little business for the floating wine-glass trade. It looked like quite a neat operation too. Your detective failed to find your missing person, after which, through the mediation of Otto Rahn, you were passed on to an apparently higher power. This service probably resulted in your paying several times as much for the privilege of finding out what was already obvious: that your loved one slept with the angels.

Yes indeed, I thought, a neat piece of theatre. I was going to enjoy putting these people away. You can sometimes forgive a man who works a line, but not the ones who prey on the grief and suffering of others. That was like stealing the cushions off a pair of crutches.

'Peter,' said Hildegard, 'I don't see that we really have much to lose.'

'No, I suppose not.'

'I'm so glad you think so,' said Vogelmann. 'One always hesitates to recommend such a thing, but I think that in this case, there is really little or no alternative.'

'What will it cost?'

'This is Emmeline's life we're talking about,' Hildegard snapped. 'How can you mention money?'

'The cost is very reasonable,' said Rahn. 'I'm quite sure you'll be entirely satisfied. But let's talk about that at a later date. The most important thing is that you meet someone who can help you.

'There is a man, a very great and gifted man, who is possessed of enormous psychic ability. He might be able to help. This man, as the last descendant of a long line of German men of wisdom, has an ancestral-clairvoyant memory that is quite unique in our time.'

'He sounds wonderful,' Hildegard breathed.

'He is,' said Vogelmann.

'Then I will arrange for you to meet him,' said Rahn. 'I happen to know that he is free this coming Thursday. Will you be available in the evening?'

'Yes. We'll be available.'

Rahn took out a notebook and started writing. When he'd finished he tore out the sheet and handed it to me.

'Here is the address. Shall we say eight o'clock? Unless you hear from me before then?' I nodded. 'Excellent.'

Vogelmann stood up to leave while Rahn bent and searched for something in his briefcase. He handed Hildegard a magazine.

'Perhaps this might also be of interest to you,' he said.

I saw them out and when I came back I found her engrossed in the magazine. I didn't need to look at the front cover to know that it was Reinhard Lange's *Urania*. Nor did I need to speak to Hildegard to know that she was convinced Otto Rahn was genuine.

20

Thursday, 3 November

The Resident Registration Office turned up an Otto Rahn, formerly of Michelstadt near Frankfurt, now living at Tiergartenstrasse 8a, Berlin West 35.

VC1, Criminal Records, on the other hand, had no trace of him.

Nor did VC2, the department that compiled the Wanted Persons List. I was just about to leave when the department director, an SS Sturmbannführer by the name of Baum, called me over to his office.

'Kommissar, did I hear you asking that officer about somebody called Otto Rahn?' he asked.

I told him that I was interested in finding out everything I could about Otto Rahn.

'Which department are you with?'

'The Murder Commission. He might be able to assist us with an inquiry.'

'So you don't actually suspect him of having committed a crime?'

Sensing that the Sturmbannführer knew something about an Otto Rahn, I decided to cover my tracks a little.

'Good grief, no,' I said. 'As I say, it's just that he may be able to put us in contact with a valuable witness. Why? Do you know someone by that name?'

'Yes, I do, as a matter of fact,' he said. 'He's more of an acquaintance really. There is an Otto Rahn who's in the SS.'

The old Hotel Prinz Albrecht Strasse was an unremarkable four-storey building of arched windows and mock Corinthian pillars, with two long, dictator-sized balconies on the first floor, surmounted by an enormous ornate clock. Its seventy rooms meant that it had never been in the same league as the big hotels like the Bristol or the Adlon, which was probably how it came to be taken over by the SS. Now called SS-Haus, and situated next door to Gestapo headquarters at number eight, it was also headquarters to Heinrich Himmler in his capacity as Reichsführer-SS.

In the Personnel Records Department on the second floor, I showed them my warrant and explained my mission.

'I'm required by the SD to obtain a security clearance for a member of the SS in order that he may be considered for promotion to General Heydrich's personal staff.'

The SS corporal on duty stiffened at the mention of Heydrich's name.

'How can I help?' he said eagerly.

'I require to see the man's file. His name is Otto Rahn.'

The corporal asked me to wait, and then went into the next room where he searched for the appropriate filing-cabinet.

'Here you are,' he said, returning after a few minutes with the file. 'I'm afraid that I'll have to ask you to examine it here. A file may be removed from this office only with the written approval of the Reichsführer himself.'

'Naturally I knew that,' I said coldly. 'But I'm sure I'll just need to take a quick look at it. This is only a formal security check.' I stepped away and stood at a lectern on the far side of the office, where I opened the file to examine its contents. It made interesting reading.

SS Unterscharführer Otto Rahn; born 18 February 1904 at Michelstadt in Odenwald; studied philology at the University of Heidelberg, graduating in 1928; joined SS, March 1936; promoted SS, Unterscharführer, April 1936; posted SS-Deaths Head Division 'Oberbayern' Dachau Concentration Camp, September 1937; seconded to Race and Resettlement Office, December 1938; public speaker and author of *Crusade Against the Grail* (1933) and *Lucifer's Servants* (1937).

There followed several pages of medical notes and character assessments, and these included an evaluation from one SS-Gruppenführer Theodor Eicke which described Rahn as 'diligent, although given to some eccentricities'. By my reckoning that could have covered just about anything, from murder to the length of his hair.

I returned Rahn's file to the desk corporal and made my way out of the building. Otto Rahn.

The more I discovered about him, the less inclined I was to believe that he was merely working some elaborate confidence trick. Here was a man interested in something else besides money. A man for whom the word 'fanatic' did not seem to be inappropriate. Driving back to Steglitz, I passed Rahn's house on Tiergartenstrasse, and I don't think I would have been surprised to see the Scarlet Woman and the Great Beast of the Apocalypse come flying out the front door.

It was dark by the time we drove to Caspar-Theyss Strasse, which runs just south of Kurfürstendamm, on the edge of Grünewald. It was a quiet street of villas which stop only a little way short of being something more grand, and which are occupied largely by doctors and dentists. Number thirty-three, next to a small cottage hospital, occupied the corner of Paulsbornerstrasse, and was opposite a large florist where visitors to the hospital could buy their flowers.

There was a touch of the Gingerbread Man about the queer-looking house to which Rahn had invited us. The basement and ground-floor brickwork was painted brown, and on the first and second floors it was cream-coloured. A septagonally shaped tower occupied the east side of the house, a timbered loggia surmounted by a balcony the centre portion, and on the west side, a moss-covered wooden gable overhung a couple of porthole windows.

'I hope you brought a clove of garlic with you,' I told Hildegard as I parked the car. I could see she didn't much care for the look of the place, but she remained obstinately silent, still convinced that everything was on the level.

We walked up to a wrought-iron gate that had been fashioned

with a variety of zodiacal symbols, and I wondered what the two SS men standing underneath one of the garden's many spruce trees and smoking cigarettes made of it. This thought occupied me for only a second before I moved on to the more challenging question of what they and the several Party staff cars parked on the pavement were doing there.

Otto Rahn answered the door, greeting us with sympathetic warmth, and directed us into a cloakroom where he relieved us of our coats.

'Before we go in,' he said, 'I should explain that there are a number of other people here for this seance. Herr Weisthor's prowess as a clairvoyant has made him Germany's most important sage. I think I mentioned that a number of leading Party members are sympathetic to Herr Weisthor's work – incidentally, this is his home – and so apart from Herr Vogelmann and myself, one of the other guests here tonight will probably be familiar to you.'

Hildegard's jaw dropped. 'Not the Führer,' she said.

Rahn smiled. 'No, not he. But someone very close to him. He has requested that he be treated just like anyone else in order to facilitate a favourable atmosphere for the evening's contact. So I'm telling you now, in order that you won't be too surprised, that it is the Reichsführer-SS, Heinrich Himmler, to whom I am referring. No doubt you saw the security men outside and were wondering what was going on. The Reichsführer is a great patron of our work and has attended many seances.'

Emerging from the cloakroom, we went through a door soundproofed in button-backed padded green leather, and into a large and simply furnished L-shaped room. Across the thick green carpet was a round table at one end, and a group of about ten people standing over a sofa and a couple of armchairs at the other. The walls, where they were visible between the light oak panelling, were painted white, and the green curtains were all drawn. There was something classically German about this room, which was the same thing as saying that it was about as warm and friendly as a Swiss Army knife.

Rahn found us some drinks and introduced Hildegard and me to the room. I spotted Vogelmann's red head first of all, nodded to him and then searched for Himmler. Since there were no uniforms to be seen, he was rather difficult to spot in his dark, double-breasted suit. Taller than I had expected, and younger too – perhaps no more than thirty-seven or thirty-eight. When he spoke, he seemed a mild-mannered sort of man, and, apart from the enormous gold Rolex, my overall impression was of a man you would have taken for a headmaster rather than the head of the German secret police. And what was it about Swiss wristwatches that made them so attractive to men of power? But a wristwatch was not as attractive to this particular man of power as was Hildegard Steininger, it seemed, and the two of them were soon deep in conversation.

'Herr Weisthor will come out presently,' Rahn explained. 'He usually needs a period of quiet meditation before approaching the spirit world. Let me introduce you to Reinhard Lange. He's the proprietor of that magazine I left for your wife.'

'Ah yes, *Urania*.'

So there he was, short and plump, with a dimple in one of his chins and a pugnaciously pendant lower lip, as if daring you to smack him or kiss him. His fair hair was well-receded, although somewhat babyish about the ears. He had hardly any eyebrows to speak of, and the eyes themselves were half-closed, slitty even. Both of these features made him seem weak and inconstant, in a Nero-like sort of way. Possibly he was neither of these two things, although the strong smell of cologne that surrounded him, his self-satisfied air, and his slightly theatrical way of speaking, did nothing to correct my first impression of him. My line of work has made me a rapid and fairly accurate judge of character, and five minutes' conversation with Lange were enough to convince me that I had not been wrong about him. The man was a worthless little queer.

I excused myself and went to the lavatory I had seen beyond the cloakroom. I had already decided to return to Weisthor's house after the seance and see if the other rooms were any more interesting than the one we were in. There didn't appear to be a dog about the place, so it seemed that all I had to do was prepare my entry. I bolted the door behind me and set about releasing the window-catch. It was stiff and I had just managed to get it open when there was a knock at the door. It was Rahn.

'Herr Steininger? Are you in there?'

'I won't be a moment.'

'We'll be starting in a moment or two.'

'I'll be right there,' I said, and, leaving the window a couple of centimetres open, I flushed the toilet and went back to rejoin the rest of the guests.

Another man had come into the room, and I realized that this must be Weisthor. Aged about sixty-five, he wore a three-piece suit of light-brown flannel and carried an ornate, ivory-handled stick with strange carvings on its shaft, some of which matched his ring. Physically he resembled an older version of Himmler, with his small smudge of a moustache, hamster-like cheeks, dyspeptic mouth and receding chin; but he was stouter, and whereas the Reichsführer reminded you of a myopic rat, Weisthor had more of the beaver about his features, an effect that was accentuated by the gap between his two front teeth.

'You must be Herr Steininger,' he said, pumping my hand. 'Permit me to introduce myself. I am Karl Maria Weisthor, and I am delighted to have already had the pleasure of meeting your lovely wife.' He spoke very formally, and with a Viennese accent. 'In that at least you are a very fortunate man. Let us hope that I may be of service to you both before the evening has ended. Otto has told me of your missing daughter Emmeline, and of how the police and our good friend Rolf Vogelmann have been unable to find her. As I said to your wife, I am sure that the spirits of our ancient German ancestors will not desert us, and that they will tell us what has become of her, as they have told us of other things before.'

He turned and waved at the table. 'Shall we be seated?' he said. 'Herr Steininger, you and your wife will sit on either side of me. Everyone will join hands, Herr Steininger. This will increase our conscious power. Try not to let go, no matter what you might see or hear, as it can cause the link to be broken. Do you both understand?'

We nodded and took our seats. When the rest of the company had sat down, I noticed that Himmler had contrived to be sitting next to Hildegard, to whom he was paying close attention. It struck me that I would tell it differently, and that it would amuse Heydrich and Nebe if I told them I spent the evening holding hands with Heinrich Himmler. Thinking about it then I almost laughed, and to cover my half-smile I turned away from Weisthor and found myself looking at a tall, urbane, Siegfried-type wearing evening dress, with the kind of warm, sensitive manner that comes only of bathing in dragon's blood.

'My name is Kindermann,' he said sternly. 'Dr Lanz Kindermann, at your service, Herr Steininger.' He glanced down at my hand as if it had been a dirty dishcloth.

'Not the famous psychotherapist?' I said.

He smiled. 'I doubt that you could call me famous,' he said, but with some satisfaction all the same. 'Nevertheless, I thank you for the compliment.'

'And are you Austrian?'

'Yes. Why do you ask?'

'I like to know something about the men whose hands I hold,' I offered, and grasped his own firmly.

'In a moment,' said Weisthor, 'I shall ask our friend Otto to turn off the electric light. But first of all, I should like us all to close our eyes and to breathe deeply. The purpose of this is to relax. Only if we are relaxed will spirits feel comfortable enough to contact us and offer us the benefit of what they are able to see.

'It may help you to think of something peaceful, such as a flower or a formation of clouds.' He paused, so that the only sounds which could be heard were the deep breathing of the people around the table and the ticking of a clock on the mantelpiece. I heard Vogelmann clear his throat, which prompted Weisthor to speak again.

'Try and flow into the person next to you so that we may feel the power of the circle. When Otto turns off the light I shall go into trance and permit my body to be taken under the control of spirit. Spirit will control my speech, my every bodily function, so that I shall be in a vulnerable position. Make no sudden noise or interruption. Speak gently if you wish to communicate with spirit, or allow Otto to speak for you.' He paused again. 'Otto? The lights, please.'

I heard Rahn stand up as if rousing himself from a deep sleep and creep across the carpet.

'From now on Weisthor will not speak unless he is under spirit,' he said. 'It will be my voice you hear speak to him in trance.' He turned off the light, and after a few seconds I heard him return to the circle.

I stared hard into the darkness at where Weisthor was sitting, but try as I might, I could see nothing but the strange shapes which play on the back of the retina when it is deprived of light. Whatever Weisthor said about flowers or clouds, I found it helped me to think of the Mauser automatic at my shoulder, and the nice formation of 9mm ammunition in the grip.

The first change that I was aware of was that of his breathing, which became progressively slower and deeper. After a while it was almost undetectable and, but for his grip, which had slackened considerably, I might have said he had disappeared.

Finally he spoke, but it was in a voice that made my flesh creep and my hair prickle.

'I have a wise king here from long, long ago,' he said, his grip tightening suddenly. 'From a time when three suns shone in the northern sky.' He uttered a long, sepulchral sigh. 'He suffered a terrible defeat in battle at the hands of Charlemagne and his Christian army.'

'Were you Saxon?' Rahn asked quietly.

'Aye, Saxon. The Franks called them pagans, and put them to death for it. Agonizing deaths, that were full of blood and pain.' He seemed to hesitate. 'It's difficult to say this. He says that blood must be paid for. He says that German paganism is grown strong again, and must be revenged on the Franks and their religion, in the name of the old gods.' Then he grunted almost as if he had been struck and went quiet again.

'Don't be alarmed,' Rahn murmured. 'Spirit can leave quite violently sometimes.'

After several minutes, Weisthor spoke again.

'Who are you?' he asked softly. 'A girl? Will you tell us your name, child? No? Come now '

'Don't be afraid,' said Rahn. 'Please come forward to us.'

'Her name is Emmeline,' said Weisthor.

I heard Hildegard gasp.

'Is your name Emmeline Steininger?' Rahn asked. 'If so, then your mother and father are here to speak to you, child.'

'She says that she is not a child,' whispered Weisthor. 'And that one of these two people is not her real parent at all.'

I stiffened. Could it be genuine after all? Did Weisthor really have mediumistic powers?

'I'm her stepmother,' said Hildegard tremulously, and I wondered if she had recognized that Weisthor should have said that neither of us was Emmeline's real parent.

'She says that she misses her dancing. But especially she misses you both.'

'We miss you too, darling.'

'Where are you, Emmeline?' I asked. There was a long silence, and so I repeated the question.

'They killed her,' said Weisthor falteringly. 'And hid her somewhere.'

'Emmeline, you must try and help us,' said Rahn. 'Can you tell us anything about where they put you?'

'Yes, I'll tell them. She says that outside the window, there's a hill. At the bottom of the hill is a pretty waterfall. What's that? A cross, or maybe something else that's high, like a tower is on top of the hill.'

'The Kreuzberg?' I said.

'Is it the Kreuzberg?' Rahn asked.

'She doesn't know the name,' whispered Weisthor. 'Where's that?

Oh how terrible. She says she's in a box. I'm sorry, Emmeline, but I don't think I can have heard you properly. Not in a box? A barrel? Yes, a barrel. A rotten smelly old barrel in an old cellar full of rotten old barrels.'

'Sounds like a brewery,' said Kindermann.

'Could you be referring to the Schultheiss Brewery?' said Rahn.

'She thinks that it must be, although it doesn't seem like a place where lots of people go. Some of the barrels are old and have holes in them. She can see out of one of them. No, my dear, it wouldn't be very good for holding beer, I quite agree.'

Hildegard whispered something that I failed to hear.

'Courage, dear lady,' Rahn said. 'Courage.' Then more loudly: 'Who was it that killed you, Emmeline? And can you tell us why?'

Weisthor groaned deeply. 'She doesn't know their names, but she thinks that it was for the Blood Mystery. How did you find out about that, Emmeline? That's one of the many thousands of things you learn about when you die, I see. They killed her like they kill their animals, and then her blood was mixed with the wine and the bread. She thinks that it must have been for religious rites, but not the sort she had ever seen before.'

'Emmeline,' said a voice which I thought must be Himmler's. 'Was it the Jews who murdered you? Was it Jews who used your blood?'

Another long silence.

'She doesn't know,' said Weisthor. 'They didn't say who or what they were. They didn't look like any of the pictures she's seen of Jews. What's that, my dear? She says that it might have been but she doesn't want to get anyone into trouble, no matter what they did to her. She says that if it was the Jews then they were just bad Jews, and that not all Jews would have approved of such a thing. She doesn't want to say any more about that. She just wants someone to go and get her out of that dirty barrel. Yes, I'm sure someone will organize it, Emmeline. Don't worry.'

'Tell her that I shall personally see to it that it happens tonight,' said Himmler. 'The child has my own word on that.'

'What's that you said? All right. Emmeline says to thank you for trying to help her. And she says to tell mother and father that she loves them very much indeed, but not to worry about her now. Nothing can bring her back. You should both get on with your lives and put what has happened behind you. Try and be happy. Emmeline has to go now.'

'Goodbye, Emmeline,' sobbed Hildegard.

'Goodbye,' I said.

Once again there was silence, but for the sound of the blood rushing in my ears. I was glad of the darkness because it hid my face, which must have shown my anger, and afforded me an opportunity to breathe my way back to a semblance of quiet sadness and resignation. If it hadn't been for the two or three minutes that elapsed from the end of Weisthor's performance and the raising of the lights, I think that I would have shot them all where they sat: Weisthor, Rahn, Vogelmann, Lange – shit, I'd have murdered the whole dirty lot of them just for the sheer satisfaction of it. I'd have made them take the barrel in their mouths and blown the backs of their heads on to each other's faces. An extra nostril for Himmler. A third eye-socket for Kindermann.

I was still breathing heavily when the lights went up again, but this was easily mistaken for grief. Hildegard's face was shiny with tears, which provoked Himmler to put his arm around her. Catching my eye he nodded grimly.

Weisthor was the last to get to his feet. He swayed for a moment as if he would fall, and Rahn took hold of him by the elbow. Weisthor smiled, and patted his friend's hand gratefully.

'I can see by your face, my dear lady, that your daughter came through.'

She nodded. 'I want to thank you, Herr Weisthor. Thank you so much for helping us.' She sniffed loudly and found her handkerchief.

'Karl, you were excellent tonight,' said Himmler. 'Quite remarkable.' There was a murmur of assent from the rest of the table, myself included. Himmler was still shaking his head in wonder. 'Quite, quite remarkable,' he repeated. 'You may all rest assured that I shall contact the proper authorities myself, and order that a squad of police be sent immediately to search the Schultheiss Brewery for the unfortunate child's body.' Himmler was staring at me now, and I nodded dumbly in response to what he was saying.

'But I don't doubt for a minute that they will find her there. I have every confidence that what we have just heard was the child speaking to Karl in order that both your minds may now be put at rest. I think that the best thing for you to do now would be to go home and wait to hear from the police.'

'Yes, of course,' I said and, walking round the table, I took Hildegard by the hand and led her away from the Reichsführer's embrace. Then we shook hands with the assembled company, accepted their condolences and allowed Rahn to escort us to the door.

'What can one say?' he said with great gravitas. 'Naturally I am very sorry that Emmeline has passed on to the other side, but as the Reichsführer himself said, it's a blessing that now you can know for sure.'

'Yes,' Hildegard sniffed. 'It's best to know, I think.'

Rahn narrowed his eyes and looked slightly pained as he grasped me by the forearm.

'I think it's also best if for obvious reasons you were to say nothing of this evening's events to the police if they should come to say that they have indeed found her. I'm afraid that they might make things very awkward for you if you seemed to know that she had been found before they did themselves. As I'm sure you will appreciate, the police aren't very enlightened when it comes to understanding this sort of thing, and might ask you all sorts of difficult questions.' He shrugged. 'I mean, we all have questions concerning what comes to us from the other side. It is indeed an enigma to everyone, and one to which we have very few answers at this stage.'

'Yes, I can see how the police might prove to be awkward,' I said. 'You may depend on me to say nothing of what transpired this evening. My wife as well.'

'Herr Steininger, I knew you would understand.' He opened the front door. 'Please don't hesitate to contact us again if at some stage you would wish to contact your daughter. But I should leave it for a while. It doesn't do to summon spirit too regularly.'

We said goodbye again, and walked back to the car.

'Get me away from here, Bernie,' she hissed as I opened the door for her. By the time I had started the engine she was crying again, only this time it was with shock and horror.

'I can't believe people could be so – so *evil*,' she sobbed.

'I'm sorry you had to go through that,' I said. 'Really I am. I'd have given anything for you to have avoided it, but it was the only way.'

I drove to the end of the street and on to Bismarkplatz, a quiet intersection of suburban streets with a small patch of grass in the middle. It was only now that I realized how close we were to Frau Lange's house in Herbertstrasse. I spotted Korsch's car, and pulled up behind it.

'Bernie? Do you think that the police will find her there?'

'Yes, I think they will.'

'But how could he fake it and know where she is? How could he know those things about her? Her love of dancing?'

'Because he, or one of those others, put her there. Probably they spoke to Emmeline and asked her a few questions before they killed her. Just for the sake of authenticity.'

She blew her nose, and then looked up. 'Why have we stopped?'

'Because I'm going back there to take a look around. See if I can find out what their ugly little game is. The car parked in front of us is driven by one of my men. His name is Korsch, and he's going to drive you home.'

She nodded. 'Please be careful, Bernie,' she said breathlessly, her head dropping forwards on to her chest.

'Are you all right, Hildegard?'

She fumbled for the door-handle. 'I think I'm going to be sick.' She fell sideways towards the pavement, vomiting into the gutter and down her sleeve as she broke her fall with her hand. I jumped out of the car and ran round to the passenger door to help her, but Korsch was there before me, supporting her by the shoulders until she could draw breath again.

'Jesus Christ,' he said, 'what happened in there?'

Crouching down beside her I mopped the perspiration from Hildegard's face before wiping her mouth. She took the handkerchief from my hand and allowed Korsch to help her sit up again.

'It's a long story,' I said, 'and I'm afraid that it's going to have to wait awhile yet. I want you to take her home and then wait for me at the Alex. Get Becker there as well. I've a feeling we're going to be busy tonight.'

'I'm sorry,' said Hildegard. 'I'm all right now.' She smiled bravely. Korsch and I helped her out and, holding her by the waist, we walked her to Korsch's car.

'Be careful, sir,' he said as he got behind the driving wheel and started the engine. I told him not to worry.

After they had driven away, I waited in the car for half an hour or so, and then walked back down Caspar-Theyss Strasse. The wind was getting up a bit and a couple of times it rose to such a pitch in the trees that lined the dark street that, had I been of a rather more fanciful disposition, I might have imagined that it was something to do with what had taken place in Weisthor's house. Disturbing the spirits and that sort of thing. As it was I was possessed of a sense of danger which the wind moaning across the cloud-tumbling sky did nothing to alleviate, and indeed, this feeling was if anything made all the more acute by seeing the gingerbread house again.

By now the staff cars were gone from the pavement outside, but I nevertheless approached the garden with caution, in case the two SS men had remained behind, for whatever reason. Having satisfied myself that the house was not guarded, I tiptoed round to the side of the house, and to the lavatory window I had left unlocked. It was well that I stepped lightly, because the light was on and from inside the small room could be heard the unmistakable sound of a man straining on the toilet-bowl. Flattening myself in the shadows against the wall, I waited until he finished, and finally, after what seemed like ten or fifteen minutes, I heard the sound of the toilet flushing, and saw the light go off.

Several minutes passed before I judged it safe to go to the window and push it up the sash. But almost immediately upon entering the lavatory, I could have wished to have been elsewhere, or at least wearing a gas-mask, since the fecal smell that greeted my nostrils was such as would have turned the stomachs of a whole clinicful of proctologists. I suppose that's what bulls mean when they say that sometimes it's a rotten job. For my money, having to stand quietly in a toilet where someone has just achieved a bowel-movement of truly Gothic proportions is about as rotten as it can get.

The terrible smell was the main reason I decided to move out into the cloakroom rather more quickly than might have been safe, and I was almost seen by Weisthor himself as he trudged wearily past the open cloakroom door and across the hallway to a room on the opposite side.

'Quite a wind tonight,' said a voice, which I recognized as belonging to Otto Rahn.

'Yes,' Weisthor chuckled. 'It all added to the atmosphere, didn't it? Himmler will be especially pleased with this turn in the weather. No doubt he will ascribe all sorts of supernatural Wagnerian notions to it.'

'You were very good, Karl,' said Rahn. 'Even the Reichsführer commented on it.'

'But you look tired,' said a third voice, which I took to be Kindermann's. 'You'd better let me take a look at you.'

I edged forward and looked through the gap between the cloakroom door and frame. Weisthor was taking off his jacket and hanging it over the back of a chair. Sitting down heavily, he allowed Kindermann to take his pulse. He seemed listless and pale, almost as if he really had been in contact with the spirit world. He seemed to hear my thoughts.

'Faking it is almost as tiring as doing it for real,' he said.

'Perhaps I should give you an injection,' said Kindermann. 'A little morphine to help you sleep.' Without waiting for a reply he produced a small bottle and a hypodermic syringe from a medical bag, and set about preparing the needle. 'After all, we don't want you feeling tired for the forthcoming Court of Honour, do we?'

'I shall want you there of course, Lanz,' said Weisthor, rolling back his own sleeve to reveal a forearm that was so bruised and scarred with puncture marks, that it looked as if he had been tattooed.

'I shan't be able to get through it without cocaine. I find it clarifies the mind wonderfully. And I shall need to be so transcendentally stimulated that the Reichsführer-SS will find what I have to say totally irresistible.'

'You know, for a moment back there I thought you were actually going to make the revelation tonight,' said Rahn. 'You really teased him with all of that stuff about the girl not wanting to get anyone into trouble. Well, frankly, he more or less believes it now.'

'Only when the time is right, my dear Otto,' said Weisthor. 'Only when the time is right. Think how much more dramatic it will be to him when I reveal it in Wewelsburg. Jewish complicity will have the force of spiritual revelation, and we will be done with this nonsense of his about respecting property and the rule of law. The Jews will get what's coming to them and there won't be one policeman to stop it.' He nodded at the syringe and watched impassively as Kindermann thrust the needle home, sighing with satisfaction as the plunger was depressed.

'And now, gentlemen, if you will kindly help an old man to his bed.'

I watched as they each took an arm and walked him up the creaking stairs.

It crossed my mind that if Kindermann or Rahn were planning to leave then they might want to put on a coat, and so I crept out of the cloakroom and went into the L-shaped room where the bogus seance had been staged, hiding behind the thick curtains in case either one of them should come in. But when they came downstairs again, they only stood in the hall and talked. I missed half of what they said, but the gist of it seemed to be that Reinhard Lange was reaching the end of his usefulness. Kindermann made a feeble attempt to apologize for his lover, but his heart didn't seem to be in it.

The smell in the lavatory was a hard act to follow, but what happened next was even more disgusting. I couldn't see exactly what took place, and there were no words to hear. But the sound of two men engaged in a homosexual act is unmistakable, and left me feeling utterly nauseated. When finally they had brought their filthy behaviour to its braying conclusion and left, chuckling like a couple of degenerate schoolboys, I felt weak enough to have to open a window for some fresh air.

In the study next door I helped myself to a large glass of Weisthor's brandy, which worked a lot better than a chestful of Berlin air, and with the curtains drawn I even felt relaxed enough to switch on the desk-lamp and take a good long look around the room before searching the drawers and cabinets.

It was worth a look, too. Weisthor's taste in decoration was no less eccentric than mad King Ludwig's. There were strange-looking calendars, heraldic coats of arms, paintings of standing stones, Merlin, the Sword in the Stone, the Grail and the Knights Templar, and photographs of castles, Hitler, Himmler, and finally Weisthor himself, in uniform: first as an officer in some regiment of Austrian infantry; and then in the uniform of a senior officer in the SS.

Karl Weisthor was in the SS. I almost said it aloud, it seemed so fantastic. Nor was he merely an NCO like Otto Rahn, but judging from the number of pips on his collar, at least a brigadier. And something else too. Why had I not noticed it before – the physical similarity between Weisthor and Julius Streicher? It was true that Weisthor was perhaps ten years older than Streicher, but the description given by the little Jewish schoolgirl, by Sarah Hirsch, could just as easily have applied to Weisthor as to Streicher: both men were heavy, with not much hair, and a small moustache; and both men had strong southern accents. Austrian or Bavarian, she had said. Well Weisthor was from Vienna. I wondered if Otto Rahn could have been the man driving the car.

Everything seemed to fall in with what I already knew, and my overhearing the conversation in the hallway confirmed my earlier suspicion that the motive behind the killings was to throw blame on to Berlin's Jews. Yet somehow there still seemed to be more to it. There had been Himmler's involvement. Was I right in thinking

that their secondary motive had been the enlistment of the Reichsführer-SS as a believer in Weisthor's powers, thereby ensuring the
latter's power-base and prospects for advancement in the SS, perhaps even at the expense of Heydrich himself?

It was a fine piece of theorizing. Now all I needed to do was
prove it, and the evidence would have to be watertight if Himmler
was going to allow his own personal Rasputin to be sent up for
multiple murder. The more so if it was likely to reveal the Reich's
chief of police as the gullible victim of an elaborate hoax.

I started to search Weisthor's desk, thinking that even if I did
find enough to nail Weisthor and his evil scheme, I wasn't about to
make a pen-pal out of the man who was arguably the most powerful man in Germany. This was not a comfortable prospect.

It turned out that Weisthor was a meticulous man with his correspondence, and I found files of letters which included copies of those
he had sent himself as well as those he had received. Sitting down at
his desk I started to read them at random. If I was looking for typed-
out admissions of guilt I was disappointed. Weisthor and his
associates had developed that talent for euphemism that working in
security or intelligence seems to encourage. These letters confirmed
everything I knew, but they were so carefully phrased, and included
several code-words, as to be open to more than one interpretation.

> K. M. Wiligut Weisthor
> Caspar-Theyss Strasse 33,
> Berlin W.

To SS-Unterscharführer Otto Rahn,
Tiergartenstrasse 8a,
Berlin W.   8 July 1938

STRICTLY CONFIDENTIAL

Dear Otto,

It is as I had suspected. The Reichsführer informs me that a press
embargo has been imposed by the Jew Heydrich in all matters

relating to Project Krist. Without newspaper coverage there will be no legitimate way for us to know who is affected as a result of Project Krist activities. In order for us to be able to offer spiritual assistance to those who are affected, and thereby bring about our objective, we must quickly devise another means of being enabled legitimately to effect our involvement.

Have you any suggestions?

Heil Hitler,
Weisthor

Otto Rahn
Tiergartenstrasse 8a,
Berlin W.

To SS-Brigadeführer K. M. Weisthor
Berlin Grünewald   10 July 1938

STRICTLY CONFIDENTIAL

Dear Brigadeführer,

I have given considerable thought to your letter and, with the assistance of SS-Hauptsturmführer Kindermann and SS-Sturmbannführer Anders, I believe that I have the solution.

Anders has some experience of police matters and is confident that in a situation created out of Project Krist, it would not be unusual for a citizen to solicit his own private agent of inquiry, police efficiency being what it is.

It is therefore proposed that through the offices and finance of our good friend Reinhard Lange, we purchase the services of a small private investigation agency, and then simply advertise in the newspapers. We are all of the opinion that the relevant parties will contact this same private detective who, after a decent interval to apparently exhaust his putative inquiries, will himself bring about our entry into this matter, by whatever means is deemed appropriate.

In the main such men are motivated only by money, and

therefore, provided that our operative is sufficiently remunerated, he will believe only what he wishes to believe, namely that we are a group of cranks. Should at any stage he prove troublesome, I am certain that we will need only to remind him of the Reichsführer's interest in this matter to guarantee his silence.

I have drawn up a list of suitable candidates, and with your permission I should like to contact these as soon as possible.

Heil Hitler,
Yours,
Otto Rahn

K. M. Wiligut Weisthor
Caspar-Theyss Strasse 33, Berlin W.

To SS-Unterscharführer Otto Rahn
Tiergartenstrasse 8a, Berlin W.   30 July 1938

STRICTLY CONFIDENTIAL

Dear Otto,

I have learnt from Anders that the police are holding a Jew on suspicion of certain crimes. Why did it not occur to any of us that the police being what they are, they would frame some person, albeit a Jew, for these crimes? At the right time in our plan such an arrest would have been most helpful, but right now, before we have had a chance to demonstrate our power for the benefit of the Reichsführer, and hope to influence him accordingly, it is nothing short of a nuisance.

However, it occurs to me that we can actually turn this to our advantage. Another Project Krist incident while this Jew is incarcerated will not only effect this man's release, but will accordingly embarrass Heydrich very badly indeed. Please see to it.

Heil Hitler,
Weisthor

SS-Sturmbannführer Richard Anders,
Order of Knights Templar, Berlin
Lumenklub, Bayreutherstrasse 22, Berlin W.

To SS-Brigadeführer K. M. Weisthor
Berlin Grünewald   27 August 1938

STRICTLY CONFIDENTIAL

Dear Brigadeführer,

My inquiries have confirmed that Police Headquarters, Alexanderplatz, did indeed receive an anonymous telephone call. Moreover a
conversation with the Reichsführer's adjutant, Karl Wolff, indicates
that it was he, and not the Reichsführer, who made the said call. He
very much dislikes misleading the police in this fashion, but he
admits that he can see no other way of assisting with the inquiry and
still preserve the necessity of the Reichsführer's anonymity.

   Apparently Himmler is very impressed.

Heil Hitler,
Yours, Richard Anders

                    SS-Hauptstürmführer Dr Lanz Kindermann
                    Am Kleinen Wannsee
                    Berlin West

To Karl Maria Wiligut
Caspar-Theyss Strasse 33,
Berlin West   29 September

STRICTLY CONFIDENTIAL

My dear Karl,

On a serious note first of all. Our friend Reinhard Lange has started
to give me cause for concern. Putting aside my own feelings for
him, I believe that he may be weakening in his resolve to assist with
the execution of Project Krist. That what we are doing is in keeping with our ancient pagan heritage no longer seems to impress him

as something unpleasant but none the less necessary. Whilst I do not for a moment believe that he would ever betray us, I feel that he should no longer be a part of those Project Krist activities which perforce must take place within this clinic.

Otherwise I continue to rejoice in your ancient spiritual heirloom, and look forward to the day when we can continue to investigate our ancestors through your autogenic clairvoyance.

Heil Hitler,
Yours, as ever,
Lanz

> The Commandant,
> SS-Brigadeführer Siegfried Taubert,
> SS-School Haus,
> Wewelsburg, near Paderborn,
> Westphalia

To SS-Brigadeführer Weisthor
Caspar-Theyss Strasse 33,
Berlin Grünewald   3 October 1938

STRICTLY CONFIDENTIAL: COURT OF HONOUR PROCEEDINGS, 6–8 NOVEMBER 1938

Herr Brigadeführer,

This is to confirm that the next Court of Honour will take place here in Wewelsburg on the above dates. As usual security will be tight and during the proceedings, beyond the usual methods of identification, a password will be required to gain admittance to the school house. At your own suggestion this is to be GOSLAR.

Attendance is deemed by the Reichsführer to be mandatory for all those officers and men listed below:

Reichsführer-SS Himmler
SS-Obergruppenführer Heydrich
SS-Obergruppenführer Heissmeyer
SS-Obergruppenführer Nebe

SS-Obergruppenführer Daluege
SS-Obergruppenführer Darre
SS-Gruppenführer Pohl
SS-Brigadeführer Taubert
SS-Brigadeführer Berger
SS-Brigadeführer Eicke
SS-Brigadeführer Weisthor
SS-Oberführer Wolff
SS-Sturmbannführer Anders
SS-Sturmbannführer von Oeynhausen
SS-Hauptsturmführer Kindermann
SS-Obersturmbannführer Diebitsch
SS-Obersturmbannführer von Knobelsdorff
SS-Obersturmbannführer Klein
SS-Obersturmbannführer Lasch
SS-Unterscharführer Rahn
Landbaumeister Bartels
Professor Wilhelm Todt

Heil Hitler,
Taubert

There were many other letters, but I had already risked too
much by staying as long as I had. More than that, I realized that,
for perhaps the first time since coming out of the trenches in 1918,
I was afraid.

21

Friday, 4 November

Driving from Weisthor's house to the Alex, I tried to make some sense out of what I had discovered.

Vogelmann's part was explained, and to some extent that of Reinhard Lange. And perhaps Kindermann's clinic was where they had killed the girls. What better place to kill someone than a hospital, where people were always coming and going feet first. Certainly his letter to Weisthor seemed to indicate as much.

There was a frightening ingenuity in Weisthor's solution. After murdering the girls, all of whom had been selected for their Aryan looks, their bodies were hidden so carefully as to be virtually impossible to find: the more so when one took into account the lack of police manpower available to investigate something as routine as a missing person. By the time the police realized that there was a mass-murderer stalking the streets of Berlin, they were more concerned with keeping things quiet so that their failure to catch the killer did not look incompetent – for at least as long as it took to find a convenient scapegoat, such as Josef Kahn.

But what of Heydrich and Nebe, I wondered. Was their attendance at this SS Court of Honour deemed mandatory merely by virtue of their senior rank? After all, the SS had its factions just like any other organization. Daluege, for instance, the head of Orpo, like his opposite number Arthur Nebe, felt as ill-disposed to Himmler and Heydrich as they felt towards him. And quite clearly of course, Weisthor and his faction were antagonistic towards 'the Jew Heydrich'. Heydrich, a Jew. It was one of those neat pieces of counter-propaganda that relies on a massive contradiction to sound convincing. I'd heard this rumour before, as had most of the bulls around the Alex, and like them I knew where it originated: Admiral Canaris, head of the Abwehr, German Military Intelligence, was Heydrich's most bitter opponent, and certainly the most powerful one.

Or was there some other reason why Heydrich was going to Wewelsburg in a few days? Nothing to do with him was ever quite what it seemed to be, although I didn't doubt for a minute that he would enjoy the prospect of Himmler's embarrassment. For him it would be nice thick icing on the cake that had as its main ingredient the arrest of Weisthor and the other anti-Heydrich conspirators within the SS.

To prove it, however, I was going to need something else besides Weisthor's papers. Something more eloquent and unequivocal, that would convince the Reichsführer himself.

It was then that I thought of Reinhard Lange. The softest excrescence on the maculate body of Weisthor's plot, it certainly wasn't going to require a clean and sharp curette to cut him away. I had just the dirty, ragged thumbnail that would do the job. I still had two of his letters to Lanz Kindermann.

Back at the Alex I went straight to the duty sergeant's desk and found Korsch and Becker waiting for me, with Professor Illmann and Sergeant Gollner.

'Another call?'

'Yes, sir,' said Gollner.

'Right. Let's get going.'

From the outside the Schultheiss Brewery in Kreuzberg, with its uniform red brick, numerous towers and turrets, as well as the fair-sized garden, made it seem more like a school than a brewery. But for the smell, which even at two a.m. was strong enough to pinch the nostrils, you might have expected to find rooms full of desks instead of beer-barrels. We stopped next to the tent-shaped gatehouse.

'Police,' Becker yelled at the nightwatchman, who seemed to like a beer himself. His stomach was so big I doubt he could have reached the pockets of his overalls, even if he had wanted to. 'Where do you keep the old beer-barrels?'

'What, you mean the empties?'

'Not exactly. I mean the ones that probably need a bit of mending.'

The man touched his forehead in a sort of salute.

'Right you are, sir. I know exactly what you mean. This way, if you please.'

We got out of the cars and followed him back up the road we had driven along. After only a short way we ducked through a green door in the wall of the brewery and went down a long and narrow passageway.

'Don't you keep that door locked?' I said.

'No need,' said the nightwatchman. 'Nothing worth stealing here. The beer's kept behind the gate.'

There was an old cellar with a couple of centuries of filth on the ceiling and the floor. A bare bulb on the wall added a touch of yellow to the gloom.

'Here you are then,' said the man. 'I guess this must be what you're looking for. This is where they puts the barrels as needs repairing. Only a lot of them never get repaired. Some of these haven't been moved in ten years.'

'Shit,' said Korsch. 'There must be nearly a hundred of them.'

'At least,' laughed our guide.

'Well, we'd better get started then, hadn't we?' I said.

'What exactly are you looking for?'

'A bottle-opener,' said Becker. 'Now be a good fellow and run along, will you?' The man sneered, said something under his breath and then waddled off, much to Becker's amusement.

It was Illmann who found her. He didn't even take the lid off.

'Here. This one. It's been moved. Recently. And the lid's a different colour from the rest.' He lifted the lid, took a deep breath and then shone his torch inside. 'It's her all right.'

I came over to where he was standing and took a look for myself, and one for Hildegard. I'd seen enough photographs of Emmeline around the apartment to recognize her immediately.

'Get her out of there as soon as you can, Professor.'

Illmann looked at me strangely and then nodded. Perhaps he heard something in my tone that made him think my interest was more than just professional. He waved in the police photographer.

'Becker,' I said.

'Yes, sir?'

'I need you to come with me.'

On the way to Reinhard Lange's address we called in at my office to collect his letters. I poured us both a large glass of schnaps and explained something of what had transpired that evening.

'Lange's the weak link. I heard them say so. What's more, he's a lemon-sucker.' I drained the glass and poured another, inhaling deeply of it to increase the effect, my lips tingling as I held it on my palate for a while before swallowing. I shuddered a little as I let it slip down my backbone and said: 'I want you to work a Vice-squad line on him.'

'Yes? How heavy?'

'Like a fucking waltzer.'

Becker grinned and finished his own drink. 'Roll him out flat? I get the idea.' He opened his jacket and took out a short rubber truncheon which he tapped enthusiastically on the palm of his hand. 'I'll stroke him with this.'

'Well, I hope you know more about using that than you do that Parabellum you carry. I want this fellow alive. Scared shitless, but alive. To answer questions. You get it?'

'Don't worry,' he said. 'I'm an expert with this little india rubber. I'll just break the skin, you'll see. The bones we can leave until another time you give the word.'

'I do believe you like this, don't you? Scaring the piss out of people.'

Becker laughed. 'Don't you?'

The house was on Lützowufer-Strasse, overlooking the Landwehr Canal and within earshot of the zoo, where some of Hitler's relations could be heard complaining about the standard of accommodation.

It was an elegant, three-storey Wilhelmine building, orange-painted and with a big square oriel window on the first floor. Becker started to pull the bell as if he was doing it on piecework. When he got tired of that he started on the door knocker. Eventually a light came on in the hall and we heard the scrape of a bolt.

The door opened on the chain and I saw Lange's pale face peer nervously round the side.

'Police,' said Becker. 'Open up.'

'What is happening?' he swallowed. 'What do you want?'

Becker took a step backwards. 'Mind out, sir,' he said, and then stabbed at the door with the sole of his boot. I heard Lange squeal as Becker kicked it again. At the third attempt the door flew open with a great splintering noise to reveal Lange hurrying up the stairs in his pyjamas.

Becker went after him.

'Don't shoot him, for Christ's sake,' I yelled at Becker.

'Oh God, help,' Lange gurgled as Becker caught him by the bare ankle and started to drag him back. Twisting round he tried to kick himself free of Becker's grip, but it was to no avail, and as Becker pulled so Lange bounced down the stairs on his fat behind. When he hit the floor Becker gripped at his face and stretched each cheek towards his ears.

'When I say open the door, you open the fucking door, right?' Then he put his whole hand over Lange's face and banged his head hard on the stair. 'You got that, queer?' Lange protested loudly, and Becker caught hold of some of his hair and slapped him twice, hard across the face. 'I said, have you got that, queer?'

'Yes,' he screamed.

'That's enough,' I said pulling him by the shoulder. He stood up breathing heavily, and grinned at me.

'You said a waltzer, sir.'

'I'll tell you when he needs some more of the same.'

Lange wiped his bleeding lip and inspected the blood that smeared the back of his hand. There were tears in his eyes but he still managed to summon up some indignation.

'Look here,' he yelled, 'what the hell is this all about? What do you mean by barging in here like this?'

'Tell him,' I said.

Becker grabbed the collar of Lange's silk dressing-gown and twisted it against his pudgy neck. 'It's a pink triangle for you, my fat little fellow,' he said. 'A pink triangle with bar if the letters to your bottom-stroking friend Kindermann are anything to go by.'

Lange wrenched Becker's hand away from his neck and stared bitterly at him. 'I don't know what you're talking about,' he hissed. 'Pink triangle? What does that mean, for God's sake?'

'Paragraph 175 of the German Penal Code,' I said.

Becker quoted the section off by heart. 'Any male who indulges in criminally indecent activities with another male, or who allows himself to participate in such activities, will be punished with gaol.' He cuffed him playfully on the cheek with the backs of his fingers. 'That means you're under arrest, you fat butt-fucker.'

'But it's preposterous. I never wrote any letters to anyone. And I'm not a homosexual.'

'You're not a homosexual,' Becker sneered, 'and I don't piss out of my prick.' From his jacket pocket he produced the two letters I'd given him, and brandished them in front of Lange's face. 'And I suppose you wrote these to the tooth-fairy?'

Lange snatched at the letters and missed.

'Bad manners,' Becker said, cuffing him again, only harder.

'Where did you get those?'

'I gave them to him.'

Lange looked at me, and then looked again. 'Wait a minute,' he said. 'I know you. You're Steininger. You were there tonight, at —' He stopped himself from saying where he'd seen me.

'That's right, I was at Weisthor's little party. I know quite a bit of what's been going on. And you're going to help me with the rest.'

'You're wasting your time, whoever you are. I'm not going to tell you anything.'

I nodded at Becker, who started to hit him again. I watched dispassionately as first he coshed him across the knees and ankles, and then lightly once, on the ear, hating myself for keeping alive the best traditions of the Gestapo, and for the cold, dehumanized brutality I felt inside my guts. I told him to stop.

Waiting for Lange to stop sobbing I walked around a bit, peering through doors. In complete contrast to the exterior, the inside of Lange's house was anything but traditional. The furniture, rugs and paintings, of which there were many, were all in the most expensive modern style – the kind that's easier to look at than to live with.

When eventually I saw that Lange had drawn himself together a bit, I said: 'This is quite a place. Not my taste perhaps, but then, I'm a little old-fashioned. You know, one of those awkward people with rounded joints, the type that puts personal comfort ahead of the worship of geometry. But I'll bet you're really comfortable here. How do you think he'll like the tank at the Alex, Becker?'

'What, the lock-up? Very geometric, sir. All those iron bars.'

'Not forgetting all those bohemian types who'll be in there and give Berlin its world-famous night-life. The rapists, the murderers, the thieves, the drunks – they get a lot of drunks in the tank, throwing-up everywhere –'

'It's really awful, sir, that's right.'

'You know, Becker, I don't think we can put someone like Herr Lange in there. I don't think he would find it at all to his liking, do you?'

'You bastards.'

'I don't think he'd last the night, sir. Especially if we were to find him something special to wear from his wardrobe. Something artistic, as befits a man of Herr Lange's sensitivity. Perhaps even a little make-up, eh, sir? He'd look real nice with a bit of lipstick and rouge.' He chuckled enthusiastically, a natural sadist.

'I think you had better talk to me, Herr Lange,' I said.

'You don't scare me, you bastards. Do you hear? You don't scare me.'

'That's very unfortunate. Because unlike Kriminalassistent Becker here, I don't particularly enjoy the prospect of human suffering. But I'm afraid I have no choice. I'd like to do this straight, but quite frankly I just don't have the time.'

We dragged him upstairs to the bedroom where Becker selected an outfit from Lange's walk-in wardrobe. When he found some rouge and lipstick Lange roared loudly and took a swing at me.

'No,' he yelled. 'I won't wear this.'

I caught his fist and twisted his arm behind him.

'You snivelling little coward. Damn you, Lange, you'll wear it and like it or so help me we'll hang you upside down and cut your throat, like all those girls your friends have murdered. And then maybe we'll just dump your carcass in a beer-barrel, or an old trunk, and see how your mother feels about identifying you after six weeks.' I handcuffed him and Becker started with the make-up. When he'd finished, Oscar Wilde by comparison would have seemed as unassuming and conservative as a draper's assistant from Hanover.

'Come on,' I growled. 'Let's get this Kit-Kat showgirl back to her hotel.'

We had not exaggerated about the night tank at the Alex. It's probably the same in every big city police station. But since the Alex is a very big city police station indeed, it followed that the tank there is also very big. In fact it is huge, as big as an average cinema theatre, except that there are no seats. Nor are there any bunks, or windows, or ventilation. There's just the dirty floor, the dirty latrine buckets, the dirty bars, the dirty people and the lice. The Gestapo kept a lot of detainees there for whom there was no room at Prinz Albrecht Strasse. Orpo put the night's drunks in there to fight, puke, and sleep it off. Kripo used the place like the Gestapo used the canal: as a toilet for its human refuse. A terrible place for a human being. Even one like Reinhard Lange. I had to keep reminding myself of what it was that he and his friends had done, of Emmeline Steininger, sitting in that barrel like so many rotten potatoes. Some of the prisoners whistled and blew kisses when they saw us bring him down, and Lange turned pale with fright.

'My God, you're not going to leave me here,' he said, clutching at my arm.

'Then unpack it,' I said. 'Weisthor, Rahn, Kindermann. A signed statement, and you can get a nice cell to yourself.'

'I can't, I can't. You don't know what they'll do to me.'

'No,' I said, and nodded at the men behind the bars, 'but I know what they'll do to you.'

The lock-up sergeant opened the enormous heavy cage and stood back as Becker pushed him into the tank.

His cries were still ringing in my ears by the time I got back to Steglitz.

Hildegard lay asleep on the sofa, her hair spread across the cushion like the dorsal fin of some exotic golden fish. I sat down, ran my hand across its smooth silkiness, and then kissed her forehead, catching the drink on her breath as I did so. Stirring, her eyes blinked open, sad and crusted with tears. She put her hand on my cheek and then on to the back of my neck, pulling me down to her mouth.

'I have to talk to you,' I said, holding back.

She pressed her finger against my lips. 'I know she's dead,' she said. 'I've done all my crying. There's no more water in the well.'

She smiled sadly, and I kissed each eyelid tenderly, smoothing her scented hair with the palm of my hand, nuzzling at her ear, chewing the side of her neck as her arms held me close, and closer still.

'You've had a ghastly evening too,' she said gently. 'Haven't you, darling?'

'Ghastly,' I said.

'I was worried about you going back to that awful house.'

'Let's not talk about it.'

'Put me to bed, Bernie.'

She put her arms around my neck and I gathered her up, folding her against my body like an invalid and carrying her into the bedroom. I sat her down on the edge of the bed and started to unbutton her blouse. When that was off she sighed and fell back against the quilt: slightly drunk I thought, unzipping her skirt and tugging it smoothly down her stockinged legs. Pulling down her slip I kissed her small breasts, her stomach and then the inside of her thighs. But her pants seemed to be too tight, or caught between her buttocks, and resisted my pulling. I asked her to lift her bottom.

'Tear them,' she said.

'What?'

'Tear them off. Hurt me, Bernie. Use me.' She spoke with breathless urgency, her thighs opening and closing like the jaws of some enormous praying mantis.

'Hildegard –'

She struck me hard across the mouth.

'Listen, damn you. Hurt me when I tell you.'

I caught her wrist as she struck again.

'I've had enough for one evening.' I caught her other arm. 'Stop it.'

'Please, you must.'

I shook my head, but her legs wrapped around my waist and my kidneys winced as her strong thighs squeezed tight.

'Stop it, for God's sake.'

'Hit me, you stupid ugly bastard. Did I tell you that you were stupid, too? A typical bone-headed bull. If you were a man you'd rape me. But you haven't got it in you, have you?'

'If it's a sense of grief you're after, then we'll take a drive down to the morgue.' I shook my head and pushed her thighs apart and then away from me. 'But not like this. It should be with love.'

She stopped writhing and for a moment seemed to recognize the truth of what I was saying. Smiling, then raising her mouth to me, she spat in my face.

After that there was nothing for it but to leave.

There was a knot in my stomach that was as cold and lonely as my apartment on Fasanenstrasse, and almost immediately I arrived home again I enlisted a bottle of brandy in dissolving it. Someone once said that happiness is that which is negative, the mere abolition of desire and the extinction of pain. The brandy helped a little. But before I dropped off to sleep, still wearing my overcoat and sitting in my armchair, I think I realized just how positively I had been affected.

22

Sunday, 6 November

Survival, especially in these difficult times, has to count as some sort of an achievement. It's not something that comes easily. Life in Nazi Germany demands that you keep working at it. But, having done that much, you're left with the problem of giving it some purpose. After all, what good is health and security if your life has no meaning?

This wasn't just me feeling sorry for myself. Like a lot of other people I genuinely believe that there is always someone who is worse off. In this case however, I knew it for a fact. The Jews were already persecuted, but if Weisthor had his way their suffering was about to be taken to a new extreme. In which case what did that say about them and us together? In what condition was that likely to leave Germany?

It's true, I told myself, that it was not my concern, and that the Jews had brought it on themselves: but even if that were the case, what was our pleasure beside their pain? Was our life any sweeter at their expense? Did my freedom feel any better as a result of their persecution?

The more I thought about it, the more I realized the urgency not only of stopping the killings, but also of frustrating Weisthor's declared aim of bringing hell down on Jewish heads, and the more I felt that to do otherwise would leave me degraded in equal measure.

I'm no knight in shining armour. Just a weather-beaten man in a crumpled overcoat on a street corner with only a grey idea of something you might as well go ahead and call Morality. Sure, I'm none too scrupulous about the things that might benefit my pocket, and I could no more inspire a bunch of young thugs to do

good works than I could stand up and sing a solo in the church
choir. But of one thing I was sure. I was through looking at my
fingernails when there were thieves in the store.

I tossed the pile of letters on to the table in front of me.

'We found these when we searched your house,' I said.

A very tired and dishevelled Reinhard Lange regarded them
without much interest.

'Perhaps you'd care to tell me how these came to be in your possession?'

'They're mine,' he shrugged. 'I don't deny it.' He sighed and
dropped his head on to his hands. 'Look, I've signed your statement. What more do you want? I've cooperated, haven't I?'

'We're nearly finished, Reinhard. There's just a loose end or two
I want tied up. Like who killed Klaus Hering.'

'I don't know what you're talking about.'

'You've got a short memory. He was blackmailing your mother
with these letters which he stole from your lover, who also happened to be his employer. He thought she'd be better for the
money, I guess. Well, to cut a long story short, your mother hired
a private investigator to find out who was squeezing her. That person was me. This was before I went back to being a bull at the
Alex. She's a shrewd lady, your mother, Reinhard. Pity you didn't
inherit some of that from her. Anyway, she thought it possible
that you and whoever was blackmailing her might be sexually
involved. And so when I found out the name, she wanted you to
decide what to do next. Of course she wasn't to know that you'd
already acquired a private investigator in the ugly shape of Rolf
Vogelmann. Or at least, Otto Rahn had, using money you provided. Coincidentally, when Rahn was looking around for a
business to buy into, he even wrote to me. We never had the pleasure of discussing his proposition, so it took me quite a while to
remember his name. Anyway, that's just by the by.

'When your mother told you that Hering was blackmailing her,
naturally you discussed the matter with Dr Kindermann, and he

recommended dealing with the matter yourselves. You and Otto Rahn. After all, what's one more wet-job when you've done so many?'

'I never killed anyone, I told you that.'

'But you went along with killing Hering, didn't you? I expect you drove the car. Probably you even helped Kindermann string up Hering's dead body and made it look like suicide.'

'No, it's not true.'

'Wearing their SS uniforms, were they?'

He frowned and shook his head. 'How could you know that?'

'I found an SS cap badge sticking in the flesh of Hering's palm. I'll bet he put up quite a struggle. Tell me, did the man in the car put up much of a fight? The man wearing the eyepatch. The one watching Hering's apartment. He had to be killed too, didn't he? Just in case he identified you.'

'No –'

'All nice and neat. Kill him, and make it look like Hering did it, and then get Hering to hang himself in a fit of remorse. Not forgetting to take away the letters of course. Who killed the man in the car? Was that your idea?'

'No, I didn't want to be there.'

I grabbed him by the lapels, picked him off his chair and started to slap him. 'Come on, I've had just about enough of your whining. Tell me who killed him or I'll have you shot within the hour.'

'Lanz did it. With Rahn. Otto held his arms while Kindermann – he stabbed him. It was horrible. Horrible.'

I let him back down on the chair. He collapsed forward on to the table and started to sob into his forearm.

'You know, Reinhard, you're in a pretty tight spot,' I said, lighting a cigarette. 'Being there makes you an accomplice to murder. And then there's you knowing about the murders of all these girls.'

'I told you,' he sniffed miserably, 'they would have killed me. I never went along with it, but I was afraid not to.'

'That doesn't explain how you got into this in the first place.' I picked up Lange's statement and glanced over it.

'Don't think I haven't asked myself the same question.'

'And did you come up with any answers?'

'A man I admired. A man I believed in. He convinced me that what we were doing was for the good of Germany. That it was our duty. It was Kindermann who persuaded me.'

'They're not going to like that in court, Reinhard. Kindermann doesn't play a very convincing Eve to your Adam.'

'But it's true, I tell you.'

'That may be so, but we're fresh out of fig-leaves. You want a defence, you better think of something to improve on that. That's good legal advice, you can depend on it. And let me tell you something, you're going to need all the good advice you can get. Because the way I see it, you're the only one who's likely to need a lawyer.'

'What do you mean?'

'I'll be straight with you, Reinhard. I've got enough in this statement of yours to send you straight to the block. But the rest of them, I don't know. They're all SS, acquainted with the Reichsführer. Weisthor's a personal friend of Himmler's, and, well, I worry, Reinhard. I worry that you'll be the scapegoat. That all of them will get away with it in order to avoid a scandal. Of course, they'll probably have to resign from the SS, but nothing more than that. You'll be the one who loses his head.'

'No, it can't be true.'

I nodded.

'Now if there was just something else besides your statement. Something that could let you off the hook on the murder charge. Of course, you'd have to take your chances on the Para 175. But you might get away with five years in a KZ, instead of an outright death sentence. You'd still have a chance.' I paused. 'So how about it, Reinhard?'

'All right,' he said after a minute, 'there is something.'

'Talk to me.'

He started hesitantly, not quite sure whether or not he was right to trust me. I wasn't sure myself.

'Lanz is Austrian, from Salzburg.'

'That much I guessed.'

'He read medicine in Vienna. When he graduated he specialized in nervous diseases and took up a post at the Salzburg Mental Asylum. Which was where he met Weisthor. Or Wiligut, as he called himself in those days.'

'Was he a doctor too?'

'God, no. He was a patient. By profession a soldier in the Austrian army. But he is also the last in a long line of German wise men which dates back to prehistoric times. Weisthor possesses ancestral clairvoyant memory which enables him to describe the lives and religious practices of the early German pagans.'

'How very useful.'

'Pagans who worshipped the Germanic god Krist, a religion which was later stolen by the Jews as the new gospel of Jesus.'

'Did they report this theft?' I lit another cigarette.

'You wanted to know,' said Lange.

'No, no. Please go on. I'm listening.'

'Weisthor studied runes, of which the swastika is one of the basic forms. In fact, crystal shapes such as the pyramid are all rune types, solar symbols. That's where the word "crystal" comes from.'

'You don't say.'

'Well, in the early 1920s Weisthor began to exhibit signs of paranoid schizophrenia, believing that he was being victimized by Catholics, Jews and Freemasons. This followed the death of his son, which meant that the line of the Wiligut wise men was broken. He blamed his wife and as time went by, became increasingly violent. Finally he tried to strangle her and was later certified insane. On several occasions during his confinement he tried to murder other inmates. But gradually, under the influence of drug treatment, his mind was brought under control.'

'And Kindermann was his doctor?'

'Yes, until Weisthor's discharge in 1932.'

'I don't get it. Kindermann knew Weisthor was a spinner and let him out?'

'Lanz's approach to psychotherapy is anti-Freudian, and he saw in Jung's work material for the history and culture of a race. His field of research has been to investigate the human unconscious mind for spiritual strata that might make possible a reconstruction of the pre-history of cultures. That's how he came to work with Weisthor. Lanz saw in him the key to his own branch of Jungian psychotherapy, which will, he hopes, enable him to set up, with Himmler's blessing, his own version of a Goering Research Institute. That's another psychotherapeutic –'

'Yes, I know it.'

'Well, at first the research was genuine. But then he discovered that Weisthor was a fake, that he was using his so-called ancestral clairvoyance as a way of projecting the importance of his ancestors in the eyes of Himmler. But by then it was too late. And there was no price that Lanz would not have paid to make sure of getting his institute.'

'What does he need an institute for? He's got the clinic, hasn't he?'

'That's not enough for Lanz. In his own field he wants to be remembered in the same breath as Freud and Jung.'

'What about Otto Rahn?'

'Gifted academically, but really little more than a ruthless fanatic. He was a guard in Dachau for a while. That's the kind of man he is.' He stopped and chewed his fingernail. 'Might I have one of those cigarettes, please?'

I tossed him the packet and watched him light one with a hand that trembled as if he had a high fever. To see him smoke it, you would have thought it was pure protein.

'Is that it?'

He shook his head. 'Kindermann still has Weisthor's medical case history, which proves his insanity. Lanz used to say that it was his insurance, to guarantee Weisthor's loyalty. You see, Himmler can't abide mental illness. Some nonsense about racial health. So if he were ever to get hold of that case history, then –'

'– then the game would be well and truly up.'

★

'So what's the plan, sir?'

'Himmler, Heydrich, Nebe – they've all gone to this SS Court of Honour at Wewelsburg.'

'Where the hell is Wewelsburg?' Becker said.

'It's quite near Paderborn,' said Korsch.

'I propose to go after them. See if I can't expose Weisthor and the whole dirty business right in front of Himmler. I'll take Lange along for the ride, just for evidentiary purposes.'

Korsch stood up and went to the door. 'Right, sir. I'll get the car.'

'I'm afraid not. I want you two to stay here.'

Becker groaned loudly. 'But that's ridiculous, it really is, sir. It's asking for trouble.'

'It may not quite go the way I'm planning. Don't forget that this Weisthor character is Himmler's friend. I doubt that the Reichsführer will take too kindly to my revelations. Worse still, he may dismiss them altogether, in which case it would be better if there was only me to take the heat. After all, he can hardly kick me off the force, since I'm only on it for as long as this case lasts and then I'm back to my own business.

'But you two have careers ahead of you. Not very promising careers, it's true.' I grinned. 'All the same, it would be a shame for you both to earn Himmler's displeasure when I can just as easily do that on my own.'

Korsch exchanged a short look with Becker, and then replied: 'Come on, sir, don't give us that cold cabbage. It's dangerous, what you're planning. We know it, and you know it too.'

'Not only that,' Becker said, 'but how will you get there with a prisoner? Who'll drive the car?'

'That's right, sir. It's over three hundred kilometres to Wewelsburg.'

'I'll take a staff car.'

'Suppose Lange tries something on the way?'

'He'll be handcuffed, so I doubt I'll have any trouble from him.' I shook my head and collected my hat and coat from the rack. 'I'm sorry, boys, but that's the way it's got to be.' I walked to the door.

'Sir?' said Korsch. He held out his hand. I shook it. Then I shook Becker's. Then I went to collect my prisoner.

Kindermann's clinic looked just as neat and well-behaved as it had the first time I'd been there, in late August. If anything, it seemed quieter, with no rooks in the trees and no boat on the lake to disturb them. There was just the sound of the wind and the dead leaves it blew across the path like so many flying locusts.

I placed my hand in the small of Lange's back and pushed him firmly towards the front door.

'This is most embarrassing,' he said. 'Coming here in handcuffs, like a common criminal. I'm well known here, you know.'

'A common criminal is what you are, Lange. Want me to put a towel over your ugly head?' I pushed him again. 'Listen, it's only my good nature that stops me from marching you in there with your prick hanging out of your trousers.'

'What about my civil rights?'

'Shit, where have you been for the last five years? This is Nazi Germany, not ancient Athens. Now shut your fucking mouth.'

A nurse met us in the hallway. She started to say hallo to Lange and then saw the handcuffs. I flapped my ID in front of her startled features.

'Police,' I said. 'I have a warrant to search Dr Kindermann's office.' This was true: I'd signed it myself. Only the nurse had been in the same holiday camp as Lange.

'I don't think you can just walk in there,' she said. 'I'll have to —'

'Lady, a few weeks ago that little swastika you see on my identity card there was considered sufficient authority for German troops to march into the Sudetenland. So you can bet it will let me march into the good doctor's underpants if I want it to.' I shoved Lange forward again. 'Come on, Reinhard, show me the way.'

Kindermann's office was at the back of the clinic. As an apartment in town it would have been considered to be on the small side, but as a doctor's private room it was just fine. There was a long, low couch, a nice walnut desk, a couple of big modern paintings of the kind that look like the inside of a monkey's mind, and enough expensively bound books to explain the country's shoe-leather shortage.

'Take a seat where I can keep an eye on you, Reinhard,' I told him. 'And don't make any sudden moves. I scare easily and then get violent to cover my embarrassment. What's the word the rattle doctors use for that?' There was a large filing cabinet by the window. I opened it and started to leaf through Kindermann's files. 'Compensatory behaviour,' I said. 'That's two words, but I guess that's what it is all right.

'You know, you wouldn't believe some of the names that your friend Kindermann has treated. This filing cabinet reads like the guest list at a Reich Chancellery gala night. Wait a minute, this looks like your file.' I picked it out and tossed it on to his lap. 'Why don't you see what he wrote about you, Reinhard? Perhaps it will explain how you got yourself in with these bastards in the first place.'

He stared at the unopened file.

'It really is very simple,' he said quietly. 'As I explained to you earlier on, I became interested in the psychic sciences as a result of my friendship with Dr Kindermann.' He raised his face to me challengingly.

'I'll tell you why you got yourself involved,' I said, grinning back at him. 'You were bored. With all your money you don't know what to be at next. That's the trouble with your kind, the kind that's born into money. You never learn its value. They knew that, Reinhard, and they played you for Johann Simple.'

'It won't work, Günther. You're talking rubbish.'

'Am I? You've read the file then. You'll know that for sure.'

'A patient ought never to see his doctor's case notes. It would be unethical of me to even open this.'

'It occurs to me that you've seen a lot more than just your doctor's case notes, Reinhard. And Kindermann learnt his ethics with the Holy Inquisition.'

I turned back to the filing cabinet and fell silent as I came across another name I recognized. The name of a girl I had once wasted a couple of months trying to find. A girl who had once been important to me. I'll admit that I was even in love with her. The job is like that sometimes. A person vanishes without trace, the world moves on, and you find a piece of information that at the right time would have cracked the case wide open. Aside of the obvious irritation you feel at remembering how wide of the mark you'd really been, mostly you learn to live with it. My business doesn't exactly suit those who are disposed to be neat. Being a private investigator leaves you holding more loose ends than a blind carpet-weaver. All the same, I wouldn't be human if I didn't admit to finding some satisfaction in tying them off. Yet this name, the name of the girl that Arthur Nebe had mentioned to me all those weeks ago when we met late one night in the ruins of the Reichstag, meant so much more than just satisfaction in finding a belated solution to an enigma. There are times when discovery has the force of revelation.

'The bastard,' said Lange, turning the pages of his own case notes. 'I was thinking the same thing myself.'

' "A neurotic effeminate",' he quoted. 'Me. How could he think such a thing about me?'

I moved down to the next drawer, only half listening to what he was saying.

'You tell me, he's your friend.'

'How could he say these things? I don't believe it.'

'Come on, Reinhard. You know how it is when you swim with the sharks. You've got to expect to get your balls bitten once in a while.'

'I'll kill him,' he said, flinging the case notes across the office.

'Not before I do,' I said, finding Weisthor's file at last. I slammed the drawer shut. 'Right. I've got it. Now we can get out of this place.'

I was about to reach for the door-handle when a heavy revolver came through the door, followed closely by Lanz Kindermann.

'Would you mind telling me what the hell's going on here?'

I stepped back into the room. 'Well, this is a pleasant surprise,' I said. 'We were just talking about you. We thought you might have gone to your Bible class in Wewelsburg. Incidentally, I'd be careful with that gun if I were you. My men have got this place under surveillance. They're very loyal, you know. That's the way we are in the police these days. I'd hate to think what they'd do if they found out that some harm had come to me.'

Kindermann glanced at Lange, who hadn't moved, and then at the files under my arm.

'I don't know what your game is, Herr Steininger, if that is your real name, but I think that you had better put those down on the desk and raise your hands, don't you?'

I laid the files down on the desk and started to say something about having a warrant, but Reinhard Lange had already taken the initiative, if that's what you call it when you're misguided enough to throw yourself on to a man who is holding a 45-calibre pistol cocked on you. His first three or four words of bellowing outrage ended abruptly as the deafening gunshot blasted the side of his neck away. Gurgling horribly, Lange twisted around like a whirling dervish, grasping frantically at his neck with his still-manacled hands, and decorating the wallpaper with red roses as he fell to the floor.

Kindermann's hands were better suited to the violin than something as big as the .45, and with the hammer down you need a carpenter's forefinger to work a trigger that heavy, so there was plenty of time for me to collect the bust of Dante that sat on Kindermann's desk and smash it into several pieces against the side of his head.

With Kindermann unconscious, I looked round to where Lange had curled himself into the corner. With his bloody forearm pressed against what remained of his jugular, he stayed alive for only a minute or so, and then died without speaking another word.

I removed the handcuffs and was transferring them to the groaning Kindermann when, summoned by the shot, two nurses burst into the office and stared in terror at the scene that met their eyes. I wiped my hands on Kindermann's necktie and then went over to the desk.

'Before you ask, your boss here just shot his pansy friend.' I picked up the telephone. 'Operator, get me Police Headquarters, Alexanderplatz, please.' I watched one nurse search for Lange's pulse and the other help Kindermann on to the couch as I waited to be connected.

'He's dead,' said the first nurse. Both of them stared suspiciously at me.

'This is Kommissar Günther,' I said to the operator at the Alex. 'Connect me with Kriminalassistent Korsch or Becker in the Murder Commission as quickly as possible, if you please.' After another short wait Becker came on to the line.

'I'm at Kindermann's clinic,' I explained. 'We stopped to pick up the medical case history on Weisthor and Lange managed to get himself killed. He lost his temper and a piece of his neck. Kindermann was carrying a lighter.'

'Want me to organize the meat wagon?'

'That's the general idea, yes. Only I won't be here when it comes. I'm sticking to my original plan, except that now I'm taking Kindermann along with me instead of Lange.'

'All right, sir. Leave it to me. Oh, incidentally, Frau Steininger called.'

'Did she leave a message?'

'No, sir.'

'Nothing at all?'

'No, sir. Sir, you know what that one needs, if you don't mind me saying?'

'Try and surprise me.'

'I reckon that she needs —'

'On second thoughts, don't bother.'

'Well, you know the type, sir.'

'Not exactly, Becker, no. But while I'm driving I'll certainly give it some thought. You can depend on it.'

I drove west out of Berlin, following the yellow signs indicating long-distance traffic, heading towards Potsdam and beyond it, to Hanover.

The autobahn branches off from the Berlin circular road at Lehnin, leaving the old town of Brandenburg to the north, and beyond Zeisar, the ancient town of the Bishops of Brandenburg, the road runs west in a straight line.

After a while I was aware of Kindermann sitting upright in the back seat of the Mercedes.

'Where are we going?' he said dully.

I glanced over my right shoulder. With his hands manacled behind his back I didn't think he'd be stupid enough to try hitting me with his head. Especially now it was bandaged, something the two nurses from the clinic had insisted on doing before allowing me to drive the doctor away.

'Don't you recognize the road?' I said. 'We're on our way to a little town south of Paderborn. Wewelsburg. I'm sure you know it. I didn't think you would want to miss your SS Court of Honour on my account.' Out of the corner of my eye I saw him smile and settle back in the rear seat, or at least, as well as he was able to.

'That suits me fine.'

'You know, you've really inconvenienced me, Herr Doktor. Shooting my star witness like that. He was going to give a special performance for Himmler. It's lucky he made a written statement back at the Alex. And, of course, you'll have to understudy.'

He laughed. 'And what makes you think I'll take to that role?'

'I'd hate to think what might happen if you were to disappoint me.'

'Looking at you, I'd say you were used to being disappointed.'

'Perhaps. But I doubt my disappointment will even compare with Himmler's.'

'My life is in no danger from the Reichsführer, I can assure you.'

'I wouldn't place too much reliance on your rank or your uniform if I were you, Hauptsturmführer. You'll shoot just as easily as Ernst Röhm and all those SA men did.'

'I knew Röhm quite well,' he said smoothly. 'We were good friends. It may interest you to know that that's a fact which is well-known to Himmler, with all that such a relationship implies.'

'You're saying he knows you're a queer?'

'Certainly. If I survived the Night of Long Knives, I think I can manage to cope with whatever inconvenience you've arranged for me, don't you?'

'The Reichsführer will be pleased to read Lange's letters, then. If only to confirm what he already knows. Never underestimate the importance to a policeman of confirming information. I dare say he knows all about Weisthor's insanity as well, right?'

'What was insanity ten years ago merely counts as a treatable nervous disorder today. Psychotherapy has come a long way in a short time. Do you seriously believe that Herr Weisthor can be the first senior SS officer to be treated? I'm a consultant at a special orthopaedic hospital at Hohenlychen, near Ravensbruck concentration camp, where many SS staff officers are treated for the prevailing euphemism that describes mental illness. You know, you surprise me. As a policeman you ought to know how skilled the Reich is in the practice of such convenient hypocrisies. Here you are hurrying to create a great big firework display for the Reichsführer with a couple of rather damp little crackers. He will be disappointed.'

'I like listening to you, Kindermann. I always like to see another man's work. I bet you're great with all those rich widows who bring their menstrual depressions to your fancy clinic. Tell me, for how many of them do you prescribe cocaine?'

'Cocaine hydrochloride has always been used as a stimulant to combat the more extreme cases of depression.'

'How do you stop them becoming addicted?'

'It's true there is always that risk. One has to be watchful for any sign of drug dependency. That's my job.' He paused. 'Why do you ask?'

'Just curious, Herr Doktor. That's my job.'

At Hohenwarhe, north of Magdeburg, we crossed the Elbe by a bridge, beyond which, on the right, could be seen the lights of the almost completed Rothensee Ship Elevator, designed to connect the Elbe with the Mittelland Canal some twenty metres above it.

Soon we had passed into the next state of Niedersachsen, and at Helmstedt we stopped for a rest, and to pick up some petroleum.

It was getting dark and looking at my watch I saw that it was almost seven o'clock. Having chained one of Kindermann's hands to the door-handle, I allowed him to take a pee, and attended to my own needs at a short distance. Then I pushed the spare wheel into the back seat beside Kindermann and handcuffed it to his left wrist, which left one hand free. The Mercedes is a big car, however, and he was far enough behind me not to worry about. All the same, I removed the Walther from my shoulder-holster, showed it to him and then laid it beside me on the big bench seat.

'You'll be more comfortable like that,' I said. 'But so much as pick your nose and you'll get this.' I started the car and drove on.

'What is the hurry?' Kindermann said exasperatedly. 'I fail to understand why you're doing this. You could just as easily stage your performance on Monday, when everyone arrives back in Berlin. I really don't see the need to drive all this way.'

'It'll be too late by then, Kindermann. Too late to stop the special pogrom that your friend Weisthor's got planned for Berlin's Jews. Project Krist, isn't that what it's called?'

'Ah, you know about that do you? You have been busy. Don't tell me that you're a Jew-lover.'

'Let's just say that I don't much care for lynch-law, and rule by the mob. That's why I became a policeman.'

'To uphold justice?'

'If you want to call it that, yes.'

'You're deluding yourself. What rules is force. Human will. And to build that collective will it must be given a focus. What we are doing is no more than a child does with a magnifying-glass when it concentrates the light of the sun on to a sheet of paper and causes it to catch alight. We are merely using a power that already exists. Justice would be a wonderful thing were it not for men. Herr —? Look here, what is your name?'

'The name is Günther, and you can spare me the Party propaganda.'

'These are facts, Günther, not propaganda. You're an anachron-
ism, do you know that? You are out of your time.'

'From the little history I know it seems to me that justice is
never very fashionable, Kindermann. If I'm out of my time, if I'm
out of step with the will of the people, as you describe it, then I'm
glad. The difference between us is that whereas you wish to use
their will, I want to see it curbed.'

'You're the worst kind of idealist: you're naïve. Do you really
think that you can stop what's happening to the Jews? You've
missed that boat. The newspapers already have the story about
Jewish ritual murder in Berlin. I doubt that Himmler and Heydrich could prevent what is going on even if they wanted to.'

'I might not be able to stop it,' I said, 'but perhaps I can try and
get it postponed.'

'And even if you do manage to persuade Himmler to consider
your evidence, do you seriously think that he'll welcome his stupidity being made public? I doubt you'll get much in the way of
justice from the Reichsführer-SS. He'll just sweep it under the
carpet and in a short while it will all be forgotten. As will the
Jews. You mark my words. People in this country have very short
memories.'

'Not me,' I said. 'I never forget. I'm a fucking elephant. Take this
other patient of yours, for instance.' I picked up one of the two
files I had brought with me from Kindermann's office and tossed it
back over the seat. 'You see, until quite recently I was a private
detective. And what do you know? It turns out that even though
you're a lump of shit we have something in common. Your patient
there was a client of mine.'

He switched on the courtesy light and picked up the file.

'Yes, I remember her.'

'A couple of years ago, she disappeared. It so happens she was in
the vicinity of your clinic at the time. I know that because she
parked my car near there. Tell me, Herr Doktor, what does your
friend Jung have to say about coincidence?'

'Er . . . meaningful coincidence, I suppose you mean. It's a principle he calls synchronicity: that a certain apparently coincidental event might be meaningful according to an unconscious knowledge linking a physical event with a psychic condition. It's quite difficult to explain in terms that you would understand. But I fail to see how this coincidence could be meaningful.'

'No, of course you don't. You have no knowledge of my unconscious. Perhaps that's just as well.'

He was quiet for a long while after that.

North of Brunswick we crossed the Mittelland Canal, where the autobahn ended, and I drove south-west towards Hildesheim and Hamelin.

'Not far now,' I said across my shoulder. There was no reply. I pulled off the main road and drove slowly for several minutes down a narrow path that led into an area of woodland.

I stopped the car and looked around. Kindermann was dozing quietly. With a trembling hand I lit a cigarette and got out. A strong wind was blowing now and an electrical storm was firing silver lifelines across the rumbling black sky. Maybe they were for Kindermann.

After a minute or two I leant back across the front seat and picked up my gun. Then I opened the rear door and shook Kindermann by the shoulder.

'Come on,' I said, handing him the key to the handcuffs, 'we're going to stretch our legs again.' I pointed down the path which lay before us, illuminated by the big headlights of the Mercedes. We walked to the edge of the beam where I stopped.

'Right that's far enough,' I said. He turned to face me. 'Synchronicity. I like that. A nice fancy word for something that's been gnawing at my guts for a long time. I'm a private man, Kindermann. Doing what I do makes me value my own privacy all the more. For instance, I would never ever write my home telephone number on the back of my business card. Not unless that someone was very special to me. So when I asked Reinhard Lange's mother just how she came to hire me in the first place instead of some other fellow, she showed me just such a card, which she got out of

Reinhard's jacket pocket before sending his suit to the cleaners. Naturally I began to start thinking. When she saw the card she was worried that he might be in trouble, and mentioned it to him. He said that he picked it off your desk. I wonder if he had a reason for doing that. Perhaps not. We'll never know, I guess. But whatever the reason, that card put my client in your office on the day she disappeared and was never seen again. Now how's that for synchronicity?'

'Look, Günther, it was an accident, what happened. She was an addict.'

'And how did she get that way?'

'I'd been treating her for depression. She'd lost her job. A relationship had ended. She needed cocaine more than seemed apparent at the time. There was absolutely no way of knowing just by looking at her. By the time I realized she was getting used to the drug, it was too late.'

'What happened?'

'One afternoon she just turned up at the clinic. In the neighbourhood, she said, and feeling low. There was a job she was going for, an important job, and she felt that she could get it if I gave her a little help. At first I refused. But she was a very persuasive woman, and finally I agreed. I left her alone for a short while. I think she hadn't used it in a long time, and had less tolerance to her usual dose. She must have aspirated on her own vomit.'

I said nothing. It was the wrong context for it to mean anything any more. Revenge is not sweet. Its true flavour is bitter, since pity is the most probable aftertaste.

'What are you going to do?' he said nervously. 'You're not going to kill me, surely. Look, it was an accident. You can't kill a man for that, can you?'

'No,' I said. 'I can't. Not for that.' I saw him breathe a sigh of relief and walk towards me. 'In a civilized society you don't shoot a man in cold blood.'

Except that this was Hitler's Germany, and no more civilized than the very pagans venerated by Weisthor and Himmler.

'But for the murders of all those poor bloody girls, somebody has to,' I said.

I pointed the gun at his head and pulled the trigger once; and then several times more.

From the narrow winding road, Wewelsburg looked like a fairly typical Westphalian peasant village, with as many shrines to the Virgin Mary on the walls and grass verges as there were pieces of farm-machinery left lying outside the half-timbered, fairy-story houses. I knew I was in for something weird when I decided to stop at one of these and ask for directions to the SS-School. The flying griffins, runic symbols and ancient words of German that were carved or painted in gold on the black window casements and lintels put me in mind of witches and wizards, and so I was almost prepared for the hideous sight that presented itself at the front door, wreathed in an atmosphere of wood smoke and frying veal.

The girl was young, no more than twenty-five and but for the huge cancer eating away at one whole side of her face, you might have said that she was attractive. I hesitated for no more than a second, but it was enough to draw her anger.

'Well? What are you staring at?' she demanded, her distended mouth, widening to a grimace that showed her blackened teeth, and the edge of something darker and more corrupt. 'And what time is this to be calling? What is it that you want?'

'I'm sorry to disturb you,' I said, concentrating on the side of her face that was unmarked by the disease, 'but I'm a little lost, and I was hoping you could direct me to the SS-School.'

'There's no school in Wewelsburg,' she said, eyeing me suspiciously.

'The SS-School,' I repeated weakly. 'I was told it was somewhere hereabouts.'

'Oh that,' she snapped, and turning in her doorway she pointed to where the road dipped down a hill. 'There is your way. The road bends right and left for a short way before you see a narrower road with a railing rising up a slope to your left.' Laughing scorn-fully, she added, 'The school, as you call it, is up there.' And with that she slammed the door shut in my face.

It was good to be out of the city, I told myself walking back to the Mercedes. Country people have so much more time for the ordinary pleasantries.

I found the road with the railing, and steered the big car up the slope and on to a cobbled esplanade.

It was easy enough to see now why the girl with the piece of coal in her mouth had been so amused, for what met my eyes was no more what one would normally have recognized as a school-house, than a zoo was a pet-shop, or a cathedral a meeting hall. Himmler's schoolhouse was in reality a decent-sized castle, com-plete with domed towers, one of which loomed over the esplanade like the helmeted head of some enormous Prussian soldier.

I drew up next to a small church a short distance away from the several troop trucks and staff cars that were parked outside what looked like the castle guard-house on the eastern side. For a moment the storm lit up the entire sky and I had a spectral black-and-white view of the whole of the castle.

By any standard it was an impressive-looking place, with rather more of the horror film about it than was entirely comfortable a proposition for the intendant trespasser. This so-called school-house looked like home from home for Dracula, Frankenstein, Orlac and a whole forestful of Wolfmen – the sort of occasion where I might have been prompted to re-load my pistol with nine millimetre cloves of snub-nosed garlic.

Almost certainly there were enough real-life monsters in the Wewelsburg Castle without having to worry about the more fan-ciful ones, and I didn't doubt that Himmler could have given Doctor X quite a few pointers.

But could I trust Heydrich? I thought about this for quite a while. Finally I decided that I could almost certainly trust him to be ambitious, and since I was effectively providing him with the means of destroying an enemy in the shape of Weisthor, I had no real alternative but to put myself and my information in his murdering white hands.

The little church bell in the clock-tower was striking midnight as I steered the Mercedes to the edge of the esplanade and beyond it, the bridge curving left across the empty moat towards the castle gate.

An SS trooper emerged from a stone sentry-box to glance at my papers and to wave me on.

In front of the wooden gate I stopped and sounded the car horn a couple of times. There were lights on all over the castle, and it didn't seem likely that I'd be waking anyone, dead or alive. A small door in the gate swung open and an SS corporal came outside to speak to me. After scrutinizing my papers in his torchlight, he allowed me to step through the door and into the arched gateway where once again I repeated my story and presented my papers, only this time it was for the benefit of a young lieutenant apparently in command of the guard-duty.

There is only one way to deal effectively with arrogant young SS officers who look as though they've been specially issued with the right shade of blue eyes and fair hair, and that is to outdo them for arrogance. So I thought of the man I had killed that evening, and fixed the lieutenant with the sort of cold, supercilious stare that would have crushed a Hohenzollern prince.

'I am Kommissar Günther,' I rapped at him, 'and I'm here on extremely pressing Sipo business affecting Reich security, which requires the immediate attention of General Heydrich. Please inform him at once that I am here. You'll find that he is expecting me, even to the extent that he has seen fit to provide me with the password to the castle during these Court of Honour proceedings.' I uttered the word and watched the lieutenant's arrogance pay homage to my own.

'Let me stress the delicacy of my mission, lieutenant,' I said, lowering my voice. 'It is imperative that at this stage only General

Heydrich or his aide be informed of my presence here in the castle. It is quite possible that Communist spies may already have infiltrated these proceedings. Do you understand?'

The lieutenant nodded curtly and ducked back into his office to make the telephone call, while I walked to the edge of the cobbled courtyard that lay open to the cold night sky.

The castle seemed smaller from the inside, with three roofed wings joined by three towers, two of them domed, and the short but wider third, castellated and furnished with a flagpole where an SS penant fluttered noisily in the strengthening wind.

The lieutenant came back and to my surprise stood to attention with a click of his heels. I guessed that this probably had more to do with what Heydrich or his aide had said than with my own commanding personality.

'Kommissar Günther,' he said respectfully, 'the general is finishing dinner and asks you to wait in the sitting-room. That is in the west tower. Would you please follow me? The corporal will attend to your vehicle.'

'Thank you, Lieutenant,' I said, 'but first I have to remove some important documents that I left on the front seat.'

Having recovered my briefcase, which contained Weisthor's medical case-history, Lange's statement and the Lange–Kindermann letters, I followed the lieutenant across the cobbled courtyard towards the west wing. From somewhere to our left could be heard the sound of men singing.

'Sounds like quite a party,' I said coldly. My escort grunted without much enthusiasm. Any kind of party is better than late-night guard-duty in November. We went through a heavy oak door and entered the great hall.

All German castles should be so Gothic; every Teutonic warlord should live and strut in such a place; each inquisitorial Aryan bully should surround himself with as many emblems of unsparing tyranny. Aside from the great heavy rugs, the thick tapestries and the dull paintings, there were enough suits of armour, musket-stands and wall-mounted cutlery to have fought a war with King Gustavus Adolphus and the whole Swedish army.

In contrast, the sitting-room, which we reached by a wooden spiral staircase, was furnished plainly and commanded a spectacular view of a small airfield's landing lights a couple of kilometres away.

'Help yourself to a drink,' said the lieutenant, opening the cabinet. 'If there's anything else you need, sir, just ring the bell.' Then he clicked his heels again and disappeared back down the staircase.

I poured myself a large brandy and tossed it straight back. I was tired after the long drive. With another glass in my hand I sat stiffly in an armchair and closed my eyes. I could still see the startled expression on Kindermann's face as the first bullet struck between the eyes. Weisthor would be missing him and his bag of drugs badly by now, I thought. I could have used an armful myself.

I sipped some more of the brandy. Ten minutes passed and I felt my head nodding.

I fell asleep and my nightmare's terrifying gallop brought me before beast men, preachers of death, scarlet judges and the outcasts of paradise.

23

Monday, 7 November

By the time I finished telling Heydrich my story the general's normally pale features were flushed with excitement.

'I congratulate you, Günther,' he said. 'This is much more than I had expected. And your timing is perfect. Don't you agree, Nebe?'

'Yes indeed, General.'

'It may surprise you, Günther,' Heydrich said, 'but Reichs-führer Himmler and myself are currently in favour of maintaining police protection for Jewish property, if only for reasons of public order and commerce. You let a mob run riot on the streets and it won't just be Jewish shops that are looted, it will be German ones too. To say nothing of the fact that the damage will have to be made good by German insurance companies. Goering will be beside himself. And who can blame him? The whole idea makes a mockery of any economic planning.

'But as you say, Günther, were Himmler to be convinced by Weisthor's scheme then he would certainly be inclined to waive that police protection. In which case I should have to go along with that position. So we have to be careful how we handle this. Himmler is a fool, but he's a dangerous fool. We have to expose Weisthor unequivocally, and in front of as many witnesses as possible.' He paused. 'Nebe?'

The Reichskriminaldirektor stroked the side of his long nose and nodded thoughtfully.

'We shouldn't mention Himmler's involvement at all, if we can possibly avoid it, General,' he said. 'I'm all for exposing Weisthor in front of witnesses. I don't want that dirty bastard to get away with it. But at the same time we should avoid embarrassing the

Reichsführer in front of the senior SS staff. He'll forgive us destroying Weisthor, but he won't forgive us making an ass of him.'

'I agree,' said Heydrich. He thought for a moment. 'This is Sipo section six, isn't it?' Nebe nodded. 'Where's the nearest SD main provincial station to Wewelsburg?'

'Bielefeld,' Nebe replied.

'Right. I want you to telephone them immediately. Have them send a full company of men here by dawn.' He smiled thinly. 'Just in case Weisthor manages to make this Jew allegation against me stick. I don't like this place. Weisthor has lots of friends here in Wewelsburg. He even officiates at some of the ludicrous SS wedding ceremonies that take place here. So we might need to mount a show of force.'

'The castle commandant, Taubert, was in Sipo prior to this posting,' said Nebe. 'I'm pretty certain we can trust him.'

'Good. But don't tell him about Weisthor. Just stick to Günther's original story about KPD infiltrators and have him keep a detachment of men on full alert. And while you're about it, you'd better have him organize a bed for the Kommissar. By God, he's earned it.'

'The room next to mine is free, General. I think it's the Henry I of Saxony Room.' Nebe grinned.

'Madness,' Heydrich laughed. 'I'm in the King Arthur and the Grail Room. But who knows? Perhaps today I shall at least defeat Morgana le Fay.'

The courtroom was on the ground floor of the west wing. With the door to one of the adjoining rooms open a crack, I had a perfect view of what went on in there.

The room itself was over forty metres long, with a bare, polished wooden floor, panelled walls and a high ceiling complete with oak beams and carved gargoyles. Dominating was a long oak table that was surrounded on all four sides with high-backed leather chairs, on each of which was a silver disk and what I presumed to be the name of the SS officer who was entitled to sit there. With the black uniforms and all the ritualistic ceremony that attended the commencement of the court proceedings, it was like spying on a meeting of the Grand Lodge of Freemasons.

First on the agenda that morning was the Reichsführer's approval of plans for the development of the derelict north tower. These were presented by Landbaumeister Bartels, a fat, owlish little man who sat between Weisthor and Rahn. Weisthor himself seemed nervous and was quite obviously feeling the lack of his cocaine.

When the Reichsführer asked him his opinion of the plans, Weisthor stammered his answer: 'In, er . . . in terms of the, er . . . cult importance of the . . . er . . . castle,' he said, 'and, er . . . its magical importance in any, er . . . in any future conflict between, er . . . East and West, er . . .'

Heydrich interrupted, and it was immediately apparent that it was not to help the Brigadeführer.

'Reichsführer,' he said coolly, 'since this is a court, and since we are all of us listening to the Brigadeführer with enormous fascination, it would I believe be unfair to you all to permit him to go any further without acquainting you of the very serious charges that have to be made against him and his colleague, Unterscharführer Rahn.'

'What charges are these?' said Himmler with some distaste. 'I know nothing of any charges pending against Weisthor. Nor even of any investigation affecting him.'

'That is because there was no investigation of Weisthor. However, a completely separate inquiry has revealed Weisthor's principal role in an odious conspiracy that has resulted in the perverted murders of seven innocent German schoolgirls.'

'Reichsführer,' roared Weisthor, 'I protest. This is monstrous.'

'I quite agree,' said Heydrich, 'and you are the monster.'

Weisthor rose to his feet, his whole body shaking.

'You lying little kike,' he spat.

Heydrich merely smiled a lazy little smile. 'Kommissar,' he said loudly, 'would you please come in here now?'

I walked slowly into the room, my shoes sounding on the

wooden floor like some nervous actor about to audition for a play. Every head turned as I came in, and as fifty of the most powerful men in Germany focused their eyes on me, I could have wished to have been anywhere else but there. Weisthor's jaw dropped as Himmler half rose to his feet.

'What is the meaning of this?' Himmler growled.

'Some of you probably know this gentleman as Herr Steininger,' Heydrich said smoothly, 'the father of one of the murdered girls. Except that he is nothing of the kind. He works for me. Tell them who you really are, Günther.'

'Kriminalkommissar Bernhard Günther, Murder Commission, Berlin-Alexanderplatz.'

'And tell these officers, if you will, why you have come here.'

'To arrest one Karl Maria Weisthor, also known as Karl Maria Wiligut, also known as Jarl Widar; Otto Rahn; and Richard Anders, all for the murders of seven girls in Berlin between 23 May and 29 September 1938.'

'Liar,' Rahn shouted, jumping to his feet, along with another officer whom I supposed to be Anders.

'Sit down,' said Himmler. 'I take it that you believe that you can prove this, Kommissar?' If I'd been Karl Marx himself he couldn't have regarded me with more hatred.

'I believe I can, sir, yes.'

'This had better not be one of your tricks, Heydrich,' Himmler said.

'A trick, Reichsführer?' he said innocently. 'If it's tricks you're looking for, these two evil men had them all. They sought to pass themselves off as mediums, to persuade weaker-minded people that it was the spirits who were informing them where the bodies of the girls they themselves had murdered were hidden away. And but for Kommissar Günther here, they would have attempted the same insane trick with this company of officers.'

'Reichsführer,' Weisthor spluttered, 'this is utterly preposterous.'

'Where is the proof you mentioned, Heydrich?'

'I said insane. I meant exactly that. Naturally there is no one here who could have fallen for such a ludicrous scheme as theirs. However, it is characteristic of those who are insane to believe in the right of what they are doing.' He retrieved the file containing Weisthor's medical case history from underneath his sheaf of papers and laid it in front of Himmler.

'These are the medical case notes of Karl Maria Wiligut, also known as Karl Maria Weisthor, which until recently were in the possession of his doctor, Hauptsturmführer Lanz Kindermann –'

'No,' yelled Weisthor, and lunged for the file.

'Restrain that man,' screamed Himmler. Immediately the two officers standing beside Weisthor caught him by the arms. Rahn reached for his holster, only I was quicker, working the Mauser's slide as I laid the muzzle against his head.

'Touch it and I'll ventilate your brain,' I said, and then relieved him of his gun.

Heydrich carried on, apparently undisturbed by any of this commotion. You had to hand it to him: he was as cool as a North Sea salmon, and just as slippery.

'In November 1924, Wiligut was committed to a lunatic asylum in Salzburg for the attempted murder of his wife. Upon examination he was declared insane and remained institutionalized under the care of Dr Kindermann until 1932. Following his release he changed his name to Weisthor, and the rest you undoubtedly know, Reichsführer.'

Himmler glanced at the file for a minute or so. Finally he sighed and said: 'Is this true, Karl?'

Weisthor, held between two SS officers, shook his head.

'I swear it's a lie, on my honour as a gentleman and an officer.'

'Roll up his left sleeve,' I said. 'The man is a drug addict. For years Kindermann has been giving him cocaine and morphine.'

Himmler nodded at the men holding Weisthor, and when they revealed his horribly black-and-blue forearm, I added: 'If you're still not convinced, I have a twenty-page statement made by Reinhard Lange.'

Himmler kept on nodding. He stepped round his chair to stand in front of his Brigadeführer, the sage of the SS, and slapped him hard across the face, then again.

'Get him out of my sight,' he said. 'He is confined to quarters until further notice. Rahn. Anders. That goes for you too.' He raised his voice to an almost hysterical pitch. 'Get out, I say. You are no longer members of this order. All three of you will return your Deaths Head rings, your daggers and your swords. I shall decide what to do with you later.'

Arthur Nebe called the guard that was waiting in readiness and, when they appeared, ordered them to escort the three men to their rooms.

By now almost every SS officer at the table was open-mouthed with astonishment. Only Heydrich stayed calm, his long face betraying no more sign of the undoubted satisfaction he was feeling at the sight of his enemies' rout than if he had been made of wax.

With Weisthor, Rahn and Anders sent out under guard, all eyes were now on Himmler. Unfortunately, his eyes were very much on me, and I holstered my gun feeling that the drama had yet to end. For several uncomfortable seconds he simply stared, no doubt remembering how at Weisthor's house I had seen him, the Reichsführer-SS and Chief of the German Police, gullible, fooled, sold – fallible. For the man who saw himself in the role of the Nazi Pope to Hitler's Antichrist, it was too much to bear. Placing himself close enough for me to smell the cologne on his closely shaven, punctilious little face, and blinking furiously, his mouth twisted into a rictus of hatred, he kicked me hard on the shin.

I grunted with pain, but stood still, almost to attention.

'You've ruined everything,' he said, shaking. 'Everything. Do you hear?'

'I did my job,' I growled. I think he might have booted me again but for Heydrich's timely interruption.

'I can certainly vouch for that,' he said. 'Perhaps, under the circumstances, it would be best if this court were postponed for an hour or so, at least until you've had a chance to recover your composure, Reichsführer. The discovery of so gross a treason within a forum that is as close to the Reichsführer's heart as this one will doubtless have come as a profound shock to him. As indeed it has been to us all.'

There was a murmur of agreement at these remarks, and Himmler seemed to regain control of himself. Colouring a little, possibly with some embarrassment, he twitched and nodded curtly.

'You're quite right, Heydrich,' he muttered. 'A terrible shock. Yes indeed. I must apologize to you, Kommissar. As you say, you merely did your duty. Well done.' And with that he turned on his not inconsiderable heel and marched smartly out of the room, accompanied by several of his officers.

Heydrich started to smile a slow, curling sort of smile that got no further than the corner of his mouth. Then his eyes found mine and steered me towards the other door. Arthur Nebe followed, leaving the remaining officers to talk loudly among themselves.

'It's not many men who live to receive a personal apology from Heinrich Himmler,' Heydrich said when the three of us were alone in the castle library.

I rubbed my shin painfully. 'Well, I'm sure I'll make a note of that in my diary tonight,' I said. 'It's all I've ever dreamed of.'

'Incidentally, you didn't mention what happened to Kindermann.'

'Let's just say that he was shot while trying to escape,' I said. 'I'm sure that you of all people must know what I mean.'

'That's unfortunate. He could still have been useful to us.'

'He got what a murderer properly has coming to him. Someone had to. I don't suppose any of those other bastards will ever get theirs. The SS brotherhood and all that, eh?' I paused and lit a cigarette. 'What will happen to them?'

'You can depend on it that they're finished in the SS. You heard Himmler say so himself.'

'Well, how ghastly for them all.' I turned to Nebe. 'Come on, Arthur. Will Weisthor get anywhere near a courtroom or a guillotine?'

'I don't like it any more than you do,' he said grimly. 'But Weisthor is too close to Himmler. He knows too much.'

Heydrich pursed his lips. 'Otto Rahn, on the other hand, is merely an NCO. I don't think the Reichsführer would mind if some sort of accident were to befall him.'

I shook my head bitterly.

'Well, at least there's an end to their dirty little plot. At least we'll be spared another pogrom, for a while anyway.'

Heydrich looked uncomfortable now. Nebe got up and looked out of the library window.

'For Christ's sake,' I yelled, 'you don't mean to say that it's going to go ahead?' Heydrich winced visibly. 'Look, we all know that the Jews had nothing to do with the murders.'

'Oh yes,' he said brightly, 'that's certain. And they won't be blamed, you have my word on it. I can assure you that –'

'Tell him,' said Nebe. 'He deserves to know.'

Heydrich thought for a moment, and then stood up. He pulled a book from off the shelf and examined it negligently.

'Yes, you're right, Nebe. I believe he probably does.'

'Tell me what?'

'We received a telex before the Court convened this morning,' said Heydrich. 'By sheer coincidence, a young Jewish fanatic has made an attempt on the life of a German diplomat in Paris. Apparently he wished to protest against the treatment of Polish Jews in Germany. The Führer has sent his own personal physician to France, but it is not expected that our man will live.

'As a result, Goebbels is already lobbying the Führer that if this diplomat should die then certain spontaneous expressions of German public outrage be permitted against Jews throughout the Reich.'

'And you'll all look the other way, is that it?'

'I don't approve of lawlessness,' said Heydrich.

'Weisthor gets his pogrom after all. You bastards.'

'Not a pogrom,' Heydrich insisted. 'Looting will not be permitted. Jewish property will merely be destroyed. The police will ensure that there is no plunder. And nothing will be permitted which in any way endangers the security of German life or property.'

'How can you control a mob?'

'Directives will be issued. Offenders will be apprehended and dealt with.'

'Directives?' I flung my cigarettes against the bookcase. 'For a mob? That's a good one.'

'Every police chief in Germany will receive a telex with guidelines.'

Suddenly I felt very tired. I wanted to go home, to be taken away from all of this. Just talking about such a thing made me feel dirty and dishonest. I had failed. But what was infinitely worse, it didn't seem as if I'd ever been meant to succeed.

A coincidence, Heydrich had called it. But a meaningful coincidence, according to Jung's idea? No. It couldn't be. There was no meaning in anything, any more.

24

Thursday, 10 November

'Spontaneous expressions of the German people's anger': that was how the radio put it.

I was angry all right, but there was nothing spontaneous about it. I'd had all night to get worked up. A night in which I'd heard windows breaking, and obscene shouts echoing up the street, and smelt the smoke of burning buildings. Shame kept me indoors. But in the morning which came bright and sunny through my curtains I felt I had to go out and take a look for myself.

I don't suppose I shall ever forget it.

Ever since 1933, a broken window had been something of an occupational hazard for any Jewish business, as synonymous with Nazism as a jackboot, or a swastika. This time, however, it was something altogether different, something much more systematic than the occasional vandalism of a few drunken SA thugs. On this occasion there had occurred a veritable Walpurgisnacht of destruction.

Glass lay everywhere, like the pieces of a huge, icy jigsaw cast down to the earth in a fit of pique by some ill-tempered prince of crystal.

Only a few metres from the front door to my building were a couple of dress shops where I saw a snail's long, silvery trail rising high above a tailor's dummy, while a giant spider's web threatened to envelop another in razor-sharp gossamer.

Further on, at the corner of Kurfürstendamm, I came across an enormous mirror that lay in a hundred pieces, presenting shattered images of myself that ground and cracked underfoot as I picked my way along the street.

For those like Weisthor and Rahn, who believed in some symbolic connection between crystal and some ancient Germanic Christ from which it derived its name, this sight must have seemed exciting enough. But for a glazier it must have looked like a licence to print money, and there were lots of people out sightseeing who said as much.

At the northern end of Fasanenstrasse the synagogue close to the S-Bahn railway was still smouldering, a gutted, blackened ruin of charred beams and burned-out walls. I'm no clairvoyant but I can say that every honest man who saw it was thinking the same thing I was. How many more buildings would end up the same way before Hitler was finished with us?

There were storm-troopers – a couple of truck-loads of them in the next street – and they were testing some more window-panes with their boots. Cautiously deciding to go another way, I was just about to turn back when I heard a voice I half-recognized.

'Get out of here, you Jewish bastards,' the young man yelled.

It was Bruno Stahlecker's fourteen-year-old son Heinrich, dressed up in the uniform of the motorized Hitler Youth. I caught sight of him just as he hurled a large stone through another shop window. He laughed delightedly at his own handiwork and said: 'Fucking Jews.' Looking around for the approval of his young comrades he saw me instead.

As I walked over to him I thought of all the things I would have said to him if I had been his father, but when I was close to him, I smiled. I felt more like giving him a good jaw-whistler with the back of my hand.

'Hallo, Heinrich.'

His fine blue eyes looked at me with sullen suspicion.

'I suppose you think you can tell me off,' he said, 'just because you were a friend of my father's.'

'Me? I don't give a shit what you do.'

'Oh? So what do you want?'

I shrugged and offered him a cigarette. He took one and I lit us both. Then I threw him the box of matches. 'Here,' I said, 'you might need these tonight. Maybe you could try the Jewish Hospital.'

'See? You are going to give me a lecture.'

'On the contrary. I came to tell you that I found the men who murdered your father.'

'You did?' Some of Heinrich's friends who were now busy looting the clothes shop yelled to him to come and help. 'I won't be long,' he called back to them. Then he said to me: 'Where are they? The men who killed my father.'

'One of them is dead. I shot him myself.'

'Good. Good.'

'I don't know what is going to happen to the other two. That all depends, really.'

'On what?'

'On the SS. Whether they decide to court-martial them or not.' I watched his handsome young face crease with puzzlement. 'Oh, didn't I tell you? Yes, these men, the ones who murdered your father in such a cowardly fashion, they were all SS officers. You see, they had to kill him because he would probably have tried to stop them breaking the law. They were evil men, you see, Heinrich, and your father always did his best to put away evil men. He was a damned good policeman.' I waved my hand at all the broken windows. 'I wonder what he would have thought of all this?'

Heinrich hesitated, a lump rising in his throat as he considered the implications of what I had told him.

'It wasn't – it wasn't the Jews who killed him then?'

'The Jews? Good gracious no.' I laughed. 'Where on earth did you get such an idea? It was never the Jews. I shouldn't believe everything you read in *Der Stürmer*, you know.'

It was with a considerable want of alacrity that Heinrich returned to his friends when he and I had finished speaking. I smiled grimly at this sight, reflecting that propaganda works both ways.

Almost a week had passed since I'd seen Hildegard. On my return from Wewelsburg I tried telephoning her a couple of times, but she was never there, or at least she never answered. Finally I decided to drive over and see her.

Driving south on Kaiserallee, through Wilmersdorf and Friedenau, I saw more of the same destruction, more of the same spontaneous expressions of the people's rage: shop signs carrying Jewish names torn down, and new anti-Semitic slogans freshly painted everywhere; and always the police standing by, doing nothing to prevent a shop being looted or to protect its owner from being beaten-up. Close to Waghäuselerstrasse I passed another synagogue ablaze, the fire-service watching to make sure the flames didn't spread to any of the adjoining buildings.

It was not the best day to be thinking of myself.

I parked close to her apartment building on Lepsius Strasse, let myself in through the main door with the street key she had given me, and walked up to the third floor. I used the door knocker. I could have let myself in but somehow I didn't think she'd appreciate that, considering the circumstances of our last meeting.

After a while I heard footsteps and the door was opened by a young SS major. He could have been something straight out of one of Irma Hanke's racial-theory classes: pale blond hair, blue eyes and a jaw that looked like it had been set in concrete. His tunic was unbuttoned, his tie was loose and it didn't look like he was there to sell copies of the SS magazine.

'Who is it, darling?' I heard Hildegard call. I watched her walk towards the door, still searching for something in her handbag, not looking up until she was only a few metres away.

She was wearing a black tweed suit, a silvery crêpe blouse and a black feathered hat that plumed off the front of her head like smoke from a burning building. It was an image that I find hard to put out of my mind. When she saw me she stopped, her perfectly lipsticked mouth slackening a little as she tried to think of something to say.

It didn't need much explaining. That's the thing about being a detective: I catch on real fast. I didn't need a reason why. Perhaps he made a better job of slapping her around than I had, him being in the SS and all. Whatever the reason, they made a handsome-looking couple, which was the way they faced me off, Hildegard threading her arm eloquently through his.

I nodded slowly, wondering whether I should mention catching her stepdaughter's murderers, but when she didn't ask, I smiled philosophically, just kept nodding, and then handed her back the keys.

I was half way down the stairs when I heard her call after me: 'I'm sorry, Bernie. Really I am.'

I walked south to the Botanical Gardens. The pale autumn sky was filled with the exodus of millions of leaves, deported by the wind to distant corners of the city, away from the branches which had once given life. Here and there, stone-faced men worked with slow concentration to control this arboreal diaspora, burning the dead from ash, oak, elm, beech, sycamore, maple, horse-chestnut, lime and weeping-willow, the acrid grey smoke hanging in the air like the last breath of lost souls. But always there were more, and more still, so that the burning middens seemed never to grow any smaller, and as I stood and watched the glowing embers of the fires, and breathed the hot gas of deciduous death, it seemed to me that I could taste the very end of everything.

Author's Note

Otto Rahn and Karl Maria Weisthor resigned from the SS in February 1939. Rahn, an experienced outdoors traveller, died from exposure while walking in the mountains near Kufstein less than one month afterwards. The circumstances of his death have never been properly explained. Weisthor was retired to the town of Goslar where he was cared for by the SS until the end of the war. He died in 1946.

A public tribunal, consisting of six Gauleiters, was convened on 13 February 1940, for the purpose of investigating the conduct of Julius Streicher. The Party tribunal concluded that Streicher was 'unfit for human leadership', and the Gauleiter of Franconia retired from public duties.

The *Kristallnacht* pogrom of 9 and 10 November 1938 resulted in 100 Jewish deaths, 177 synagogues burnt down and the destruction of 7,000 Jewish businesses. It has been estimated that the amount of glass destroyed was equal to half the annual plate-glass production of Belgium, whence it had originally been imported. Damages were estimated to be in the hundreds of millions of dollars. Where insurance monies were paid to Jews, these were confiscated as compensation for the murder of the German diplomat, von Rath, in Paris. This fine totalled $250 million.

A GERMAN REQUIEM

For Jane,
and in memory of my father

It is not what they built. It is what they knocked down.
It is not the houses. It is the spaces between the houses.
It is not the streets that exist. It is the streets that no longer exist.
It is not your memories which haunt you.
It is not what you have written down.
It is what you have forgotten, what you must forget.
What you must go on forgetting all your life.

From 'A German Requiem', by James Fenton

PART ONE

BERLIN, 1947

These days, if you are a German you spend your time in Purgatory before you die, in earthly suffering for all your country's unpunished and unrepented sins, until the day when, with the aid of the prayers of the Powers – or three of them, anyway – Germany is finally purified.

For now we live in fear. Mostly it is fear of the Ivans, matched only by the almost universal dread of venereal disease, which has become something of an epidemic, although both afflictions are generally held to be synonymous.

I

It was a cold, beautiful day, the kind you can best appreciate with a fire to stoke and a dog to scratch. I had neither, but then there wasn't any fuel about and I never much liked dogs. But thanks to the quilt I had wrapped around my legs I was warm, and I had just started to congratulate myself on being able to work from home – the sitting-room doubled as my office – when there was a knock at what passed for the front door.

I cursed and got off my couch.

'This will take a minute,' I shouted through the wood, 'so don't go away.' I worked the key in the lock and started to pull at the big brass handle. 'It helps if you push it from your side,' I shouted again. I heard the scrape of shoes on the landing and then felt a pressure on the other side of the door. Finally it shuddered open.

He was a tall man of about sixty. With his high cheekbones, thin short snout, old-fashioned side-whiskers and angry expression, he reminded me of a mean old king baboon.

'I think I must have pulled something,' he grunted, rubbing his shoulder.

'I'm sorry about that,' I said, and stood aside to let him in. 'There's been quite a bit of subsidence in the building. The door needs rehanging, but of course you can't get the tools.' I showed him into the sitting-room. 'Still, we're not too badly off here. We've had some new glass, and the roof seems to keep out the rain. Sit down.' I pointed to the only armchair and resumed my position on the couch.

The man put down his briefcase, took off his bowler hat and sat down with an exhausted sigh. He didn't loosen his grey overcoat and I didn't blame him for it.

'I saw your little advertisement on a wall on the Kurfürstendamm,' he explained.

'You don't say,' I said, vaguely recalling the words I had used on a small square of card the previous week. Kirsten's idea. With all the notices advertising life-partners and marriage-markets that covered the walls of Berlin's derelict buildings, I had supposed that nobody would bother to read it. But she had been right after all.

'My name is Novak,' he said. 'Dr Novak. I am an engineer. A process metallurgist, at a factory in Wernigerode. My work is concerned with the extraction and production of non-ferrous metals.'

'Wernigerode,' I said. 'That's in the Harz Mountains, isn't it? In the Eastern Zone?'

He nodded. 'I came to Berlin to deliver a series of lectures at the university. This morning I received a telegram at my hotel, the Mitropa —'

I frowned, trying to remember it.

'It's one of those bunker-hotels,' said Novak. For a moment he seemed inclined to tell me about it, and then changed his mind. 'The telegram was from my wife, urging me to cut short my trip and return home.'

'Any particular reason?'

He handed me the telegram. 'It says that my mother is unwell.'

I unfolded the paper, glanced at the typewritten message, and noted that it actually said she was dangerously ill.

'I'm sorry to hear it.'

Dr Novak shook his head.

'You don't believe her?'

'I don't believe my wife ever sent this,' he said. 'My mother may indeed be old, but she is in remarkably good health. Only two days ago she was chopping wood. No, I suspect that this has been cooked up by the Russians, to get me back as quickly as possible.'

'Why?'

'There is a great shortage of scientists in the Soviet Union. I think that they intend to deport me to work in one of their factories.'

I shrugged. 'Then why allow you to travel to Berlin in the first place?'

'That would be to grant the Soviet Military Authority a degree of efficiency which it simply does not possess. My guess is that an order for my deportation has only just arrived from Moscow, and that the SMA wishes to get me back at the earliest opportunity.'

'Have you telegraphed your wife? To have this confirmed?'

'Yes. She replied only that I should come at once.'

'So you want to know if the Ivans have got her.'

'I've been to the military police here in Berlin,' he said, 'but —'

His deep sigh told me with what success.

'No, they won't help,' I said. 'You were right to come here.'

'Can you help me, Herr Günther?'

'It means going into the Zone,' I said, half to myself, as if I needed some persuasion, which I did. 'To Potsdam. There's someone I know I can bribe at the headquarters of the Group of Soviet Forces in Germany. It'll cost you, and I don't mean a couple of candy-bars.'

He nodded solemnly.

'You wouldn't happen to have any dollars, I suppose, Dr Novak?'

He shook his head.

'Then there's also the matter of my own fee.'

'What would you suggest?'

I nodded at his briefcase. 'What have you got?'

'Just papers, I'm afraid.'

'You must have something. Think. Perhaps something at your hotel.'

He lowered his head and uttered another sigh as he tried to recall a possession that might be of some value.

'Look, Herr Doktor, have you asked yourself what you will do if it turns out your wife is being held by the Russians?'

'Yes,' he said gloomily, his eyes glazing over for a moment.

This was sufficiently articulate. Things did not look good for Frau Novak.

'Wait a moment,' he said, dipping his hand inside the breast of his coat, and coming up with a gold fountain-pen. 'There's this.'

He handed me the pen.

'It's a Parker. Eighteen carat.'

I quickly appraised its worth. 'About fourteen hundred dollars on the black market,' I said. 'Yes, that'll take care of Ivan. They love fountain-pens almost as much as they love watches.' I raised my eyebrows suggestively.

'I'm afraid I couldn't part with my watch,' said Novak. 'It was a present – from my wife.' He smiled thinly as he perceived the irony.

I nodded sympathetically and decided to move things along before guilt got the better of him.

'Now, as to my own fee. You mentioned metallurgy. You wouldn't happen to have access to a laboratory, would you?'

'But of course.'

'And a smelter?'

He nodded thoughtfully, and then more vigorously as the light dawned. 'You want some coal, don't you?'

'Can you get some?'

'How much do you want?'

'Fifty kilos would be about right.'

'Very well.'

'Be back here in twenty-four hours,' I told him. 'I should have some information by then.'

Thirty minutes later, after leaving a note for my wife, I was out of the apartment and on my way to the railway station.

In late 1947 Berlin still resembled a colossal Acropolis of fallen masonry and ruined edifice, a vast and unequivocal megalith to the waste of war and the power of 75,000 tonnes of high explosive. Unparalleled was the destruction that had been rained on the capital of Hitler's ambition: devastation on a Wagnerian scale with the Ring come full circle – the final illumination of that twilight of the gods.

In many parts of the city a street map would have been of little more use than a window-cleaner's leather. Main roads meandered like rivers around high banks of debris. Footpaths wound precipitously over shifting mountains of treacherous rubble which sometimes, in warmer weather, yielded a clue unmistakable to the nostrils that something other than household furniture was buried there.

With compasses in short supply you needed a lot of nerve to find your way along facsimile streets on which only the fronts of shops and hotels remained standing unsteadily like some abandoned film-set; and you needed a good memory for the buildings where people still lived in damp cellars, or more precariously on the lower floors of apartment blocks from which a whole wall had been neatly removed, exposing all the rooms and life inside, like some giant doll's house: there were few who risked the upper floors, not least because there were so few undamaged roofs and so many dangerous staircases.

Life amidst the wreckage of Germany was frequently as unsafe as it had been in the last days of the war: a collapsing wall here, an unexploded bomb there. It was still a bit of a lottery.

At the railway station I bought what I hoped might just be a winning ticket.

2

That night, on the last train back to Berlin from Potsdam, I sat in a carriage by myself. I ought to have been more careful, only I was feeling pleased with myself for having successfully concluded the doctor's case: but I was also tired, since this business had taken almost the whole day and a substantial part of the evening.

Not the least part of my time had been taken up in travel. Generally this took two or three times as long as it had done before the war; and what had once been a half-hour's journey to Potsdam now took nearer two. I was closing my eyes for a nap when the train started to slow, and then juddered to a halt.

Several minutes passed before the carriage-door opened and a large and extremely smelly Russian soldier climbed aboard. He mumbled a greeting at me, to which I nodded politely. But almost immediately I braced myself as, swaying gently on his huge feet, he unslung his Mosin Nagant carbine and operated the bolt action. Instead of pointing it at me, he turned and fired his weapon out of the carriage window, and after a brief pause my lungs started to move again as I realized that he had been signalling to the driver.

The Russian burped, sat down heavily as the train started to move again, swept off his lambskin cap with the back of his filthy hand and, leaning back, closed his eyes.

I pulled a copy of the British-run *Telegraf* out of my coat-pocket. Keeping one eye on the Ivan, I pretended to read. Most of the news was about crime: rape and robbery in the Eastern Zone were as common as the cheap vodka which, as often as not, occasioned their commission. Sometimes it seemed as if Germany was still in the bloody grip of the Thirty Years' War.

I knew just a handful of women who could not describe an incident in which they had been raped or molested by a Russian. And even if one makes an allowance for the fantasies of a few neurotics, there was still a staggering number of sex-related crimes. My wife knew several girls who had been attacked only quite recently, on the eve of the thirtieth anniversary of the Russian Revolution. One of these girls, raped by no less than five Red Army soldiers at a police station in Rangsdorff, and infected with syphilis as a result, tried to bring criminal charges, but found herself subjected to a forcible medical examination and charged with prostitution. But there were also some who said that the Ivans merely took by force that which German women were only too willing to sell to the British and the Americans.

Complaints to the Soviet Kommendatura that you had been robbed by Red Army soldiers were equally in vain. You were likely to be informed that 'all the German people have is a gift from the people of the Soviet Union'. This was sufficient sanction for indiscriminate robbery throughout the Zone, and you were sometimes lucky if you survived to report the matter. The depredations of the Red Army and its many deserters made travel in the Zone only slightly less dangerous than a flight on the *Hindenburg*. Travellers on the Berlin–Magdeburg railway had been stripped naked and thrown off the train; and the road from Berlin to Leipzig was so dangerous that vehicles often drove in convoy: the *Telegraf* had reported a robbery in which four boxers, on their way to a fight in Leipzig, had been held up and robbed of everything except their lives. Most notorious of all were the seventy-five robberies committed by the Blue Limousine Gang, which had operated on the Berlin–Michendorf road, and which had included among its leaders the vice-president of the Soviet-controlled Potsdam police.

To people who were thinking of visiting the Eastern Zone, I said 'don't'; and then if they still wanted to go, I said 'Don't wear a wristwatch – the Ivans like to steal them; don't wear anything but your oldest coat and shoes – the Ivans like quality; don't argue or answer back – the Ivans don't mind shooting you: if you must talk to them speak loudly of American fascists; and don't read any newspaper except their own *Taegliche Rundschau*.'

This was all good advice and I would have done well to have taken it myself, for suddenly the Ivan in my carriage was on his feet and standing unsteadily over me.

'*Vi vihodeetye* (are you getting off)?' I asked him.

He blinked crapulously and then stared malevolently at me and my newspaper before snatching it from my hands.

He was a hill-tribesman type, a big stupid Chechen with almond-shaped black eyes, a gnarled jaw as broad as the steppes and a chest like an upturned church-bell: the kind of Ivan we made jokes about – how they didn't know what lavatories were and how they put their food in the toilet bowls thinking that they were refrigerators (some of these stories were even true).

'*Lzhy* (lies),' he snarled, brandishing the paper in front of him, his open, drooling mouth showing great yellow kerbstones of teeth. Putting his boot on the seat beside me, he leaned closer. '*Lganyo,*' he repeated in tones lower than the smell of sausage and beer which his breath carried to my helplessly flaring nostrils. He seemed to sense my disgust and rolled the idea of it around in his grizzled head like a boiled sweet. Dropping the *Telegraf* to the floor he held out his horny hand.

'*Ya hachoo padarok,*' he said, and then slowly in German, '. . . I want present.'

I grinned at him, nodding like an idiot, and realized that I was going to have to kill him or be killed myself. '*Padarok,*' I repeated. '*Padarok.*'

I stood up slowly and, still grinning and nodding, gently pulled back the sleeve of my left arm to reveal my bare wrist. The Ivan was grinning too by now, thinking he was on to a good thing. I shrugged.

'*Oo menya nyet chasov,*' I said, explaining that I didn't have a watch to give him.

'*Shto oo vas yest* (what have you got)?'

'*Nichto,*' I said, shaking my head and inviting him to search my coat pockets. 'Nothing.'

'*Shto oo vas yest*?' he said again, more loudly this time.

It was, I reflected, like me talking to poor Dr Novak, whose wife I had been able to confirm was indeed being held by the MVD. Trying to discover what he could trade.

'*Nichto*,' I repeated.

The grin disappeared from the Ivan's face. He spat on the carriage floor.

'*Vroon* (liar),' he growled, and pushed me on the arm.

I shook my head and told him that I wasn't lying.

He reached to push me again, only this time he checked his hand and took hold of the sleeve with his dirty finger and thumb. '*Doraga* (expensive),' he said, appreciatively, feeling the material.

I shook my head, but the coat was black cashmere – the sort of coat I had no business wearing in the Zone – and it was no use arguing: the Ivan was already unbuckling his belt.

'*Ya hachoo vashi koyt*,' he said, removing his own well-patched greatcoat. Then, stepping to the other side of the carriage, he flung open the door and informed me that either I would hand over the coat or he would throw me off the train.

I had no doubt that he would throw me out whether I gave him my coat or not. It was my turn to spit.

'*Nu, nyelzya* (nothing doing),' I said. 'You want this coat? You come and get it, you stupid fucking *svinya*, you ugly, dumb *kryestyan'in*. Come on, take it from me, you drunken bastard.'

The Ivan snarled angrily and picked up his carbine from the seat where he had left it. That was his first mistake. Having seen him signal to the engine-driver by firing his weapon out of the window, I knew that there could not be a live cartridge in the breech. It was a deductive process he made only a moment behind me, but by the time he was working the bolt action a second time I had buried the toe of my boot in his groin.

The carbine clattered to the floor as the Ivan doubled over painfully, and with one hand reached between his legs: with the other he lashed out hard, catching me an agonizing blow on the thigh that left my leg feeling as dead as mutton.

As he straightened up again I swung with my right, and found my fist caught firmly in his big paw. He snatched at my throat and I head-butted him full in the face, which made him release my fist as he instinctively cupped his turnip-sized nose. I swung again and this time he ducked and seized me by the coat lapels. That was his second mistake, but for a brief, puzzled half-second I did not realize it. Unaccountably he cried out and staggered back from me, his hands raised in the air in front of him like a scrubbed-up surgeon, his lacerated fingertips pouring with blood. It was only then that I remembered the razor-blades I had sewn under my lapels many months before, for just this eventuality.

My flying tackle carried him crashing to the floor and half a torso's length beyond the open door of the fast-moving train. Lying on his bucking legs I struggled to prevent the Ivan pulling himself back into the carriage. Hands that were sticky with blood clawed at my face and then fastened desperately round my neck. His grip tightened and I heard the air gurgle from my own throat like the sound of an espresso-machine.

I punched him hard under the chin, not once but several times, and then pressed the heel of my hand against it as I sought to push him back into the racing night air. The skin on my forehead tightened as I gasped for breath.

A terrible roaring filled my ears, as if a grenade had burst directly in front of my face, and, for a second his fingers seemed to loosen. I lunged at his head and connected with the empty space that was now mercifully signalled by an abruptly terminated stump of bloody human vertebra. A tree, or perhaps a telegraph pole, had neatly decapitated him.

My chest a heaving sack of rabbits, I collapsed back into the carriage, too exhausted to yield to the wave of nausea that was beginning to overtake me. But after only a few seconds more I could no longer resist it and summoned forward by the sudden contraction of my stomach, I vomited copiously over the dead soldier's body.

It was several minutes before I felt strong enough to tip the corpse out of the door, with the carbine quickly following. I picked the Ivan's malodorous greatcoat off the seat to throw it out as well, but the weight of it made me hesitate. Searching the pockets I found a Czechoslovakian-made .38 automatic, a handful of wristwatches – probably all stolen – and a half-empty bottle of Moscowskaya. After deciding to keep the gun and the watches, I uncorked the vodka, wiped the neck, and raised the bottle to the freezing night-sky.

'*Alla rasi bo sun* (God save you),' I said, and swallowed a generous mouthful. Then I flung the bottle and the greatcoat off the train and closed the door.

Back at the railway station snow floated in the air like fragments of lint and collected in small ski-slopes in the angle between the station wall and the road. It was colder than it had been all week and the sky was heavy with the threat of something worse. A fog lay on the white streets like cigar smoke drifting across a well starched tablecloth. Close by, a streetlight burned with no great intensity, but it was still bright enough to light up my face for the scrutiny of a British soldier staggering home with several bottles of beer in each hand. The bemused grin of intoxication on his face changed to something more circumspect as he caught sight of me, and he swore with what sounded like fright.

I limped quickly past him and heard the sound of a bottle breaking on the road as it slipped from nervous fingers. It suddenly occurred to me that my hands and face were covered with the Ivan's blood, not to mention my own. I must have looked like Julius Caesar's last toga.

Ducking into a nearby alley I washed myself with some snow. It seemed to remove not only the blood but the skin as well, and probably left my face looking every bit as red as before. My icy toilette completed, I walked on, as smartly as I was able, and reached home without further adventure.

It had gone midnight by the time I shouldered open my front door – at least it was easier getting in than out. Expecting my wife to be in bed, I was not surprised to find the apartment in darkness, but when I went into the bedroom I saw that she was not there.

I emptied my pockets and prepared for bed.

Laid out on the dressing-table, the Ivan's watches – a Rolex, a Mickey Mouse, a gold Patek and a Doxas – were all working and adjusted to within a minute or two of each other. But the sight of so much accurate time-keeping seemed only to underline Kirsten's lateness. I might have been concerned for her but for the suspicion I held as to where she was and what she was doing, and the fact that I was worn through to my tripe.

My hands trembling with fatigue, my cortex aching as if I had been pounded with a meat-tenderizer, I crawled to bed with no more spirit than if I had been driven from among men to eat grass like an ox.

3

I awoke to the sound of a distant explosion. They were always dynamiting dangerous ruins. A wolf's howl of wind whipped against the window and I pressed myself closer to Kirsten's warm body while my mind slowly decoded the clues that led me back into the dark labyrinth of doubt: the scent on her neck, the cigarette smoke sticking to her hair.

I had not heard her come to bed.

Gradually a duet of pain between my right leg and my head began to make itself felt, and closing my eyes again I groaned and rolled wearily on to my back, remembering the awful events of the previous night. I had killed a man. Worst of all I had killed a Russian soldier. That I had acted in self-defence would, I knew, be a matter of very little consequence to a Soviet-appointed court. There was only one penalty for killing soldiers of the Red Army.

Now I asked myself how many people might have seen me walking from Potsdamer Railway Station with the hands and face of a South American headhunter. I resolved that, for several months at least, it might be better if I were to stay out of the Eastern Zone. But staring at the bomb-damaged ceiling of the bedroom I was reminded of the possibility that the Zone might choose to come to me: there was Berlin, an open patch of lathing on an otherwise immaculate expanse of plasterwork, while in the corner of the bedroom was the bag of black-market builder's gypsum with which I was one day intending to cover it over. There were few people, myself included, who did not believe that Stalin was intent on a similar mission to cover over the small bare patch of freedom that was Berlin.

I rose from my side of the bed, washed at the ewer, dressed, and went into the kitchen to find some breakfast.

On the table were several grocery items that had not been there the night before: coffee, butter, a tin of condensed milk and a couple of bars of chocolate – all from the Post Exchange, or PX, the only shops with anything in them, and shops that were restricted to American servicemen. Rationing meant that the German shops were emptied almost as soon as the supplies came in.

Any food was welcome: with cards totalling less than 3,500 calories a day between Kirsten and me, we often went hungry – I had lost more than fifteen kilos since the end of the war. At the same time I had my doubts about Kirsten's method of obtaining these extra supplies. But for the moment I put away my suspicions and fried a few potatoes with ersatz coffee-grounds to give them some taste.

Summoned by the smell of cooking Kirsten appeared in the kitchen doorway.

'Enough there for two?' she asked.

'Of course,' I said, and set a plate in front of her.

Now she noticed the bruise on my face. 'My god, Bernie, what the hell happened to you?'

'I had a run-in with an Ivan last night.' I let her touch my face and demonstrate her concern for a brief moment before sitting down to eat my breakfast. 'Bastard tried to rob me. We slugged it out for a minute and then he took off. I think he must have had a busy evening. He left some watches behind.' I wasn't going to tell her that he was dead. There was no sense in us both feeling anxious.

'I saw them. They look nice. Must be a couple of thousand dollars' worth there.'

'I'll go up to the Reichstag this morning and see if I can't find some Ivans to buy them.'

'Be careful he doesn't come there looking for you.'

'Don't worry. I'll be all right.' I forked some potatoes into my mouth, picked up the tin of American coffee and stared at it impassively. 'A bit late last night, weren't you?'

'You were sleeping like a baby when I got home.' Kirsten checked her hair with the flat of her hand and added, 'We were very busy yesterday. One of the Yanks took the place over for his birthday party.'

'I see.'

My wife was a schoolteacher, but worked as a waitress at an American bar in Zehlendorf which was open to American service-men only. Underneath the overcoat which the cold obliged her to wear about our apartment, she was already dressed in the red chintz frock and tiny frilled apron that was her uniform.

I weighed the coffee in my hand. 'Did you steal this lot?'

She nodded, avoiding my eye.

'I don't know how you get away with it,' I said. 'Don't they bother to search any of you? Don't they notice a shortage in the store-room?'

She laughed. 'You've no idea how much food there is in that place. Those Yanks are on over 4,000 calories a day. A GI eats your monthly meat ration in just one night, and still has room for ice-cream.' She finished her breakfast and produced a packet of Lucky Strike from her coat pocket. 'Want one?'

'Did you steal those as well?' But I took one anyway and bowed my head to the match she was striking.

'Always the detective,' she muttered, adding, rather more irri-tatedly, 'As a matter of fact these were a present, from one of the Yanks. Some of them are just boys, you know. They can be very kind.'

'I'll bet they can,' I heard myself growl.

'They like to talk, that's all.'

'I'm sure your English must be improving.' I smiled broadly to defuse any sarcasm that was in my voice. This was not the time. Not yet anyway. I wondered if she would say anything about the bottle of Chanel that I had recently found hidden in one of her drawers. But she did not mention it.

Long after Kirsten had gone to the snack bar there was a knock at the door. Still nervous about the death of the Ivan I put his automatic in my jacket pocket before going to answer it.

'Who's there?'

'Dr Novak.'

Our business was swiftly concluded. I explained that my informer from the headquarters of the GSOV had confirmed with one telephone call on the landline to the police in Magdeburg, which was the nearest city in the Zone to Wernigerode, that Frau Novak was indeed being held in 'protective custody' by the MVD. Upon Novak's return home both he and his wife were to be deported immediately for 'work vital to the interests of the peoples of the Union of Soviet Socialist Republics' to the city of Kharkov in the Ukraine.

Novak nodded grimly. 'That would follow,' he sighed. 'Most of their metallurgical research is centred there.'

'What will you do now?' I asked.

He shook his head with such a look of despondency that I felt quite sorry for him. But not as sorry as I felt for Frau Novak. She was stuck.

'Well, you know where to find me if I can be of any further service to you.'

Novak nodded at the bag of coal I had helped him carry up from his taxi and said, 'From the look of your face, I should imagine that you earned that coal.'

'Let's just say that burning it all at once wouldn't make this room half as hot.' I paused. 'It's none of my business Dr Novak, but will you go back?'

'You're right, it's none of your business.'

I wished him luck anyway, and when he was gone carried a shovelful of coal into the sitting-room, and with a care that was only disturbed by my growing anticipation of being once more warm in my home, I built and lit a fire in the stove.

I spent a pleasant morning laid up on the couch, and was almost inclined to stay at home for the rest of the day. But in the afternoon I found a walking-stick in the cupboard and limped up to the Kurfürstendamm where, after queuing for at least half an hour, I caught a tram eastwards.

'Black market,' shouted the conductor when we came within sight of the old ruined Reichstag, and the tram emptied itself.

No German, however respectable, considered himself to be above a little black-marketeering now and again, and with an average weekly income of about 200 marks — enough to buy a packet of cigarettes — even legitimate businesses had plenty of occasions to rely on black-market commodities to pay employees. People used their virtually useless Reichsmarks only to pay the rent and to buy their miserable ration allowances. For the student of classical economics, Berlin presented the perfect model of a business cycle that was determined by greed and need.

In front of the blackened Reichstag on a field the size of a football pitch as many as a thousand people were standing about in little knots of conspiracy, holding what they had come to sell in front of them, like passports at a busy frontier: packets of saccharine, cigarettes, sewing-machine needles, coffee, ration coupons (mostly forged), chocolate and condoms. Others wandered around, glancing with deliberate disdain at the items held up for inspection, and searching for whatever it was they had come to buy. There was nothing that couldn't be bought here: anything from the title-deeds to some bombed-out property to a fake denazification certificate guaranteeing the bearer to be free of Nazi 'infection' and therefore employable in some capacity that was subject to Allied control, be it orchestra conductor or road-sweeper.

But it wasn't just Germans who came to trade. Far from it. The French came to buy jewellery for their girlfriends back home, and the British to buy cameras for their seaside holidays. The Americans bought antiques that had been expertly faked in one of the many workshops off Savignyplatz. And the Ivans came to spend their months of backpay on watches; or so I hoped.

I took up a position next to a man on crutches whose tin leg stuck out of the top of the haversack he was carrying on his back. I held up my watches by their straps. After a while I nodded amicably at my one-legged neighbour who apparently had nothing which he could display, and asked him what he was selling.

He jerked the back of his head at his haversack. 'My leg,' he said without any trace of regret.

'That's too bad.'

His face registered quiet resignation. Then he looked at my watches. 'Nice,' he said. 'There was an Ivan round here about fifteen minutes ago who was looking for a good watch. For 10 per cent I'll see if I can find him for you.'

I tried to think how long I might have to stand there in the cold before making a sale. 'Five,' I heard myself say. 'If he buys.'

The man nodded, and lurched off, a moving tripod, in the direction of the Kroll Opera House. Ten minutes later he was back, breathing heavily and accompanied by not one but two Russian soldiers who, after a great deal of argument, bought the Mickey Mouse and the gold Patek for $1,700.

When they had gone I peeled nine of the greasy bills off the wad I had taken from the Ivans and handed them over.

'Maybe you can hang on to that leg of yours now.'

'Maybe,' he said with a sniff, but later on I saw him sell it for five cartons of Winston.

I had no more luck that afternoon, and having fastened the two remaining watches to my wrists, I decided to go home. But passing close to the ghostly fabric of the Reichstag, with its bricked-up windows and its precarious-looking dome, my mind was changed by one particular piece of graffiti that was daubed there, reproducing itself on the lining of my stomach: 'What our women do makes a German weep, and a GI come in his pants.'

The train to Zehlendorf and the American sector of Berlin dropped me only a short way south of Kronprinzenallee and Johnny's American Bar where Kirsten worked, less than a kilometre from US Military Headquarters.

It was dark by the time I found Johnny's, a bright, noisy place with steamed-up windows, and several jeeps parked in front. A sign above the cheap-looking entrance declared that the bar was only open to First Three Graders, whatever they were. Outside the door was an old man with a stoop like an igloo – one of the city's many thousands of tip-collectors who made a living from picking up cigarette-ends: like prostitutes each tip-collector had his own beat, with the pavements outside American bars and clubs the most coveted of all, where on a good day a man or woman could recover as many as a hundred butts a day: enough for about ten or fifteen whole cigarettes, and worth a total of about five dollars.

'Hey, uncle,' I said to him, 'want to earn yourself four Winston?' I took out the packet I had bought at the Reichstag and tapped four into the palm of my hand. The man's rheumy eyes travelled eagerly from the cigarettes to my face.

'What's the job?'

'Two now, two when you come and tell me when this lady comes out of here.' I gave him the photograph of Kirsten I kept in my wallet.

'Very attractive piece,' he leered.

'Never mind that.' I jerked my thumb at a dirty-looking café further up Kronprinzenallee, in the direction of the US Military HQ. 'See that café?' He nodded. 'I'll be waiting there.'

The tip-collector saluted with his finger and quickly trousering the photograph and the two Winston, he started to turn back to scan his flagstones. But I held him by the grubby handkerchief he wore tied round his stubbly throat. 'Don't forget now, will you?' I said, twisting it tight. 'This looks like a good beat. So I'll know where to go looking if you don't remember to come and tell me. Got that?'

The old man seemed to sense my anxiety. He grinned horribly. 'She might have forgotten you, sir, but you can rest assured that I won't.' His face, a garage floor of shiny spots and oily patches, reddened as for a moment I tightened my grip.

'See that you don't,' I said and let him go, feeling a certain amount of guilt for handling him so roughly. I handed him another cigarette by way of compensation and, discounting his exaggerated endorsements of my own good character, I walked up the street to the dingy café.

For what felt like hours, but wasn't quite two, I sat silently nursing a large and inferior-tasting brandy, smoking several cigarettes and listening to the voices around me. When the tip-collector came to fetch me his scrofulous features wore a triumphant grin. I followed him outside and back into the street.

'The lady, sir,' he said, pointing urgently towards the railway station. 'She went that way.' He paused as I paid him the balance of his fee, and then added, 'With her *schätzi*. A captain, I think. Anyway, a handsome young fellow, whoever he is.'

I didn't stay to hear any more and walked as briskly as I was able in the direction which he had indicated.

I soon caught sight of Kirsten and the American officer who accompanied her, his arm wrapped around her shoulders. I followed them at a distance, the full moon affording me a clear view of their leisurely progress, until they came to a bombed-out apartment block, with six layers of flaky-pastry floors collapsed one on top of the other. They disappeared inside. Should I go in after them, I asked myself. Did I need to see everything?

Bitter bile percolated up from my liver to break down the fatty doubt that lay heavy in my gut.

Like mosquitoes I heard them before I saw them. Their English was more fluent than my understanding, but she seemed to be explaining that she could not be late home two nights in a row. A cloud drifted across the moon, darkening the landscape, and I crept behind an enormous pile of scree, where I thought I might get a better view. When the cloud sailed on, and the moonlight shone undiminished through the bare rafters of the roof, I had a clear sight of them, silent now. For a moment they were a facsimile of innocence as she knelt before him while he laid his hands upon her head as if delivering holy benediction. I puzzled as to why Kirsten's head should be rocking on her shoulders, but when he groaned my understanding of what was happening was as swift as the feeling of emptiness which accompanied it.

I stole silently away and drank myself stupid.

4

I spent the night on the couch, an occurrence which Kirsten, asleep in bed by the time I finally staggered home, would have wrongly attributed to the drink on my breath. I feigned sleep until I heard her leave the apartment, although I could not escape her kissing me on the forehead before she went. She was whistling as she stepped down the stairs and into the street. I got up and watched her from the window as she walked north up Fasanen-strasse towards Zoo Station and her train to Zehlendorf.

When I lost sight of her I set about trying to salvage some rem-nant of myself with which I could face the day. My head throbbed like an excited Dobermann, but after a wash with an ice-cold flan-nel, a couple of cups of the captain's coffee and a cigarette, I started to feel a little better. Still, I was much too preoccupied with the memory of Kirsten frenching the American captain and thoughts of the harm I could bring to him to even remember the harm I had already caused a soldier of the Red Army, and I was not as careful in answering a knock at the door as I should have been.

The Russian was short and yet he stood taller than the tallest man in the Red Army, thanks to the three gold stars and light-blue braid border on his greatcoat's silver epaulettes identifying him as a palkovnik, a colonel, of the MVD – the Soviet secret political police.

'Herr Günther?' he asked politely.

I nodded sullenly, angry with myself for not having been more careful. I wondered where I had left the dead Ivan's gun, and if I dared to make a break for it. Or would he have men waiting at the foot of the stairs for just such an eventuality?

The officer took off his cap, clicked his heels like a Prussian and head-butted the air. 'Palkovnik Poroshin, at your service. May I come in?' He did not wait for an answer. He wasn't the type who was used to waiting for anything other than his own wind.

No more than about thirty years old, the colonel wore his hair long for a soldier. Pushing it clear of his pale blue eyes and back over his narrow head, he rendered the veneer of a smile as he turned to face me in my sitting-room. He was enjoying my discomfort.

'It is Herr Bernhard Günther, is it not? I have to be sure.'

Knowing my name like that was a bit of a surprise. And so was the handsome gold cigarette-case which he flicked open in front of me. The tan on the ends of his cadaverous fingers suggested that he didn't bother with selling cigarettes as much as smoking them. And the MVD didn't normally bother to share a smoke with a man they were about to arrest. So I took one and owned up to my name.

He fed a cigarette into his lantern jaw and produced a matching Dunhill to light us both.

'And you are a —' he winced as the smoke billowed into his eye '— *sh'pek* . . . what is the German word —?'

'Private detective,' I said, translating automatically and regretting my alacrity almost at the very same moment.

Poroshin's eyebrows lifted on his high forehead. 'Well, well,' he remarked with a quiet surprise that turned quickly first to interest and then sadistic pleasure, 'you speak Russian.'

I shrugged. 'A little.'

'But that is not a common word. Not for someone who only speaks a little Russian. *Sh'pek* is also the Russian word for salted pig fat. Did you know that as well?'

'No,' I said. But as a Soviet prisoner of war I had eaten enough of it smeared on coarse black bread to know it only too well. Did he guess that?

'*Nye shooti* (seriously)?' he grinned. 'I bet you do. Just as I'd bet you know that I'm MVD, eh?' Now he laughed out loud. 'Do you see how good at my job I am? I haven't been talking to you for five minutes and already I'm able to say that you are keen to conceal that you speak good Russian. But why?'

'Why don't you tell me what you want, Colonel?'

'Come now,' he said. 'As an Intelligence officer it is only natural for me to wonder why. You of all people must understand that kind of curiosity, yes?' Smoke trailed from his shark's fin of a nose as he pursed his lips in a rictus of apology.

'It doesn't do for Germans to be too curious,' I said. 'Not these days.'

He shrugged and wandered over to my desk and looked at the two watches that were lying on it. 'Perhaps,' he murmured thoughtfully.

I hoped that he wouldn't presume to open the drawer where I now remembered I had put the dead Ivan's automatic. Trying to steer him back to whatever it was he had wanted to see me about, I said: 'Isn't it true that all private detective and information agencies are forbidden in your zone?'

At last he came away from the desk.

'*Vyerno* (quite right), Herr Günther. And that is because such institutions serve no purpose in a democracy –'

Poroshin tut-tutted as I started to interrupt.

'No, please don't say it, Herr Günther. You were going to say that the Soviet Union can hardly be called a democracy. But if you did, the Comrade Chairman might hear you and send terrible men like me to kidnap you and your wife.

'Of course we both know that the only people making a living in this city now are the prostitutes, the black-marketeers and the spies. There will always be prostitutes, and the black-marketeers will last only for as long as the German currency remains unreformed. That leaves spying. That's the new profession to be in, Herr Günther. You should forget about being a private detective when there are so many new opportunities for people like yourself.'

'That sounds almost as if you are offering me a job, Colonel.'

He smiled wryly. 'Not a bad idea at that. But it isn't why I came.' He looked behind him at the armchair. 'May I sit down?'

'Be my guest. I'm afraid I can't offer you much besides coffee.'

'Thank you, no. I find it a rather excitable drink.'

I arranged myself on the couch and waited for him to start.

'There is a mutual friend of ours, Emil Becker, who has got himself into the devil's kitchen, as you say.'

'Becker?' I thought for a moment and recalled a face from the Russian offensive of 1941; and before that, in the Reichskriminal police – the Kripo. 'I haven't seen him in a long time. I wouldn't call him a friend exactly, but what's he done? What are you holding him for?'

Poroshin shook his head. 'You misunderstand. He isn't in trouble with us, but with the Americans. To be precise, their Vienna military police.'

'So if you haven't got him, and the Americans have, he must have actually committed a crime.'

Poroshin ignored my sarcasm. 'He has been charged with the murder of an American officer, an army captain.'

'Well, we've all felt like doing that at some time.' I shook my head at Poroshin's questioning look. 'No, it doesn't matter.'

'What matters here is that Becker did not kill this American,' he said firmly. 'He is innocent. Nevertheless, the Americans have a good case, and he will certainly hang if someone does not help him.'

'I don't see what I can do.'

'He wishes to engage you in your capacity as a private detective, naturally. To prove him innocent. For this he will pay you generously. Win or lose, the sum of $5,000.'

I heard myself whistle. 'That's a lot of money.'

'Half to be paid now, in gold. The balance payable upon your arrival in Vienna.'

'And what's your interest in all this, Colonel?'

He flexed his neck across the tight collar of his immaculate tunic. 'As I said, Becker is a friend.'

'Do you mind explaining how?'

'He saved my life, Herr Günther. I must do whatever I can to help him. But it would be politically difficult for me to assist him officially, you understand.'

'How do you come to be so familiar with Becker's wishes in this affair? I can hardly imagine that he telephones you from an American gaol.'

'He has a lawyer, of course. It was Becker's lawyer who asked me to try and find you; and to ask you to help your old comrade.'

'He was never that. It's true we once worked together. But "old comrades", no.'

Poroshin shrugged. 'As you wish.'

'Five thousand dollars. Where does Becker get $5,000?'

'He is a resourceful man.'

'That's one word for it. What's he doing now?'

'He runs an import and export business, here and in Vienna.'

'A nice enough euphemism. Black-market, I suppose.'

Poroshin nodded apologetically and offered me another cigarette from his gold case. I smoked it with slow deliberation, wondering what small percentage of all this might be on the level.

'Well, what do you say?'

'I can't do it,' I said eventually. 'I'll give you the polite reason first.'

I stood up and went to the window. In the street below stood a shiny new BMW with a Russian pennant on the bonnet; leaning on it was a big, tough-looking Red Army soldier.

'Colonel Poroshin, it wouldn't have escaped your attention that it's not getting any easier to get in or out of this city. After all, you have Berlin surrounded with half the Red Army. But quite apart from the ordinary travel restrictions affecting Germans, things do seem to have got quite a lot worse during the last few weeks, even for your so-called allies. And with so many displaced persons trying to enter Austria illegally, the Austrians are quite happy that journeys there should be discouraged. All right. That's the polite reason.'

'But none of this is a problem,' Poroshin said smoothly. 'For an old friend like Emil I will gladly pull a few wires. Rail warrants, a pink pass, tickets – it can all be easily fixed. You can trust me to handle all the necessary arrangements.'

'Well, I suppose that's the second reason why I'm not going to do it. The less polite reason. I don't trust you, Colonel. Why should I? You talk about pulling a few strings to help Emil. But you could just as easily pull them the other way. Things are rather fickle on your side of the fence. I know a man who came back from the war to find Communist Party officials living in his house – officials for whom nothing was simpler than to pull a few strings in order to ensure his committal to a lunatic asylum just so they could keep the house.

'And, only a month or two ago, I left a couple of friends drinking in a bar in your sector of Berlin, only to learn later that minutes after I had gone Soviet forces surrounded the place and pressed everyone in the bar into a couple of weeks of forced labour.

'So I repeat, Colonel: I don't trust you and see no reason why I should. For all I know I might be arrested the minute I step into your sector.'

Poroshin laughed out loud. 'But why? Why should you be arrested?'

'I never noticed that you need much of a reason.' I shrugged exasperatedly. 'Maybe because I'm a private detective. For the MVD that's as good as being an American spy. I believe that the old concentration camp at Sachsenhausen which your people took over from the Nazis is now full of Germans who've been accused of spying for the Americans.'

'If you will permit me one small arrogance, Herr Günther: do you seriously believe that I, an MVD palkovnik, would consider that the matter of your deception and arrest was more important than the affairs of the Allied Control Council?'

'You're a member of the Kommendatura?' I was surprised.

'I have the honour to be Intelligence officer to the Soviet Deputy Military Governor. You may inquire at the council headquarters in Elsholzstrasse if you don't believe me.' He paused, waiting for some reaction from me. 'Come now. What do you say?'

When I still said nothing, he sighed and shook his head. 'I'll never understand you Germans.'

'You speak the language well enough. Don't forget, Marx was a German.'

'Yes, but he was also a Jew. Your countrymen spent twelve years trying to make those two circumstances mutually exclusive. That's one of the things I can't understand. Change your mind?'

I shook my head.

'Very well.'

The Colonel showed no sign of being irritated at my refusal. He looked at his watch and then stood up.

'I must be going,' he said. Taking out a notebook he started to write on a piece of paper. 'If you do change your mind you can reach me at this number in Karlshorst. That's 55-16-44. Ask for General Kaverntsev's Special Security Section. And there's my home telephone number as well: 05-00-19.'

Poroshin smiled and nodded at the note as I took it from him. 'If you should be arrested by the Americans, I wouldn't let them see that if I were you. They'll probably think you're a spy.'

He was still laughing about that as he went down the stairs.

5

For those who had believed in the Fatherland, it was not the defeat which gave the lie to that patriarchal view of society, but the rebuilding. And with the example of Berlin, ruined by the vanity of men, could be learned the lesson that when a war has been fought, when the soldiers are dead and the walls are destroyed, a city consists of its women.

I walked towards a grey granite canyon which might have concealed a heavily worked mine, from where a short train of brick-laden trucks was even now emerging under the supervision of a group of rubble-women. On the side of one of their trucks was chalked 'No time for love'. You didn't need reminding in view of their dusty faces and wrestlers' bodies. But they had hearts as big as their biceps.

Smiling through their catcalls and whistles of derision – where were my hands now that the city needed to be reconstructed? – and waving my walking-stick like a sick-note, I carried on until I came to Pestalozzistrasse where Friedrich Korsch (an old friend from my days with Kripo, and now a Kommissar with Berlin's Communist-dominated police force) had told me that I could find Emil Becker's wife.

Number 21 was a damaged five-storey building of basin-flats with paper windows, and inside the front doorway, smelling heavily of burnt toast, was a sign which warned 'Unsafe Staircase! In use at visitor's own risk'. Fortunately for me, the names and apartment-numbers that were chalked on the wall inside the door told me that Frau Becker lived on the ground floor.

I walked down a dark, dank corridor to her door. Between it and the landing washbasin an old woman was picking large chunks of fungus off the damp wall and collecting them in a cardboard box.

'Are you from the Red Cross?' she asked.

I told her I wasn't, knocked at the door and waited.

She smiled. 'It's all right, you know. We're really quite well-off here.' There was a quiet insanity in her voice.

I knocked again, more loudly this time, and heard a muffled sound, and then bolts being drawn on the other side of the door.

'We don't go hungry,' said the old woman. 'The Lord provides.' She pointed at her shards of fungus in the box. 'Look. There are even fresh mushrooms growing here.' And so saying she pulled a piece of fungus from the wall and ate it.

When the door finally opened, I was momentarily unable to speak from disgust. Frau Becker, catching sight of the old woman, brushed me aside and stepped smartly into the corridor, where with many loud insults she shooed the old woman away.

'Filthy old baggage,' she muttered. 'She's always coming into this building and eating that mould. The woman's mad. A complete spinner.'

'Something she ate no doubt,' I said queasily.

Frau Becker fixed me with the awl of her bespectacled eye. 'Now who are you and what do you want?' she asked brusquely.

'My name is Bernhard Günther –' I started.

'Heard of you,' she snapped. 'You're with Kripo.'

'I was.'

'You'd better come in.' She followed me into the icy-cold sitting-room, slammed the door shut and closed the bolts as if in mortal fear of something. Noticing how this took me aback, she added by way of explanation: 'Can't be too careful these days.'

'No indeed.'

I looked around at the loathsome walls, the threadbare carpet and the old furniture. It wasn't much but it was neatly kept. There was little she could have done about the damp.

'Charlottenburg's not too badly off,' I offered by way of mitigation, 'in comparison with some areas.'

'Maybe so,' she said, 'but I can tell you, if you'd come after dark and knocked till kingdom come, I wouldn't have answered. We get all sorts of rats round here at night.' So saying she picked up a large sheet of plywood from off the couch, and for a moment in the gloom of the place I thought she was working on a jigsaw-puzzle. Then I saw the numerous packets of Olleschau cigarette papers, the bags of butts, the piles of salvaged tobacco, and the serried ranks of re-rolls.

I sat down on the couch, took out my Winston and offered her one.

'Thanks,' she said grudgingly, and threaded the cigarette behind her ear. 'I'll smoke it later.' But I didn't doubt that she would sell it with the rest.

'What's the going rate for one of those re-cycled nails?'

'About 5 marks,' she said. 'I pay my collectors five US for 150 tips. That rolls about twenty good ones. Sell them for about ten US. What, are you writing an article about it for the *Tagesspiegel*? Spare me the Victor Gollancz–Save Berlin routine, Herr Günther. You're here about that lousy husband of mine, aren't you? Well, I haven't seen him in a long while. And I hope I never clap eyes on him again. I expect you know he's in a Viennese gaol, do you?'

'Yes, I do.'

'You may as well know that when the American MPs came to tell me he'd been arrested, I was glad. I could forgive him for deserting me, but not our son.'

There was no telling if Frau Becker had turned witch before or after her husband had jumped his wife's bail. But on first acquaintance she wasn't the type to have persuaded me that her absconding husband had made the wrong choice. She had a bitter mouth, prominent lower jaw and small sharp teeth. No sooner had I explained the purpose of my visit than she started to chew the air around my ears. It cost me the rest of my cigarettes to placate her enough to answer my questions.

'Exactly what happened? Can you tell me?'

'The MPs said that he shot and killed an American army captain in Vienna. They caught him red-handed apparently. That's all I was told.'

'What about this Colonel Poroshin? Do you know anything about him?'

'You want to know if you can trust him or not. That's what you want to know. Well, he's an Ivan,' she sneered. 'That's all you should need to know.' She shook her head and added, impatiently: 'Oh, they knew each other here in Berlin because of one of Emil's rackets. Penicillin, I think it was. Emil said that Poroshin caught syphilis off some girl he was keen on. More like the other way round, I thought. Anyway this was the worst kind of syphilis: the sort that makes you swell up. Salvarsan didn't seem to work. Emil got them some penicillin. Well, you know how rare that is, the good stuff I mean. That could be one reason why Poroshin's trying to help Emil. They're all the same, these Russians. It's not just their brains that are in their balls. It's their hearts too. Poroshin's gratitude comes straight from his scrotum.'

'And another reason?'

Her brow darkened.

'You said that could be one reason.'

'Well of course. It can't simply be a matter of pulling Poroshin's tail out of the fire, can it? I wouldn't be at all surprised if Emil had been spying for him.'

'Got any evidence for that? Did he see much of Poroshin when he was still here in Berlin?'

'I can't say he did, I can't say he didn't.'

'But he's not charged with anything besides murder. He's not been charged with spying.'

'What would be the point? They've got enough to hang him as it is.'

'That's not the way it works. If he had been spying, they would have wanted to know everything. Those American MPs would have asked you a lot of questions about your husband's associates. Did they?'

She shrugged. 'Not that I can remember.'

'If there was any suspicion of spying they would have investigated it, if only to find out what sort of information he might have got hold of. Did they search this place?'

Frau Becker shook her head. 'Either way, I hope he hangs,' she said bitterly. 'You can tell him that if you see him. I certainly won't.'

'When did you last see him?'

'A year ago. He came back from a Soviet POW camp in July and he legged it three months later.'

'And when was he captured?'

'February 1943, at Briansk.' Her mouth tightened. 'To think that I waited three years for that man. All those other men who I turned away. I kept myself for him, and look what happened.' A thought seemed to occur to her. 'There's your evidence for spying, if you need any. How was it that he managed to get himself released, eh? Answer me that. How did he get home when so many others are still there?'

I stood up to leave. Perhaps the situation with my own wife made me more inclined to take Becker's part. But I had heard enough to realize that he would need all the help he could get – possibly more, if this woman had anything to do with it.

I said: 'I was in a Soviet prisoner-of-war camp myself, Frau Becker. For less time than your husband, as it happens. It didn't make me a spy. Lucky maybe, but not a spy.' I went to the door, opened it, and hesitated. 'Shall I tell you what it did make me? With people like the police, with people like you, Frau Becker, with people like my own wife, who's hardly let me touch her since I came home. Shall I tell you what it made me? It made me unwelcome.'

6

It is said that a hungry dog will eat a dirty pudding. But hunger doesn't just affect your standards of hygiene. It also dulls the wits, blunts the memory – not to mention the sex-drive – and generally produces a feeling of listlessness. So it was no surprise to me that there had been a number of occasions during the course of 1947 when, with senses pinched from want of nourishment, I had nearly met with an accident. It was for this very reason I decided to reflect upon my present, rather irrational inclination, which was to take Becker's case after all, with the benefit of a full stomach.

Formerly Berlin's finest, most famous hotel, the Adlon was now little more than a ruin. Somehow it remained open to guests, with fifteen available rooms which, because it was in the Soviet sector, were usually taken by Russian officers. A small restaurant not only survived in the basement, but did brisk business too, a result of it being exclusive to Germans with food coupons who might therefore lunch or dine there without fear of being thrown off a table in favour of some more obviously affluent Americans or British, as happened in most other Berlin restaurants.

The Adlon's improbable entrance was underneath a pile of rubble on Wilhelmstrasse, only a short distance away from the Führerbunker where Hitler had met his death, and which could be toured for the price of a couple of cigarettes in the hand of any one of the policemen who were supposed to keep people out of it. All Berlin's bulls were doubling as touts since the end of the war.

I ate a late lunch of lentil soup, turnip 'hamburger' and tinned fruit; and having sufficiently turned over Becker's problem in my metabolized mind, I handed over my coupons and went up to what passed for the hotel reception desk to use the telephone.

My call to the Soviet Military Authority, the SMA, in Karlshorst was connected quickly enough, but I seemed to wait forever to be put through to Colonel Poroshin. Nor did speaking in Russian speed the progress of my call; it merely earned me a look of suspicion from the hotel porter. When finally I got through to Poroshin he seemed genuinely pleased that I had changed my mind and told me that I should wait by the picture of Stalin on Unter den Linden, where his staff car would collect me in fifteen minutes.

The afternoon had turned as raw as a boxer's lip and I stood in the door of the Adlon for ten minutes before heading back up the small service stairs and towards the top of the Wilhelmstrasse. Then, with the Brandenburg Gate at my back, I walked up to the house-sized picture of the Comrade Chairman that dominated the centre of the avenue, flanked by two smaller plinths, each bearing the Soviet hammer and sickle.

As I waited for the car, Stalin seemed to watch me, a sensation which, I supposed, was intended: the eyes were as deep, black and unpleasant as the inside of a postman's boot, and under the cockroach moustaches the smile was hard permafrost. It always amazed me that there were people who referred to this murdering monster as 'Uncle' Joe: he seemed to me to be about as avuncular as King Herod.

Poroshin's car arrived, its engine drowned by the noise of a squadron of YAK 3 fighters passing overhead. I climbed aboard, and rolled helplessly in the back seat as the broad-shouldered, Tatar-faced driver hit the BMW's accelerator, sending the car speeding east towards Alexanderplatz, and beyond to the Frankfurter Allee and Karlshorst.

'I always thought that German civilians were forbidden to ride in staff cars,' I said to the driver in Russian.

'True,' he said, 'but the colonel said that if we are stopped I'm just to say that you're being arrested.'

The Tatar laughed uproariously at my look of obvious alarm, and I could only console myself with the fact that while we were driving at such a speed, it was unlikely that we could be stopped by anything other than an anti-tank gun.

We reached Karlshorst minutes later.

A villa colony with a steeplechase course, Karlshorst, nick-named 'the little Kremlin', was now a completely isolated Russian enclave which Germans could only enter by special permit. Or the kind of pennant on the front of Poroshin's car. We were waved through several checkpoints and finally drew up alongside the old St Antonius Hospital on Zeppelin Strasse now housing the SMA for Berlin. The car ground to a halt in the shadow of a five-metre-high plinth on top of which was a big red Soviet star. Poroshin's driver sprang out of his seat, opened my door smartly and, ignor-ing the sentries, squired me up the steps to the front door. I paused in the doorway for a moment, surveying the shiny new BMW cars and motorcycles in the car park.

'Someone been shopping?' I said.

'From the BMW factory at Eisenbach,' said my driver proudly. 'Now Russian.'

With this depressing thought he left me in a waiting-room that smelled strongly of carbolic. The room's only concession to decor-ation was another picture of Stalin with a slogan underneath that read: 'Stalin, the wise teacher and protector of the working people'. Even Lenin, portrayed in a smaller frame alongside the wise one, seemed from his expression to have one or two problems with that particular sentiment.

I met these same two popular faces hanging on the wall of Poro-shin's office on the top floor of the SMA building. The young colonel's neatly pressed olive-brown tunic was hanging on the back of the glass door, and he was wearing a Circassian-style shirt, belted with a black strap. But for the polish on his soft calf-leather boots he might have passed for a student at Moscow University. He set down his mug and stood up from behind his desk as the Tatar ushered me into his office.

'Sit down, please, Herr Günther,' said Poroshin, pointing at a bentwood chair. The Tatar waited to be dismissed. Poroshin lifted his mug and held it up for my inspection. 'Would you like some Ovaltine, Herr Günther?'

'Ovaltine? No, thanks, I hate the stuff.'

'Do you?' He sounded surprised. 'I love it.'

'It's kind of early to be thinking of going to bed, isn't it?'

Poroshin smiled patiently. 'Perhaps you would prefer some vodka.' He pulled open his desk drawer and took out a bottle and a glass, which he placed on the desk in front of me.

I poured myself a large one. Out of the corner of my eye I saw the Tatar rub his thirst with the back of his paw. Poroshin saw it too. He filled another glass and laid it on the filing cabinet so that it was immediately next to the man's head.

'You have to train these Cossack bastards like dogs,' he explained. 'For them drunkenness is an almost religious ordinance. Isn't that so, Yeroshka?'

'Yes, sir,' he said blankly.

'He smashed a bar up, assaulted a waitress, punched a sergeant, and but for me he might have been shot. Still might be shot, eh, Yeroshka? The minute you touch that glass without my permission. Understand?'

'Yes, sir.'

Poroshin produced a big, heavy revolver and laid it on the desk to emphasize his point. Then he sat down again.

'I imagine you know quite a lot about discipline with your record, Herr Günther? Where did you say you served during the war?'

'I didn't say.'

He leaned back in his chair and swung his boots on to the desk. The vodka trembled over the edge of my glass as they thudded down on the blotter.

'No, you didn't, did you? But I imagine that with your qualifications you would have served in some Intelligence capacity.'

'What qualifications?'

'Come now, you're being too modest. Your spoken Russian, your experience with Kripo. Ah yes, Emil's lawyer told me about that. I'm told that you and he were once part of the Berlin Murder Commission. And you a Kommissar, too. That's quite senior, isn't it?'

I sipped my vodka and tried to keep calm. I told myself that I ought to have expected something like this.

'I was just an ordinary soldier, obeying orders,' I said. 'I wasn't even a Party member.'

'So few were, it would now seem. I find that really quite remarkable.' He smiled and raised a salutary index finger. 'Be as coy as you like Herr Günther, but I shall find out about you. Mark my words. If only to satisfy my curiosity.'

'Sometimes curiosity is a bit like Yeroshka's thirst,' I said, '– best left unsatisfied. Unless it's the disinterested, intellectual kind of curiosity that belongs properly to the philosophers. Answers have a habit of disappointing.' I finished the glass and laid it on the blotter next to his boots. 'But I didn't come here with a cipher in my socks to play your afternoon's vexed question, Colonel. So how about you feed me with one of those Lucky Strikes you were smoking this morning and satisfy *my* curiosity at least as far as telling me one or two facts about this case?'

Poroshin leaned forward and knocked open a silver cigarette box on the desk. 'Help yourself,' he said.

I took one and lit it with a fancy silver lighter that was cast in the shape of a field gun; then I looked at it critically, as if judging its value in a pawnshop. He had irritated me and I wanted to kick back at him somehow. 'You've got some nice loot,' I said. 'This is a German field gun. Did you buy it, or was there nobody at home when you called?'

Poroshin closed his eyes, snorted a little laugh, then got up and went over to the window. He drew up the sash and unbuttoned his fly. 'That's the trouble with drinking all that Ovaltine,' he said, apparently unperturbed by my attempt to insult him. 'It goes straight through you.' When he started to pee, he glanced back across his shoulder at the Tatar who remained standing by the filing cabinet and the glass of vodka which stood on it. 'Drink it and get out, pig.'

The Tatar didn't hesitate. He emptied the glass with one jerk of his head and stepped swiftly out of the office, closing the door behind him.

'If you saw how peasants like him leave the toilets here, you would understand why I prefer to piss out of the window,' said Poroshin, buttoning himself. He closed the window and resumed his seat. The boots thudded back on to the blotter. 'My fellow Russians can make life in this sector rather trying at times. Thank God for people like Emil. He is a most amusing man to have around on occasion. And very resourceful too. There is simply nothing that he cannot get hold of. What is the word you have for these black-market types?'

'Swing Heinis.'

'Yes, swings. If one wanted entertainment, Emil would be the swing to arrange it.' He laughed fondly at the thought of him, which was more than I could do. 'I never met a man who knew so many girls. Of course they are all prostitutes and chocoladies, but that is not such a great crime these days, is it?'

'It depends on the chocolady,' I said.

'Also, Emil is most ingenious at getting things across the border – the Green Frontier you call it, don't you?'

I nodded. 'Through the woods.'

'An accomplished smuggler. He's made a great deal of money. Until this happened he was living very well in Vienna. A big house, a fine car and an attractive girlfriend.'

'Have you ever made use of his services? And I don't mean his acquaintance with chocoladies.'

Poroshin confined himself to repeating that Emil could get hold of anything.

'Does that include information?'

He shrugged. 'Now and again. But whatever Emil does, he does for money. I find it hard to believe he would not have also been doing things for the Americans.

'In this case, however, he had a job from an Austrian. A man called König, who was in the advertising and publicity business. The company was called Reklaue & Werbe Zentrale, and they had offices here in Berlin and in Vienna. König wanted Emil to collect layouts from the Vienna office to bring to Berlin, on a regular basis. He said that the work was too important to trust to the post or to a courier, and König couldn't go himself as he was awaiting denazification. Of course Emil suspected that the parcels contained things besides advertisements, but the money was good enough for him to ask no questions, and since he came to and from Berlin on a fairly regular basis anyway, it wasn't going to cause him any extra problems. Or so he thought.

'For a while Emil's deliveries went without a problem. When he was bringing cigarettes or some such contraband into Berlin he would also bring one of König's parcels. He handed them over to a man called Eddy Holl and collected his money. It was as simple as that.

'Well, one night Emil was in Berlin and went to a nightclub in Berlin–Schönberg called the Gay Island. By accident he met this man, Eddy Holl. He was drunk and introduced him to an American army captain called Linden. Eddy described Emil to Captain Linden as "their Vienna courier". The next day Eddy telephoned Emil and apologized for being drunk and suggested that it would be better for all their sakes if Emil forgot all about Captain Linden.

'Several weeks later, when Emil was back in Vienna, he got a call from this Captain Linden, who said that he would like to meet him again. So they met at some bar and the American started to ask questions about the advertising firm, Reklaue & Werbe. There wasn't much that Emil could tell him, but Linden's being there worried him. He thought that if Linden was in Vienna that there might not be any more need for his own services. It would be a shame, he thought, to see the end of such easy money. So he followed Linden around Vienna for a while. After a couple of days Linden met another man, and followed by Emil they went to an old film studio. Minutes later Emil heard a shot and the man came out, alone. Emil waited until this man was gone. Then he went in and found Captain Linden's dead body, and a load of stolen tobacco. Naturally enough he did not inform the police. Emil tries to have as little to do with them as possible.

'The next day, König and a third man came to see him. Don't

ask me his name, I don't know. They said that an American friend had gone missing, and that they were worried something might have happened to him. In view of the fact that Emil had once been a detective with Kripo, would he, for a substantial reward, look into it for them. Emil agreed, seeing an easy way to make some money, and perhaps an opportunity to help himself to some of the tobacco.

'After a day or so, and having had the studio watched for a while, Emil and a couple of his boys decided it was safe to go back there with a van. They found the International Patrol waiting for them. Emil's boys were a couple of pleasure-shooters and got themselves killed. Emil was arrested.'

'Does he know who tipped them off?'

'I asked my people in Vienna to find that out. It seems the tip-off was anonymous.' Poroshin smiled appreciatively. 'Now here's the good part. Emil's gun is a Walther P38. He took it with him to the studio. But when he was arrested and surrendered it he noticed that it wasn't his P38 after all. This one had a German eagle on the handgrip. And there was another important difference. The local ballistics expert quickly identified this as the same gun that had shot and killed Captain Linden.'

'Someone switched it for Becker's own gun, eh?' I said. 'Yes, it's not the sort of thing you'd notice right away, is it? Very neat. A man, conveniently carrying the murder weapon, returns to the scene of the crime, ostensibly to collect his stolen tobacco. Quite a strong case there I'd say.'

I took a last puff of my cigarette before extinguishing it in Poroshin's silver desk-ashtray and helping myself to another. 'I'm not sure what I would be able to do,' I said. 'Turning water into wine isn't in my normal line of work.'

'Emil is anxious, so his lawyer, Dr Liebl, tells me, that you should find this man König. He seems to have disappeared.'

'I'll bet he has. Do you think it was König who made the switch, when he came to Becker's house?'

'It certainly looks that way. König or perhaps the third man.'

'Do you know anything about König, or this publicity firm?'

'*Nyet.*'

There was a knock at the door and an officer came into Poroshin's office.

'We have Am Kupfergraben on the line, sir,' he announced in Russian. 'They say it's urgent.'

I pricked up my ears. Am Kupfergraben was the location of Berlin's biggest MVD gaol. With so many displaced and missing persons in my line of work, it paid to keep your ears open.

Poroshin glanced at me, almost as if he knew what I was thinking, and then said to the other officer, 'It will have to wait, Jegoroff. Any other calls?'

'Zaisser from K−5.'

'If that Nazi bastard wants to speak to me he can damn well wait outside my door. Tell him that. Now leave us please.' He waited until the door had closed behind his subordinate. 'K−5 mean anything to you, Günther?'

'Should it?'

'Not yet, no. But in time, who knows?' He did not elaborate, but instead glanced at his wristwatch. 'We really must get on. I have an appointment this evening. Jegoroff will arrange all your necessary papers – pink pass, travel permit, a ration card, an Austrian identity card – do you have a photograph? Never mind. Jegoroff will have one taken. Oh yes, I think it would be a good idea if you were to have one of our new tobacco permits. It allows you to sell cigarettes throughout the Eastern Zone, and obliges all Soviet personnel to be of assistance to you wherever it is possible. It might just get you out of any trouble.'

'I thought the black market was illegal in your zone,' I said, curious as to the reason for this blatant piece of official hypocrisy.

'It is illegal,' Poroshin said, without any trace of embarrassment. 'This is an officially licensed black market. It allows us to raise some foreign currency. Rather a good idea don't you think? Naturally we will supply you with a few cartons of cigarettes to make it look convincing.'

'You seem to have thought of everything. What about my money?'

'It will be delivered to your home at the same time as your papers. The day after tomorrow.'

'And where is the money coming from? This Dr Liebl, or from your cigarette concessions?'

'Liebl will be sending me money. Until then this matter will be handled by the SMA.'

I didn't like this much, but there wasn't much of an alternative. Take money from the Russians, or go to Vienna and trust that the money would be paid in my absence.

'All right,' I said. 'Just one more thing. What do you know about Captain Linden? You said that Becker met him in Berlin. Was he stationed here?'

'Yes. I was forgetting him, wasn't I?' Poroshin stood up and went over to the filing cabinet on which the Tatar had left his empty glass. He opened one of the drawers and fingered his way across the tops of his files until he found the one he was searching for.

'Captain Edward Linden,' he read, coming back to his chair. 'Born Brooklyn, New York, 22 February 1907. Graduated Cornell University, with a degree in German, 1930; serving 970th Counter-Intelligence Corps; formerly 26th Infantry, stationed at Camp King Interrogation Centre, Oberusel as denazification officer; currently attached to US Documents Centre in Berlin as Crowcass liaison officer. Crowcass is the Central Registry of War Crimes and Security Suspects of the United States Army. It's not very much, I'm afraid.'

He dropped the file open in front of me. The strange, Greek-looking letters covered no more than half a sheet of paper.

'I'm not much good with Cyrillic,' I said.

Poroshin did not look convinced.

'What exactly is the United States Documents Centre?'

'It's a building in the American sector, near the edge of the Grünewald. The Berlin Documents Centre is the depository for Nazi ministerial and party documents captured by the Americans and the British towards the end of the war. It's quite comprehensive. They've got the complete NSDAP membership records, which makes it easy to find out when people lie on their denazification questionnaires. I'll bet they've even got your name there somewhere.'

'Like I said, I was never a Party member.'

'No,' he grinned, 'of course not.' Poroshin took the file and returned it to the filing cabinet. 'You were only obeying orders.'

It was plain he didn't believe me any more than he believed that I was unable to decipher St Cyril's Byzantine alphabet: in that at least he would have been justified.

'And now, if you have no more questions, I really must leave you. I am due at the State Opera in the Admiralspalast in half an hour.' He took off his belt and, yelling the names of Yeroshka and Jegoroff, slipped into his tunic.

'Have you ever been to Vienna?' he asked, fixing the cross belt under his epaulette.

'No, never.'

'The people are just like the architecture,' he said, inspecting his appearance in the window's reflection. 'They are all front. Everything that's interesting about them seems to be on the surface. Inside they're very different. Now there's a people I could really work with. All Viennese were born to be spies.'

7

'You were late again last night,' I said.

'I didn't wake you, did I?' She slid naked out of bed and went over to the full-length mirror in the corner of our bedroom. 'Anyway, you were kind of late yourself the other night.' She started to examine her body. 'It's so nice having a warm house again. Where on earth did you find the coal?'

'A client.'

Watching her standing there, stroking her pubic hair and flattening her stomach with the palm of her hand, lifting her breasts, scrutinizing her tight, finely-lined mouth with its waxy sheen, concave cheeks and shrinking gums, and finally twisting around to assess her gently sagging bottom, her bony hand with the rings on the fingers slightly looser than before, pulling at the flesh of one buttock, I didn't need to be told what was going through her mind. She was an attractive, mature woman intent on making full use of what time she had left.

Feeling hurt and irritated, I jack-knifed out of bed to find my leg buckling beneath me.

'You look fine,' I said wearily, and limped into the kitchen.

'That sounds a little short for a love sonnet,' she called out.

There were some more PX goods on the kitchen table: a couple of cans of soup, a bar of real soap, a few saccharine cards and a packet of condoms.

Still naked, Kirsten followed me into the kitchen and watched me examining her haul. Was it just the one American? Or were there more?

'I see you've been busy again,' I said, picking up the packet of Parisians. 'How many calories are these?'

She laughed behind her hand. 'The manager keeps a load under the counter.' She sat down on a chair. 'I thought it would be nice. You know, it's been quite a while since we did anything.' She let her thighs yawn as if to let me see a little more of her. There's time now, if you want.'

It was quickly done, expedited with an almost professional non-chalance on her part, as if she had been administering an enema. No sooner had I finished than she was heading towards the bath-room with hardly a blush on her cheek, carrying the used Parisian as if it were a dead mouse she had found under the bed.

Half an hour later, dressed and ready to leave for work, she paused in the sitting-room where I had stoked the ashes in the stove and was now adding some more coal. For a moment she watched me bring the fire to life again.

'You're good at that,' she said. I couldn't tell whether any sarcasm was intended. Then she gave me a peremptory kiss and went out.

The morning was colder than a mohel's knife, and I was glad to start the day in a reading library on Hardenbergstrasse. The library assistant was a man with a mouth so badly scarred that it was impossible to say where his lips were until he started to speak.

'No,' he said, in a voice that belonged properly to a sea-lion, 'there are no books about the BDC. But there have been a couple of newspaper articles published in the last few months. One in the *Telegraf*, I think, and the other in the *Military Government Informa-tion Bulletin*.'

He collected his crutches and shouldered his one-legged way to a cabinet housing a large card-index where, as he had remembered, he found references for both these articles: one, published in the *Telegraf* in May, an interview with the Centre's commanding offi-cer, a Lieutenant-Colonel Hans W. Helm; the other an account of the Centre's early history, written by a junior staff member in August.

I thanked the assistant, who told me where to find the library's copies of both publications.

'Lucky for you that you came today,' he said. 'I'm travelling to Giessen tomorrow, to have my artificial leg fitted.'

Reading the articles I realized that I had never thought the Americans were capable of such efficiency. Admittedly, there had been a certain amount of luck involved in the accumulation of some of the Centre's documentary collections. For example, troops of the US Seventh Army had stumbled on the complete Nazi Party membership records at a paper mill near Munich, where they were about to be pulped. But staff at the Centre had set about the creation and organization of the most comprehensive archive, so that it could be determined with complete accuracy exactly who was a Nazi. As well as the NSDAP master files, the Centre included in its collection the NSDAP membership applications, Party correspondence, SS service records, Reich Security Office records, SS racial records, proceedings of the Supreme Party Court and the People's Court – everything from the membership files of the National Socialist Schoolteachers' Organization to a file detailing expulsions from the Hitler Youth.

Another thought occurred to me as I left the library and made my way to the railway station. I would never have believed that the Nazis could have been stupid enough to have recorded their own activities in such comprehensive and incriminating detail.

I left the U–Bahn – a stop too early as it turned out – at a station in the American sector which, for no reason to do with their occupation of the city, was called Uncle Tom's Hut, and walked down Argentinische Allee.

Surrounded by the tall fir trees of the Grünewald, and only a short distance from a small lake, the Berlin Documents Centre stood in well-guarded grounds at the end of Wasserkäfersteig, a cobblestoned cul-de-sac. Inside a wire fence the Centre comprised a number of buildings, but the main part of the BDC appeared to be a two-storey affair at the end of a raised pathway, painted white and with green shutters on the windows. It was a nice-looking place, although I soon remembered it as the headquarters of the old Forschungsamt – the Nazis' telephone-tapping centre.

The soldier at the gatehouse, a big, gap-toothed Negro, eyed me suspiciously as I halted at his checkpoint. He was probably more used to dealing with people in cars, or military vehicles, than with a lone pedestrian.

'What do you want, Fritzy?' he said, clapping his woolly gloves together and stamping his boots to keep warm.

'I was a friend of Captain Linden's,' I said in my halting English. 'I have just heard the terrible news, and I came to say how sorry my wife and I were. He was kind to us both. Gave us PX, you know.' From my pocket I produced the short letter I had composed on the train. 'Perhaps you would be kind enough to deliver this to Colonel Helm.'

The soldier's tone changed immediately.

'Yes sir, I'll give it to him.' He took the letter and regarded it awkwardly. 'Very kind of you to think of him.'

'It is just a few marks, for some flowers,' I said, shaking my head. 'And a card. My wife and I wanted something on Captain Linden's grave. We would go to the funeral if it was in Berlin, but we thought that his family would be taking him home.'

'Well, no, sir,' he said. 'The funeral's in Vienna, this Friday morning. Family wanted it that way. Less trouble than shipping a body all the way home I guess.'

I shrugged. 'For a Berliner that might as well be in America. Travel is not easy these days.' I sighed and glanced at my watch. 'I had better be getting along. I have quite a walk ahead of me.' When I turned to walk away, I groaned, and clutching my knee and affecting a broad grimace, I sat squarely down on the road in front of the barrier, my stick clattering on the cobbles beside me. Quite a performance. The soldier side-stepped his checkpoint.

'Are you all right?' he said, collecting my stick and helping me to my feet.

'A bit of Russian shrapnel. It gives me some trouble now and again. I'll be all right in a minute or two.'

'Hey, come on in to the gatehouse and sit down for a couple of minutes.' He led me round the barrier and through the little door of his hut.

'Thank you. It is very kind of you.'

'Kind, nothing. Any friend of Captain Linden's . . .'

I sat down heavily and rubbed my almost painless knee. 'Did you know him well?'

'Me, I'm just a Pfc. I can't say I knew him, but I used to drive him now and again.'

I smiled and shook my head. 'Could you speak more slowly please? My English is not so good.'

'I drove him now and again,' the soldier said more loudly, and he imitated the action of turning a steering-wheel. 'You say that he gave you PX?'

'Yes, he was very kind.'

'Yeah, that sounds like Linden. Always had plenty of PX to give away.' He paused as a thought occurred to him. 'There was one particular couple – well, he was like a son to them. Always taking them Care packages. Perhaps you know them. The Drexlers?'

I frowned and rubbed my jaw thoughtfully. 'Not the couple who live in –' I snapped my fingers as if the street name were on the tip of my tongue '– where is it now?'

'Steglitz,' he said, prompting me. 'Handjery Strasse.'

I shook my head. 'No, I must be thinking of someone else. Sorry.'

'Hey, don't mention it.'

'I suppose the police must have asked you a lot of questions about Captain Linden's murder.'

'Nope. They asked us nothing, on account of the fact that they already got the guy who did it.'

'They've got someone? That is good news. Who is he?'

'Some Austrian.'

'But why did he do it? Did he say?'

'Nope. Crazy, I guess. How d'you meet the captain, anyway?'

'I met him at a nightclub. The Gay Island.'

'Yeah, I know it. Never go there myself. Me, I prefer those places down on the Ku-damm: Ronny's Bar, and the Club Royale. But Linden used to go to the Gay Island a lot. He had a lot of German friends, I guess, and that's where they liked to go.'

'Well, he spoke such good German.'

'That he did, sir. Like a native.'

'My wife and I used to wonder why he never had a regular girl. We even offered to introduce him to some. Nice girls, from good families.'

The soldier shrugged. 'Too busy, I guess.' He chuckled. 'He sure had plenty of others. Gee, that man liked to frat.'

After a moment I realized he meant fraternize, which was the euphemism in general military usage for what another American officer was doing to my wife. I squeezed my knee experimentally and stood up.

'Sure you're all right now?' said the soldier.

'Yes, thank you. You have been most kind.'

'Kind, nothing. Any friend of Captain Linden's . . .'

8

I inquired after the Drexlers at the Steglitz local post office on Sintenis Platz, a quiet, peaceful square, once covered in grass and now given over to the cultivation of things edible.

The postmistress, a woman with an enormous Ionic curl on either side of her head, informed me crisply that her office knew of the Drexlers and that like most people in the area they collected their mail from the office. Therefore, she explained, their precise address on Handjery Strasse was not known. But she did add that the Drexlers' usually considerable mail was now even larger in view of the fact that it was several days since they had bothered to collect it. She used the word 'bothered' with more than a little distaste, and I wondered if there was some reason she should have disliked the Drexlers. My offer to deliver their mail was swiftly rebuffed. That would not have been proper. But she told me that I could certainly remind them to come and take it away as it was becoming a nuisance.

Next I decided to try at the Schönberg Police Praesidium on nearby Grünewald Strasse. Walking there, under the uneasy shadow of gorgonzola walls that leaned forwards as if permanently on tiptoe, past buildings otherwise unscathed but with just a corner balustrade missing, like an illicitly sampled wedding cake, took me right by the Gay Island nightclub, where Becker had reportedly met Captain Linden. It was a dreary, cheerless-looking place with a cheap neon sign, and I felt almost glad that it was closed.

The bull on the desk at the Police Praesidium had a face as long as a mandarin's thumbnail, but he was an obliging sort of fellow and while he consulted the local registration records he told me that the Drexlers were not unknown to the Schönberg police.

'They're a Jewish couple,' he explained. 'Lawyers. Quite well known around here. You might even say that they were notorious.'

'Oh? Why's that?'

'It's not that they break any laws, you understand.' The sergeant's wurst-sized finger found their name in his ledger and traversed the page to the street and the number. 'Here we are. Handjery Strasse. Number seventeen.'

'Thank you, Sergeant. So what is it about them?'

'Are you a friend of theirs?' He sounded circumspect.

'No, I'm not.'

'Well sir, it's just that people don't like that kind of thing. They want to forget about what happened. I don't think there's any good in raking over the past like that.'

'Forgive me, Sergeant, but what is it that they do exactly?'

'They hunt so-called Nazi war-criminals, sir.'

I nodded. 'Yes, I can see how that might not make them very popular with the neighbours.'

'It was wrong what happened. But we have to rebuild, start again. And we can hardly do that if the war follows us around like a bad smell.'

I needed some more information from him, so I agreed. Then I asked about the Gay Island.

'It's not the sort of place I'd let my missus catch me in, sir. It's run by a sparkler called Kathy Fiege. The place is full of them. But there's never any trouble there, apart from the occasional drunken Yank. Not that you can call that trouble. And if the rumours are true we'll all be Yanks soon – leastways all of us in the American sector, eh?'

I thanked him and walked to the station door. 'One more thing, sergeant,' I said, turning on my heels. 'The Drexlers? Do they ever find any war-criminals?'

The sergeant's long face took on an amused, sly aspect.

'Not if we can help it, sir.'

The Drexlers lived a short way south from the Police Praesidium, in a recently renovated building close to the S–Bahn line and opposite a small school. But there was no reply when I knocked at the door of their top-floor apartment.

I lit a cigarette to rid my nostrils of the strong smell of disinfectant that hung about the landing, and knocked again. Glancing down I saw two cigarette-ends lying, unaccountably uncollected, on the floor close to the door. It didn't look as if anyone had been through the door in a while. Bending down to pick them up I found the smell even stronger. Dropping into a press-up position I pushed my nose up to the gap between floor and door and retched as the air inside the apartment caught my throat and lungs. I rolled quickly away and coughed half my insides on to the stairs below.

When I had recovered my breath I stood up and shook my head. It seemed hardly possible that anyone could live in such an atmosphere. I glanced down the stairwell. There was nobody about.

I stepped back from the door and kicked hard at the lock with my better leg, but it budged hardly at all. Once more I checked the stairwell to see if the noise had drawn anyone out of their apartment and, finding myself undetected, I kicked again.

The door sprang open and a terrible, pestilent smell flew forth, so strong that I reeled back for a moment and almost fell downstairs. Pulling my coat lapel across my nose and mouth I bounded into the darkened apartment, and, spying the faint outline of a curtain valance, I tore the heavy velvet drapes aside and threw open the window.

Cold air stripped the tears from my eyes as I leaned into the fresh air. Children on their way home from school waved to me and weakly I waved back at them.

When I was sure that the draught between the door and the window had ventilated the room I ducked inside to find whatever I would find. I didn't think it was the kind of smell that was meant to take care of any pest smaller than a rogue elephant.

I went over to the front door and pushed it back and forwards on its hinges to fan some more clean air through while I surveyed the desk, the chairs, the bookcases, the filing cabinets and the piles of books and papers that filled the little room. Beyond was an open door, and the edge of a brass bedstead.

My foot kicked something on the floor as I moved towards the bedroom. A cheap tin tray of the kind you find in a bar or a café.

But for the congestion in the two faces that lay side by side on their pillows, you might have thought they were still sleeping. If your name is on someone's death-card, there are worse ways than asphyxia while asleep to collect it.

I pulled back the quilt and undid Herr Drexler's pyjama top, revealing a well-swollen stomach marbled with veins and blebs like a piece of blue cheese. I pressed it with my forefinger: it felt tight. Sure enough, a harder pressure with my hand produced a fart from the corpse, indicating a gaseous disruption of the internal organs. It appeared as if the pair of them had been dead for at least a week.

I drew the quilt over them again and returned to the front room. For a while I stared hopelessly at the books and papers which lay on the desk, even making a desultory attempt to find some clue or other, but since I had as yet only the vaguest appreciation of the puzzle, I soon abandoned this as a waste of time.

Outside, under a mother-of-pearl-coloured sky, I was just starting up the street towards the S–Bahn when something caught my eye. There was so much discarded military equipment still lying about Berlin that, but for the manner of the Drexlers' death, I should have paid the thing no regard. Lying on a heap of rubble that had collected in the gutter was a gas-mask. An empty tin can rolled to my feet as I tugged at the rubber strap. Rapidly colouring in the outline scenario of the murder, I abandoned the mask and squatted down on to the backs of my legs to read the label on the rusting metallic curve.

'Zyklon–B. Poisonous gas! Danger! Keep cool and dry! Protect from the sun and from naked flame. Open and use with extreme caution. Kaliwerke A. G. Kolin.'

In my mind's eye I pictured a man standing outside the Drexlers' door. It was late at night. Nervously he half-smoked a couple of cigarettes before pulling on the gas-mask, checking the straps to make sure he had a tight fit. Then he opened the can of crystallized prussic acid, tipped the pellets – already liquefying on contact with the air – on to the tray he had brought with him, and quickly slid it under the door, into the Drexlers' apartment. The sleeping couple breathed deeply, lapsing into unconsciousness as the Zyklon–B gas, first used on human beings in the concentration camps, started to block the uptake of oxygen in their blood. Small chance that the Drexlers would have left a window open in this weather. But perhaps the murderer laid something – a coat or a blanket – across the bottom of the door to prevent a draught of fresh air into the apartment, or to prevent anyone else in the building from being killed. One part in two thousand of the gas was lethal. Finally, after fifteen or twenty minutes, when the pellets were fully dissolved, and the murderer was satisfied that the gas had done its silent, deadly work – that two more Jews had, for whatever reason, joined the six million – he would have collected up his coat, his mask and his empty can (perhaps he hadn't meant to leave the tray: not that it mattered, he would surely have worn gloves to handle the Zyklon–B), and walked into the night.

You could almost admire its simplicity.

9

Somewhere, further up the street, a jeep grumbled off into the snow-charged blackness. I wiped the condensation off the window with my sleeve, and saw the reflection of a face that I recognized.

'Herr Günther,' he said, as I turned in my seat, 'I thought it was you.' A thin layer of snow covered the man's head. With its squared-off skull and prominent, perfectly round ears, it reminded me of an ice-bucket.

'Neumann,' I said, 'I thought you were dead for sure.'

He wiped his head and took off his coat. 'Mind if I join you? My girl hasn't turned up yet.'

'When did you ever have a girl, Neumann? At least, one you hadn't already paid for.'

He twitched nervously. 'Look, if you're going to be –'

'Relax,' I said. 'Sit down.' I waved to the waiter. 'What will you have?'

'Just a beer, thanks.' He sat down and with narrowed eyes regarded me critically. 'You haven't changed much, Herr Günther. Older-looking, a bit greyer, and rather thinner than you used to be, but still the same.'

'I hate to think what I'd be like if you thought I looked any different,' I said pointedly. 'But what you say sounds like a fairly accurate description of eight years.'

'Is that how long it's been? Since we last met?'

'Give or take a world war. You still listening at keyholes?'

'Herr Günther, you don't know the half of it,' he snorted. 'I'm a prison warder at Tegel.'

'I don't believe it. You? You're as bent as a stolen rocking-chair.'

'Honest, Herr Günther, it's true. The Yanks have got me guarding Nazi war-criminals.'

'And you're the hard-labour, right?'

Neumann twitched again.

'Here comes your beer.'

The waiter laid the glass in front of him. I started to speak but the Americans at the next table burst into loud laughter. Then one of them, a sergeant, said something else and this time even Neumann laughed.

'He said that he doesn't believe in fraternization,' Neumann explained. 'He said he doesn't want to treat any fräulein the way he'd treat his brother.'

I smiled and looked over at the Americans. 'Did you learn to speak English working in Tegel?'

'Sure. I learn a lot of things.'

'You were always a good informer.'

'For instance,' he lowered his voice, 'I heard that the Soviets stopped a British military train at the border to take off two cars containing German passengers. The word is that it's in retaliation for the establishment of Bizonia.' He meant the merging of the British and American zones of Germany. Neumann drank some of his beer and shrugged. 'Maybe there will be another war.'

'I don't see how,' I said. 'Nobody's got much stomach for another dose of it.'

'I dunno. Maybe.'

He set his glass down and produced a box of snuff which he offered to me. I shook my head and grimaced as I watched him take a pinch and slide it under his lip.

'Did you see any action during the war?'

'Come on, Neumann, you should know better. Nobody asks a question like that these days. Do you hear me asking how you got a denazification certificate?'

'I'll have you know that I got that quite legitimately.' He fished out his wallet and unfolded a piece of paper. 'I was never involved in anything. Free from Nazi infection this says, and that's what I am, and proud of it. I didn't even join the army.'

'Only because they wouldn't have you.'

'Free from Nazi infection,' he repeated angrily.

'Must be about the only infection you never had.'

'What are you doing here anyway?' he sneered back.

'I love coming to the Gay Island.'

'I've never seen you here before, and I've been coming here a while.'

'Yes, it looks like the kind of place you'd feel comfortable in. But how do you afford it, on a warder's pay?'

Neumann shrugged evasively.

'You must do a lot of errands for people,' I suggested.

'Well, you have to, don't you.' He smiled thinly. 'I'll bet you're here on a case, aren't you?'

'Maybe.'

'I might be able to help. Like I say, I come here a lot.'

'All right then.' I took out my wallet and held up a five-dollar bill. 'You ever hear of a man called Eddy Holl? He comes in here sometimes. He's in the advertising and publicity business. A firm called Reklaue & Werbe Zentrale.'

Neumann swallowed and stared dismally at the bill. 'No,' he said reluctantly, 'I don't know him. But I could ask around. The barman's a friend. He might –'

'I already tried him. Not the talkative type. But from what he did say, I don't think he knew Holl.'

'This advertising mob. What did you say they were called?'

'Reklaue & Werbe Zentrale. They're in Wilmersdorfer Strasse. I was there this afternoon. According to them Herr Eddy Holl is at the offices of their parent company in Pullach.'

'Well, maybe he is. In Pullach.'

'I've never even heard of it. I can't imagine the headquarters of anything being in Pullach.'

'Well, you'd be wrong.'

'All right,' I said. 'I'm ready to be surprised.'

Neumann smiled and nodded at the five dollars I was slipping back into my wallet. 'For five dollars I could tell you everything I know about it.'

'No cold cabbage.'

He nodded and I tossed him the bill. 'This had better be good.'

'Pullach is a small suburb of Munich. It is also the headquarters of the Postal Censorship Authorities of the United States Army. The mail for all the GIs at Tegel has to go through there.'

'Is that it?'

'What do you want, the average rainfall?'

'All right, I'm not sure what that tells me, but thanks anyway.'

'Maybe I can keep my eyes open for this Eddy Holl.'

'Why not? I'm off to Vienna tomorrow. When I get there I'll telegraph you with the address where I'll be staying in case you get something. Cash on delivery.'

'Christ, I wish I was going. I love Vienna.'

'You never struck me as the cosmopolitan type, Neumann.'

'I don't suppose you fancy delivering a few letters when you're there, do you? I've got quite a few Austrians on my landing.'

'What, play postman for Nazi war-criminals? No thanks.' I finished my drink and looked at my watch. 'You think she's coming, this girl of yours?' I stood up to leave.

'What time is it?' he said, frowning.

I showed him the face of the Rolex on my wrist. I had more or less decided not to sell it. Neumann winced as he saw the time.

'I expect she got held up,' I said.

He shook his head sadly. 'She won't come now. Women.'

I gave him a cigarette. 'These days the only woman you can trust is another man's wife.'

'It's a rotten world, Herr Günther.'

'Yeah, well, don't tell anyone, will you.'

10

On the train to Vienna I met a man who talked about what we had done to the Jews.

'Look,' he said, 'they can't blame us for what happened. It was preordained. We were merely fulfilling their own Old Testament prophecy: the one about Joseph and his brothers. There you have Joseph, a repressive father's youngest and most favoured son, and whom we can take to be symbolic of the whole Jewish race. And then you have all the other brothers, symbolic of gentiles everywhere, but let's assume they are Germans who are quite naturally jealous of the little velvet boy. He's better looking than they are. He has a coat of many colours. My God, no wonder they hate him. No wonder they sell him into slavery. But the important point to note is that what the brothers do is as much a reaction against a stern and authoritarian father – a fatherland if you like – as it is against an apparently over-privileged brother.' The man shrugged and started to knead the lobe of one of his question-mark shaped ears thoughtfully. 'Really, when you think about it, they ought to thank us.'

'How do you work that out?' I said, with considerable want of faith.

'Had it not been for what Joseph's brothers did, the children of Israel would never have been enslaved in Egypt, would never have been led to the Promised Land by Moses. Similarly, had it not been for what we Germans did, the Jews would never have gone back to Palestine. Why even now, they are on the verge of establishing a new state.' The man's little eyes narrowed as if he had been one of the few allowed a peek in God's desk-diary. 'Oh yes,' he said, 'it was a prophecy fulfilled, all right.'

'I don't know about any prophecy,' I growled, and jerked my thumb at the scene skimming by the carriage window: an apparently

endless Red Army troop convoy, moving south along the autobahn, parallel to the railway line, 'but it certainly looks like we
ended up in the Red Sea.'

It was well named, this infinite column of savage, omnivorous
red ants, ravaging the land and gathering all that they could carry –
more than their individual body weights – to take back to their
semi-permanent, worker-run colonies. And like some Brazilian
planter who had seen his coffee crop devastated by these social
creatures, my hatred of the Russians was tempered by an equal
measure of respect. For seven long years I had fought them, killed
them, been imprisoned by them, learned their language and finally
escaped from one of their labour camps. Seven thin ears of corn
blasted with the east wind, devouring the seven good ears.

At the outbreak of the war I had been a Kriminalkommissar in
Section 5 of the RSHA, the Reich Main Security Office, and
automatically ranked as a full lieutenant in the SS. Apart from the
oath of loyalty to Adolf Hitler, my being an SS-Obersturmführer
had not seemed much of a problem until June 1941, when Arthur
Nebe, formerly the director of the Reichs Criminal Police, and
newly promoted SS-Gruppenführer, was given command of an
Action Group as part of the invasion of Russia.

I was just one of the various police personnel who were drafted
to Nebe's group, the aim of which, so I believed, was to follow the
Wehrmacht into occupied White Russia and combat lawbreak-
ing and terrorism of whatever description. My own duties at the
Group's Minsk headquarters had involved the seizure of the
records of the Russian NKVD and the capture of an NKVD
death-squad that had massacred hundreds of White Russian political prisoners to prevent them from being liberated by the German
Army. But mass murder is endemic in any war of conquest, and it
soon became apparent to me that my own side was also arbitrarily
massacring Russian prisoners. Then came the discovery that the
primary purpose of the Action Groups was not the elimination of
terrorists but the systematic murder of Jewish civilians.

In all my four years' service in the first, Great War, I never saw anything which had a more devastating effect on my spirit than what I witnessed in the summer of 1941. Although I was not personally charged with the task of commanding any of these mass-execution squads, I reasoned that it could only be a matter of time before I was so ordered, and, as an inevitable corollary, before I was shot for refusing to obey. So I requested an immediate transfer to the Wehrmacht and the front line.

As the commanding general of the Action Group, Nebe could have had me sent to a punishment battalion. He could even have ordered my execution. Instead he acceded to my request for a transfer, and after several more weeks in White Russia, during which time I assisted General Gehlen's Foreign Armies East Intelligence Section with the organization of the captured NKVD records, I was transferred, not to the front line, but to the War Crimes Bureau of the Military High Command in Berlin. By that time Arthur Nebe had personally supervised the murders of over 30,000 men, women and children.

After my return to Berlin I never saw him again. Years later I met an old friend from Kripo who told me that Nebe, always an ambiguous sort of Nazi, had been executed in early 1945 as one of the members of Count Stauffenberg's plot to kill Hitler.

It always gave me a strange kind of feeling to know that I very possibly owed my life to a mass-murderer.

To my great relief, the man with the curious line in hermeneutics left the train at Dresden, and I slept between there and Prague. But most of the time I thought about Kirsten and the abruptly worded note I had left her, explaining that I would be away for several weeks and accounting for the presence of the gold sovereigns in the apartment, which constituted half of my fee for taking Becker's case, and which Poroshin had taken it upon himself to deliver the previous day.

I cursed myself for not writing more, for failing to say that there was nothing I wouldn't have done for her, no Herculean labour I would not have gladly performed on her behalf. All of this she knew of course, made manifest as it was in the packet of extravagantly worded letters that she kept in her drawer. Next to her unmentioned bottle of Chanel.

The journey between Berlin and Vienna is a long time to spend brooding about the infidelity of your wife, so it was just as well that Poroshin's aide had got me a ticket on a train that took the most direct route – nineteen and a half hours, via Dresden, Prague and Brno – as opposed to the twenty-seven-and-a-half-hour train which went via Leipzig and Nuremberg. With a screech of wheels the train drew slowly to a halt in Franz Josefs Bahnhof, mantling the platform's few occupants in a steamy limbo.

At the ticket barrier I presented my papers to an American MP and, having explained my presence in Vienna to his satisfaction, walked into the station, dropped my bag and looked around for some sign that my arrival was both expected and welcomed by someone in the small crowd of waiting people.

The approach of a medium-sized, grey-haired man signalled that I was correct in the first of these calculations, although I was soon to be apprised of the vanity of the second. He informed me that his name was Dr Liebl and that he had the honour of acting as Emil Becker's legal representative.

'I have a taxi waiting,' he said, glancing uncertainly at my luggage. 'Even so, it isn't very far to my offices and had you brought a smaller bag we might have walked there.'

'I know it sounds pessimistic,' I said, 'but I rather thought I'd have to stay overnight.'

I followed him across the station floor.

'I trust that you had a good journey, Herr Günther.'

'I'm here, aren't I?' I said, forcing an affable sort of chuckle. 'How else does one define a good journey these days?'

'I really couldn't say,' he said crisply. 'Myself, I never leave Vienna.' He waved his hand dismissively at a group of ragged-looking DPs who seemed to have camped out in the station. 'Today, with the whole world on some kind of journey, it seems imprudent that I should expect God to look out for the kind of traveller who would only wish to be able to return from whence he started.'

He ushered me to a waiting taxi, and I handed my bag to the driver and climbed into the back seat, only to find the bag come after me again.

'There's an extra charge for luggage carried outside,' Liebl explained, pushing the bag on to my lap. 'As I said, it's not very far and taxis are expensive. While you're here I recommend that you use the tramways – it's a very good service.' The car moved away at speed, the first corner pressing us together like a couple of lovers in a cinema theatre. Liebl chuckled. 'It's also a lot safer, Viennese drivers being what they are.'

I pointed to our left. 'Is that the Danube?'

'Good God, no. That's the canal. The Danube is in the Russian sector, further east.' He pointed to our right, at a grim-looking building. 'That's the police prison, where our client is currently residing. We have an appointment there first thing tomorrow, after which you may wish to attend Captain Linden's funeral at the Central Cemetery.' Liebl nodded back at the prison. 'Herr Becker is not long in there, as it happens. The Americans were initially disposed to treat the case as a matter of military security and as a result they held him in their POW cage at the Stiftskaserne – the headquarters of their military police in Vienna. I had the very devil of a job getting in and out of there, I can tell you. However, the Military Government Public Safety Officer has now decided that the case is one for the Austrian courts, and so he'll be held there until the trial, whenever that may be.'

Liebl leaned forwards, tapped the driver on the shoulder and told him to make a right and head towards the General Hospital.

'Now that we're paying for this, we may as well drop your bag off,' he said. 'It's only a short detour. At least you've seen where your friend is, so you can appreciate the gravity of his situation.

'I don't wish to be rude, Herr Günther, but I should tell you that I was against you coming to Vienna at all. It isn't as if there aren't any private detectives here. There are. I've used many of them myself, and they know Vienna better than you. I hope you won't mind me saying that. I mean, you don't know this city at all, do you?'

'I appreciate your frankness, Dr Liebl,' I said, not appreciating it much at all. 'And you're right, I don't know this city. As a matter of fact I've never been here in my life. So let me speak frankly. With twenty-five years of police work behind me I'm not particularly disposed to give much of a damn what you think. Why Becker should hire me instead of some local sniffer is his business. The fact that he's prepared to pay me generously is mine. There's nothing in between, for you or anyone else. Not now. When you get to court I'll sit on your lap and comb your hair if you want me to. But until then you read your lawbooks and I'll worry about what you're going to say that'll get the stupid bastard off.'

'Good enough,' Liebl growled, his mouth teetering on the edge of a smile. 'Veracity becomes you rather well. Like most lawyers I have a sneaking admiration for people who seem to believe what they say. Yes, I have a high regard for the probity of others, if only because we lawyers are so brimful of artifice.'

'I thought you spoke plainly enough.'

'A mere feint, I asssure you,' he said loftily.

We left my luggage at a comfortable-looking pension in the 8th Bezirk, in the American sector, and drove on to Liebl's office in the inner city. Like Berlin, Vienna was divided among the Four Powers, with each of them controlling a separate sector. The only difference was that Vienna's inner city, surrounded by the wide open boulevard of grand hotels and palaces that was called the Ring, was under the control of all four Powers at once in the shape of the International Patrol. Another, more immediately noticeable difference was in the Austrian capital's state of repair. It was true the city had been bombed about a bit, but compared with Berlin Vienna looked tidier than an undertaker's shop window.

When at last we were sitting in Liebl's office, he found Becker's files and ran through the facts of the case with me.

'Naturally, the strongest piece of evidence against Herr Becker is his possession of the murder weapon,' Liebl said, handing me a couple of photographs of the gun which had killed Captain Linden.

'Walther P38,' I said. 'SS handgrip. I used one myself in the last year of the war. They rattle a bit, but once the unusual trigger pull is mastered you can generally shoot them fairly accurately. I never much cared for the external hammer though. No, I prefer the PPK myself.' I handed back the pictures. 'Do you have any of the pathologist's snaps of the captain?'

Liebl passed me an envelope with evident distaste.

'Funny how they look when they're all cleaned up again,' I said as I looked at the photographs. 'You shoot a man in the face with a .38 and he looks no worse than if he'd had a mole removed. Good-looking son of a bitch, I'll say that much for him. Did they find the bullet?'

'Next picture.'

I nodded as I found it. Not much to kill a man, I thought.

'The police also found several cartons of cigarettes at Herr Becker's home,' said Liebl. 'Cigarettes of the same kind that were in the old studio where Linden was shot.'

I shrugged. 'He likes to smoke. I don't see what a few boxes of nails can pin on him.'

'No? Then let me explain. These were cigarettes stolen from the tobacco factory on Thaliastrasse, which is quite near the studio. Whoever stole the cigarettes was using the studio to store them. When Becker first found Captain Linden's body he helped himself to a few cartons before he went home.'

'That sounds like Becker, all right,' I sighed. 'He always did have long fingers.'

'Well, it's the length of his neck that matters now. I need not remind you that this is a capital case, Herr Günther.'

'You can remind me of it as often as you think fit, Herr Doktor. Tell me, who owned the studio?'

'Drittemann Film und Senderaum GMBH. At least that was the name of the company on the lease. But nobody seems to remember any films being made there. When the police searched the place they didn't find so much as an old spotlight.'

'Could I get a look inside?'

'I'll see if I can arrange it. Now, if you have any more questions, Herr Günther, I suggest that you save them until tomorrow morning when we see Herr Becker. Meanwhile, there are one or two arrangements that you and I must conclude, such as the balance of your fee, and your expenses. Please excuse me for a moment while I get your money from the safe.' He stood up and went out of the room.

Liebl's practice, in Judengasse, was on the first floor of a shoemaker's shop. When he came back into his office carrying two bundles of banknotes, he found me standing at the window.

'Two thousand five hundred American dollars, in cash, as agreed,' he said coolly, 'and 1,000 Austrian schillings to cover your expenses. Any more will need to be authorized by Fräulein Braunsteiner – she's Herr Becker's girlfriend. The costs of your accommodation will be taken care of by this office.' He handed me a pen. 'Will you sign this receipt, please?'

I glanced over the writing and signed. 'I'd like to meet her,' I said. 'I'd like to meet all Becker's friends.'

'My instructions are that she will contact you at your pension.'

I pocketed the money and returned to the window.

'I trust that if the police pick you up with all those dollars, I may rely on your discretion? There are currency regulations which –'

'I'll leave your name out of it, don't worry. As a matter of interest, what's to stop me taking the money and returning home?'

'You merely echo my own warning to Herr Becker. In the first place, he said that you were an honourable man, and that if you were paid to do a job, you would do it. Not the type to leave him to hang. He was quite dogmatic about it.'

'I'm touched,' I said. 'And in the second place?'

'Can I be frank?'

'Why stop now?'

'Very well. Herr Becker is one of the worst racketeers in Vienna. Despite his present predicament he is not entirely without influence in certain, shall we say, more nefarious quarters of this city.' His face looked pained. 'I should be reluctant to say any more at the risk of sounding like a common thug.'

'That's quite candid enough, Herr Doktor. Thank you.'

He came over to the window. 'What are you looking at?'

'I think I'm being followed. Do you see that man —?'

'The man reading the newspaper?'

'I'm sure I saw him at the railway station.'

Liebl removed his spectacles from his top pocket and bent them round his furry old ears. 'He doesn't look Austrian,' he pronounced finally. 'What paper is he reading?'

I squinted for a moment. 'The *Wiener Kurier*.'

'Hmm. Not a Communist, anyway. He's probably an American, a field agent from the Special Investigation Section of their military police.'

'Wearing plainclothes?'

'I believe that they are no longer required to wear uniform. At least in Vienna.' He removed his glasses and turned away. 'I dare say it'll be something routine. They'll want to know all about any friend of Herr Becker. You should expect to be pulled in sometime, for questioning.'

'Thanks for the warning.' I started to move away from the window but found my hand lingered on the big shutter, with its solid-looking cross bar. 'They certainly knew how to build these old places, didn't they? This thing looks as if it was meant to keep out an army.'

'Not an army, Herr Günther. A mob. This was once the heart of the ghetto. In the fifteenth century, when the house was built, they had to be prepared for the occasional pogrom. Nothing changes so very much, does it?'

I sat down opposite him and smoked a Memphis from the packet I had brought from Poroshin's supplies. I waved the packet at Liebl who took one and put it carefully into a cigarette-case. He and I hadn't had the best of starts. It was time to repair a few bridges. 'Keep the pack,' I told him.

'You're very kind,' he said, handing me an ashtray in return.

Watching him light one now, I wondered what genealogy of debauch had jaspered his once handsome face. His grey cheeks were heavily wrinked with almost glacial striations, and his nose was slightly puckered, as if someone had told a sick joke. His lips were very red and very thin and he smiled like a wily old snake, which only served to enhance the look of dissipation that the years, and, most probably, the war had etched on his features. He himself provided an explanation.

'I was in a concentration camp for a while. Before the war I was a member of the Christian Social Party. You know, people prefer to forget, but there was a very great feeling for Hitler in Austria.' He coughed a little as the first smoke filled his lungs. 'It is very convenient for us that the Allies decided that Austria was a victim of Nazi aggression instead of a collaborator with it. But it is also absurd. We are perfect bureaucrats, Herr Günther. It is remarkable the number of Austrians who came to occupy crucial roles in the organization of Hitler's crimes. And many of these same men – and quite a few Germans – are living right here in Vienna. Even now the Security Directorate for Upper Austria is investigating the theft of a number of identity cards from the Vienna State Printing Office. So you can see that for those who wish to stay here, there is always a means of doing so. The truth is that these men, these Nazis, enjoy living in my country. They have five hundred years of Jew-hatred to make them feel at home.

'I mention these things because as a *pifke –*' he smiled apologetically '– as a Prussian, you may find that you encounter a certain amount of hostility in Vienna. These days Austrians tend to reject everything German. They work very hard at being Austrian. An accent like yours might serve to remind some Viennese that for seven years they were National Socialists. An unpalatable fact that most people now prefer to believe was little more than a bad dream.'

'I'll bear it in mind.'

When I finished my meeting with Liebl I went back to the pension in Skodagasse, where I found a message from Becker's girlfriend to say that she would drop by around six to make sure that I was comfortable. The Pension Caspian was a first-class little place. I had a bedroom with a small adjoining sitting-room and bathroom. There was even a tiny covered veranda where I might have sat in summer. The place was warm and there seemed to be a never-ending supply of hot water – an unaccustomed luxury. I had not long finished a bath, the duration of which even Marat might have baulked at, when there was a knock at my sitting-room door, and, glancing at my wristwatch, I saw that it was almost six. I slipped into my overcoat and opened the door.

She was small and bright-eyed, with a child's rosy cheeks and dark hair that looked as if it rarely felt a comb. Her well-toothed smile straightened a little as she saw my bare feet.

'Herr Günther?' she said, hesitantly.

'Fräulein Traudl Braunsteiner.'

She nodded.

'Come in. I'm afraid I spent rather longer in the bath than I should have, but the last time I had really hot water was when I came back from the Soviet labour camp. Have a seat while I throw on some clothes.'

When I came back into the sitting-room I saw that she had brought a bottle of vodka and was pouring two glasses out on a table by the French window. She handed me my drink and we sat down.

'Welcome to Vienna,' she said. 'Emil said I should bring you a bottle.' She kicked the bag by her leg. 'Actually I brought two. They've been hanging out of the window of the hospital all day, so the vodka is nice and cold. I don't like vodka any other way.'

We clinked glasses and drank, the bottom of her glass beating my own to the table-top.

'You're not unwell, I hope? You mentioned a hospital.'

'I'm a nurse, at the General. You can see it if you walk to the top of the street. That's partly why I booked you in here – because it's so near. But also because I know the owner, Frau Blum-Weiss. She was a friend of my mother's. Also I thought you'd prefer to stay close to the Ring, and to the place where the American captain was shot. That's in Dettergasse, on the other side of Vienna's outer ring, the Gürtel.'

'This place suits me very nicely. To be honest it's a lot more comfortable than what I'm used to at home, back in Berlin. Things are quite hard there.' I poured us another drink. 'Exactly how much do you know about what happened?'

'I know everything that Dr Liebl has told you; and everything that Emil will tell you tomorrow morning.'

'What about Emil's business?'

Traudl Braunsteiner smiled coyly and uttered a little snigger. 'There's not much I don't know about Emil's business either.' Noticing a button that was hanging by a thread from her crumpled raincoat, she tugged it off and pocketed it. She was like a fine lace handkerchief that was in need of laundering. 'Being a nurse, I guess I'm a little relaxed about that sort of thing: black market. I've stolen a few drugs myself, I don't mind admitting it. Actually, all the girls do it at some time or another. For some it's a simple choice: sell penicillin or sell your body. I guess we are lucky enough to have something else to sell.' She shrugged and swallowed her second vodka. 'Seeing people suffering and dying doesn't breed a very healthy respect for law and order.' She laughed apologetically. 'Money's no good if you're not fit to spend it. God, what are the Krupp family worth? Billions probably. But they've got one of them at an insane asylum here in Vienna.'

'It's all right,' I said. 'I wasn't asking you to justify it to me.' But plainly she was trying to justify it to herself.

Traudl tucked her legs underneath her behind. She sat carelessly in the armchair, not seeming to mind any more than I did that I could see her stocking-tops and garters, and the edge of her smooth, white thighs.

'What can you do?' she said, biting her fingernail. 'Now and again everyone in Vienna has to buy something that's a bit Ressel

Park.' She explained that this was the city's main centre for the black market.

'It's the Brandenburg Gate in Berlin,' I said. 'And in front of the Reichstag.'

'How funny,' she chuckled mischievously. 'There would be a scandal in Vienna if that sort of thing went on outside our parliament.'

'That's because you have a parliament. Here the Allies just supervise. But they actually govern in Germany.' My view of her underwear disappeared now as she tugged at the hem of her skirt.

'I didn't know that. Not that it would matter. There would still be a scandal in Vienna, parliament or no parliament. Austrians are such hypocrites. You would think they would feel easier about these things. There's been a black market here since the Habsburgs. It wasn't cigarettes then of course, but favours, patronage. Personal contacts still count for a lot.'

'Speaking of which, how did you meet Becker?'

'He fixed some papers for a friend of mine, a nurse at the hospital. And we stole some penicillin for him. That was when there was still some about. This wasn't long after my mother died.' Her bright eyes widened as if she was struggling to comprehend something. 'She threw herself under a tram.' Forcing a smile and a bemused sort of laugh, she managed to contain her feelings. 'My mother was a very Viennese type of Austrian, Bernie. We're always committing suicide, you know. It's a way of life for us.

'Anyway, Emil was very kind and great fun. He took me away from my grief, really. I've no other family, you see. My father was killed in an air-raid. And my brother died in Yugoslavia, fighting the partisans. Without Emil I really don't know what might have become of me. If something were to happen to him now –' Traudl's mouth stiffened as she pictured the fate that seemed most likely to befall her lover. 'You will do your best for him, won't you? Emil said you were the only person he could trust to find something that might give him half a chance.'

'I'll do everything I can for him, Traudl, you have my word on that.' I lit us both a cigarette and handed one to her. 'It may interest you to know that normally I'd convict my own mother if she were standing over a dead body with a gun in her hand. But for what it's worth I believe Becker's story, if only because it's so plausibly bad. At least until I've heard it from him. That may not surprise you very much, but it sure as hell impresses me.

'Only look at my fingertips. They're a little short on saintly aura. And the hat on the sideboard there? It wasn't meant for stalking deer. So if I'm to guide him out of that condemned cell your boyfriend is going to have to find me a ball of thread. Tomorrow morning, he'd better have something to say for himself or this show won't be worth the price of the greasepaint.'

12

The Law's most terrible punishment is always what happens in a man's own imagination: the prospect of one's own, judicially executed killing is food for thought of the most ingeniously masochistic kind. To put a man on trial for his life is to fill his mind with thoughts crueller than any punishment yet devised. And naturally enough the idea of what it must be like to drop metres through a trap-door, to be brought up short of the ground by a length of rope tied round the neck takes its toll on a man. He finds it hard to sleep, loses his appetite, and not uncommonly his heart starts to suffer under the strain of what his own mind has imposed. Even the most dull, unimaginative intellect need only roll his head around on his shoulders, and listen to the crunching gristle sound of his vertebrae in order to appreciate, in the pit of his stomach, the ghastly horror of hanging.

So I was not surprised to find Becker a thinner, etiolated sketch of his former self. We met in a small, barely furnished interview room at the prison on Rossauer Lände. When he came into the room he silently shook me by the hand before turning to address the warder who had stationed himself against the door.

'Hey, Pepi,' Becker said jovially, 'do you mind?' He reached inside his shirt pocket and retrieved a packet of cigarettes which he tossed across the room. The warder called Pepi caught them with the tips of his fingers and inspected the brand. 'Have a smoke outside the door, OK?'

'All right,' said Pepi, and left.

Becker nodded appreciatively as the three of us seated ourselves round the table bolted to the yellow-tiled wall.

'Don't worry,' he said to Dr Liebl. 'All the warders are at it in here. Much better than the Stiftskaserne, I can tell you. None of those fucking Yanks could be greased. There's nothing those bastards want that they can't get for themselves.'

'You're telling me,' I said, and found my own cigarettes. Liebl shook his head when I offered him one. 'These come from your friend Poroshin,' I explained as Becker slipped one out of the pack.

'Quite a fellow, isn't he?'

'Your wife thinks he's your boss.'

Becker lit us both and blew a cloud of smoke across my shoulder. 'You spoke to Ella?' he said, but he didn't sound surprised.

'Apart from the five thousand, she's the only reason I'm here,' I said. 'With her on your case I decided you probably needed all the help you could get. As far as she's concerned you're already swinging.'

'Hates me that bad, eh?'

'Like a cold sore.'

'Well she's got the right, I guess.' He sighed and shook his head. Then he took a long, nervous drag of his cigarette that barely left the paper on the tobacco. For a moment he stared at me, his bloodshot eyes blinking hard through the smoke. After several seconds he coughed and smiled all at once. 'Go ahead and ask me.'

'All right. Did you kill Captain Linden?'

'As God is my witness, no.' He laughed. 'Can I go now, sir?' He took another desperate suck at his smoke. 'You do believe me, don't you, Bernie?'

'I believe you'd have a better story if you were lying. I credit you with that much sense. But as I was saying to your girlfriend –'

'You've met Traudl? Good. She's great, isn't she?'

'Yes, she is. Christ only knows what she sees in you.'

'She enjoys my after-dinner conversation of course. That's why she doesn't like to see me locked up in here. She misses our little fireside chats about Wittgenstein.' The smile disappeared as his hand reached across the table and clutched at my forearm. 'Look, you've got to get me out of here, Bernie. The five thousand was just to get you in the game. You prove that I'm innocent and I'll treble your fee.'

'We both know that it isn't going to be easy.'

Becker misunderstood.

'Money's not a problem: I've got plenty of money. There's a car parked in a garage in Hernals with $30,000 in the boot. It's yours if you get me off.'

Liebl winced as his client continued to demonstrate his apparent lack of business acumen. 'Really, Herr Becker, as your lawyer I must protest. This is not the way to –'

'Shut up,' Becker said savagely. 'When I want your advice I'll ask for it.'

Liebl gave a diplomatic sort of shrug, and leaned back on his chair.

'Look,' I said, 'let's talk about a bonus when you're out. The money's fine. You've already paid me well. I wasn't talking about the money. No, what I'd like now are a few ideas. So how about you start by telling me about Herr König: where you met him, what he looks like and whether you think he likes cream in his coffee, OK?'

Becker nodded and ground his cigarette out on the floor. He clasped and unclasped his hands and started to squeeze his knuckles uncomfortably. Probably he had been over the story too many times to feel happy about repeating it.

'All right. Well then, let's see. I met Helmut König in the Koralle. That's a nightclub in the 9th Bezirk. Porzellangasse. He just came up and introduced himself. Said he'd heard of me, and wanted to buy me a drink. So I let him. We talked about the usual things. The war, me being in Russia, me being in Kripo before the SS, same as you really. Only you left, didn't you, Bernie?'

'Just keep to the point.'

'He said he'd heard of me from friends. He didn't say who. There was some business he'd like to put my way: a regular delivery across the Green Frontier. Cash money, no questions asked. It was easy. All I had to do was collect a small parcel from an office here in Vienna and take it to another office in Berlin. But only when I was going anyway, with a lorry load of cigarettes, that kind of thing. If I'd been picked up they probably wouldn't even have noticed König's parcel. At first I thought it was drugs. But then I opened one of the parcels. It was just a few files: Party files, army files, SS files. The old stuff. I couldn't see what made it worth money to them.'

'Was it always just files?'

He nodded.

'Captain Linden worked for the US Documents Centre in Berlin,' I explained. 'He was a Nazi-hunter. These files – do you remember any names?'

'Bernie, they were tadpoles, small fry. SS corporals and army pay-clerks. Any Nazi-hunter would just have thrown them back. Those fellows are after the big fish, people like Bormann and Eichmann. Not fucking little pay-clerks.'

'Nevertheless, the files were important to Linden. Whoever it was that killed him also arranged to have a couple of amateur detectives he knew murdered. Two Jews who had survived the camps and were out to settle a few scores. I found them dead a few days ago. They'd been that way a while. Perhaps the files were for them. So it would help if you could try and remember some of the names.'

'Sure, anything you say, Bernie. I'll try to fit it into my busy schedule.'

'You do that. Now tell me about König. What did he look like?'

'Let's see: he was about forty, I'd say. Well-built, dark, thick moustache, weighed about ninety kilos, one-ninety tall; wore a good tweed suit, smoked cigars and always had a dog with him – a little terrier. He was Austrian for sure. Sometimes he had a girl around. Her name was Lotte. I don't know her surname, but she worked at the Casanova Club. Good-looking bitch, blonde. That's all I remember.'

'You said that you talked about the war. Didn't he tell you how many medals he won?'

'Yes, he did.'

'Then don't you think you should tell me?'

'I didn't think it was relevant.'

'I'll decide what's relevant. Come on, unpack it, Becker.'

He stared at the wall and then shrugged. 'As far as I remember, he said he had joined the Austrian Nazi Party when it was still illegal, in 1931. Later he got himself arrested for putting up posters. So he escaped to Germany to avoid arrest and joined the Bavarian police in Munich. He joined the SS in 1933, and stayed in until the end of the war.'

'Any rank?'

'He didn't say.'

'Did he give you any indication of where he served and in what sort of capacity?'

Becker shook his head.

'Not much of a conversation you two had. What were you reminiscing about, the price of bread? All right. What about the second man – the one who came to your home with König and asked you to look for Linden?'

Becker squeezed his temples. 'I've tried to remember his name, but it just won't come,' he said. 'He was a bit more of the senior officer type. You know, very stiff and proper. An aristocrat, maybe. Again he was aged about forty, tall, thin, clean-shaven, balding. Wore a Schiller jacket and a club-tie.' He shook his head. 'I'm not very good on club-ties. It could have been Herrenklub, I don't know.'

'And the man you saw come out of the studio where Linden was killed: what did he look like?'

'He was too far away for me to see much, except that he was quite short and very stocky. He wore a dark hat and coat and he was in a hurry.'

'I'll bet he was,' I said. 'The publicity firm, Reklaue & Werbe Zentrale. It's on Mariahilferstrasse, isn't it?'

'Was,' Becker said gloomily. 'It closed not long after I was arrested.'

'Tell me about it anyway. Was it always König you saw there?'

'No. It was usually a fellow called Abs, Max Abs. He was an academic-looking type, chin-beard, little glasses, you know.'

Becker helped himself to another of my cigarettes. 'There was one thing I was meaning to tell you. One time I was there I heard Abs take a telephone call, from a stonemason called Pichler. Maybe he had a funeral. I thought that maybe you could find Pichler and find out about Abs when you go to Linden's funeral this morning.'

'At twelve o'clock,' Liebl said.

'I thought that it might be worth a look, Bernie,' Becker explained.

'You're the client,' I said.

'See if any of Linden's friends show up. And then see Pichler. Most of Vienna's stonemasons are along the wall of the Central Cemetery, so it shouldn't be all that difficult to find him. Maybe you can discover if Max Abs left an address when he ordered his piece of stone.'

I didn't much care for having Becker describe my morning's work for me like this, but it seemed easier to humour him. A man facing a possible death sentence can demand certain indulgences of his private investigator. Especially when there's cash up front. So I said, 'Why not? I love a good funeral.' Then I stood up and walked about his cell a bit, as if I were the one who was nervous about being caged in. Maybe he was just more used to it than me.

'There's one thing still puzzling me here,' I said after a minute's thoughtful pacing.

'What's that?'

'Dr Liebl told me that you're not without friends and influence in this city.'

'Up to a point.'

'Well, how is it that none of your so-called friends tried to find König? Or for that matter his girlfriend Lotte?'

'Who's saying they didn't?'

'Are you going to keep it to yourself, or do I have to give you a couple of bars of chocolate?'

Becker's tone turned placatory. 'Now, it's not certain what happened here, Bernie, so I don't want you getting the wrong idea about this job. There's no reason to suppose that —'

'Cut the cold cabbage and just tell me what happened.'

'All right. A couple of my associates, fellows who knew what they were doing, asked around about König and the girl. They checked a few of the nightclubs. And . . .' he winced uncomfortably '. . . they haven't been seen since. Maybe they double-crossed me. Maybe they just left town.'

'Or maybe they got the same as Linden,' I suggested.

'Who knows? But that's why you're here, Bernie. I can trust you. I know the kind of fellow you are. I respect what you did back in Minsk, really I did. You're not the kind to let an innocent man hang.' He smiled meaningfully. 'I can't believe I'm the only one who's had a use for a man of your qualifications.'

'I do all right,' I said quickly, not caring much for flattery, least of all from clients like Emil Becker. 'You know, you probably deserve to hang,' I added. 'Even if you didn't kill Linden, there must have been plenty of others.'

'But I just didn't see it coming. Not until it was too late. Not like you. You were clever, and got out while you still had a choice. I never had that chance. It was obey orders, or face a court martial and a firing squad. I didn't have the courage to do anything other than what I did.'

I shook my head. I really didn't care any more. 'Perhaps you're right.'

'You know I am. We were at war, Bernie.' He finished his cigarette and stood up to face me in the corner where I was leaning. He lowered his voice, as if he meant Liebl not to hear.

'Look,' he said, 'I know this is a dangerous job. But only you can do it. It needs to be done quietly, and privately, the way you do it best. Do you need a lighter?'

I had left the gun I'd taken off the dead Russian in Berlin, having had no wish to risk arrest for crossing a border with a pistol. I doubted that Poroshin's cigarette pass could have sorted that out. So I shrugged and said, 'You tell me. This is your city.'

'I'd say you'll need one.'

'All right,' I said, 'but for Christ's sake make it a clean one.'

When we were outside the prison again Liebl smiled sarcastically and said: 'Is a lighter what I think it is?'

'Yes. But it's just a precaution.'

'The best precaution you can take while you're in Vienna is to stay out of the Russian sector. Especially late at night.'

I followed Liebl's gaze across the road and beyond, to the other side of the canal, where a red flag fluttered in the early morning breeze.

'There are a number of kidnapping gangs working for the Ivans in Vienna,' he explained. 'They snatch anyone they think might be spying for the Americans, and in return they're given black-market concessions to operate out of the Russian sector, which effectively puts them beyond the reach of the law. They took one woman out of her own house rolled up in a carpet, just like Cleopatra.'

'Well, I'll be careful not to fall asleep on the floor,' I said. 'Now, how do I get to the Central Cemetery?'

'It's in the British sector. You need to take a 71 from Schwarzenbergplatz, only your map calls it Stalinplatz. You can't miss it: there's an enormous statue to the Soviet soldier as liberator that we Viennese call the Unknown Plunderer.'

I smiled. 'Like I always say, Herr Doktor, we can survive defeat, but heaven help us from another liberation.'

13

'The city of the other Viennese' was how Traudl Braunsteiner had described it. This was no exaggeration. The Central Cemetery was bigger than several towns of my acquaintance and quite a bit more affluent too. There was no more chance of the average Austrian doing without a headstone than there was of him staying out of his favourite coffee house. It seemed there was nobody who was too poor for a decent piece of marble, and for the first time I began to appreciate the attractions of the undertaking business. A piano keyboard, an inspired muse, the introductory bars of a famous waltz – there was nothing too ornate for Vienna's craftsmen, no flatulent fable or overstated allegory that was beyond the dead hand of their art. The huge necropolis even mirrored the religious and political divisions of its living counterpart, with its Jewish, Protestant and Catholic sections, not to mention those of the Four Powers.

There was quite a turnover of services at the first-wonder-of-the-world-sized chapel where Linden's obsequies were heard, and I found that I had missed the captain's mourners there by only a few minutes.

The little cortège wasn't difficult to spot as it drove slowly across the snowbound park to the French sector where Linden, a Catholic, was to be buried. But for one on foot, as I was, it was rather more difficult to catch up: by the time I did the expensive casket was already being lowered slowly into the dark-brown trench like a dinghy let down into a dirty harbour. The Linden family, arms interlinked in the manner of a squad of riot-police, faced its grief as indomitably as if there had been medals to be won.

The colour party raised their rifles and took aim at the floating snow. It gave me an uncomfortable feeling as they fired, and for just a moment I was back in Minsk when, on a walk to staff head-quarters, I had been summoned by the sound of gunshots: climbing up an embankment I had seen six men and women kneeling at the edge of a mass grave already filled with innumerable bodies, some of whom were still alive, and behind them an SS firing squad commanded by a young police officer. His name was Emil Becker.

'Are you a friend of his?' said a man, an American, appearing behind me.

'No,' I said. 'I came over because you don't expect to hear gunfire in a place like this.' I couldn't tell if the American had been at the funeral already or if he had followed me from the chapel. He didn't look like the man who had been standing outside Liebl's office. I pointed at the grave. 'Tell me, who's the –'

'A fellow called Linden.'

It is difficult for someone who does not speak German as a first language, so I might have been mistaken, but there seemed to be no trace of emotion in the American's voice.

When I had seen enough, and having ascertained that there was nobody even vaguely resembling König among the mourners – not that I really expected to see him there – I walked quietly away. To my surprise I found the American walking alongside me.

'Cremation is so much kinder to the thoughts of the living,' he said. 'It consumes all sorts of hideous imaginings. For me the putrefaction of a loved one is quite unthinkable. It remains in the thoughts with the persistence of a tapeworm. Death is quite bad enough without letting the maggots make a meal of it. I should know. I've buried both parents and a sister. But these people are Catholics. They don't want anything to jeopardize their chances of bodily resurrection. As if God is going to bother with –' he waved his arm at the whole cemetery '– all this. Are you a Catholic, Herr –?'

'Sometimes,' I said. 'When I'm hurrying to catch a train, or trying to sober up.'

'Linden used to pray to St Anthony,' said the American. 'I believe he's the patron saint of lost things.'

Was he trying to be cryptic, I wondered. 'Never use him myself,' I said.

He followed me on to the road that led back to the chapel. It was a long avenue of severely pruned trees on which the gobbets of snow sitting on the sconce-like ends of the branches resembled the stumps of melted candles from some outsized requiem.

Pointing at one of the parked cars, a Mercedes, he said: 'Like a lift to town? I've got a car here.'

It was true that I wasn't much of a Catholic. Killing men, even Russians, wasn't the kind of sin that was easy to explain to one's maker. All the same I didn't have to consult St Michael, the patron saint of policemen, to smell an MP.

'You can drop me at the main gate, if you like,' I heard myself reply.

'Sure, hop in.'

He paid the funeral and the mourners no more attention. After all he had me, a new face, to interest him now. Perhaps I was some-one who might shed some light on a dark corner of the whole affair. I wondered what he would have said if he could have known that my intentions were the same as his own; and that it was in the vague hope of just such an encounter that I had allowed myself to be persuaded to come to Linden's funeral in the first place.

The American drove slowly, as if he were part of the cortège, no doubt hoping to spin out his chance to discover who I was and why I was there.

'My name is Shields,' he volunteered. 'Roy Shields.'

'Bernhard Günther,' I answered, seeing no reason to tease him with it.

'Are you from Vienna?'

'Not originally.'

'Where, originally?'

'Germany.'

'No, I didn't think you were Austrian.'

'Your friend – Herr Linden,' I said, changing the subject. 'Did you know him well?'

The American laughed and found some cigarettes in the top pocket of his sports jacket. 'Linden? I didn't know him at all.' He pulled one clear with his lips and then handed me the packet. 'He got himself murdered a few weeks back, and my chief thought it would be a good idea if I were to represent our department at the funeral.'

'And what department is that?' I asked, although I was almost certain I already knew the answer.

'The International Patrol.' Lighting his cigarette he mimicked the style of the American radio broadcasters. 'For your protection, call A29500.' Then he handed me a book of matches from somewhere called the Zebra Club. 'Waste of valuable time if you ask me, coming all the way down here like this.'

'It's not that far,' I told him; and then: 'Perhaps your chief was hoping that the murderer would put in an appearance.'

'Hell, I should hope not,' he laughed. 'We've got that guy in gaol. No, the chief, Captain Clark, is the kind of fellow who likes to observe the proper protocols.' Shields turned the car south towards the chapel. 'Christ,' he muttered, 'this place is like a god-damned gridiron.

'You know, Günther, that road we just turned off is almost a kilometre, as straight as an arrow. I caught sight of you when you were still a couple of hundred metres short of Linden's funeral, and it looked to me like you were in a hurry to join us.' He grinned, to himself it seemed. 'Am I right?'

'My father is buried only a short way from Linden's grave. When I got there and saw the colour party I decided to come back a little later, when it's quieter.'

'You walked all that way and you didn't bring a wreath?'

'Did you bring one?'

'Sure did. Cost me fifty schillings.'

'Cost you, or cost your department?'

'I guess we did pass a hat round at that.'

'And you need to ask me why I didn't bring a wreath.'

'Come on, Günther,' Shields laughed. 'There isn't one of you people who isn't involved in some kind of a racket. You're all exchanging schillings for dollar scrip, or selling cigarettes on the black market. You know, I sometimes think that the Austrians are making more from breaking the rules than we are.'

'That's because you're a policeman.'

We passed through the main gate on Simmeringer Hauptstrasse and drew up in front of the tram stop, where several men were already clinging to the outside of the packed tram car like a litter of hungry piglets on a sow's belly.

'Are you sure you don't want that lift into town?' said Shields.

'No thanks. I have some business with some of the stone-masons.'

'Well, it's your funeral,' he said with a grin, and sped away.

I walked along the high wall of the cemetery, where it seemed that most of Vienna's market gardeners and stonemasons had their premises, and found a pathetic old woman standing in my way. She held up a penny candle and asked me if I had a light.

'Here,' I said, and gave her Shields' book of matches.

When she made as if to take only one I told her to keep the whole book. 'I can't afford to pay you for it,' she said, with real apology.

Just as surely as you know that a man waiting for a train will look at his watch, I knew that I would be seeing Shields again. But I wished him back right then and there so that I could have shown him one Austrian who didn't have the price of a match, let alone a fifty-schilling wreath.

Herr Josef Pichler was a fairly typical Austrian: shorter and thinner than the average German, with pale, soft-looking skin, and a sparse, immature sort of moustache. The hangdog expression on his drawn-out muzzle of a face gave him the appearance of one who had consumed too much of the absurdly young wine that Austrians apparently consider drinkable. I met him standing in his yard, comparing the sketch-plan of a stone's inscription with its final execution.

'God's greeting to you,' he said sullenly. I replied in kind.

'Are you Herr Pichler, the celebrated sculptor?' I asked. Traudl had advised me that the Viennese have a passion for overblown titles and flattery.

'I am,' he said, with a slight swell of pride. 'Does the gallant gentleman wish to consider ordering a piece?' He spoke as if he had been the curator of an art-gallery on Dorotheergasse. 'A fine head-stone perhaps.' He indicated a large slice of polished black marble on which names and a date had been inscribed and painted in gold. 'Something marmoreal? A carved figure? A statue perhaps?'

'To be honest, I am not entirely sure, Herr Pichler. I believe you recently created a fine piece for a friend of mine, Dr Max Abs. He was so delighted with it that I wondered if I might have something similar.'

'Yes, I think I remember the Herr Doktor.' Pichler took off his little chocolate cake of a hat and scratched the top of his grey head. 'But the particular design escapes me for the moment. Do you remember what kind of piece it was he had?'

'Only that he was delighted with it, I'm afraid.'

'No matter. Perhaps the honourable gentleman would care to return tomorrow, by which time I should have been able to find the Herr Doktor's specifications. Permit me to explain.' He showed me the sketch in his hand, one for a deceased whose inscription described him as an 'Engineer of Urban Conduits and Conservancy'.

'Take this customer,' he said, warming to the theme of his own business. 'I have a design with his name and order number here. When this piece is completed the drawing will be filed away according to the nature of the piece. From then on I must consult my sales book to find the name of the customer. But right now I'm in something of a hurry to complete this piece and really –' he patted his stomach '– I'm dead today.' He shrugged apologetically. 'Last night, you understand. I'm short of staff, too.'

I thanked him and left him to his Engineer of Urban Conduits and Conservancy. That was presumably what you called yourself if you were one of the city's plumbers. What sort of title, I wondered, did the private investigators give themselves? Balanced on the outside of the tram car back to town, I kept my mind off my precarious position by constructing a number of elegant titles for my rather vulgar profession: Practitioner of Solitary Masculine Lifestyle; Non-metaphysical Inquiry Agent; Interrogative Intermediary to the Perplexed and Anxious; Confidential Solicitor for the Displaced and the Misplaced; Bespoke Grail-Finder; Seeker after Truth. I liked the last one best of all. But, at least as far as my client in the particular case before me was concerned, there was nothing which seemed properly to reflect the sense of working for a lost cause that might have deterred even the most dogmatic Flat Earther.

14

According to all the guidebooks, the Viennese love dancing almost as passionately as they love music. But then the books were all written before the war, and I didn't think that their authors could ever have spent a whole evening at the Casanova Club in Dorotheergasse. There the band was led in a way that put you in mind of the most ignominious retreat, and the shit-kicking that passed for something approximately terpsichorean looked as if it might have been performed more in imitation of a polar bear kept in a very small cage. For passion you had to look to the sight of the ice yielding noisily to the spirit in your glass.

After an hour in the Casanova I was feeling as sour as a eunuch in a bathful of virgins. Counselling myself to be patient, I leaned back into my red velvet-and-satin booth and stared unhappily at the tent-like drapes on the ceiling: the last thing to do, unless I wanted to end up like Becker's two friends (whatever he said, I hadn't much doubt that they were dead), was to bounce around the place asking the regulars if they knew Helmut König, or maybe his girlfriend Lotte.

On its ridiculously plush surface, the Casanova didn't look like the kind of place which a fearful angel might have preferred to avoid. There were no extra-large tuxedoes at the door, nor anyone about who looked as if he could be carrying anything more lethal than a silver toothpick, and the waiters were all commendably obsequious. If König no longer frequented the Casanova it wasn't because he was afraid of having his pocket fingered.

'Has it started turning yet?'

She was a tall, striking girl with the sort of exaggeratedly made body that might have adorned a sixteenth-century Italian fresco: all breasts, belly and backside.

'The ceiling,' she explained, jerking her cigarette-holder vertically.

'Not yet, anyway.'

'Then you can buy me a drink,' she said, and sat down beside me. 'I was starting to worry you wouldn't show up.'

'I know, I'm the kind of girl you've been dreaming about. Well, here I am now.'

I waved to the waiter and let her order herself a whisky and soda.

'I'm not one for dreaming much,' I told her.

'Well, that's a pity, isn't it?'

She shrugged.

'What do you dream about?'

'Listen,' she said, shaking her head of long, shiny brown hair, 'this is Vienna. It doesn't do to describe your dreams to anyone here. You never know, you might just be told what they really mean, and then where would you be?'

'That sounds almost as if you have something to hide.'

'I don't see you wearing sandwich boards. Most people have something to hide. Especially these days. What's in their heads most of all.'

'Well, a name ought to be easy enough. Mine's Bernie.'

'Short for Bernhard? Like the dog that rescues mountaineers?'

'More or less. Whether or not I do any rescuing depends on how much brandy I'm carrying. I'm not as loyal when I'm loaded.'

'I never met a man who was.' She jerked her head down at my cigarette. 'Can you spare me one of those?'

I handed her a pack and watched as she screwed one into her holder. 'You didn't tell me your name,' I said, thumb-nailing a match alight for her.

'Veronika, Veronika Zartl. Pleased to meet you, I'm sure. I don't think I've ever seen your face in here. Where are you from? You sound like a *pifke*.'

'Berlin.'

'I thought so.'

'Anything wrong with that?'

'Not if you like *pifkes*. Most Austrians don't, as it happens.' She spoke in the slow, almost yokelish drawl that seemed typical of the modern Viennese. 'But I don't mind them. I get mistaken for a *pifke* myself sometimes. That's because I won't speak like the rest of them.' She chuckled. 'It's so funny when you hear some lawyer or dentist speaking like he was a tram-driver or a miner just so as he doesn't get mistaken for a German. Mostly they only do it in shops, to make sure that they get the good service that all Austrians think that they are entitled to. You want to try it yourself, Bernie, and see the difference it makes to the way you're treated. Viennese is quite easy, you know. Just speak like you're chewing something and add "ish" onto the end of everything you say. Cleverish, eh?'

The waiter returned with her drink which she regarded with some disapproval. 'No ice,' she muttered as I tossed a banknote on to the silver tray and left the change under Veronika's questioning eyebrow.

'With a tip like that you must be planning on coming back here.'

'You don't miss much, do you?'

'Are you? Planning on coming back here, I mean.'

'It could be that I am. But is it always like this? The trade here's about as busy as an empty fireplace.'

'Just wait until it gets crowded, and then you'll wish it was like this again.' She sipped her drink and leaned back on the red-velvet-and-gilt chair, stroking the buttonback satin upholstery that covered the wall of our booth with the palm of her outstretched hand.

'You should be grateful for the quiet,' she told me. 'It gives us a chance to get to know each other. Just like those two.' She waved her holder meaningfully at a couple of girls who were dancing with each other. With their gaudy outfits, tight buns and flashing paste necklaces they looked like a pair of circus horses. Catching Veronika's eye they smiled and then whinnied a little confidence to each other at a coiffure's distance.

I watched them turn in elegant little circles. 'Friends of yours?'

'Not exactly.'

'Are they – together?'

She shrugged. 'Only if you made it worth their while.' She laughed some smoke out of her pert little nose. 'They're just giving their high-heels some exercise, that's all.'

'Who's the taller one?'

'Ibolya. That's Hungarian for a violet.'

'And the blonde?'

'That's Mitzi.' Veronika was bristling a little as she named the other girl. 'Maybe you'd prefer to talk to them.' She took out her powder-compact and scrutinized her lipstick in the tiny mirror. 'I'm expected soon anyway. My mother will be getting worried.'

'There's no need to play the Little Red Riding Hood with me,' I told her. 'We both know that your mother doesn't mind if you leave the path and walk through the woods. And as for those two sparklers over there, a man can look in the window, can't he?'

'Sure, but there's no need to press your nose up against it. Not when you're with me, anyway.'

'It seems to me, Veronika,' I said, 'that you wouldn't have to try very hard to sound like someone's wife. Frankly, it's the sort of sound that drives a man to a place like this in the first place.' I smiled just to let her know I was still friendly. 'And then along you come with the rolling-pin in your voice. Well, it could put a man right back to where he was when he walked through the door.'

She smiled back at me. 'I guess you're right at that,' she said.

'You know, it strikes me that you're new at this chocolady thing.'

'Christ,' she said, her smile turning bitter, 'isn't everyone?'

But for the fact that I was tired I might have stayed longer at the Casanova, might even have gone home with Veronika. Instead I gave her a packet of cigarettes for her company and told her that I would be back the following evening.

On the town, late at night, was not the best time to compare Vienna to any metropolis, with the possible exception of the lost city of Atlantis. I had seen a moth-eaten umbrella stay open for longer than Vienna. Veronika had explained, over several more drinks, that Austrians preferred to spend their evenings at home, but that when they did choose to make a night of it, they traditionally made an early start – as early as six or seven o'clock. Which left me trailing back to the Pension Caspian along an empty street at only 10.30, with just my shadow and the sound of my half-intoxicated footsteps for company.

After the combusted atmosphere of Berlin, Vienna's air tasted as pure as birdsong. But the night was a cold one, and shivering inside my overcoat I quickened my step, disliking the quiet, and remembering Dr Liebl's warning about the Soviet predilection for nocturnal kidnappings.

At the same time, however, crossing Heldenplatz in the direction of the Volksgarten, and beyond the Ring, Josefstadt and home, it was easy to find one's thoughts turning to the Ivans. As far away from the Soviet sector as I was, there was still ample evidence of their omnipresence. The Imperial Palace of the Habsburgs was one of the many public buildings in the internationally run city centre that was occupied by the Red Army. Over the main door was a colossal red star in the centre of which was a picture of Stalin in profile, set against a significantly dimmer one of Lenin.

It was as I passed the ruined Kunsthistorische that I felt there was someone behind me, someone hanging back between the shadows and the piles of rubble. I stopped in my tracks, looked around and saw nothing. Then, about thirty metres away, next to a statue of which only the torso remained, like something I had once seen in a mortuary drawer, I heard a noise, and a moment later saw some small stones roll down a high bank of rubble.

'Are you feeling a bit lonely?' I called out, having drunk just enough not to feel stupid asking such a ridiculous question. My voice echoed up the side of the ruined museum. 'If it's the museum you're interested in, we're closed. Bombs, you know: dreadful things.' There was no reply, and I found myself laughing. 'If you're a spy, you're in luck. That's the new profession to be in. Especially if you're a Viennese. You don't have to take my word for it. One of the Ivans told me.'

Still laughing to myself, I turned and walked away. I didn't bother to see if I was followed, but crossing onto Mariahilfer-strasse I heard footsteps again as I paused to light a cigarette.

As anyone who knows Vienna could have told you, this wasn't exactly the most direct route back to Skodagasse. I even told myself. But there was a part of me, probably the part most affected by alcohol, that wanted to find out exactly who was following me and why.

The American sentry who stood out in front of the Stifts-kaserne was having a cold time of it. He watched me carefully as I passed by on the other side of the empty street and I reflected that he might even recognize the man on my tail as a fellow American and member of the Special Investigations Section of his own military police. Probably they were in the same baseball team or whatever game it was that American soldiers played when they weren't eating or chasing women.

Further up the slope of the wide street I glanced to my left and through a doorway saw a narrow covered passage that seemed to lead down several flights of steps to an adjoining street. Instinctively I ducked inside. Vienna might not have been blessed with a fabulous nightlife but it was perfect for anyone on foot. A man who knew his way around the streets and the ruins, who could remember these convenient passages, would, I thought, provide even the most determined police cordon with a better chase than Jean Valjean.

Ahead of me, beyond my sight, someone else was making his way down the steps, and thinking that my tail might take these for my own footsteps, I pressed myself against a wall and waited for him in the dark.

After less than a minute I heard the approaching sound of a man running lightly. Then the footsteps halted at the top of the passageway as he stood trying to judge whether or not it was safe to come after me. Hearing the other man's footsteps, he started forward.

I stepped out of the shadows and punched him hard in the

stomach — so hard I thought I would have to bend down and
retrieve my knuckles — and while he lay gasping on the steps where
he had fallen, I tugged his coat off his shoulders and pulled it down
to hold his arms. He wasn't carrying a gun, so I helped myself to
the wallet in his breast pocket and picked out an ID card.

' "Captain John Belinsky",' I read. ' "430th United States CIC".
What's that? Are you one of Mr Shields' friends?'

The man sat up slowly. 'Fuck you, kraut,' he said biliously.

'Have you orders to follow me?' I tossed the card on to his lap
and searched the other compartments of his wallet. 'Because you'd
better ask for another assignment, Johnny. You're not very good at
this sort of thing — I've seen less conspicuous striptease dancers
than you.' There wasn't much of interest in his wallet: some dollar
scrip, a few Austrian schillings, a ticket for the Yank Movie Theatre,
some stamps, a room card from Sacher's Hotel and a photograph
of a pretty girl.

'Have you finished with that?' he said in German.

I tossed him the wallet.

'That's a nice-looking girl you have there, Johnny,' I said. 'Did
you follow her as well? Maybe I should give you my snapshot.
Write my address on the back. Make it easier for you.'

'Fuck you, kraut.'

'Johnny,' I said, starting back up the steps to Mariahilferstrasse,
'I'll bet you say that to all the girls.'

15

Pichler lay under a massive piece of stone like some primitive car mechanic repairing a neolithic stone-axle, with the tools of his trade – a hammer and a chisel – held tight in his dusty, blood-stained hands. It was almost as if while carving the black rock's inscription he had paused for a moment to draw breath and decipher the words that seemed to emerge vertically from his chest. But no mason ever worked in such a position, at right angles to his legend. And draw breath he never would again, for although the human chest is sufficiently strong a cage for those soft, mobile pets that are the heart and lungs, it is easily crushed by something as heavy as half a tonne of polished marble.

It looked like an accident, but there was one way to be sure. Leaving Pichler in the yard where I had found him, I went into the office.

I retained very little memory of the dead man's description of his business-accounting system. To me, the niceties of double-entry bookkeeping are about as useful as a pair of brogue galoshes. But as someone who ran a business himself, albeit a small one, I had a rudimentary knowledge of the petty, fastidious way in which the details of one ledger are supposed to correspond with those in another. And it didn't take William Randolph Hearst to see that Pilcher's books had been altered, not by any subtle account-ing, but by the simple expedient of tearing out a couple of pages. There was only one financial analysis that was worth a spit, and that was that Pichler's death had been anything but accidental.

Wondering whether his murderer had thought to steal the sketch-design for Dr Max Abs' headstone, as well as the relevant pages from the ledgers, I went back into the yard to see if I might be able to find it. I had a good look round, and after a few minutes discovered a number of dusty art-files propped up against a wall in the workshop at the back of the yard. I untied the first file and started to sort through the draughtsman's drawings, working quickly since I had no wish to be found searching the premises of a man who lay crushed to death less than ten metres away. And when at last I found the drawing I was looking for I gave it no more than a cursory glance before folding it up and slipping it into my coat pocket.

I caught a 71 back to town and went to the Café Schwarzenberg, close to the tram terminus on the Kärtner Ring. I ordered a mélange and then spread the drawing out on the table in front of me. It was about the size of a double-page spread in a newspaper, with the customer's name – Max Abs – clearly marked on an order copy stapled to the top right-hand corner of the paper.

The mark-up for the inscription read: 'SACRED TO THE MEMORY OF MARTIN ALBERS, BORN 1899, MAR-TYRED 9 APRIL 1945. BELOVED OF WIFE LENI, AND SONS MANFRED AND ROLF. BEHOLD, I SHEW YOU A MYSTERY; WE SHALL NOT ALL SLEEP, BUT WE SHALL ALL BE CHANGED, IN A MOMENT, IN THE TWINKLING OF AN EYE, AT THE LAST TRUMP: FOR THE TRUMPET SHALL SOUND, AND THE DEAD SHALL BE RAISED INCORRUPTIBLE, AND WE SHALL BE CHANGED. I CORINTHIANS 15: 51–52.'

On Max Abs' order was written his address, but beyond the fact that the doctor had paid for a headstone in the name of a man who was dead – a brother-in-law perhaps? – and which had now occasioned the murder of the man who had carved it, I could not see that I had learned very much.

The waiter, wearing his grey frizzy hair on the back of his bald-ing head like a halo, returned with the small tin tray that carried my mélange and the glass of water customarily served with coffee in Viennese cafés. He glanced down at the drawing before I folded it away to make room for the tray, and said, with a sympathetic sort of smile: 'Blessed are they that mourn, for they shall be comforted.'

I thanked him for his kind thought and, tipping him generously, asked him first from where I might send a telegram, and then where Berggasse was.

'The Central Telegraph Office is on Börseplatz,' he answered, 'on the Schottenring. You'll find Berggasse just a couple of blocks north of there.'

An hour or so later, after sending my telegrams to Kirsten and to Neumann, I walked up to Berggasse, which ran between the police prison where Becker was locked up and the hospital where his girlfriend worked. This coincidence was more remarkable than the street itself, which seemed largely to be occupied by doctors and dentists. Nor did I think it particularly remarkable to discover from the old woman who owned the building in which Abs had occupied the mezzanine floor that only a few hours earlier he had told her he was leaving Vienna for good.

'He said his job urgently required him to go to Munich,' she explained in the kind of tone that left me feeling she was still a bit puzzled by this sudden departure. 'Or at least somewhere near Munich. He mentioned the name but I'm afraid that I've forgotten it.'

'It wasn't Pullach, was it?'

She tried to look thoughtful but only succeeded in looking bad-tempered. 'I don't know if it was or if it wasn't,' she said finally. The cloud lifted from her face as she returned to her normal bovine expression. 'Anyway, he said he would let me know where he was when he got himself settled.'

'Did he take all his things with him?'

'There wasn't much to take,' she said. 'Just a couple of suitcases. The apartment is furnished, you see.' She frowned again. 'Are you a policeman or something?'

'No, I was wondering about his rooms.'

'Well why didn't you say? Come in, Herr —?'

'It's Professor, actually,' I said with what I thought sounded like a typically Viennese punctiliousness. 'Professor Kurtz.' There was also the possibility that by giving myself the academic handle

I might appeal to the snob in the woman. 'Dr Abs and myself are mutually acquainted with a Herr König, who told me that he thought the Herr Doktor might be about to vacate some excellent rooms at this address.'

I followed the old woman through the door and into the big hallway which led to a tall glass door. Beyond the open door lay a courtyard with a solitary plane tree growing there. We turned up the wrought-iron staircase.

'I trust you will forgive my discretion,' I said. 'Only I wasn't sure how much credence to place on my friend's information. He was most insistent that they were excellent rooms, and I'm sure I don't have to tell you, madam, how difficult it can be for a gentleman to find an apartment of any quality in Vienna these days. Perhaps you know Herr König?'

'No,' she said firmly. 'I don't think I ever met any of Dr Abs' friends. He was a very quiet man. But your friend is well informed. You won't find a better set of rooms for 400 schillings a month. This is a very good neighbourhood.' At the door to the apartment she lowered her voice. 'And entirely Jew-free.' She produced a key from the pocket of her jacket and slipped it into the keyhole of the great mahogany door. 'Of course, we had a few of them here before the Anschluss. Even in this house. But by the time the war came most of them had gone away.' She opened the door and showed me into the apartment.

'Here we are,' she said proudly. 'There are six rooms in total. It's not as big as some of the apartments in the street, but then not as expensive either. Fully furnished as I think I said.'

'Lovely,' I said looking about me.

'I'm afraid that I haven't yet had time to clean the place,' she apologized. 'Doctor Abs left a lot of rubbish to throw out. Not that I mind really. He gave me four weeks' money in lieu of notice.' She pointed at one door which was closed. 'There's still quite a bit of bomb damage showing in there. We had an incendiary in the courtyard when the Ivans came, but it's due to be repaired very soon.'

'I'm sure it's fine,' I said generously.

'Right then. I'll leave you to have a little look around on your own, Professor Kurtz. Let you get a feel for the place. Just lock up after you and knock on my door when you've seen everything.'

When the old woman had gone I wandered among the rooms, finding only that for a single man Abs seemed to have received an extraordinarily large number of Care parcels, those food parcels that came from the United States. I counted the empty cardboard boxes that bore the distinctive initials and the Broad Street, New York address and found that there were over fifty of them.

It didn't look like Care so much as good business.

When I had finished looking around I told the old woman that I was looking for something bigger and thanked her for allowing me to see the place. Then I strolled back to my pension in Skodagasse.

I wasn't back very long before there was a knock at my door.

'Herr Günther?' said the one wearing the sergeant's stripes.

I nodded.

'I'm afraid you'll have to come with us, please.'

'Am I being arrested?'

'Excuse me, sir?'

I repeated the question in my uncertain English. The American MP shifted his chewing-gum around impatiently.

'It will be explained to you down at headquarters, sir.'

I picked up my jacket and slipped it on.

'You will remember to bring your papers, won't you, sir?' he smiled politely. 'Save us coming back for them.'

'Of course,' I said, collecting my hat and coat. 'Have you got transport? Or are we walking?'

'The truck's right outside the front door.'

The landlady caught my eye as we came through her lobby. To my surprise she looked not at all perturbed. Maybe she was used to her guests getting pulled in by the International Patrol. Or perhaps she just told herself that someone else was paying for my room whether I slept there or in a cell at the police prison.

We climbed into the truck and drove a few metres north before a short turn to the right took us south down Lederergasse, away from the city centre and the headquarters of the IMP.

'Aren't we going to Kärtnerstrasse?' I said.

'It isn't an International Patrol matter, sir,' the sergeant explained. 'This is American jurisdiction. We're going to the Stiftskaserne, on Mariahilferstrasse.'

'To see who? Shields or Belinsky?'

'It will be explained –'

'– when we get there, right.'

The mock-baroque entrance to the Stiftskaserne, the headquarters of the 796th Military Police, with its half-relief Doric columns, griffins and Greek warriors, was situated, somewhat incongruously, between the twin entrances of Tiller's department store, and was part of a four-storey building that fronted onto Mariahilferstrasse. We passed through the massive arch of this entrance and beyond the rear of the main building and a parade ground to another building, which housed a military barracks.

The truck drove through some gates and pulled up outside the barracks. I was escorted inside and up a couple of flights of stairs to a big bright office which commanded an impressive view of the anti-aircraft tower that stood on the other side of the parade ground.

Shields stood up from behind a desk and grinned like he was trying to impress the dentist.

'Come on in and sit down,' he said as if we were old friends. He looked at the sergeant. 'Did he come peaceably, Gene? Or did you have to beat the shit out of his ass?'

The sergeant grinned a little and mumbled something which I didn't catch. It was no wonder that one could never understand their English, I thought: Americans were forever chewing something.

'You better stick around a while, Gene,' Shields added. 'Just in case we have to get tough with this guy.' He uttered a short laugh and, hitching up his trousers, sat squarely in front of me, his heavy legs splayed apart like some samurai lord, except that he was probably twice as large as any Japanese.

'First of all, Günther, I have to tell you that there's a Lieutenant Canfield, a real asshole Brit, down at International Headquarters who would love somebody to help him with a little problem he's got. It seems like some stonemason in the British sector got himself killed when a rock fell on his tits. Mostly everyone, including the lieutenant's boss, believes that it was probably an accident. Only the lieutenant's the keen type. He's read Sherlock Holmes and he wants to go to detective school when he leaves the army. He's got this theory that someone tampered with the dead man's books. Now I don't know if that's sufficient motive to kill a man or not, but I do remember seeing you go into Pichler's office yesterday morning after Captain Linden's funeral.' He chuckled. 'Hell, I admit it, Günther. I was spying on you. Now what do you say to that?'

'Pichler's dead?'

'How about it you try it with a little more surprise? "Don't tell me Pichler is dead!" or "My God, I don't believe what you are telling me!" You wouldn't know what happened to him, would you, Günther?'

I shrugged. 'Maybe the business was getting on top of him.'

Shields laughed at that one. He laughed like he had once taken a few classes in laughing, showing all his teeth, which were mostly bad, in a blue boxing-glove of a jaw that was wider than the top of his dark and balding head. He seemed loud, like most Americans, and then some. He was a big, brawny man with shoulders like a rhinoceros, and wore a suit of light-brown flannel with lapels that were as broad and sharp as two Swiss halberds. His tie deserved to hang over a café terrace, and his shoes were heavy brown Oxfords. Americans seemed to have an attraction for stout shoes in the same way that Ivans loved wristwatches: the only difference was that they generally bought them in shops.

'Frankly, I don't give a damn for that lieutenant's problems,' he said. 'It's shit in the British backyard, not mine. So let them sweep it up. No, I'm merely explaining your need to cooperate with me. You may have nothing at all to do with Pichler's death, but I'm sure that you don't want to waste a day explaining that to Lieutenant Canfield. So you help me and I'll help you: I'll forget I ever saw you go into Pichler's shop. Do you understand what I'm saying to you?'

'There's nothing wrong with your German,' I said. All the same it struck me with what venom he attacked the accent, tackling the consonants with a theatrical degree of precision, almost as if he regarded the language as one which needed to be spoken cruelly. 'I don't suppose it would matter if I said that I know absolutely nothing about what happened to Herr Pichler?'

Shields shrugged apologetically. 'As I said, it's a British problem, not mine. Maybe you are innocent. But like I say, it sure would be a pain in the ass explaining it to those British. I swear they think every one of you krauts is a goddam Nazi.'

I threw up my hands in defeat. 'So how can I help you?'

'Well, naturally, when I heard that before coming to Captain Linden's party you visited his murderer in prison, my inquiring nature could not be constrained.' His tone grew sharper. 'Come on, Günther. I want to know what the hell is going on between you and Becker.'

'I take it you know Becker's side of the story.'

'Like it was engraved on my cigarette-case.'

'Well, Becker believes it. He's paying me to investigate it. And, he hopes, to prove it.'

'You're investigating it, you say. So what does that make you?'

'A private investigator.'

'A shamus? Well, well.' He leaned forwards on his chair, and taking hold of the edge of my jacket, felt the material with his finger and thumb. It was fortunate that there were no razor blades sewn on that particular number. 'No, I can't buy that. You're not half greasy enough.'

'Greasy or not, it's true.' I took out my wallet and showed him my ID. And then my old warrant disc. 'Before the war I was with the Berlin Criminal Police. I'm sure I don't have to tell you that Becker was too. That's how I know him.' I took out my cigarettes. 'Mind if I smoke?'

'Smoke, but don't let it stop your lips moving.'

'Well, after the war I didn't want to go back to the police. The force was full of Communists.' I was throwing him a line with that one. There wasn't one American I had met who seemed to like Communism. 'So I set up in business on my own. Actually, I had a period out of the force during the mid-thirties, and did a bit of private work then. So I'm not exactly new at this game. With so many displaced persons since the war, most people can use an honest bull. Believe me, thanks to the Ivans they're few and far between in Berlin.'

'Yeah, well it's the same here. Because the Soviets got here first they put all their own people in the top police jobs. Things are so bad that the Austrian government had to look to the chief of the Vienna Fire Service when they were trying to find a straight man to become the new vice-president of police.' He shook his head. 'You're one of Becker's old colleagues. How about that? What kind of cop was he, for Christ's sake?'

'The crooked kind.'

'No wonder this country's in such a mess. I suppose you were SS as well then?'

'Briefly. When I found out what was going on I asked for a transfer to the front. People did, you know.'

'Not enough of them. Your friend didn't, for one.'

'He's not exactly a friend.'

'So why did you take the case?'

'I needed the money. And I needed to get away from my wife for a while.'

'Do you mind telling me why?'

I paused, realizing that it was the first time I had talked about it. 'She's been seeing someone else. One of your brother officers. I thought that if I wasn't around for a while she might decide what was more important: her marriage or this *schätzi* of hers.'

Shields nodded and then made a sympathetic-sounding grunt.

'Naturally all your papers are in order?'

'Naturally.' I handed them over and watched him examine my identity card and my pink pass.

'I see you came through the Russian Zone. For a man who doesn't like Ivans you must have some pretty good contacts in Berlin.'

'Just a few dishonest ones.'

'Dishonest Russkies?'

'What other kind is there? Sure I had to grease some people, but the papers are genuine.'

Shields handed them back. 'Do you have your *Fragebogen* with you?'

I fished my denazification certificate out of my wallet and handed it over. He only glanced at it, having no desire to read through the 133 questions and answers it recorded. 'An exonerated person, eh? How come you weren't classed as an offender? All SS were automatically arrested.'

'I saw out the end of the war in the army. On the Russian front. And, like I said, I got a transfer out of the SS.'

Shields grunted and handed back the *Fragebogen*. 'I don't like SS,' he growled.

'That makes two of us.'

Shields examined the big fraternity ring which gracelessly adorned one of his well-tufted fingers. He said: 'We checked Becker's story, you know. There was nothing in it.'

'I don't agree.'

'And what makes you think that?'

'Do you think he'd be willing to pay me $5,000 to dig around if his story were just hot air?'

'Five thousand?' Shields let out a whistle.

'Worth it if your head's in a noose.'

'Sure. Well, maybe you can prove that the guy was somewhere else when we actually caught him. Maybe you can find something that'll persuade the judge that his friends didn't shoot at us. Or that he wasn't carrying the gun that shot Linden. You got any bright ideas yet, shamus? Like maybe the one that took you to see Pichler?'

'It was a name that Becker remembered as having been mentioned by someone at Reklaue & Werbe Zentrale.'

'By who?'

'Dr Max Abs?'

Shields nodded, recognizing the name.

'I'd say it was him who killed Pichler. Probably he went to see him not long after I did and found out that someone claiming to be a friend of his had been asking questions. Maybe Pichler told him that he'd said I should come back the following day. So before I did Abs killed him and took away the paperwork with his name and address on. Or so he thought. He forgot something which led me to his address. Only by the time I got there he'd cleared out. According to his landlady he's halfway to Munich by now. You know, Shields, it might not be a bad idea if you were to have someone meet him off that train.'

Shields stroked his poorly-shaven jaw. 'It might not be at that.'

He stood up and went behind his desk where he picked up the telephone and proceeded to make a number of calls, but using a vocabulary and an accent that I was unable to comprehend. When finally he replaced the receiver in its cradle, he looked at his wristwatch and said: 'The train to Munich takes eleven and a half hours, so there's plenty of time to make sure he gets a warm hello when he gets off.'

The telephone rang. Shields answered it, staring at me openmouthed and unblinking, as if there wasn't much of my story he had believed. But when he put down the telephone a second time he was grinning.

'One of my calls was to the Berlin Documents Centre,' he said. 'I'm sure you know what that is. And that Linden worked there?'

I nodded.

'I asked them if they had anything on this Max Abs guy. That was them calling back just now. It seems that he was SS too. Not actually wanted for any war crimes, but something of a coincidence, wouldn't you say? You, Becker, Abs, all former pupils of Himmler's little Ivy League.'

'A coincidence is all it is,' I said wearily.

Shields settled back in his chair. 'You know, I'm perfectly pre-pared to believe that Becker was just the trigger-man for Linden. That your organization wanted him dead because he had found out something about you.'

'Oh?' I said without much enthusiasm for Shields' theory. 'And which organization is that?'

'The Werewolf Underground.'

I found myself laughing out loud. 'That old Nazi fifth-column story? The stay-behind fanatics who were going to continue a guer-rilla war against our conquerors? You have to be joking, Shields.'

'Something wrong with that, you think?'

'Well, they're a bit late for a start. The war's been over for nearly three years. Surely you Americans have screwed enough of our women by now to realize that we never planned to cut your throats in bed. The Werewolves . . .' I shook my head pityingly. 'I thought they were something that your own intelligence people had dreamed up. But I must say I certainly never thought there was anyone who actually believed that shit. Look, maybe Linden did find out something about a couple of war-criminals, and maybe they wanted him out of the way. But not the Werewolf Under-ground. Let's try and find something a little more original, can we?' I started another cigarette and watched Shields nod and think his way through what I had said.

'What does the Berlin Documents Centre have to say about Linden's work?' I said.

'Officially, he was no more than the Crowcass liaison officer – the Central Registry of War Crimes and Security Suspects of the United States Army. They insist that Linden was simply an admin-istrator and not a field agent. But then, if he were working in Intelligence, those boys wouldn't tell us anyway. They've got more secrets than the surface of Mars.'

He got up from behind the desk and went to the window.

'You know, the other day I had eyes of a report that said as many as two out of every thousand Austrians were spying for the Soviets. Now there are over 1.8 million people in this city, Günther. Which means that if Uncle Sam has as many spies as Uncle Joe there are over 7,000 spies right on my doorstep. To say nothing of what the British and the French are doing. Or what the Vienna state police get up to – that's the Commie-run political police, not the ordinary Vienna police, although they're a bunch of Communists as well of course. And then only a few months ago we had a whole bunch of Hungarian state police infiltrated into Vienna in order to kidnap or murder a few of their own dissident nationals.'

He turned away from the window and came back to the seat in front of me. Grasping the back of it as if he were planning to pick it up and crash it over my head, he sighed and said: 'What I'm trying to say, Günther, is that this is a rotten town. I believe Hitler called it a pearl. Well, he must have meant one that was as yellow and worn as the last tooth in a dead dog. Frankly, I look out of that window and I see about as much that's precious about this place as I can see blue when I'm pissing in the Danube.'

Shields straightened up. Then he leaned across and took hold of my jacket lapels, pulling me up to my feet.

'Vienna disappoints me, Günther, and that makes me feel bad. Don't you do the same, old fellow. If you turn up something I think I should know about and you don't come and tell me, I'll get real sore. I can think of a hundred good reasons to haul your ass out of this town even when I'm in a good mood, like I am now. Am I making myself clear?'

'Like you were made of crystal.' I brushed his hands off my jacket and straightened it on my shoulders. Halfway to the door I stopped and said: 'Does this new cooperation with the American Military Police extend as far as removing the tail you put on me?'

'Someone's following you?'

'He was until I took a poke at him last night.'

'This is a weird city, Günther. Maybe he's queer for you.'

'That must be why I presumed he was working for you. The man's an American named John Belinsky.'

Shields shook his head, his eyes innocently wide. 'I never heard of him. Honest to God, I never ordered anyone to tail you. If someone's following you it has nothing to do with this office. You know what you should do?'

'Surprise me.'

'Go home to Berlin. There's nothing here for you.'

'Maybe I would, except that I'm not sure that there's anything there either. That's one of the reasons I came, remember?'

16

It was late by the time I got to the Casanova Club. The place was full of Frenchmen and they were full of whatever it is that Frenchmen drink when they want to get good and stiff. Veronika had been right after all: I did prefer the Casanova when it was quiet. Failing to spot her in the crowd I asked the waiter I had tipped so generously the previous night if she had been in the place.

'She was here only ten, fifteen minutes ago,' he said. 'I think she went to the Koralle, sir.' He lowered his voice, and dipped his head towards me. 'She doesn't much care for Frenchmen. And to tell the truth, neither do I. The British, the Americans, even the Russians, one can at least respect armies that took a hand in our defeat. But the French? They are bastards. Believe me, sir, I know. I live in the 15th Bezirk, in the French sector.' He straightened the table-cloth. 'And what will the gentleman have to drink?'

'I think I might take a look at the Koralle myself. Where is it, do you know?'

'It's in the 9th Bezirk sir. Porzellangasse, just off Berggasse, and close to the police prison. Do you know where that is?'

I laughed. 'I'm beginning to.'

'Veronika is a nice girl,' the waiter added. 'For a chocolady.'

Rain blew into the Inner City from the east and the Russian sector. It turned to hail in the cold night air and stung the four faces of the International Patrol as they pulled up outside the Casanova. Nodding curtly to the doorman, and without a word, they passed me by and went inside to look for soldierly vice, that compromising manifestation of lust exacerbated by a combination of a foreign country, hungry women and a never-ending supply of cigarettes and chocolate.

At the now-familiar Schottenring I crossed on to Währinger Strasse and headed north across Rooseveltplatz in the moonlit shadow of the twin towers of the Votivkirche which, despite its enormous, sky-piercing height, had somehow survived all the bombs. I was turning into Berggasse for the second time that day when, from a large ruined building on the opposite side of the road, I heard a cry for help. Telling myself that it was none of my business I stopped for only a brief moment, intending to keep to my route. But then I heard it again: an almost recognizably contralto voice.

I felt fear crawl across my skin as I walked quickly in the direction of the sound. A high bank of rubble was piled against the building's curved wall and, having climbed to the top of it, I stared through an empty arched window into a semi-circular room that was of the proportions of a small-sized theatre.

There were three of them struggling in a little spot of moonlight against a straight wall that faced the windows. Two were Russian soldiers, filthy and ragged and laughing uproariously as they attempted forcibly to strip the clothes from the third figure, which was a woman. I knew it was Veronika even before she lifted her face to the light. She screamed and was slapped hard by the Russian who held her arms and the two flap sides of her dress that his comrade, kneeling on her toes, had torn open.

'*Pakazhitye, dushka* (show me, darling),' he guffawed, wrenching Veronika's underwear down over her knocking knees. He sat back on his haunches to admire her nakedness. '*Pryekrasnaya* (beautiful),' he said, as if he had been looking at a painting, and then pushed his face into her pubic hair. '*Vkoosnaya, tozhe* (tasty, too),' he growled.

The Russian looked round from between her legs as he heard my footfall on the debris that littered the floor, and seeing the length of lead pipe in my hand he stood up beside his friend, who now pushed Veronika aside.

'Get out of here, Veronika,' I shouted.

Needing little encouragement, she grabbed her coat and ran

towards one of the windows. But the Russian who had licked her seemed to have other ideas, and snatched at her mane of hair. In the same moment I swung the pipe, which hit the side of his lousy-looking head with an audible clang, numbing my hand with the vibration from the blow. The thought was just crossing my mind that I had hit him much too hard when I felt a sharp kick in the ribs, and then a knee thudded into my groin. The pipe fell on to the brick-strewn floor and there was a taste of blood in my mouth as I slowly followed it. I drew my legs up to my chest and tensed myself as I waited for the man's great boot to smash into my body again and finish me. Instead I heard a short, mechanical punch of a sound, like the sound of a rivet-gun, and when the boot swung again it was well over my head. With one leg still in the air, the man staggered for a second like a drunken ballet-dancer and then fell dead beside me, his forehead neatly trepanned with a well-aimed bullet. I groaned and for a moment shut my eyes. When I opened them again and raised myself on to my forearm, there was a third man squatting in front of me, and for a chilling moment he pointed the silenced barrel of his Luger at the centre of my face.

'Fuck you, kraut,' he said, and then, grinning broadly, helped me to my feet. 'I was going to belt you myself, but it looks like those two Ivans have saved me the trouble.'

'Belinsky,' I wheezed, holding my ribs. 'What are you, my guardian angel?'

'Yeah. It's a wonderful life. You all right, kraut?'

'Maybe my chest would feel better if I quit smoking. Yes, I'm all right. Where the hell did you come from?'

'You didn't see me? Great. After what you said about tailing someone I read a book about it. I disguised myself as a Nazi so as you wouldn't notice me.'

I looked around. 'Did you see where Veronika went?'

'You mean you know that lady?' He meandered over to the soldier I had felled with the pipe, and who lay senseless on the floor. 'I thought you were just the Don Quixote type.'

'I only met her last night.'

'Before you met me, I guess. Belinsky stared down at the soldier for a moment, then levelled the Luger at the back of the man's head and pulled the trigger. 'She's outside,' he said with no more emotion than if he had shot at a beer-bottle.

'Shit,' I breathed, appalled at this display of callousness. 'They could certainly have used you in an Action Group.'

'What?'

'I said I hope I didn't make you miss your tram last night. Did you have to kill him?'

He shrugged and started to unscrew the Luger's silencer. 'Two dead is better than one left alive to testify in court. Believe me, I know what I'm talking about.' He kicked the man's head with the toe of his shoe. 'Anyway, these Ivans won't be missed. They're deserters.'

'How do you know?'

Belinsky pointed out two bundles of clothes and equipment that lay near the doorway, and next to them the remains of a fire and a meal.

'It looks like they've been hiding here for a couple of days. I guess they got bored and fancied some —' he searched for the right word in German and then, shaking his head, completed the sentence in English '— cunt.' He holstered the Luger and dropped the silencer into his coat pocket. 'If they're found before the rats eat them up, the local boys will just figure that the MVD did it. But my bet is on the rats. Vienna's got the biggest rats you ever saw. They come straight up out of the sewers. Come to think of it, from the smell of these two, I'd say they'd been down there themselves. The main sewer comes out in the Stadt Park, just by the Soviet Kommendatura and the Russian sector.' He started towards the window. 'Come on, kraut, let's find this girl of yours.'

Veronika was standing a short way back down Währinger Strasse and looked ready to make a run for it if it had been the two Russians who came out of the building. 'When I saw your friend go in,' she explained, 'I waited to see what would happen.'

She had buttoned her coat to the neck, and, but for a slight bruise on her cheek and the tears in her eyes, I wouldn't have said she looked like a girl who had narrowly missed being raped. She glanced nervously back at the building with a question in her eyes.

'It's all right,' said Belinsky. 'They won't bother us no more.'

When Veronika had finished thanking me for saving her, and Belinsky for saving me, he and I walked her home to the half-ruin in Rotenturmstrasse where she had her room. There she thanked us some more and invited us both to come up, an offer which we declined, and only after I had promised to visit her in the morning could she be persuaded to close the door and go to bed.

'From the look of you I'd say that you could use a drink,' Belinsky said. 'Let me buy you one. The Renaissance Bar is just around the corner. It's quiet there, and we can talk.'

Close by St Stephen's Cathedral, which was now being restored, the Renaissance in Singerstrasse was an imitation Hungarian tavern with gypsy music. The kind of place you see depicted on a jigsaw-puzzle, it was no doubt popular with the tourists, but just a concertina-squeeze too premeditated for my simple, gloomy taste. There was one significant compensation, as Belinsky explained. They served Cscreszne, a clear Hungarian spirit made from cherries. And for one who had recently been subjected to a kicking, it tasted even better than Belinsky had promised.

'That's a nice girl,' he said, 'but she ought to be a bit more careful in Vienna. So should you for that matter. If you're going to go around playing Errol-fucking-Flynn you should have more than just a bit of hair under your arm.'

'I guess you're right.' I sipped at my second glass. 'But it seems strange you telling me that, you being a bull and all. Carrying a gun's not strictly legal for anyone but Allied personnel.'

'Who said I was a bull?' He shook his head. 'I'm CIC. The Counter-Intelligence Corps. The MPs don't know shit about what we get up to.'

'You're a spy?'

'No, we're more like Uncle Sam's hotel detectives. We don't run spies, we catch them. Spies and war-criminals.' He poured some more of the Csereszne.

'So why are you following me?'

'It's hard to say, really.'

'I'm sure I could find you a German dictionary.'

Belinsky withdrew a ready-filled pipe from his pocket and while he explained what he meant he suck-started the thing into yielding a steady smoke.

'I'm investigating the murder of Captain Linden,' he said.

'What a coincidence. So am I.'

'We want to try and find out what it was that brought him to Vienna in the first place. He liked to keep things pretty close to his chest. Worked on his own a lot.'

'Was he in the CIC too?'

'Yes, the 970th, stationed in Germany. I'm 430th. We're stationed in Austria. Really he should have let us know he was coming on to our patch.'

'And he didn't send so much as a postcard, eh?'

'Not a word. Probably because there was no earthly reason why he should have come. If he was working on anything that affected this country he should have told us.' Belinsky let out a balloon of smoke and waved it away from his face. 'He was what you might call a desk-investigator. An intellectual. The sort of fellow you could let loose on a wall full of files with instructions to find Himmler's optical prescription. The only problem is that because he was such a bright guy, he kept no case notes.' Belinsky tapped his forehead with the stem of his pipe. 'He kept everything up here. Which makes it a nuisance to find out what he was investigating that got him a lead lunch.'

'Your MPs think that the Werewolf Underground might have had something to do with it.'

'So I heard.' He inspected the smouldering contents of his cherry-wood pipe bowl, and added: 'Frankly, we're all scraping around in the dark a bit on this one. Anyway, that's where you walk into my life. We thought maybe you'd turn up something that we couldn't manage ourselves, you being a native, comparatively speaking. And if you did, I'd be there for the cause of free democracy.'

'Criminal investigation by proxy, eh? It wouldn't be the first time that it's happened. I hate to disappoint you, only I'm kind of in the dark myself.'

'Maybe not. After all, you already got the stonemason killed. In my book that rates as a result. It means you got someone upset, kraut.'

I smiled. 'You can call me Bernie.'

'The way I figure it, Becker wouldn't bring you into the game without dealing you a few cards. Pichler's name was probably one of them.'

'You might be right,' I conceded. 'But all the same it's not a hand I'd care to put my shirt on.'

'Want to let me take a peek?'

'Why should I?'

'I saved your life, kraut,' he growled.

'Too sentimental. Be a little more practical.'

'All right then, maybe I can help.'

'Better. Much better.'

'What do you need?'

'Pichler was more than likely murdered by a man named Abs, Max Abs. According to the MPs he used to be SS, but small-time. Anyway, he boarded a train to Munich this afternoon and they were going to have someone meet him: I expect that they'll tell me what happens. But I need to find out more about Abs. For instance, who this fellow was.' I took out Pichler's drawing of Martin Albers' gravestone and spread it on the table in front of Belinsky. 'If I can find out who Martin Albers was and why Max Abs was willing to pay for his headstone I might be on my way to establishing why Abs thought it necessary to kill Pichler before he spoke to me.'

'Who is this Abs guy? What's his connection?'

'He used to work for an advertising firm here in Vienna. The same place that König managed. König's the man that briefed

Becker to run files across the Green Frontier. Files that went to Linden.'

Belinsky nodded.

'All right then,' I said. 'Here's my next card. König had a girl-friend called Lotte who hung around the Casanova. It could be that she sparkled there a bit, nibbled a little chocolate, I don't know yet. Some of Becker's friends crashed around there and a few other places and didn't come home for tea. My idea is to put the girl on to it. I thought I'd have to get to know her a bit first of all. But of course now that she's seen me on my white horse and wear-ing my Sunday suit of armour I can hurry that along.'

'Suppose Veronika doesn't know this Lotte. What then?'

'Suppose you think of a better idea.'

Belinsky shrugged. 'On the other hand, your scheme has its points.'

'Here's another thing. Both Abs and Eddy Holl, who was Beck-er's contact in Berlin, are working for a company that's based in Pullach, near Munich. The South German Industries Utilization Company. You might like to try and find out something about it. Not to mention why Abs and Holl decided to move there.'

'They wouldn't be the first two krauts to go and live in the American Zone,' said Belinsky. 'Haven't you noticed? Relations are starting to get a shade difficult with our Communist allies. The news from Berlin is that they've started to tear up a lot of the roads connecting the east and west sectors of the city.' His face made plain his lack of enthusiasm, and then added: 'But I'll see what I can turn up. Anything else?'

'Before I left Berlin I came across a couple of amateur Nazi-hunters named Drexler. Linden used to take them Care parcels now and again. I wouldn't be surprised if they were working for him: everyone knows that's how the CIC pays its way. It would help if we knew who they had been looking for.'

'Can't we ask them?'

'It wouldn't do much good. They're dead. Someone slipped a tray-load of Zyklon–B pellets underneath their door.'

'Give me their address anyway.' He took out a notepad and pencil.

When I had given it to him he pursed his lips and rubbed his jaw. His was an impossibly broad face, with thick horns of eyebrows that curved halfway round his eye-sockets, some small animal's skull for a nose and intaglio laugh-lines which, added to his square chin and sharply angled nostrils, completed a perfectly septagonal figure: the overall impression was of a ram's head resting on a V-shaped plinth.

'You were right,' he admitted. 'It's not much of a hand, is it? But it's still better than the one I folded on.'

With the pipe clenched tight between his teeth, he crossed his arms and stared down at his glass. Perhaps it was his choice of drink, or perhaps it was his hair, styled longer than the crewcut favoured by the majority of his countrymen, but he seemed curiously un-American.

'Where are you from?' I said eventually.

'Williamsburg, New York.'

'Belinsky,' I said, measuring each syllable. 'What kind of a name is that for an American?'

The man shrugged, unperturbed. 'I'm first-generation American. My dad's from Siberia originally. His family emigrated to escape one of the Tsar's Jewish pogroms. You see, the Ivans have got a tradition of anti-Semitism that's almost as good as yours. Belinsky was Irving Berlin's name before he changed it. And as names for Americans go, I don't think a yid-name like that sounds any worse than a kraut-name like Eisenhower, do you?'

'I guess not.'

'Talking of names, if you do speak to the MPs again it might be better if you didn't mention me, or the CIC, to them. On account of the fact that they recently screwed up an operation we had going. The MVD managed to steal some US Military Police uniforms from the battalion HQ at the Stiftskaserne. They put them on and persuaded the MPs at the 19th Bezirk station to help them arrest one of our best informers in Vienna. A couple of days later another informant told us that the man was being interrogated at

MVD headquarters in Mozartgasse. Not long after that we learned he had been shot. But not before he talked and gave away several other names.

'Well, there was an almighty row, and the American High Commissioner had to kick some ass for the poor security of the 796th. They court-martialled a lieutenant and broke a sergeant back to the ranks. As a result of which me being CIC is tantamount to having leprosy in the eyes of the Stiftskaserne. I suppose you might find that hard to understand, you being German.'

'On the contrary,' I said. 'I'd say being treated like lepers is something we krauts understand only too well.'

17

The water arriving in the tap from the Styrian Alps tasted cleaner than the squeak of a dentist's fingers. I carried a glassful of it from the bathroom to answer the telephone ringing in my sitting-room, and sipped some more while I waited for Frau Blum-Weiss to switch the call through.

'Well, good-morning,' Shields said with affected enthusiasm. 'I hope I got you out of bed.'

'I was just cleaning my teeth.'

'And how are you today?' he said, still refusing to come to the point.

'A slight headache, that's all.' I had drunk too much of Belinsky's favourite liquor.

'Well, blame it on the föhn,' suggested Shields, referring to the unseasonably warm and dry wind that occasionally descended on Vienna from the mountains. 'Everyone else in this city blames all kinds of strange behaviour on it. But all I notice is that it makes the smell of horseshit even worse than usual.'

'It's nice to talk to you again, Shields. What do you want?'

'Your friend Abs didn't get to Munich. We're pretty sure he got on the train, only there was no sign of him at the other end.'

'Maybe he got off somewhere else.'

'The only stop that train makes is in Salzburg, and we had that covered too.'

'Perhaps someone threw him off. While the train was still moving.' I knew only too well how that happened.

'Not in the American Zone.'

'Well, that doesn't start until you get to Linz. There's over a hundred kilometres of Russian Lower Austria between here and your zone. You said yourself that you're sure he got on the train.

So what else does that leave?' Then I recalled what Belinsky had said about the poor security of the US Military Police. 'Of course, it's possible he simply gave your men the slip. That he was too clever for them.'

Shields sighed. 'Sometime, Günther, when you're not too busy with your old Nazi comrades, I'll drive you out to the DP camp at Auhof and you can see all the illegal Jewish emigrants who thought they were too smart for us.' He laughed. 'That is, if you're not scared that you might be recognized by someone from a concentration camp. It might even be fun to leave you there. Those Zionists don't have my sense of humour about the SS.'

'I'd certainly miss that, yes.'

There was a soft, almost furtive knock at the door.

'Look, I've got to go.'

'Just watch your step. If I so much as think that I can smell shit on your shoes I'll throw you in the cage.'

'Yes, well, if you do smell something it'll probably just be the föhn.'

Shields laughed his ghost-train laugh and then hung up.

I went to the door and let in a short, shifty-looking type who brought to mind the print of a portrait by Klimt that was hanging in the breakfast-room. He wore a brown, belted raincoat, trousers that seemed a little short of his white socks and, barely covering his head of long fair hair, a small, black Tyrolean that was loaded with badges and feathers. Somewhat incongruously, his hands were enclosed in a large woollen muff.

'What are you selling, swing?' I asked him.

The shifty look turned suspicious. 'Aren't you Günther?' he drawled in an improbable voice that was as low as a stolen bassoon.

'Relax,' I said, 'I'm Günther. You must be Becker's personal gunsmith.'

'S'right. Name's Rudi.' He glanced around and grew easier. 'You alone in this watertight?'

'Like a hair on a widow's tit. Have you brought me a present?'

Rudi nodded and with a sly grin pulled one of his hands out of the muff. It held a revolver and it was pointed at my morning croissant. After a short, uncomfortable moment his grin widened and he released the handgrip to let the gun hang by the trigger-guard on his forefinger.

'If I stay in this city I'm going to have to shop for a new sense of humour,' I said, taking the revolver from him. It was a .38 Smith with a six-inch barrel and the words 'Military and Police' clearly engraved in the black finish. 'I suppose the bull who owned this let you have it for a few packets of cigarettes.' Rudi started to answer, but I got there first. 'Look, I told Becker a clean gun, not Exhibit A in a murder trial.'

'That's a new gun,' Rudi said indignantly. 'Squeeze your eye down the barrel. It's still greased: hasn't been fired yet. I swear them at the top don't even know it's missing.'

'Where did you get it?'

'The Arsenal Warehouse. Honest, Herr Günther, that gun's as clean as they come these days.'

I nodded reluctantly. 'Did you bring any ammunition?'

'There's six in it,' he said, and taking his other hand out of the muff laid a miserly handful of cartridges on to the sideboard, next to my two bottles from Traudl. 'And these.'

'What, did you buy them off the ration?'

Rudi shrugged. 'All I could get for the moment, I'm afraid.' Eyeing the vodka he licked his lips.

'I've had my breakfast,' I told him, 'but you help yourself.'

'Just to keep the cold out, eh?' he said and poured a nervous glassful, which he quickly swallowed.

'Go ahead and have another. I never stand between a man and a good thirst.' I lit a cigarette and went over to the window. Outside, a Pan's pipes of icicles hung from the edge of the terrace roof. 'Especially on a day as chilly as this one.'

'Thanks,' said Rudi, 'thanks a lot.' He smiled thinly, and poured a second, steadier glass, which he sipped at slowly. 'So how's it coming along? The investigation, I mean.'

'If you've got any ideas I'd love to hear them. Right now the fish aren't exactly jumping on to the riverbank.'

Rudi flexed his shoulders. 'Well, the way I see it is that this Ami captain, the one that took the 71 –'

He paused while I made the connection: the number 71 was the tram that went to the Central Cemetery. I nodded for him to continue.

'Well, he must have been involved in some kind of racket. Think about it,' he instructed, warming to his subject. 'He goes to a warehouse with some coat, and the place is stacked high with nails. I mean, why did they go there in the first place? It couldn't have been because the killer planned to shoot him there. He wouldn't have done it near his stash, would he? They must have gone to look at the merchandise, and had an argument.'

I had to admit there was something in what he said. I thought for a minute. 'Who sells cigarettes in Austria, Rudi?'

'Apart from everyone?'

'The main black-siders.'

'Excepting Emil, there's the Ivans; a mad American staff sergeant who lives in a castle near Salzburg; a Romanian Jew here in Vienna; and an Austrian named Kurtz. But Emil was the biggest. Most people have heard the name of Emil Becker in that particular connection.'

'Do you think it's possible that one of them could have framed Emil, to take him out of competition?'

'Sure. But not at the expense of losing all those nails. Forty cases of cigarettes, Herr Günther. That's a big loss for someone to take.'

'When exactly was this tobacco factory on Thaliastrasse robbed?'

'Months ago.'

'Didn't the MPs have any idea who could have done it? Didn't they have any suspects?'

'Not a chance. Thaliastrasse is in the 16th Bezirk, part of the French sector. The French MPs couldn't catch drip in this city.'

'What about the local bulls – the Vienna police?'

Rudi shook his head firmly. 'Too busy fighting with the state police. The Ministry of the Interior has been trying to have the state mob absorbed into the regular force, but the Russians don't like it and are trying to fuck the thing up. Even if it means wrecking the whole force.' He grinned. 'I can't say I'd be sorry. No, the locals are almost as bad as the Frenchies. To be honest, the only bulls that are worth a damn in this city are the Amis. Even the Tommies are pretty stupid if you ask me.'

Rudi glanced at one of the several watches he had strapped to his arm. 'Look, I've got to go, otherwise I'll miss my pitch at Ressel. That's where you'll find me every morning if you need to, Herr Günther. There, or at the Hauswirth Café on Favoritenstrasse during the afternoon.' He drained his glass. 'Thanks for the drink.'

'Favoritenstrasse,' I repeated, frowning. 'That's in the Russian sector, isn't it?'

'True,' said Rudi. 'But it doesn't make me a Communist.' He raised his little hat and smiled. 'Just prudent.'

18

The sad aspect to her face, with its downcast eyes and the tilt of her thickening jaw, not to mention her cheap and secondhand-looking clothes, made me think that Veronika could not have made much out of being a prostitute. And certainly there was nothing about the cold, cavern-sized room she rented in the heart of the city's red-light district that indicated anything other than an eked-out, hand-to-mouth kind of existence.

She thanked me again for helping her and, having inquired solicitously after my bruises, proceeded to make a pot of tea while she explained that one day she was planning to become an artist. I looked through her drawings and watercolours without much enjoyment.

Profoundly depressed by my gloomy surroundings, I asked her how it was that she had ended up on the sledge. This was foolish, because it never does to challenge a whore about anything, least of all her own immorality, and my only excuse was that I felt genuinely sorry for her. Had she once had a husband who had seen her frenching an Ami in a ruined building for a couple of bars of chocolate?

'Who said I was on the sledge?' she responded tartly.

I shrugged. 'It's not coffee that keeps you up half the night.'

'Maybe so. All the same, you won't find me working in one of those places on the Gürtel where the numbers just walk up the stairs. And you won't find me selling it on the street outside the American Information Office, or the Atlantis Hotel. Chocolady I may be, but I'm no sparkler. I have to like the gentleman.'

'That won't stop you getting hurt. Like last night, for instance. Not to mention venereal disease.'

'Listen to yourself,' she said with amused contempt. 'You sound just like one of those bastards in the vice squad. They pick you up, have a doctor examine you for a dose and then give you a lecture on the perils of drip. You're beginning to sound like a bull.'

'Maybe the police are right. Ever think of that?'

'Well, they never found anything wrong with me. Nor will they.' She smiled a shrewd little smile. 'Like I said, I'm careful. I have to like the gentleman. Which means I won't do Ivans or niggers.'

'Nobody ever heard of an Ami or a Tommy with syphilis, I suppose.'

'Look, you play the percentages.' She scowled. 'What the hell do you know about it anyway? Saving my ass doesn't give you the right to read me the Ten Commandments, Bernie.'

'You don't have to be a swimmer to throw someone a life-preserver. I've met enough snappers in my time to know that most of them started out as selective as you. Then someone comes along and beats the shit out of them, and the next time, with the land-lord chasing for his rent, they can't afford to be quite as choosy. You talk about percentages. Well, there's not much percentage in french for ten schillings when you're forty. You're a nice girl, Veronika. If there were a priest around he'd maybe think you were worth a short homily, but since there isn't you'll have to make do with me.'

She smiled sadly and stroked my hair. 'You're not so bad. Not that I have any idea why you think it necessary. I'm really quite all right. I've got money saved. Soon I'll have enough to get myself into an art-school somewhere.'

I thought it just as likely that she would win a contract to repaint the Sistine Chapel, but I felt my mouth force its way up to a politely optimistic sort of smile. 'Sure you will,' I said. 'Look, maybe I can help. Maybe we can help each other.' It was a hope-lessly flat-footed way of manoeuvring the conversation back to the main purpose of my visit.

'Maybe,' she said, serving the tea. 'One more thing and then you can give me a blessing. The vice squad has got files on over 5,000 girls in Vienna. But that's not even half of it. These days everyone has to do things that were once unthinkable. You too, probably. There's not much percentage in going hungry. And even less in going back to Czechoslovakia.'

'You're Czech?'

She sipped some of her tea, then took a cigarette from the packet I had given her the night before and collected a light.

'According to my papers I was born in Austria. But the fact is that I'm Czech: a Sudeten German-Jew. I spent most of the war hiding out in lavatories and attics. Then I was with the partisans for a while, and after that a DP camp for six months before I escaped across the Green Frontier.

'Have you heard of a place called Wiener Neustadt? No? Well, it's a town about fifty kilometres outside Vienna, in the Russian Zone, with a collection centre for Soviet repatriations. There are 60,000 of them waiting there at any one time. The Ivans screen them into three groups: enemies of the Soviet Union are sent to labour camps; those they can't actually prove are enemies are sent to work outside the camps – so either way you end up as some kind of slave labour; unless, that is, you're the third group and you're sick or old or very young, in which case you're shot right away.'

She swallowed hard and took a long drag of her cigarette. 'Do you want to know something? I think I would sleep with the whole of the British Army if it meant that the Russians couldn't claim me. And that includes the ones with syphilis.' She tried a smile. 'But as it happens I have a medical friend who got me a few bottles of penicillin. I dose myself with it now and again just to be on the safe side.'

'That sounds expensive.'

'Like I said, he's a friend. It costs me nothing that could be spent on the reconstruction.' She picked up the teapot. 'Would you like some more tea?'

I shook my head. I was anxious to be out of that room. 'Let's go somewhere,' I suggested.

'All right. It beats staying here. How's your head for heights? Because there's only one place to go on a Sunday in Vienna.'

The amusement park of the Prater, with its great wheel, merry-go-rounds and switchback-railway, was somehow incongruous in that part of Vienna which, as the last to fall to the Red Army, still showed the greatest effects of the war and the clearest evidence of our being in an otherwise less amusing sector. Broken tanks and guns still littered the nearby meadows, while on every one of the dilapidated walls of houses all along the Ausstellungsstrasse was the faded chalk outline of the Cyrillic word '*Atak'ivat*' (searched), which really meant 'looted'.

From the top of the big wheel Veronika pointed out the piers of the Red Army Bridge, the star on the Soviet obelisk close by it and, beyond these, the Danube. Then, as the cabin carrying the two of us started its slow descent to the ground, she reached inside my coat and took hold of my balls, but snatched her hand away again when I sighed uncomfortably.

'It could be that you would have preferred the Prater before the Nazis,' she said peevishly, 'when all the dolly-boys came here to pick up some trade.'

'That's not it at all,' I laughed.

'Maybe that's what you meant when you said that I could help you.'

'No, I'm just the nervous type. Try it again sometime when we're not sixty metres up in the air.'

'Highly strung, eh? I thought you said you had a head for heights.'

'I lied. But you're right, I do need your help.'

'If vertigo's your problem, then getting horizontal is the only treatment I'm qualified to prescribe.'

'I'm looking for someone, Veronika: a girl who used to hang around the Casanova Club.'

'Why else do men go to the Casanova except to look for a girl?'

'This is one particular girl.'

'Maybe you hadn't noticed. None of the girls at the Casanova are that particular.' She threw me a narrow-eyed look, as if she suddenly distrusted me. 'I thought you sounded like them at the top. All that shit about drip and all. Are you working with that American?'

'No, I'm a private investigator.'

'Like the Thin Man?'

She laughed when I nodded.

'I thought that stuff was just for the films. And you want me to help you with something you're investigating, is that it?'

I nodded again.

'I never saw myself quite like Myrna Loy,' she said, 'but I'll help you if I can. Who is this girl you're looking for?'

'Her name is Lotte. I don't know her last name. You might have seen her with a man called König. He wears a moustache and has a small terrier.'

Veronika nodded slowly. 'Yes, I remember them. Actually I used to know Lotte reasonably well. Her name is Lotte Hartmann, but she hasn't been around in a few weeks.'

'No? Do you know where she is?'

'Not exactly. They went skiing together – Lotte and Helmut König, her *schätzi*. Somewhere in the Austrian Tyrol, I believe.'

'When was this?'

'I don't know. Two, three weeks ago. König seems to have plenty of money.'

'Do you know when they're coming back?'

'I have no idea. I do know she said she'd be away for at least a month if things worked out between them. Knowing Lotte, that means it would depend on how much of a good time he showed her.'

'Are you sure she's coming back?'

'It would take an avalanche to stop her coming back here. Lotte's Viennese right up to her earlobes; she doesn't know how to live anywhere else. I guess you want me to keep my eye close to the keyhole for them.'

'That's about the size of it,' I said. 'Naturally I'll pay you.'

She shrugged. 'There's no need,' she said, and pressed her nose against the windowpane. 'People who save my life get themselves all sorts of generous discounts.'

'I ought to warn you. It could be dangerous.'

'You don't have to tell me,' she said coolly. 'I've met König. He's all smooth and charming at the club but he doesn't fool me. Helmut's the kind of man who takes his brass knuckles to confession.'

When we were on the ground again I used some of my coupons to buy us a bag of lingos, a Hungarian snack of fried dough sprinkled with garlic, from one of the stalls near the great wheel. After this modest lunch we took the Lilliput Railway down to the Olympic Stadium and walked back in the snow through the woods on Hauptallee.

Much later on, when we were in her room again, she said, 'Are you still feeling nervous?'

I reached for her gourd-like breasts and found her blouse damp with perspiration. She helped me to unbutton her and while I enjoyed the weight of her bosom in my hand she unfastened her skirt. I stood back to give her room to step out of it. And when she had laid it over the back of a chair I took her by the hand and drew her towards me.

For a brief moment I held her tight, enjoying her short, husky breath on my neck, before searching down for the curve of her girdled behind, her membrane-tight stocking-tops, and then the soft, cool flesh between her gartered thighs. And after she had engineered the subtraction of what little remained to cover her, I kissed her and allowed an intrepid finger to enjoy a short exploration of her hidden places.

In bed she held a smile on her face as slowly I strove to fathom her. Catching sight of her open eyes, which were no more than dreamy, as if she was unable to forget my satisfaction in search of her own, I found that I was too excited to care much beyond what seemed polite. When at last she felt the wound I was making in her become more urgent, she raised her thighs on to her chest and, reaching down, spread herself open with the flats of her hands, as if holding taut a piece of cloth for the needle of a sewing-machine, so that I might see myself periodically drawn tight into her. A moment later I flexed against her as life worked its independent and juddering propulsion.

It snowed hard that night, and then the temperature fell into the sewers, freezing the whole of Vienna, to preserve it for a better day. I dreamed, not of a lasting city, but of the city which was to come.

PART TWO

19

'A date for Herr Becker's trial has now been set,' Liebl told me, 'which makes it absolutely imperative that we make all haste with the preparation of our defence. I trust you will forgive me, Herr Günther, if I impress upon you the urgent need for evidence to substantiate our client's account. While I have faith in your ability as a detective, I should very much like to know exactly what progress you have made so far, in order that I may best advise Herr Becker how we are to conduct his case in court.'

This conversation took place several weeks after my arrival in Vienna – but it was not the first time that Liebl had pressed me for some indication of my progress.

We were sitting in the Café Schwarzenberg, which had become the nearest thing I'd had to an office since before the war. The Viennese coffee house resembles a gentleman's club, except in so far as that a day's membership costs little more than the price of a cup of coffee. For that you can stay for as long as you like, read the papers and magazines that are provided, leave messages with waiters, receive mail, reserve a table for appointments and generally run a business in total confidence before all the world. The Viennese respect privacy in the same way that Americans worship antiquity, and a fellow patron of the Schwarzenberg would no more have stuck his nose over your shoulder than he would have stirred a cup of mocha with his forefinger.

On previous occasions I had told Liebl that an exact idea of progress was not something that existed in the world of the private investigator: that it was not the kind of business in which one might report that a specific course of action would definitely occur within a certain period. That's the trouble with lawyers. They expect the rest of the world to work like the Code Napoléon. On this particular occasion however, I had rather more to tell Liebl.

'König's girlfriend, Lotte, is back in Vienna,' I said.

'She's returned from her skiing holiday at long last?'

'It looks like that.'

'But you haven't yet found her.'

'Someone I know from the Casanova Club has a friend who spoke to her just a couple of days ago. She may even have been back for a week or so.'

'A week?' Liebl repeated. 'Why has it taken so long to find that out?'

'These things take time,' I shrugged provocatively. I was fed up with Liebl's constant quizzing and had started to take a childish delight in teasing him with these displays of apparent insouciance.

'Yes,' he grumbled, 'so you've said before.' He did not sound convinced.

'It's not like we have addresses for these people,' I said. 'And Lotte Hartmann hasn't been near the Casanova since she's been back. The girl who spoke to her said that Lotte had been trying to get a small part in a film at Sievering Studios.'

'Sievering? Yes, that's in the 19th Bezirk. The studio is owned by a Viennese called Karl Hartl. He used to be a client of mine. Hartl's directed all the great stars: Pola Negri, Lya de Putti, Maria Corda, Vilma Banky, Lilian Harvey. Did you see *The Gypsy Baron*? Well that was Hartl.'

'You don't suppose he could know anything about the film studio where Becker found Linden's body?'

'Drittemann Film?' Liebl stirred his coffee absently. 'If it were a legitimate film company, Hartl would know about it. There's not much that happens in Viennese film-production that Hartl doesn't know about. But this wasn't anything more than a name on a lease. There weren't actually any films made there. You checked it out yourself, didn't you?'

'Yes,' I said, recalling the fruitless afternoon I had spent there two weeks before. It turned out that even the lease had expired, and that the property had now reverted to the state. 'You're right. Linden was the first and last thing to be shot there.' I shrugged. 'It was just a thought.'

'So what will you do now?'

'Try and trace Lotte Hartmann at Sievering. That shouldn't be too difficult. You don't go after a part in a film without leaving an address where you can be contacted.'

Liebl sipped his coffee noisily, and then dabbed daintily at his mouth with a spinnaker-sized handkerchief.

'Please waste no time in tracing this person,' he said. 'I'm sorry to have to press you like this, but until we discover Herr König's whereabouts, we have nothing. Once you find him we might at least try and oblige him to be called as a material witness.'

I nodded meekly. There was more I could have told him but his tone irritated me, and any further explanation would have generated questions I was simply not equipped to answer yet. I could, for instance, have given him an account of what I had learned from Belinsky, at that same table in the Schwarzenberg, about a week after he had saved my skin – information that I was still turning over in my mind, and trying to make sense of. Nothing was as straightforward as Liebl somehow imagined.

'First of all,' Belinsky had explained, 'the Drexlers were what they seemed. She survived Matthausen Concentration Camp, while he came out of the Lodz Ghetto and Auschwitz. They met in a Red Cross hospital after the war, and lived in Frankfurt for a while before they went to Berlin. Apparently they worked pretty closely with the Crowcass people and the public prosecutor's office. They maintained a large number of files on wanted Nazis and pursued many cases simultaneously. Consequently our people in Berlin weren't able to determine if there had been any one investigation which related to their deaths, or to Captain Linden's. The local police are baffled, as they say. Which is probably the way they prefer it. Frankly, they don't give much of a damn who killed the Drexlers, and the American MP investigation doesn't look as if it's going to get anywhere.

'But it doesn't seem likely that the Drexlers would have been very interested in Martin Albers. He was SS and SD clandestine operations chief in Budapest until 1944, when he was arrested for his part in Stauffenberg's plot to kill Hitler, and hanged at Flossenburg Concentration Camp in April 1945. But I dare say he had it coming to him. From all accounts, Albers was a bit of a bastard, even if he did try and get rid of the Führer. A lot of you guys were a hell of a long time about that, you know. Our Intelligence people even think that Himmler knew about the plot all along and let it go ahead in the hope that he could take Hitler's place himself.

'Anyway, it turns out that this Max Abs guy was Albers' servant, driver and general dogsbody, so it kind of looks as if he was honouring his old boss. The Albers family was killed in an air-raid, so I guess there was no one else to erect a stone in his memory.'

'Rather an expensive gesture, wouldn't you say?'

'You think so? Well, I'd sure hate to get killed minding your ass, kraut.'

Then Belinsky told me about the Pullach company.

'It's an American-sponsored organization, run by the Germans, set up with the aim of rebuilding German commerce throughout Bizonia. The whole idea is that Germany should become economically self-supporting as quickly as possible so that Uncle Sam won't have to keep baling you all out. The company itself is located at an American mission called Camp Nicholas, which until a few months ago was occupied by the postal censorship authorities of the US Army. Camp Nicholas is a big compound that was originally built for Rudolf Hess and his family. But after he went AWOL Bormann had it for a while. And then Kesselring and his staff. Now it's ours. There's just enough security about the place to convince the locals that the camp is home to some kind of technical research establishment, but that's no surprise given the history of the place. Anyway, the good people of Pullach give it a wide berth, preferring not to know too much about what's happening there, even if it is something as harmless as an economic and commercial think-tank. I guess they're good at that, what with Dachau just a few miles away.'

That seemed to take care of Pullach, I thought. But what of Abs? It didn't seem to be in character for a man who wished to commemorate the memory of a hero of the German Resistance (such as it had existed), to kill an innocent man merely in order to remain anonymous. And how could Abs be connected with Linden, the Nazi-hunter, except as some kind of informer? Was it possible that Abs had also been killed, just like Linden and the Drexlers?

I finished my coffee, lit a cigarette and for the present moment I was content that these and other questions could not be asked in any forum other than my own mind.

The number 39 ran west along Sieveringer Strasse into Döbling and stopped just short of the Vienna Woods, a spur of the Alps which reaches as far as the Danube.

A film studio is not a place where you are likely to see any great evidence of industry. Equipment lies forever idle in the vans hired to transport it. Sets are never more than half-built even when they are finished. But mostly there are lots of people, all drawing a wage, who seem to do little more than stand around, smoking cigarettes and nursing cups of coffee; and these only stand because they are not considered important enough to be provided with a seat. For anyone foolish enough to have financed such an apparently profligate undertaking, film must seem like the most expensive length of material since Chinese silk, and would, I reflected, surely have driven Dr Liebl half-mad with impatience.

I inquired after the studio manager from a man with a clipboard, and he directed me to a small office on the first floor. There I found a tall, paunchy man with dyed hair, wearing a lilac-coloured cardigan and having the manner of an eccentric maiden aunt. He listened to my mission with one hand clasped on top of the other as if I had been requesting the hand of his warded niece.

'What are you, some kind of policeman?' he said combing an unruly eyebrow with his fingernail. From somewhere in the building came the sound of a very loud trumpet, which caused him to wince noticeably.

'A detective,' I said, disingenuously.

'Well, we always like to cooperate with them at the top, I'm sure. What did you say this girl was casting for?'

'I didn't. I'm afraid I don't know. But it was in the last two or three weeks.'

He picked up the telephone and pressed a switch.

'Willy? It's me, Otto. Could you be a love and step into my office for a moment?' He replaced the receiver, and checked his hair. 'Willy Reichmann's a production manager here. He may be able to help you.'

'Thanks,' I said and offered him a cigarette.

He threaded it behind his ear. 'How kind. I'll smoke it later.'

'What are you filming at the moment?' I inquired while we waited. Whoever was playing the trumpet hit a couple of high notes that didn't seem to match.

Otto emitted a groan and stared archly at the ceiling. 'Well, it's called *The Angel with the Trumpet*,' he said with a conspicuous lack of enthusiasm. 'It's more or less finished now, but this director is such a perfectionist.'

'Would that be Karl Hartl?'

'Yes. Do you know him?'

'Only *The Gypsy Baron*.'

'Oh,' he said sourly. 'That.'

There was a knock at the door and a short man with bright red hair came into the office. He reminded me of a troll.

'Willy, this is Herr Günther. He's a detective. If you're willing to forgive the fact that he liked *The Gypsy Baron* you might like to give him some assistance. He's looking for a girl, an actress who was at a casting session here not so long ago.'

Willy smiled uncertainly, revealing small uneven teeth that looked like a mouthful of rock salt, nodded and said in a high-pitched voice: 'You'd best come into my office, Herr Günther.'

'Don't keep Willy too long, Herr Günther,' Otto instructed as

I followed Willy's diminutive figure into the corridor. 'He has an appointment in fifteen minutes.'

Willy turned on his heel and looked blankly at the studio manager. Otto sighed exasperatedly. 'Don't you ever write anything in your diary, Willy? We've got that Englishman coming from London Films. Mr Lyndon-Haynes? Remember?'

Willy grunted something and then closed the door behind us. He led the way along the corridor to another office, and ushered me inside.

'Now, what is this girl's name?' he said, pointing me to a chair.

'Lotte Hartmann.'

'I don't suppose you know the name of the production company?'

'No, but I know that she came here within the last couple of weeks.'

He sat down and opened one of the desk drawers. 'Well, there were only three films casting here this past month, so it shouldn't be too difficult.' His short fingers picked out three files which he laid on the blotter and started to sort through their contents. 'Is she in trouble?'

'No. It's just that she may know someone who can help the police with an inquiry we are making.' This was true at least.

'Well if she's been up for a part this last month or so, she'll be in one of these files. We may be short of attractive ruins in Vienna, but one thing we've got plenty of is actresses. Half of them are chocoladies, mind you. Even at the best of times an actress is just a chocolady by another name.' He came to the end of one pile of papers and started on another.

'I can't say I miss your lack of ruins,' I remarked. 'I'm from Berlin myself. We've got ruins on an epic scale.'

'Don't I know it. But this Englishman I have to see wants lots of ruins here in Vienna. Just like Berlin. Just like Rosellini.' He sighed disconsolately. 'I ask you: what is there apart from the Ring and the Opera district?'

I shook my head sympathetically.

'What does he expect? The war's been over for three years.

Does he imagine that we delayed rebuilding just in case an English film crew turned up? Perhaps these things take longer in England than in Austria. It wouldn't surprise me, considering the amount of red-tape the British generate. Never known such a bureaucratic lot. Christ knows what I'm going to tell this fellow. By the time they start filming they'll be lucky to find a broken window.'

He skimmed a sheet of paper across the desk. Pinned to its top left-hand corner was a passport-sized photograph. 'Lotte Hartmann,' he announced.

I glanced at the name and the photograph. 'It looks like it.'

'Actually I remember her,' he said. 'She wasn't quite what we were looking for on that occasion, but I said I could probably find her something in this English production. Good-looking, I'll say that much for her. But to be frank with you, Herr Günther, she isn't much of an actress. A couple of walk-on parts at the Burg-theater during the war and that's about it. Still, the English are making a film about the black market and so they want lots of chocoladies. In view of Lotte Hartmann's particular experience I thought she could be one of them.'

'Oh? What experience is that?'

'She used to be a greeter at the Casanova Club. And now she's a croupier at the Casino Oriental. At least that's what she told me. For all I know she could be one of the exotic dancers they have there. Anyway, if you're looking for her, that's the address she gave.'

'Mind if I borrow this sheet?'

'Be my guest.'

'One more thing: if for any reason Fräulein Hartmann gets in contact with you I'd be grateful if you would keep this under your hat.'

'Like it was a new toupee.'

I stood up to leave. 'Thanks,' I said, 'you've been very helpful. Oh, and good luck with your ruins.'

He grinned wryly. 'Yes, well, if you see any weak walls, give them a shove, there's a good fellow.'

I was at the Oriental that evening, just in time for the first show at 8.15. The girl dancing naked on the pagoda-like dance floor, to the accompaniment of a six-piece orchestra, had eyes that were as cold and hard as the blackest piece of Pichler's porphyry. Contempt was written into her face as indelibly as the birds tattooed on her small, girlish breasts. A couple of times she had to stifle a yawn, and once she grimaced at the gorilla who was detailed to watch over her in case anyone wanted to show the girl his appreciation. When after forty-five minutes she came to the end of her act, her curtsy was a mockery of those of us who had watched it.

I waved to a waiter and transferred my attention to the club itself. 'The wonderful Egyptian Night Cabaret' was how the Oriental described itself on the book of matches I had collected from the brass ashtray, and it was certainly greasy enough to have passed for something Middle Eastern, at least in the clichéd eye of some set-designer from Sievering Studios. A long, curving stairway led down into the Moorish-style interior with its gilt pillars, cupola'd ceiling and many Persian tapestries on the mock-mosaic walls. The dank, basement smell, cheap Turkish tobacco-smoke and number of prostitutes only added to the authentic Oriental atmosphere. I half expected to see the thief of Baghdad sit down at the wooden marquetry table I had taken. Instead I got a Viennese garter-handler.

'You looking for a nice girl?' he asked.

'If I were I wouldn't have come here.'

The pimp read this the wrong way up, and pointed out a big redhead who was seated at the anachronistic American bar. 'I can get you nice and cosy with that one there.'

'No thanks. I can smell her pants from here.'

'Listen, *pifke*, that little chocolady is so clean you could eat your supper off her crotch.'

'I'm not that hungry.'

'Perhaps something else, then. If it's drip you're worried about, I know where I can find some nice fresh snow, with no footprints. Know what I mean?' He leaned forwards across the table. 'A girl who hasn't even finished school yet. How does a splash like that sound to you?'

'Disappear, swing, before I shut your flap.'

He leaned back suddenly. 'Slow your blood down, *pifke*,' he sneered. 'I was only trying to –' He yelped with pain as he found himself drawn to his feet by one sideburn held between Belinsky's forefinger and thumb.

'You heard my friend,' he said with quiet menace, and pushing the man away he sat down opposite me. 'God, I hate pimps,' he muttered, shaking his head.

'I'd never have guessed,' I said, and waved again at the waiter, who seeing the pimp's manner of departure approached the table with more obsequiousness than an Egyptian houseboy. 'What'll you have?' I asked the American.

'A beer,' he said.

'Two Gossers,' I told the waiter.

'Immediately, gentlemen,' he said, and scuttled away.

'Well that's certainly made him more attentive,' I observed.

'Yeah, well, you don't come to the Casino Oriental for ritzy service. You come to lose money on the tables or in a bed.'

'What about the floor-show? You forgot the show.'

'The hell I did.' He laughed obscenely and proceeded to explain that he usually tried to catch the show at the Oriental at least once a week.

When I told him about the girl with the tattoos on her breasts he shook his head with worldly indifference, and for a while I was obliged to listen to him tell me about the strippers and exotic dancers he'd seen in the Far East, where a girl with a tattoo was considered nothing to write home about. This kind of conversation was of little interest to me, and when after several minutes Belinsky ran out of unholy anecdote, I was glad to be able to change the subject.

'I found König's girlfriend, Fräulein Hartmann,' I announced.

'Yes? Where?'

'In the next room. Dealing cards.'

'The croupier? The blonde piece with the tan and the icicle up her ass?'

I nodded.

'I tried to buy her a drink,' he said, 'only I might as well have been selling brushes. If you're going to ingratiate yourself with that one you've got your work cut out, kraut. She's so cold her perfume makes your nostrils ache. Perhaps if you were to kidnap her you might stand some chance.'

'I was thinking along similar lines. Seriously, how low is your credit with the MPs here in Vienna?'

Belinsky shrugged. 'It's a real snake's ass. But say what you've got in mind and I'll tell you for sure.'

'How's this then? The International Patrol comes in here one night and arrests me and the girl on some pretext. Then they take us down to Kärtnerstrasse where I start talking tough about how a mistake has been made. Maybe some money even changes hands to make it look really convincing. After all, people like to believe that all police are corrupt, don't they? So she and König might appreciate that little bit of fine detail. Anyway, when the police let us go I make out to Lotte Hartmann that the reason I helped her was because I find her attractive. Well naturally she's grateful and would like me to know it, only she's got this gentleman friend. Maybe he can repay me somehow or other. Put some business my way, that kind of thing.' I paused and lit a cigarette. 'Well, what do you think?'

'In the first place,' Belinsky said thoughtfully, 'the IP isn't allowed in this joint. There's a big sign at the front door to that effect. Your ten-schilling entrance buys a night's membership to what is, after all, a private club, which means the IP just can't come marching in here dirtying the carpet and scaring the flower-lady.'

'All right then,' I said, 'they wait outside and work a spot-check on people as they leave the club. Surely there's nothing to stop them doing that? They pull Lotte and me in on suspicion: her of being a chocolady, and me of working some racket.'

The waiter arrived with our beers. Meanwhile the second show was starting. Belinsky swallowed a mouthful of his drink and sat back in his seat to watch.

'I like this one,' he growled, lighting his pipe. 'She's got an ass like the west coast of Africa. Just you wait until you see it.' Puffing contentedly, his pipe fixed between his grinning teeth, Belinsky kept his eyes on the girl peeling off her brassière.

'It might just work at that,' he said eventually. 'Only forget trying to bribe one of the Americans. No, if it's grease you're trying to simulate then it really has to be an Ivan or a Frenchy. As it happens the CIC has turned a Russian captain in the IP. Apparently he's trying to work his passage to the United States, so he's good for service manuals, identity-papers, tip-offs, the usual kind of thing. A fake arrest ought to be within his abilities. And by a happy coincidence the Russians are in the chair this month, so it should be easy enough to arrange a night when he's on duty.'

Belinsky's grin widened as the dancing girl eased her pants over her substantial backside to reveal a tiny G-string.

'Oh, will you look at that?' he chuckled, with schoolboyish glee. 'Put a nice frame around her ass and I could hang it on my wall.' He tossed back his beer and winked lasciviously at me. 'I'll say one thing for you krauts. You build your women every bit as well as you build your automobiles.'

20

My clothes actually seemed to fit me better. My trousers had
stopped hanging loose around my waist like a clown's pantaloons.
Slipping into my jacket was no longer reminiscent of a schoolboy
optimistically trying on his dead father's suits. And my shirt-collar
was as snug about my neck as the bandage on a coward's arm.
There was no doubt that a couple of months in Vienna had put
some weight on me, so that I now looked more like the man who
had gone to a Soviet POW camp and less like the man who had
returned from one. But while this pleased me, I saw it as no excuse
to get out of condition, and I had resolved to spend less time sitting in the Café Schwarzenberg, and to take more exercise.

It was the time of year when winter's denuded trees were starting to bud, and when the decision to wear an overcoat was no
longer automatic. With only a chalk-mark of cloud on an otherwise uniformly blue board of sky, I decided to take a walk around
the Ring and expose my pigments to the warm spring sunshine.

Like a chandelier that is too big for the room in which it hangs,
so the official buildings on the Ringstrasse, built at a time of overbearing Imperial optimism, were somehow too grand, too opulent
for the geographical realities of the new Austria. A country of six
million people, Austria was little more than the butt-end of a very
large cigar. It wasn't a Ring I went walking on so much as a wreath.

The American sentry outside the US-requisitioned Bristol
Hotel had his pink face lifted up to catch the rays of the morning
sun. His Russian counterpart guarding the similarly requisitioned
Grand Hotel next door looked as if he had spent his whole life
outdoors, so dark were his features.

Crossing on to the south side of the Ring in order to be close to
the park as I came up the Schubertring, I found myself near the

Russian Kommendatura, formerly the Imperial Hotel, as a large Red Army staff car drew up outside the enormous red star and four caryatids that marked the entrance. The car door opened and out stepped Colonel Poroshin.

He did not seem in any way surprised to see me. Indeed, it was almost as if he had expected to find me walking there, and for a moment he simply looked at me as if it had been only a few hours since I had sat in his office in the little Kremlin in Berlin. I suppose my jaw must have dropped, because after a second he smiled, murmured '*Dobraye ootra* (Good-morning)', and then carried on into the Kommendatura followed closely by a couple of junior officers who stared suspiciously back at me, while I stood there, simply lost for words.

More than a little puzzled as to why Poroshin should have turned up in Vienna now, I wandered back across the road to the Café Schwarzenberg, narrowly escaping being hit by an old lady on a bicycle who rang her bell furiously at me.

I sat down at my usual table to give some thought to Poroshin's arrival on the scene, and ordered a light snack, my new fitness resolution already ruined.

The colonel's presence in Vienna seemed easier to explain with some coffee and cake inside of me. There was, after all, no reason why he should not have come. As an MVD colonel he could probably go wherever he liked. That he had not said more to me or inquired as to how my efforts were going on behalf of his friend I thought was probably due to the fact that he had no wish to discuss the matter in front of the two other officers. And he had only to pick up the telephone and ring the headquarters of the International Patrol in order to discover if Becker was still in prison or not.

All the same I had a feeling on the sole of my shoe that Poroshin's arrival from Berlin was connected with my own investigation, not necessarily for the better. Like a man who has breakfasted on prunes, I told myself I was certain to notice something before very long.

21

Each one of the Four Powers took administrative responsibility for the policing of the Inner City for a month at a time. 'In the chair' was how Belinsky had described it. The chair in question was located in a meeting-room at the combined forces headquarters in the Palais Auersperg, although it also affected who sat next to the driver in the International Patrol vehicle. But though the IP was an instrument of the Four Powers and subject in theory to orders from the combined forces, for all practical purposes it was American operated and supplied. All vehicles, petrol and oil, radios, radio spares, maintenance of the vehicles and the radios, operation of the radio network system and organization of the patrols were the responsibility of the US 796th. This meant that the American member of the patrol always drove the vehicle, operated the radio and performed the first-echelon maintenance. Thus, at least as far as the patrol itself was concerned, the idea of 'the chair' was a bit of a movable feast.

Although the Viennese referred to 'the four men in the jeep', or sometimes 'the four elephants in the jeep', in reality 'the jeep' had long been abandoned as too small to accommodate a patrol of four men, their short-wave transmitter, not to mention any prisoners; and a three-quarter-ton Command and Reconnaissance vehicle was now the favoured mode of transport.

All this I learned from the Russian corporal commanding the IP truck parked a short distance from the Casino Oriental on Petersplatz, in which I sat under arrest, waiting for the kapral's colleagues to pick up Lotte Hartmann. Speaking neither French nor English, and with only a smattering of German, the kapral was delighted to find someone with whom he could have a conversation, even if it was a Russian-speaking prisoner.

'I'm afraid I can't tell you very much about why you're being arrested, apart from the fact that it's for black-marketeering,' he apologised. 'You'll find out more when we get to the Kärtner-strasse. We'll both find out, eh? All I can tell you about is the procedure. My captain will fill out an arrest-form, in duplicate – everything's in duplicate – and leave both copies with the Austrian police. They'll forward one copy to the Military Government Public-Safety Officer. If you're held for trial in a military court, a charge sheet will be prepared by my captain; and if you're held for trial in an Austrian court, the local police will be instructed accordingly.' The kapral frowned. 'To be honest with you, we don't bother much with black-market offences these days. Or vice for that matter. It's smugglers we're generally after, or illegal emigrants. Those other three bastards think I've gone mad, I can tell. But I've got my orders.'

I smiled sympathetically and said how I appreciated him explaining. I was thinking of offering him a cigarette when the door of the truck opened and the French patrolman helped a very pale-looking Lotte Hartmann to climb up beside me. Then he and the Englishman came after her, locking the door from the inside. The smell of her fear was only marginally weaker than the cloying scent of her perfume.

'Where are they taking us?' she whispered to me.

I told her we were going to the Kärtnerstrasse.

'No talking is allowed,' said the English MP in appalling German. 'Prisoners will keep quiet until we reach headquarters.'

I smiled quietly to myself. The language of bureaucracy was the only second language that an Englishman would ever be capable of speaking well.

The IP was headquartered in an old palace within a cigarette-end's flick of the State Opera. The truck drew up outside and we were marched through huge glass doors and into a baroque-style hall, where an assortment of atlantes and caryatids showed the omnipresent hand of the Viennese stonemason. We went up a staircase that was as wide as a railway track, past urns and busts of forgotten noblemen, through a pair of doors that were longer than the legs of a circus tall-man and into an arrangement of glass-fronted offices. The Russian kapral opened the door of one of them, ushered his two prisoners inside and told us to wait there.

'What did he say?' Fräulein Hartmann asked as he closed the door behind him.

'He said to wait.' I sat down, lit a cigarette and looked about the room. There was a desk, four chairs and on the wall a large wooden noticeboard of the kind you see outside churches, except that this one was in Cyrillic, with columns of chalked numbers and names, headed 'Wanted Persons', 'Absentees', 'Stolen Vehicles', 'Express Messages', 'Part I Orders' and 'Part II Orders'. In the column headed 'Wanted Persons' appeared my own name and that of Lotte Hartmann. Belinsky's pet Russian was making things look very convincing.

'Have you any idea what this is all about?' she asked tremulously.

'No,' I lied. 'Have you?'

'No, of course not. There must be some kind of mistake.'

'Evidently.'

'You don't seem all that concerned. Or maybe you just don't understand that it's the Russians who ordered us to be brought here.'

'Do you speak Russian?'

'No, of course not,' she said impatiently. 'The American MP who arrested me said that this was a Russian call and nothing to do with him.'

'Well, the Ivans are in the chair this month,' I said reflectively. 'What did the Frenchman say?'

'Nothing. He just kept looking down the front of my dress.'

'He would.' I smiled at her. 'It's worth a look.'

She gave me a sarcastic sort of smile. 'Yes, well, I don't think they brought me here just to see the wood stacked in front of the cabin, do you?' She spoke with crisp distaste, but accepted the cigarette I offered her all the same.

'I can't think of a better reason.'

She swore under her breath.

'I've seen you, haven't I?' I said. 'At the Oriental?'

'What were you during the war – an air spotter?'

'Be nice. Maybe I can help you.'

'Better help yourself first.'

'You can depend on that.'

When the office door finally opened it was a tall, burly-looking Red Army officer who came into the room. He introduced himself as Captain Rustaveli and took a seat behind the desk.

'Look here,' demanded Lotte Hartmann, 'would you mind telling me why I've been brought here in the middle of the night? What the hell is going on?'

'All in good time, Fräulein,' he replied in flawless German. 'Please sit down.'

She slumped on to a chair beside me and regarded him sullenly. The captain looked at me.

'Herr Günther?'

I nodded and told him in Russian that the girl spoke only German. 'She'll think I'm a more impressive son-of-a-bitch if you and I confine ourselves to a language she can't understand.'

Captain Rustaveli stared coldly back at me and for a brief moment I wondered if something had gone wrong and Belinsky had not managed to make it clear to this Russian officer that our arrests were a put-up job.

'Very well,' he said after a long moment. 'Nevertheless, we shall at least have to go through the motions of an interrogation. May I see your papers please, Herr Günther?' From his accent I took him for a Georgian. The same as Comrade Stalin.

I reached inside my jacket and handed over my identity card into which, at Belinsky's suggestion, I had inserted two $100 bills while sitting in the truck. Rustaveli quickly slipped the money into his breeches pocket without blinking, and out of the corner of my eye I saw Lotte Hartmann's jaw drop on to her lap.

'Very generous,' he murmured, turning over my identity card

in his hairy fingers. Then he opened a file with my name on it. 'Although quite unnecessary, I can assure you.'

'There's her feelings to think of, Captain. You wouldn't want me to disappoint her prejudice, would you?'

'No indeed. Good-looking, wouldn't you say?'

'Very.'

'A whore, do you think?'

'That, or something pretty close to it. I'm only guessing of course, but I'd say she was the type that likes to strip a man of a lot more than ten schillings and his underwear.'

'Not the sort of girl to fall in love with, eh?'

'It would be like putting your tail on an anvil.'

It was warm in Rustaveli's office and Lotte started to fan herself with her jacket, allowing the Russian several glimpses of her ample cleavage.

'It's rare that an interrogation is quite so amusing,' he said, and looking down at his papers added: 'She has nice tits. That's the kind of truth I can really respect.'

'I guess it's a lot easier for you Russians to look at.'

'Well, whatever this little show has been laid on to achieve, I hope you get to have her. I can't think of a better reason to go to all this trouble. Me, I've got a sexual disease: my tail swells up every time I see a woman.'

'I guess that makes you a fairly typical Russian.'

Rustaveli smiled wryly. 'Incidentally, you speak excellent Russian, Herr Günther. For a German.'

'So do you, Captain. For a Georgian. Where are you from?'

'Tbilisi.'

'Stalin's birthplace?'

'No, thank God. That's Gori's misfortune.' Rustaveli closed my file. 'That should be enough to impress her, don't you think?'

'Yes.'

'What shall I tell her?'

'You have information that she's a whore,' I explained, 'so you're reluctant to let her go. But you let me talk you into it.'

'Well, that seems to be in order, Herr Günther,' Rustaveli said, reverting to German again. 'My apologies for having detained you. Now you may leave.'

He handed back my identity card, and I stood up and made for the door.

'But what about me?' Lotte moaned.

Rustaveli shook his head. 'I'm afraid you must stay, Fräulein. The vice squad doctor will be here shortly. He will question you regarding your work at the Oriental.'

'But I'm a croupier,' she wailed, 'not a chocolady.'

'That is not our information.'

'What information?'

'Your name has been mentioned by several other girls.'

'What other girls?'

'Prostitutes, Fräulein. Possibly you may have to submit yourself for a medical examination.'

'A medical? What for?'

'For venereal disease, of course.'

'Venereal disease —?'

'Captain Rustaveli,' I said above Lotte's rising cry of outrage, 'I can vouch for this woman. I wouldn't say I knew her very well, but I've known her long enough to be able to state, quite categorically, that she is not a prostitute.'

'Well —' he cavilled.

'I ask you: does she look like a prostitute?'

'Frankly, I've yet to meet an Austrian girl who isn't selling it.' He closed his eyes for a second, and then shook his head. 'I can't go against the protocol. These are serious charges. Many Russian soldiers have been infected.'

'As I recall, the Oriental where Fräulein Hartmann was arrested is off limits to the Red Army. I was under the impression that your men tended to go to the Moulin Rouge in Walfischgasse.'

Rustaveli pursed his lips and shrugged. 'That is true. But nevertheless —'

'Perhaps if I were to meet you again, Captain, we might discuss the possibility of me compensating the Red Army for any embarrassment regarding a breach of the protocol. In the meantime, would you be able to accept my personal surety for the Fräulein's good character?'

Rustaveli scratched his stubble thoughtfully. 'Very well,' he said, 'your personal surety. But remember, I have your addresses. You can always be re-arrested.' He turned to Lotte Hartmann and told her that she was also free to leave.

'Thank God,' she breathed, and sprang to her feet.

Rustaveli nodded at the kapral standing guard on the other side of the grimy glass door, and then ordered him to escort us out of the building. Then the captain clicked his heels and apologized for 'the mistake', as much for the benefit of his kapral as for any effect it might have had on Lotte Hartmann.

She and I followed the kapral back down the big staircase, our steps echoing up to the ornate cornice-work on the high ceiling, and through the arched glass doors into the street where he leaned over the pavement and spat copiously into the gutter.

'A mistake, eh?' He uttered a bitter laugh. 'Mark my words, I'll be the one that gets the blame for it.'

'I hope not,' I said, but the man just shrugged, adjusted his lambskin hat and trudged wearily back into his headquarters.

'I suppose I ought to thank you,' Lotte said, tying up the collar of her jacket.

'Forget it,' I said, and started walking towards the Ring. She hesitated for a moment and then tripped after me.

'Wait a minute,' she said.

I stopped and faced her again. Frontally her face was even more attractive than its profile, as the length of her nose seemed less noticeable. And she was not cold at all. Belinsky had been wrong about that, mistaking cynicism for general indifference. Indeed, I thought she seemed more apt to entice men, although an evening of watching her in the Casino had established that she was probably one of those unsatisfactory women who dangle intimacy, only to withdraw it at a later stage.

'Yes? What is it?'

'Look, you've already been very kind,' she said, 'but would you mind walking me home? It is very late for a decent girl to be on the streets, and I doubt if I'll be able to find a taxi at this time of night.'

I shrugged and looked at my watch. 'Where do you live?'

'It's not very far. The 3rd Bezirk, in the British sector.'

'All right.' I sighed with a conspicuous lack of enthusiasm. 'Lead the way.'

We walked eastwards, along streets that were as quiet as a house of Franciscan tertiaries.

'You haven't explained why you helped me,' she said, breaking the silence after a while.

'I wonder if that's what Andromeda said when Perseus had saved her from the sea-monster.'

'You seem a little less obviously heroic, Herr Günther.'

'Don't be fooled by my manners,' I told her. 'I've got a whole chestful of medals down at my local pawnshop.'

'So you're not the sentimental type either.'

'No, I like sentiment. It looks fine on needlework and Christmas cards. Only it doesn't make much of an engraving on the Ivans. Or perhaps you weren't looking.'

'Oh, I was looking all right. It was very impressive the way you handled him. I never knew the Ivans could be greased like that.'

'You just have to know the right spot on the axle. That kapral would probably have been too scared to take some drop, and a major too proud. Not to mention the fact that I'd met our Captain Rustaveli before, when he was plain Lieutenant Rustaveli and both he and his girlfriend had a dose of drip. I got them some good penicillin, for which he was very grateful.'

'You don't look like any swing Heini.'

'I don't look like a swing, I don't look like a hero. What are you, the head of casting at Warner Brothers?'

'I only wish I were,' she murmured. And then: 'Anyway, you started it. You said to that Ivan that I didn't look like a chocolady. Coming from you I'd say it almost sounded like a compliment.'

'Like I said, I've seen you at the Oriental, selling nothing worse than bad luck. Incidentally, I hope you're a good card-player, because I'm supposed to go back and give him something for your liberty. Assuming you actually want to stay out of the cement.'

'How much will that be?'

'A couple of hundred dollars ought to do it.'

'A couple of hundred?' Her words echoed around Schwarzen-bergplatz as we came past a great fountain, and crossed onto Rennweg. 'Where am I going to get that kind of mouse?'

'Same place you got the suntan and nice jacket, I imagine. Failing that you could ask him to the club and deal him a few aces off the bottom of the deck.'

'I could if I were that good. But I'm not.'

'That's too bad.'

She was quiet for a moment as she gave the matter some thought. 'Maybe you could persuade him to take less. After all, you seem to speak pretty good Russkie.'

'Maybe,' I allowed.

'I don't suppose it would do much good to go to court and pro-test my innocence, would it?'

'With the Ivans?' I laughed harshly. 'You might just as well appeal to the goddess Kali.'

'No, I didn't think so.'

We came up a side street or two and stopped outside an apart-ment building that was close by a small park.

'Would you like to come in for a drink?' She fumbled in her handbag for her key. 'I know I could use one.'

'I could suck one out of the rug,' I said, and followed her through the door, upstairs and into a cosy, solidly furnished apartment.

There was no ignoring the fact that Lotte Hartmann was attract-ive. Some women, you look at them and calculate what modest length of time you would be willing to settle for. Generally, the better-looking the girl the less time with which you tell yourself you would be satisfied. After all, a really attractive woman might have to accommodate a lot of similar wishes. Lotte was the kind of girl with whom you could have been persuaded to settle for five steamy, unfettered minutes. Just five minutes for her to let you and your imagination do what you wanted. Not too much to ask, you would have thought. The way things happened, though, it looked like she might actually have granted me rather longer than that. Perhaps even the full hour. But I was dog-tired, and perhaps I drank a little too much of her excellent whisky to pay much attention to the way she bit her bottom-lip and stared at me through those black-widow eyelashes. I was probably supposed to lie quietly on her bed with my muzzle resting on her impressively convex lap and let her fold my big, floppy ears, only I ended up falling asleep on the sofa.

When I awoke later that same morning, I scribbled my address and telephone number on a piece of paper and, leaving Lotte asleep in bed, I caught a taxi back to my pension. There I washed, changed my clothes and ate a large breakfast, which did much to restore me. I was reading the morning's *Wiener Zeitung* when the telephone rang.

A man's voice, with only the smallest trace of a Viennese accent, asked me if it was speaking to Herr Bernhard Günther. When I identified myself the voice said:

'I'm a friend of Fräulein Hartmann. She tells me that you very kindly helped her out of an awkward spot last night.'

'She's not exactly out of it yet,' I said.

'Quite so. I was hoping that we could meet and discuss the matter. Fräulein Hartmann mentioned the sum of $200 for this Russian captain. Also that you had offered to act as her intermediary.'

'Did I? I suppose I might have.'

'I was hoping I might give you the money to give to this wretched fellow. And I should like to thank you, personally.'

I felt sure that this was König, but I stayed silent for a moment, not wishing to seem too eager to meet him.

'Are you still there?'

'Where do you suggest?' I asked reluctantly.

'Do you know the Amalienbad, on Reumannplatz?'

'I'll find it.'

'Shall we say in one hour? In the Turkish baths?'

'All right. But how will I recognize you? You haven't even told me your name yet.'

'No I haven't,' he said mysteriously, 'but I'll be whistling this tune.' And with that he proceeded to whistle it down the line.

'Bella, bella, bella Marie,' I said, recognizing a melody that had been irritatingly ubiquitous some months before.

'Precisely that,' said the man, and hung up.

It seemed a curiously conspiratorial mode of recognition, but I told myself that if it was König, he had good reason to be cautious.

The Amalienbad was in the 10th Bezirk, in the Russian sector, which meant catching a number 67 south down Favoritenstrasse. The district was a working-class quarter with lots of dirty old factories, but the municipal baths on Reumannplatz was a seven-storeyed building of comparatively recent construction which, without any apparent exaggeration, advertised itself as the largest and most modern baths in Europe.

I paid for a bath and a towel, and after I had changed I went to find the men's steam-room. This was at the far end of a swimming pool that was as big as a football field, and possessed only a few Viennese who, wrapped in their bath-sheets, were trying to sweat off some of the weight that was rather easy to gain in the Austrian capital. Through the steam, at the far end of the luridly-tiled room, I heard someone whistling intermittently. I walked towards the source of the tune, and took it up as I approached.

I came upon the seated figure of a man with a uniformly white body and a uniformly brown face: it looked almost as if he had blacked-up, like Jolson, but of course this disparity in colour was a souvenir of his recent skiing holiday.

'I hate that tune,' he said, 'but Fräulein Hartmann is always humming it and I couldn't think of anything else. Herr Günther?'

I nodded, circumspectly, as if I had come there only reluctantly.

'Permit me to introduce myself. My name is König.' We shook hands and I sat down beside him.

He was a well-built man, with thick dark eyebrows and a large, flourishing moustache: it looked like some rare species of marten that had escaped on to his lip from some colder, more northerly clime. Drooping over König's mouth, this small sable completed a generally lugubrious expression which started with his melancholy brown eyes. He was much as Becker had described him but for the absence of the small dog.

'I hope you like a Turkish bath, Herr Günther?'

'Yes, when they're clean.'

'Then it's lucky I chose this one,' he said, 'instead of the Diana-bad. Of course the Diana's war-damaged, but the place does seem to attract rather more than its fair share of incurables and other assorted lower humans. They go for the thermal pools they have there. You take a dip at your peril. You could go in with eczema and come out with syphilis.'

'It doesn't sound very healthy.'

'I dare say that I'm exaggerating a little,' König smiled. 'You're not from Vienna, are you?'

'No, I'm from Berlin,' I said. 'I come and go from Vienna.'

'How is Berlin these days? From what one hears the situation there is getting worse. The Soviet delegation walked out of the Control Commission, did it not?'

'Yes,' I said, 'soon the only way in or out will be by military air transport.'

König made a tutting noise and rubbed his big hairy chest wearily. 'Communists,' he sighed, 'that's what happens when you make deals with them. It was terrible what happened at Potsdam and Yalta. The Amis just let the Ivans take what they wanted. A great mistake, which makes another war a virtual certainty.'

'I doubt if anyone's got the stomach for another one,' I said, repeating the same line I had used on Neumann in Berlin. This was a fairly automatic reaction with me, but I genuinely believed it to be true.

'Not yet, maybe. But people forget, and in time –' he shrugged '– who knows what may happen? Until then, we carry on with our lives and our businesses, doing the best that we can.' For a moment he rubbed his scalp furiously. Then he said: 'What business are you in? The only reason I ask is that I hoped that there might be some way in which I could repay you for helping Fräulein Hartmann. Such as putting a little business your way, perhaps.'

I shook my head. 'It's not necessary. If you really want to know, I'm in imports and exports. But to be frank with you, Herr König, I helped her because I liked the smell of her scent.'

He nodded appreciatively. 'That's natural enough. She is very lovely.' But slowly, rapture gave way to perplexity. 'Strange though, don't you think? The way you were both picked up like that.'

'I can't answer for your friend, Herr König, but in my line of work there are always business rivals who would be glad to see me out of the way. An occupational hazard, you might say.'

'By Fräulein Hartmann's account, it's a hazard to which you seem more than equal. I heard that you handled that Russian captain quite expertly. And she was most impressed that you could speak Russian.'

'I was a plenny,' I said, 'a POW in Russia.'

'That would certainly explain it. But tell me, do you believe that this Russian can be serious? That there were charges made against Fräulein Hartmann?'

'I'm afraid he was very serious.'

'Have you any idea where he could have got his information?'

'No more than I have about how he came to have my name. Perhaps the lady has someone with a tooth against her.'

'Maybe you could find out who. I'd be prepared to pay you.'

'Not my line,' I said, shaking my head. 'The chances are that it was an anonymous tip-off. Probably done out of spite. You'd be wasting your money. If you'll take my advice you'll just give the Ivan what he wants and pay up. Two hundred is not a lot of coal to get a name off a file. And when the Ivans decide to keep a dog away from a bitch it's best to settle the account without any trouble.'

König smiled and then nodded. 'Perhaps you are right,' he said. 'But you know, it has occurred to me that you and this Ivan are in it together. It would after all be a nice way of raising money, wouldn't it? The Russian puts the squeeze on innocent people, and you offer to act as intermediary.' He kept on nodding as he surveyed the subtlety of his own scheme. 'Yes, it could be very profitable for someone with the right kind of background.'

'Keep going,' I laughed. 'Maybe you can make an ox out of an egg.'

'Surely you admit that it's possible.'

'Anything is possible in Vienna. But if you think I'm trying to give you some chocolate for a lousy two hundred, that's your affair. It may have escaped your attention, König, but it was your ladyfriend who asked me to walk her home, and you who asked me to come here. Frankly, I've got better things to polish.' I stood up and made as if to leave.

'Please, Herr Günther,' he said, 'accept my apologies. Perhaps I was allowing my imagination to run away with me. But I must confess that this whole affair has me intrigued. And even at the best of times, I find myself suspicious with regard to so many things that happen today.'

'Well, that sounds like a recipe for a long life,' I said, sitting down again.

'In my own particular line of work, it pays to be a little sceptical.'

'What line of work is that?'

'I used to be in advertising. But that is an odious, unrewarding business, full of very small minds with no real vision. I dissolved the company I owned and moved into business research. The flow of accurate information is essential in all walks of commerce. But it is something that one must treat with a degree of caution. Those who wish to be well-informed must first equip themselves with doubt. Doubt breeds questions, and questions beg answers. These things are essential to the growth of any new enterprise. And new enterprise is essential to the growth of a new Germany.'

'You sound like a politician.'

'Politics.' He smiled wearily, as if the subject was too childish for him to contemplate. 'A mere sideshow to the main event.'

'Which is?'

'Communism against the free world. Capitalism is our only hope of withstanding the Soviet tyranny, wouldn't you agree?'

'I'm no friend of the Ivans,' I said, 'but capitalism comes with its own particular faults.'

But König was hardly listening. 'We fought the wrong war,' he said, 'the wrong enemy. We should have fought the Soviets, and only the Soviets. The Amis know that now. They know the mistake they made in letting Russia have a free hand in Eastern Europe. And they're not about to let Germany or Austria go the same way.'

I stretched my muscles in the heat and yawned wearily. König was beginning to bore me.

'You know,' he said, 'my company could use a man with your special talents. A man with your background. Which part of the SS was it that you were in?' Noting the surprise that must have appeared on my face, he added: 'The scar under your arm. Doubtless you too were keen to remove your SS tattoo before being captured by the Russians.' He lifted his own arm to reveal an almost identical scar in his armpit.

'I was with Military Intelligence – the Abwehr – when the war ended,' I explained, 'not the SS. That was much earlier.'

But he had been right about the scar, the result of an obliterating and excruciatingly painful burn sustained from the muzzle flash of an automatic pistol I had fired underneath my upper arm. It had been that or risk discovery and death at the hands of the NKVD.

König himself offered no explanation for the removal of his own tattoo. Instead he proceeded to expand on his offer of employment.

This was all much more than I had hoped for. But I still had to be careful: it was only a few minutes since he had all but accused me of working in consort with Captain Rustaveli.

'It's not that working for someone else gives me the livers or anything,' I said, 'but right now I've got another bottle to finish.' I shrugged. 'Maybe when that's empty . . . who knows? But thanks anyway.'

He did not seem offended that I had declined his offer, and merely shrugged philosophically.

'Where can I find you if I ever change my mind?'

'Fräulein Hartmann at the Casino Oriental will know where to contact me.' He collected a folded newspaper from beside his thigh and handed it to me. 'Open it carefully when you get outside. There are two $100 bills to pay off the Ivan, and one for your trouble.'

At that moment he groaned and took hold of his face, baring incisors and canines that were as even as a row of tiny milk bottles. Observing my eyebrows and mistaking their inquiry for concern he explained that he was quite all right but that he had recently been fitted with two dental plates.

'I can't seem to get used to having them in my mouth,' he said, and briefly allowed the blind, slow worm that was his tongue to squirm along the upper and lower galleries of his jaw. 'And when I see myself in a mirror, it's like having some perfect stranger grinning back at me. Most disconcerting.' He sighed and shook his head sadly. 'A pity really. I always had such perfect teeth.'

He stood up, adjusting the sheet around his chest, and then shook my hand.

'It was a pleasure meeting you, Herr Günther,' he said with easy Viennese charm.

'No, the pleasure was all mine,' I replied.

König chuckled. 'We'll make an Austrian out of you yet, my friend.' Then he walked off into the steam, whistling that same maddening tune.

23

There's nothing the Viennese love more than getting 'cosy'. They look to achieve this conviviality in bars and restaurants, to the accompaniment of a musical quartet comprising a bass, a violin, an accordion and a zither – a strange instrument which resembles an empty box of chocolates with thirty or forty strings that are plucked like a guitar. For me, this omnipresent combination embodies everything that was phoney about Vienna, like the syrupy sentiment and the affected politeness. It did make me feel cosy. Only it was the kind of cosiness you might have experienced after you had been embalmed, sealed in a lead-lined coffin, and tidily deposited in one of those marble mausoleums up at the Central Cemetery.

I was waiting for Traudl Braunsteiner, in the Herrendorf, a restaurant on Herrengasse. The place was her choice, but she was late. When at last she arrived her face was red because she had been running, and also because of the cold.

'You have a less than Catholic air about you, the way you sit there in the shadows,' she said, sitting down at the dinner table.

'I work at that,' I said. 'Nobody wants a detective who looks as honest as the village postmaster. Being dimly lit is good for business.'

I waved to a waiter and we quickly ordered.

'Emil's upset that you haven't been to see him lately,' Traudl said, giving up her menu.

'If he wants to know what I've been doing, tell him I'll be sending him a bill for a shoe-repair. I've walked all over this damned city.'

'You know he goes to trial next week, don't you?'

'I'm not likely to be able to forget it, what with Liebl telephoning nearly every day.'

'Emil's not about to forget it either.' She spoke quietly, obviously upset.

'I'm sorry,' I said, 'that was a stupid thing to say. Look, I do have some good news. I've finally spoken to König.'

Her face lit up with excitement. 'You have?' she said. 'When? Where?'

'This morning,' I said. 'At the Amalienbad.'

'What did he say?'

'He wanted me to work for him. I think it might not be a bad idea, as a way of getting close enough to him to find some sort of evidence.'

'Couldn't you just tell the police where he is so that they can arrest him?'

'On what charge?' I shrugged. 'As far as the police are concerned they've already got their man cold. Anyway, even if I could persuade them to do it, König wouldn't be so easy to clip. The Americans can't go into the Russian sector and arrest him, even if they wanted to. No, Emil's best chance is that I gain König's confidence as quickly as possible. And that's why I turned down his offer.'

Traudl bit her lip with exasperation. 'But why? I don't understand.'

'I have to make sure that König believes I don't want to work for him. He was slightly suspicious of the way in which I got to meet his girlfriend. So here's what I want to do. Lotte's a croupier at the Oriental. I want you to give me some money to lose there tomorrow night. Enough to make it look like I've been cleaned out. Which would give me a reason to reconsider König's offer.'

'This counts as legitimate expenses, does it?'

'I'm afraid it does.'

'How much?'

'Three or four thousand schillings ought to do it.'

She thought for a minute and then the waiter arrived with a bottle of Riesling. When he had filled our glasses Traudl sipped some of her wine and said: 'All right then. But only on one condition: that I'm there to watch you lose it.'

From the set of her jaw I judged her to be quite determined. 'I don't suppose it would do much good to remind you that it could be dangerous. It's not as if you could accompany me. I can't afford to be seen with you in case somebody recognizes you as Emil's girl. If this weren't such a quiet place I would have insisted that we met at your house.'

'Don't worry about me,' she said firmly. 'I'll treat you like you were a sheet of glass.'

I started to speak again, but she held her hands over her small ears.

'No, I'm not listening to any more. I'm coming, and that's final. You're a spinner if you think that I'm just going to hand over 4,000 schillings without keeping an eye on what happens to it.'

'You have a point.' I stared at the limpid disc of wine in my glass for a moment, and then said, 'You love him a lot, don't you?'

Traudl swallowed hard, and nodded vigorously. After a short pause, she added, 'I'm carrying his child.'

I sighed and tried to think of something encouraging to say to her.

'Look,' I mumbled, 'don't worry. We'll get him out of this mess. There's no need to be the cockroach. Come on, come out of the dumps. Everything will work out, for you and the baby, I'm sure of it.' A pretty inadequate speech I thought and lacking any real conviction.

Traudl shook her head, and smiled. 'I'm all right, really I am. I was just thinking how the last time I was here was with Emil, when I told him that I was pregnant. We used to come here a lot. I never meant to fall in love with him, you know.'

'Nobody ever means to do it.' I noticed that my hand was on hers. 'It just happens that way. Like a car accident.' But looking at her elfin face I wasn't sure if I agreed with what I was saying. Her beauty wasn't the kind that's left smeared on your pillowcase in the morning, but the kind that would make a man proud that his child should have such a mother. I realized how much I envied Becker this woman, how much I myself would have wanted to fall in love with her if she had come my way. I let go her hand and quickly lit a cigarette to hide behind some smoke.

24

The next evening found me hurrying from its sharp edge and hint of snow, although the calendar suggested something less inclement, and into the warm, lubricious fug of the Casino Oriental, my pockets packed tight with wads of Emil Becker's easy money.

I bought quite a lot of the highest denomination chips and then wandered over to the bar to await Lotte's arrival at one of the card-tables. Having ordered a drink, all I had to do was shoo away the sparklers and the chocoladies that buzzed around, intent on keeping me and my wallet company, which left me with a keener appreciation of what it must be like to be a horse's ass in high summer. It was ten o'clock before Lotte showed up at one of the tables, by which time the flick of my tail was becoming more apathetic. I delayed another few minutes for appearance's sake before carrying my drink over to Lotte's stretch of green baize and sitting down directly opposite her.

She surveyed the pile of chips that I neatly arranged in front of me and made an equally neat purse of her lips. 'I didn't figure you for a quirk,' she said, meaning a gambler. 'I thought you had more sense.'

'Maybe your fingers will be lucky for me,' I said brightly.

'I wouldn't bet on it.'

'Yes, well, I'll certainly bear that in mind.'

I'm not much of a card-player. I couldn't even have named the game I was playing. So it was with some considerable surprise that, at the end of twenty minutes' play, I realized that I had almost doubled my original stock of chips. It seemed a perverse logic that trying to lose money at cards should be every bit as difficult as trying to win it.

Lotte dealt from the shoe and once again I won. Glancing up

from the table I noticed Traudl seated opposite me, nursing a small pile of chips. I hadn't seen her come into the club, but by now the place was so busy that I would have missed Rita Hayworth.

'I guess it's my lucky night,' I remarked to no one in particular as Lotte raked my winnings towards me. Traudl merely smiled politely as if I had been a stranger to her, and prepared to make her next modest bet.

I ordered another drink and, concentrating hard, tried to make a go of being a real loser, taking a card when I should have stayed, betting when I should have folded and generally trying to sidestep luck at every available opportunity. Now and again I tried to play sensibly in order to make what I was doing appear less obvious. But after another forty minutes I had succeeded in losing all of what I had won, as well as half my original capital. When Traudl left the table, having seen me lose enough of her boyfriend's money to be satisfied that it had been used for the purpose I had stated, I finished my drink and sighed exasperatedly.

'It looks as if it's not my lucky night after all,' I said grimly.

'Luck's got nothing to do with the way you play,' Lotte murmured. 'I just hope you were more skilful in dealing with that Russian captain.'

'Oh, don't worry about him, he's taken care of. You won't have any more problems there.'

'I'm glad to hear it.'

I gambled my last chip, lost it and then stood up from the table saying that maybe I was going to be grateful for König's offer of a job after all. Smiling ruefully, I walked back to the bar where I ordered a drink and for a while watched a topless girl dancing in a parody of a Latin American step on the floor to the tinny, jerking sound of the Oriental's jazz band.

I didn't see Lotte leave the table to make a telephone call but after a while König came down the stairs into the club. He was accompanied by a small terrier, which stayed close to his heels, and a taller, more distinguished-looking man who was wearing a

Schiller jacket and a club-tie. This second man disappeared through a bead curtain at the back of the club while König made a pantomime of catching my eye.

He walked over to the bar, nodding to Lotte and producing a fresh cigar from the top pocket of his green tweed suit as he came.

'Herr Günther,' he said, smiling, 'how nice to meet you again.'

'Hello, König,' I said. 'How are your teeth?'

'My teeth?' His smile vanished as if I had asked him how his chancre was.

'Don't you remember?' I explained. 'You were telling me about your plates.'

His face relaxed. 'So I was. They're much better, thank you.' Tipping in a smile again, he added, 'I hear you've had some bad luck at the tables.'

'Not according to Fräulein Hartmann. She told me that luck has nothing at all to do with the way I play cards.'

König finished lighting his four-schilling corona and chuckled. 'Then you must allow me to buy you a drink.' He waved the barman over, ordered a scotch for himself and whatever I was drinking. 'Did you lose much?'

'More than I could afford,' I said unhappily. 'About 4,000 schillings.' I drained my glass and pushed it across the bartop for a refill. 'Stupid, really. I shouldn't play at all. I have no real aptitude for cards. So I'm cleaned out now.' I toasted König silently and swallowed some more vodka. 'Thank God I had the good sense to pay my hotel bill well in advance. Apart from that, there's very little to feel happy about.'

'Then you must allow me to show you something,' he said, and puffed at his cigar vigorously. He blew a large smoke ring into the air above his terrier's head and said, 'Time for a smoke, Lingo,' whereupon, and much to its owner's amusement, the brute leaped up and down, sniffing excitedly at the tobacco-enriched air like the most craven nicotine addict.

'That's a neat trick,' I smiled.

'Oh, it's no trick,' said König. 'Lingo loves a good cigar almost as much as I do.' He bent down and patted the dog's head. 'Don't you, boy?' The dog barked by way of reply.

'Well, whatever you call it, it's money, not laughs I need right now. At least until I can get back to Berlin. You know it's fortunate you happened to come along. I was sitting here wondering how I might manage to broach the subject of that job with you again.'

'My dear fellow, all in good time. There's someone I want you to meet first. He is the Baron von Bolschwing and he runs a branch of the Austrian League for the United Nations here in Vienna. It's a publishing house called Österreichischer Verlag. He's an old comrade too, and I know he would be interested to meet a man like yourself.'

I knew König was referring to the SS.

'He wouldn't be associated with this research company of yours, would he?'

'Associated? Yes, associated,' he allowed. 'Accurate information is essential to a man like the Baron.'

I smiled and shook my head wryly. 'What a town this is for saying "going-away party" when what you really mean is "a requiem mass". Your "research" sounds rather like my "imports and exports", Herr König: a fancy ribbon round a rather plain cake.'

'I can't believe that a man who served with the Abwehr could be much of a stranger to these necessary euphemisms, Herr Günther. However, if you wish me to do so, I will, as the saying goes, uncover my batteries for you. But let us first move away from the bar.' He led me to a quiet table and we sat down.

'The organization of which I am a member is fundamentally an association of German officers, the primary aim and purpose of which is the collection of research – excuse me, intelligence – as to the threat that the Red Army poses to a free Europe. Although military ranks are seldom used, nevertheless we exist under military discipline and we remain officers and gentlemen. The fight against Communism is a desperate one, and there are times when we must do things we may find unpleasant. But for many old comrades struggling to adjust to civilian life, the satisfaction of continuing to serve in the creation of a new free Germany outweighs such considerations. And there are of course generous rewards.'

It sounded as if König had said these words or their equivalent on a number of other occasions. I was beginning to think that there were more old comrades whose struggle to adjust to civilian life was remedied by the simple expedient of continuing under a form of military discipline than I could guess at. He spoke a lot more, most of which went in one ear and out of the other, and after a while he drained the remainder of his drink and said that if I were interested in his proposition then I should meet the Baron. When I told him that I was very much interested, he nodded satisfiedly and steered me towards the bead curtain. We came along a corridor and then went up two flights of stairs.

'These are the premises of the hat shop next door,' explained König. 'The owner is a member of our Org, and allows us to use them for recruiting.'

He stopped outside a door and knocked gently. Hearing a shout, he ushered me into a room which was lit only by a lamppost outside. But it was enough to make out the face of the man seated at a desk by the window. Tall, thin, clean-shaven, dark-haired and balding, I judged him to be about forty.

'Sit down, Herr Günther,' he said and pointed at a chair on the other side of the desk.

I removed the stack of hat-boxes that lay on it while König went over to the window behind the Baron and sat on the deep sill.

'Herr König believes you might make a suitable representative for our company,' said the Baron.

'You mean an agent, don't you?' I said and lit a cigarette.

'If you like,' I saw him smile. 'But before that can happen it's up to me to learn something of your personality and circumstances. To question you in order that we might determine how best to use you.'

'Like a *Fragebogen?* Yes, I understand.'

'Let's start with your joining the SS,' said the Baron.

I told him all about my service with Kripo and the RSHA, and how I had automatically become an officer in the SS. I explained that I had gone to Minsk as a member of Arthur Nebe's Action Group, but, having no stomach for the murder of women and children, I had asked for a transfer to the front and how instead I had been sent to the Wehrmacht War Crimes Bureau. The Baron questioned me closely but politely, and he seemed the perfect Austrian gentleman. Except that there was also about him an air of false modesty, a surreptitious aspect to his gestures and a way of speaking that seemed to indicate something of which any true gentleman might have felt less than proud.

'Tell me about your service with the War Crimes Bureau.'

'This was between January 1942 and February 1944,' I explained. 'I had the rank of Oberleutnant conducting investigations into both Russian and German atrocities.'

'And where was this, exactly?'

'I was based in Berlin, in Blumeshof, across from the War Ministry. From time to time I was required to work in the field. Specifically in the Crimea and the Ukraine. Later on, in August 1943, the OKW moved its offices to Torgau because of the bombing.'

The Baron smiled a supercilious smile and shook his head. 'Forgive me,' he said, 'it's just that I had no idea that such an institution had existed within the Wehrmacht.'

'It was no different to what happened within the Prussian Army during the Great War,' I told him. 'There have to be some accepted humanitarian values, even in wartime.'

'I suppose there do,' sighed the Baron, but he did not sound convinced of this. 'All right. Then what happened?'

'With the escalation of the war it became necessary to send all the able-bodied men to the Russian front. I joined General Schorner's northern army in White Russia in February 1944, promoted Hauptmann. I was an Intelligence officer.'

'In the Abwehr?'

'Yes. I spoke a fair bit of Russian by then. Some Polish too. The work was mostly interpreting.'

'And you were finally captured where?'

'Königsberg, in East Prussia. April 1945. I was sent to the copper mines in the Urals.'

'Where exactly in the Urals, if you don't mind?'

'Outside Sverdlovsk. That's where I perfected my Russian.'

'Were you questioned by the NKVD?'

'Of course. Many times. They were very interested in anyone who had been an Intelligence officer.'

'And what did you tell them?'

'Frankly, I told them everything I knew. The war was over by that stage and so it didn't seem to matter much. Naturally I left out my previous service with the SS, and my work with the OKW. The SS were taken to a separate camp where they were either shot or persuaded to work for the Soviets in the Free Germany Committee. That seems to be how most of the German People's Police were recruited. And I dare say the Staatspolizei here in Vienna.'

'Quite so.' His tone was testy. 'Do carry on, Herr Günther.'

'One day a group of us were told that we were to be transferred to Frankfurt an der Oder. This would be in December 1946. They said they were sending us to a rest camp there. As you can imagine we thought that was pretty funny. Well, on the transport train I overheard a couple of the guards say that we were bound for a uranium mine in Saxony. I don't suppose either of them realized I could speak Russian.'

'Can you remember the name of this place?'

'Johannesgeorgenstadt, in the Erzebirge, on the Czech border.'

'Thank you,' the Baron said crisply, 'I know where it is.'

'I jumped the train as soon as I saw a chance, not long after we crossed the German–Polish border, and then I made my way back to Berlin.'

'Were you at one of the camps for returning POWs?'

'Yes. Staaken. I wasn't there for very long, thank God. The nurses there didn't think much of us plennys. All they were interested in was American soldiers. Fortunately the Social Welfare Office of the Municipal Council found my wife at my old address almost immediately.'

'You've been very lucky, Herr Günther,' said the Baron. 'In several respects. Wouldn't you say so, Helmut?'

'As I told you Baron, Herr Günther is a most resourceful man,' said König, stroking his dog absently.

'Indeed he is. But tell me, Herr Günther, did no one debrief you about your experiences in the Soviet Union?'

'Like who, for instance?'

It was König who answered. 'Members of our Organization have interrogated a great many returning plennys,' he said. 'Our people present themselves as social workers, historical researchers, that kind of thing.'

I shook my head. 'Perhaps if I had been officially released, instead of escaping . . .'

'Yes,' said the Baron. 'That must be the reason. In which case you must count yourself as doubly fortunate, Herr Günther. Because if you had been officially released we should now almost certainly have been obliged to take the precaution of having you shot, in order to protect the security of our group. You see, what you said about the Germans who were persuaded to work for the Free Germany Committee was absolutely right. It is these traitors who were usually released first of all. Sent to a uranium mine in Erzebirge as you were, eight weeks is as long as you could have been expected to have lived. Being shot by the Russians would have been easier. So you see we can now be confident of you, knowing that the Russians were happy for you to die.'

The Baron stood up now, the interrogation evidently over. I saw that he was taller than I had supposed. König slid off his window sill and stood beside him.

I pushed myself off my chair and silently shook the Baron's outstretched hand, and then König's. Then König smiled and handed me one of his cigars. 'My friend,' he said, 'welcome to the Org.'

25

During the next couple of days König met me at the hat shop next to the Oriental on several occasions in order to school me in the many elaborate and secret working methods of the Org. But first I had to sign a solemn declaration agreeing, on my honour as a German officer, not to disclose anything of the Org's covert activities. The declaration also stipulated that any breach of secrecy would be severely punished, and König said that I would be well-advised to conceal my new employment not only from any friends and relatives but 'even' – and these were his precise words – 'even from our American colleagues'. This, and one or two other remarks he made, led me to believe that the Org was in fact fully funded by American Intelligence. So when my training – considerably shortened in view of my experience with the Abwehr – was complete I irately demanded of Belinsky that we should talk as quickly as possible.

'What's eating you, kraut?' he said when we met at a table I had reserved for us in a quiet corner at the Café Schwarzenberg.

'If I'm not in my plate, it's only because you've been showing me the wrong map.'

'Oh? And how's that?' He set to work with one of his clove-scented toothpicks.

'You know damned well. König's part of a German Intelligence organization set up by your own people, Belinsky. I know because they've just finished recruiting me. So either you put me in the picture or I go to the Stiftskaserne and explain how I now believe that Linden was murdered by an American-sponsored organization of German spies.'

Belinsky looked around for a moment and then leaned purposefully across the table, his big arms framing it as if he was planning to pick it up and drop it on my head.

'I don't think that would be a very good idea,' he said quietly.

'No? Perhaps you think you can stop me. Like the way you stopped that Russian soldier. I might just mention that as well.'

'Perhaps I will kill you, kraut,' he said. 'It shouldn't be too difficult. I have a gun with a silencer. I could probably shoot you in here and nobody would notice. That's one of the nice things about the Viennese. With someone's brains spattered in their coffee cups, they'd still try and mind their own fucking business.' He chuckled at the idea and then shook his head, talking over me when I tried to reply.

'But what are we talking about?' he said. 'There's no need for us to fall out. No need at all. You're right. Maybe I should have explained before now, but if you have been recruited by the Org then you've undoubtedly been obliged to sign a secrecy declaration. Am I right?'

I nodded.

'Maybe you don't take it very seriously, but at least you can understand when I tell you that my government required me to sign a similar declaration, and that I take it very seriously indeed. It's only now that I can take you into my complete confidence, which is ironic: I'm investigating the very same organization which your membership of now enables me to treat you as someone who no longer poses a security risk. How's that for a bit of cock-eyed logic?'

'All right,' I said. 'You've given me your excuse. Now how about telling me the whole story.'

'I mentioned Crowcass before now, right?'

'The War Crimes Commission? Yes.'

'Well, how shall I put it? The pursuit of Nazis and the employment of German intelligence personnel are not exactly separate considerations. For a long time the United States has been recruiting former members of the Abwehr to spy on the Soviets. An independent organization was set up at Pullach, headed by a senior German officer, to gather intelligence on behalf of CIC.'

'The South German Industrial Utilization Company?'

'The same. When the Org was set up they had explicit instructions about exactly who they might recruit. This is supposed to be a clean operation, you understand. But for some time now we've had the suspicion that the Org is also recruiting SS, SD and Gestapo personnel in violation of its original mandate. We wanted intelligence people, for God's sake, not war-criminals. My job is to find out the level of penetration that these outlawed classes of personnel have achieved within the Org. You with me?'

I nodded. 'But where did Captain Linden fit into this?'

'As I explained before, Linden worked in records. It's possible that his position at the US Documents Centre enabled him to act as a consultant to members of the Org with regard to recruitment. Checking out people to see if their stories matched what could be discovered from their service records, that kind of thing. I am sure I don't have to tell you that the Org is keen to avoid any possible penetration by Germans who may have already been recruited by the Soviets in their prison camps.'

'Yes,' I said, 'I've already had that explained to me in no uncertain terms.'

'Maybe Linden even advised them on who might have been worth recruiting. But that's the bit we're not sure about. That and what this stuff was your friend Becker was playing courier with.'

'Maybe he lent them some files when they were interrogating potential recruits who might have been under some suspicion,' I suggested.

'No, that simply couldn't have happened. Security at the Centre is tighter than a clam's ass. You see, after the war the army was scared your people might try to take the contents of the centre back. That or destroy them. You just don't walk out of that place with an armful of files. All documentary examinations are on-site and must be accounted for.'

'Then perhaps Linden altered some of the files.'

Belinsky shook his head. 'No, we've already thought of that and checked back from the original log to every single one of the files which Linden had sight of. There's no sign of anything having been removed or destroyed. It seems our best chance of finding out what the hell he was up to depends on your membership of the Org, kraut. Not to mention your best chance of finding something that will put your friend Becker in the clear.'

'I'm almost out of time with that. He goes to trial at the beginning of next week.'

Belinsky looked thoughtful. 'Maybe I could help you to cut a few corners with your new colleagues. If I were to provide you with some high-grade Soviet intelligence it could put you well in with the Org. Of course it would have to be stuff that my people had seen already, but the boys in the Org wouldn't know that. If I dressed it up with the right kind of provenance, that would make you look like a pretty good spy. How does that sound?'

'Good. While you're in such an inspired mood you can help me out of another fix. After König had got through instructing me in the use of the dead-letter box, he gave me my first assignment.'

'He did? Good. What was it?'

'They want me to kill Becker's girlfriend, Traudl.'

'That pretty little nurse?' He sounded quite outraged. 'The one at the General Hospital? Did they say why?'

'She came into the Casino Oriental to oversee me losing her boyfriend's money. I warned her about it, but she wouldn't listen. I guess it must have made them nervous or something.'

But this wasn't the reason that König had given me.

'A bit of wet-work is often used as an early test of loyalty,' Belinsky explained. 'Did they say how to do it?'

'I'm to make it look like an accident,' I said. 'So naturally I'll need to get her out of Vienna as quickly as possible. And that's where you come in. Can you organize a travel warrant and a rail ticket for her?'

'Sure,' he said, 'but try and persuade her to leave as much behind as possible. We'll drive her across the zone and get her on a train at Salzburg. That way we can make it look as if she's disappeared, maybe dead. Which would help you, right?'

'Let's just make sure that she gets safely out of Vienna,' I told him. 'If anyone has to take risks I'd rather it was me than her.'

'Leave it to me, kraut. It'll take a few hours to arrange, but the little lady is as good as out of here. I suggest that you go back to your hotel and wait for me to bring her papers. Then we'll go and pick her up. In which case, perhaps it would be better if you didn't speak to her before then. She might not want to leave your friend Becker to face the music on his own. It would be better if we could just pick her up and drive out of here. That way if she decides to protest about it there won't be much that she can do.'

After Belinsky had left to make the necessary arrangements, I wondered if he would have been so willing to help get Traudl safely out of Vienna if he had seen the photograph which König had given to me. He had told me that Traudl Braunsteiner was an MVD agent. Knowing the girl as I did it seemed utterly absurd. But for anyone else — most of all a member of CIC — looking at the photograph that had been taken in a Vienna restaurant, in which Traudl was evidently enjoying the company of a Russian colonel of MVD, whose name was Poroshin, things might have seemed rather less than clear-cut.

26

There was a letter from my wife waiting for me when I returned to the Pension Caspian. Recognizing the tight, almost child-like writing on the cheap manilla envelope, crushed and grimy from a couple of weeks at the mercy of a haphazard postal service, I balanced it on the mantelpiece in my sitting-room and stared at it for a while, recollecting the letter to her that I had positioned similarly on our own mantelpiece at home in Berlin, and regretting its peremptory tone.

Since then I had sent her only two telegrams: one to say that I had arrived safely in Vienna and giving my address; and the other telling her that the case might take a little longer than I had first anticipated.

I dare say a graphologist could easily have analysed Kirsten's hand and made a pretty good job of convincing me that it indicated the letter inside had been written by an adulterous woman who was in the frame of mind to tell her inattentive husband that despite his having left her $2,000 in gold she nevertheless intended divorcing him and using the money to emigrate to the United States with her handsome American *schätzi*.

I was still looking at the unopened envelope with some trepidation when the telephone rang. It was Shields.

'And how are we doing today?' he asked in his over-precise German.

'I am doing very well, thank you,' I said, mocking his way of speaking, but he didn't seem to notice. 'Exactly how may I be of service to you, Herr Shields?'

'Well, with your friend Becker about to go to trial, frankly I wondered what kind of detective you were. I was asking myself whether you had come up with anything pertinent to the case: if your client was going to get his $5,000 worth?'

He paused, waiting for me to reply, and when I said nothing he continued, rather more impatiently.

'So? What's the answer? Have you found the vital piece of evidence that will save Becker from the hangman's noose? Or does he take the drop?'

'I've found Becker's witness, if that's what you mean, Shields. Only I haven't got anything that connects him with Linden. Not yet anyway.'

'Well, you had better work fast, Günther. When trials commence in this city they're apt to be a mite quick. I'd hate to see you get round to proving a dead man innocent. That looks bad all round, I'm sure you would agree. Bad for you, bad for us, but worst of all for the man on the rope.'

'Suppose I could set this other fellow up for you to arrest him as a material witness.' It was an almost desperate suggestion, but I thought it worth a try.

'There's no other way he'd show up in court?'

'No. At least it would give Becker someone to point the finger at.'

'You're asking me to make a dirty mark on a shiny floor.' Shields sighed. 'I hate not to give the other side a chance, you know. So I tell you what I'm going to do. I'll have a word with my Executive Officer, Major Wimberley, and see what he recommends. But I can't promise anything. Chances are, the major will tell me to go balls out and get a conviction, and to hell with your man's witness. There's a lot of pressure on us to get a quick result here, you know. The Brig doesn't like it when American officers are murdered in his city. That's Brigadier-General Alexander O. Gorder, commanding the 796th. One tough son-of-a-bitch. I'll be in touch.'

'Thanks, Shields. I appreciate it.'

'Don't thank me yet, mister,' he said.

I replaced the receiver and picked up my letter. After I'd fanned myself with it, and used it to clean my fingernails, I tore it open.

Kirsten was never much of a letter-writer. She was more one for a postcard, only a postcard from Berlin was no longer likely to inspire much in the way of wishful thinking. A view of the ruined

Kaiser-Wilhelm church? Or one of the bombed-out Opera House? The execution shed at Plotzensee? I thought that it would be a good long while before there were any postcards sent from Berlin. I unfolded the paper and started to read:

Dear Bernie,

I hope this letter reaches you, but things are so difficult here that it may not, in which case I may also try to send you a telegram, if only to tell you that everything is all right. Sokolovsky has demanded that the Soviet military police should control all traffic from Berlin to the West, and this may mean that the mail does not get through.

The real fear here is that this will all turn into a full-scale siege of the city in an effort to push the Americans, the British and the French out of Berlin – although I don't suppose anyone would mind if we saw the back of the French. Nobody objects to the Amis and the Tommies bossing us around – at least they fought and beat us. But Franz? They are such hypocrites. The fiction of a victorious French army is almost too much for a German to bear.

People say that the Amis and the Tommies won't stand by and see Berlin fall to the Ivans. I'm not so sure about the British. They've got their hands full in Palestine right now (all books on Zionist Nationalism have been removed from Berlin bookshops and libraries, which seems only too familiar). But just when you think that the British have more important things to do, one hears that they've been destroying more German shipping. The sea is full of fish for us to eat, and they're blowing up boats! Do they want to save us from the Russians in order that they can starve us?

One still hears rumours of cannibalism. There's a story going around Berlin that the police were called to a house in Kreuzberg where downstairs neighbours had heard the sounds of a terrible commotion, and found blood seeping through their ceiling. They burst in and found an old couple dining off the raw flesh of a pony that they had dragged off the street and killed with rocks. It may or may not be true, but I have the terrible feeling that it is. What is certain is that morale has sunk to new depths. The skies are full of transport planes and troops of all four Powers are increasingly jumpy.

You remember Frau Fersen's son, Karl? He came back from a Russian POW camp last week, but in very poor health. Apparently the doctor says that his lungs are finished, poor boy. She was telling me what he'd said about his time in Russia. It sounds awful! Why ever didn't you talk to me about it, Bernie? Perhaps I would have been more understanding. Perhaps I could have helped. I am conscious that I haven't been much of a wife to you since the war. And now that you are no longer here, this seems harder to bear. So when you come back I thought that maybe we could use some of the money you left – so much money! did you rob a bank? – to go on holiday somewhere. To leave Berlin for a while, and spend time together.

Meanwhile, I have used some of the money to repair the ceiling. Yes, I know you had planned on doing it yourself, but I know how you kept putting it off. Anyway, it's done now, and it looks very nice.

Come home and see it soon. I miss you.

Your loving wife,
Kirsten.

So much for my imaginary graphologist, I reflected happily, and poured myself the last of Traudl's vodka. This had the immediate effect of melting my nervousness of telephoning Liebl to report on my almost imperceptible progress. To hell with Belinsky, I said to myself, and resolved to solicit Liebl's opinion as to whether Becker would or would not be best served by trying to obtain König's immediate arrest in order that he be forced to give evidence.

When Liebl finally came on the line he sounded like a man who had just come to the telephone after falling down a flight of stairs. His normally forthright and irascible manner was cowed and his voice was balanced precariously at the very edge of breakdown.

'Herr Günther,' he said, and swallowed his way to a more

decorous silence. Then I heard him take a deep breath as he took control of himself again. 'There's been the most terrible accident. Fräulein Braunsteiner has been killed.'

'Killed?' I repeated dumbly. 'How?'

'She was run over by a car,' Liebl said quietly.

'Where?'

'It happened virtually on the doorstep of the hospital where she worked. Apparently it was instantaneous. There was nothing they could do for her.'

'When was this?'

'Just a couple of hours ago, when she was coming off duty. Unfortunately the driver did not stop.'

That part I could have guessed for myself.

'He was scared probably. Possibly he had been drinking. Who knows? Austrians are such bad drivers.'

'Did anyone see the – the accident?' The words sounded almost angry in my mouth.

'There are no witnesses so far. But someone seems to recollect having seen a black Mercedes driving rather too fast much farther along Alser Strasse.'

'Christ,' I said weakly, 'that's just around the corner. To think I might even have heard the squeal of those car-tyres.'

'Yes, indeed, quite so,' Liebl murmured. 'But there was no pain. It was so quick that she could not have suffered. The car struck her in the middle of her back. The doctor I spoke to said that her spine was completely shattered. Probably she was dead before she hit the ground.'

'Where is she now?'

'In the morgue at the General Hospital,' Liebl sighed. I heard him light a cigarette and take a long drag of smoke. 'Herr Günther,' he said, 'we shall of course have to inform Herr Becker. Since you know him so much better than I –'

'Oh no,' I said quickly, 'I get enough rotten jobs without contracting to do that one as well. Take her insurance policy and her will along if it makes it any easier for you.'

'I can assure you that I'm every bit as upset about this as you are, Herr Günther. There's no need to be –'

'Yes, you're right. I'm sorry. Look, I hate to sound callous, but let's see if we can't use this to get an adjournment.'

'I don't know if this quite qualifies as compassionate,' Liebl hummed. 'It's not as if they were married or anything.'

'She was going to have his baby, for Christ's sake.'

There was a brief, shocked silence. Then Liebl spluttered, 'I had no idea. Yes, you're right, of course. I'll see what I can do.'

'Do that.'

'But however am I going to tell Herr Becker?'

'Tell him she was murdered,' I said. He started to say something, but I was not in a mood to be contradicted. 'It was no accident, believe me. Tell Becker it was his old comrades who did it. Tell him that precisely. He'll understand. See if it doesn't jog his memory a little. Perhaps now he'll remember something he should have told me earlier. Tell him that if this doesn't make him give us everything he knows then he deserves a crushed windpipe.' There was a knock at the door. Belinsky with Traudl's travel papers. 'Tell him that,' I snapped and banged the receiver back onto its cradle. Then I crossed the floor of the room and hauled the door open.

Belinsky held Traudl's redundant travel papers in front of him and gave them a jaunty wave as he came into the room, too pleased with himself to notice my mood.

'It took a bit of doing, getting a pink as quickly as this,' he said, 'but old Belinsky managed it. Just don't ask me how.'

'She's dead,' I said flatly, and watched his big face fall.

'Shit,' he said, 'that's too bad. What the hell happened?'

'A hit-and-run driver.' I lit a cigarette and slumped into the armchair. 'Killed her outright. I've just had Becker's lawyer on the phone telling me. It happened not far from here, a couple of hours ago.'

Belinsky nodded and sat down on the sofa opposite me. Although I avoided his eye I still felt it trying to look into my soul. He shook his head for a while and then produced his pipe which he set about filling with tobacco. When he had finished he started to light the thing and in between fire-sustaining sucks of air, he said, 'Forgive me – for asking – but you didn't – change your mind – did you?'

'About what?' I growled belligerently.

He removed the pipe from his mouth and glanced into the bowl before replacing it between his big irregular teeth. 'I mean, about killing her yourself.'

Finding the answer on my rapidly colouring face he shook his head quickly. 'No, of course not. What a stupid question. I'm sorry.' He shrugged. 'All the same, I had to ask. You must agree, it's a bit of a coincidence, isn't it? The Org asks you to arrange an accident for her, and then almost immediately she gets herself knocked down and killed.'

'Maybe you did it,' I heard myself say.

'Maybe.' Belinsky sat forward on the sofa. 'Let's see now: I waste all afternoon getting this unfortunate little fräulein a pink and a ticket out of Austria. Then I knock her down and kill her in cold blood on my way here to see you. Is that it?'

'What kind of car do you drive?'

'A Mercedes.'

'What colour?'

'Black.'

'Someone saw a black Mercedes speeding further up the street from the scene of the accident.'

'I dare say. I've yet to see the car which drives slowly in Vienna. And in case you hadn't noticed, just about every other non-military vehicle in this city is a black Mercedes.'

'All the same,' I persisted, 'maybe we should take a look at the front fenders, and check for dents.'

He spread his hands innocently, as if he had been about to give the sermon on the mount. 'Be my guest. Only you'll find dents all over the car. There seems to be a law against careful driving here.' He sucked some more of his pipe smoke. 'Look, Bernie, if you don't mind me saying so I think we're in danger of throwing the handle after the axe-head here. It's a real shame that Traudl's dead, but there's no sense in you and me falling out over it. Who knows? Maybe it was an accident. You know it's true what I said about Viennese drivers. They're worse than the Soviets, and they take some beating. Jesus, it's like a chariot race on these roads. Now I agree that it's a hell of a coincidence, but it's not an impossible one, by any stretch of the imagination. You must admit that, surely.'

I nodded slowly. 'All right. I admit it's not impossible.'

'On the other hand maybe the Org briefed more than one agent to kill her so that if you missed, somebody else was bound to get her. It's not unusual for assassinations to be handled that way. Certainly not in my own experience, anyway.' He paused, and then pointed his pipe at me. 'You know what I think? I think that the next time you see König, you should simply keep quiet about it. If he mentions it then you can assume that it probably was an accident and feel confident of taking the credit for it.' He searched in his jacket pocket and drew out a buff-coloured envelope which he threw into my lap. 'It makes this a little less necessary, but that can't be helped.'

'What's this?'

'From an MVD station near Sopron, close to the Hungarian border. It's the details of MVD personnel and methods throughout Hungary and Lower Austria.'

'And how am I supposed to account for this little lot?'

'I rather thought that you could handle the man who gave it to us. Frankly it's just the sort of material that they're keen on. The man's name is Yuri. That's all you need to know. There are map references and the location of the dead-letter box he's been using. There's a railway bridge near a little town called Mattersburg. On the bridge is a footpath and about two-thirds of the way along the handrail is broken. The top part is hollow cast metal. All you have to do is collect your information from there once a month, and leave some money and instructions.'

'How do I account for my relationship with him?'

'Until quite recently Yuri was stationed in Vienna. You used to buy identity papers for him. But now he's getting more ambitious, and you haven't the money to buy what he's got to offer. So you can offer him to the Org. CIC has already assessed his worth. We've had all we're going to get out of him, at least in the short term. There's no harm done if he gives all the same stuff to the Org.' Belinsky re-lit his pipe and puffed vigorously while he awaited my reaction.

'Really,' he said, 'there's nothing to it. An operation of this sort is hardly deserving of the word "intelligence". Believe me, very few of them are. But all in all a source like this and an apparently successful bit of murder leaves you pretty well accredited, old man.'

'You'll forgive my lack of enthusiasm,' I said drily, 'only I'm beginning to lose sight of what I'm doing here.'

Belinsky nodded vaguely. 'I thought you wanted to clear your old pitman.'

'Maybe you haven't been listening. Becker was never my friend. But I really think he is innocent of Linden's murder. And so did Traudl. So long as she was alive this case really felt as if it was worthwhile, there seemed to be some point in trying to prove Becker innocent. Now I'm not so sure.'

'Come on, Günther,' Belinsky said. 'Becker's life without his girl is still better than no life at all. Do you honestly think that Traudl would have wanted you to give up?'

'Maybe, if she knew the kind of crap he was into. The kind of people he was dealing with.'

'You know that's not true. Becker was no altar-boy, that's for sure. But from what you've told me about her I'd bet she knew that. There's not much innocence left any more. Not in Vienna.'

I sighed and rubbed my neck wearily. 'Maybe you're right,' I conceded. 'Maybe it's just me. I'm used to having things being a little more well-defined than this. A client came along, paid my fee and I'd point my suit in whatever direction seemed appropriate. Sometimes I even got to solve a case. That's a pretty good feeling, you know. But right now it's like there are too many people near me, telling me how to work. As if I've lost my independence. I've stopped feeling like a private investigator.'

Belinsky rocked his head on his shoulders like a man who has sold out of something. Explanations probably. He made a stab at one all the same. 'Come on, surely you must have worked under-cover before now.'

'Sure,' I said. 'Only it was with a sharper sense of purpose. At least I got to see a criminal's picture. I knew what was right. But this isn't clear-cut any more, and it's beginning to peel my reed.'

'Nothing stays the same, kraut. The war changed everything for everyone, private investigators included. But if you want to see criminals' photographs I can show you a hundred. Thousands probably. War-criminals, all of them.'

'Photographs of krauts? Listen, Belinsky, you're an American and you're a Jew. It's a lot easier for you to see the right here. Me? I'm a German. For one brief, dirty moment I was even in the SS. If I met one of your war-criminals he'd probably shake me by the hand and call me an old comrade.'

He had no answer for that.

I found another cigarette and smoked it in silence. When it was finished I shook my head ruefully. 'Maybe it's just Vienna. Maybe it's being away from home for so long. My wife wrote to me. We weren't getting along too well when I left Berlin. Frankly I couldn't wait to leave, and so I took this case against my better judgement. Anyway she says that she hopes we can start again. And do you know, I can't wait to get back to her and give it a try. Maybe –' I shook my head. 'Maybe I need a drink.'

Belinsky grinned enthusiastically. 'Now you're talking, kraut,' he said. 'One thing I've learned in this job: if in doubt, pickle it in alcohol.'

27

It was late when we drove back from the Melodies Bar, a nightclub in the 1st Bezirk. Belinsky drew up outside my pension and as I got out of the car a woman stepped quickly out of the shadow of a nearby doorway. It was Veronika Zartl. I smiled thinly at her, having drunk rather too much to care for any company.

'Thank God you've come,' she said. 'I've waited hours.' Then she flinched as through the open car door we both heard Belinsky utter an obscene remark.

'What's the matter?' I asked her.

'I need your help. There's a man in my room.'

'So what's new?' said Belinsky.

Veronika bit her lip. 'He's dead, Bernie. You've got to help me.'

'I'm not sure what I can do,' I said uncertainly, wishing that we'd stayed longer in the Melodies. I said to myself: 'A girl ought not to trust anyone these days.' To her I said: 'You know, it's really a job for the police.'

'I can't tell the police,' she groaned impatiently. 'That would mean the vice squad, the Austrian criminal police, public health officials and an inquest. I'd probably lose my room, everything. Don't you see?'

'All right, all right. What happened?'

'I think he had a heart attack.' Her head dropped. 'I'm sorry to bother you, only there is no one else I can turn to.'

I cursed myself again and then stuck my head back into Belinsky's car. 'The lady needs our help,' I grunted, without much enthusiasm.

'That's not all she needs.' But he started the engine and added: 'Come on, hop in, the pair of you.'

He drove to Rotenturmstrasse and parked outside the bomb-damaged building where Veronika had her room. When we got out of the car I pointed across the darkened cobbles of Stephansplatz to the partly restored cathedral.

'See if you can't find a tarpaulin over on the building site,' I told Belinsky. 'I'll go up and take a look. If there's something suitable, bring it up to the second floor.'

He was too drunk to argue. Instead he nodded dully and walked back towards the Cathedral scaffolding, while I turned and followed Veronika up the stairs to her room.

A large, lobster-coloured man of about fifty lay dead in her big oak bed. Vomiting is quite common in cases of congestive heart failure. It covered his nose and mouth like a bad facial burn. I pressed my fingers against the man's clammy neck.

'How long has he been here?'

'Three or four hours.'

'It's lucky you kept him covered up,' I told her. 'Close that window.' I stripped the bedclothes from the dead man's body and started to raise the upper part of his torso. 'Give me a hand here,' I ordered.

'What are you doing?' She helped me to bend the torso over the legs as if I had been trying to shut an overstuffed suitcase.

'I'm keeping this bastard in shape,' I said. 'A bit of chiropractic ought to slow up the stiffening and make it easier for us to get him in and out of the car.' I pressed down hard on the back of his neck, and then, blowing hard from my exertions, pushed the man back against the puke-strewn pillows. 'Uncle here's been getting extra food-stamps,' I breathed. 'He must weigh more than a hundred kilos. It's lucky we've got Belinsky along to help.'

'Is Belinsky a policeman?' she asked.

'Sort of,' I said, 'but don't worry, he's not the kind of bull who cares much for the crime figures. Belinsky's got other fish to fry. He hunts Nazi war-criminals.' I started to bend the dead man's arms and legs.

'What are you going to do with him?' she said nauseously.

'Drop him on the railway line. With him being naked it will

look like the Ivans gave him a little party and then threw him off a train. With any luck the express will go over him and fit him with a good disguise.'

'Please don't,' she said weakly. '. . . He was very kind to me.'

When I'd finished with the body I stood up and straightened my tie. 'This is hard work on a vodka supper. Now where the hell is Belinsky?' Spotting the man's clothes which were laid neatly over the back of a dining-chair by the grimy net curtains, I said: 'Have you been through his pockets yet?'

'No, of course not.'

'You *are* new at this game, aren't you?'

'You don't understand at all. He was a good friend of mine.'

'Evidently,' Belinsky said coming through the door. He held up a length of white material. 'I'm afraid that this was all I could find.'

'What is it?'

'An altar-cloth, I think. I found it in a cupboard inside the cathedral. It didn't look like it was being used.'

I told Veronika to help Belinsky wrap her friend in the cloth while I searched his pockets.

'He's good at that,' Belinsky told her. 'He went through my pockets once while I was still breathing. Tell me, honey, were you and fat boy actually doing it when he was scythed out?'

'Leave her alone, Belinsky.'

'Blessed are the dead which die in the Lord from henceforth,' he chuckled. 'But me? I just hope I die in a good woman.'

I opened the man's wallet and thumbed a fold of dollar bills and schillings on to the dressing-table.

'What are you looking for?' asked Veronika.

'If I'm going to dispose of a man's body I like to know at least a little more about him than just the colour of his underwear.'

'His name was Karl Heim,' she said quietly.

I found a business card. 'Dr Karl Heim,' I said. 'A dentist, eh? Is he the one who got you the penicillin?'

'Yes.'

'A man who liked to take precautions, eh?' Belinsky murmured.

'From the look of this room, I can understand why.' He nodded at the money on the dressing-table. 'You had better keep that money, sweetheart. Get yourself a new decorator.'

There was another business card in Heim's wallet. 'Belinsky,' I said. 'Have you ever heard of a Major Jesse P. Breen? From something called the DP Screening Project?'

'Sure I have,' he said, coming over and taking the card out of my fingers. 'The DPSP is a special section of the 430th. Breen is the CIC's local liaison officer for the Org. If any of the Org's men get into trouble with the US military police, Breen is supposed to try and help them sort it out. That is unless it's anything really serious, like a murder. And I wouldn't put it past him to fix that as well, providing the victim was anyone but an American or an Englishman. It looks as if our fat friend might have been one of your old comrades, Bernie.'

While Belinsky talked I quickly searched Heim's trouser pockets and found a set of keys.

'In that case it might be an idea if you and I were to take a look around the good doctor's surgery,' I said. 'I've got a feeling in my socks that we might just find something interesting there.'

We dumped Heim's naked body on a quiet stretch of railway track near the Ostbahnhof in the Russian sector of the city. I was keen to leave the scene as quickly as possible, but Belinsky insisted on sitting in the car and waiting to see the train finish the job. After about fifteen minutes a goods train bound for Budapest and the Orient came rumbling by, and Heim's corpse was lost under its many hundreds of pairs of wheels.

'For all flesh is grass,' Belinsky intoned, 'and all the goodliness thereof is as the flower of the field: The grass withereth, and the flower fadeth.'

'Cut that out, will you?' I said. 'It makes me nervous.'

'But the souls of the righteous are in the hand of God and there shall no torment touch them. Anything you say, kraut.'

'Come on,' I said. 'Let's get away from here.'

We drove north to Währing in the 18th Bezirk, and an elegant three-storey house on Türkenschanzplatz, close to a decent-sized park which was bisected by a small railway line.

'We could have dropped our passenger out here,' said Belinsky, 'on his own doorstep. And saved ourselves a trip into the Russian sector.'

'This is the American sector,' I reminded him. 'The only way to get thrown off a train round here is to travel without a ticket. They even wait until the train stops moving.'

'That's Uncle Sam for you, hey? No, you're right, Bernie. He's better off with the Ivans. It wouldn't be the first time they threw one of our people off a train. But I'd sure hate to be one of their trackmen. Damned dangerous, I'd say.'

We left the car and walked towards the house.

There was no sign that anyone was at home. Above the broad, toothy grin of a short wooden fence the darkened windows on the white stuccoed house stared back like the empty sockets in a great skull. A tarnished brass plate on the gatepost which, with typical Viennese exaggeration, bore the name of Dr Karl Heim, Consultant Orthodontic Surgeon, not to mention most of the letters of the alphabet, indicated two separate entrances: one to Heim's residence, and the other to his surgery.

'You look in the house,' I said, opening the front door with the keys. 'I'll go round the side and check the surgery.'

'Anything you say.' Belinsky produced a flashlight from his overcoat pocket. Seeing my eyes fasten on the torch, he added: 'What's the matter? You scared of the dark or something?' He laughed. 'Here, you take it. I can see in the dark. In my line of work you have to.'

I shrugged and relieved him of the light. Then he reached inside his jacket and took out his gun.

'Besides,' he said, screwing on the silencer. 'I like to keep one hand free for turning door-handles.'

'Just watch who you shoot,' I said and walked away.

Round the side of the house I let myself in through the surgery door and, after closing it quietly behind me again, switched on the torch. I kept the light on the linoleum floor and away from the windows in case a nosy neighbour happened to be keeping an eye on the place.

I found myself in a small reception and waiting area which was home to a number of potted plants and a tankful of terrapins: it made a change from goldfish, I told myself, and mindful of the fact that their owner was now dead, I sprinkled some of the foul smelling food that they ate on to the surface of their water. That was my second good deed of the day. Charity was beginning to be a bit of a habit with me.

Behind the reception desk I opened the appointment-book and pointed the torch beam on to its pages. It didn't look like Heim had much of a practice to leave to his competition, always assuming he had any. There wasn't a lot of spare money around for curing toothache these days, and I didn't doubt that Heim would have made a better living selling drugs on the black market. Turning back the pages I could see that he averaged no more than two or three appointments a week. Several months back in the book I came across two names I knew: Max Abs and Helmut König. Both of them were marked down for full extractions within a few days of each other. There were lots of other names listed for full extractions, but none that I recognized.

I went over to the filing cabinets and found them mostly empty, with the exception of one that contained details only of patients prior to 1940. The cabinet didn't look as if it had been opened since then, which struck me as odd as dentists tend to be quite meticulous about such things; and indeed, the Heim of pre-1940 had been conscientious with his patients' records, detailing residual teeth, fillings and denture-fitting marks for each one of them. Had he just got sloppy, I wondered, or had an inadequate volume of business ceased to make such careful records worthwhile? And why so many full extractions of late? It was true, the war had left a great many men, myself included, with poor teeth. In my case this was one legacy of a year's starvation as a Soviet prisoner. But nevertheless I had still managed to keep a full set. And there were plenty of others like me. What need for König then, who I remembered telling me that he had had such good teeth, to have had all of his teeth extracted? Or did he simply mean that his teeth had been good before they went bad? While none of this was enough for Conan Doyle to have turned into a short story, it certainly left me puzzled.

The surgery itself was much like any other I had ever been in. A little dirtier perhaps, but then nothing was as clean as it had been before the war. Beside the black-leather chair stood a large cylinder of anaesthetic gas. I turned the tap at the neck of the bottle and, hearing a hissing sound, switched it off again. Everything looked like it was in proper working order.

Beyond a locked door was a small store-room, and it was there that Belinsky found me.

'Find anything?' he said.

I told him about the lack of records.

'You're right,' Belinsky said with what sounded like a smile, 'that doesn't sound at all German.'

I flashed the torch over the shelves in the store-room.

'Hello,' he said, 'what have we got here?' He reached out to touch a steel drum on the side of which was painted in yellow the chemical formula H_2SO_4.

'I wouldn't, if I were you,' I said. 'That stuff's not from a schoolboy's chemistry set. Unless I'm very much mistaken, it's sulphuric acid.' I moved the torch beam up the side of the drum to where the words EXTREME CAUTION were also painted. 'Enough to turn you into a couple of litres of animal fat.'

'Kosher, I hope,' Belinsky said. 'What does a dentist want with a drum-load of sulphuric acid?'

'For all I know he soaks his false teeth in it overnight.'

On a shelf beside the drum, piled one on top of the other, were several kidney-shaped steel trays. I picked one of them up and brought it under the beam of the torch. The two of us stared at what looked like a handful of odd-shaped peppermints, all stuck together as if they had been half-sucked and then saved by some disgusting small boy. But there was also dried blood on some of them.

Belinsky's nose wrinkled with disgust. 'What the hell are these?'

'Teeth.' I handed him the torch and picked one of the spiky white objects out of the tray to hold it up to the light. 'Extracted teeth. And several mouthfuls of them too.'

'I hate dentists,' Belinsky hissed. He fumbled in his waistcoat and found one of his picks to chew.

'I'd say these normally end up in the drum of acid.'

'So?' But Belinsky had noticed my interest.

'What kind of dentist does nothing but full extractions?' I asked. 'The appointment-book is booked for nothing but full extractions.' I turned the tooth in my fingers. 'Would you say that there was much wrong with this molar? It hasn't even been filled.'

'It looks like a perfectly healthy tooth,' agreed Belinsky.

I stirred the sticky mass in the tray with my forefinger. 'Same as the rest of them,' I observed. 'I'm no dentist, but I don't see the point of pulling teeth that haven't even been filled yet.'

'Maybe Heim was on some kind of piece work. Maybe the guy just liked to pull teeth.'

'Better than he liked keeping records. There are no records for any of his recent patients.'

Belinsky picked up another kidney-tray and inspected its contents. 'Another full set,' he reported. But something rolled in the next tray. It looked like several tiny ball bearings. 'Well, what have we here?' He picked one up and regarded it with fascination. 'Unless I'm very much mistaken, I should say each one of these little confections contains a dose of potassium cyanide.'

'Lethal pills?'

'That's right. They were very popular with some of your old comrades, kraut. Especially the SS and senior state and party officials who might have had the guts to prefer suicide to being captured by the Ivans. I believe that these were originally developed for German secret agents, but Arthur Nebe and the SS decided that the top brass had a greater need of them. A man would have his dentist make him a false tooth, or use an existing cavity, and then put this little baby inside. Nice and snug – you'd be surprised. When he was captured he might even have a decoy cyanide brass cartridge in his pocket, which meant our people wouldn't bother with a dental examination. And then, when the man had decided the right time had come, he would work off the false tooth, tongue out this capsule and chew the thing until it broke. Death is almost instantaneous. That's how Himmler killed himself.'

'Goering too, I heard.'

'No,' said Belinsky, 'he used one of the decoys. An American officer smuggled it back to him while he was in gaol. How about that, eh? One of our own people going soft on the fat bastard like that.' He dropped the capsule back into the tray and handed it to me.

I poured a few into my hand to get a closer look. It seemed almost astonishing that things which were so small could also be so deadly. Four tiny seed pearls for the deaths of four men. I did not think I could have carried one in my mouth, false tooth or not, and still enjoyed my dinner.

'You know what I think, kraut? I think we've got ourselves a lot of toothless Nazis running round Vienna.' I followed him back into the surgery. 'I take it that you're familiar with dental techniques for the identification of the dead.'

'As familiar as the next bull,' I said.

'It was damned useful after the war,' he said. 'The best way we had of establishing the identity of a corpse. Naturally enough there were many Nazis who were keen for us to believe that they were dead. And they went to a great deal of trouble to try and persuade us of it. Half-charred bodies carrying false papers, you know the sort of thing. Well of course the first thing we did was have a dentist take a look at a corpse's teeth. Even if you don't have a man's dental records you can at least determine his age from his teeth: periodontosis, root resorption, etc. – you can say for sure that a corpse isn't who it is supposed to be.'

Belinsky paused and looked about the surgery. 'You finished looking around in here?'

I told him I was and asked if he had found anything in the house. He shook his head and said he hadn't. Then I said that we had better get the hell out of there.

He resumed his explanation as we climbed into the car.

'Take the case of Heinrich Müller, chief of the Gestapo. He was last seen alive in Hitler's bunker in April 1945. Müller was supposed to have been killed in the battle for Berlin in May 1945. But when after the war his body was exhumed, a dental expert specializing in jawbone surgery at a Berlin hospital in the British sector couldn't identify the teeth in the corpse as those belonging to a forty-four-year-old male. He thought that the corpse was more probably that of a man of no more than twenty-five.' Belinsky turned the ignition, gunned the engine for a second or two, and then slipped the car into gear.

Crouched over the steering-wheel, he drove badly for an American, double-declutching, missing his gears and generally over-steering. It was clear to me that driving required all of his attention, but he continued with his calm explanation, even after we had almost killed a passing motorcyclist.

'When we catch up with some of these bastards, they've got false papers, new hairstyles, moustaches, beards, glasses, you name it. But teeth are as good as a tattoo, or sometimes a fingerprint. So if any of them have had all their teeth pulled it removes yet another possible means of identification. After all, a man who can explode a cartridge under his arm to remove an SS number probably wouldn't baulk at wearing false teeth, would he?'

I thought of the burn scar under my own arm and reflected that he was probably right. To disguise myself from the Russians I would certainly have resorted to having my teeth out, assuming that I would have the same opportunity for painless extraction as Max Abs and Helmut König.

'No, I guess not.'

'You can bet your life on it. Which is why I stole Heim's appointment-book.' He patted the breast of his coat where I assumed he was now keeping it. 'It might be interesting to find out who these men with bad teeth really are. Your friend König, for instance. And Max Abs too. I mean, why would a little SS chauffeur feel the need to disguise what he had in his mouth? Unless he wasn't an SS corporal at all.' Belinsky chuckled enthusiastically at the thought of it. 'That's why I have to be able to see in the dark. Some of your old comrades really know how to mix the maps. You know, I wouldn't be at all surprised if we're still chasing some of these Nazi bastards when their kids are having to sugar their strawberries for them.'

'All the same,' I said, 'the longer it is before you catch them, the harder it will be to get a positive identification.'

'Don't you worry,' he snarled vindictively. 'There won't be a shortage of witnesses willing to come forward and testify against these shits. Or perhaps you think people like Müller and Globocnik should be allowed to get away with it?'

'Who's Globocnik, when he's having a party?'

'Odilo Globocnik. He headed up Operation Reinhard, establishing most of the big death camps in Poland. Another one who is supposed to have committed suicide in '45. So come on, what do you think? There's a trial going on in Nuremberg right now. Otto Ohlendorf, commander of one of those SS special action groups. Do you think he should hang for his war crimes?'

'War crimes?' I repeated wearily. 'Listen, Belinsky, I worked in the Wehrmacht's War Crimes Bureau for three years. So don't think you can lecture me about fucking war crimes.'

'I'm just interested to know where you stand, kraut. Exactly what kind of war crimes did you Jerries investigate anyway?'

'Atrocities, by both sides. You've heard of Katyn Forest?'

'Of course. You investigated that?'

'I was part of the team.'

'How about that?' He seemed genuinely surprised. Most people were.

'Frankly, I think that the idea of charging fighting men with war crimes is absurd. The murderers of women and children should be punished, yes. But it wasn't just Jews and Poles who were killed by people like Müller and Globocnik. They murdered Germans, too. Perhaps if you'd given us half a chance we could have brought them to justice ourselves.'

Belinsky turned off Währinger Strasse and drove south, past the long edifice of the General Hospital and on to Alser Strasse where, encountering the same recollection as myself, he slowed the car to a more respectful pace. I could tell he had been about to answer my point, but now he grew quiet, almost as if he felt obliged to avoid giving me any cause for offence. Drawing up outside my pension, he said: 'Did Traudl have any family?'

'Not that I know of. There's just Becker.' I wondered at that, though. The photograph of her and Colonel Poroshin still preyed on my mind.

'Well, that's all right. I'm not going to lose any sleep worrying about his grief.'

'He's my client, in case you'd forgotten. In helping you I'm supposed to be working to prove him innocent.'

'And you're convinced of that?'

'Yes, I am.'

'But surely you must know he's on the Crowcass list.'

'You're pretty cute,' I said dumbly, 'letting me make all the running like this, only to tell me that. Supposing that I do get lucky and win the race, am I going to be allowed to collect the prize?'

'Your friend is a murdering Nazi, Bernie. He commanded an execution squad in the Ukraine, massacring men, women and children. I'd say that he deserved to hang whether he killed Linden or not.'

'You're pretty cute, Belinsky,' I repeated bitterly, and started to get out of the car.

'But as far as I'm concerned, he's small fry. I'm after bigger fish than Emil Becker. You can help me. You can try and repair some of the damage that your country has done. A symbolic gesture, if you like. Who knows – if enough Germans do the same then maybe the account could be settled.'

'What are you talking about?' I said, from the road. 'What account?'

I leaned on the car door and bent forward to see Belinsky take out his pipe.

'God's account,' he said quietly.

I laughed and shook my head in disbelief.

'What's the matter? Don't you believe in God?'

'I don't believe in trying to make a deal with him. You speak about God as if he sells secondhand cars. I've misjudged you. You're much more of an American than I thought you were.'

'Now that's where you're wrong. God likes making deals. Look at that covenant he made with Abraham, and with Noah. God's a huckster, Bernie. Only a German could mistake a deal for a direct order.'

'Get to the point, will you? There is a point, isn't there?' His manner seemed to indicate as much.

'I'm going to level with you —'

'Oh? I seem to remember you doing that a little earlier on.'

'Everything I told you was true.'

'There's just more to come, right?'

Belinsky nodded and lit his pipe. I felt like smacking it out of his mouth. Instead I got back into the car and closed the door.

'With your penchant for selective truth, you should get a job in an advertising agency. Let's hear it.'

'Just don't make a hot throat at me until I'm through, right?'

I nodded curtly.

'All right. For a start, we — Crowcass — believe Becker is innocent of Linden's murder. You see, the gun which killed him was used to kill somebody else in Berlin almost three years ago. The ballistics people matched that bullet with the one that killed Linden, and they were both fired from the same gun. For the time of the first killing Becker has a pretty good alibi: he was a Russian prisoner of war. Of course he could have acquired the gun since then, but I haven't come to the interesting part yet, the part that actually makes me want Becker to be innocent.

'The gun was a Standard SS-issue Walther P38. We traced the serial-number records held at the US Documents Centre and discovered that this same pistol was one of a batch that was issued to senior officers within the Gestapo. This particular weapon was given to Heinrich Müller. It was a long shot but we compared the bullet that killed Linden with the one that killed the man we dug up who was supposed to be Müller, and what do you know? Jackpot. Whoever killed Linden might also have been responsible for putting a false Heinrich Müller in the ground. Do you see, Bernie? It's the best clue that we've ever had that Gestapo Müller is still alive. It means that only a few months ago he might have been right here in Vienna, working for the Org, of which you are now a member. He may even still be here.

'Do you know how important that is? Think about it, please. Müller was the architect of the Nazi terror. For ten years he controlled the most brutal secret police the world has ever known. This was a man almost as powerful as Himmler himself. Can you imagine how many people he must have tortured? How many deaths he must have ordered? How many Jews, Poles – even how many Germans he must have killed? Bernie, this is your opportunity to help avenge all those dead Germans. To see that justice is done.'

I laughed scornfully. 'Is that what you call it when you let a man hang for something he didn't do? Correct me if I'm wrong, Belinsky, but isn't that part of your plan: to let Becker take the drop?'

'Naturally I hope that it doesn't come to that. But if it's necessary, then so be it. So long as the military police have Becker, Müller won't be spooked. And if that includes hanging him, yes. Knowing what I know about Emil Becker, I won't lose much sleep.' Belinsky watched my face carefully for some sign of approval. 'Come on, you're a cop. You appreciate how these things work. Don't tell me you've never had to nail a man for one thing because you couldn't prove another. It all evens up, you know that.'

'Sure, I've done it. But not when a man's life was involved. I've never played games with a man's life.'

'Provided you help us to find Müller we're prepared to forget about Becker.' The pipe emitted a short smoke signal, which seemed to bespeak a growing impatience on its owner's part. 'Look, all I'm suggesting is that you put Müller in the dock instead of Becker.'

'And if I do find Müller, what then? He's not about to let me walk up and put the cuffs on him. How am I supposed to bring him in without getting my head blown off?'

'You can leave that to me. All you have to do is establish exactly where he is. Telephone me and my Crowcass team will do the rest.'

'How will I recognize him?'

Belinsky reached behind his seat and brought back a cheap leather briefcase. He unzipped it and took out an envelope from which he removed a passport-sized photograph.

'That's Müller,' he said. 'Apparently he speaks with a very pronounced Munich accent, so even if he should have radically changed his appearance, you'll certainly have no trouble recognizing his voice.' He watched me turn the photograph towards the streetlight and stare at it for a while.

'He'd be forty-seven now. Not very tall, big peasant hands. He may still even be wearing his wedding ring.'

The photograph didn't say much about the man. It wasn't a very revealing face; and yet it was a remarkable one. Müller had a squarish skull, a high forehead, and tense, narrow lips. But it was the eyes that really got to you, even on that small photograph. Müller's eyes were like the eyes of a snowman: two black, frozen coals.

'Here's another one,' Belinsky said. 'These are the only two photographs of him known to exist.'

The second picture was a group shot. There were five men seated round an oak table as if they had been having dinner in a comfortable restaurant. Three of them I recognized. At the head of the table was Heinrich Himmler, playing with his pencil and smiling at Arthur Nebe on his right. Arthur Nebe: my old comrade, as Belinsky would have said. On Himmler's left, and apparently hanging on every one of the Reichsführer-SS's words, was Reinhard Heydrich, chief of the RSHA, assassinated by Czech terrorists in 1942.

'When was this picture taken?' I asked.

'November 1939.' Belinsky leaned across and tapped one of the two other men in the picture with the stem of his pipe. 'That's Müller there,' he said, 'sitting beside Heydrich.'

Müller's hand had moved in the same half-second that the camera-shutter had opened and closed: it was blurred as if covering the order paper on the table, but even so, the wedding ring was clearly visible. He was looking down, almost not listening to Himmler at all. By comparison with Heydrich, Müller's head was small. His hair was closely cropped, shaven even until it reached the very top of the cranium, where it had been permitted to grow a little in a small, carefully tended allotment.

'Who's the man sitting opposite Müller?'

'The one taking notes? That's Franz Josef Huber. He was chief of the Gestapo here in Vienna. You can hang on to those pictures if you want. They're only prints.'

'I haven't agreed to help you yet.'

'But you will. You have to.'

'Right now I ought to tell you to go and fuck yourself, Belinsky. You see, I'm like an old piano – I don't much like being played. But I'm tired. And I've had a few. Maybe I'll be able to think a little more clearly tomorrow.' I opened the car door and got out again.

Belinsky was right: the body work of the big black Mercedes was covered in dents.

'I'll call you in the morning,' he said.

'You do that,' I said, and slammed the door shut.

He drove away like he was the devil's own coachman.

28

I did not sleep well. Troubled by what Belinsky had said, my thoughts made my limbs restless, and after only a few hours I woke before dawn in a cold sweat and did not sleep again. If only he hadn't mentioned God, I said to myself.

I was not a Catholic until I became a prisoner in Russia. The regime in the camp was so hard that it seemed to me that there was an even chance it would kill me, and, wishing to make my peace with the back of my mind, I had sought out the only churchman among my fellow prisoners, a Polish priest. I had been brought up as a Lutheran, but religious denomination seemed like a matter of small account in that dreadful place.

Becoming a Catholic in the full expectation of death only made me more tenacious of life, and after I'd escaped and returned to Berlin I continued to attend mass and to celebrate the faith that had apparently delivered me.

My newfound Church did not have a good record in its relation to the Nazis, and had now also distanced itself from any imputation of guilt. It followed that if the Catholic Church was not guilty, nor were its members. There was, it seemed, some theological basis for a rejection of German collective guilt. Guilt, said the priests, was really something personal between a man and his God, and its attribution to one nation by another was blasphemy, for this could only be a matter of divine prerogative. After that, all that there remained to do was pray for the dead, for those who had done wrong, and for the whole dreadful and embarrassing epoch to be forgotten as quickly as possible.

There were many who remained uneasy at the way the moral dirt was swept under the carpet. But it is certain that a nation cannot feel collective guilt, that each man must encounter it personally.

Only now did I realize the nature of my own guilt – and perhaps it was really not much different from that of many others: it was that I had not said anything, that I had not lifted my hand against the Nazis. I also realized that I had a personal sense of grievance against Heinrich Müller, for as chief of the Gestapo he had done more than any other man to achieve the corruption of the police force of which I had once been a proud member. From that had flowed wholesale terror.

Now it seemed it was not too late to do something after all. It was just possible that, by seeking out Müller, the symbol not just of my own corruption but Becker's too, and bringing him to justice, I might help to clear my own guilt for what had happened.

Belinsky rang early, almost as if he had already guessed my decision, and I told him that I would help him to find Gestapo Müller not for Crowcass, nor for the United States Army, but for Germany. But mostly, I told him, I would help him to get Müller for myself.

29

First thing that morning, after telephoning König and arranging a meeting to hand over Belinsky's ostensibly secret material, I went to Liebl's office in Judengasse in order that he might arrange for me to see Becker at the police prison.

'I want to show him a photograph,' I explained.

'A photograph?' Liebl sounded hopeful. 'Is this a photograph that might become an item of evidence?'

I shrugged. 'That depends on Becker.'

Liebl made a couple of swift telephone calls, trading on the death of Becker's fiancée, the possibility of new evidence and the proximity of the trial, which gained us almost immediate access to the prison. It was a fine day and we made our way there by foot, with Liebl walking his umbrella like a colour sergeant in an imperial regiment of guards.

'Did you tell him about Traudl?' I asked.

'Last night.'

'How did he take it?'

The grey brow on the old lawyer's head shifted uncertainly. 'Surprisingly well, Herr Günther. Like you, I had supposed our client would be devastated by the news.' The brow shifted again, more in consternation this time. 'But he was not. No, it was his own unfortunate situation that seemed to preoccupy him. As well as your progress, or lack of it. Herr Becker does seem to have an extraordinary amount of faith in your powers of detection. Powers for which, if I may be frank with you, sir, I have seen little or no evidence.'

'You're entitled to your opinion, Dr Liebl. I guess you're like most lawyers I've met: if your own sister sent you an invitation to her wedding you'd be happy only if it was signed under seal and in the presence of two witnesses. Perhaps if our client had been a little more forthcoming . . .'

'You suspect he's been holding something back? Yes, I remember you said as much on the telephone yesterday. Without knowing quite what you were talking about I did not feel able to take advantage of Herr Becker's –' he hesitated for a second while he debated whether or not he could reasonably use the word, and then decided that he could '– grief, to make such an allegation.'

'Very sensitive of you, I'm sure. But perhaps this photograph will jog his memory.'

'I do hope so. And perhaps his bereavement will have sunk in, and he will make a better show of his grief.'

It seemed like a very Viennese sort of sentiment.

But when we saw Becker he appeared hardly affected. After a packet of cigarettes had persuaded the guard to leave the three of us alone in the interview room I tried to find out why.

'I'm sorry about Traudl,' I said. 'She was a really lovely girl.'

He nodded expressionlessly, as if he had been listening to some boring point of legal procedure as explained by Liebl.

'I must say you don't seem very upset by it,' I remarked.

'I'm dealing with it in the best way I know how,' he said quietly. 'There's not a lot I can do here. Chances are they won't even let me attend the funeral. How do you think I feel?'

I turned to Liebl and asked him if he wouldn't mind leaving the room for a minute. 'There's something I wish to say to Herr Becker in private.'

Liebl glanced at Becker, who nodded curtly back at him. Neither of us spoke until the heavy door had closed behind the lawyer.

'Spit it out, Bernie,' Becker said, half-yawning at the same time. 'What's on your mind?'

'It was your friends in the Org who killed your girl,' I said, watching his long thin face closely for some sign of emotion. I wasn't sure if this was true or not, but I was keen to see what it might make him reveal. But there was nothing. 'They actually asked me to kill her.'

'So,' he said, with his eyes narrowing, 'you're in the Org.' His tone was cautious. 'When did this happen?'

'Your friend König recruited me.'

His face seemed to relax a little. 'Well, I guessed it was only a matter of time. To be honest, I wasn't at all sure whether or not you were in the Org when you first came to Vienna. With your background you're the kind of man they're quick to recruit. If you're in now, you have been busy. I'm impressed. Did König say why he wanted you to kill Traudl?'

'He told me she was an MVD spy. He showed me a photograph of her talking to Colonel Poroshin.'

Becker smiled sadly. 'She was no spy,' he said, shaking his head, 'and she was not my girlfriend. She was Poroshin's girl. Originally she posed as my fiancée so that I could stay in contact with Poroshin while I was in prison. Liebl knew nothing about it. Poroshin said that you hadn't been all that keen to come to Vienna. Said you didn't seem to have a very good opinion of me. He wondered if you would stay very long when you did come. So he thought it would be a good idea if Traudl worked on you a little and persuaded you that there was someone who loved me on the outside, someone who needed me. He's a shrewd judge of character, Bernie. Go on, admit it, she's half the reason why you've stuck to my case. Because you thought that mother and baby deserved the benefit of the doubt, even if I didn't.'

It was Becker who was watching me now, looking for some reaction. Oddly enough, I found I wasn't angry at all. I was used to discovering that at any one time I only ever had half the truth.

'So I don't suppose she was a nurse at all.'

'Oh, she was a nurse all right. She used to steal penicillin for me to sell on the black market. It was me who introduced her to Poroshin.' He shrugged. 'I didn't know about the two of them for a while. But I wasn't surprised. Traudl liked a good time, like most of the women in this city. She and I were even lovers for a brief while, but nothing like that lasts for very long in Vienna.'

'Your wife said that you got Poroshin some penicillin for a dose of drip? Was that true?'

'I got him some penicillin, sure, but it wasn't for him. It was for his son. He had cerebro-spinal fever. There's quite an epidemic of it, I believe. And a shortage of antibiotics, especially in Russia. There's a shortage of everything but manpower in the Soviet Union.

'After that, Poroshin did me one or two favours. Fixed papers, gave me a cigarette concession, that sort of thing. We became quite friendly. And when the Org's people got round to recruiting me, I told him all about it. Why not? I thought König and his friends were a bunch of spinners. But I was happy to make money from them, and frankly I wasn't much involved with the Org beyond that odd bit of courier-work to Berlin. Poroshin was keen that I get closer to them however, and when he offered me a lot of money, I agreed to try. But they're absurdly suspicious, Bernie, and when I expressed some interest in doing more work for them they insisted that I subject myself to an interrogation about my service with the SS and my imprisonment in a Soviet POW camp. It bothered them a lot that I was released. They didn't say anything about it at the time, but in view of what has happened since, I guess they must have decided that they couldn't trust me, and put me out of the way.' Becker lit one of his cigarettes and leaned back on the hard chair.

'Why didn't you tell this to the police?'

He laughed. 'You think I didn't? When I told them about the Org those stupid bastards thought I was telling them about the Werewolf Underground. You know, that shit about a Nazi terrorist group.'

'So that's where Shields got the idea.'

'Shields?' Becker snorted. 'He's a fucking idiot.'

'All right, why didn't you tell me about the Org?'

'Like I said, Bernie, I wasn't sure if they hadn't already recruited you in Berlin. Ex-Kripo, ex-Abwehr, you'd have been exactly what they were looking for. But if you hadn't been in the Org and I'd told you, you might well have gone round Vienna asking questions about it, in which case you would have ended up dead, like my two business partners. And if you were in the Org I thought that maybe that would just be in Berlin. Here in Vienna you'd be just another detective, albeit one I knew and trusted. Do you see?'

I grunted an affirmative and found my own cigarettes.

'You still should have told me.'

'Perhaps.' He drew fiercely on his cigarette. 'Listen, Bernie. My original offer still stands. Thirty thousand dollars if you can dig me out of this hole. So if you've got anything up your sleeve . . .'

'There's this,' I said, cutting across him. I produced Müller's photograph, the one that was passport-sized. 'Do you recognize him?'

'I don't think so. But I've seen this picture before, Bernie. At least I think I have. Traudl showed it to me before you came to Vienna.'

'Oh? Did she say how she came by it?'

'Poroshin, I guess.' He studied the picture more carefully. 'Oak-leaf collar patches, silver braid on the shoulders. An SS-Brigadeführer by the look of him. Who is it, anyway?'

'Heinrich Müller.'

'Gestapo Müller?'

'Officially he's dead, so I'd like you to keep quiet about all this for the moment. I've teamed up with this American agent from the War Crimes Commission who is interested in the Linden case. He worked for the same department. Apparently the gun that was used to kill Linden belonged to Müller, and was used to kill the man who was supposed to be Müller. Which might leave Müller still alive. Naturally the War Crimes people are anxious to get hold of Müller at any price. Which leaves you firmly on the spot I'm afraid, at least for the moment.'

'I wouldn't mind if it was firmly. But the particular spot they have in mind has hinges on it. Do you mind explaining what this means exactly?'

'It means they're not prepared to do anything that might scare Müller out of Vienna.'

'Assuming he's here.'

'That's right. Because this is an intelligence operation, they're not prepared to let the military police in on it. If the charges against you were to be dropped now, it might persuade the Org that the case was about to be reopened.'

'So where does that leave me, for Christ's sake?'

'This American agent I'm working with has promised to let you go if we can put Müller in your place. We're going to try and draw him out into the open.'

'Until then they're just going to let the trial go ahead, maybe even the sentence too?'

'That's about the size of it.'

'And you're asking me to keep my mouth shut in the meantime.'

'What can you say? That Linden was possibly murdered by a man who's been dead for three years?'

'It's just so –' Becker flung his cigarette into the corner of the room '– so damned callous.'

'Do you want to take that biretta off your head? Look, they know about what you did in Minsk. Playing a game with your life isn't something they feel squeamish about. To be honest, they don't much care whether you swing or not. This is your only chance, and you know it.'

Becker nodded sullenly. 'All right,' he said.

I stood up to leave, but a sudden thought stopped me from walking to the door.

'As a matter of interest,' I said, 'why did they release you from the Soviet POW camp?'

'You were a prisoner. You know what it was like. Always scared they were going to find out you were in the SS.'

'That's why I'm asking.'

He hesitated for a moment. Then he said: 'There was a man who was due to be released. He was very sick, and would have died soon enough. What was the point in repatriating him?' He shrugged, and looked me square in the eye. 'So I strangled him. Ate some camphor to make myself sick – damn near killed myself – and took his place.' He stared me out. 'I was desperate, Bernie. You remember what it was like.'

'Yes, I remember.' I tried to conceal my distaste, and failed. 'All the same, if you'd told me that before today I'd have let them hang you.' I reached for the door-handle.

'There's still time. Why don't you?'

If I'd told him the truth Becker wouldn't have understood what I was talking about. He probably thought that metaphysics was something you used to manufacture cheap penicillin for the black market. So instead I shook my head, and said, 'Let's just say that I made a deal with someone.'

30

I met König at the Café Sperl in Gumpendorfer Strasse, which was in the French sector but close to the Ring. It was a big, gloomy place which the many art nouveau-style mirrors on the walls did nothing to brighten, and was home to several half-size billiard tables. Each one of these was illuminated by a light which was fixed to the yellowing ceiling above with a brass fitting that looked like something out of an old U-boat.

König's terrier sat a short way off from its master like the dog on the record label, watching him play a solitary but thoughtful game. I ordered a coffee and approached the table.

He judged his shot at a careful cue's length, and then applied a screw of chalk to the tip, silently acknowledging my presence with a short nod of his head.

'Our own Mozart was particularly fond of this game,' he said, lowering his eyes to the felt. 'Doubtless he found it a very congenial facsimile of the very precise dynamism of his intellect.' He fixed his eye on the cue-ball like a sniper taking aim, and after a long, painstaking moment, rifled the white on to one red and then the other. This second red coasted down the length of the table, teetered on the lip of the pocket and, enticing a small murmur of satisfaction from its translator – for there exists no more graceful manifestation of the laws of gravity and motion – slipped noiselessly out of sight.

'I, on the other hand, enjoy the game for rather more sensuous reasons. I love the sound of the balls hitting each other, and the way they run so smoothly.' He retrieved the red from the pocket and replaced it to his own satisfaction. 'But most of all I love the colour green. Did you know that among Celtic peoples the colour green is considered unlucky? No? They believe green is followed by black. Probably because the English used to hang Irishmen for wearing green. Or was it the Scots?' For a moment König stared almost insanely at the surface of the billiard table, as if he could have licked it with his tongue.

'Just look at it,' he breathed. 'Green is the colour of ambition, and of youth. It's the colour of life, and of eternal rest. *Requiem aeternam dona eis.*' Reluctantly he laid his cue down on the cloth, and conjuring a large cigar from one of his pockets, turned away from the table. The terrier stood up expectantly. 'You said on the telephone that you had something for me. Something important.'

I handed him Belinsky's envelope. 'Sorry it's not in green ink,' I said, watching him take out the papers. 'Do you read Cyrillic?'

König shook his head. 'I'm afraid it might as well be in Gaelic.' But he went ahead and spread the papers out on the billiard table and then lit his cigar. When the dog barked he ordered it to be quiet. 'Perhaps you would be good enough to explain exactly what I am looking at?'

'These are details of MVD dispositions and methods in Hungary and Lower Austria.' I smiled coolly and sat down at an adjacent table where the waiter had just laid my coffee.

König nodded slowly, stared uncomprehendingly at the papers for another few seconds, then scooped them up, replaced them in their envelope and slipped the papers inside his jacket pocket.

'Very interesting,' he said, sitting down at my table. 'Assuming for a moment that they're genuine –'

'Oh, they're genuine all right,' I said quickly.

He smiled patiently, as if I could have had no idea of the lengthy process whereby such information was properly verified. 'Assuming they're genuine,' he repeated firmly, 'how exactly did you come by them?'

A couple of men came over to the billiard table and started a game. König drew his chair away and jerked his head at me to follow him. 'It's all right,' said one of the players. 'There's plenty of room to get by.' But we moved our chairs anyway. And when we were at a more discreet distance from the table I started to give him the story I had rehearsed with Belinsky. Only now König shook his head firmly and picked up his dog, which licked his ear playfully.

'This isn't the right time or place,' he said. 'But I'm impressed at how busy you have been.' He raised his eyebrows and watched the two men at the billiard table with an air of distraction. 'I learned this morning that you had been successful in procuring some petrol coupons for that medical friend of mine. The one at the General Hospital.' I realized that he was talking about Traudl's murder. 'And so soon after we had discussed the matter too. It really was most efficient of you, I'm sure.' He puffed smoke at the dog on his lap which sniffed and then sneezed. 'It's so difficult to obtain reliable supplies of anything in Vienna these days.'

I shrugged. 'You just have to know the right people, that's all.'

'As you clearly do, my friend.' He patted the breast pocket of his green tweed suit, where he had put Belinsky's documents. 'In these special circumstances I feel I ought to introduce you to someone in the company who will be better able than I to judge the quality of your source. Someone who, as it happens, is keen to meet you, and decide how best a man of your skills and resourcefulness may be used. We had thought to wait a few weeks before making the introduction, but this new information changes everything. However, first I must make a telephone call. I shall be a few minutes.' He looked down the café and pointed to one of the other free billiard tables. 'Why don't you try a few shots while I'm away?'

'I've not much use for games of skill,' I said. 'I distrust a game that relies on anything but luck. That way I needn't blame myself if I lose. I have a tremendous capacity for self-recrimination.'

A twinkle came into König's eye. 'My dear fellow,' he said standing up from the table, 'that seems hardly German.'

I watched him as he walked into the back of the café to use the phone, the terrier trotting faithfully after him. I wondered who it was that he was calling: the one who was better able to judge the quality of my source might even be Müller. It seemed too much to hope for so soon.

When König returned a few minutes later, he seemed excited. 'As I thought,' he said, nodding enthusiastically, 'there is someone who is keen to have immediate sight of this material, and to meet you. I have a car outside. Shall we go?'

König's car was a black Mercedes, like Belinsky's. And like Belinsky he drove too fast for safety on a road that had seen a heavy morning rain. I said that it would be better to arrive late than not to arrive at all, but he paid no attention. My feeling of discomfort was made worse by König's dog, which sat on his master's lap and barked excitedly at the road ahead for the whole of the journey, as if the brute had been giving directions on where we were going. I recognized the road as the one which led to Sievering Studios, but at that same moment the road forked and we turned north again on to Grinzinger Allee.

'Do you know Grinzing?' König shouted over the dog's incessant barking. I said that I did not. 'Then you really don't know the Viennese,' he opined. 'Grinzing is famous for its wine production. In the summer everyone comes up here in the evening to go to one of the taverns selling the new vintage. They drink too much, listen to a Schrammel quartet and sing old songs.'

'It sounds very cosy,' I said, without much enthusiasm.

'Yes, it is. I own a couple of vineyards up here myself. Just two small fields you understand. But it's a start. A man must have some land, don't you think? We'll come back here in the summer and then you can taste the new wine yourself. The lifeblood of Vienna.'

Grinzing seemed hardly a suburb of Vienna at all, more a charming little village. But because of its proximity to the capital, its cosy country charm somehow appeared as false as one of the film sets they built over at Sievering. We drove up a hill on a narrow winding lane which led between old Heurige Inns and cottage gardens, with König declaring how pretty he thought it all was now that spring was here. But the sight of so much storybook provinciality merely served to stimulate my city-bred parts to contempt, and I restricted myself to a sullen grunt and a muttered sentence about tourists. To one more used to the perennial sight of rubble,

Grinzing with its many trees and vineyards looked very green. However I made no mention of this impression for fear that it might set König off on one of his queer little monologues about that sickly colour.

He stopped the car in front of a high yellow-brick wall which enclosed a large, yellow-painted house and a garden that looked as if it had spent all day in the beauty parlour. The house itself was a tall, three-storey building with a high-dormered roof. Apart from its bright colour, there was a certain austerity of detail about the façade which lent the house an institutional appearance. It looked like a rather opulent sort of town hall.

I followed König through the gates and up an immaculately bordered path to a heavy studded oak door of the kind that expected you to be holding a battle-axe when you knocked. We walked straight into the house and on to a creaking wooden floor that would have given a librarian a heart attack.

König led me into a small sitting-room, told me to wait there and then left, closing the door behind him. I took a good look round, but there wasn't much to see beyond the fact of the owner's bucolic taste in furniture. A rough-hewn table blocked the French window, and a couple of cartwheel farmhouse chairs were ranged in front of an empty fireplace that was as big as a mineshaft. I sat down on a slightly more comfortable-looking ottoman and re-tied my shoelaces. Then I polished my toes with the edge of the threadbare rug. I must have waited there for an indifferent half-hour before König came back to fetch me. He led me through a maze of rooms and corridors and up a flight of stairs to the back of the house, with the manner of a man whose jacket is lined with oak panelling. Hardly caring if I insulted him or not now that I was about to meet someone more important, I said, 'If you changed that suit you'd make someone a wonderful butler.'

König did not turn around, but I heard him bare his dentures and utter a short, dry laugh. 'I'm glad you think so. You know, although I like a sense of humour I would not advise you to exercise it with the general. Frankly, his character is most severe.' He opened a door and we came into a bright, airy room with a fire in the grate and hectares of empty bookshelves. Against the broad window, behind a long library table, stood a grey-suited figure with a closely-cropped head I half recognized. The man turned and smiled, his hooked nose unmistakably belonging to a face from my past.

'Hello, Günther,' said the man.

König looked quizzically at me as I blinked speechlessly at the grinning figure.

'Do you believe in ghosts, Herr König?' I said.

'No. Do you?'

'I do now. If I'm not mistaken, the gentleman by the window was hanged in 1945 for his part in the plot to kill the Führer.'

'You can leave us, Helmut,' said the man at the window. König nodded curtly, turned on his heel and left.

Arthur Nebe pointed at a chair in front of the table on which Belinsky's documents lay spread out beside a pair of spectacles and a fountain pen. 'Sit down,' he said. 'Drink?' He laughed. 'You look as though you need one.'

'It's not every day I get to see a man raised from the dead,' I said quietly. 'Better make it a large one.'

Nebe opened a large carved-wood drinks cabinet, revealing a marble interior filled with several bottles. He took out a bottle of vodka and two small glasses, which he filled to the top.

'To old comrades,' he said, raising his glass. I smiled uncertainly. 'Drink up. It won't make me disappear again.'

I tossed the vodka back and breathed deeply as it hit my stomach. 'Death agrees with you, Arthur. You look well.'

'Thanks. I've never felt better.'

I lit a cigarette and left it on my lip for a while.

'Minsk, wasn't it?' he said. 'In 1941. The last time we saw each other?'

'That's right. You got me transferred to the War Crimes Bureau.'

'I ought to have had you put on a charge for what you asked. Even had you shot.'

'From what I hear, you were keen on shooting that summer.'
Nebe let that one pass. 'So why didn't you?'

'You were a damned good policeman. That's why.'

'So were you.' I sucked hard at my cigarette. 'At least, you were
before the war. What made you change, Arthur?'

Nebe savoured his drink for a moment and then finished it with
one swallow. 'This is good vodka,' he remarked quietly, almost to
himself. 'Bernie, don't expect me to give you an explanation. I
had my orders to carry out, and so it was them or me. Kill or be
killed. That's how it always was with the SS. Ten, twenty, thirty
thousand – after you've calculated that to save your own life you
must kill others then the number makes little or no difference.
That was my final solution, Bernie: the final solution to the pressing problem of my own continued survival. You were fortunate
that you were never required to make that same calculation.'

'Thanks to you.'

Nebe shrugged modestly, before pointing at the papers spread
before him. 'I'm rather glad that I didn't have you shot, now that
I've seen this lot. Naturally this material will have to be assessed by
an expert, but on the face of it you appear to have won the lottery.
All the same, I'd like to hear more about your source.'

I repeated my story, after which Nebe said:

'Can he be trusted, do you think? Your Russian?'

'He never let me down before,' I said. 'Of course, he was just
fixing papers for me then.'

Nebe refilled our glasses and frowned.

'Is there a problem?' I asked.

'It's just that in the ten years I've known you Bernie, I can't find
anything that can persuade me that you're now a common black-
marketeer.'

'That shouldn't be any more difficult than the problem I have
persuading myself that you're a war-criminal, Arthur. Or for that
matter, accepting that you're not dead.'

Nebe smiled. 'You have a point. But with so many opportunities
presented by the vast number of displaced persons, I'm surprised

you didn't return to your old trade and become a private investigator again.'

'Private investigation and the black market are not mutually exclusive,' I said. 'Good information is just like penicillin or cigarettes. It has its price. And the better, the more illicit the information, the higher that price. It's always been like that. Incidentally, my Russian will want to be paid.'

'They always do. Sometimes I think that the Ivans have more confidence in the dollar than the Americans themselves.' Nebe clasped his hands and laid both forefingers along the length of his shrewd-looking nose. Then he pointed them at me as if he had been holding a pistol. 'You've done very well, Bernie. Very well indeed. But I must confess I am still puzzled.'

'About me as a black Peter?'

'I can accept the idea of that rather more easily than I can accept the idea of you killing Traudl Braunsteiner. Murder was never in your line.'

'I didn't kill her,' I said. 'König told me to do it, and I thought I could, because she was a Communist. I learned to hate them while I was in a Soviet prison-camp. Even enough to kill one. But when I thought about it, I realized I couldn't do it. Not in cold blood. Maybe I could have done it if it had been a man, but not a girl. I was going to tell him that this morning, but when he congratulated me on having done it, I decided to keep my mouth shut and take the credit. I figured there might be some money in it.'

'So somebody else killed her. How very intriguing. You've no idea who, I suppose?'

I shook my head.

'A mystery, then.'

'Just like your resurrection, Arthur. How exactly did you manage it?'

'I'm afraid that I can't take any of the credit,' he said. 'It was something the Intelligence people dreamed up. In the last few months of the war they simply doctored the service records of senior SS and party personnel, to the effect that we were dead.

Most of us were executed for our part in Count Stauffenberg's plot to kill the Führer. Well, what were another hundred or so executions on a list that was already thousands of names long? And then some of us were listed as killed in a bombing raid, or in the battle for Berlin. Then all that remained was to make sure that these records fell into the hands of the Americans.

'So the SS transported the records to a paper mill near Munich, and the owner – a good Nazi – was briefed to wait until the Amis were on his doorstep before he started to destroy anything.' Nebe laughed. 'I remember reading in the newspaper how pleased with themselves the Amis were. What a coup they thought they had scored. Of course, most of what they captured was genuine enough. But for those of us who were most at risk from their ridiculous war-crimes investigations, it provided a real breathing space, and enough time to establish a new identity. There's nothing quite like being dead for giving one a little room.' He laughed again. 'Anyway, that US Documents Centre of theirs in Berlin is still working for us.'

'How do you mean?' I asked, wondering if I was about to learn something that would throw light on why Linden had been killed. Or perhaps he had simply found out that the records had been doctored before they fell into Allied hands? Wouldn't that have been enough to justify killing him?

'No, I've said enough for the moment.' Nebe drank some more vodka and licked his lips appreciatively. 'These are interesting times we live in, Bernie. A man can be whoever he wants to be. Take me: my new name is Nolde, Arthur Nolde, and I make wine on this estate. Resurrected, you said. Well you're not so very far away from it there. Only our Nazi dead are raised incorruptible. We're changed, my friend. It's the Russians who are wearing the black hats and trying to take over the town. Now that we're working for the Americans, we're the good boys. Dr Schneider – he's the man who set the Org up with the help of their CIC – he has regular meetings with them at our headquarters in Pullach. He's even been to the United States to meet their Secretary of State.

Can you imagine it? A senior German officer working with the President's number two? You don't get more incorruptible than that, not these days.'

'If you don't mind,' I said, 'I find it hard to think of the Amis as saints. When I got back from Russia my wife was getting an extra ration from an American captain. Sometimes I think they're no better than the Ivans.'

Nebe shrugged. 'You're not the only one in the Org who thinks that,' he said. 'But for my part, I never heard of the Ivans asking a lady's permission or giving her a few bars of chocolate first. They're animals.' He smiled as a thought came into his head. 'All the same, I will admit that some of those women ought to be grateful to the Russians. But for them, they might never have known what it was like.'

It was a poor joke, and in bad taste, but I laughed along with him anyway. I was still sufficiently nervous of Nebe to want to be good company for him.

'So what did you do, about your wife and this American captain?' he asked when his laughter had subsided.

Something made me check myself before I replied. Arthur Nebe was a clever man. Before the war, as chief of the criminal police, he had been Germany's most outstanding policeman. It would have been too risky to give an answer which suggested that I had wanted to kill an American Army captain. Nebe saw common factors worthy of investigation where other men only saw the hand of a capricious god. I knew him too well to believe that he would have forgotten how once he had assigned Becker to a murder inquiry I was leading. Any hint of an association, no matter how accidental, between the death of one American officer affecting Becker and the death of another affecting me and I didn't doubt that Nebe would have given orders to have had me killed. One American officer was bad enough. Two would have been too much of a coincidence. So I shrugged, lit a cigarette and said: 'What can you do but make sure it's her and not him who gets the slap in the mouth? American officers don't take kindly to being

socked, least of all by krauts. It's one of the small privileges of conquest that you don't have to take any shit from your defeated
enemy. I can't imagine you've forgotten that, Herr Gruppenführer.
You of all people.'

I watched his grin with an extra curiosity. It was a cunning
smile, in an old fox's face, but his teeth looked real enough.

'That was very wise of you,' he said. 'It doesn't do to go around
killing Americans.' Confirming my nervousness of him, he added,
after a long pause: 'Do you remember Emil Becker?'

It would have been stupid to have tried to affect a show of pro-
tracted remembering. He knew me better than that.

'Of course,' I said.

'It was his girlfriend that König told you to kill. One of his
girlfriends anyway.'

'But König said she was MVD,' I frowned.

'And so she was. So was Becker. He killed an American officer.
But not before he'd tried to infiltrate the Org.'

I shook my head slowly. 'A crook, maybe,' I said, 'but I can't see
Becker as one of Ivan's spies.' Nebe nodded insistently. 'Here in
Vienna?' He nodded again. 'Did he know about you being alive?'

'Of course not. We used him to do a little courier work now
and again. It was a mistake. Becker was a black-marketeer, like
you, Bernie. Rather a successful one, as it happens. But he had
delusions regarding his own worth to us. He thought he was at the
centre of a very big pond. But he was nowhere near it. Quite
frankly if a meteorite had landed in the middle of it, Becker
wouldn't even have noticed the fucking ripple.'

'How did you find out about him?'

'His wife told us,' Nebe said. 'When he came back from a Soviet
POW camp, our people in Berlin sent someone round to his house
to see if we could recruit him to the Org. Well, they missed him,
and by the time they got to speak to Becker's wife he had left home
and was living here in Vienna. The wife told them about Becker's
association with a Russian colonel of MVD. But for one reason
and another – actually it was sheer bloody inefficiency – it was

quite a while before that information reached us here in Vienna section. And by that time he had been recruited by one of our collectors.'

'So where is he now?'

'Here in Vienna. In gaol. The Americans are putting him on trial for murder, and he will most certainly hang.'

'That must be rather convenient for you,' I said, sticking my neck out a little way. 'Rather too convenient, if you ask me.'

'Professional instinct, Bernie?'

'Better just call it a hunch. That way, if I'm wrong it won't make me look like an amateur.'

'Still trusting your guts, eh?'

'Most of all now that I've got something inside them again, Arthur. Vienna's a fat city after Berlin.'

'So you think we killed the American?'

'That would depend on who he was, and if you had a good reason. Then all you would have to do is make sure they got someone's coat for it. Someone you might want out of the way. That way you could get to hit two flies with one swat. Am I right?'

Nebe inclined his head to one side a little. 'Perhaps. But don't ever try to remind me of just how good a detective you were by doing something as stupid as proving it. It's still a very sore point with some people in this section, so it might be best if you were to nail your beak about it altogether.

'You know, if you really felt like playing detective, you might like to give us the benefit of your advice as to how we should go about finding one of our own missing persons. His name is Dr Karl Heim and he's a dentist. A couple of our people were supposed to take him to Pullach early this morning, but when they went to his house there was no sign of him. Of course he may just have gone on the local cure,' Nebe meant a tour of the bars, 'but in this city there is always the possibility that the Ivans have snatched him. There are a couple of freelance gangs that the Russians have working here. In return they get concessions to sell black-market cigarettes. As far as we've been able to find out, both these gangs report to Becker's Russian colonel. That's probably how he got most of his supplies in the first place.'

'Sure,' I said, unnerved by this latest revelation of Becker's involvement with Colonel Poroshin. 'What do you want me to do?'

'Speak to König,' Nebe instructed, 'give him some advice on how he might try and find Heim. If you get time, you could even give him some help.'

'That's simple enough,' I said. 'Anything else?'

'Yes, I'd like you to come back here tomorrow morning. There's one of our people who has specialized in all matters relating to the MVD. I have a feeling that he will be especially keen to talk to you about this source of yours. Shall we say ten o'clock?'

'Ten o'clock,' I repeated.

Nebe stood up and came round the table to shake my hand. 'It's good to see an old face, Bernie, even if it does look like my conscience.'

I smiled weakly and clasped his hand. 'What's past is past,' I said.

'Exactly so,' he said, dropping a hand on to my shoulder. 'Until tomorrow then. König will drive you back to town.' Nebe opened the door and led the way down the stairs back to the front of the house. 'I'm sorry to hear about that problem with your wife. I could arrange to have her sent some PX if you wanted.'

'Don't bother,' I said quickly. The last thing I wanted was anyone from the Org turning up at my apartment in Berlin and asking Kirsten awkward questions she wouldn't know how to answer. 'She works in an American café and gets all the PX she needs.'

In the hallway we found König playing with his dog.

'Women,' Nebe laughed. 'It was a woman who bought König his dog, isn't that so, Helmut?'

'Yes, Herr General.'

Nebe bent down to tickle the dog's stomach. It rolled over and presented itself submissively to Nebe's fingers.

'And do you know why she bought him a dog?' I caught König's embarrassed little crease of a smile, and I sensed that Nebe was about to crack a joke. 'To teach the man obedience.'

I laughed right along with the two of them. But after only a few days' closer acquaintance with König I thought that Lotte Hartmann would as soon have taught her boyfriend to recite the Torah.

31

The sky was grey by the time I got back to my rooms. I heard a handful of rain against the french windows, and seconds later there was a short flash and a huge clap of thunder that sent the pigeons on my terrace flying for cover. I stood and watched the storm as it rocked the trees and flooded the drains, discharging the atmosphere of all its surplus electrical energy until the air was clear and comfortable again.

Ten minutes later the birds were singing in the trees, as if in celebration of the purgative squall. There seemed much to envy them in this swift climatic cure, and I wished the pressure I felt on my own nerves could have been as easily resolved. Trying to keep one step ahead of all the lies, my own included, I was rapidly coming to the end of my own ingenuity, and I was in danger of losing the tempo of the whole affair. Not to mention my life.

It was about eight o'clock when I called Belinsky at Sacher's, a hotel on Philharmonikerstrasse requisitioned by the military. I thought it might be too late to catch him, but he was there. He sounded relaxed, like he'd known all along that the Org would take his bait.

'I said I'd call,' I reminded him. 'It's a bit late, but I've been busy.'

'No problem. Did they buy it? The information?'

'Damn near took my hand off. König drove me to a house in Grinzing. Possibly it's their headquarters here in Vienna, I'm not sure. It's certainly grand enough.'

'Good. Did you see anything of Müller?'

'No. But I saw someone else.'

'Oh? And who was that?' Belinsky's voice got cool.

'Arthur Nebe.'

'Nebe? Are you sure of that?' He was excited now.

'Of course I'm sure. I knew Nebe before the war. I thought he was dead. But this afternoon we spoke for almost an hour. He wants me to help König find our dentist friend, and to go back to Grinzing for a meeting tomorrow morning to discuss your Russian's love letters. I've a hunch that Müller's going to be there.'

'How do you make that out?'

'Nebe said that there would be someone there who specialized in all matters relating to the MVD.'

'Yes, coming from Arthur Nebe that description might well fit Müller. What time is this meeting?'

'Ten o'clock.'

'That only gives me tonight to get things organized. Let me think for a minute.' He was silent for so long that I wondered if he was still on the line. But then I heard him take a deep breath. 'How far is the house from the road?'

'Twenty or thirty metres at the front and the north side. Behind the house to the south is a vineyard. I couldn't tell you how far the road is on that side. There's a row of trees between the house and the vineyard. Some outbuildings as well.' I gave him directions to the house as best I remembered them.

'All right,' he said briskly. 'Here's what we'll do. After ten, I'll start to have my men surround the place at a discreet distance. If Müller is there, you signal to us and we'll close in and pick him up. That's going to be the difficult part because they'll be watching you closely. While you were there, did you happen to use the lavatory?'

'No, but I walked past one on the first floor. If the meeting is in the library where I met Nebe, as I imagine it will be, that will be the one in use. It faces north, towards Josefstadt and the road. And there's a window, with a beige roller blind. Perhaps I could use the blind to signal.'

There was another short silence. Then he said: 'Twenty minutes past the hour, or as near as you can manage, you go to the music-room. When you're in there you pull the blind down and count for five seconds, and then push it up for five seconds. Do it three times. I'll be watching the place through binoculars, and when I see your signal I'll sound the car horn three times. That will be the signal for my men to move in. Then you rejoin the meeting, sit tight and wait for the cavalry.'

'It sounds simple enough. A bit too simple really.'

'Look, kraut, I would suggest that you hang your ass out of the window and whistle "Dixie" but that might attract attention.' He gave an irritated sort of sigh. 'A swoop like this needs a lot of paperwork, Günther. I have to work out code names and get all kinds of special authorizations for a major field operation. And then there's an investigation if the whole thing turns out to be a false alarm. I hope you're right about Müller. You know, I'm going to be up all night arranging this little party.'

'That really knocks over the heap,' I said. 'I'm the one on the beach and you're bitching about some sand in the oil. Well, I'm really blue about your damned paperwork.'

Belinsky laughed. 'Come on, kraut. Don't get a hot throat about it. I just meant that it would be nice if we could be sure that Müller will be there. Be reasonable. We still don't know for sure that he's part of the Org's set-up in Vienna.'

'Sure we do,' I lied. 'This morning I went to the police prison and showed Emil Becker one of Müller's snapshots. He identified him immediately as the man who was with König when he asked Becker to try and find Captain Linden. Unless Müller is just sweet on König, that means he must be part of the Org's Vienna section.'

'Shit,' said Belinsky, 'why didn't I think of doing that? It's so simple. He's certain it was Müller?'

'No doubt whatsoever.' I strung him along like that for a while until I was sure of him. 'All right, slow your blood down. As a matter of fact, Becker didn't identify him at all. But he had seen the photograph before. Traudl Braunsteiner showed it to him. I just wanted to make sure it wasn't you who gave it to her.'

'You still don't trust me yet, do you, kraut?'

'If I'm going to walk into the lion's den for you, I'm entitled to give you an eye-test beforehand.'

'Yes, well that still leaves us with the problem of where Traudl Braunsteiner got hold of a picture of Gestapo Müller.'

'From a Colonel Poroshin of MVD, I expect. He gave Becker a cigarette concession here in Vienna in return for information and the occasional bit of kidnapping. When Becker was approached by the Org he told Poroshin all about it and agreed to try and find out everything he could. After Becker was arrested, Traudl was their go-between. She just posed as his girlfriend.'

'You know what this means, kraut?'

'It means the Ivans are after Müller as well, right?'

'But have you thought what would happen if they got him? Frankly there's not much chance of him going on trial in the Soviet Union. Like I said before, Müller's made a special study of Soviet police methods. No, the Russians want Müller because he can be very useful to them. He could, for instance, tell them who all the Gestapo's agents in the NKVD were. Men who are probably still in place in the MVD.'

'Let's hope he's there tomorrow then.'

'You'd better tell me how to find this place.'

I gave him clear directions, and told him not to be late. 'These bastards scare me,' I explained.

'Hey, you want to know something? All you krauts scare me. But not as much as the Russians.' He chuckled in a way that I had almost started to like. 'Goodbye, kraut,' he said, 'and good luck.'

Then he hung up, leaving me staring at the purring receiver with the curious sensation that the disembodied voice to which I had been speaking belonged nowhere outside my own imagination.

32

Smoke drifted up to the vaulted ceiling of the nightclub like the thickest underworld fog. It wreathed the solitary figure of Belinsky like Bela Lugosi emerged from a churchyard as he strode up to the table where I sat. The band I had been listening to could hold a beat about as well as a one-legged tap-dancer, but somehow he managed to walk to the rhythm it was generating. I knew he was still angry with me for doubting him, and that he was well aware of how, even now, I was trying to fathom why it was that he hadn't thought to show Müller's photograph to Becker. So I wasn't very surprised when he took hold of my hair and banged my head twice on the table, telling me that I was just a suspicious kraut. I got up and staggered away from him towards the door, but found my exit blocked by Arthur Nebe. His presence there was so unexpected that I was momentarily unable to resist Nebe grasping me by both ears and banging my skull once against the door, and then once again for good luck, saying that if I hadn't killed Traudl Braunsteiner then perhaps I ought to find out who had. I twisted my head free of his hands and said that I might as soon have guessed that Rumpelstiltskin's name was Rumpelstiltskin.

I shook my head again, unwillingly, and blinked hard at the dark. There was another knock at the door, and I heard a half-whispered voice.

'Who is it?' I said, reaching for the bedside light, and then my watch. The name made no impression on me as I swung my legs out of bed and went into the sitting-room.

I was still swearing as I opened the door a little wider than was safe. Lotte Hartmann stood in the corridor, in the glistening black evening dress and astrakhan jacket I remembered her wearing from our last evening together. She had a questioning, impertinent sort of look in her eye.

'Yes?' I said. 'What is it? What do you want?'

She sniffed with cool contempt and pushed the door lightly with her gloved hand, so I stepped back into the room. She came in, closed the door behind her and, leaning on it, looked around while my nostrils got a little exercise thanks to the smell of smoke, alcohol and perfume she carried on her venal body. 'I'm sorry if I woke you up,' she said. She didn't look at me so much as the room.

'No you're not,' I said.

Now she took a little trip around the floor, peering into the bedroom and then the bathroom. She moved with an easy grace and as confidently as any woman who is used to the constant sensation of having a man's eyes fixed on her behind.

'You're right,' she grinned, 'I'm not sorry at all. You know, this place isn't as bad as I thought it would be.'

'Do you know what time it is?'

'Very late.' She giggled. 'Your landlady wasn't impressed with me at all. So I had to tell her I was your sister and that I had come all the way from Berlin to give you some bad news.' She giggled again.

'And you're it?'

She pouted for a moment. But it was just an act. She was still too amused with herself to take much umbrage. 'When she asked me if I had any luggage I said that the Russians had stolen it on the train. She was extremely sympathetic, and really rather sweet. I hope you're not going to be different.'

'Oh? I thought that's why you were here. Or are the vice squad giving you problems again?'

She ignored the insult, always supposing she had even bothered to notice it. 'Well, I was just on my way home from the Flottenbar – that's on Mariahilferstrasse, do you know it?'

I didn't say anything. I lit a cigarette and fixed it in a corner of my mouth to stop me snarling something at her.

'Anyway, it's not far from here. And I thought that I'd just drop by. You know –' her tone grew softer and more seductive '– I haven't had a chance to thank you properly,' she let that one hang in the air for a second, and I suddenly wished that I was wearing a dressing-gown, 'for getting me out of that little spot of bother with the Ivans.' She untied the ribbon of her jacket and let it slip to the floor. 'Aren't you even going to offer me a drink?'

'I'd say you've had enough.' But I went ahead and found a couple of glasses anyway.

'Don't you think you'd like to find that out for yourself?' She laughed easily and sat down without any hint of unsteadiness. She looked like the type who could take the stuff through the vein and still walk a chalk line without so much as a hiccup.

'Do you want anything in it?' I held a glass of vodka up as I asked the question.

'Perhaps,' she said ruminatively, 'after I've had my drink.'

I handed her the drink and put one quickly down into the pit of my stomach to hold the fort. I took another drag on my cigarette and hoped that it might fill me up enough to kick her out.

'What's the matter?' she said, almost triumphantly. 'Do I make you nervous or something?'

I guessed it was probably the something. 'Not me,' I said, 'just my pyjamas. They're not used to mixed company.'

'From the look of them I'd say they were more used to mixing concrete.' She helped herself to one of my cigarettes and blew a cord of smoke straight at my groin.

'I could get rid of them if they bothered you,' I said, stupidly. My lips were dry when they sucked at my cigarette again. Did I want her to leave or not? I wasn't making a very good job of throwing her out on her perfect little ear.

'Let's talk a little first. Why don't you sit down?'

I sat down, relieved that I could still fold in the middle.

'All right,' I said, 'how about you tell me where your boyfriend is tonight?'

She grimaced. 'Not a good subject, Perseus. Pick another.'

'You two have a rattle?'

She groaned. 'Do we have to?'

I shrugged. 'It doesn't make me itch a lot.'

'The man's a bastard,' she said, 'but I still don't want to talk about it. Especially today.'

'What's so special about today?'

'I got a part in a movie.'

'Congratulations. What's the role?'

'It's an English film. Not a very big part, you understand. But there are going to be some big stars in it. I play the role of a girl at a nightclub.'

'Well, that sounds simple enough.'

'Isn't it exciting?' she squealed. 'Me acting with Orson Welles.'

'*The War of the Worlds* fellow?'

She shrugged blankly. 'I never saw that film.'

'Forget it.'

'Of course they're not actually sure about Welles. But they think there's a good chance they can persuade him to come to Vienna.'

'That all sounds very familiar to me.'

'What's that?'

'I didn't even know you were an actress.'

'You mean I didn't tell you? Listen, that job at the Oriental is just temporary.'

'You seem pretty good at it.'

'Oh, I've always been good with numbers and money. I used to work in the local tax department.' She leaned forward and her expression became just a little too quizzical, as if she meant to question me about my year-end business expenses. 'I've been meaning to ask you,' she said, 'that night when you dropped all that mouse. What were you trying to prove?'

'Prove? I'm not sure I follow you.'

'No?' She turned her smile up a couple of stops to shoot me a knowing, conspiratorial sort of look. 'I see a lot of quirks, mister. I get to recognize the types. One day I'm even going to write a book about it. Like Franz Josef Gall. Ever hear of him?'

'I can't say that I have.'

'He was an Austrian doctor who founded the science of phrenology. Now you've heard of that, haven't you?'

'Sure,' I said. 'And what can you tell from the bumps I'm wearing on my head?'

'I can tell you're not the kind to drop that sort of money without a good reason.' She stretched an eyebrow of draughtsman's quality up her smooth forehead. 'I've got an idea about that too.'

'Let's hear it,' I urged, and poured myself another drink. 'Maybe you'll make a better go of reading my mind than you did of reading my cranium.'

'Don't act so hard to get,' she told me. 'We both know you're the kind of man that likes to make an impression.'

'And did I? Make an impression?'

'I'm here, aren't I? What do you want – Tristan and Isolde?'

So that was it. She thought that I had lost the money for her benefit. To look like a big-shot.

She drained her glass, stood up and handed it back to me. 'Pour me some more of that love potion of yours while I powder my nose.'

While she was in the bathroom I refilled the glasses with hands that were none too steady. I didn't particularly like the woman, but I had nothing against her body: it was just fine. I had an idea that my head was going to object to this little skylark when my libido had released the controls, but at that particular moment I could do nothing more than sit back and enjoy the flight. Even so, I was unprepared for what happened next.

I heard her open the bathroom door and say something ordinary about the perfume she was wearing, but when I turned round with the drinks I saw that the perfume was all that she was wearing. Actually she had kept her shoes on, but it took my eyes a little while to work their way down past her breasts and her pubic equilateral. Except for those high-heels, Lotte Hartmann was as naked as an assassin's blade, and probably just as treacherous.

She stood in the doorway of my bedroom, her hands hanging by her bare thighs, glowing with delight as my tongue licked my lips rather too obviously for me to have contemplated using it on anything but her. Maybe I could have given her a pompous little lecture at that. I'd seen enough naked women in my time, some of them in fair shape too. I ought to have tossed her back like a fish, but the sweat starting out on my palms, the flare of my nostrils, the lump in my throat and the dull, insistent ache in my groin told me that the machina had other ideas as to the next course of action than the deus which called it home.

Delighted with the effect she was having on me, Lotte smiled happily and took the glass from my hand.

'I hope you don't mind me undressing,' she said, 'only the gown is an expensive one and I had the strangest feeling that you were about to tear it off my back.'

'Why should I mind? It's not as if I haven't finished reading the evening paper. Anyway, I like having a naked woman about the place.' I watched the slight wobble of her behind as she walked lazily to the other side of the sitting-room where she swallowed her drink and dropped the empty glass on to the sofa.

Suddenly I wanted to see her bottom shaking like a jelly against the rut of my abdomen. She seemed to sense this and, bending forwards, took hold of the radiator like a wrestler pulling against the ring ropes in his corner. Then she stood with her feet a short way apart and stood quietly with her backside towards me, as if waiting for a thoroughly unnecessary body-search. She glanced back over her shoulder, flexed her buttocks and then faced the wall again.

I'd had more eloquent invitations, but with the blood buzzing in my ears and battering those few brain cells not yet affected by alcohol or adrenalin, I really couldn't remember when. Probably I didn't even care. I tore off my pyjamas and stalked after her.

I'm no longer young enough, nor quite thin enough, to share a single bed with anything other than a hangover or a cigarette. So it was perhaps a sense of surprise that woke me from an unexpectedly comfortable sleep at around six o'clock. Lotte, who might otherwise have caused me a restless night, was no longer lying in the crook of my arm and for a brief, happy moment I supposed that she must have gone home. It was then that I heard a small, stifled sob coming from the sitting-room. Reluctantly I slipped out from under the covers and into my overcoat, and went to see what was wrong.

Still naked, Lotte had made a little ball of herself on the floor by the radiator where it was warm. I squatted down beside her and asked why she was crying. A fat tear rolled down a stained cheek and hung on her top lip like a translucent wart. She licked it away and sniffed as I handed her my handkerchief.

'What do you care?' she said bitterly. 'Now that you've had your fun.'

She had a point, but I went ahead and protested, enough to be polite. Lotte heard me out and when her vanity was satisfied she tried a crippled sort of smile that reminded me of the way an unhappy child will cheer up when you hand over 50 pfennigs or a penny-chew.

'You're very sweet,' she allowed finally, and wiped her red eyes. 'I'll be all right now, thank you.'

'Do you want to tell me about it?'

Lotte glanced at me out of the corner of one eye. 'In this town? Better tell me your rates first, doctor.' She blew her nose and then uttered a short, hollow laugh. 'You might make a good screw doctor.'

'You seem quite sane to me,' I said, helping her to an armchair.

'I wouldn't bet on it.'

'Is that your professional advice?' I lit a couple of cigarettes and handed her one. She smoked it desperately, and without much apparent pleasure.

'That's my advice as a woman who's mad enough to have been having an affair with a man who just slapped her round like a circus clown.'

'König? I never saw him as the violent type.'

'If he seems urbane that's only the morphine he uses.'

'He's an addict?'

'I don't know if he's an addict exactly. But whatever it was he did while he was in the SS, he needed morphine to get through the war.'

'So why did he paste you?'

She bit her lip fiercely. 'Well, it wasn't because he thought I could use a little colour.'

I laughed. I had to hand it to her, she was a tough one. I said, 'Not with that tan anyway.' I picked up the astrakhan jacket from the floor where she had dropped it and draped it around her shoulders. Lotte drew it close to her throat and smiled bitterly.

'Nobody puts his hand on my jaw,' she said, 'not if he ever wants to put his hand any place else. Tonight was the first and last time that he'll give me a pair of slaps, so help me.' She blew smoke from her nostrils as fiercely as a dragon. 'That's what you get when you try to help someone, I guess.'

'Help who?'

'König came into the Oriental at around ten last night,' she explained. 'He was in a foul mood and when I asked him why, he wanted to know if I remembered a dentist who used to come into the club and gamble a bit.' She shrugged. 'Well, I did remember him. A bad player but certainly not half as bad as you like to pretend you are.' Her eyes flicked at me uncertainly.

I nodded, urgently. 'Go on.'

'Helmut wanted to know if Dr Heim, the dentist, had been in the place during the last couple of days. I told him I didn't think he had. Then he wanted me to ask some of the girls if they remembered him being there. Well, there was one particular girl I said he should be sure to speak to. A bit of a hard-luck case, but pretty with it. The doctors always went for her. I guess it was because she always looked that little bit more vulnerable, and there are some men who quite like that sort of thing. It so happened she was sitting at the bar, so I pointed her out to him.'

I felt my stomach turning to quicksand. 'What was this girl's name?' I asked.

'Veronika something,' she said, and noticing my concern, added, 'Why? Do you know her?'

'A little,' I said. 'What happened then?'

'Helmut and one of his friends took Veronika next door.'

'To the hat shop?'

'Yes.' Her voice was soft now and just a little ashamed. 'Helmut's temper –' she flinched at the memory of it '– I was worried. Veronika's a nice girl. A doofy, but nice, you know. She's had a bit of a hard life but she's got plenty of guts. Perhaps too many for her own good. I thought with Helmut the way he was, the mood he was in, it would be better for her to tell him if she knew anything or not, and to tell him quickly. He's not a very patient man. Just in case he turned nasty.' She grimaced. 'Not much of a corner to turn, when you know Helmut.

'So I went after them. Veronika was crying when I found them. They'd already slapped her around quite hard. She'd had enough, and I told them to stop it. That was when he slapped me. Twice.' She held her cheeks as if the pain lingered with the memory. 'Then he shoved me out into the corridor and told me to mind my own business and stay out of his.'

'What happened after that?'

'I went to the Ladies, a couple of bars and came here, in that order.'

'Did you see what happened to Veronika?'

'They left with her, Helmut and the other man.'

'You mean they took her away somewhere?'

Lotte shrugged glumly. 'I guess so.'

'Where would they have taken her?' I stood up and walked into the bedroom.

'I don't know.'

'Try and think.'

'You're going after her?'

'Like you said, she's been through a lot already.' I started to dress. 'And what's more, I got her into this.'

'You. How come?'

While I finished dressing I described how, coming back from Grinzing with König, I had explained how I would have gone about trying to find a missing person, in this case Dr Heim.

'I told him how we could check Heim's usual haunts if he could tell me where they were,' I told her. But I left out how I had thought it would never have got that far: how I assumed that with Müller – possibly Nebe and König too – arrested by Belinsky and the people from Crowcass, the need actually to look for Heim would never have arisen: how I thought that I had stalled König into waiting until the meeting at Grinzing was over before we started to look for his dead dentist.

'Why should they have thought that you could find her?'

'Before the war I was a detective with the Berlin police.'

'I should have known,' she snorted.

'Not really,' I said, straightening my tie, and jabbing a cigarette into my sour-tasting mouth, 'but I should certainly have known that your boyfriend was arrogant enough to go and look for Heim on his own. It was stupid of me to think that he would wait.' I climbed back into my overcoat and picked up my hat. 'Do you think they would have taken her to Grinzing?' I asked her.

'Now I come to think of it, I had the idea they were going to Veronika's room, wherever that is. But if she's not there, Grinzing would be as good a place to look as any.'

'Well, let's hope she's home.' But even as I said it, I knew in my guts that this was unlikely.

Lotte stood up. The jacket covered her chest and her upper torso, but left bare the burning bush which earlier had spoken so persuasively and left me feeling as sore as a skinned rabbit.

'What about me?' she said quietly. 'What shall I do?'

'You?' I nodded down at her nakedness. 'Put the magic away and go home.'

33

The morning was bright, clear and chilly. Crossing the park in front of the new town hall on my way to the Inner City, a couple of squirrels bounded up to say hello and check me out for breakfast. But before they got close they caught the cloud on my face and the smell of fear on my socks. Probably they even made a mental note of the heavy shape in my coat pocket and thought better of it. Smart little creatures. After all, it wasn't so very long since small mammals were being shot and eaten in Vienna. So they hurried on their way, like living scribbles of fur.

At the dump where Veronika lived they were used to people, mostly men, coming and going at all hours of the day and night, and even if the landlady had been the most misanthropic of lesbians, I doubt she would have paid me much attention if she had met me on the stairs. But as it happened there was nobody about, and I made my way up to Veronika's room unchallenged.

I didn't need to break the door in. It was wide open, just like all the drawers and cupboards. I wondered why they had bothered when all the evidence they needed was still hanging on the back of the chair where Doctor Heim had left it.

'The stupid bitch,' I muttered angrily. 'What's the point of getting rid of a man's body if you leave his suit in your room?' I slammed a drawer shut. The force dislodged one of Veronika's pathetic sketches from off the chest of drawers, and it floated to the floor like a huge dead leaf. König had probably turned the place over out of pure spite. And then taken her to Grinzing. With an important meeting there that morning I couldn't see that they would have gone anywhere else. Assuming that they didn't kill her outright. On the other hand, if Veronika told them the truth about what had happened – that a couple of friends had helped her to dispose of Heim's body after his suffering a heart attack, then (if she had omitted mentioning Belinsky's name and my own) perhaps they would let her go. But there was a real possibility that they might still kick her around to make sure she had told them everything she knew: that by the time I arrived to try and help her I would already be exposed as the man who had dumped Heim's body.

I remembered how Veronika had told me about her life as a Sudeten Jew during wartime. How she had hid in lavatories, dirty basements, cupboards and attics. And then a DP camp for six months. 'A bit of hard life,' was how Lotte Hartmann had described it. The more I thought about it, the more it seemed to me that she'd had very little of what could properly be called life at all.

I glanced at my wristwatch and saw that it was seven o'clock. There were still three hours to go before the meeting started: longer before Belinsky could be expected with 'the cavalry', as he put it. And because the men who had taken Veronika were who they were, I began to think that there was a real possibility that she wouldn't live that long. It looked as if I had no choice but to go and get her myself.

I took out my revolver, thumbed open the six-shot cylinder and checked that it was fully loaded before heading back downstairs. Outside, I hailed a taxi at the rank on Kärtnerstrasse and told the driver to go to Grinzing.

'Whereabouts in Grinzing?' he asked, accelerating away from the kerb.

'I'll tell you when we get there.'

'You're the boss,' he said, speeding on to the Ring. 'Only reason I asked was that everything there will be shut at this time of the morning. And you don't look like you're going hill-walking. Not in that coat.' The car shuddered as we hit a couple of enormous potholes. 'And you're no Austrian. I can tell that from your accent. You sound like a *pifke*, sir. Am I right?'

'Skip the university-of-life class, will you? I'm not in the mood.'

'That's all right, sir. Only reason I asked was in case you were looking for a little bit of fun. You see, sir, only a few minutes further on from Grinzing, on the road to Cobenzl, there's this hotel – the Schloss-Hotel Cobenzl.' He wrestled with the wheel as the car hit another pothole. 'Right now it's being used as a DP camp. There's girls there you can have for just a few cigarettes. Even at this hour of the morning if you fancy it. A man wearing a good coat like yours could have two or three together maybe. Get them to put a nice show on for you between themselves if you know what I mean.' He laughed coarsely. 'Some of these girls, sir. They've grown up in DP camps. Got the morals of rabbits, so they have. They'll do anything. Believe me, sir, I know what I'm talking about. I keep rabbits myself.' He chuckled warmly at the thought of it all. 'I could arrange something for you, sir. In the back of the car. For a small commission of course.'

I leaned forwards on the seat. I don't know why I bothered with him. Maybe I just don't like garter-handlers. Maybe I just didn't much care for his Trotsky lookalike face.

'That would be just great,' I said, very tough. 'If it weren't for a Russian table-trap I found in the Ukraine. Partisans put a tension-release grenade behind a drawer that they left half-open with a bottle of vodka in there, just to get your attention. I came along, pulled the drawer, the pressure was released and the grenade detonated. It took the meat and two vegetables clean off at my belly. I nearly died of shock, then I nearly died from loss of blood. And when finally I came out of the coma I nearly died of grief. I tell you if I so much as see a bit of plum I'm liable to go mad with the frustration of it. I'd probably kill the nearest man to me out of plain envy.'

The driver glanced back over his shoulder. 'Sorry,' he said nervously, 'I didn't mean to –'

'Forget it,' I said, almost smiling now.

When we came past the yellow house I told the driver to keep going to the top of the hill. I had decided to approach Nebe's house from the back, through the vineyards.

Because the meters on Vienna's taxis were old and out of date, it was customary to multiply the tariff shown by five to give the total sum payable. There were six schillings on the clock when I told him to stop, and this was all the driver asked me for, his hand trembling as he took the money. The car was already roaring away by the time I realized he had forgotten his arithmetic.

I stood there, on a muddy track by the side of the road, wondering why I hadn't kept my mouth shut, having intended to tell the man to wait a while. Now if I did find Veronika, I would have the problem of how to get away. Me and my smart mouth, I thought. The poor bastard was only offering a service, I told myself. But he was wrong about one thing. There was something open, a café further up Cobenzlgasse: the Rudelshof. I decided that if I was going to get shot I'd prefer to collect it with something in my stomach.

The café was a cosy little place if you didn't mind taxidermy. I sat down under the beady eye of an anthraxic-looking weasel and waited for the badly stuffed proprietor to shamble up to my table.

'God's greeting to you, sir,' he said. 'It's a lovely morning.'

I reeled away from his distilled breath. 'I can tell you're already enjoying it,' I said, using my smart mouth yet again. He shrugged, uncomprehending, and took my order.

The five-schilling Viennese breakfast I gobbled tasted like the taxidermist had cooked it during his time off between jobs: the coffee had grounds in it, the roll was about as fresh as a piece of scrimshaw and the egg was so hard it might have come from a quarry. But I ate it. I had so much on my mind I'd probably have eaten the weasel if only they'd sat it on a slice of toast.

Outside the café I walked down the road awhile and then climbed over a wall into what I thought must be Arthur Nebe's vineyard.

There wasn't much to see. The vines themselves, planted in neat rows, were still only young shoots, hardly higher than my knee. Here and there on high trolleys were what looked like abandoned jet engines but were in fact the rapid burners they used at night to heat the atmosphere around the shoots and protect them from late frost. They were still warm to the touch. The field itself was perhaps a hundred metres square and offered little in the way of cover.

I wondered exactly how Belinsky would manage to deploy his men. Apart from crawling the length of the field on your belly, you could only stay close to the wall while you worked your way down to the trees immediately behind the yellow house and its outbuildings.

When I got as far as the trees I looked for some sign of life, and seeing none I edged my way forwards until I heard voices. Next to the largest of the outbuildings, a long half-timbered affair that resembled a barn, two men, neither of whom I recognized, were standing talking. Each man wore a metal drum on his back, and this was connected by a rubber hose to a long thin tube of metal he held in his hand which I presumed to be some kind of crop-spraying contraption.

At last they finished their conversation and walked towards the opposite side of the vineyard, as if to start their attack on the bacteria, fungi and insects which plagued their lives. I waited until they were well across the field before leaving the cover of the trees and entering the building.

A musty fruit smell hit my nostrils. Large oak vats and storage tanks were ranged under the open rafters of the ceiling like enormous cheeses. I walked the length of the stone floor and emerged at the other end of this first building to be faced with the door to another, built at right angles to the house.

This second outhouse contained hundreds of oak barrels, which lay on their sides as if awaiting the giant St Bernard dogs to come and collect them. Stairs led down into the darkness. It seemed like a good place to imprison someone, so I switched on the light and went downstairs to take a look. But there were only thousands of bottles of wine, each rack marked by a small blackboard on which were chalked a few numbers that must have meant something to somebody. I came back upstairs, switched off the light and stood by the barrel-room window. It was beginning to look as if Veronika might be in the house after all.

From where I was standing I had a clear view across a short cobbled yard, to the west side of the house. In front of an open door a big black cat sat staring at me. Beside the door was the window of what looked like the kitchen. There was a large, shiny shape on the kitchen ledge which I thought was probably a pot or a kettle. After a while the cat walked slowly up to the outbuilding where I was hiding and mewed loudly at something beside the window where I was standing. For a second or two it fixed me with its green eyes, and then for no apparent reason ran off. I looked back towards the house and continued to watch the kitchen door and window. After a few more minutes I judged it safe to leave the barrel room, and started across the yard.

I had not gone three paces when I heard the ratchet sound of an automatic-slide and almost simultaneously felt the cold steel of a gun muzzle pressed hard against my neck.

'Clasp your hands behind your head,' said a voice, none too distinctly.

I did as I was told. The gun pressed under my ear felt heavy enough to be a .45. Enough to dispose of a large part of my skull. I winced as he screwed the gun between my jaw and my jugular vein.

'Twitch and you're tomorrow morning's pig swill,' he said, smacking my pockets, and relieving me of my revolver.

'You'll find that Herr Nebe is expecting me,' I said.

'Don't know a Herr Nebe,' he said thickly, almost as if his mouth didn't work properly. Naturally I was reluctant to turn round and take a good look to make sure.

'Yes, that's right, he changed his name, didn't he?' I tried hard to remember Nebe's new surname. Meanwhile I heard the man behind me step back a couple of steps.

'Now walk to your right,' he told me. 'Towards the trees. And don't trip on your shoelaces or anything.'

He sounded big and not too bright. And it was a strangely accented German he spoke: like Prussian, but different; more like the Old Prussian I had heard my grandfather speak; almost like the German I had heard spoken in Poland.

'Look, you're making a mistake,' I said. 'Why don't you check with your boss? My name is Bernhard Günther. There's a meeting at ten o'clock this morning. I'm supposed to be at it.'

'It's not even eight yet,' grunted my captor. 'If you're here for a meeting, how come you're so early? And how come you don't come to the front door like normal visitors? How come you walk across the fields? How come you snoop around in the outhouses?'

'I'm early because I own a couple of wineshops in Berlin,' I said. 'I thought it might be nice to take a look around the estate.'

'You were taking a look all right. You're a snooper.' He chuckled cretinously. 'I got orders to shoot snoopers.'

'Now wait a minute –' I turned into a clubbing blow from his gun, and as I fell I caught a glimpse of a big man with a shaven head and a lopsided sort of jaw. He grabbed me by the scruff of my neck and hauled me back on to my feet, and I wondered why I had never thought to sew a razor blade under that part of my coat collar. He pushed me through the line of trees and down a slope to a small clearing where several large dustbins were standing. A trail of smoke and a sweet sickly smell arose through the roof of a small brick hut: it was where they incinerated the rubbish. Next to several bags of what looked like cement, a sheet of rusting corrugated iron lay on some bricks. The man ordered me to draw it aside.

Now I had it. He was a Latvian. A big, stupid Latvian. And I decided that if he was working for Arthur Nebe he was probably from a Latvian SS division, that had served in one of the Polish death camps. They had used a lot of Latvians at places like Auschwitz. Latvians were enthusiastic anti-Semites when Moses Mendelssohn was one of Germany's favourite sons.

I hauled the iron sheet away from what was revealed as some kind of old drain, or cesspit. Certainly it smelt every bit as bad. It was then that I saw the cat again. It emerged from between two paper sacks labelled calcium oxide close by the pit. It mewed contemptuously, as if to say, 'I warned you there was someone standing in that yard, but you wouldn't listen to me.' An acrid, chalky smell came up from the pit and made my skin crawl. 'You're right,' mewed the cat, like something from Edgar Allan Poe, 'calcium oxide is a cheap alkali for treating acid soil. Just the sort of thing you would expect to see in a vineyard. But it's also called quicklime, and that's an extremely efficient compound for speeding human decomposition.'

With horror I realized that the Latvian really did mean to kill me. And there I was trying to place his accent like some sort of philologist, and to recall the chemical formulas I had learned at school.

Then I got my first good look at him. He was big and as burly as a circus horse, but you hardly noticed that for looking at his face: its whole right side was crooked like he had a big chew of tobacco in his cheek; his right eye stared wide as if it had been made of glass. He could probably have kissed his own earlobe. Starved of affection, as any man with such a face would have been, he probably had to.

'Kneel down by the side of the pit,' he snarled, sounding like a Neanderthal short of a couple of vital chromosomes.

'You're not going to kill an old comrade, are you?' I said desperately trying to remember Nebe's new name, or even one of the Latvian regiments. I considered shouting for help except that I knew he would have shot me without hesitation.

'You're an old comrade?' he sneered, without much apparent difficulty.

'Obersturmführer with the First Latvian,' I said with a poor show of nonchalance.

The Latvian spat into the bushes and regarded me blankly with his pop eye. The gun, a big blue steel Colt automatic, remained pointed squarely at my chest.

'First Latvian, eh? You don't sound like a Lat.'

'I'm Prussian,' I said. 'Our family lived in Riga. My father was a shipworker from Danzig. He married a Russian.' I offered a few words of Russian by way of confirmation, although I could not remember if Riga was predominantly Russian or German-speaking.

His eyes narrowed, one rather more than the other. 'So what year was the First Latvian founded?'

I swallowed hard and racked my memory. The cat mewed

encouragingly. Reasoning that the raising of a Latvian SS regiment would have to have followed Operation Barbarossa in 1941, I said, '1942.'

He grinned horribly, and shook his head with slow sadism. '1943,' he said, advancing a couple of paces. 'It was 1943. Now get down on your knees or I'll give it to you in the guts.'

Slowly I sank down on my knees on the edge of the pit, feeling the ground wet through the material of my trousers. I had seen more than enough of SS murder to know what he intended: a shot in the back of the neck, my body collapsing neatly into a ready-made grave, and a few spadefuls of quicklime on top. He came around behind me in a wide circle. The cat settled down to watch, its tail wrapping neatly around its behind as it sat. I closed my eyes and waited.

'Rainis,' said a voice, and several seconds passed. I hardly dared to look around and see if I had been saved.

'It's all right, Bernie. You can get up now.'

My breath came out in one huge burp of fright. Weakly, my knees knocking, I picked myself up from the edge of the pit and turned to see Arthur Nebe standing a few metres behind the Latvian ugly. To my annoyance he was grinning.

'I'm glad you find it so amusing, Dr Frankenstein,' I said. 'Your fucking monster nearly killed me.'

'What on earth were you thinking of, Bernie?' Nebe said. 'You should know better. Rainis here was only doing his job.'

The Latvian nodded sullenly and holstered his Colt. 'He was snooping,' he said dully. 'I caught him.'

I shrugged. 'It's a nice morning. I thought I'd take a look at Grinzing. I was just admiring your estate when Lon Chaney here stuck a gun in my ear.'

The Latvian took my revolver out of his jacket pocket and handed it to Nebe. 'He was carrying a lighter, Herr Nolde.'

'Planning to shoot small game, is that it, Bernie?'

'You can't be too careful these days.'

'I'm glad you think so,' said Nebe. 'It saves me the trouble of apologizing.' He weighed my gun in his hand and then pocketed it. 'All the same, I'll hang on to this for now if you don't mind. Guns make some of our friends nervous. Remind me to return it to you before you leave.' He turned to the Latvian.

'All right, Rainis, that's all. You were only doing your job. I suggest that you go and get yourself some breakfast.'

The monster nodded and walked back towards the house, with the cat following him.

'I'll bet he can eat his weight in peanuts.'

Nebe smiled thinly. 'Some people keep savage dogs to protect them. I have Rainis.'

'Yes, well I hope he's house-trained.' I took off my hat and wiped my brow with my handkerchief. 'Me, I wouldn't let him past the front door. I'd keep him on a chain in the yard. Where does he think he is? Treblinka? The bastard couldn't wait to shoot me, Arthur.'

'Oh, I don't doubt it. He enjoys killing people.'

Nebe shook his head to my offer of a cigarette, but he had to help me light mine as my hand was shaking like it was talking to a deaf Apache.

'He's a Latvian,' Nebe explained. 'He was a corporal at the Riga concentration camp. When the Russians captured him they stamped on his head and broke his jaw with their boots.'

'Believe me, I know how they must have felt.'

'They paralysed half his face, and left him slightly soft in the head. He was always a brutal killer. But now he's more like an animal. And just as loyal as any dog.'

'Well, naturally I was thinking he'd have his good points too. Riga eh?' I jerked my head at the open pit and the incinerator. 'I bet that little waste-disposal set-up makes him feel quite at home.' I sucked gratefully at my cigarette and added, 'If it comes to that, I bet it makes you both feel at home.'

Nebe frowned. 'I think you need a drink,' he said quietly.

'I wouldn't be at all surprised. Just make sure it doesn't have any lime in it. I think I lost my taste for lime, for ever.'

34

I followed Nebe into the house and up to the library where we had talked the day before. He fetched me a brandy from the drinks-cabinet and set it down on the table in front of me.

'Forgive me for not joining you,' he said, watching me down it quickly. 'Normally I quite enjoy a cognac with my breakfast but this morning I must keep a clear head.' He smiled indulgently as I replaced the empty glass on the table. 'Better now?'

I nodded. 'Tell me, have you found your missing dentist yet? Dr Heim?' Now that I no longer had to worry about my own immediate prospects for survival, Veronika was once again at the front of my mind.

'He's dead, I'm afraid. That's bad enough, but it's not half as bad as not knowing what had happened to him was. At least we now know that the Russians haven't got him.'

'What did happen to him?'

'He had a heart attack.' Nebe uttered the familiar, dry little laugh I remembered from my days at the Alex, the headquarters of Berlin's criminal police. 'It seems that he was with a girl at the time. A chocolady.'

'You mean it was while they were —?'

'I mean precisely that. Still, I can think of worse ways to go, can't you?'

'After what I've just been through, that's not particularly difficult for me, Arthur.'

'Quite.' He smiled almost sheepishly.

I spent a moment searching for a frame of words that might enable me to innocently inquire as to Veronika's fate. 'So what did she do? The chocolady, I mean. Phone the police?' I frowned. 'No, I expect not.'

'Why do you say that?'

I shrugged at the apparent simplicity of my explanation. 'I can't imagine she'd have risked a run-in with the vice squad. No, I'll bet she tried to have him dumped somewhere. Got her garter-handler to do it.' I raised my eyebrows questioningly. 'Well? Am I right?'

'Yes, you're right.' He sounded almost as if he admired my thinking. 'As usual.' Then he uttered a wistful sort of sigh. 'What a pity that we're no longer with Kripo. I can't tell you how much I miss it all.'

'Me too.'

'But you, you could rejoin. Surely you're not wanted for anything, Bernie?'

'And work for the Communists? No thanks.' I pursed my lips and tried to look rueful. 'Anyway, I'd rather stay out of Berlin for a while. A Russian soldier tried to rob me on a train. It was self-defence, but I'm afraid I killed him. I was seen leaving the scene of the crime covered in blood.'

' "The scene of the crime",' quoted Nebe, rolling the phrase round his mouth like a fine wine. 'It's good to talk to a detective again.'

'Just to satisfy my professional curiosity, Arthur: how did you find the chocolady?'

'Oh, it wasn't me, it was König. He tells me that it was you who told him how best to go about looking for poor Heim.'

'It was just routine stuff, Arthur. You could have told him.'

'Maybe so. Anyway, it seems that König's girlfriend recognized Heim from a photograph. Apparently he used to frequent the nightclub where she works. She remembered that Heim used to be especially keen on one of the snappers who worked there. All Helmut had to do was persuade her to come clean about it. It was as simple as that.'

'Getting information out of a snapper is never "as simple as that",' I said. 'It can be like getting a curse out of a nun. Money is the only way to get a party-girl to talk that doesn't leave a bruise.' I waited for Nebe to contradict me, but he said nothing. 'Of course, a bruise is cheaper, and leaves no margin for error.' I grinned at him as if to say that I had no particular scruples when it came to slapping a chocolady in the interests of efficient investigation. 'I'd say König wasn't the type to waste money: am I right?'

To my disappointment, Nebe merely shrugged and then glanced at his watch. 'You'd better ask him yourself when you see him.'

'Is he coming to this meeting too?'

'He'll be here.' Nebe consulted his watch again. 'I'm afraid I have to leave you now. I've still one or two things to do before ten. Perhaps it would be better if you stayed in here. Security is tight today, and we wouldn't want another incident, would we? I'll have someone bring you some coffee. Build a fire if you like. It's rather cold in here.'

I tapped my glass. 'I can't say that I'm noticing it much now.'

Nebe regarded me patiently. 'Yes, well, do help yourself to some more brandy, if you think you need it.'

'Thanks,' I said, reaching for the decanter, 'I don't mind if I do.'

'But stay sharp. You'll be asked a lot of questions about your Russian friend. I wouldn't like your opinion of his worth to be doubted merely because you had too much to drink.' He walked across the creaking floor to the door.

'Don't worry about me,' I said, surveying the empty shelves, 'I'll read a book.'

Nebe's considerable nose wrinkled with disapproval. 'Yes, it's such a pity that the library is gone. Apparently the previous owners left a superb collection, but when the Russians came they used them all as fuel for the boiler.' He shook his head sadly. 'What can you do with subhumans like that?'

When Nebe had left the library I did as he had suggested and built a fire in the grate. It helped me to focus my mind on my next course of action. As the flames took hold of the small edifice of logs and sticks I had constructed, I reflected that Nebe's apparent amusement at the circumstances of Heim's death seemed to indicate that the Org was satisfied Veronika had told the truth.

It was true, I was no wiser as to where she might be, but I had gained the impression that König was not yet at Grinzing, and without my gun I did not see that I could now leave and look for her elsewhere. With only two hours to go before the Org's meeting, it appeared that my best course of action was to wait for König to arrive, and hope that he could put my mind at rest. And if he had killed or injured Veronika, I would settle his account personally when Belinsky arrived with his men.

I collected the poker off the hearth and stoked the fire negligently. Nebe's man arrived with the coffee, but I paid him no attention, and after he had gone again I stretched out on the sofa and closed my eyes.

The fire stirred, clapped its hands a couple of times, and warmed my side. Behind my closed lids, bright red turned to deep purple, and then something more restful . . .

'Herr Günther?'

I jerked my head up from the sofa. Sleeping in an awkward position, even for only a few minutes, had made my neck as stiff as new leather. But when I looked at my watch I saw that I had been sleeping for more than an hour. I flexed my neck.

Sitting beside the sofa was a man wearing a grey flannel suit. He leaned forward and held out his hand for me to shake. It was a broad, strong hand and surprisingly firm for such a short man. Gradually I recognized his face, although I had never met him before.

'I am Dr Moltke,' he said. 'I've heard a great deal about you, Herr Günther.' You could have blown froth from the top of his accent it was so Bavarian.

I nodded uncertainly. There was something about his gaze I found deeply disconcerting. His were the eyes of a music-hall hypnotist.

'I'm pleased to meet you, Herr Doktor.' Here was another one who had changed his name. Another one who was supposed to be dead, like Arthur Nebe. And yet this was no ordinary Nazi fugitive from justice, if indeed justice existed anywhere in Europe during 1948. It gave me a strange feeling to consider that I had just shaken hands with a man who, but for the mysterious circumstances surrounding his 'death', might well have been the world's most wanted man. This was 'Gestapo' Heinrich Müller, in person.

'Arthur Nebe has been telling me about you,' he said. 'You know, you and I are quite alike it seems. I was a police detective, like yourself. I began on the beat and I learnt my profession in the hard school of ordinary police work. Like you I also specialized: while you worked for the murder commission, I was led to the surveillance of Communist Party functionaries. I even made a special study of Soviet Russian police methods. I found much there to admire. As a policeman yourself, you would surely appreciate their professionalism. The MVD, which used to be the NKVD, is probably the finest secret police force anywhere in the world. Better even than the Gestapo. For the simple reason, I think, that National Socialism was never able to offer a faith capable of commanding such a consistent attitude towards life. And do you know why?'

I shook my head. His broad Bavarian speech seemed to suggest a natural geniality which I knew the man himself could not possibly have possessed.

'Because, Herr Günther, unlike Communism, we never really appealed to the intellectuals as well as to the working classes. You know, I myself did not join the Party until 1939. Stalin does these things better. Today I see him in quite a different light than I did of old.'

I frowned, wondering whether this was Müller's idea of a test, or a joke. But he seemed to be perfectly serious. Pompously so.

'You admire Stalin?' I asked, almost incredulously.

'He stands head and shoulders above any of our Western leaders. Even Hitler was a small man by comparison. Just think what Stalin and his Party have stood up to. You were in one of their camps. You know what they're like. Why, you even speak Russian. You always know where you are with the Ivans. They put you up against a wall and shoot you, or they give you the Order of Lenin. Not like the Americans or the British.' Müller's face suddenly took on an expression of intense dislike. 'They talk about morality and justice and yet they allow Germany to starve. They write about ethics and yet they hang old comrades one day, and recruit them for their own security services the next. You can't trust people like that, Herr Günther.'

'Forgive me, Herr Doktor, but I was under the impression that we were working for the Americans.'

'That is wrong. We work *with* the Americans. But in the end we are working *for* Germany. For a new Fatherland.'

Looking more thoughtful now, he got up and went over to the window. His manner of expressing deliberation was a silent rhapsody more characteristic of a peasant priest wrestling with his conscience. He folded his thick hands thoughtfully, unclasped them again and finally pressed his temples between both fists.

'There is nothing to admire in America. Not like Russia. But the Amis do have power. And what gives them this power is the dollar. That is the only reason why we must oppose Russia. We need the American dollars. All that the Soviet Union can give us is an example: an example of just what loyalty and dedication can achieve, even without money. So then, think what Germans might do with similar devotion and American cash.'

I tried and failed to stifle a yawn. 'Why are you telling me this Herr – Herr Doktor?' For one ghastly second I had almost called him Herr Müller. Did anyone but Arthur Nebe, and perhaps von Bolschwing, who had interrogated me, know who Moltke really was?

'We are working for a new tomorrow, Herr Günther. Germany may be divided between them now. But there will come a time when we are a great power again. A great economic power. So long as our Organization works alongside the Amis to oppose Communism, they will be persuaded to allow Germany to rebuild herself. And with our industry and our technology we shall achieve what Hitler could never have achieved. And what Stalin – yes, even Stalin with his massive five-year plans – what he can still only dream of. The German may never rule militarily, but he can do it economically. It is the mark, not the swastika, that will conquer Europe. You doubt what I say?'

If I looked surprised it was only because the idea of German industry being on top of anything but a scrapheap seemed perfectly ludicrous.

'It's just that I wonder if everyone in the Org thinks the same way as you?'

He shrugged. 'Not precisely, no. There are a variety of opinions as to the worth of our allies, and the evil of our enemies. But all are agreed on one thing, and that is the new Germany. Whether it takes five years, or fifty-five years.'

Absently, Müller started to pick his nose. It occupied him for several seconds, after which he inspected his thumb and forefinger and then wiped them on Nebe's curtains. It was, I considered, a poor indicator of the new Germany he had been speaking of.

'Anyway, I just wanted this opportunity to thank you personally for your initiative. I've had a good look at the documents that your friend has provided, and there's no doubt in my mind – it's first-class material. The Americans will be beside themselves with excitement when they see it.'

'I'm pleased to hear it.'

Müller strolled back to his chair by my sofa and sat down again. 'How confident are you that he can carry on providing this sort of high-grade material?'

'Very confident, Herr Doktor.'

'Excellent. You know, this couldn't have come along at a better time. The South German Industries Utilization Company is applying to the American State Department for increased funding. Your man's information will be an important part of that case. At this morning's meeting I shall be recommending that the exploitation of this new source be given top priority here in Vienna.'

He collected the poker off the hearth and jabbed violently at the glowing embers of the fire. It wasn't too difficult to imagine him doing the same to some human subject. Staring into the flames, he added: 'With a matter of such personal interest to me, I have a favour to ask, Herr Günther.'

'I'm listening, Herr Doktor.'

'I must confess I had hoped to persuade you to let me run this informer myself.'

I thought for a minute. 'Naturally I should have to ask his opinion. He trusts me. It might take a little time.'

'Of course.'

'And as I told Nebe, he'll want money. Lots of it.'

'You can tell him I'll organize everything. A Swiss bank account. Whatever he wants.'

'Right now what he wants most is a Swiss watch,' I said, improvising. 'A Doxas.'

'No problem,' Müller grinned. 'You see what I mean about the Russian? He knows exactly what he wants. A nice watch. Well, leave that to me.' Müller replaced the poker on its stand and sat back contentedly. 'Then I can assume you have no objections to my proposal? Naturally you will be well-rewarded for bringing us such an important informer.'

'Since you mention it, I do have a figure in mind,' I said.

Müller raised his hands and beckoned me to name it.

'You may or may not know that I suffered a heavy loss at cards quite recently. I lost most of my money, about 4,000 schillings. I thought that you might like to make that up to 5,000.'

He pursed his lips and started nodding slowly. 'That sounds not unreasonable. In the circumstances.'

I smiled. It amused me that Müller was so concerned to protect his area of expertise within the Org that he was willing to buy me out of my involvement with Belinsky's Russian. It was easy to see that in this way the reputation of Gestapo Müller as the authority on all matters relating to the MVD would be ensured. He slapped both his knees decisively.

'Good. I'm glad that's settled. I've enjoyed our little chat. We'll talk again after this morning's meeting.'

We certainly will, I said to myself. Only it would probably be at the Stiftskaserne, or wherever the Crowcass people were likely to interrogate Müller.

'Of course we'll have to discuss the procedure for contacting your source. Arthur tells me you already have a dead-letter arrangement.'

'It's all written down,' I said to him. 'I'm sure you'll find everything is in order.' I glanced at my watch and saw that it was already past ten o'clock. I got up and straightened my tie.

'Oh, don't worry,' Müller said, clapping me on the shoulder. He seemed almost jovial now that he had got what he wanted. 'They will wait for us, I can assure you.'

But almost at the same moment the library door opened and the slightly irritated face of the Baron von Bolschwing peered into the room. He raised his wristwatch significantly and said, 'Herr Doktor, we really must get on now.'

'It's all right,' Müller boomed, 'we've finished. You can tell everyone to come in now.'

'Thank you very much.' But the Baron's voice was peevish.

'Meetings,' sneered Müller. 'One after another in this organization. There's no end to the pain of it. Like wiping your arse with a car tyre. It's as if Himmler were still alive.'

I smiled. 'That reminds me. I have to hit the spot.'

'It's just along the corridor,' he said.

I went to the door, excusing myself first to the Baron and then to Arthur Nebe as I shouldered past the men coming into the library. These were Old Comrades all right. Men with hard eyes, flabby smiles, well-fed stomachs and a certain arrogance, as if none of them had ever lost a war or done anything for which they ought to have been in any way ashamed. This was the collective face of the new Germany that Müller had droned on about.

But of König there was still no sign.

In the sour-smelling toilet I bolted the door carefully, checked my watch and stood at the window trying to see the road beyond the trees at the side of the house. With the wind stirring the leaves it was difficult to distinguish anything very clearly, but in the distance I thought that I could just about make out the fender of a big black car.

I reached for the cord of the blind and, hoping that the thing was attached to the wall rather more firmly than the blind in my own bathroom back in Berlin, I pulled it gently down for five seconds, then let it roll up again for another five seconds. When I had done this three times as arranged, I waited for Belinsky's signal and felt very relieved when I heard three blasts of a car horn from far away. Then I flushed the toilet, and opened the door.

Halfway back along the corridor leading back to the library I saw König's dog. He stood in the middle of the corridor sniffing the air and regarding me with something like recognition. Then he turned away and trotted downstairs. I didn't think there was a quicker way of finding König than by letting his crapper do it for me. So I followed.

At a door on the ground floor the dog stopped and whined a little bark. As soon as I opened it, he was off again, scampering along another corridor towards the back of the house. He stopped once more and made a show of trying to burrow under another door, to what looked like the cellar. For several seconds I hesitated to open it, but when the dog barked I decided that it was wiser to let him through rather than risk that the noise would summon König. I turned the handle, pushed, and, when the door didn't budge, pulled. It came towards me with only a gentle creak, largely concealed by what sounded at first like a cat mewing somewhere down in the cellar. Cool air and the horrible realization that this was no cat touched my face, and I felt myself shiver involuntarily. Then the dog twisted round the edge of the door and disappeared down the bare wooden stairs.

Even before I had tiptoed to the bottom of the flight, where a large rack of wine concealed me from immediate discovery, I had recognized the painful voice as belonging to Veronika. The scene required very little analysis. She was sitting in a chair, stripped to the waist, her face deathly pale. A man sat immediately in front of her; his sleeves were rolled up and he was torturing her knee with some bloodstained metal object. König stood behind her, steadying the chair and periodically stifling her screams with a length of rag.

There was no time to worry about my lack of a gun, and it was fortunate that König was momentarily distracted by the arrival of his dog. 'Lingo,' he said looking down at the brute, 'how did you get down here? I thought I locked you out.' He bent down to pick the dog up and in the same moment I stepped smartly round the wine rack and ran forwards.

The man in the chair was still in his seat as I clapped both his ears with my cupped hands as hard as I could. He screamed and fell on to the floor, clutching both sides of his head and writhing desperately as he tried to contain the pain of what were almost certainly burst eardrums. It was then that I saw what he had been doing to Veronika. Sticking out of her knee joint at a right angle was a corkscrew.

König's gun was even now halfway out of his shoulder-holster. I leaped at him, punched hard at his exposed armpit and then chopped him across the upper lip with the edge of my hand. The two blows together were enough to disable him. He staggered back from Veronika's chair, blood pouring from his nose. I needn't have hit him again, but now that his hand no longer covered her mouth, her loud cries of excruciating pain persuaded me to deliver a third, more vicious blow with my forearm, aimed at the centre of his sternum. He was unconscious before he hit the ground. Immediately the dog stopped its furious barking and set about trying to revive him with its tongue.

I picked König's gun off the floor, slipped it into my trouser pocket and quickly started untying Veronika. 'It's all right,' I said, 'we're getting out of here. Belinsky will be here any minute with the police.'

I tried not to look at the mess they had made of her knee. She moaned pitiably as I pulled the last of the cords away from her bloodstained legs. Her skin was cold and she was shaking all over, clearly going into shock. But when I took off my jacket and put it about her shoulders, she held my hand firmly and said through gritted teeth, 'Get it out, for God's sake get it out of my knee.'

With one eye on the cellar stairs in case one of Nebe's men should come looking for me now that my presence upstairs was overdue, I knelt down in front of her and surveyed the wound and the instrument that had caused it. It was an ordinary-looking corkscrew, with a wooden handle now sticky with blood. The sharp business end had been screwed into the side of her knee-joint to a depth of several millimetres, and there seemed no way of removing it without causing her almost as much pain as had been caused by screwing it in. The slightest touch of the handle made her cry out.

'Please take it out,' she urged, sensing my indecision.

'All right,' I said, 'but hold on to the seat of your chair. This is going to hurt.' I drew the other chair close enough to prevent her kicking me in the groin and sat down. 'Ready?' She closed her eyes and nodded.

The first anti-clockwise twist turned her face a bright shade of scarlet. Then she screamed, with every particle of air in her lungs. But with the second twist, mercifully she passed out. I surveyed the thing in my hand for a brief second and then hurled it at the man whose ears I had boxed. Lying in a corner, breathing stertorously between groans, Veronika's torturer looked to be in a bad way. The blow had been a cruel one, and although I had never used it before, I knew from my army training that sometimes it even caused a fatal brain haemorrhage.

Veronika's knee was bleedily heavily. I searched around for something with which to bandage her wound, and decided to make do with the shirt of the man I had deafened. I went over to him and tore it off his back.

Having folded the body of the shirt, I pressed it hard against the knee and then used the sleeves to tie it tightly. When the dressing was finished it was a good-looking piece of first-aid work. But her breathing had turned shallow now, and I didn't doubt that she would need a stretcher out of there.

By this time, almost fifteen minutes had elapsed since my signal to Belinsky, and yet there was no sound that anything had yet happened. How long could it take his men to move in? I hadn't heard so much as a shout to indicate that they might have encountered some resistance. With people like the Latvian around, it seemed too much to expect that Müller and Nebe could have been arrested without a fight.

König moaned and moved his leg feebly like a swatted insect. I kicked the dog aside and bent down to take a look at him. The skin underneath his moustache had turned a dark, livid colour, and from the amount of blood that had rolled down his cheeks, I judged that I had probably separated his nose cartilage from the upper section of his jaw.

'I guess it'll be a while before you enjoy another cigar,' I said grimly.

I took König's Mauser out of my pocket and checked the breech. Through the inspection hole I saw the familiar glint of a centre-fire cartridge. One in the chamber. I hauled out the magazine and saw another six neatly ranged like so many cigarettes. I slammed the magazine back up the handle with the heel of my hand and thumbed back the hammer. It was time to find out what had happened to Belinsky.

I went back up the cellar stairs, waited behind the door for a moment and listened. Briefly I thought I heard breathing and then realized that it was my own. I brought the gun up beside my head, slipped the safety off with my thumbnail, and came through the door.

For a split second I saw the Latvian's black cat, and then felt what seemed like the whole ceiling collapsing on top of me. I heard a small popping noise like a champagne cork, and almost laughed as I realized that it was all the sound of the gun firing involuntarily in my hand that my concussed brain was able to decode. Stunned like a landed salmon I lay on the floor. My body hummed like a telephone cable. Too late I remembered that for a big man the Latvian was remarkably light on his feet. He knelt down beside me, grinned into my face before wielding the cosh again.

Then the darkness came.

35

There was a message waiting for me. It was written in capital letters as if to emphasize its importance. I struggled to make my eyes focus, only the message kept moving. Blearily, I picked out the individual letters. It was laborious, but I had no choice. Finally I pieced the letters together. The message read: 'CARE USA'. It seemed important somehow, although I failed to understand why. But then I saw that this was only one part of the message, and the second half at that. I swallowed nauseously and struggled through the first part of the message, which was coded: 'GR. WT 26lbs. CU.FT. o'10".' What could it all mean? I was still trying to understand the code when I heard footsteps and then the sound of a key turning in the lock.

My head cleared agonizingly as I was hauled up by two pairs of strong hands. One of the men kicked the empty cardboard Care package out of the way as they frogmarched me through the doorway.

My neck and shoulder were hurting so bad that my skin turned to gooseflesh the second they held me under my arms, which I now realized were handcuffed in front of me. I retched desperately and tried to get back on to the floor where I had felt comparatively comfortable. But I remained supported and struggling merely made the pain more intense; and so I allowed myself to be dragged along a short, damp passageway, past a couple of broken barrels and up some steps to a big oak vat. The two men sat me roughly in a chair.

A voice, Müller's voice, told them to give me some wine. 'I want him to be fully conscious when we question him.'

Someone put a glass to my lips, and tilted my head painfully. I drank. When the glass was empty I could taste blood in my mouth.

I spat in front of me, I didn't care where. 'Cheap stuff,' I heard myself croak. 'Cooking wine.'

Müller laughed, and I turned my head towards the sound. The bare lightbulbs burned only dimly but even so they managed to hurt my eyes. I squeezed the lids hard shut, and then opened them again.

'Good,' said Müller. 'You've still got something left in you. You'll need it to answer all my questions, Herr Günther, I can assure you.'

Müller was sitting on a chair with his legs crossed and his arms folded. He looked like a man who was about to watch an audition. Seated beside him, and looking rather less relaxed than the former Gestapo chief, was Nebe. Next to him sat König, wearing a clean shirt, and holding his nose and mouth with a handkerchief as if he had a bad attack of hayfever. On the stone floor at their feet lay Veronika. She was unconscious, and but for the bandage round her knee quite naked. Like me she was also handcuffed, although her pallor indicated that this was an entirely redundant precaution.

I turned my head to the right. A few metres away stood the Latvian and another thug whom I hadn't seen before. The Latvian was grinning excitedly, no doubt in anticipation of my further humiliation.

We were in the largest of the outhouses. Beyond the windows the night looked in on the proceedings with dark indifference. Somewhere I could hear the low throb of a generator. It hurt to move my head or my neck, and it was actually more comfortable to look back at Müller.

'Ask anything you like,' I said, 'you'll get nothing out of me.' But even as I spoke I knew that in Müller's expert hands there was no more chance of my not telling him everything than there was of me naming the next Pope.

He found my bravado sufficiently absurd as to laugh and shake his head. 'It's quite a few years since I conducted an interrogation,' he said with what sounded like nostalgia. 'However, I think you'll find that I haven't lost my touch.' Müller looked to Nebe and König as if seeking their approbation, and each man nodded grimly.

'I bet you won prizes for it, you half-sized bastard.'

At this utterance, the Latvian was prompted to strike me hard across the cheek. The sudden jerk of my head sent an agonizing pain down to my toenails and made me cry out.

'No, no, Rainis,' Müller said like a father to a child, 'we must allow Herr Günther to talk. He may insult us now, but eventually he will tell us what we want to hear. Please don't hit him again unless I order you to do it.'

Nebe spoke. 'It's no use, Bernie. Fräulein Zartl has now told us all about how you and this American fellow disposed of poor Heim's body. I wondered why you were so inquisitive about her. Now we know.'

'In fact we now know a great deal,' said Müller. 'While you have been having a nap, Arthur here posed as a policeman in order to gain access to your rooms.' He smiled smugly. 'It wasn't too difficult for him. Austrians are such docile, law-abiding people. Arthur, tell Herr Günther what you discovered.'

'Your photographs, Heinrich. I imagine that the American must have given them to him. What do you say, Bernie?'

'Go to hell.'

Nebe continued, unperturbed. 'There was also a drawing of Martian Albers' headstone. You remember that unfortunate business, Herr Doktor?'

'Yes,' said Müller, 'that was very careless of Max.'

'I dare say you must have guessed that Max Abs and Martin Albers were one and the same person, Bernie. He was an old-fashioned, rather sentimental kind of man. He just couldn't pretend to be dead like the rest of us. No, he had to have a stone to commemorate his passing, to make it look respectable. Really, a typical Viennese, wouldn't you say? I should think you were probably the person who tipped off the MPs in Munich that Max was due to arrive there. Of course, you weren't to know that Max was carrying several sets of papers and travel warrants. You see, documents were Max's speciality. He was a master forger. As the former head of SD clandestine operations section in Budapest, he was one of the very best in his field.'

'I suppose he was another bogus conspirator against Hitler,' I said. 'Another fake entry on the list of all those who were executed. Just like you, Arthur. I have to hand it to you: you've been very clever.'

'That was Max's idea,' said Nebe. 'Ingenious, yes, but with König's help not very difficult to organize. You see, König commanded the execution squad at Plotzensee, and hanged conspirators by the hundreds. He supplied all the details.'

'As well as the butcher's hooks and piano wire, no doubt.'

'Herr Günther,' said König indistinctly through the handkerchief he kept pressed to his nose, 'I hope to be able to do the same for you.'

Müller frowned. 'We're wasting time,' he said briskly. 'Nebe told your landlady that the Austrian police thought you had been kidnapped by the Russians. After that she was most helpful. Apparently your rooms are being paid for by Dr Ernst Liebl. This man is now known to us as Emil Becker's advocate at law. Nebe is of the opinion that you were retained by him to come to Vienna and attempt to clear him of the murder of Captain Linden. I myself am of this opinion. Everything fits, so to speak.'

Müller nodded at one of the uglies, who stepped forward and collected up Veronika in his pylon-sized arms. She made no movement, and but for her breathing which became louder and more difficult as her head lolled back on her neck, one might have thought that she was dead. She looked as if they had drugged her.

'Why don't you leave her out of this, Müller,' I said. 'I'll tell you whatever it is you want to know.'

Müller pretended to look puzzled. 'That surely is what remains to be seen.' He stood up, as did Nebe and König. 'Bring Herr Günther along, Rainis.'

The Latvian hauled me to my feet. Just the effort of being made to stand made me feel suddenly faint. He dragged me a few metres to the side of a sunken circular oak vat which was of the dimensions of a good-sized fish-pond. The vat itself was joined to a rectangular steel plate which had two wooden semicircular wings like the leaves of a large dining table, by a thick steel column which went up to the ceiling. The thug carrying Veronika stepped down in the vat and laid her on the bottom. Then he got out and drew down the two oak leaves of the plate to form a perfect, deadly circle.

'This is a wine press,' Müller said matter-of-factly.

I struggled weakly in the Latvian's big arms, but there was nothing I could do. It felt like my shoulder or collarbone was broken. I called them several filthy words and Müller nodded approvingly.

'Your concern for this young woman is encouraging,' he said.

'It was her you were looking for this morning,' said Nebe. 'When you walked into Rainis, wasn't it?'

'Yes, all right, it was. Now let her go, for God's sake. I give you my word, Arthur, she knows absolutely nothing.'

'Yes, that's true,' Müller admitted. 'Or at least not much. So König tells me anyway, and he is a most persuasive person. But you'll be flattered to learn that she still managed to conceal the part which you played in Heim's disappearance for quite a while. Isn't that so, Helmut?'

'Yes, General.'

'But in the end she told us everything,' Müller continued. 'Even before your impossibly heroic arrival on the scene. She told us that you and she had enjoyed a sexual relationship, and that you had been kind to her. Which was why she had asked you for help when it came to getting rid of Heim's body. Which was why you came looking for her when König took her away. Incidentally, I must compliment you. You killed one of Nebe's men quite expertly. It's a great pity that a man of your formidable skills will never work for our Organization after all. But a number of things remain a puzzle, and I expect you, Herr Günther, to enlighten us.' He glanced around and saw that the man who had laid Veronika into the vat was now standing by a small panel of electric switches on the wall.

'Do you know anything about making wine?' he asked, walking round the vat. 'The crushing, as the word suggests, is the process whereby the grape is squeezed, bursting its skin and releasing the juice. As you will no doubt be aware it was once done by treading the grapes in huge casks. But most modern presses are pneumatic or electrically operated machines. The crushing is repeated several times, and thus is an indication of the quality of the wine, with the first press being the best of all. Once every bit of juice has been squeezed out, the residue – I believe Nebe calls it "the cake" – is supplied to a distillery; or, as is the case on this small estate, it is turned into fertilizer.' Müller looked across at Arthur Nebe. 'There, Arthur, did I get that right?'

Nebe smiled indulgently. 'Perfectly right, Herr General.'

'I hate to mislead anyone,' Müller said with good humour. 'Even a man who is going to die.' He paused and looked down into the vat. 'Of course at this precise moment it is not your life which is the most pressing issue, if I may be permitted that one tasteless little joke.'

The big Latvian guffawed in my ear, and my head was suddenly enveloped with the stink of his garlicky breath.

'So I advise you to make your answers quickly and accurately, Herr Günther. Fräulein Zartl's life depends on it.' He nodded at the man by the control panel who pressed a button which initiated a mechanical noise, gradually increasing in pitch.

'Don't think too harshly of us,' said Müller. 'These are hard times. There are shortages of everything. If we had any sodium pentathol we should give it to you. We should even look to buy it on the black market. But I think you'll agree that this method is every bit as effective as any truth drug.'

'Ask your damned questions.'

'Ah, you're in a hurry to answer. That's good. Tell me then: who is this American policeman? The one who helped you dispose of Heim's body.'

'His name is John Belinsky. He works for Crowcass.'

'How did you meet him?'

'He knew that I was working to prove Becker's innocence. He approached me with an offer to work in tandem. Initially he said that he wanted to find out why Captain Linden had been murdered, but then after a while he told me that he really wanted to find out about you. If you had anything to do with Linden's death.'

'So the Americans aren't happy that they have the right man?'

'No. Yes. The military police are. But the Crowcass people aren't. The gun used to kill Linden was one which they traced back to a killing in Berlin. A corpse which was supposed to be you, Müller. And the gun checked back to SS records at the Berlin Documents Centre. Crowcass didn't inform the military police for fear that they might spook you out of Vienna.'

'And you were encouraged to infiltrate the Org on their behalf?'

'Yes.'

'Are they so certain that I'm here?'

'Yes.'

'But until this morning you had never seen me before. Explain how they know, please.'

'The information that I supplied on the MVD was designed to draw you out. They know you like to consider yourself an expert in these matters. The thinking was that with information of such quality, you yourself would take charge of the debrief. If I saw you at this morning's meeting I was to signal to Belinsky from the toilet window. I had to pull down the blind three times. He would be watching the window through binoculars.'

'And then what?'

'He was supposed to have brought agents to surround the house. He was meant to have arrested you. The deal was that if they were successful in arresting you, then they would let Becker go free.'

Nebe glanced over at one of his men, and jerked his head at the door. 'Get some men to check the grounds. Just in case.'

Müller shrugged. 'So you're saying that the only reason they know I'm here in Vienna is because you made some signal to them from a lavatory window. Is that it?' I nodded. 'But then why didn't this Belinsky have his men move in and arrest me, as you had planned?'

'Believe me, I've been asking myself the same question.'

'Come now, Herr Günther. This is inconsistent, is it not? I ask you to be fair. How am I supposed to believe this?'

'Would I have gone looking for the girl if I didn't think there were going to be agents arriving?'

'What time were you supposed to make your signal?' asked Nebe.

'Twenty minutes into the meeting I was supposed to excuse myself.'

'At 10.20 then. But you were looking for Fräulein Zartl before seven o'clock this morning.'

'I decided that she might not be able to wait until the Americans showed up.'

'You're asking us to believe that you would have risked a whole operation for one –' Müller's nose wrinkled with disgust '– for one little chocolady?' He shook his head. 'I find that very hard to believe.' He nodded at the man controlling the wine press. This man pushed a second button and the machine's hydraulics cranked into gear. 'Come now, Herr Günther. If what you say is true, why didn't the Americans come when you signalled to them?'

'I don't know,' I shouted.

'Then speculate,' said Nebe.

'They never meant to arrest you,' I said, putting into words my own suspicions. 'All they wanted to know was that you were alive and working for the Org. They used me, and after they found out what they wanted, they dumped me.'

I tried to wrestle free of the Latvian as the press began its slow descent. Veronika lay unconscious, her chest swelling gently as she continued breathing, oblivious to the descending plate. I shook my head. 'Look, I honestly don't know why they didn't turn up.'

'So,' said Müller, 'let's get this clear. The only evidence that they have of my continued existence, apart from this rather tenuous piece of ballistic evidence you mentioned, is your own signal.'

'Yes, I suppose so.'

'One more question. Do you – do the Amis – know why Captain Linden was killed?'

'No,' I said, and then reasoning that negative answers were not what was wanted, added: 'We figured that he was being supplied with information about war-criminals in the Org. That he came to Vienna to investigate you. At first we thought that König was supplying him with the information.' I shook my head, trying to recall some of the theories I had come up with to explain Linden's death. 'Then we thought that he might somehow have been supplying the Org with information in order to help you to recruit new members. Switch that machine off, for God's sake.'

Veronika disappeared from sight as the press closed over the edge of the vat. There were only two or three metres of life left to her.

'We didn't know why, damn you.'

Müller's voice was slow and calm, like a surgeon's. 'We must be sure, Herr Günther. Let me repeat the question –'

'I don't know –'

'Why was it necessary for us to kill Linden?'

I shook my head desperately.

'Just tell me the truth. What do you know? You're not being fair to this young woman. Tell us what you found out.'

The shrill whine of the machine grew louder. It reminded me of the sound of the elevator in my old offices in Berlin. Where I should have stayed.

'Herr Günther,' Müller's voice contained a gramme of urgency, 'for the sake of this poor girl, I beg you.'

'For God's sake . . .'

He glanced over at the thug by the control panel and shook his squarely-cropped head.

'I can't tell you anything,' I shouted.

The press shuddered as it encountered its living obstacle. The mechanical whine briefly rose a couple of octaves as the resistance to the hydraulic force was dealt with, and then returned to its old pitch before finally the press came to the end of its cruel journey. The noise died away at another nod from Müller.

'Can't, or won't, Herr Günther?'

'You bastard,' I said, suddenly weak with disgust, 'you vicious, cruel bastard.'

'I don't think she'll have felt much,' he said with studied indifference. 'She was drugged. Which is more than you will be when we repeat this little exercise in say –' he glanced at his wristwatch '– twelve hours. You have until then to think it over.' He looked over the edge of the vat. 'I can't promise to kill you outright, of course. Not like this girl. I might want to squeeze you two or three times before we spread you on the fields. Just like the grapes.

'On the other hand, if you tell me what I wish to know, I can promise you a rather less painful death. A pill would be so much less distressing for you, don't you think?'

I felt my lip curl. Müller winced fastidiously as I started to swear, and then shook his head.

'Rainis,' he said, 'you may hit Herr Günther just once before returning him to his quarters.'

36

Back in my cell I massaged the floating rib above my liver which Nebe's Latvian had selected for one stunningly painful punch. At the same time I tried to douse the lights on the memory of what had just happened to Veronika, but without success.

I had met men who had been tortured by the Russians during the war. I remembered them describing how the most awful part of it was the uncertainty – whether you would die, whether you could withstand the pain. That part was certainly true. One of them had described a way of reducing the pain. Breathing deeply and gulping could induce a light-headedness that was partly anaesthetic. The only trouble was that it had also left my friend prone to bouts of chronic hyperventilation which eventually caused him to suffer a fatal heart-attack.

I cursed myself for my selfishness. An innocent girl, already a victim of the Nazis, had been killed because of her association with me. Somewhere inside of me a voice replied that it was she who had asked for my help, and that they might well have tortured and killed her irrespective of my own involvement. But I was in no mood to go easy on myself. Wasn't there anything else I could have told Müller about Linden's death that might have satisfied him? And what would I tell him when it came to my own turn? Selfish again. But there was no avoiding my egotism's snake's eyes. I didn't want to die. More importantly, I didn't want to die on my knees begging for mercy like an Italian war-hero.

They say impending pain offers the mind the purest aid to concentration. Doubtless Müller would have known that. Thinking about the lethal pill he had promised me if I told him whatever it was he wanted to hear helped me to remember something vital. Twisting round my handcuffs, I reached down into my trouser pocket, and tugged out the lining with my little finger, allowing the two pills I had taken from Heim's surgery to roll into my palm.

I wasn't even sure why I had taken them at all. Curiosity perhaps. Or maybe it was some subconscious prompt which had told me I might have need of a painless exit myself. For a long time I just stared at the tiny cyanide capsules with a mixture of relief and horrific fascination. After a while I hid one pill in my trouser-turnup, which left the one I had decided I would keep in my mouth – the one that would in all probability kill me. With an appreciation of irony that was much exaggerated by my situation, I reflected that I had Arthur Nebe to thank for diverting these lethal pills from the secret agents for whom they had been created to the top brass in the SS, and from them to me. Perhaps the pill in my hand had been Nebe's own. It is of such speculations, however improbable, that a man's philosophy consists during his last remaining hours.

I slipped the pill into my mouth and held it gingerly between my back molars. When the time came, would I even have the guts to chew the thing? My tongue pushed the pill over the edge of my tooth and into the corner of my cheek. I rubbed my fingers over my face and could feel it through the flesh. Would anyone see it? The only light in the cell came from a bare bulb fixed to one of the wooden rafters seemingly with nothing but cobwebs. All the same I couldn't help thinking that the outline of the pill in my mouth was very much visible.

When a key scraped in the mortice, I realized that I would soon find out.

The Latvian came through the door holding his big Colt in one hand and a small tray in the other.

'Get away from the door,' he said thickly.

'What's this?' I said, sliding backwards on my backside. 'A meal? Perhaps you could tell the management that what I'd like most is a cigarette.'

'Lucky to get anything at all,' he growled. Carefully he squatted down and laid the tray on the dusty floor. There was a jug of coffee and a large slice of strudel. 'The coffee's fresh. The strudel is home-made.'

For a brief, stupid second I considered rushing him, before reminding myself that a man in my weakened condition could rush about as quickly as a frozen waterfall. And I would have had no more chance of overpowering the huge Latvian than I had of engaging him in Socratic dialogue. He seemed to sense some flicker of hope on my face however, even though the pill resting on my gum remained undetected. 'Go ahead,' he said, 'try something. I wish you would; I'd like to blow your kneecap off.' Laughing like a retarded grizzly bear he backed out of my cell and closed the door with a loud bang.

From the size of him, I judged Rainis to be the kind who enjoyed his food. When he wasn't killing or hurting people it was probably his only real pleasure. Perhaps he was even something of a glutton. It occurred to me that if I were to leave the strudel untouched, Rainis might be unable to resist eating it himself. That if I were to put one of my cyanide capsules inside the filling then later on, perhaps long after I myself was dead, the dumb Latvian would eat my cake and die. It might, I reflected, be a comforting thought as I left the world, that he would be swiftly following me.

I decided to drink the coffee while I thought about it. Was a lethal pill hot-water-soluble? I didn't know. So I popped the capsule out of my mouth, and thinking that it might as well be that pill which I used to put my pathetic plan into action, I pushed it into the fruit filling with my forefinger.

I could happily have eaten it myself, pill and all, I was so hungry. My watch told me that over fifteen hours had passed since my Viennese breakfast, and the coffee tasted good. I decided that it could only have been Arthur Nebe who had instructed the Latvian to bring me supper.

Another hour passed. There were eight to go before they would come to take me back upstairs. I would wait until there was no hope, no possibility of reprieve before I took my own life. I tried to sleep, but without much success. I was beginning to understand what Becker must have felt like, facing the gallows. At least I was better off than he was: I still had my lethal pill.

It was almost midnight when I heard the key in the lock again. Quickly I transferred my second pill from my trouser turnup to my cheek in case they decided to search my clothes. But it was not Rainis who came to fetch my tray but Arthur Nebe. He held an automatic in his hand.

'Don't force me to use this, Bernie,' he said. 'You know I won't hesitate to shoot you if I have to. You'd best get back against that far wall.'

'What's this? A social call?' I dragged myself back from the door. He tossed a packet of cigarettes and some matches after me.

'You might say that.'

'I hope you're not here to talk about old times, Arthur. I'm not feeling very sentimental right now.' I looked at the cigarettes. Winston. 'Does Müller know you're smoking American nails, Arthur? Be careful. You might get into trouble: he's got some strange ideas about the Amis.' I lit one and inhaled with slow satisfaction. 'Still, bless you for this.'

Nebe drew a chair round the door and sat down. 'Müller has his own ideas of where the Org is going,' he said. 'But there's no doubting his patriotism or his determination. He's quite ruthless.'

'I can't say I'd noticed.'

'He has an unfortunate tendency to judge other people by his own insensitive standards, however. Which means that he really does believe you are capable of keeping your mouth shut and allowing that girl to die.' He smiled. 'I, of course, know you rather better than that. Günther is a sentimental sort of man, I told him. Even a little bit of a fool. It would be just like him to risk his neck for someone he hardly knew. Even a chocolady. It was the same in Minsk, I said. He was perfectly prepared to go to the front line rather than kill innocent people. People to whom he owed nothing.'

'That doesn't make me a hero, Arthur. Just a human being.'

'It makes you someone Müller is used to dealing with: a man

with a principle. Müller knows what men will take and still stay silent. He's seen lots of people sacrifice their friends and then themselves in order to keep silent. He's a fanatic. Fanaticism is the only thing he understands. And as a result he thinks you're a fanatic. He's convinced there's a possibility that you might be holding out on him. As I said, I know you rather better than that. If you had known why Linden was killed I think you would have said so.'

'Well, it's nice to know somebody believes me. It'll make being turned into this year's vintage all the more bearable. Look, Arthur, why are you telling me this? So I can tell you that you're a better judge of character than Müller?'

'I was thinking: if you were to tell Müller exactly what he wants to hear, then it might save you a lot of pain. I'd hate to see an old friend suffer. And believe me, he'll make you suffer.'

'I don't doubt it. It's not this coffee that's helped to keep me awake, I can tell you. Come on, what is this? The old friend and foe routine? Like I said, I don't know why Linden was canned.'

'No, but I could tell you.'

I winced as the cigarette smoke stung my eyes. 'Let me get this straight,' I said uncertainly. 'You're going to tell me what happened to Linden, in order that I can spill it to Müller, and thereby save myself from a fate worse than death, right?'

'That's about the size of it.'

I shrugged, painfully. 'I don't see that I've got anything to lose.' I grinned. 'Of course, you could just let me escape, Arthur. For old times' sake.'

'We weren't going to talk about old times, you said so yourself. Anyway, you know too much. You've seen Müller. You've seen me. I'm dead, remember?'

'Nothing personal, Arthur, but I wish you were.' I took another cigarette and lit myself with the butt of the first. 'All right, unpack it. Why was Linden killed?'

'Linden had a German–American background. He even read German at Cornell University. During the war he had some minor intelligence role, and afterwards worked as a denazification officer.

He was a clever man, and soon had a nice racket going for himself, selling Persil certificates, clearances for Old Comrades, you know the sort of thing. Then he joined the CIC as a desk-investigator and Crowcass liaison officer at the Berlin Documents Centre. Naturally he kept up his old black-market contacts and by this time he had become known to us in the Org as someone sympathetic to our cause. We contacted him in Berlin and offered him a sum of money to perform a small service, on an occasional basis.

'You remember I told you about how a number of us faked our deaths? Gave ourselves new identities? Well, that was Albers – the Max Abs you were interested in. His idea. But of course the fundamental weakness of any new identity, especially when it has to be done so quickly, is that one lacks a past. Think of it, Bernie: world war, every able-bodied German between the ages of twelve and sixty-five under arms, and no service record for me, Alfred Nolde. Where was I? What was I doing? We thought we were very clever in killing off our real identities, letting the records fall into the hands of the Amis, but instead it merely created new questions. We had no idea that the Documents Centre would prove to be quite so comprehensive. Its effect has been to make it possible to check every answer on a man's denazification questionnaire.

'Many of us were working for the Americans by this stage. Naturally it suits them now to turn a blind eye to the pasts of our Org members. But what about tomorrow? Politicians have a habit of changing policy. Right now we're friends in the fight against Communism. But will the same hold true in five or ten years' time?

'So Albers came up with a new scheme. He created old documentation for our more senior personnel in their new identities, himself included. We were all of us given smaller, less culpable roles in the SS and Abwehr than were possessed by our real selves. As Alfred Nolde I was a sergeant in the SS Personnel Section. My file contains all my personal details: even dental records. I led a quiet, fairly blameless kind of war. It's true I was a Nazi, but never a war-criminal. That was somebody else. The fact that I happen to resemble someone called Arthur Nebe is neither here nor there.

'Security at the Centre is tight, however. It's impossible to take files out. But it is comparatively easy to take files in. Nobody is searched when they go into the Centre, only when they leave. This was Linden's job. Once a month Becker would deliver new files, forged by Albers, to Berlin. And Linden would file them in the archive. Naturally this was before we found out about Becker's Russian friends.'

'Why were the forgeries done here and not in Berlin?' I asked. 'That way you could have cut out the need for a courier.'

'Because Albers refused to go anywhere near Berlin. He liked it here in Vienna, not least because Austria is the first step on the rat-line. It's easy to get across the border into Italy, and then the Middle East, South America. There were lots of us who came south. Like birds in winter, eh?'

'So what went wrong?'

'Linden got greedy, that's what went wrong. He knew the material he was getting was forged, but he couldn't understand what it amounted to. At first I think it was mere curiosity. He started photographing the stuff we were giving him. And then he enlisted the help of a couple of Jewish lawyers – Nazi-hunters – to try and establish the nature of the new files, who these men were.'

'The Drexlers.'

'They were working with the Joint Army Group on war crimes. Probably the Drexlers had no idea that Linden's motives for seeking their help were purely personal and for profit. And why should they have done? His credentials were unquestionable. Anyway, I think they noted something about all these new SS personnel and Party records: that we kept the same initials as our old identities; it's an old trick with building a new legend. Makes you feel more comfortable with your new name. Something as instinctive as initialling a contract becomes safe. I think Drexler must have compared these new names with the names of comrades who were missing or presumed dead and suggested that Linden might like to compare the details of a file held on Alfred Nolde with the file on

Arthur Nebe, Heinrich Müller with Heinrich Moltke, Max Abs with Martin Albers etc.'

'So that's why you had the Drexlers killed.'

'Exactly. That was after Linden turned up here in Vienna, looking for more money. Money to keep his mouth shut. It was Müller who met him and who killed him. We knew that Linden had already made contact with Becker, for the very simple reason that Linden told us. So we decided to kill two flics with one swat. First we left several cases of cigarettes around the warehouse where Linden was killed in order to incriminate Becker. Then König went to see Becker and told him that Linden was missing. The idea was that Becker would start going round asking questions about Linden, looking for him at his hotel and generally getting himself noticed. At the same time König switched Müller's gun for Becker's. Then we informed the police that Becker had shot and killed Linden. It was an unlooked-for bonus that Becker already knew where Linden's body was, and that he should return to the scene of the crime with the aim of taking away the cigarettes. Of course the Amis were waiting for him and caught him red-handed. The case was watertight. All the same, if the Amis had been even half efficient they would have discovered the link between Becker and Linden in Berlin. But I don't think they even bothered to take the investigation outside of Vienna. They're happy with what they've got. Or at least we thought they were until now.'

'With what Linden knew, why didn't he take the precaution of leaving a letter with someone? Informing the police of what had happened in the event of his death.'

'Oh, but he did,' said Nebe. 'Only the particular lawyer he chose in Berlin was also a member of the Org. On Linden's death he read the letter and passed it across to the head of the Berlin section.' Nebe stared levelly at me, and nodded seriously. 'That's it, Bernie. That's what Müller wants to find out if you know or not. Well, now that you do know, you can tell him, and save yourself from being tortured. Naturally, I would prefer it if this conversation remained a secret.'

'As long as I live, Arthur, you can depend on it. And thanks.' I felt my voice crack a little. 'I appreciate it.'

Nebe nodded in acknowledgement and stared around him uncomfortably. Then his gaze fell upon the uneaten slice of strudel.

'You weren't hungry?'

'I've not got much of an appetite,' I said. 'One or two things on my mind, I guess. Give it to Rainis.' I lit a third cigarette. Was I wrong, or had he really licked his lips? That would have been too much to hope for. But it was surely worth a try.

'Or help yourself if you're feeling hungry.'

Nebe really did lick his lips now.

'May I?' he asked politely.

I nodded negligently.

'Well, if you're sure,' he said, picking the plate up off the tray on the floor. 'My housekeeper made it. She used to work for Demel. The best strudel you ever tasted in your life. It would be a pity to waste it, eh?' He took a big bite.

'I never had much of a sweet tooth myself,' I lied.

'That's nothing short of tragic in Vienna, Bernie. You are in the greatest city in the world for cake. You should have come here before the war: Gerstner's, Lehmann's, Heiner's, Aida, Haag, Sluka's, Bredendick's – pastrycooks like you never tasted before.' He took another large mouthful. 'To come to Vienna without a sweet tooth? Why, that's like a blind man taking a trip on the Big Wheel in the Prater. You don't know what you're missing. Why don't you try a little?'

I shook my head firmly. My heart was beating so quickly that I thought he must hear it. Suppose he didn't finish it?

'I really couldn't eat anything.'

Nebe shook his head pityingly, and bit once more. The teeth could not be real, I thought, surveying their white evenness. Nebe's own teeth had been much more stained.

'Anyway,' I said, nonchalantly, 'I'm supposed to be watching my weight. I've put on several kilos since coming to Vienna.'

'Me too,' he said. 'You know, you should really –'

He never finished the sentence. He coughed and choked all in one jerk of his head. Stiffening suddenly, he made a dreadful blowing noise through his lips as if he had been trying to play a tuba, and fragments of half-chewed cake rolled out of his mouth. The plate of strudel clattered on to the floor, followed by Nebe himself. Scrabbling on top of him, I tried to wrestle the automatic from his grasp before he could fire it and bring Müller and his thugs down on my head. To my horror I saw that the gun was cocked, and in the same half second Nebe's dying finger pulled the trigger.

But the hammer clicked harmlessly. The safety was still on.

Nebe's legs jerked feebly. One eyelid flickered shut while the other stayed perversely open. His last breath was a long mucoid gurgle smelling strongly of almonds. Finally he lay still, his face already turning a blueish colour. Disgusted, I spat the lethal pill out of my own mouth. I had little sympathy for him. In a few hours he might have watched the same thing happening to me.

I prised the gun free from Nebe's dead hand, which was now grey-skinned with cyanosis, and having unsuccessfully searched his pockets for the key to my handcuffs, I stood up. My head, shoulder, rib, even my penis it seemed were hurting terribly, but I felt a lot better for the grip of the Walther P38 in my hand. The kind of gun that had killed Linden. I thumb-cocked the hammer for semi-automatic operation, as Nebe himself had done before coming into my cell, slipped off the safety, as he had forgotten to do, and stepped carefully out of the cell.

I walked to the end of the damp passageway and climbed the stairs to the pressing and fermentation room where Veronika had died. There was only one light near the front door and I went towards it, hardly daring to glance at the wine press. If I had seen him I would have ordered Müller into the machine and squeezed him out of his Bavarian skin. In another body I might have risked the guards and gone up to the house, where possibly I could have tried to arrest him: probably I would just have shot him. It had been that kind of day. Now it would be as much as I could do to escape with my life.

Switching out the light I opened the front door. Without a jacket, I shivered. The night was a cold one. I crept along to the line of trees where the Latvian had tried to execute me and hid in some bushes.

The vineyard was bright with the lights of the rapid burners. Several men were busy pushing the tall trolleys which carried the burners up and down the furrows to positions which they apparently judged important. From where I sat, their long flames looked like giant fireflies moving slowly through the air. It seemed as if I would have to choose another route to escape from Nebe's estate.

I returned to the house and moved stealthily along the wall, past the kitchen towards the front garden. None of the ground-floor lights were on, but one at an upper-floor window lay reflected on the lawn like a big square swimming-pool. I halted by the corner and sniffed the air. Someone was standing in the porch, smoking a cigarette.

After what seemed like forever, I heard the man's footsteps on the gravel, and glancing quickly round the corner I saw the unmistakable figure of Rainis lumbering down the path towards the open gates where a large grey BMW was parked facing the road.

I walked on to the front lawn staying out of the light from the house, and followed him until he got to the car. He opened the car boot and started to rummage around as if looking for something. By the time he closed it again, I had put less than five metres between us. He turned and froze as he saw the Walther levelled at his misshapen head.

'Put those car keys in the ignition,' I said softly.

The Latvian's face turned even uglier at the prospect of my escaping. 'How did you get out?' he sneered.

'There was a key hidden in the strudel,' I said, and jerked the gun at the car keys in his hand. 'The car keys,' I repeated. 'Do it. Slowly.'

He stepped back and opened the driver's door. Then he bent inside and I heard the rattle of keys as he slipped them into the ignition. Straightening again, he rested his foot almost carelessly on the running-board, and leaning on the roof of the car, smiled a grin that was the shape and colour of a rusting tap.

'Want me to wash it before you go?'

'Not this time, Frankenstein. What I would like you to do is give me the keys for these.' I showed him my still-manacled wrists.

'Keys for what?'

'Keys for handcuffs.'

He shrugged, and kept on grinning. 'I got no keys for no handcuffs. Don't believe me, you search me, you find out.'

Hearing him speak, I almost winced. Latvian and soft in the head he may have been, but Rainis had no idea of German grammar. He probably thought a conjunction was a gypsy dealing three cards on a street-corner.

'Sure you've got keys, Rainis. It was you who cuffed me, remember? I saw you put them in your vest pocket.'

He stayed silent. I was beginning to want to kill him badly.

'Look, you stupid Latvian asshole. If I say "jump" again you'd better not look down for a skipping-rope. This is a gun, not a fucking hairbrush.' I stepped forward a pace and snarled through clenched teeth. 'Now find them or I'll fit your ugly face with the kind of hole that doesn't need a key.'

Rainis made a little show of patting his pockets and then produced a small silver key from his waistcoat. He held it up like a minnow.

'Drop it on the driver's seat and step away from the car.'

Now that he was closer to me, Rainis could see by the expression on my face that I had a lot of hate in my mind. This time he didn't hesitate to obey, and tossed the little key on to the seat. But if I had thought him stupid, or suddenly obedient, I made a mistake. It was fatigue, probably.

He nodded down at one of the wheels. 'You'd better let me fix that slack tyre,' he said.

I glanced downwards and then quickly up again as the Latvian sprint-started towards me, his big hands reaching for my neck like a savage tiger. A half second later I pulled the trigger. The Walther fed and cycled another round into the firing chamber in less time than it took for me to blink. I fired again. The shots echoed across the garden and up the sky as if the twin sounds had been bearing the Latvian's soul to final judgement. I didn't doubt that it would be heading earthwards and below ground fairly quickly again. His big body crashed face first on to the gravel and lay still.

I ran to the car and jumped into the seat, ignoring the handcuff key underneath my backside. There was no time to do anything but start the car. I turned the key in the ignition and the big car, new by the smell of it, roared into life. Behind me, I heard shouts. Collecting the gun off my lap, I leaned out and fired a couple of rounds back at the house. Then I threw it on the passenger seat beside me, rammed the gear stick forward, hauled the door shut and stamped on the accelerator. The rear tyres gouged at the driveway as the BMW skidded forward. For the moment it didn't matter that my hands were still manacled: the road ahead lay straight and down a hill.

But the car veered dangerously from side to side as I released the steering for a brief second, and wrestled the gear into second. My hands back on the wheel I swerved to avoid a parked car and almost put the BMW into the side of a fence. If I could only get to Stifstkaserne and Roy Shields I would tell him all about Veronika's murder. If the Amis were quick they could at least get them for that. Explanations about Müller and the Org could come later. When the MPs had Müller in the cage, there would be no limit to the embarrassment I was going to cause Belinsky, Crowcass, CIC – the whole rotten bunch of them.

I looked in the wing mirror and saw the headlights of a car. I wasn't sure if it was chasing me or not but I pushed the already screaming engine even further and almost immediately braked, pushing the wheel up hard to the right. The car hit the kerb and bounced back on to the road. My foot touched the floor again, the engine complaining loudly against the lower gear. But I couldn't risk changing into third now that there were more bends in the road to negotiate.

At the junction of Billrothstrasse and the Gürtel I almost had to lean over in order to steer the car sharp right, past a van hosing down the street. I didn't see the roadblock until it was too late, and but for the truck parked behind the makeshift barrier that had been erected I don't suppose I would have bothered to try and swerve or stop. As it was, I turned hard left and lost the back wheels on the water on the road.

For a moment I had a camera obscura's eye view as the BMW spun out of control: the barrier, the US military policemen waving their arms or chasing after me, the road I had just driven down, the car that had been following me, a row of shops, a plate glass window. The car danced sideways on two wheels like a mechanical Charlie Chaplin and then there was a cataract of glass as I crashed into one of the shops. I rolled helplessly across the passenger seat and hit the door as something solid came through the other side. I felt something sharp underneath my elbow, then my head hit the frame and I must have blacked out.

It could only have been for a few seconds. One moment there was noise, movement, pain and chaos; and the next there was just quiet, with only the sound of a wheel spinning slowly to tell me that I was still alive. Mercifully the car had stalled so my first worry, which was of the car catching fire, was allayed.

Hearing footsteps on shards of glass and American voices announcing that they were coming to get me I shouted my encouragement, but to my surprise it came out as little more than a whisper. And when I tried to raise my arm to reach for the doorhandle I lost consciousness again.

37

'Well, how are we feeling today?' Roy Shields leaned forward on the chair beside my bed and tapped the plaster cast on my arm. A wire and pulley kept it high in the air. 'That must be pretty handy,' he said. 'A permanent Nazi salute? Shit, you Germans can even make a broken arm look patriotic.'

I took a short look around. It appeared to be a fairly normal hospital ward but for the bars on the windows and the tattoos on the nurses' forearms.

'What kind of hospital is this?'

'You're in the military hospital at the Stiftskaserne,' he said. 'For your protection.'

'How long have I been here?'

'Almost three weeks. You had quite a bump on your square head. Fractured your skull. Busted collarbone, broken arm, broken ribs. You've been delirious since you came in.'

'Yes? Well, blame it on the föhn, I guess.'

Shields chuckled and then his face grew more sombre. 'Better hold on to that sense of humour,' he said. 'I've got some bad news for you.'

I riffled through the card index inside my head. Most of the cards had been thrown on the floor, but the ones I picked up first seemed somehow especially relevant. Something I had been working on. A name.

'Emil Becker,' I said, recalling a manic face.

'He was hanged, the day before yesterday,' Shields shrugged apologetically. 'I'm sorry. Really I am.'

'Well you certainly didn't waste any time,' I remarked. 'Is that good old American efficiency? Or has one of your people cornered the market in rope?'

'I wouldn't lose any sleep about it, Günther. Whether he murdered Linden or not, Becker earned that collar.'

'That doesn't sound like a very good advert for American justice.'

'Come on, you know it was an Austrian court that dropped his cue-ball.'

'You handed them the stick and the chalk, didn't you?'

Shields looked away for a moment and then rubbed his face with irritation. 'Aw, what the hell. You're a cop. You know how it is. These things happen with any system. Just because your shoes pick up a bit of shit doesn't mean you have to buy a new pair.'

'Sure, but you learn to stay on the path instead of taking shortcuts across the field.'

'Wise guy. I don't even know why we're having this conversation. You've still not given me a shred of evidence why I should accept that Becker didn't kill Linden.'

'So you can order a retrial?'

'A file is never quite complete,' he said with a shrug. 'A case is never really closed, even when all the participants are dead. I still have one or two loose ends.'

'I'm all cut up about your loose ends, Shields.'

'Perhaps you should be, Herr Günther.' His tone was stiffer now. 'Perhaps I ought to remind you that this is a military hospital, and under American jurisdiction. And if you remember, I once had occasion to warn you about meddling in this case. Now that you've done exactly that, I'd say you've still got some explaining to do. Possession of a firearm by a German or Austrian national. Well, that's contrary to the Austrian Military Government's Public Safety Manual for a start. You could get five years for that alone. Then there's the car you were driving. Quite apart from the fact that you were wearing handcuffs and that you don't appear to be in possession of a valid driving licence, there's the small matter of driving through a military checkpoint.' He paused and lit a cigarette. 'So what's it to be: information or incarceration?'

'Neatly put.'

'I'm a neat kind of fellow. All policemen are. Come on. Let's have it.'

I sank back on my pillow resignedly. 'I'm warning you, Shields, you're likely to have as many loose ends as you started with. I doubt if I could prove half of what I could tell you.'

The American folded his brawny arms and leaned back on his chair. 'Proof is for the courtroom, my friend. I'm a detective, remember? This is for my own private casebook.'

I told him nearly everything. When I had finished his face adopted a lugubrious expression and he nodded sagely. 'Well, I can certainly suck a bit of that.'

'That's good,' I sighed, 'but my tits are getting a little sore right now, babe. If you've got questions, how about you save them till next time. I'd like to take a little nap.'

Shields stood up. 'I'll be back tomorrow. But just one question for now: this guy from Crowcass –'

'Belinsky?'

'Belinsky, yeah. How come that he quit the game before the period was up?'

'Your guess is as good as mine.'

'Better maybe.' He shrugged. 'I'll ask around. Our relations with the Intelligence boys have improved since this Berlin thing. The American Military Governor has told them and us that we need to present a united front in case the Soviets try the same thing here.'

'What Berlin thing?' I said. 'In case they try what here?'

Shields frowned. 'You don't know about that? No, of course, you wouldn't, would you?'

'Look, my wife is in Berlin; hadn't you better tell me what's happened?'

He sat down again, only on the edge of the chair, which added to his obvious discomfort. 'The Soviets have imposed a complete military blockade on Berlin,' he said. 'They're not letting any-thing in or out of the Zone. So we're supplying the city by plane. Happened the day your friend got his own personal airlift. 24 June.'

He smiled thinly. 'It's kind of tense up there from what I hear. Lots of folk think that there's going to be one almighty great showdown between us and the Russkies. Me, I wouldn't be at all surprised. We should have kicked their asses a long time ago. But we're not about to abandon Berlin, you can depend on it. Provided everybody keeps their heads, we should get through it all right.'

Shields lit a cigarette and put it between my lips. 'I'm sorry about your wife,' he said. 'You been married long?'

'Seven years.' I said. 'What about you? Are you married?'

He shook his head. 'I guess I never met the right girl. Do you mind me asking: has it worked out all right for you both? You being a detective and all.'

I thought for a minute. 'Yes,' I said, 'it's worked out just fine.'

Mine was the only occupied bed in the hospital. That night a barge slipping down the canal woke me with its bovine-sounding horn, and then abandoned me to stare sleeplessly at the dark as the echo of it fled into eternity like the bray of the last trump. Staring into the void of the pitch-black darkness, my whispered breathing serving only to remind me of my own mortality, it seemed that, seeing nothing, I could see beyond to what was most tangible: death itself, a lean, moth-eaten figure shrouded in heavy black velvet, ever ready to press the silent, chloroformed pad over the victim's nose and mouth, and to carry him to a waiting black sedan to some dreadful zone and DP camp where darkness never ends and whence no one ever escapes. As light returned to press against the window bars, so too did courage, although I knew that Death's Ivans held no high regard for those who met them without fear. Whether a man is ready to die or not, his requiem always sounds the same.

It was several days before Shields returned to the hospital. This time he was accompanied by two other men who from their haircuts and well-fed faces I took to be Americans. Like Shields they wore loudly cut suits. But their faces were older and wiser. Bing

Crosby types with briefcases, pipes and emotions restricted to their supercilious eyebrows. Lawyers, or investigators. Or Corps. Shields handled the introductions.

'This is Major Breen,' he said, indicating the older of the two men. 'And this is Major Medlinskas.'

Investigators then. But for which organization?

'What are you,' I said, 'the medical students?'

Shields grinned uncertainly. 'They'd like to ask you a few questions. I'll help with the translating.'

'Tell them I'm feeling a lot better, and thank them for the grapes. And perhaps one of them could fetch me the pot.'

Shields ignored me. They drew up three chairs and sat down like a team of judges at a dog show, with Shields nearest to me. Briefcases were opened, and notepads produced.

'Maybe I should have my twister here.'

'Is that really necessary?' said Shields.

'You tell me. Only I look at these two and I don't think they're a couple of American tourists who want to know the best places in Vienna to nudge a pretty girl.'

Shields translated my concern to the other two, the older of whom grunted and said something about criminals.

'The Major says that this is not a criminal matter,' reported Shields. 'But if you want a lawyer, one will be fetched.'

'If this is not a criminal matter, then how come I'm in a military hospital?'

'You were wearing handcuffs when they picked you out of that car,' sighed Shields. 'There was a pistol on the floor and a machine-gun in the trunk. They weren't about to take you to the maternity hospital.'

'All the same, I don't like it. Don't think that this bandage on my head gives you the right to treat me like an idiot. Who are these people anyway? They look like spies to me. I can recognize the type. I can smell the invisible ink on their fingers. Tell them that. Tell them that people from CIC and Crowcass give me an acid stomach on account of the fact that I trusted one of their people before and got my fingers clipped. Tell them that I wouldn't be lying here now if it wasn't for an American agent called Belinsky.'

'That's what they want to talk to you about.'

'Yeah? Well maybe if they were to put away those notebooks I'd feel a little easier.'

They seemed to understand this. They shrugged simultaneously and returned the notebooks to the briefcases.

'One more thing,' I said. 'I'm an experienced interrogator myself. Remember that. If I start to get the impression that I'm being rinsed and stacked for criminal charges then the interview will be over.'

The older man, Breen, shifted in his chair and clasped his hands across his knee. It didn't make him look any cuter. When he spoke, his German wasn't as bad as I had imagined it would be. 'I don't see any objections to that,' he said quietly.

And then it began. The major asked most of the questions, while the younger man nodded and occasionally interrupted in his bad German to ask me to clarify a remark. For the best part of two hours I answered or parried their questions, only refusing to reply directly on a couple of occasions when it seemed to me that they had stepped across the line of our agreement. Gradually, however, I perceived that most of their interest in me lay in the fact that neither the 970th CIC in Germany, nor the 430th CIC in Austria knew anything about a John Belinsky. Nor indeed was there a John Belinsky attached, however tenuously, to the Central Registry of War Crimes and Security Suspects of the United States Army. The military police had no one by that name; nor the army. There was however a John Belinsky in the Air Force, but he was nearly fifty; and the Navy had three John Belinskys, all of whom were at sea. Which was just how I felt.

Along the way the two Americans sermonized about the importance of keeping my mouth shut with regard to what I had learned about the Org and its relation to the CIC. Nothing could have suited me more and I counted this as a strong hint that as soon as I was well again, I would be permitted to leave. But my relief was tempered by a great deal of curiosity as to who John Belinsky had really been, and what he had hoped to achieve. Neither of my interrogators gave me the benefit of their opinions. But naturally I had my own ideas.

Several times in the following weeks Shields and the two Americans came to the hospital to continue with their inquiry. They were always scrupulously polite, almost comically so; and the questions were always about Belinsky. What had he looked like? Which part of New York had he said that he came from? Could I remember the number of his car?

I told them everything I could remember about him. They checked his room at Sacher's and found nothing: he had cleared out on the very day that he was supposed to have come to Grinzing with the cavalry. They staked out a couple of the bars he had said he favoured. I think they even asked the Russians about him. When they tried to speak to the Georgian officer in the IP, Captain Rustaveli, who had arrested Lotte Hartmann and me on Belinsky's instructions, it transpired that he had been suddenly recalled to Moscow.

Of course it was all too late. The cat had already fallen into the stream, and what was now clear was that Belinsky had been working for the Russians all along. No wonder he had played up the rivalry between the CIC and the military police, I said to my new American friends of truth. I thought myself a very clever sort of coat to have spotted that as early on as I had. By now he had presumably told his MVD boss all about America's recruitment of Heinrich Müller and Arthur Nebe.

But there were several subjects about which I remained silent. Colonel Poroshin was one: I didn't like to think what might have happened had they discovered that a senior officer in the MVD had arranged my coming to Vienna. Their curiosity about my travel documents and cigarette permit was quite uncomfortable enough. I told them that I had had to pay a great deal of money to bribe a Russian officer, and they seemed satisfied with that explanation.

Privately I wondered if my meeting with Belinsky had always

been part of Poroshin's plan. And the circumstances of our deciding to work together: was it possible that Belinsky had shot those two Russian deserters as a demonstration for my benefit, as a way of impressing upon me his ruthless dislike for all things Soviet?

There was another thing about which I kept resolutely silent, and that was Arthur Nebe's explanation of how the Org had sabotaged the US Documents Centre in Berlin with the help of Captain Linden. That, I decided, was their problem. I did not think I cared to help a government that was prepared to hang Nazis on Mondays, Tuesdays, and Wednesdays, and to recruit them for its own security services on Thursdays, Fridays, and Saturdays. Heinrich Müller had at least got that part right.

As for Müller himself, Major Breen and Captain Medlinskas were adamant that I must have been mistaken about him. The former Gestapo chief was long dead, they assured me. Belinsky, they insisted, for reasons best known to himself, had almost certainly shown me someone else's picture. The military police had made a very careful search of Nebe's wine estate in Grinzing, and discovered only that the owner, one Alfred Nolde, was abroad on business. No bodies were found, nor any evidence that anyone had been killed. And while it was true that there existed an organization of former German servicemen which was working alongside the United States to prevent the further spread of international Communism, it was, they insisted, quite inconceivable that this organization could have included fugitive Nazi war-criminals.

I listened impassively to all this nonsense, too exhausted by the whole business to care much what they believed or, for that matter, what they wanted me to believe. Suppressing my first reaction in the face of their indifference to the truth, which was to tell them to go to hell, I merely nodded politely, my manners verging on the truly Viennese. Agreeing with them seemed to be the best possible way of expediting my freedom.

Shields was less complaisant however. His help with translation grew more surly and uncooperative as the days went by, and it became obvious that he was unhappy with the way in which the two officers appeared to be more concerned to conceal rather than to reveal the implications of what I had first told him, and certainly he had believed. Much to Shields' annoyance, Breen pronounced himself content that the case of Captain Linden had been brought to a satisfactory conclusion. Shields' only satisfaction might have come from the knowledge that the 796th military police, still smarting as a result of the scandal involving Russians posing as American MPs, now had something to throw back at the 430th CIC: a Russian spy, posing as a member of the CIC, with the proper identity card, staying at a hotel requisitioned by the military, driving a vehicle registered to an American officer and generally coming and going as he pleased through areas restricted to American personnel. I knew that this would only have been a small consolation for a man like Roy Shields: a policeman with a common enough fetish for neatness. It was easy for me to sympathize. I'd often encountered that same feeling myself.

For the last two interrogations, Shields was replaced by another man, an Austrian, and I never saw him again.

Neither Breen nor Medlinskas told me when at last they had concluded their inquiry. Nor did they give me any indication that they were satisfied with my answers. They just left the matter hanging. But such are the ways of people in the security services.

Over the next two or three weeks I made a full recovery from my injuries. I was both amused and shocked to learn from the prison doctor, however, that on my first being admitted to the hospital after my accident, I had been suffering from gonorrhoea.

'In the first place, you're damned lucky that they brought you here,' he said, 'where we have penicillin. If they'd taken you anywhere but an American Military Hospital they'd have used Salvarsan, and that stuff burns like Lucifer's spitball. And in the second, you're lucky it was just drip and not Russian syphilis. These local whores are full of it. Haven't any of you Jerries ever heard of French letters?'

'You mean Parisians? Sure we have. But we don't wear them. We give them to the Nazi fifth column who prick holes in them and sell them to GIs to make them sick when they screw our women.'

The doctor laughed. But I could tell that in a remote part of his soul he believed me. This was just one of many similar incidents I encountered during my recovery, as my English slowly improved, enabling me to talk with the two Americans who were the prison hospital's nurses. For as we laughed and joked it always seemed to me that there was something strange in their eyes, but which I was never able to identify.

And then, a few days before I was discharged, it came to me in a sickening realization. Because I was a German these Americans were actually chilled by me. It was as if, when they looked at me, they ran newsreel film of Belsen and Buchenwald inside their heads. And what was in their eyes was a question: how could you have allowed it to happen? How could you have let that sort of thing go on?

Perhaps, for several generations at least, when other nations look us in the eye, it will always be with this same unspoken question in their hearts.

38

It was a pleasant September morning when, wearing an ill-fitting suit lent to me by the nurses at the military hospital, I returned to my pension in Skodagasse. The owner, Frau Blum-Weiss greeted me warmly, informed me that my luggage was stored safely in her basement, handed me a note which had arrived not half an hour before, and asked me if I would care to have some breakfast. I told her I would, and having thanked her for looking after my belongings, inquired if I owed any money.

'Dr Liebl settled everything, Herr Günther,' she said. 'But if you would like to take your old rooms again, that will be all right. They are vacant.'

Since I had no idea when I might be able to return to Berlin, I said I would.

'Did Dr Liebl leave me any message?' I asked, already knowing the answer. He had made no attempt to contact me during my stay in the military hospital.

'No,' she said, 'no message.'

Then she showed me back to my old rooms and had her son bring my luggage up to me. I thanked her again and said that I would breakfast just as soon as I had changed into my own clothes.

'Everything's there,' she said as her son heaved my bags on to the luggage stand. 'I had a receipt for the few things that the police took away: papers, that kind of thing.' Then she smiled sweetly, wished me another pleasant stay, and closed the door behind her. Typically Viennese, she showed no desire to know what had befallen me since last I had stayed in her house.

As soon as she had left the room, I opened my bags and found, almost to my astonishment and much to my relief, that I was still in possession of my $2,500 in cash and my several cartons of cigarettes. I lay on the bed and smoked a Memphis with something approaching delight.

I opened the note while I ate my breakfast. There was only one short sentence and that was written in Cyrillic: 'Meet me at the Kaisergruft at eleven o'clock this morning.' The note was unsigned but then it hardly needed to be. When Frau Blum Weiss returned to my table to clear away the breakfast things, I asked her who had delivered it.

'It was just a schoolboy, Herr Günther,' she said, collecting the crockery on a tray, 'an ordinary schoolboy.'

'I have to meet someone,' I explained. 'At the Kaisergruft. Where is that?'

'The Imperial Crypt?' She wiped a hand on a well-starched pinafore as if she had been about to meet the Kaiser himself, and then crossed herself. Mention of royalty always seemed to make the Viennese doubly respectful. 'Why, it's at the Church of the Capuchins on the west side of Neuer Markt. But go early, Herr Günther. It's only open in the morning, from ten to twelve. I'm sure you'll find it very interesting.'

I smiled and nodded gratefully. There was no doubting that I was likely to find it very interesting indeed.

Neuer Markt hardly looked like a market square at all. A number of tables had been laid out like a café terrace. There were customers who weren't drinking coffee, waiters who did not seem inclined to serve them and little sign of any café from where coffee might have been obtained. It seemed quite makeshift, even by the easy standards of a reconstructed Vienna. There were also a few people just watching, almost as if a crime had occurred and everyone was waiting for the police. But I paid it little regard and, hearing the eleven o'clock chimes of the nearby clock tower, hurried on to the church.

It was as well for whichever zoologist who had named the famous monkey that the Capuchin monks' style of habit was rather more remarkable than their plainish church in Vienna. Compared with most other places of worship in that city, the Kapuzinerkirche looked as if they must have been flirting with Calvinism at the time that it was built. Either that or the Order's treasurer had run off with the money for the stonemasons; there wasn't one carving on it. The church was sufficiently ordinary for me to walk past the place without even recognizing it. I might have done so again but for a group of American soldiers who were hanging around in a doorway and from whom I overheard a reference to 'the stiffs'. My new acquaintance with English as it was spoken by the nurses at the military hospital told me that this group was intent on visiting the same place as I was.

I paid a schilling entrance to a grumpy old monk and entered a long, airy corridor that I took to be a part of the monastery. A narrow stairwell led down into the vault.

It was in fact, not one vault, but eight interconnecting vaults and much less gloomy than I had expected. The interior was simple, being in plain white with the walls faced partly in marble, and contrasted strongly with the opulence of its contents.

Here were the remains of over a hundred Habsburgs and their famous jaws, although the guidebook which I had thought to bring with me said that their hearts were pickled in urns located underneath St Stephen's Cathedral. It was as much evidence for royal mortality as you could have found anywhere north of Cairo. Nobody, it seemed, was missing except the Archduke Ferdinand, who was buried at Graz, no doubt piqued at the rest of them for having insisted that he visit Sarajevo.

The cheaper end of the family, from Tuscany, were stacked in simple lead coffins, one on top of the other like bottles in a wine-rack, at the far end of the longest vault. I half expected to see an old man prising a couple of them open to try out a new mallet and set of stakes. Naturally enough the Habsburgs with the biggest egos rated the grandest sarcophagi. These huge, morbidly ornamented copper caskets seemed to lack nothing but caterpillar tracks and gun turrets for them to have captured Stalingrad. Only the Emperor Joseph II had shown anything like restraint in his choice of box; and only a Viennese guidebook could have described the copper casket as 'excessively simple'.

I found Colonel Poroshin in the Franz Joseph vault. He smiled warmly when he saw me and clapped me on the shoulder: 'You see, I was right. You can read Cyrillic, after all.'

'Maybe you can read my mind as well.'

'For sure,' he said. 'You are wondering what we could possibly have to say to each other, given all that has happened. Least of all in this place. You are thinking that in a different place, you might try to kill me.'

'You should be on the stage, Palkovnik. You could be another Professor Schaffer.'

'You are mistaken, I think. Professor Schaffer is a hypnotist, not a mind-reader.' He slapped his gloves on his open palm with the air of one who had scored a point. 'I am not a hypnotist, Herr Günther.'

'Don't underestimate yourself. You managed to make me believe that I was a private investigator and that I should come here to Vienna to try and clear Emil Becker of murder. A hypnotic fantasy if ever I heard one.'

'A powerful suggestion, perhaps,' said Poroshin, 'but you were acting under your own free will.' He sighed. 'A pity about poor Emil. You're wrong if you think that I didn't hope you could prove him innocent. But to borrow a chess term, it was my Vienna gambit: it has a peaceable first appearance, but the sequel is full of subtleties and aggressive possibilities. All that one requires is a strong and valiant knight.'

'That was me, I suppose.'

'*Tochno* (exactly). And now the game is won.'

'Do you mind explaining how?'

Poroshin pointed to the casket on the right of the more elevated one containing the Emperor Franz Joseph.

'The Crown Prince Rudolf,' he said. 'He committed suicide in the famous hunting lodge at Mayerling. The general story is well-known but the details and the motives remain unclear. Just about the only thing we can be certain of is that he lies in this very tomb. For me, to know this for sure is enough. But not everyone whom we believe to have committed suicide is really quite as dead as poor Rudolf. Take Heinrich Müller. To prove him still alive, now that was something worthwhile. The game was won when we knew that for sure.'

'But I lied about that,' I said insouciantly. 'I never saw Müller. The only reason I signalled to Belinsky was because I wanted him and his men to come and help me save Veronika Zartl, the choco-lady from the Oriental.'

'Yes, I admit that Belinsky's arrangements with you were less than perfect in their concept. But as it happens I know that you are lying now. You see, Belinsky really was at Grinzing with a team of agents. They were not of course Americans, but my own men. Every vehicle leaving the yellow house in Grinzing was followed including, I may say, your own. When Müller and his friends discovered your escape they were so panic-stricken that they fled almost immediately. We simply tailed them, at a discreet distance, until they thought that they were safe again. Since then we have been able to positively identify Herr Müller for ourselves. So you see? You did not lie.'

'But why didn't you just arrest him? What good is he to you if he's left at liberty?'

Poroshin made his face look shrewd.

'In my business, it is not necessarily politic always to arrest a man who is my enemy. Sometimes he can be many times more valuable if he is allowed to remain at large. From as early as the beginning of the war, Müller was a double agent. Towards the end of 1944 he was naturally anxious to disappear from Berlin altogether and come to Moscow. Well, can you imagine it, Herr Günther? The head of the fascist Gestapo living and working in the capital of democratic socialism? If the British or American intelligence agencies were to have discovered such a thing they would undoubt-edly have leaked this information to the world's press at some politically opportune moment. Then they would have sat back and watched us squirm with embarrassment. So, it was decided that Müller could not come.

'The only problem was that he knew so much about us. Not to mention the whereabouts of dozens of Gestapo and Abwehr spies throughout the Soviet Union and Eastern Europe. He had first to be neutralized before we could turn him away from our door. So we tricked him into giving us the names of all these agents, and at the same time started to feed him with new information which, while of no help to the German war-effort, might prove of considerable interest to the Americans. It goes without saying that this information was also false.

'Anyway, all this time we continued to put off Müller's defection, telling him to wait just a little longer, and that he had nothing to worry about. But when we were ready we allowed him to discover that for various political reasons his defection could not be sanctioned. We hoped that this would now persuade him to offer his services to the Americans, as others had done. General Gehlen for example. Baron von Bolschwing. Even Himmler – although he was simply too well known for the British to accept his offer. And too crazy, yes?

'Perhaps we miscalculated. Perhaps Müller left it too late and was unable to escape the eye of Martin Bormann and the SS who guarded the Führerbunker. Who knows? Anyway, Müller apparently committed suicide. This he faked, but it was quite a while before we could prove this to our own satisfaction. Müller is a very clever man.

'When we learned about the Org we thought that it wouldn't be long before Müller turned up again. But he stayed persistently in the shadows. There was the occasional, unconfirmed sighting, but nothing for certain. And then when Captain Linden was shot, we noticed from the reports that the serial number of the murder weapon was one which had been originally issued to Müller. But this part you already know, I think.'

I nodded. 'Belinsky told me.'

'A most resourceful man. The family is Siberian, you know. They returned to Russia after the Revolution, when Belinsky was still a boy. But by then he was all-American, as they say. The whole family were soon working for NKVD. It was Belinsky's idea to pose as a Crowcass agent. Not only do Crowcass and CIC often work at cross purposes, but Crowcass is often staffed with CIC personnel. And it is quite common for the American military police to be left in ignorance of CIC/Crowcass operations. The Americans are even more Byzantine in their organizational structures than we are ourselves. Belinsky was plausible to you; but he was also plausible, as an idea, to Müller: enough to scare him out into the open when you told him that a Crowcass agent was on his trail; but not enough to scare him as far as South America, where he could be of no use to us. After all, there are others in CIC, less fastidious about employing war-criminals than the people in Crowcass, whose protection Müller could seek out.

'And so it has proved. Even as we speak Müller is exactly where we want him: with his American friends in Pullach. Being useful to them. Giving them the benefit of his massive knowledge of Soviet intelligence structures and secret police methods. Boasting about the network of loyal agents he still believes are in place. This was the first stage of our plan – to disinform the Americans.'

'Very clever,' I said, with genuine admiration, 'and the second?'

Poroshin's face adopted a more philosophical expression. 'When the time is right, it is we who shall leak some information to the world's press: that Gestapo Müller is a tool of American Intelligence. It is we who will sit back and watch them squirm with embarrassment. It may be in ten years' time, or even twenty. But, provided Müller stays alive, it will happen.'

'Suppose the world's press don't believe you?'

'The proof will not be so hard to obtain. The Americans are great ones for keeping files and records. Look at that Documents Centre of theirs. And we have other agents. Provided that they know where and what to look for, it will not be too difficult to find the evidence.'

'You seem to have thought of everything.'

'More than you will ever know. And now that I have answered your question, I have one for you, Herr Günther. Will you answer it, please?'

'I can't imagine what I can tell you, Palkovnik. You're the player, not me. I'm just a knight in your Vienna gambit, remember?'

'Nevertheless, there is something.'

I shrugged. 'Fire away.'

'Yes,' he said, 'to return to the chess board for a moment. One expects to make sacrifices. Becker, for example. And you of course. But sometimes one encounters the unexpected loss of material.'

'Your queen?'

He frowned for a moment. 'If you like. Belinsky told me that it was you who killed Traudl Braunsteiner. But he was a very determined man in this whole affair. The fact that I had a personal interest in Traudl was of no special account to him. I know this to be true. He would have killed her without a second thought. But you –

'I had one of my people in Berlin check you out at the US Documents Centre. You told the truth. You were never a Party member. And the rest of it is there too. How you asked for a transfer out of the SS. That could have got you shot. So a sentimental fool, maybe. But a killer? I will tell you straight, Herr Günther: my intellect says that you did not kill her. But I must know it here too.' He slapped his stomach. 'Perhaps here most of all.'

He fixed me with his pale blue eyes, but I did not flinch or look away.

'Did you kill her?'

'No.'

'Did you run her down?'

'Belinsky had a car, not me.'

'Say that you had no part in her murder.'

'I was going to warn her.'

Poroshin nodded. '*Da*,' he said, '*dagavareelees* (that's agreed). You are speaking the truth.'

'*Slava bogu* (Thank God).'

'You are right to thank him.' He slapped his stomach once again. 'If I had not felt it, I would have had to kill you as well.'

'As well?' I frowned. Who else was dead? 'Belinsky?'

'Yes, most unfortunate. It was smoking that infernal pipe of his. Such a dangerous habit, smoking. You should give it up.'

'How?'

'It's an old Cheka way. A small quantity of tetryl in the mouth-piece attached to a fuse which leads to a point below the bowl. When the pipe is lit, so is the fuse. Quite simple, but also quite deadly. It blew his head off.' Poroshin's tone was almost indifferent. 'You see? My mind told me that it was not you who killed her. I merely wanted to be sure that I would not have to kill you as well.'

'And now you are sure?'

'For sure,' he said. 'Not only will you walk out of here alive –'

'You would have killed me down here?'

'It is a suitable enough place, don't you think?'

'Oh yes, very poetic. What were you going to do? Bite my neck? Or had you wired one of the caskets?'

'There are many poisons, Herr Günther.' He held out a small flick-knife in his palm. 'Tetrodotoxin on the blade. Even the smallest scratch, and bye-bye.' He pocketed the knife in his tunic and gave a sheepish little shrug. 'I was about to say that not only may you now walk out of here alive, but that if you go to the Café Mozart now, you will find someone waiting there for you.'

My look of puzzlement seemed to amuse him. 'Can you not guess?' he said delightedly.

'My wife? You got her out of Berlin?'

'*Kanyeshna* (Of course). I don't know how else she would have got out. Berlin is surrounded by our tanks.'

'Kirsten is waiting at the Mozart Café now?'

He looked at his watch and nodded. 'For fifteen minutes already,' he said. 'You'd best not keep her waiting much longer.

An attractive woman like that, on her own in a city like Vienna? One must be so careful nowadays. These are difficult times.'

'You're full of surprises, Colonel,' I told him. 'Five minutes ago you were ready to kill me on nothing more tangible than your indigestion. And now you're telling me that you've brought my wife from Berlin. Why are you helping me like this? *Ya nye pan-eemayoo* (I don't understand).'

'Let us just say that it was part of the whole futile romance of Communism, *vot i vsyo* (that's all).' He clicked his heels like a good Prussian. 'Goodbye, Herr Günther. Who knows? After this Berlin thing, we may meet again.'

'I hope not.'

'That is too bad. A man of your talents —' Then he turned and strode off.

I left the Imperial Crypt with as much spring in my step as Lazarus. Outside, on Neuer Markt, there were still more people watching the strange little café-terrace that had no café. Then I saw the camera and the lights, and at the same time I spotted Willy Reichmann, the little red-haired production manager from Sievering Film Studios. He was speaking English to another man who was holding a megaphone. This was surely the English film that Willy had told me about: the one for which Vienna's increasingly rare ruins had been a prerequisite. The film in which Lotte Hartmann, the girl who had given me a well-deserved dose of drip, had been given a part.

I stopped to watch for a few moments, wondering if I might catch sight of König's girlfriend, but there was no sign of her. I thought it unlikely that she would have left Vienna with him and passed up her first screen role.

One of the onlookers around me said, 'What on earth are they doing?' and another answered saying, 'It's supposed to be a café — the Mozart Café.' Laughter rippled through the crowd. 'What, here?' said another voice. 'Apparently they like the view better here,' replied a fourth. 'It's what they call poetic licence.'

The man with the megaphone asked for quiet, ordered the cameras to roll and then called for action. Two men, one of them carrying a book as if it was some kind of religious icon, shook hands and sat down at one of the tables.

Leaving the crowd to watch what happened next, I walked quickly south, towards the real Mozart Café and the wife who was waiting there for me.

Author's Note

In 1988 Ian Sayer and Douglas Botting, who were compiling a history of the American Counter-Intelligence Corps entitled *America's Secret Army: The Untold Story of the Counter-Intelligence Corps*, were asked by a US government investigative agency to verify a file consisting of documents signed by CIC agents in Berlin towards the end of 1948 in connection with the employment of Heinrich Müller as a CIC advisor. The file indicated that Soviet agents had concluded that Müller had not been killed in 1945 and that he was possibly being used by Western Intelligence agencies. Sayer and Botting rejected the material as a forgery 'counterfeited by a skilful but rather confused person'. This view was corroborated by Colonel E. Browning, who was CIC Operations Chief in Frankfurt at the time the documents were supposed to have been produced. Browning indicated that the whole idea of something as sensitive as the employment of Müller as a CIC advisor was ludicrous. 'Regretfully,' wrote the two authors, 'we have to conclude that the fate of the chief of the Gestapo in the Third Reich remains shrouded in mystery and speculation, as it has always been, and probably always will be.'

Attempts by a leading British newspaper and an American news magazine to investigate the story in detail have so far come to nothing.

He just wanted a decent book to read ...

Not too much to ask, is it? It was in 1935 when Allen Lane, Managing
Director of Bodley Head Publishers, stood on a platform at Exeter railway
station looking for something good to read on his journey back to London.
His choice was limited to popular magazines and poor-quality paperbacks –
the same choice faced every day by the vast majority of readers, few of
whom could afford hardbacks. Lane's disappointment and subsequent anger
at the range of books generally available led him to found a company – and
change the world.

'We believed in the existence in this country of a vast reading public for intelligent
books at a low price, and staked everything on it'
Sir Allen Lane, 1902–1970, founder of Penguin Books

The quality paperback had arrived – and not just in bookshops. Lane was
adamant that his Penguins should appear in chain stores and tobacconists,
and should cost no more than a packet of cigarettes.

Reading habits (and cigarette prices) have changed since 1935, but
Penguin still believes in publishing the best books for everybody to
enjoy. We still believe that good design costs no more than bad design,
and we still believe that quality books published passionately and responsibly
make the world a better place.

So wherever you see the little bird – whether it's on a piece of
prize-winning literary fiction or a celebrity autobiography, political tour
de force or historical masterpiece, a serial-killer thriller, reference book,
world classic or a piece of pure escapism – you can bet that it represents
the very best that the genre has to offer.

Whatever you like to read – trust Penguin.